READER'S DIGEST
BOOKS

With the exception of actual personages identified as such, the characters and incidents in the fictional selections in this volume are entirely the product of the authors' imaginations and have no relation to any person or event in real life.

www.readersdigest.co.uk

The Reader's Digest Association Limited 11 Westferry Circus Canary Wharf London E14 4HE

For information as to ownership of copyright in the material of this book, and acknowledgments, see last page.

Printed in France
ISBN 0 276 42865 X

READER'S DIGEST BOOKS

Selected and condensed by Reader's Digest

THE READER'S DIGEST ASSOCIATION LIMITED, LONDON

CONTENTS

Ancient Rome is brought vividly to life in this exciting new novel set in AD 79. When the great Augusta aqueduct fails, engineer Marcus Attilius is under pressure to safeguard the water supply to Pompeii and the rest of the Bay of Naples. The fault in the aqueduct seems to lie on the flanks of Vesuvius and, as Attilius heads out to the volcano, he discovers there are forces at work that even the might of the Roman Empire cannot control.

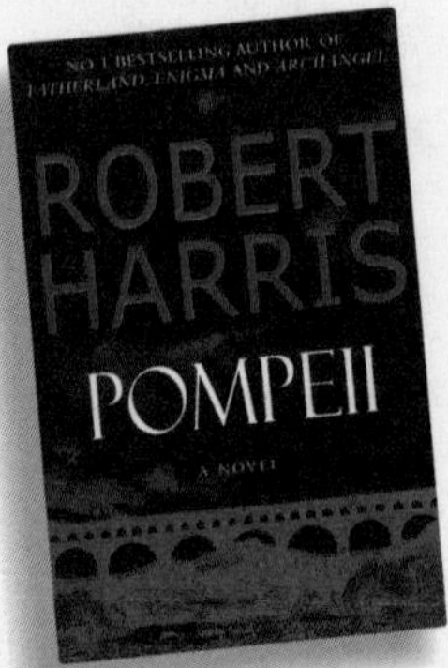

PUBLISHED BY HUTCHINSON

In 1954, two US marshals take a ferry to Shutter Island's high-security mental hospital, charged with discovering the fate of a missing patient. After questioning staff, inmates and the chief of staff, Teddy Daniels fears that he and his partner are being spun a yarn. Then, as a huge storm develops, cutting off all communication with the mainland, the terrifying realisation dawns that those who run Shutter Island may not want Teddy and Chuck to leave.

PUBLISHED BY BANTAM PRESS

THE RUNNER

page 293

Peter May

When a weightlifter dies in the arms of his mistress, Detective Li Yan of the Beijing police is ordered to cover up the scandal. Aware that this is just one of several recent deaths in the Olympic team, Li shares his concerns with his American partner, Margaret. The two of them are soon probing the city's secretive and corrupt underworld—only to be brought face to face with a sinister scientific mastermind. A compulsive page-turner.

PUBLISHED BY HODDER & STOUGHTON

THE CRUELLEST MILES

page 437

Gay and Laney Salisbury

In the winter of 1925, a diphtheria epidemic broke out in the gold-rush town of Nome, Alaska, just as supplies of antitoxin were running dangerously low. The port was icebound, the nearest railway was hundreds of miles away, and planes could not fly in the extreme weather. There was only one way left to bring in supplies. Read how it was done in this gripping true-life account of human bravery and endurance.

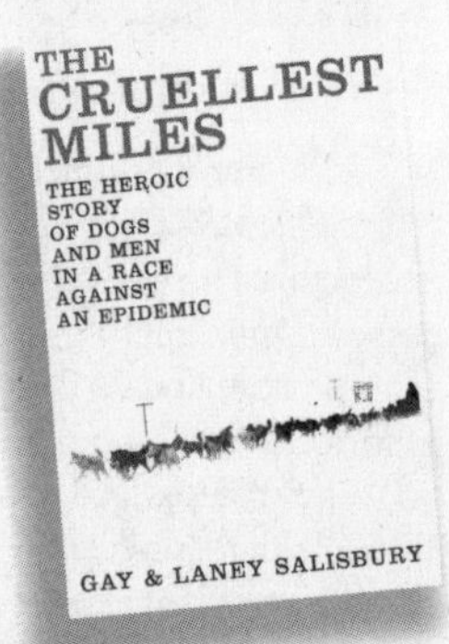

PUBLISHED BY BLOOMSBURY

ROBERT HARRIS

POMPEII

AUGUST, AD 79. ALL ALONG THE BAY OF NAPLES, THE WEALTHY INHABITANTS OF POMPEII ARE RELAXING IN THE SWELTERING HEAT, OBLIVIOUS TO ANYTHING BEYOND THE WALLS OF THEIR LUXURIOUS VILLAS.

DISASTER IS JUST DAYS AWAY.

Author's note: the Romans divided the day into twelve hours. The first, *hora prima*, began at sunrise. The last, *hora duodecima*, ended at sunset. The night was divided into eight watches: *Vespera*, *Prima fax*, *Concubia* and *Intempesta* before midnight; *Inclinatio*, *Gallicinium*, *Conticinium* and *Diluculum* after it. The days of the week were Moon, Mars, Mercury, Jupiter, Venus, Saturn and Sun.

MARS

August 22: Two days before the eruption

Conticinium — 04:21 hours

They left the aqueduct two hours before dawn, climbing by moonlight into the hills overlooking the port—six men in single file, the engineer leading. He had turfed them out of their beds himself—all stiff limbs and sullen, bleary faces—and now he could hear them complaining about him behind his back, their voices carrying louder than they realised in the warm, still air.

'A fool's errand,' somebody muttered.

'Boys should stick to their books,' said another.

He lengthened his stride. Let them prattle, he thought.

Already he could feel the heat of the morning beginning to build, the promise of another day without rain. He was younger than most of his work gang, and shorter than any of them: a compact, muscular figure with cropped brown hair. The shafts of the tools he carried slung across his shoulder—a heavy, bronze-headed axe and a wooden shovel—chafed against his sunburnt neck. Still, he forced himself to stretch his legs as far as they could reach, mounting swiftly from foothold to foothold, and only when he was high above Misenum, at a place where the track forked, did he set down his burdens and wait for the others to catch up.

He wiped the sweat from his eyes on the sleeve of his tunic. Such shimmering, feverish heavens they had here in the south! Even this close to daybreak, a great hemisphere of stars swept down to the horizon. He could see the horns of Taurus, and the belt and sword of the Hunter; there was the constellation they called the Vintager, which always rose for Caesar on the twenty-second day of August and signalled that it was time to harvest the wine. Tomorrow night the moon would be full. He raised his hand to the sky, his blunt-tipped fingers black and sharp against the glittering constellations.

From down in the harbour came the splash of oars as the night watch rowed between the moored triremes. A dog barked and another answered. And then the voices of the labourers slowly climbing the path beneath him: the harsh local accent of Corax the overseer—*Look, our new aquarius is waving at the stars!*—and the slaves and the free men, equals for once in their resentment if nothing else, panting for breath and laughing sycophantically.

The engineer dropped his hand. 'At least,' he said, 'with such a sky, we have no need of torches.' He stooped to collect his tools, and frowned into the darkness. One path would take them west, skirting the edge of the naval base. The other led north, towards the seaside resort of Baiae. 'I think this is where we turn.'

'He thinks,' sneered Corax.

The engineer had decided the previous day that the best way to treat the overseer was to ignore him. Without a word he put his back to the sea, and began ascending the black mass of the hillside.

The path here was steeper and he had to scramble up it sideways, his feet skidding. He had to admit it did not look promising. People stared at these brown, scorched hills and thought they were as dry as deserts, but the engineer knew differently. He tried to remember how the path had appeared in the glare of the afternoon, when he had first reconnoitred it. Swaths of scorched grass. And then, at a place where the ground levelled, flecks of pale green in the blackness—signs of life that turned out to be shoots of ivy.

He stopped and turned slowly in a full circle. Either his eyes were getting used to it, or dawn was close now, in which case they were almost out of time. The others had halted behind him. He could hear their heavy breathing. Here was another story for them to take back to Misenum—how their new young aquarius had turfed them from their beds and marched them into the hills in the middle of the night, and all *on a fool's errand*. There was a taste of ash in his mouth.

'Are we lost, pretty boy?' Corax's mocking voice again.

He made the mistake of rising to the bait: 'I'm looking for a rock.'

This time they did not even try to hide their laughter.

'He's running around like a mouse in a pisspot!'

'I know it's here somewhere. I marked it with chalk.'

More laughter—and at that he wheeled on them: the squat, broad-shouldered Corax; Becco, the long-nose, who was a plasterer; the chubby Musa, whose skill was laying bricks; and the two slaves, Polites and Corvinus. 'Laugh. Good. But I promise you: either we find it before dawn or we shall all be back here tomorrow night. Including you, Gavius Corax. Only next time make sure you're sober.'

Corax spat and took a half-step forward and the engineer braced himself for a fight. They had been building up to this for three days now, ever since he had arrived in Misenum. Not an hour had passed without Corax trying to undermine him in front of the men.

And if we fight, thought the engineer, he will win—it's five against one—and they will throw my body over the cliff and say I slipped in the darkness. But how will that go down in Rome—if a second aquarius of the Aqua Augusta is lost in less than a fortnight?

They faced one another, no more than a pace between them, so close that the engineer could smell the stale wine on the older man's breath. But then Becco gave an excited shout and pointed.

Just visible behind Corax's shoulder was a rock, marked neatly in its centre by a thick white cross.

ATTILIUS WAS the engineer's name—Marcus Attilius Primus, to lay it out in full, but plain Attilius would have satisfied him. After all, what name was more honourable in the history of his profession than that of the Attilii, aqueduct engineers for four generations? His great-grandfather had been recruited by Marcus Agrippa from the ballista section of Legion XII and set to work building the Aqua Julia. His grandfather had planned the Anio Novus. His father had completed the Aqua Claudia, bringing her over seven miles of arches, and laying her, on the day of her dedication, like a silver carpet at the feet of the Emperor. Now he, at twenty-seven, had been sent south to Campania and given command of the Aqua Augusta.

The Augusta was one of the greatest feats of engineering ever accomplished. Somewhere, high in the pine-forested mountains of the Appenninus, the aqueduct captured the springs of the Serinus river and bore the water westwards—channelled it along underground passages, carried it over ravines on top of tiered arcades, forced it across valleys through massive siphons—all the way down to the plains of Campania, then round the far side of Mount

Vesuvius, then south to the coast at Neapolis, and finally along the Misenum peninsula to the dusty naval town, a distance of sixty miles, with a mean drop of just two inches every one hundred yards. She was the longest aqueduct in the world, longer than the great aqueducts of Rome and far more complex, for whereas her sisters in the north fed one city only, the Augusta's serpentine conduit—the matrix, as they called it: the mother line—suckled no fewer than nine towns round the Bay of Neapolis: Pompeii first, then Nola, Acerrae, Atella, Neapolis, Puteoli, Cumae, Baiae and finally Misenum.

And this was the problem, the engineer thought. She had to do too much. Rome had more than half a dozen aqueducts: if one failed the others could make up the deficit. But there was no reserve supply down here, especially not in this drought, now dragging into its third month. Wells that had provided water for generations had turned into tubes of dust. Streams had dried up. Even the Augusta was showing signs of exhaustion, the level of her enormous reservoir dropping hourly, and it was this that had brought him out onto the hillside when he ought to have been in bed.

From the leather pouch on his belt Attilius withdrew a small block of polished cedar with a chin rest carved into one side. The grain of the wood had been rubbed smooth and bright by the skin of his ancestors. His great-grandfather was said to have been given it as a talisman by Vitruvius, architect to the Divine Augustus, and the old man had maintained that the spirit of Neptune, god of water, lived within it. Attilius had no time for gods. He placed his faith instead in stones and water, and in the daily miracle that came from mixing two parts of slaked lime to five parts of puteolanum—the local red sand—to produce a substance that would set under water with a consistency harder than rock.

But still, it was a fool who denied the existence of luck, and if this family heirloom could bring him that . . . He would try anything once.

He had left his rolls of Vitruvius behind in Rome. Not that it mattered. They had been hammered into him since childhood, as other boys learned their Virgil. He could still recite entire passages by heart.

'These are the growing things to be found which are signs of water: slender rushes, wild willow, alder, chaste berry, ivy, and other things of this sort, which cannot occur on their own without moisture . . .'

'Corax there,' ordered Attilius. 'Corvinus there. Becco, take the pole and mark the place I tell you. You two: keep your eyes open.'

Corax gave him a look as he passed.

'Later,' said Attilius. There would be time to settle their quarrel when they got back to Misenum. Now they would have to hurry.

A grey gauze had filtered out the stars. The moon had dipped. Fifteen miles to the east, across the bay, the forested pyramid of Mount Vesuvius was becoming visible. The sun would rise behind it.

'This is how to test for water: lie face down, before sunrise, in the places where the search is to be made, and with your chin propped on the ground, survey these regions. In this way the line of sight will not wander higher than it should, because the chin will be motionless . . .'

Attilius knelt on the singed grass and arranged the block in line with the chalk cross, fifty paces distant. Then he set his chin on the rest. The ground was still warm from yesterday. Particles of ash wafted into his face as he stretched out. No dew. Seventy-eight days without rain. The world was burning up. To his right, Vesuvius darkened and light shot from its edge. A shaft of heat struck Attilius's cheek. He had to bring up his hand to shield his face from the dazzle as he squinted across the hillside.

'Where moisture can be seen curling and rising into the air, dig on the spot, because this sign cannot occur in a dry location...'

You saw it quickly, his father used to tell him, or you did not see it at all. He tried to scan the ground methodically, shifting his gaze from one section to the next. But it all seemed to run together—parched browns and greys and streaks of reddish earth, already beginning to waver in the sun.

There! As thin as a fishing line it was—not 'curling' or 'rising' as Vitruvius promised, but snagging, close to the ground, as if a hook were caught on a rock and someone were jerking it. It zigzagged towards him. And vanished. He pointed—'There, Becco!'—and the plasterer lumbered towards the spot. 'Back. Yes. There. Mark it.'

He scrambled to his feet and hurried towards them. The three had gathered round the place and Becco was trying to jam the pole into the earth, but the ground was too hard to sink it far enough.

Attilius was triumphant. 'You saw it? You must have.'

They stared at him blankly.

'It rose like this.' He made horizontal chops at the air with his hand. 'Like steam coming off a cauldron that's being shaken.'

'Smoke.' Corax stamped his foot on the dry earth, raising a cloud of dust. 'A brush fire can burn underground for days.'

'I know smoke. I know vapour. This was vapour.'

Attilius dropped to his knees and started digging with his bare hands, working his fingers under the rocks and tossing them aside. Something had emerged from here. He was sure of it. Why had the ivy come back to life so quickly if there was no spring?

He said, without turning round, 'Fetch the tools.'

THEY DUG ALL MORNING, as the sun climbed slowly above the blue furnace of the bay, melting from yellow disc to gaseous white star.

The crater they eventually excavated was twice as deep as a man's height, and broad enough for two of them to work in. And there was a spring there, right enough, but it retreated whenever they came close. They would dig. The rusty soil at the bottom of the hole would turn damp. And then it would bake dry again in the sunlight. They would excavate another layer and the same process would recur.

Only at the tenth hour, when the sun had passed its zenith, did Attilius at last acknowledge defeat. He collected his tools and set off without waiting for the others. They could find their own way back. When he reached the coastal path, Misenum appeared beneath him, shimmering in the haze of heat.

The headquarters of the western imperial fleet was a triumph of Man over Nature, for by rights no town should exist here. There was no river to support her, few wells or springs. Yet the Divine Augustus had decreed that the Empire needed a port from which to control the Mediterranean, and here she was, the embodiment of Roman power: the golden beaks and fantail sterns of fifty warships glinting in the sun, the dusty parade ground of the military school, the red-tiled roofs and the whitewashed walls of the civilian town rising above the shipyard. Ten thousand sailors and another ten thousand citizens were crammed into a narrow strip of land with no fresh water to speak of. Only the aqueduct had made Misenum possible.

Hora Undecima — 17:42 hours

At the Villa Hortensia, the great coastal residence on the northern outskirts of Misenum, they were preparing to put a slave to death. They were going to feed him to the eels.

It was not an unknown practice round the Bay of Neapolis. The new owner of the Villa Hortensia, the millionaire Numerius Popidius Ampliatus, had first heard the story as a boy—of how the Augustan aristocrat, Vedius Pollio, would hurl clumsy servants into his eel pond as a punishment for breaking dishes—and he would often refer to it admiringly as the perfect illustration of what it was to have power. Power, and imagination, and wit, and a certain *style*.

So when, years later, Ampliatus, too, came to possess a fishery—and when one of his slaves also destroyed something of value, the precedent naturally came to mind. Ampliatus had been born a slave himself; this was how he thought an aristocrat ought to behave.

The poor fellow was duly stripped to his loincloth, had his hands tied behind his back and was marched down to the sea. A knife was run down both his calves, to draw blood, and he was doused with vinegar, which was said to drive the eels mad.

The eels had their own pen, away from the other fishponds, reached by a concrete gangway. These eels were morays, notorious for their aggression, their bodies as long as a man's and as wide as a human trunk, with flat heads, wide snouts and razor teeth. The villa's fishery was 150 years old and nobody knew how many scores lurked in the labyrinth of tunnels at the bottom of the pond. The more ancient eels were monsters and several wore jewellery. One, which had a gold earring fitted to its pectoral fin, was said to have been a favourite of the Emperor Nero.

At the eleventh hour, Ampliatus himself promenaded down from the villa to watch, attended by his teenage son, Celsinus, together with his household steward, Scutarius, a few of his business clients, and a crowd of about 100 of his other male slaves who he had decided would profit by witnessing the spectacle. His wife and daughter he had ordered to remain indoors: this was not a sight for women. A large chair was set up for him, with smaller ones for his guests. He did not even know the errant slave's name. He had come as part of a job lot with the fishponds when Ampliatus had bought the villa earlier in the year.

All manner of fish were kept, at vast expense, along the shoreline of the house—sea bass; grey mullet, that required high walls around their pond to prevent them leaping to freedom; flatfish and parrot-fish and giltheads; lampreys and congers and hake.

But by far the most expensive of Ampliatus's aquatic treasures were the red mullet, the delicate and whiskered goatfish, notoriously difficult to keep, whose colours ran from pale pink to orange. And it was these that the slave had killed—whether by malice or incompetence, Ampliatus did not know or care, but there they were: a multi-hued carpet floating on the surface of their pond, discovered earlier that afternoon. Poisoned, every one.

The slave was screaming as they dragged and prodded him towards the edge of the pool. It was not his fault, he was shouting. It was not the food. It was the water. They should fetch the aquarius.

The piercing cries of the slave teetering on the side of the eel pond carried up from the seafront and into the silent house where the women were hiding.

Corelia Ampliata had run to her bedroom, thrown herself down on the mattress, and pulled her pillow over her head, but there was no escaping the sound. Unlike her father, she knew the slave's name—Hipponax, a Greek—and also the name of his mother, Atia, who worked in the kitchens, and whose lamentations, once they started, were even more terrible than his. Unable to bear the screams, she sprang up and ran through the deserted villa to find the wailing woman, who had sunk against a column in the cloistered garden.

Seeing Corelia, Atia clutched at her young mistress's hem and began weeping at her feet, repeating over and over that her son was innocent, that he had shouted to her as he was being carried away—it was the water, there was something wrong with the water.

Corelia stroked Atia's grey hair. There was little else she could do. Useless to appeal to her father for clemency—he listened to nobody, least of all to a woman, and least of all women to his daughter, from whom he expected unquestioning obedience—an intervention from her would only make the death of the slave doubly certain.

The old woman suddenly broke away. 'I must find help.'

'Atia, Atia,' said Corelia gently, 'who will give it?'

'He shouted for the aquarius. Didn't you hear? I shall fetch him.'

'And where is he?'

'Maybe at the aqueduct down the hill, where the watermen work.'

'I'll come with you,' Corelia said, and she gathered up her skirts with one hand, grabbed the old woman's wrist with the other and together they fled through the garden, past the empty porter's stool, out of the side door, and into the dazzling heat of the public road.

THE TERMINUS of the Aqua Augusta was a vast underground reservoir, a few hundred paces south of the Villa Hortensia, hewn into the slope overlooking the port and known, for as long as anyone could remember, as the Piscina Mirabilis—The Pool of Wonders.

Viewed from the outside, there was nothing particularly wonderful about her. She appeared on the surface as a low, flat-roofed building of red brick, festooned with pale green ivy, a city block long and half a block wide, surrounded by shops and storerooms, bars and apartments, hidden away in the dusty backstreets above the naval base.

Only at night, when the noise of traffic and shouts of tradesmen had fallen silent, was it possible to hear the subterranean thunder of falling water, and only if you went into the yard, unlocked the door and descended a few steps into the Piscina itself was it possible to appreciate the reservoir's full glory. The vaulted roof was supported by forty-eight pillars, each more than fifty feet high—though most of their length was submerged by the waters of the reservoir—and the echo of the aqueduct was enough to shake your bones.

Attilius's first thought on coming down from the hills and into the yard at the end of that afternoon was to check the level of the reservoir. But when he tried the door he found it was locked and then he remembered that Corax was carrying the key on his belt. He thought no more about it. He could hear the distant rumble of the Augusta—she was running: that was all that counted.

So he turned away from the reservoir and glanced around the deserted yard. The previous evening he had ordered that the space be tidied and swept while he was away, and he was pleased to see that this had been done.

He went into the stores, dropped his tools on the earth floor and re-entered the yard just as the others trooped in. They headed straight for the drinking fountain without bothering to acknowledge him, taking turns to gulp the water—Corax, then Musa, then Becco. The two slaves squatted patiently in the shade, waiting until the free men had finished. Attilius shouted to Corax that the men could finish work for the day, then started to climb the narrow wooden staircase to his living quarters.

The yard was a quadrangle. Its northern side was taken up by the wall of the Piscina Mirabilis. To the west and south were storerooms and the administrative offices of the aqueduct. To the east was the living accommodation: a barracks for the slaves on the ground floor, and an apartment for the aquarius above it. Corax and the other free men lived in the town with their families.

Attilius, who had left his mother and sister behind in Rome, thought that in due course he would move them down to Misenum as well and rent a house, which his mother could keep for him. But for the time being he was sleeping in the cramped bachelor accommodation of his predecessor, Exomnius, whose few possessions he had had moved into the small spare room at the end of the passage.

What had happened to Exomnius? Naturally, that had been Attilius's first question when he arrived in the port. But nobody had had an answer. It seemed that old Exomnius, a Sicilian who had run the Augusta for nearly twenty years, had simply walked out one morning more than two weeks ago and had not been heard of since.

Ordinarily, the department of the Curator Aquarum in Rome, which administered the aqueducts in regions one and two (Latium and Campania), would have been willing to let matters lie for a while. But given the drought, and the strategic importance of the Augusta, and the fact that the Senate had risen for its summer recess and half its members were at their holiday villas around the bay, it had been thought prudent to dispatch an immediate replacement.

Attilius had received the summons on the Ides of August, at dusk, just as he was finishing off some routine maintenance work on the Anio Novus. Conducted into the presence of the Curator Aquarum himself, Acilius Aviola, at his official residence on the Palatine Hill, he had been offered the commission. Attilius was bright, energetic, dedicated—the senator knew how to flatter a man when he wanted something—with no wife or children to detain him in Rome. Could he leave the next day? And, of course, Attilius had accepted at once, for this was a great opportunity to advance his career.

He sat on the edge of the hard wooden bed. His household slave, Phylo, had put out a jug of water and a basin, some fruit, a loaf, a pitcher of wine and a slice of hard white cheese. He washed, ate, mixed some wine into the water and drank. Then, too exhausted even to remove his shoes and tunic, he lay down on the mattress, closed his eyes and slipped at once into that hinterland between sleeping and waking which his dead wife endlessly roamed, her voice calling out to him—pleading, urgent: 'Aquarius! Aquarius!'

HIS WIFE HAD BEEN just twenty-two when he watched her body consigned to the flames of her funeral pyre. This woman was younger—eighteen, perhaps. Still, there was enough of the dream still lingering in his mind, and enough of Sabina about the girl in the yard for his heart to jump. The same darkness of hair. The same whiteness of skin. The same voluptuousness of figure.

She was standing beneath his window and shouting up. 'Aquarius!'

The sound of raised voices had drawn some of the men from the shadows and by the time he reached the bottom of the stairs they had formed a gawping half-circle around her. She was wearing a loose white tunica, open wide at the neck and sleeves—a dress to be worn in private, which showed a little more of the milky plumpness of her bare white arms and breasts than a respectable lady would have risked in public. He saw now that she was not alone. A slave attended her—a skinny, trembling, elderly woman.

She was gabbling something about a pool of red mullet that had died in her father's fish ponds, and poison in the water, and a man who was being fed to the eels, and how he must come at once.

He held up his hand to interrupt her and asked her name.

'I am Corelia Ampliata, daughter of Numerius Popidius Ampliatus.' At the mention of her father, Attilius noticed Corax and some of the men exchange looks. 'Are you the aquarius?'

Corax said, 'The aquarius isn't here.'

The engineer waved him away. 'I am in charge of the aqueduct.'

'Then come with me.' She began walking towards the gate. The men were starting to laugh at her. Musa did an impersonation of her swaying hips, tossing his head grandly: '"Oh, Aquarius, come with me!"'

'Corelia Ampliata,' said Attilius patiently, 'I believe red mullet to be sea-water fish. And I have no responsibility for the sea.'

'My father is putting a man to death. The slave was screaming for the aquarius. You are his only hope. Will you come or not?'

'Wait,' said Attilius. He nodded towards the older woman, who had her hands pressed to her face and was crying. 'Who is this?'

'She's his mother.'

The men were quiet now.

'Come,' she said quietly. 'Please. A few hundred paces. No distance at all.' She tugged at his arm, and he allowed himself to be pulled along. She was not an easy woman to resist. Perhaps he ought at least to walk her back to her family? It was hardly safe for a woman of her age and class to be out in the streets of a naval town.

IT WAS THE TIME of day, an hour or so before dusk, when the people of Misenum began emerging from their houses. Not that the town had lost much of its heat. The stones were like bricks from a kiln. Old women sat on stools beside their porches, fanning themselves, while the men stood at the bars, drinking and talking.

Corelia was mounting steps quickly, skirts gathered in either hand, the slave woman running ahead. Attilius loped behind.

'"A few hundred paces,"' he muttered to himself. '"No distance at all"—yes, but every foot of the way uphill!' His tunic was glued to his back by his sweat.

They came at last to level ground. Before them was a long high wall, dun-coloured, with an arched gate set into it, surmounted by two wrought-iron dolphins leaping to exchange a kiss. The women hurried through the unguarded entrance, and Attilius followed—plunging from noisy, dusty reality into a silent world of blue that knocked away his breath. Turquoise, lapis lazuli, indigo, sapphire—every jewelled blue that Mother Nature had ever bestowed—rose in layers before him, from crystal shallows, to deep water, to sharp horizon, to sky. The villa sprawled below on a series of terraces, its back to the hillside, its face to the bay, built for this sublime panorama. Moored to a jetty was a twenty-oared luxury cruiser, painted crimson and gold.

Corelia led him down, past statues, fountains, watered lawns, across a mosaic floor inlaid with a design of sea creatures and out onto a terrace with a swimming pool, also blue, projecting towards the sea. He was struck by how deserted the great house seemed and when Corelia gestured to the balustrade, and he laid his hands cautiously on the stone parapet and leaned over, he saw why. Most of the household was gathered along the seashore.

It took a while for his mind to assemble all the elements of the scene. The setting was a fishery, a series of concrete walls enclosing rectangular pools. Dead fish dappled the surface of one. Around the most distant, a group of men was staring at something in the water, an object that one of them was prodding with a boat hook.

Behind him, the old woman started making a noise—a soft ululation of grief and despair. He took a step backwards and turned towards Corelia, shaking his head. He wanted to escape from this place. There was nothing he could do.

But she was in his way, standing very close. 'Please. Help her.'

Her eyes were even bluer than Sabina's had been. They seemed to collect the blueness of the bay and fire it back at him. He hesitated, set his jaw, then turned and reluctantly looked to sea again.

He forced his gaze to skirt what was happening at the pool, let it travel back towards the shore, tried to appraise the whole thing with a professional eye. He saw wooden sluice gates. Metal lattices over some of the ponds to keep the fish from escaping. Gangways. Pipes.

He cocked his head, beginning to understand—the pipes must

carry fresh water down from the land, to mix with the sea water, to make it brackish. As in a lagoon. An artificial lagoon. The perfect conditions for rearing fish. And the most sensitive of fish to rear, a delicacy reserved only for the very rich, were red mullet.

He said quietly, 'Where does the aqueduct connect to the house?'

Corelia shook her head. 'I don't know.'

It would have to be big, he thought. A place this size . . .

He knelt beside the swimming pool, scooped up a palmful of the warm water, swilled it round in his mouth. It was clean, as far as he could judge. But then again, that might mean nothing. He tried to remember when he had last checked the outflow of the aqueduct. Not since the previous evening, before he went to bed.

'At what time did the fish die?'

Corelia glanced at the slave woman, but she was lost to their world. 'I don't know. Perhaps two hours ago?'

Two hours! He vaulted over the balustrade onto the lower terrace beneath and started to stride towards the shore.

DOWN AT THE WATER'S EDGE, the entertainment had not lived up to its promise. But then nowadays, what did? Ampliatus felt increasingly that he had reached some point—age, was it, or wealth?—when the arousal of anticipation was invariably more exquisite than the emptiness of relief. The voice of the victim cries out, the blood spurts and then—what? Just another death.

Ampliatus took off his straw hat, fanned his face, looked around at his son. Celsinus at first appeared to be staring straight ahead, but when you looked again you saw his eyes were closed, which was typical of the boy. He always seemed to be doing what you wanted. But then you realised he was only obeying mechanically, with his body: his attention was elsewhere.

What was in his mind? Some Eastern rubbish, presumably. When the boy was six—twelve years ago—Ampliatus had built a temple in Pompeii, dedicated to the cult of Isis. He had presented the building in Celsinus's name, with the aim of getting the boy onto Pompeii's ruling council. And it had worked. What he had not anticipated was that Celsinus would take it seriously. That was what he would be brooding about now, no doubt—about Osiris, the Sun god, husband to Isis, who is slain each evening by his treacherous brother, Set, the bringer of darkness. And how men, when they die, are judged by the Ruler of the Kingdom of the Dead, and if found worthy are granted eternal life. Did Celsinus really believe all this twaddle?

Ampliatus was distracted by a shout from behind him. There was a stir among the assembled slaves and Ampliatus shifted round in his chair. A man whom he did not recognise was striding down the steps from the villa waving his arm above his head and calling out.

THE PRINCIPLES OF ENGINEERING were simple, universal, impersonal—in Rome, in Gaul, in Campania—which was what Attilius liked about them. Even as he ran, he was envisaging what he could not see. The main line of the aqueduct would be up in that hill at the back of the villa, buried a yard beneath the surface, running down to the Piscina Mirabilis. Whoever had owned the villa when the Aqua Augusta was built, more than a century ago, would almost certainly have run two spurs off it. One to a big cistern to feed the house, the swimming pool, the garden fountains; if there was contamination on the matrix, it might take a day or more for that to make its presence felt, depending on the size of the tank. But the other spur would channel a share of the Augusta's water directly down to the fishery. Any problem with the aqueduct and the impact there would be immediate.

Ahead of him, the tableau of the kill was beginning to assume an equally clear shape: the master of the household—Ampliatus, presumably—rising from his chair, the spectators now with their backs to the pool, all eyes on him as he sprinted down the final flight of steps. He ran onto the concrete ramp of the fishery.

'Pull him out!' he said as he ran past Ampliatus.

Ampliatus, his thin face livid, shouted something at his back and Attilius turned, still running, trotting backwards now, holding up his palms: 'Please. Just pull him out.'

Ampliatus's mouth gaped open, but then, still staring intently at Attilius, he slowly raised his hand, setting off a chain of activity. The steward of the household put two fingers to his mouth and whistled at the slave with the boat hook, and made an upwards motion with his hand, at which the slave hooked something and began to drag it in.

Attilius was almost at the pipes. They were terracotta. A pair. More than a foot each in diameter. They emerged from the slope, traversed the ramp together, then parted company at the edge of the water, running in opposite directions along the side of the fishery. A crude inspection plate was set into each of them—a loose piece of pipe, two feet long, cut crossways.

Attilius knelt and lifted the cover away. His face was over the running water and he smelt it at once. Released from the confined space of the pipe, it was strong enough to make him want to retch. An unmistakable smell of rotten eggs. The breath of Hades. Sulphur.

THE SLAVE WAS DEAD. Attilius, crouching beside the open pipe, saw the remains hauled out of the eel pond and covered with a sack. He saw the audience disperse and begin traipsing back up to the villa, at the same time as the grey-headed slave woman threaded her way between them, down towards the sea. As she reached the dead man she flung up her hands to the sky and began rocking silently from side to side. Ampliatus did not notice her. He was walking purposefully towards Attilius. Corelia was behind him and a young man who looked just like her—her brother, presumably—and a few others. A couple of the men had knives at their belts.

He returned his attention to the water. Was it his imagination or was the pressure slackening? The smell was certainly much less obvious, now that the surface was open to the air. He plunged his hands into the flow, frowning, trying to gauge the strength of it.

A voice said, 'You are on my property.'

Attilius looked up to find Ampliatus staring down at him. He was in his middle fifties. Short, but broad-shouldered and powerful.

'Your property, yes. But the Emperor's water.' He stood. The waste of so much precious liquid, in the middle of a drought, to pamper a rich man's fish, made him angry. 'You need to close the sluices to the aqueduct. There's sulphur in the matrix and red mullet abominate all impurities. *That*'—he emphasised the word—'is what killed your precious fish.'

Ampliatus tilted his head back slightly, sniffing the insult. He had a fine, rather handsome face. His eyes were the same shade of blue as his daughter's. 'And who are you?'

'Attilius. Aquarius of the Aqua Augusta.'

The millionaire frowned. 'What happened to Exomnius?'

'I wish I knew. I have to get back to town. We have an emergency on the aqueduct.'

He made to go, but Ampliatus moved to one side, blocking his way. 'You insult me,' he said. 'On my property. In front of my family. And now you try to leave without offering an apology?' He brought his face close to Attilius's. 'Who gave you permission to come here?'

'If I have in any way offended you—' began Attilius. But then he remembered the wretched bundle in its shroud of sacking and the apology choked in his throat. 'Get out of my way.'

He tried to push his way past, but Ampliatus grabbed his arm and someone drew a knife.

'He came because of me, Father. I invited him.'

'What?'

Ampliatus wheeled round on Corelia. What he might have done, whether he would have struck her, Attilius would never know, for at that instant a terrible screaming started. Advancing along the ramp came the grey-headed woman. She had smeared her face, her arms, her dress with her son's blood and her hand was pointing straight ahead, the first and last of her bony brown fingers rigidly extended. She was shouting in a language Attilius did not understand, although in truth he did not need to, for a curse is a curse in any tongue, and this one was directed straight at Ampliatus.

He let go of Attilius's arm and turned to face her, absorbing the full force of it, with an expression of indifference. And then, as the torrent of words began to slacken, he laughed. There was silence for a moment, then the others began to laugh as well. Attilius glanced at Corelia, who gave an almost imperceptible nod and gestured with her eyes to the villa—*I shall be all right*, she seemed to be saying, *go*—and that was the last that he saw or heard, as he turned his back on the scene and started mounting the path up to the house.

Hora Duodecima — 18:48 hours

Attilius carried one faint hope: that somehow the sulphur was confined to the Villa Hortensia; that the leak was in the pipework beneath the house; and that Ampliatus's property was merely an isolated pocket of foulness on the beautiful curve of the bay.

That hope lasted for as long as it took him to sprint down the hill to the Piscina Mirabilis, to roust Corax from the barracks where he was playing a game of bones with Musa and Becco, to explain what had happened and to wait impatiently while the overseer unlocked the door to the reservoir—at which moment it evaporated completely, wafted away by the rank smell of sulphur.

'Dog's breath!' Corax blew out his cheeks in disgust.

Attilius descended a couple of steps, the back of his hand pressed to his nose. Beyond the pillars, he could hear the aqueduct disgorging into the reservoir, but with nothing like its normal percussive force. As he had suspected at the fishery, the pressure was dropping.

He called up to the Greek slave, Polites, who was waiting at the top of the steps, that he wanted a few things fetched—a torch, a plan of the aqueduct's main line and one of the stoppered bottles from the storeroom, which they used for taking water samples. Polites trotted off obediently and Attilius peered into the gloom.

'How long have you worked on the Augusta, Corax?'

'Twenty years.'

'Anything like this ever happened before?'

'Never. You've brought us all bad luck.'

Keeping one hand on the wall, Attilius made his way cautiously down the remaining steps to the reservoir's edge. The smell, together with the melancholy light of the day's last hour, made him feel as if he were descending into hell. There was even a rowing boat moored at his feet: a suitable ferry to carry him across the Styx.

Polites appeared in the doorway, holding a taper and a torch. He ran down and handed them to Attilius, who touched the glowing tip to the mass of tow and pitch. It ignited with a *wumph* and a gust of oily heat. Their shadows danced on the concrete walls.

Attilius stepped into the boat, holding the torch aloft, then turned to collect the rolled-up plans and the glass bottle. The boat was light and shallow-bottomed, used for maintenance work in the reservoir, and when Corax climbed aboard it dipped low into the water.

'If Exomnius was here, what would he do?'

'I don't know. But I tell you one thing. He knew this water better than any man alive. He would have seen this coming.'

'Perhaps he did, and that was why he ran away.'

'Exomnius was no coward. He didn't run anywhere.'

'Then where is he, Corax?'

'I've told you, pretty boy, I don't know.'

The overseer leaned across, untied the rope from its mooring ring and pushed them away from the steps, then turned to sit facing Attilius and took up the oars. His face in the torchlight was swarthy, guileful, older than his forty years. He had a wife and a brood of children crammed into an apartment across the street from the reservoir. Attilius wondered why Corax hated him so much. Was it simply that he had coveted the post of aquarius for himself and resented the arrival of a younger man from Rome? Or was there something more?

He told Corax to row them towards the centre of the reservoir, and when they reached it he handed him the torch, uncorked one of the bottles and rolled up the sleeves of his tunic. How often had he seen his father do this, in the reservoir of the Claudia and the Anio Novus on the Esquiline Hill? The old man had shown him how each of the matrices had its own flavour, as distinct from one another as different vintages of wine. A good aquarius, his father had said, should know more than just the solid laws of architecture and hydraulics—he should have a taste, a nose, a feel for water, and for the rocks and soils through which it had passed on its journey to the surface. Lives might depend on this skill.

An image of his father flashed into his mind. Killed before he was fifty by the lead he had worked with all his life, leaving Attilius as head of the family.

Attilius stretched over the side and plunged the bottle in as far as he could stretch, then slowly turned it under water, letting the air escape in a stream of bubbles. He recorked it and withdrew it.

Settled back in the boat, he opened the bottle again and passed it back and forth beneath his nose. He took a mouthful, gargled and swallowed. It had a bitter flavour, but it was drinkable, just. He passed it to Corax who swapped it for the torch and gulped the whole lot down. 'It'll do,' he said, 'if you mix it with enough wine.'

The boat bumped against a pillar and Attilius noticed the widening line between the dry and damp concrete—sharply defined, already a foot above the surface of the reservoir.

She was draining away faster than the Augusta could fill her.

'What's the capacity of the Piscina?'

'Two hundred and eighty quinariae.'

He raised the torch towards the roof, which disappeared into the shadows about fifteen feet above them. So that meant the water was perhaps thirty-five feet deep, the reservoir two-thirds full. Suppose it held 200 quinariae. At Rome, they worked on the basis that one quinaria was roughly the daily requirement for 200 people. The naval garrison at Misenum was 10,000 strong, plus, say, another ten thousand civilians. A simple calculation.

They had water for two days. Assuming they could ration the flow to perhaps an hour at dawn and another at dusk.

Attilius glanced towards the northern end of the reservoir, where the Augusta emerged. 'We should check the pressure.'

Corax began to row with powerful strokes, steering them expertly around the labyrinth of pillars, towards the falling water. Attilius held the torch in one hand and with the other he unrolled the plans.

The whole of the western end of the bay, from Neapolis to Cumae, was sulphurous, he knew that much. Green translucent lumps of sulphur were dug from the mines in the Leucogaei Hills, two miles north of the aqueduct's main line. Then there were the hot sulphur springs around Baiae, to which convalescents came from across the Empire. It must be somewhere in this smouldering region that the Augusta had become polluted.

They had reached the aqueduct's tunnel. Attilius laid aside the plans and raised the torch. It lit the giant head of Neptune, carved in stone, from whose mouth the Augusta normally gushed in a jet-black torrent. But even in the time it had taken to row from the steps the flow had dwindled. By now it was scarcely more than a trickle.

Corax gave a soft whistle. 'I never thought I'd live to see the Augusta dry. You were right to be worried, pretty boy.'

It was not possible, the engineer thought. Aqueducts did not just fail—not like this, not in a matter of hours. The matrices were walled with brick, rendered with waterproof cement, and surrounded by a concrete casing a foot and a half thick. The usual problems—structural flaws, leaks, lime deposits that narrowed the channel—all these needed months to develop. It had taken the Claudia a full decade gradually to close down.

He was interrupted by a shout from the slave, Polites. 'Aquarius!'

He half turned his head. 'What is it?'

'There's a rider in the yard, Aquarius! He has a message that the aqueduct has failed!'

Attilius reached for the plans again. 'Where has he come from?'

He expected the slave to shout back Baiae or Cumae. Puteoli at the very worst. Neapolis would be a disaster.

But the reply was like a punch in the stomach. 'Nola!'

THE MESSENGER was so rimed with dust he looked more ghost than man. And even as he told his story—of how the water had failed in Nola's reservoir at dawn and of how the failure had been preceded by a sharp smell of sulphur that had started in the middle of the night—a fresh sound of hoofs was heard in the road outside and a second horse trotted into the yard.

The rider offered Attilius a rolled papyrus. A message from the city fathers at Neapolis. The Augusta had gone down there at noon.

Attilius read it carefully, managing to keep his face expressionless. There was quite a crowd in the yard by now. Two horses, a pair of riders, surrounded by the gang of aqueduct workers who had abandoned their evening meal to listen to what was going on. The commotion was beginning to attract the attention of passers-by in the street, as well as some of the local shopkeepers. 'Hey, Waterman!' shouted the owner of the snack bar opposite. 'What's going on?'

It would not take much, thought Attilius, for panic to take hold like a hillside fire. He called to a couple of slaves to close the gates to the yard and told Polites to see that the messengers were given food and drink. 'Musa, Becco—get a cart and start loading it. Quicklime, puteolanum, tools—everything we might need to repair the matrix. As much as a couple of oxen can pull.'

He strode towards the aqueduct's office. He ducked through the low entrance into the small cubicle. Exomnius had left the Augusta's records in chaos. Bills of sale, letters, engineers' reports and storeroom inventories, orders from the naval commander in Misenum—some of them twenty or thirty years old—spilled out of chests, across a table and over the concrete floor. Attilius swept the table clear with his forearm and unrolled the plans.

Nola. How was this possible? Nola was thirty miles to the east of Misenum, and nowhere near the sulphur fields. With a cart and oxen it would take them the best part of two days merely to reach it. If Nola had gone down at dawn, then Acerrae and Atella would have followed in the middle of the morning. If Neapolis, twelve miles round the coast from Misenum, had lost its supply at noon, then Puteoli's must have gone at the eighth hour, Cumae's at the ninth, Baiae's at the tenth. And now, at last, at the twelfth, it was their turn.

Eight towns, with only Pompeii unaccounted for. More than 200,000 people without water.

He was aware of the entrance behind him darkening, of Corax coming up and leaning against the door frame, watching him.

He rolled up the map and tucked it under his arm. 'Give me the key to the sluices. I'm going to shut off the reservoir.'

'But that's the Navy's water. You can't do that. Not without the authority of the admiral.'

'Then why don't you get the authority of the admiral? The Piscina Mirabilis is a strategic reserve. It's there to be shut off in an emergency. Now give me the key, or you'll answer for it in Rome.'

'Have it your way, pretty boy.' Corax removed the key from the ring on his belt. 'I'll go and see the admiral all right. I'll tell him what's been going on. And then we'll see who answers for what.'

Attilius grabbed the key and edged sideways past him, out into the yard. He shouted to the nearest slave, 'Close the gates after me. No one is to be let in without my permission.'

'Yes, Aquarius.'

In the street, he turned left, then left again and down a steep flight of steps. The building that housed the sluice gate was a small red-brick cube, barely taller than a man. He turned the key in the lock and tugged at the heavy wooden door.

He was level now with the floor of the Piscina Mirabilis. Water from the reservoir poured down a tunnel in the wall, through a bronze grille, swirled in the open conduit at his feet, and then was channelled into three pipes that fanned out and disappeared under the flagstones behind him, carrying the supply down to Misenum. The flow was controlled by a sluice gate worked by a wooden handle and attached to an iron wheel. It was stiff from lack of use, but when he put his back into it, it began to turn. The gate descended, gradually choking off the flow of water until it ceased altogether.

He had done it now, he thought. Deprived the Navy of its water, without authority, three days into his first command. Men had been sent to the treadmills for less; he had been a fool to let Corax be the first to get to the admiral. Even now the overseer would be making sure who got the blame. Locking the door to the sluice chamber, he headed down a narrow alley towards the harbour.

THE ADMIRAL'S VILLA was on the far side of Misenum, and to reach it the engineer had to travel the best part of half a mile—across the narrow causeway and over the revolving wooden bridge that separated the two natural harbours of the naval base.

He had been warned about the admiral before he left Rome. 'The commander in chief is Gaius Plinius,' said the Curator Aquarum. 'Pliny. You'll come across him sooner or later. He thinks he knows everything about everything. You should take a look at his latest book. The *Natural History*. Every known fact about Mother Nature in thirty-seven volumes.'

There was a copy in the public library at the Porticus of Octavia. The engineer had time to read no further than the table of contents.

The world, its shape, its motion. Eclipses, Thunderbolts. Music from the stars. Sky portents. Sky-beams, sky-yawning, colours of the sky,

sky-flames, sky-wreaths, sudden rings. Showers of stones . . .

There were other books by Pliny in the library. Six volumes on oratory. Eight on grammar. Twenty on the war in Germany, in which he had commanded a cavalry unit. Attilius wondered how he managed to write so much and rise so high in the imperial administration at the same time.

The sky was red with the setting sun and to his left, in the outer harbour, a passenger ferry was approaching through the golden glow, her sails furled, a dozen oars on either side dipping slowly in unison as she steered between the anchored triremes of the imperial fleet. She was too late to be the nightly arrival from Ostia, which meant she was probably a local service. The weight of the passengers crammed on her open deck was pressing her low to the surface.

He was moving more quickly than the water pipes were emptying and when he passed through the triumphal arch that marked the entrance to the port he could see that the big public fountain at the crossroads was still flowing. Around it was grouped the usual twilight crowd—sailors dousing their befuddled heads, ragged children shrieking and splashing, a line of women and slaves with earthenware pots, waiting to collect their water for the night.

The overloaded ferry had come alongside the quay, and the passengers were scrambling ashore. Attilius called across the street to ask one of the men where was the ferry from, and he shouted back, 'Neapolis, my friend—and before that, Pompeii.'

Pompeii. Attilius checked his stride. Odd, he thought, that they had heard no word from Pompeii, the first town on the matrix. He stepped into the path of the oncoming crowd. 'Any of you from Pompeii? Was anyone in Pompeii this morning?' But nobody took any notice. They were thirsty after the voyage—and, of course they would be, he realised, if they had come from Neapolis, where the water had failed at noon—and most of them passed to either side of him in their eagerness to reach the fountain, all except for one, an elderly holy man, with the conical cap and curved staff of an augur.

'I was in Pompeii this morning,' he said. 'Why? Is there something I can do to help you, my son? I am practised in the interpretation of all the usual phenomena—thunderbolts, entrails, bird omens, unnatural manifestations. My rates are reasonable.'

'May I ask, holy father,' said the engineer, 'when you left Pompeii?'

'At first light.'

'And were the fountains playing? Was there water?'

'Yes, there was water. But when I arrived in Neapolis the streets were dry and in the baths I smelled sulphur. That is why I decided to return to the ferry and come on here. Sulphur is a terrible omen.'

'True enough,' agreed Attilius. 'But are you certain? And are you sure the water was running?'

'Yes, my son. I'm sure.'

There was a commotion around the fountain and both men turned to look. It was nothing much to start with, just some pushing and shoving, but quickly punches were being thrown. The crowd seemed to contract, to rush in on itself and become denser. Wriggling between the backs at the edge of the mob, a man in a Greek tunic emerged, clutching a waterskin tightly to his chest. Blood was pouring from a gash in his temple. He disappeared into an alleyway.

And so it starts, thought the engineer. First this fountain, and then the others all around the port, and then the big basin in the forum. And then the public baths, and then the villas—nothing emerging from the empty pipes except the whistle of rushing air . . .

Vespera — 20:07 hours

The admiral's official residence was set high on the hillside overlooking the harbour. It was dusk by the time Attilius reached it and all around the bay, in the seaside villas, torches, oil lamps and braziers were being lit, so that gradually a broken thread of yellow light had begun to emerge, wavering for mile after mile, picking out the curve of the coast, before vanishing in the haze towards Capri.

A marine centurian was hurrying away as the engineer arrived on the terrace and the remains of a large meal were being cleared from a stone table beneath a trellised pergola. The instant the slave announced him—'Marcus Attilius Primus, aquarius of the Aqua Augusta!'—a stocky man in his middle fifties at the far end of the terrace turned and came waddling towards him, trailed by what he assumed were the guests of his abandoned dinner party: four men in togas, at least one of whom, judging by the purple stripe on his formal dress, was a senator. Behind them came Corax.

Attilius had for some reason imagined that the famous scholar would be thin, but Pliny was fat, his belly protruding sharply. He was dabbing at his forehead with his napkin.

'Shall I arrest you now, Aquarius? I could, you know.' He had a fat man's voice: a high-pitched wheeze, which became hoarser as he counted off the charges on his pudgy fingers. 'Incompetence to start with—who can doubt that? Negligence—where were you when the sulphur infected the water? Insubordination—on what authority did you shut off our supply? Treason—yes, I could make a charge of treason stick. What about fomenting rebellion in the imperial dockyards? I've had to order out a century of marines—fifty to break some heads in the town and restore public order, the other fifty to the reservoir, to guard whatever water's left—'

He broke off, short of breath. With his puffed-out cheeks, pursed lips and sparse grey curls plastered down with sweat, he had the appearance of an elderly, furious cherub, fallen from some painted ceiling. The youngest of his guests—a pimply lad in his late teens—stepped forward to support his arm, but Pliny shrugged him away.

At the back of the group Corax grinned. He had been even more effective at spreading poison than Attilius had expected.

Attilius noticed that a star had come out above Vesuvius. He had never really looked properly at the mountain before, certainly not from this angle. The sky was dark but the mountain was darker, rising massively above the bay to a pointed summit. And there was the source of the trouble, he thought. Somewhere on the mountain.

'Who are you anyway?' Pliny eventually managed to rasp out. 'I don't know you. What's happened to the proper aquarius? Well? Speak up! What have you to say for yourself?'

Attilius straightened his back. 'I need,' he said, 'to borrow a ship.'

HE SPREAD out his map on the table in Pliny's library, weighing down either side with a couple of pieces of magnetite that he took from a display cabinet. An elderly slave shuffled behind the admiral's back, lighting an elaborate bronze candelabrum.

The admiral nodded at the engineer. 'All right. Let's hear it.'

Attilius glanced around at the faces of his audience, intent in the candlelight. He had been told their names before they sat down: Pedius Cascus, a senior senator who had been a consul years ago and who owned a big villa along the coast at Herculaneum; Pomponianus, an old army comrade of Pliny's, rowed over for dinner from his villa at Stabiae; and Antius, captain of the imperial flagship, the *Victoria*. The pimply youth was Pliny's nephew, Gaius Caecilius.

He put his finger on the map and they all leaned forwards, even

Corax. 'This is where I thought originally that the break must be, Admiral—here, in the burning fields around Cumae. That would explain the sulphur. But then we learned that the supply had gone down in Nola as well—over here, to the east. That was at dawn. The timing is crucial, because according to a witness who was in Pompeii at first light, the fountains there were still running this morning. As you can see, Pompeii is some distance back up the matrix from Nola, so logically the Augusta should have failed there in the middle of the night. The fact that it didn't can only mean one thing. The break has to be here'—he circled the spot—'somewhere here, on this five-mile stretch, where she runs close to Vesuvius.'

Pliny frowned at the map. 'And the ship? Where does that come in?'

'I believe we have two days' worth of water left. If we set off overland from Misenum to discover what's happened it will take us at least that long simply to find where the break has occurred. But if we go by sea to Pompeii—if we travel light and pick up most of what we need in the town—we should be able to start repairs tomorrow.'

Pliny said, 'How many men do you have?'

'Fifty altogether, but most of those are spread out along the length of the matrix, maintaining the settling tanks and the reservoirs in the towns. I have a dozen altogether in Misenum. I'd take half of those with me. Any other labour we need, I'd hire locally in Pompeii.'

'We could let him have a liburnian, Admiral,' said Antius. 'If he left at first light he could be in Pompeii by the middle of the morning.'

Corax seemed to be panicked by the mere suggestion. 'But with respect, this is just more of his moonshine, Admiral. For a start, I'd like to know how he's so sure the water's still running in Pompeii.'

'I met a man on the quayside, Admiral, on my way here. The local ferry had just docked. He told me he was in Pompeii this morning.'

'All right,' said Corax. 'Let's say this is where the break is. This part of the matrix is five miles long and every foot is underground. It will take us more than a day just to find out where she's gone down.'

'That's not true,' objected Attilius. 'With that much water escaping from the matrix, a blind man could find the break.'

'With that much water backed up in the tunnel, how do we get inside it to make the repairs?'

'Listen,' said the engineer. 'When we get to Pompeii, we split into three groups. The first group goes out to the Augusta—follows the spur from Pompeii to its junction with the matrix and then works westwards. I can assure you, finding where the break is will not be a great problem. The second group stays in Pompeii and puts together enough men and materials to carry out the repairs. A third group rides into the mountains, to the springs at Abellinum, with instructions to shut off the Augusta.'

The senator looked up. 'Can that be done? In Rome, when an aqueduct has to be closed for repairs, it stays shut down for weeks.'

'According to the drawings, Senator, yes—it can be done. I have never seen the springs of the Serinus myself, but it appears from this plan that they flow into a basin with two channels. Most of the water comes west, to us. But a smaller channel runs north, to feed Beneventum. If we send all the water north, and let the western channel drain off, we can get inside to repair it. The point is, we don't have to dam it and build a temporary diversion, which is what we have to do with the aqueducts of Rome, before we can even start on the maintenance. We can work much more quickly.'

The senator transferred his eyes to Corax. 'Is this true, Overseer?'

'Maybe,' conceded Corax grudgingly. 'However, I still maintain he's talking moonshine, Admiral, if he thinks we can get all this done in a day or two. I know this stretch. We had problems here nearly twenty years ago, at the time of the great earthquake. Exomnius was the aquarius, new in the job, and we worked on it together. All right—it didn't block the matrix completely, I grant you that—but it still took us weeks to render all the cracks in the tunnel.'

'What great earthquake?' Attilius had never heard mention of it.

'Actually, it was seventeen years ago,' Pliny's nephew piped up. 'Seneca describes the incident. You must have read it, Uncle?'

'Yes, Gaius, thank you,' said the admiral. He stared at the map. 'I wonder—' he muttered. He shouted at the slave. 'Dromo! Bring me my glass of wine.' He returned his attention to the map. 'So is this what has damaged the Augusta? An earthquake?'

'Then surely we would have felt it?' objected Antius. 'That last quake brought down a good part of Pompeii. They're still rebuilding. We've had no reports of anything on that scale.'

The slave had shuffled up beside Pliny, carrying a tray, in the centre of which stood a large goblet of clear glass, three-quarters full.

Pliny set the glass carefully on the table. 'Watch.'

As the engineer studied the glass he saw that the surface of the wine was vibrating slightly. Tiny ripples radiated out from the centre, like the quivering of a plucked string. Pliny picked up the glass and the movement ceased; he replaced it and the motion resumed.

'I noticed it during dinner. The shaking is not continuous. See now—the wine is still.'

'Why does it stop and start?' asked the senator.

'I have no answer, Cascus. Aquarius—what do you think?'

'I'm an engineer, Admiral,' said Attilius tactfully, 'not a philosopher.' In his view, they were wasting time. 'All I can tell you is that the matrix of an aqueduct is built to withstand extreme forces. Where the Augusta runs underground, which is most of the way, she's six feet high and three feet wide, and she rests on a base of concrete one and a half feet thick, with walls of the same dimensions. Whatever force breached that must have been powerful.'

Pliny sat back in his chair. 'Very well, Aquarius. I shall give you your ship.' He turned to the captain. 'Antius—which is the fastest liburnian in the fleet?'

'That would be the *Minerva*, Admiral. Torquatus's ship.'

'Have her made ready to sail at first light.'

'Yes, Admiral.'

'And I want notices posted on every fountain telling the citizens that rationing is now in force. Water will only be allowed to flow twice each day, for one hour exactly, at dawn and dusk.'

Antius winced. 'Aren't you forgetting that tomorrow is a public holiday, Admiral? It's Vulcanalia, if you recall?'

'I'm perfectly aware it's Vulcanalia. Gaius—draft a letter for me to sign to the aediles of Pompeii, asking them to provide whatever men and materials may be necessary for the repair of the aqueduct. Corax—it's clear that you know the terrain around Vesuvius better than anyone else. You should be the one to ride out and locate the fault, while the aquarius assembles the main expedition in Pompeii.'

The overseer's mouth flapped open in dismay.

'What's the matter? Do you disagree?'

'No, Admiral.' Corax hid his anxiety quickly. 'I don't mind looking for the break. But would it not make more sense for one of us to remain at the reservoir to supervise the rationing—'

Pliny cut him off impatiently. 'Rationing will be the Navy's responsibility. It's primarily a question of public order.'

For a moment Corax looked as if he might be on the point of arguing, but then he bowed his head, frowning.

He doesn't want me to go to Pompeii, thought Attilius. This whole performance tonight has been to keep me away from Pompeii.

A woman's coiffeured head appeared at the doorway. She must

have been about sixty. The pearls at her throat were the largest Attilius had ever seen. She crooked her finger at the senator. 'Cascus, darling, how much longer are you planning to keep us waiting?'

'Forgive us, Rectina,' said Pliny. 'We've almost finished. Does anyone have anything else to add?' He glanced at each of them in turn. 'No? In that case, I for one propose to finish my dinner.'

Nocte Intempesta — 23:22 hours

Two hours later—sleepless, naked, stretched out on his narrow wooden bed—the engineer lay waiting for the dawn. First the aquarius disappears and then the water. The more he considered it, the more convinced he was that these must be connected.

He swung his bare feet onto the warm floor. He picked up the oil lamp that flickered on the nightstand and went out into the passage, shielding the flame with his hand. Drawing back the curtain opposite, he shone the light into the cubicle where Exomnius's possessions were stored. A couple of wooden chests, a pair of bronze candelabra, a cloak, sandals, a pisspot. It was not much to show for a lifetime. Neither of the chests was locked, he noticed.

Still holding the lamp, he lifted the lid of the nearest chest and began to rummage through it with his free hand. Clothes—old clothes mostly—two tunics, loincloths, a toga, neatly folded. He closed the lid and raised the other. Not much in this chest, either. A clay beaker for throwing dice. The dice themselves. A few glass jars containing various herbs and unguents. A couple of plates. A small bronze goblet, badly tarnished.

He picked up the goblet. Was it really bronze? Now he examined it more closely, he was not so sure. He weighed it in his hand, turned it over, breathed on it and rubbed the bottom with his thumb. A smear of gold appeared and part of an engraved letter *P*. He rubbed again until he could make out all the initials. *N. P. N. l. A.*

The *l* stood for *libertus* and showed it to be the property of a freed slave. A slave who had been freed by an owner whose family name began with a P.

Her voice was suddenly as clear in his mind as if she had been standing beside him. *'My name is Corelia Ampliata, daughter of Numerius Popidius Ampliatus . . .'*

THE MOONLIGHT SHONE on the smooth stones of the narrow street and silhouetted the lines of the flat roofs. It seemed almost as hot as it had been in the late afternoon; the moon as bright as the sun. As he mounted the steps between the shuttered, silent houses, he could picture her darting before him—the movement of her hips beneath the plain white dress.

He came to the level ground and the high wall of the great villa. The glinting metal dolphins leapt and kissed above the chained gate. He rattled the iron bars and pressed his face to the warm metal. The porter's room was shuttered and barred. There was not a light to be seen.

He was remembering Ampliatus's reaction when he turned up on the seashore: '*What happened to Exomnius?*' There had been surprise in his voice and, now he came to think about it, possibly something more: alarm.

'Corelia!' He called her name softly. 'Corelia Ampliata!'

No response. And then a whisper in the darkness, so low he almost missed it: 'Gone.'

A woman's voice. It came from somewhere to his left. He stepped back from the gate and peered into the shadows. He could make out nothing except a small mound of rags piled in a drift against the wall. He moved closer and saw that the shreds of cloth were moving slightly. A skinny foot protruded. It was the mother of the dead slave. He went down on one knee and cautiously touched the rough fabric of her dress. She shivered, then groaned and muttered something. He withdrew his hand. His fingers were sticky with blood.

He lifted her carefully until she was sitting, propped against the wall. Her swollen head dropped forwards and he saw that her matted hair had left a damp mark on the stone. She had been whipped and badly beaten, and thrown out of the household to die.

N. P. N. l. A: Numerius Popidius Numerii libertus Ampliatus. Granted his freedom by the family Popidii. It was a fact of life that there was no crueller master than an ex-slave.

He threaded one arm under the crook of her knees and with the other he grasped her round her shoulders. It cost him no effort to rise. She was mere rags and bones. Somewhere, in the streets close to the harbour, the night watchman was calling the fifth division of the darkness: 'Media noctis inclinatio'—midnight.

The engineer straightened his back and set off down the hill as the day of Mars turned into the day of Mercury.

MERCURY

August 23: The day before the eruption

Diluculum — 06:00 hours

At the top of the great stone lighthouse on the southern headland the slaves were dousing the fires to greet the dawn. Attilius watched the glow fade beyond the promontory, while in the harbour the outlines of warships took shape against the pearl-grey sky.

He turned and walked back along the quay to where the others were waiting. He could make out their faces at last—Musa, Becco, Corvinus, Polites. No sign yet of Corax.

The ship the admiral had promised was moored before them: the *Minerva*, named for the goddess of wisdom, with an owl, the symbol of her deity, carved into her prow. A liburnian. Smaller than the big triremes. Built for speed. She was deserted.

Attilius heard a hundred pairs of feet, doubling along the road from the military school. Then a couple of torches appeared and the unit swung into the street leading to the harbour front. They came on, three officers wearing body armour and crested helmets in the lead. At a first shout of command the column halted; at a second, it broke and the sailors moved towards the ship. In their sleeveless tunics, the hugely muscular shoulders and arms of the oarsmen appeared grotesquely out of proportion to their lower bodies.

'Look at them,' drawled the tallest of the officers. 'The cream of the Navy: human oxen.' He turned to Attilius and raised his fist in salute. 'Torquatus, captain of the *Minerva*.'

'Marcus Attilius. Engineer. Let's go.'

IT DID NOT take long to load the ship. Attilius had seen no point in dragging the heavy amphorae of quicklime and sacks of puteolanum down from the reservoir and ferrying them across the bay. If Pompeii was, as they described her, swarming with builders, he would use the admiral's letter to commandeer what he needed. Tools, though, were a different matter. A man should always use his own tools. By the time they had finished it was light and the ship was ready to sail.

Attilius walked up the gangplank and jumped down to the deck. A line of marines with boat hooks was waiting to push her away from the quay. From his platform beneath the sternpost, next to the helmsman, Torquatus shouted down, 'Are you ready, Engineer?' and Attilius called back that he was. The sooner they left, the better.

'But Corax isn't here,' objected Becco.

To hell with him, thought Attilius. It was almost a relief. He would manage the job alone. 'That's Corax's lookout.'

The mooring ropes were cast off.

'There he is!' shouted Becco. 'Look! It's Corax!'

The overseer saw them, and started to run. He moved fast for a man in his forties. The gap between the ship and the quay was widening quickly and it seemed impossible that he could make it, but when he reached the edge he leapt, and a couple of the marines stretched out and caught his arms and hauled him aboard.

The *Minerva* was swinging out from the harbour and sprouting oars, two dozen on either side of her narrow hull. A drum sounded below deck, and the blades dipped. It sounded again and the ship glided forwards—picking up speed as the tempo of the drum beats quickened. The helmsman swung hard on the huge oar that served as a rudder, steering a course between two anchored triremes.

THE *MINERVA* PASSED between the great concrete moles that protected the entrance to the harbour and out into the bay. Attilius could see the Villa Hortensia. The terraces, the garden paths, the slope where Ampliatus had set up his chair to watch the execution, the gantries between the fish-pens—all deserted. The villa's crimson-and-gold cruiser was no longer moored at the end of the jetty.

It was exactly as the old woman had said: they had gone.

She had still not recovered her senses when he left the reservoir before dawn. He had lain her on a straw mattress in one of the rooms beside the kitchen, and had told the domestic slave, Phylo, to summon a doctor and to see that she was cared for. If she recovered—then, as far as he was concerned, she could stay. He would have to buy another slave in any case, to look after his food and clothes. His needs were few; the work would be light.

Musa said, 'I hear he paid ten million for it.'

Attilius acknowledged the remark with a grunt, without taking his eyes off the house. 'Well, he's not there now.'

'Ampliatus? He has houses everywhere. Mostly, he's in Pompeii.'

'Pompeii?' Now the engineer looked round.

Musa was sitting crosslegged, eating a fig. 'That's where he comes from. Pompeii's where he made his money.'

'And yet he was born a slave.'

'So it goes these days,' said Musa bitterly. 'Your slave dines off silver plate, while your honest, freeborn citizen works from dawn till nightfall for a pittance.'

Musa uncorked his waterskin and took a swig, then wiped the top and offered it up to Attilius. The engineer took it and squatted beside him. The water had a vaguely bitter taste. Sulphur. He swallowed a little, wiped the top in return and handed it back.

'You're right, Musa,' he said carefully. 'How old is Ampliatus? Not even fifty. Yet he's gone from slave to master of the Villa Hortensia in the time it would take you or I to scrape together enough to buy some bug-infested apartment. How could any man do that honestly?'

'An honest millionaire? As rare as hen's teeth! The way I hear it,' said Musa, 'he really started coining it just after the earthquake. He'd been left his freedom in old man Popidius's will. He was a good-looking lad, Ampliatus, and there was nothing he wouldn't do for his master. The old man was a lecher—I don't think he'd leave the dog alone. And Ampliatus looked after his wife for him, too, if you know what I mean.' Musa winked. 'Anyway, Ampliatus got his freedom, and a bit of money from somewhere, and then Jupiter decided to shake things up a bit. This was back in Nero's time. It was a very bad quake—the worst anyone could remember. I was in Nola, and I thought my days were up, I can tell you. But you know what they say: one man's loss is another's gain. Pompeii caught it worst of all. But while everyone else was getting out, talking about the town being finished, Ampliatus was going round, buying up the ruins. Got hold of some of those big villas for next to nothing, fixed them up, divided them into three or four, then sold them off for a fortune.'

'Nothing illegal about that, though.'

'Maybe not. But did he really own them when he sold them? That's the thing.' Musa tapped the side of his nose. 'Owners dead. Owners missing. Legal heirs on the other side of the Empire. Half the town was rubble, don't forget. The Emperor sent a commissioner down from Rome to sort out who owned what. Suedius Clementius.'

'And Ampliatus bribed him?'

'Let's just say Suedius left a richer man than he arrived. So they say.'

'And what about Exomnius? He was the aquarius at the time of the earthquake—he must have known Ampliatus.'

Attilius could see at once that he had made a mistake. The eager light of gossip was immediately extinguished in Musa's eyes. 'I don't know anything about that,' he muttered. 'He was a fine man, Exomnius. He was good to work for.'

THE *MINERVA* PUSHED ON steadily as the heat of the morning settled over the bay. For two hours the oarsmen kept up the same remorseless pace. Clouds of steam curled from the terraces of the open-air baths in Baiae. In the hills above Puteoli, the fires of the sulphur mines burned pale green.

The engineer sat apart, his hands clasped round his knees, his hat pulled low to shield his eyes, watching the coast slide by, searching the landscape for some clue as to what had happened to the Augusta.

The farther east they rowed, the more Vesuvius dominated the bay. Her lower slopes were a mosaic of cultivated fields and villas, but from her halfway point rose virgin forest. A few wisps of cloud hung round her tapering peak. Torquatus declared that the hunting up there was excellent—boar, deer, hare. He had been out many times with his dogs and net, and also with his bow. But one had to look out for the wolves. In winter, the top was snowcapped.

Squatting next to Attilius he took off his helmet and wiped his forehead. 'Hard to imagine,' he said, 'snow in this heat.'

'And is she easy to climb?' Attilius asked.

'Not too hard. Easier than she looks. The top's fairly flat when you get up there. When the skies are clear you can see for fifty miles.'

They had passed the city of Neapolis and were parallel with a stately town that Torquatus said was Herculaneum. She was at the foot of the luxuriant mountain, her windows facing out to sea. Brightly coloured pleasure craft bobbed in the shallows. Music, and the sounds of children playing, wafted across the placid water.

'Now that's the greatest villa on the bay,' said Torquatus. He nodded towards an immense, colonnaded property that sprawled along the shoreline and rose in terraces above the sea. 'That's the Villa Calpurnia. I had the honour to take the new Emperor there last month, on a visit to the former consul, Pedius Cascus.'

Attilius pictured the lizard-like senator from the previous evening, in his purple-striped toga. 'I had no idea he was so rich.'

'Inherited through his wife, Rectina. The admiral comes here often, to use the library. Do you see that group of figures, reading in the shade beside the pool? They are philosophers.' Torquatus found this very funny. 'Some men breed birds as a pastime, others have dogs. The senator keeps philosophers!'

'And what species are these philosophers?'

'Followers of Epicurus. According to Cascus, they hold that man is mortal, the gods are indifferent to his fate, and therefore the only thing to do in life is enjoy oneself.'

'I could have told him that for nothing.'

Torquatus laughed again, then put on his helmet and tightened the chin-strap. 'Not long to Pompeii now, Engineer. Another half-hour should do it.' He walked back towards the stern.

Attilius reached for the leather sack in which he carried what he needed—Pliny's letter to the aediles of Pompeii, a small bag of gold coins and the map of the Augusta.

He unrolled the plan, and felt a stir of anxiety. The proportions of the sketch, he realised, were not at all accurate. It failed to convey the immensity of Vesuvius, which must surely, now he looked at it, be seven or eight miles across. What had seemed a mere thumb's-width on the map was in reality half a morning's trek.

He pushed himself to his feet and made his way over to the men, who were playing dice. Corax had his hand cupped over the beaker and was shaking it hard. 'Come on, Fortuna, you old whore,' he muttered and rolled the dice. He threw all aces—a dog—and groaned. Becco gave a cry of joy and scooped up the pile of copper coins.

'My luck was good,' said Corax, 'until he appeared.' He jabbed his finger at Attilius. 'He's worse than a raven, lads. You mark my words—he'll lead us all to our deaths.'

'I'll tell you what,' said the engineer, squatting beside them. 'Let's play a different game. When we get to Pompeii, Corax is going out first to the far side of Vesuvius, to find the break on the Augusta. Someone must go with him. Why don't you throw for the privilege?'

'Whoever wins goes with Corax!' exclaimed Musa.

'No,' said Attilius. 'Whoever loses.'

'Whoever loses!' Becco laughed. 'That's a good one!'

They took it in turns to roll the dice.

Musa went last, and threw a dog. He looked crestfallen.

'All right,' said Attilius, 'the dice settle it. Corax and Musa will locate the fault.'

'And what about the others?' grumbled Musa.

'Becco and Corvinus will ride to Abellinum and close the sluices. Polites stays with me in Pompeii and organises tools and transport.'

POMPEII CAME INTO VIEW slowly from behind a headland, a fortress-city, built to withstand a siege, set back a quarter of a mile from the sea, on higher ground, her port spread out beneath her.

It was only as they drew closer that Attilius saw that her walls were no longer continuous—that the long years of the Roman peace had persuaded the city fathers to drop their guard. Houses had been allowed to emerge above the ramparts, and to spill, in widening, palm-shaded terraces, down towards the docks.

Activity everywhere. People swarming along the road in front of the town—on foot, on horseback, in chariots and on the backs of wagons—throwing up a haze of dust and clogging the steep paths that led up from the port to the two big city gates. As the *Minerva* turned into the narrow entrance of the harbour the din of the crowd grew louder—a holiday crowd, by the look of it, coming into town from the countryside to celebrate the festival of Vulcan. Attilius scanned the dockside for fountains but could see none.

He turned to Corax. 'Where does the water come into the town?'

'On the other side of the city,' said Corax, staring intently at the town. 'Beside the Vesuvius Gate. *If* it's still flowing.'

'Who works there?'

'Just some town slave. You won't find him much help.'

'Why not?'

Corax grinned but would not say. A private joke.

They were inside the harbour now. Warehouses and cranes crowded against the water's edge. The oars were shipped; and they glided alongside the wharf, no more than a foot of clear water between the deck and the quay. Two groups of sailors carrying mooring cables jumped ashore and wound them quickly round the stone posts. A moment later the ropes snapped taut and, with a jerk that almost knocked Attilius off his feet, the *Minerva* came to rest.

He saw it as he was recovering his balance. A big stone plinth with a head of Neptune gushing water from his mouth into a bowl shaped like an oyster-shell, and the bowl *overflowing*, cascading down to rinse the cobbles, and wash, unregarded, into the sea. Nobody was queuing to drink. Nobody was paying it any attention. Why should they? It was just an ordinary miracle. He vaulted over the side of the warship and walked towards it. He dropped his sack and put his hands into the clear arc of water, cupped them, raised them to his lips. It tasted sweet and pure and he almost laughed aloud with pleasure and relief.

Hora Quarta — 09:48 hours

A man could buy anything he needed in the harbour of Pompeii. Horses were as easy to come by as flies. Half a dozen dealers hung around outside the customs shed. The nearest sat on a stool beneath a crudely drawn sign of the winged Pegasus, bearing the slogan 'Baculus: Horses Swift Enough for the Gods'.

'I need five,' Attilius told the dealer. 'Good, strong beasts, capable of working all day. And I need them now.'

'That's no problem, citizen.' Baculus was a small, bald man, with the brick-red face and glassy eyes of a heavy drinker.

'And I also want oxen. Two teams and two wagons.'

He clicked his tongue. 'That, I think, will take longer. Two hours. Maybe three.'

Attilius agreed on a price and told the dealer to bring round four of the horses immediately to the Vesuvius Gate. He pushed his way back through the traders towards the *Minerva*.

By now the crew had been allowed up on deck. Most had peeled off their sodden tunics and the stench of sweat was strong enough to compete with the stink of the nearby fish-sauce factory, where liquefying offal was decomposing in vats in the sunshine. Corvinus and Becco were carrying the tools, throwing them over the side to Musa and Polites. Corax stood with his back to the boat, peering towards the town, occasionally rising on tiptoe to see over the heads of the crowd. He noticed Attilius and stopped.

Attilius waved to the others to stop what they were doing and to gather round. It was agreed that they would leave Polites to finish the unloading and to guard the tools on the dockside; Attilius would send word to him about where to meet up later. Then the remaining five set off towards the nearest gate, Corax trailing behind, and whenever Attilius looked back it seemed that he was searching for someone, his head craning from side to side.

The engineer led them up the ramp from the harbour towards the city wall, and into the dark tunnel of the gate. A customs official gave them a cursory glance to check they were not carrying anything they might sell, then nodded them into the town.

The forum was imposing for a provincial town: basilica, covered market, temples, a public library; three or four dozen statues of emperors and local worthies high up on their pedestals. Not all of it was finished. A webwork of wooden scaffolding covered some of the large buildings. The high walls acted to trap the noise of the crowd and reflect it back at them—the flutes and drums of the buskers, the cries of the beggars and hawkers, the sizzle of cooking food. Fruit-sellers were offering green figs and pink slices of melon. Slaves, bowed under the weight of bundles of wood, were hurrying in relays to pile them onto the big bonfire being built in the centre of the forum for the evening sacrifice to Vulcan.

The engineer took off his hat and wiped his forehead. Already there was something about the place he did not much like. A hustler's town, he thought. She would welcome a visitor for exactly as long as it took to fleece him.

'You know the way to the Vesuvius Gate,' he shouted to Corax. 'You lead.'

Water was pumping through the city. As they fought their way towards the far end of the forum he could hear it washing clear the big public latrine beside the Temple of Jupiter and bubbling in the streets beyond. He kept close behind Corax, and once or twice he found himself splashing through the little torrents that were running in the gutters. He counted seven fountains, all overflowing. The Augusta's failure was clearly Pompeii's gain. The aqueduct had nowhere to run except here. So while the other towns round the bay were baking dry in the heat, the children of Pompeii paddled in the streets.

It was hard work, toiling up the hill, and by the time they reached the big northern gate Baculus was already waiting for them with their horses. He had hitched them to a post beside a small building that backed onto the city wall.

Attilius said, 'The castellum aquae?' Corax nodded. The engineer took it in at a glance—the same red-brick construction as the Piscina Mirabilis, the same muffled sound of rushing water. Looking back down the hill he could see the water towers that regulated the pressure of the flow. He sent Musa inside the castellum to fetch out the water slave while he counted out a small pile of gold coins and gave them to Baculus, who tested each one with his teeth. 'And the oxen?'

These, Baculus promised, would be ready by the seventh hour. He would attend to it immediately. He wished them all the blessings of Mercury on their journey, and took his leave—but only as far, Attilius noticed, as the bar across the street.

He assigned the horses on the basis of their strength. The best he gave to Becco and Corvinus, on the grounds that they would have the most riding to do, and he was still explaining his reasons to an aggrieved Corax when Musa reappeared to announce that the castellum aquae was deserted.

'What?' Attilius wheeled round. 'Nobody there at all?'

Corax said, 'I told you he'd be no help.'

Attilius cleared his throat. 'All right. You all know what you have to do? Becco, Corvinus—have either of you ever been up to Abellinum before?'

'I have,' said Becco.

'What's the set-up?'

'The springs rise beneath a temple dedicated to the water goddesses, and flow into a basin within the nymphaeum. The aquarius in charge is Probus, who also serves as priest.'

'An aquarius as priest!' Attilius laughed and shook his head. 'Well, you can tell this heavenly engineer, whoever he is, that the goddesses, in their celestial wisdom, require him to close his main sluice and divert all his water to Beneventum. Make sure it's done the moment you arrive. Becco—you are to remain behind in Abellinum and see it stays closed for twelve hours. Then you open it again. Got that?'

Becco nodded.

'And if, by any remote chance, we can't make the repairs in twelve hours,' said Corax sarcastically, 'what then?'

'I've thought of that. As soon as the water is closed off, Corvinus leaves Becco at the basin and follows the course of the Augusta back down the mountains until he reaches the rest of us north east of Vesuvius. By that time it will be clear how much work needs to be done. If we can't fix the problem in twelve hours, he can take word back to Becco to keep the sluice gate closed until we've finished.'

'Twelve hours!' repeated Corax, shaking his head. 'That's going to mean working through the night.'

'What's the matter, Corax? Scared of the dark? When you locate the problem, make an assessment of how much material we'll need, and how many men. You stay there and send Musa back with a report. I'll requisition everything we need from the aediles. Once I've loaded up the wagons, I'll wait at the castellum aquae to hear from you.'

'And what if I don't locate the problem?'

It occurred to Attilius that the overseer, in his bitterness, might even try to sabotage the entire mission. 'Then we'll set out anyway, and get to you before nightfall. So don't try to screw me around.'

HE SAW THEM OFF from the pomoerium, the sacred zone just beyond the Vesuvius Gate, kept clear of buildings in honour of the city's guardian deities.

The road ran round the town like a racetrack, passing beside a bronze works and through a big cemetery. As the men mounted their horses Attilius felt he ought to say something—some speech like Caesar's, on the eve of battle—but before he could think of anything they were kicking their heels into the sides of their horses and wheeling away through the crowds thronging into the city—Corax and Musa to the left, to pick up the trail to Nola; Becco and Corvinus right, towards Nuceria and Abellinum. As they trotted into the necropolis, only Corax looked back—not at Attilius, but over his head, towards the walls of the city. His glance swept along the ramparts and watchtowers for a final time, then he planted himself more firmly in the saddle and turned in the direction of Vesuvius.

The engineer followed the progress of the riders as they disappeared behind the tombs, leaving only a blur of brown dust above the white sarcophagi to show where they had passed. He stood for a few moments, then he retraced his steps towards the city gate.

It was only as he joined the pedestrians queuing at the gate that he noticed the slight hump in the ground where the tunnel of the aqueduct passed beneath the city wall. He stopped and swivelled, following the line of it towards the nearest manhole, and saw that its course pointed directly at the summit of Vesuvius. It was impossible, he thought, that the spur should actually run all the way onto Vesuvius itself. It must swerve off to the east at the edge of the lower slopes to join up with the Augusta's main line. He wondered where exactly.

He went back through the shadowy gate and into the glare of the small square. He walked round the side of the castellum aquae and along the short alley that led to its entrance. 'Is anyone there?'

No answer. He could hear the rush of the aqueduct much more clearly here, and when he pushed open the low wooden door he was hit at once by the drenching spray and that sharp, coarse, sweet smell—of fresh water on warm stone.

He went inside. Fingers of light from two small windows set high above his head pierced the darkness. But he did not need light to know how the castellum was arranged for he had seen dozens of them over the years—all identical, all laid out according to the principles of Vitruvius. The tunnel of the Pompeii spur was smaller than the Augusta's main matrix, but still big enough for a man to squeeze along it, stooping, in order to make repairs. The water jetted from the mouth through a bronze mesh screen into a shallow concrete reservoir divided by wooden gates, which in turn fed a set of three big lead pipes. The central conduit would carry the supply for the fountains; that to its left would be for private houses; that to its right for the public baths. What was unusual was the force of the flow. It was not only drenching the walls, it had also swept a mass of debris along the tunnel, trapping it against the metal screen. He could make out leaves and twigs and even a few small rocks. Slovenly maintenance, he thought. No wonder Corax had said the water slave was useless.

He swung one leg over the concrete wall of the reservoir and then the other, and lowered himself into the swirling pool. The water came up almost to his waist. He waded the few paces to the grille and ran his hands under water, round the edge of the mesh frame, feeling for its fastenings. When he found them, he unscrewed them. There were two more at the top. He undid those as well, lifted away the grille, and stood aside to let the rubbish swirl past him.

'Is somebody there?'

The voice startled him. A young man stood in the doorway. 'Of course there's somebody here, you idiot.'

'What are you doing?'

'Are you the water slave? Then I'm doing your job for you—that's what I'm doing. Wait there.' Attilius swung the grille back into place and refastened it, waded over to the side of the reservoir and hauled himself out. 'I'm Marcus Attilius. The new aquarius of the Augusta. And what do they call you, apart from a lazy fool?'

'Tiro, Aquarius.' The boy's eyes were open wide in alarm, his pupils darting from side to side. 'Forgive me.' He dropped to his knees. 'The public holiday, Aquarius—I slept late—I—'

'All right. Never mind that.' The boy was only about sixteen—a scrap of humanity, as thin as a stray dog—and Attilius regretted his roughness. 'Come on. Get up off the floor. I need you to take me to the magistrates.' He held out his hand but the slave ignored it, his eyes still flickering wildly back and forth. Attilius waved his palm in front of Tiro's face, and said in surprise, 'You're blind?'

'Yes, Aquarius.'

No wonder Corax had smiled when Attilius had asked about him. 'But how do you attend to your duties if you can't see?'

'I can hear better than any man.' Despite his nervousness, Tiro spoke with a trace of pride. 'I can tell by the sound of the water how well it flows, if it's obstructed. I can smell it, and taste it for impurities.' He lifted his head, sniffing the air. 'There's no need for me to adjust the gates this morning. I've never heard the flow so strong.'

'That's true.' The engineer realised he had underestimated the boy. 'The main line is blocked somewhere between here and Nola. That's why I've come, to get help to repair it. You're the property of the town?' Tiro nodded. 'Who are the magistrates?'

'Marcus Holconius and Quintus Brittius,' said Tiro promptly. 'The aediles are Lucius Popidius and Gaius Cuspius.'

'Which one is in charge of the water supply?'

'Popidius.'

'Where's his house?'

'Straight down the hill, Aquarius, towards the Stabian Gate. I can take you.'

THEY DESCENDED into the town together. It tumbled away below them, a jumble of terracotta roofs sloping down to the glinting sea. Framing the view to the left was the blue ridge of the Surrentum peninsula; to the right was the tree-covered flank of Vesuvius. Attilius found it hard to imagine a more perfect spot in which to build a city, high enough above the bay to be wafted by breeze, close enough to the shore to enjoy the benefits of the Mediterranean trade. No wonder it had risen again so quickly after the earthquake.

The street was lined with houses, narrow-fronted, windowless dwellings. The only relief from the monotony of the drab walls were election slogans daubed in red paint.

THE ENTIRE MASS HAVE APPROVED THE CANDIDACY OF CUSPIUS FOR THE OFFICE OF AEDILE.

THE FRUIT DEALERS URGE THE ELECTION OF MARCUS HOLCONIUS PRISCUS AS MAGISTRATE.

HIS NEIGHBOURS URGE THE ELECTION OF LUCIUS POPIDIUS SECUNDUS AS AEDILE.

'Your whole town appears to be obsessed with elections, Tiro. It's worse than Rome.'

'The free men vote for the new magistrates each March, Aquarius.'

They were walking quickly, Tiro keeping a little ahead of Attilius, threading along the crowded pavement. The engineer had to ask him to slow down. Tiro apologised. He did not need to feel his way, he said. He knew it by instinct. He had been blind from birth, had been dumped on the refuse tip outside the city walls and left to die, but someone had picked him up; he'd lived by running errands for the town since he was six years old.

'This aedile, Popidius,' said Attilius, as they passed his name for the third time, 'his must have been the family that once had Ampliatus as a slave.'

But Tiro, despite the keenness of his ears, seemed for once not to have heard.

They came to a big crossroads, dominated by an enormous triumphal arch, resting on four marble pillars. A team of four horses, frozen in stone, plunged and reared against the brilliant sky, hauling the figure of Victory in her golden chariot. The monument was dedicated to yet another Holconius—Marcus Holconius Rufus, dead these past sixty years. Always the same few names, he thought. Holconius, Popidius, Cuspius.

The engineer was about to put his foot down to cross the street when he suddenly pulled it back. It appeared to him that the large stones were rippling slightly. A great dry wave was passing through the town. An instant later he lurched and had to grab at Tiro's arm to stop himself falling. A few people screamed; a horse shied. For a few moments the centre of Pompeii was almost silent. And then, gradually, activity began again. Breath was exhaled. Conversations resumed. The driver flicked his whip over the back of his frantic horse and the cart jumped forwards.

'Don't worry, Aquarius,' Tiro said cheerfully. 'It happens all the time this summer. Five times, ten times, even, in the past two days. The ground is complaining of the heat!'

Tiro offered his hand—the blind man guiding the sighted—but Attilius, still shaken by the tremor, ignored it and mounted the high pavement unaided. He said irritably, 'Where's this bloody house?'

'There.' Tiro gestured vaguely to a doorway across the street. It did not look much. The usual blank walls. A bakery on one side. Above the big door of the house was another of the ubiquitous, red-painted slogans: HIS NEIGHBOURS URGE THE ELECTION OF LUCIUS POPIDIUS SECUNDUS AS AEDILE.

'Aquarius, may I ask you something?'

'Of course.'

'What has become of Exomnius?'

'Nobody knows, Tiro. He's vanished.'

The slave absorbed this, nodding slowly. 'Exomnius did not like the shaking, either. He said it reminded him of the time before the big earthquake, many years ago. The year I was born.'

'Exomnius was in Pompeii recently?'

'Of course. He lived here.'

'He lived *here*? In Pompeii?'

Attilius felt bewildered, and yet he also grasped immediately that it must be true. It explained why Exomnius's quarters at Misenum had been so devoid of personal possessions, and why Corax had not wanted him to come here, and why the overseer had behaved so strangely in Pompeii—all that looking around, searching the crowds for a familiar face.

'He had rooms at Africanus's place,' said Tiro.

'And how long ago did you speak to him?'

'I can't remember.'

'Try to remember, Tiro. It could be important. After the Festival of Neptune, or before?' Neptunalia was on the twenty-third day of July: the most sacred date in the calendar for the men of the aqueducts.

'After. Definitely. Perhaps two weeks ago?'

'Two weeks? Then you must have been one of the last to talk to him. And he was worried about the tremors?' Tiro nodded again. 'And Ampliatus? He was a great friend of Ampliatus, was he not? Were they often together?'

The slave gestured to his eyes. 'I cannot see—'

No, thought Attilius, but I bet you heard them. He glanced across the street at the house of Popidius. 'All right, Tiro. You can go back to the castellum. Do your day's work. I'm grateful for your help.'

'Thank you, Aquarius.' Tiro turned and began climbing back up the hill towards the Vesuvius Gate.

Hora Quinta — 11:07 hours

The house had a heavy-studded double door. Attilius hammered on it with his fist. Almost at once it opened and the porter appeared—a Nubian, immensely tall and broad. He wore a sleeveless, crimson tunic. His thick black arms and neck were as solid as tree trunks.

Attilius said, 'A keeper worthy of his gate, I see.'

The porter did not smile. 'State your business.'

'Marcus Attilius, aquarius of the Aqua Augusta, wishes to present his compliments to Lucius Popidius Secundus.'

'It's a public holiday. He's not at home.'

Attilius opened his bag, and pulled out the admiral's letter. 'Do you see this seal? Give it to him. Tell him it's from the commander in chief of the imperial fleet at Misenum. Tell him I need to see him on the Emperor's business.'

A man's voice behind the porter cut in: 'The Emperor's business, did he just say, Massavo? You had better let him in.' The Nubian stepped back, and the engineer slipped quickly through the opening. The door was closed behind him.

The man who had spoken wore the same crimson uniform as the porter. He had a bunch of keys attached to his belt—the household steward, presumably. He took the letter and ran his thumb across the seal, checking to see if it was broken. Satisfied, he studied Attilius. 'Lucius Popidius is entertaining guests for Vulcanalia. But I shall see that he receives it.'

'No,' said Attilius. 'I shall give it to him myself. Immediately.'

'Very well,' the steward said. He gave Attilius the letter. 'Follow me.'

He led the way down the narrow corridor of the vestibule towards a sunlit atrium, and for the first time Attilius realised the immensity of the old house. The narrow façade was an illusion. He could see beyond the shoulder of the steward straight through into the interior, 150 feet or more, successive vistas of light and colour—the shaded passageway with its black and white mosaic floor, the dazzling brilliance of the atrium with its marble fountain; a tablinum for receiving visitors, guarded by two bronze busts; and then a colonnaded swimming pool, its pillars wrapped with vines.

They came into the atrium and the steward said, 'Wait here,' before disappearing behind a curtain that screened a narrow passageway. The sun was almost directly overhead, shining through the square aperture in the atrium's roof. From this position Attilius could see most of the swimming pool. At the far end, four women reclined on couches. The curtain parted and the steward reappeared, beckoning.

Attilius knew at once, by the humidity and by the smell of oil, that he was being shown into the house's private baths. The steward took him into the changing room and told him to remove his shoes, then they went back out into the passageway and into the tepidarium, where an immensely fat old man lay face down, naked, on a table, being worked on by a young masseur.

The steward slid open a door, releasing a billow of vapour from the dimly lit interior, then stood aside to let the engineer through.

It was hard at first to see very much in the caldarium, for the only light came from a couple of torches mounted on the wall, and the glowing coals of the brazier that had created the steam that filled the room. But gradually Attilius made out a large sunken bath, with three dark heads of hair, seemingly floating in the greyness. There was a splash as a hand was raised and gently waved.

'Over here, Aquarius,' said a languid voice. 'You have a message for me, I believe, from the Emperor?'

Another head was stirring. 'Fetch us a torch!' it commanded. 'Let us at least see who is disturbing us on a feast day.'

A slave in the corner of the room, who Attilius had not noticed, took down one of the torches from the wall and held it close to the engineer's face so that he could be inspected. Attilius could feel the pores of his skin opening, the sweat running freely down his body.

The heat of the torch on his cheek was unbearable. 'This is no place to conduct the Emperor's business,' he said stiffly and pushed the slave's arm away. 'To whom am I speaking?'

'I am Lucius Popidius,' said the languid voice, 'and these gentlemen are Gaius Cuspius and Marcus Holconius. And our friend in the tepidarium is Quintus Brittius. Now do you know who we are?'

'You're the four elected magistrates of Pompeii.'

'Correct,' said Popidius. 'And this is our town, Aquarius, so guard your tongue.'

Attilius knew how the system worked. As aediles, Popidius and Cuspius would hand out the licences for all the businesses, from the brothels to the baths; they were responsible for keeping the streets clean, the water flowing, the temples open. Holconius and Brittius were the duoviri—the commission of two men—who presided over the court in the basilica and dispensed the Emperor's justice: a flogging here, a crucifixion there, and no doubt a fine to fill the city's coffers whenever possible. He would not be able to accomplish much without them. He forced himself to stand quietly, waiting.

'Well,' said Popidius after a while. 'I suppose I have cooked for long enough.' He sighed and stood, a ghostly figure in the steam, and held out his hand for a towel. The slave replaced the torch in its holder, knelt before his master and wrapped a cloth round his waist. 'All right then. Where's this letter?' He took it and padded into the adjoining room. Attilius followed.

Brittius was on his back and the young slave had obviously been giving him more than a massage. The old man batted away the slave's hands, and reached for a towel. He scowled at Attilius. His face was scarlet. 'Who's this then, Popi?'

'The new aquarius of the Augusta. Exomnius's replacement. He's come from Misenum.' Popidius broke open the seal and unrolled the letter. He was in his early forties, with delicately handsome features. The dark hair slicked back over his small ears emphasised his aquiline profile as he bent forwards to read.

The others were now coming in from the caldarium, curious to find out was happening, slopping water over the floor.

Brittius propped himself on his elbow. 'What does it say, Popi?'

'It's from Pliny. It seems the aqueduct has failed somewhere near Vesuvius. All the towns from Nola westwards are dry. He says he wants us—"orders" us, he says—to "provide immediately sufficient men and materials from the colony of Pompeii to effect repairs to the Aqua Augusta, under the command of Marcus Attilius Primus, engineer, of the Department of the Curator Aquarum, Rome".'

'Look at this,' said one of the other men. He was in his middle twenties, with a muscular body but a small head, which seemed to wear an expression of permanent puzzlement. Attilius guessed he must be the second junior magistrate, the aedile, Cuspius.

The young man turned the tap above the circular basin and water gushed out. 'There's no drought here—d'you see? So I say this: what's it to do with us? You want men and materials, Aquarius? Go to one of these towns that has no water. Go to Nola. We're swimming in it! Look!'

Popidius smiled and rolled up the papyrus. 'I think you have our answer, Aquarius.'

'Now listen to me, your honours,' Attilius said. 'From midnight tonight, Pompeii will also lose her water. The entire supply is being diverted to Beneventum, so we can get inside the tunnel of the aqueduct to repair it. I've already sent my men into the mountains to close the sluices.' There was a mutter of anger. He held up his hand. 'If you refuse to help me, I'll send to Rome for a commissioner to come down and investigate the abuse of the imperial aqueduct. I'll make you pay for every extra cupful you've taken beyond your proper share!'

'Such insolence,' shouted Brittius as the curtain was swished aside to reveal another man: Numerius Popidius Ampliatus.

What most astonished Attilius, once he had recovered from the shock of seeing him again, was how much they all deferred to him. Even Brittius swung his plump legs over the side of the table and straightened his back, as if it were somehow disrespectful to be caught lying down in the presence of this former slave.

The engineer remembered the pulpy remains of the slave in the eel pool, the lacerated back of the slave woman.

'So what's all this, gentlemen?' Ampliatus suddenly grinned and pointed at Attilius. 'Arguing in the baths? On a religious festival? That's unseemly. Where were you all brought up?'

Popidius said, 'This is the new aquarius of the aqueduct.'

'I know Marcus Attilius. We've met, haven't we, Aquarius? May I see that?' He took Pliny's letter from Popidius and scanned it quickly, then glanced at Attilius. 'What is your plan?'

'To follow the spur from Pompeii back to its junction with the Augusta, then to work my way along the main line towards Nola until I find the break.'

'And what is it you need?'

'I don't know yet exactly. Perhaps a dozen amphorae of lime. Twenty baskets of puteolanum. Fifty paces of timber and five hundred bricks. As many torches as you can spare. Ten strong pairs of hands. I may need less, I may need more. It depends how badly the aqueduct is damaged.'

'How soon will you know?'

'One of my men will report back this afternoon.'

Ampliatus nodded. 'Well, gentlemen, I think we should do all in our power to help. Never let it be said that Pompeii turned its back on an appeal from the Emperor. What do you say?'

The magistrates exchanged uneasy glances. Eventually Popidius said, 'It may be that we were overhasty—'

Ampliatus cut him off. 'That's settled then. I can let you have all you need, if you'll just be so good as to wait outside.'

The engineer collected his shoes and walked out of the tepidarium, into the gloomy passageway. He pulled on his shoes, opened the curtain and stepped back out into the dazzling sunlight. Across the atrium, the surface of the pool was rocking from the impact of a dive. The wives of the magistrates were still gossiping at the other end and they had been joined by a dowdy middle-aged woman who sat demurely apart, her hands folded in her lap. A couple of slaves carrying trays laden with dishes passed behind them. There was a smell of cooking. A huge feast was clearly in preparation.

His eye was caught by a flash of darkness beneath the glittering water and an instant later the swimmer broke the surface.

'Corelia Ampliata!'

He said her name aloud, unintentionally. She did not hear him. She shook her head, and stroked her black hair away from her closed eyes, gathering it behind her with both hands.

'Corelia!' He whispered it, not wanting to attract the attention of the other women, and this time she turned. She began wading towards him. She was wearing a shift of thin material that came down almost to her knees and as her body emerged from the water she placed one dripping arm across her breasts and the other between her thighs. He walked towards the pool.

'Aquarius,' she hissed, 'you must leave this place!' She was standing on the circular steps that led out of the pool. 'Get out! Go! My father is here, and if he sees you—'

'Too late for that. We've met.' But he drew back slightly, so that he was hidden from the view of the women at the other end of the pool. I ought to look away, he thought. It would be the honourable thing to do. But he could not take his eyes off her. 'What are you doing here?'

'"What am I doing here?"' She regarded him as if he were an idiot. 'Where else should I be? My father owns this house.'

'But I was told that Lucius Popidius lived here.'

'He does.'

He was still confused. 'Then—?'

'We are to be married.' She said it flatly and shrugged, and there was something terrible in the gesture, an utter hopelessness, and suddenly all was clear to him—the reason for Ampliatus's unannounced appearance, Popidius's deference to him, the way the others had followed his lead. Somehow Ampliatus had contrived to buy the roof from over Popidius's head and now he was going to extend his ownership completely, by marrying off his daughter to his former master. The thought of that ageing playboy sharing a bed with Corelia filled him with an unexpected anger, even though he told himself it was none of his business.

'But surely a man of Popidius's age is already married?'

'He was. He's been forced to divorce.'

'And what does Popidius think of such an arrangement?'

'He thinks it is contemptible, of course, to make a match so far beneath him—as you do, clearly.'

'Not at all, Corelia,' he said quickly. He saw that she had tears in her eyes. 'On the contrary. I should say you were worth a hundred Popidii. A thousand.'

'I hate him,' she said.

From the passage came the sound of rapid footsteps and Ampliatus's voice, yelling, 'Aquarius! You take advantage of my good nature!' Ampliatus was advancing across the tablinum. 'I told you to wait for me, that was all.' He glared at Corelia—'You should know better, after what I told you yesterday!'—then he shouted across the pool—'Celsia!'—and the mousy woman Attilius had noticed earlier jerked up in her chair. 'Get our daughter out of the pool! It's unseemly for her to show her tits in public! I'll be back in an hour! Don't dish up without me!' And with a gesture to Attilius that he should fall in behind him, the master of the House of the Popidii turned on his heel and strode towards the door.

Hora Sexta — 12:00 hours

Ampliatus had a litter and eight slaves waiting outside on the pavement, dressed in the same crimson livery as the porter and steward. They scrambled to attention as their master appeared, but he walked straight past them, just as he ignored the small crowd of petitioners squatting in the shade of the wall across the street, despite the public holiday, who called out his name in a ragged chorus.

'We'll walk,' he said, and set off up the slope towards the crossroads. Attilius followed at his shoulder. It was noon, the air scalding, the roads quiet. The few pedestrians who were about mostly hopped into the gutter as Ampliatus approached or drew back into the shop doorways. He nodded an occasional greeting, and when the engineer looked back he saw that they were trailing a retinue that would have done credit to a senator—first, at a discreet distance, the slaves with the litter, and behind them the little straggle of supplicants.

About halfway up the hill to the Vesuvius Gate—the engineer counted three city blocks—Ampliatus turned right, crossed the street, and opened a little wooden door set into a wall. He put his hand on Attilius's shoulder to usher him inside.

Ampliatus closed the door behind them and Attilius found himself standing in a big, deserted space, a building site, occupying the best part of the entire block. To the left was a brick wall surmounted by a sloping, red-tiled roof—the back of a row of shops. To the right, a complex of new buildings, very nearly finished, with large modern windows looking out across the expanse of scrub and rubble. A rectangular tank was being excavated directly beneath the windows.

Ampliatus had his hands on his hips and was studying the engineer's reaction. 'What do you think I'm building?'

'Baths.'

'That's it. What do you think?'

'It's impressive,' said Attilius. It was at least as good as anything he had seen under construction in Rome in the past ten years.

'We had to demolish almost the whole block to make way for it,' said Ampliatus, 'and that was unpopular. But it will be worth it. It will be the finest baths outside Rome.' He cupped his hands to his mouth and bellowed, 'Januarius!'

A tall man appeared at the top of a flight of stairs on the other side of the yard. He ran across the yard, bowing.

'Januarius—this is my friend, the aquarius of the Augusta.'

'Honoured,' said Januarius, and he gave Attilius another bow.

'Januarius is one of my foremen. Where are the lads?'

'In the barracks, sir.' He looked terrified. 'It's the holiday—'

'Forget the holiday! We need them here now. Ten did you say you needed, Aquarius? Better make it a dozen. Januarius, send for a dozen of the strongest men we have. Brebix's gang. They're to bring food and drink for a day. What else was it you needed?'

'Quicklime,' began Attilius, 'puteolanum—'

'That's it. All that stuff. Timber. Bricks. Torches—don't forget torches. He's to have everything he needs. And you'll require transport, won't you? A couple of teams of oxen?'

'I've already hired them. They should be arriving down at the harbour by now. I have a slave waiting there with our tools.'

'Fetch the men from the barracks, Januarius, and send a boy to the docks to have the aquarius's wagons brought here for loading. I'll show you around while we're waiting, Aquarius.'

BATHS WERE NOT a luxury. Baths were the foundation of civilisation. Baths were what raised even the meanest citizen of Rome above the level of the wealthiest, hairy-arsed barbarian. Was it not to feed the baths that the aqueducts had been invented in the first place? Had not the baths spread the Roman ethos across Europe, Africa and Asia as effectively as the legions, so that in whatever town in this far-flung empire a man might find himself, he could at least be sure of finding this one precious piece of home?

Such was the essence of Ampliatus's lecture as he conducted Attilius around the empty shell of his dream. The rooms smelt strongly of fresh paint and stucco and their footsteps echoed as they passed through the cubicles into the main part of the building. Here, the frescoes were already in place. Views of the green Nile flowed into scenes from the lives of the gods. Triton swam beside the Argonauts. Neptune transformed his son into a swan. The pool in the caldarium was built to take twenty-eight paying customers at a time, and as the bathers lay on their backs they would gaze up at a sapphire ceiling swimming with every species of marine life, and believe themselves to be floating in an undersea grotto.

To attain the luxury he demanded, Ampliatus was employing the most modern techniques, the best materials, the most skilful craftsmen in Italy. It was built to withstand an earthquake. All the fittings were of brass. The lavatory seats were Phrygian marble, with elbow rests carved in the shape of dolphins and chimeras. Hot and cold running water throughout. *Civilisation.*

'How soon before you're finished?'

'I should say a month. I need to bring in the carpenters. I want some shelves, a few cupboards. I thought of putting down wood in the changing room. I was considering pine.'

'No,' said Attilius. 'Use alder.'

'Alder? Why?'

'It won't rot in contact with water. I'd use pine—or perhaps a cypress—for the shutters. But it would need to be something from the lowlands, where the sun shines. Don't touch pine from the mountains. Not for a building of this quality. But you probably know all that.'

'Not at all. I've built a lot, it's true, but I've never understood much about wood and stone. It's money I understand.' He looked at the engineer. 'And you, Aquarius?' he said quietly. 'What is it you know?'

'Water.'

'Well, that's important. Water is at least as valuable as money.'

'Is it? Then why aren't I a rich man?'

'Perhaps you could be.' He made the remark lightly, left it floating in the air for a moment and then went on: 'Do you ever stop to think how curiously the world is ordered, Aquarius? When this place is open, I shall make another fortune. But without your aqueduct, I could not build my baths. That's a thought, is it not? Without Attilius: no Ampliatus.'

'Except that it's not my aqueduct. It belongs to the Emperor.'

'True.' Ampliatus sniffed the air. 'This wet paint makes my head ache. Come, let me show you my plans for the grounds.'

Outside, the luminous air felt almost solid with the heat, but Ampliatus did not appear to feel it. He climbed the open staircase easily and stepped onto the small sun deck. From here he had a commanding view of his little kingdom. That would be the exercise yard, he said. He would plant trees around it for shade. He patted the stone parapet. 'This was the site of my first property,' he said. 'Seventeen years ago I bought it. If I told you how little I paid for it, you wouldn't believe me. Mark you, there was not much left of it after the earthquake. Never been so happy. Repaired it, rented it out, bought another, rented that. Some of these big old houses from the time of the Republic were huge. I split them up and fitted ten families into them. I've gone on doing it ever since.'

'You had been freed by the Popidii by then?'

Ampliatus shot him a look. However hard he tries to be affable, thought Attilius, those eyes will always betray him.

'If that was meant as an insult, Aquarius, forget it. Everyone knows that I was born a slave and I'm not ashamed of it. Yes, I was free, manumitted in my master's will when I was twenty. Lucius, his son—the one you met—made me his household steward. Then I did some debt-collecting for an old money-lender called Jucundus. He taught me a lot. But I never would have been rich if it hadn't been for the earthquake. By the time it had finished this town was rubble. It didn't matter then who had been born free and who had been born a slave.'

'Who was in charge of rebuilding the town?'

'Nobody! That was the disgrace of it. All the richest families ran away to their country estates. They were all convinced there was going to be another earthquake.'

'Including Popidius?'

'Especially Popidius!' He wrung his hands, and whined, '"Oh, Ampliatus, the gods are punishing us!" They came creeping back, of course, once they saw it was safe, but by then things had started to change. *Salve lucrum!* "Hail profit!" That's the motto of the new Pompeii. Not money, mark you—any fool can inherit money. Profit. That takes skill. Lucius Popidius! What skill does he have? He can drink in cold water and piss out hot, and that's about it. Whereas you, I think, are a man of some ability. I could use a fellow like you.'

'Use me?'

'Here, for a start. These baths need a man who understands water.

In return for your advice, I could cut you in on the profits.'

Attilius shook his head, smiling. 'I don't think so.'

Ampliatus smiled back. 'Ah, you drive a hard bargain! I admire that in a man. Very well—a share of the ownership, too.'

'No. Thank you. I'm flattered. But my family has worked the imperial aqueducts for a century. I was born to be an engineer on the matrices, and I shall die doing it.'

'Why not do both? Run the aqueduct, and advise me as well. No one need ever know.'

Attilius looked at him closely. Beneath the money, the violence and the lust for power, he was really nothing bigger than a small-town crook. 'No,' he said coldly, 'that would be impossible.'

The contempt must have shown in his face because Ampliatus retreated at once. 'You're right,' he said. From down in the street came a rumble of heavy wooden wheels on stone. 'Listen—I think I can hear your wagons coming. We'd better go down and let them in.'

Ampliatus dodged across the rubble-strewn yard and swung open the heavy gates. Polites led the first team of oxen into the site. A man Attilius did not recognise was leading the second team; a couple more sat on the back of the empty cart, their legs dangling over the side. They jumped down immediately when they noticed Ampliatus and stood looking respectfully at the ground.

'Well done, lads,' said Ampliatus. 'I'll see you're rewarded for working a holiday. But it's an emergency and we've all got to rally round and help fix the aqueduct. For the common good—isn't that right, Aquarius?' He pinched the cheek of the nearest man. 'You're under his command now. Serve him well. Aquarius: take as much as you want. It's all in the yard. Torches are inside the storeroom. I'd stay and help you load myself, but you know how it is. We're dining early because of the festival and I mustn't show my low birth by keeping all those fine gentlemen and their ladies waiting.' He held out his hand. 'So! I wish you luck, Aquarius.'

Attilius took it and nodded. 'Thank you.'

Ampliatus grunted, and turned away. Outside in the street his litter was waiting for him and this time he clambered straight into it. At a gesture from Ampliatus, the slaves hoisted the bronze-capped poles—first to waist height, and then onto their shoulders. Attilius stood in the gateway and watched him go, the crimson canopy swaying as it moved off down the hill, the little crowd of weary petitioners trudging after it.

It was all there, as Ampliatus had promised—the bricks, just big enough to fit a man's grasp; the baskets of powdery red puteolanum, always heavier and denser than you expected; the timber; and finally the quicklime, in its bulbous clay amphorae.

He began loading the carts with the other men, then went into the bathhouse to look for the torches. He found them in the largest storeroom and even these were of a superior sort—tightly wadded flax and resin impregnated with tar. Next to them were open wooden crates of oil lamps and enough candles to light a large temple. Clearly, this was going to be a most luxurious establishment.

He was suddenly curious and with his arms full of torches he looked into some of the other storerooms. Piles of towels in one, jars of scented massage oil in another, lead exercise weights and coils of rope in a third. Everything ready and waiting for use; everything here except chattering, sweating humanity to bring it all to life. And water, of course. It would use a lot of water, this place. Four or five pools, showers, flush-latrines, a steam room . . . Only public facilities, such as the fountains, were connected to the aqueduct free of charge, as the gift of the Emperor. But private baths like these would cost a small fortune in water taxes. And if Ampliatus had made his money by buying big properties, subdividing them, and renting them out, then his overall consumption of water must be huge. He wondered how much he was paying for it. Presumably he could find out once he returned to Misenum and tried to bring some order to the chaos in which Exomnius had left the Augusta's records.

Perhaps he wasn't paying anything at all. He stood there in the bathhouse, turning the possibility over in his mind. The aqueducts had always been wide open to corruption. Farmers tapped into the main lines where they crossed their land. Citizens ran an extra pipe or two and paid the water inspectors to look the other way. Materials went missing. If the Augusta's accounts were in such a mess, might it be because they had been tampered with?

The weight of the torches was making his arms ache. He went outside and stacked them on the back of one of the wagons, then leaned against it, thinking. More of Ampliatus's men had arrived. The loading had finished and they were sprawled in the shade, waiting for orders. The oxen stood placidly, flicking their tails, their heads in clouds of flies. He made up his mind and beckoned to Polites.

'Go in and fetch a coil of rope. Then take the wagons and the men up to the castellum aquae, next to the Vesuvius Gate, and wait for me. Corax should be coming back soon. And while you're at it, see if you can buy some food for us all.' He gave the slave his bag. 'There's money in there. Look after it for me. I shan't be long.'

He glanced up at the cloudless sky. The sun had passed its zenith. Becco and Corvinus should have reached Abellinum by now. The sluice gates might already be closed, the Augusta starting to drain dry. He did not have much time. He brushed the residue of brick dust from the front of his tunic and walked out of the open gate.

Hora Septa — 14:10 hours

Ampliatus's banquet was just entering its second hour. It was stiflingly hot, even with one wall of the dining room entirely open to the air, and with three slaves in their crimson livery stationed round the table waving fans of peacock feathers.

There were four diners to each couch. This was at least one too many, in the judgment of Lucius Popidius. It meant that one was too close to one's fellow diners. Popidius, for example, reclined between Ampliatus's dreary wife, Celsia, and his own mother, Taedia—close enough to feel the heat of their bodies.

And the food! Did Ampliatus not understand that hot weather called for simple, cold dishes, and that all these sauces, all this elaboration, had gone out of fashion back in Claudius's time? The first of the hors d'oeuvres had not been too bad—oysters, olives, sardines, and eggs seasoned with chopped anchovies—altogether acceptable. But then had come lobster, sea urchins and, finally, mice rolled in honey and poppy seeds.

Roast wild boar filled with live thrushes that flapped helplessly across the table as the belly was carved open, shitting as they went. Then the delicacies: the tongues of storks and flamingos (not too bad), but the tongue of a parrot had always looked to Popidius like nothing so much as a maggot and it had indeed tasted as he imagined a maggot might taste if doused in vinegar. Then a stew of nightingales' livers . . .

He glanced around at his fellow guests. Even fat Brittius, whose motto was Seneca's—'eat to vomit, vomit to eat'—was starting to look green. He caught Popidius's eye and mouthed something at him. Popidius could not quite make it out. He cupped his ear and

Brittius repeated it, shielding his mouth from Ampliatus with his napkin and emphasising every syllable: 'Tri-mal-chi-o.'

Popidius almost burst out laughing. Trimalchio! Very good! The freed slave of monstrous wealth in the satire by Titus Petronius, who subjects his guests to exactly such a meal and cannot see how vulgar and ridiculous he is showing himself. Ha-ha! Trimalchio!

Popidius looked across at his former slave, presiding at the head of the table. He was still not entirely sure how it had happened. There had been the earthquake, of course. Suddenly Ampliatus was everywhere—rebuilding the town, controlling the elections, even buying the house next door. Popidius had never had a head for figures, so when Ampliatus had told him he could make some money, too, he had signed the contracts without even reading them. And somehow the money had been lost, and then it turned out that the family house was surety, and his only escape from the humiliation of eviction was to marry Ampliatus's daughter. Imagine: his own ex-slave as his father-in-law! The shame of it.

Not that he would mind sharing a bed with Corelia. He watched her hungrily, as she whispered to her brother. His gaze met Brittius's again. What a funny fellow. He winked and gestured with his eyes to Ampliatus and mouthed again, 'Trimalchio!'

'What's that you're saying, Popidius?'

Ampliatus's voice cut across the table like a whip. Popidius cringed.

'He was saying, "What a feast!"' Brittius raised his glass. 'That's what we're all saying, Ampliatus. What a magnificent feast.' A murmur of assent went round the table.

'And the best is yet to come,' said Ampliatus. He clicked his fingers and one of the slaves hurried out in the direction of the kitchen.

Popidius forced a smile. 'I for one have left room for dessert, Ampliatus.' In truth he felt like vomiting, and he would not have needed the usual cup of warm brine and mustard to do it, either.

'Oh, it's not yet time for dessert, my dear Popidius. Or may I—if it's not too premature—call you "son"?' Ampliatus grinned and by a superhuman effort, Popidius succeeded in hiding his revulsion.

There was a sound of scuffling footsteps and then four slaves appeared, bearing on their shoulders a model trireme, as long as a man and cast in silver. The diners broke into applause. The slaves approached the table on their knees and slid the trireme, prow first, across the table. It was entirely filled by an enormous eel. Its eyes had been removed and replaced by rubies. Its jaws were propped open and filled with ivory. Clipped to its pectoral fin was a diamond ring.

'From my own fishery at Misenum,' said Ampliatus proudly. 'A moray. It must be thirty years old if it's a day. You see the ring? I do believe, Popidius, that this is the creature your friend Nero used to sing to.' He picked up a large silver knife. 'Now who will have the first slice? You, Corelia—I think you should try it first.'

Now that was a nice gesture, thought Popidius. Up till this point, her father had conspicuously ignored her, and he had begun to suspect ill feeling between them, but here was a mark of favour. So it was with some astonishment that he saw the girl flash a look of undiluted hatred at her father, throw down her napkin, rise from her couch, and run sobbing from the table.

THE FIRST COUPLE of pedestrians Attilius approached swore they had never heard of Africanus's place. But at the crowded bar of Hercules, a little farther down the street, the man behind the counter gave him a shifty look and then provided directions in a quiet voice before saying, 'But be careful who you talk to, citizen.'

Attilius could guess what that meant and sure enough, from the moment he left the main road, the street curved and narrowed, the houses became meaner and more crowded. The brightly coloured dresses of the prostitutes bloomed in the gloom like blue and yellow flowers. So this was where Exomnius had chosen to spend his time!

At the end of the street, a first-floor balcony jutted over the pavement, reducing the road to scarcely more than a passageway. He shouldered his way past a group of loitering men, through the nearest open door, and into a dingy vestibule. There was a sharp, almost feral stink of sweat and semen. From upstairs came the sound of a flute, a thump on the floorboards, male laughter. On either side of him, from curtained cubicles, came the noises of the night—grunts, whispers, a child's whimper.

In the semidarkness, an elderly woman in a short green dress sat on a stool with her legs wide apart. She stood as she heard him enter and came towards him eagerly, vermilion lips cracked into a smile.

Attilius said, 'Africanus?'

'Not here,' she said. She had a thick accent. Cilician, perhaps.

'What about Exomnius?' At the mention of his name her painted mouth split wide. She tried to block his path, but he moved her out of his way, gently, his hands on her bare shoulders, and moved towards one of the cubicles on the opposite side of the vestibule. But the whore beat him to it, extending her arms to block his way.

'No,' she said. 'No trouble. He not here.'

'Where, then?'

She hesitated. 'Above.' She gestured with her chin towards the ceiling. 'I show,' she said, quickly. 'This way.'

She ushered him towards a second door. Attilius stepped into the street. She followed and pointed to the staircase a few paces farther on. She hurried back inside. As he started to mount the stone steps he heard her give a low whistle. When he reached the top of the staircase he did not bother to knock but flung open the door.

His quarry was already halfway out of the window, presumably tipped off by the whistle from the elderly whore. But the engineer was across the room and had him by his belt before he could drop down to the flat roof below. He was light and scrawny and Attilius hauled him back as easily as an owner might drag a dog back by his collar. He deposited him on the carpet and planted his foot firmly in the middle of Africanus's back.

'Good.' Attilius nodded. He smiled. He bent and grabbed Africanus by his belt again and dragged him out of the door.

'TEENAGE GIRLS!' said Ampliatus, as the sound of Corelia's footsteps died away. 'It's all just nerves before her wedding.'

He stuck his knife into the side of the eel, then gestured irritably to the nearest slave to carve. He watched the dexterous hand of the slave as he piled their plates with lumps of bony grey meat. Nobody wanted to eat it yet nobody wanted to be the first to refuse.

He was served first but he waited until the others all had their golden dishes set in front of them before breaking off a piece of fish. He raised it to his lips, paused, and glanced around the table, until, one by one, they wearily followed his example.

He had been anticipating this moment all day. Vedius Pollio had thrown his slaves to his eels not only to enjoy the novelty of seeing a man torn apart under water rather than by beasts in the arena, but also because, as a gourmet, he maintained that human flesh gave the morays a more piquant flavour. Ampliatus chewed carefully yet he tasted nothing. The meat was bland and leathery—inedible.

He scooped the fish out of his mouth with his fingers and threw it back on his plate in disgust. His guests were coughing politely into their napkins or picking the tiny bones out of their teeth and he knew they would all be laughing about him for days afterwards.

He noticed his steward, Scutarius, approaching the dining room carrying a small box. The steward hesitated, clearly not wanting to disturb his master with a business matter during a meal. Ampliatus screwed up his napkin, got to his feet, nodded curtly to his guests, and beckoned to Scutarius to follow him into the tablinum. Once they were out of sight he flexed his fingers. 'Give it here.'

The lock on the box had been broken. Ampliatus flipped open the lid. Inside were a dozen small rolls of papyri. He pulled out one at random. It was covered in columns of figures and for a moment Ampliatus squinted at it, baffled, but then the figures assumed a shape—he always did have a head for numbers—and he understood. 'Where is the man who brought this?'

'Waiting in the vestibule, master.'

'Take him into the old garden. Have the kitchen serve dessert and tell my guests I shall return shortly.'

Ampliatus took the back route, behind the dining room and up the wide staircase into the large courtyard of his old house. This was the place he had bought ten years earlier, deliberately settling himself next door to the ancestral home of the Popidii. What a pleasure it had been to live on an equal footing with his former masters and to bide his time, knowing even then that one day, somehow, he would punch a hole in the thick garden wall and swarm through to the other side, like an avenging army capturing an enemy city.

He sat himself on the circular stone bench in the centre of the garden, beneath the shade of a rose-covered pergola. This was where he liked to conduct his most private business. He could always talk here undisturbed. No one could approach him without being seen. He opened the box again and took out each of the papyri, then glanced up at the wide uncorrupted sky. He could hear Corelia's goldfinches, chirruping in their rooftop aviary and, beyond them, the drone of the city coming back to life after the long siesta.

He did not look up as he heard his visitor approach.

'So,' he said, 'it seems we have a problem.'

CORELIA HAD BEEN GIVEN the finches not long after the family had moved into the house, on her tenth birthday. She had fed them with scrupulous attention, tended them when they were sick, watched them hatch, mate, flourish, die, and now, whenever she wanted to be alone, it was to the aviary that she came. It occupied half of the small balcony outside her room, above the cloistered garden. The top of the cage was sheeted as protection against the sun.

She was sitting, drawn up tightly in the shady corner, her arms clasped round her legs, when she heard someone come into the courtyard. She edged forward and peered over the balustrade. Her father had settled himself onto the circular stone bench, and was reading through some papers. He laid the last one aside and stared at the sky, turning in her direction. She ducked her head back quickly.

She heard him say, 'So, it seems we have a problem.'

She had discovered as a child that the cloisters played a peculiar trick. The walls and pillars seemed to capture the sound of voices and funnel them upwards, so that even whispers, barely audible at ground level, were as distinct up here as speeches from the rostrum on election day. Most of what she heard when she was growing up had meant nothing to her—contracts, boundaries, rates of interest—the thrill had simply been to have a private window on the adult world. It was here, a month ago, that she had heard her own future being bargained away by her father with Popidius: so much to be discounted on the announcement of the betrothal, the full debt to be discharged once the marriage was transacted, a premium payable on account of virginity, virginity attested by the surgeon, Pumponius Magonianus, payment waived on signing of contracts within the stipulated period . . .

'I always say,' her father had whispered, 'speaking man to man here, Popidius, you can't put a price on a good fuck.'

'It seems we have a problem . . .'

A man's voice—harsh, not one she recognised—replied, 'Yes, we have a problem right enough. And his name is Marcus Attilius.'

She leaned forwards again so as not to miss a word.

ATTILIUS MARCHED Africanus down the staircase. 'I am an official here on the Emperor's business. I need to see where Exomnius lived. Take me to his room.'

'It's locked.'

'Where's the key?'

'Downstairs.'

'Get it.'

When they reached the street he pushed the brothel keeper back into the gloomy hallway and stood guard as he fetched his cash-box from its hiding place. The prostitute in the short green dress had returned to her stool: Zmyrina, Africanus called her—'Zmyrina, which is the key to Exomnius's room?'—his hands shaking so much that when finally he managed to open the cash-box and take out the keys he dropped them and she had to stoop and retrieve them for him. She picked out a key from the bunch and held it up.

'What are you so scared about?' asked Attilius.

'I don't want any trouble,' said Africanus. He took the key and led the way to the bar next door. It was a cheap place, with the same fetid smell as the brothel, and he thought that Exomnius must have fallen a long way—the corruption must have really entered his soul—for him to have ended up here.

Africanus scuttled through the bar and up the rickety wooden staircase to the landing. He turned towards the door with the key outstretched and then gave a little cry of surprise. He gestured to the lock and when Attilius stepped up next to him he saw that it was broken. The interior of the room was dark. Africanus went and unfastened the shutters. The afternoon light flooded a shambles of strewn clothes and upended furniture. Africanus gazed around him in dismay. 'This was nothing to do with me—I swear.'

Attilius took it all in at a glance. There had not been much in the room to start with—bed and thin mattress with a pillow and a coarse brown blanket, a washing jug, a pisspot, a chest, a stool—but nothing had been left untouched. Even the mattress had been slashed; its stuffing of horsehair bulged out in tufts.

'I believe you,' said Attilius. Africanus would hardly have broken his own lock when he had a key. On a little table was a lump of white and green marble that turned out, on closer inspection, to be a half-eaten loaf of bread. There was a fresh smear of fingerprints in the dust. Attilius touched the surface of the table and inspected the blackened tip of his finger. This had been done recently, he thought. The dust had not had time to resettle. Perhaps this was why Ampliatus had been so keen to show him the new baths—to keep him occupied while the rooms were searched? What a fool he had been, chattering on about lowland pine. He said, 'When did you last see Exomnius?'

Africanus spread his hands. How was he supposed to remember?

'When did he pay his rent?'

'In advance. On the calends of every month.'

'So he paid you at the beginning of August?' Africanus nodded. Then one thing was certain, Attilius thought. Whatever else had happened to him, Exomnius had not planned to disappear. The man was clearly a miser. He would never have paid for a room he had no intention of using. 'Leave me,' he said. 'I'll straighten it up.'

Africanus seemed about to argue, but when Attilius took a step towards him he held up his hands in surrender and retreated to the landing. The engineer closed the broken door.

So who had done this? He went round the room, reassembling it so that he could get an impression of how it had looked, as if by doing so he might get some clue as to what had happened.

A floorboard creaked on the landing. He turned to look at the door. The moving shadows of a pair of feet showed clearly beneath the cheap wood. 'Who's there?' he called, and then the door opened slowly and he saw it was only Zmyrina.

She gazed round the room and put her hands to her mouth in horror. 'Who done this?'

'You tell me.'

'He said when come back he take care for me.'

'Who?'

'Aelianus. He said.'

It took him a while to work out who she meant—Exomnius. Exomnius Aelianus. She was the first person he had met who had used the aquarius's given, rather than his family, name. That just about summed him up. His only intimate—a whore. 'Well, he obviously isn't coming back,' he said roughly.

She passed the back of her hand under her nose a couple of times and he realised that she was crying. 'He dead?'

'He might not be.' Attilius softened his tone. 'No one knows.'

'Buy me from Africanus. He said. No whore everyone. Special him. Understand?' She touched her chest and gestured to Attilius.

'Yes, I understand.'

He looked at Zmyrina with new interest. It was not uncommon, he knew, especially in this part of Italy. The foreign sailors, when they left the Navy after their twenty-five years' service and were granted Roman citizenship—the first thing most of them did with their demob money was head for the nearest slave market and buy themselves a wife. The prostitute was kneeling now, picking up clothes.

'He had the money, did he? Enough money to buy you? Only you wouldn't think it, to look at this place.'

'Not *here*.' She sat back on her heels and looked up at him with scorn. 'Not safe money *here*. Money hidden. Some place clever. Nobody find. He said. Nobody.'

'Well, it looks as though someone has had a good try.'

'Money not here.'

She was emphatic, and he thought, Yes, I bet you searched it yourself often enough when he wasn't around. 'I don't suppose he told you where this place was?'

She stared him, her vermilion mouth wide open, and suddenly she bent her head. Her shoulders were shaking. He thought at first she was crying but when she turned he saw that the glint in her eyes was from tears of laughter. 'No!' She clapped her hands. It was the funniest thing she had ever heard, and he had to agree—the idea of Exomnius confiding in a whore of Africanus where he had hidden his money—it was funny. He began laughing himself.

ATTILIUS HURRIED BACK up the hill towards the Vesuvius Gate. He had a feeling that he might be being followed and looked back over his shoulder but no one was paying him any attention. As he approached the small square in front of the castellum aquae he could see the oxen and the fully laden carts, and a small crowd of men sprawled in the dirt outside a bar. The horse he had hired was tethered to its post. And here was Polites—the most trustworthy member of the work gang—advancing to meet him.

'Where is Musa?' Attilius asked.

'Still not here, Aquarius.'

'What?' Attilius swore and cupped his hand to his eyes to check the position of the sun. It must be five hours since the others had ridden off. He had expected to receive some word by now.

'How many men do we have?'

'Twelve,' Polites said, rubbing his hands together uneasily.

'What's the matter with you?'

'They're a rough-looking lot, aquarius. And they've been drinking for an hour.'

'Then they'd better stop.'

He crossed the square to the bar. Ampliatus had promised a dozen of his strongest slaves and he had more than kept his word. It looked as if he had supplied a troop of gladiators. A flagon of wine was being passed round, from one pair of tattooed arms to another.

The engineer spoke loudly. 'I am Marcus Attilius, aquarius of the Aqua Augusta, and you men are under my command now. That's enough drinking. We're moving out.'

The man whose turn it was with the wine regarded Attilius with indifference. He raised the clay jar to his mouth, threw back his head and drank. Wine dribbled down his chin and onto his chest. There was an appreciative cheer and Attilius felt the anger ignite inside himself. 'Who is the senior man among you?'

The drinker lowered the flagon. '"The senior man,"' he mocked. 'What is this? The army?'

'You are drunk,' said Attilius quietly, 'and no doubt stronger than I. But I am sober, and in a hurry. Now *move*.' He lashed out with his foot and caught the flagon, knocking it out of the drinker's hand. It spun away and landed on its side, where it lay, unbroken, emptying itself across the stones. For a moment, in the silence, the glug-glug-glug of the wine was the only sound, and then there was a rush of activity—the men rising, shouting, the drinker lunging forwards, with the apparent intention of sinking his teeth into Attilius's leg. Through all this commotion, one booming voice rang louder than the rest—'Stop!'—and an enormous man, well over six feet tall, moved with surprising speed to plant himself between Attilius and the others. He had a coarse red beard, trimmed, shovel-shaped. He spread out his arms to keep them back.

'I am Brebix,' he said. 'A freed man.' He had a coarse red beard, trimmed, shovel-shaped. 'If anyone is senior, I am.'

Attilius nodded. This man, he saw, actually *was* a gladiator, or rather an ex-gladiator. He had the brand of his troop on his arm, a snake drawing back to strike. 'Tell these men that if they have any complaints, they should take them to Ampliatus. Tell them that none has to come with me, but any who stay behind will have to answer for it to their master. Now get those wagons out through the gate. I'll meet you on the other side of the city wall. Polites!'

'Yes?' The slave eased his way through the mob.

'Fetch me my horse. We've wasted enough time here. We'll meet up with Musa on the road.'

As Polites hurried away, Attilius glanced down the hill. Pompeii was like a frontier garrison. A boom town. Ampliatus was rebuilding it in his own image. He would not be sorry if he never saw it again—apart from Corelia. He wondered what she was doing, but even as the image of her wading towards him through the glittering pool began to form in his mind he forced himself to banish it. Get out of here, get to the Augusta, get the water running, and then get back to Misenum and check the aqueduct's records to see if there was some evidence there of what Exomnius had been up to. Those were his priorities. To think of anything else was foolish.

THE PUBLIC SUNDIAL showed it was well into the ninth hour when Attilius passed on horseback beneath the long vault of the Vesuvius Gate. The customs official poked his head out of his booth, yawned and turned away.

The engineer had never been a natural rider. For once, though, he was glad to be mounted: it gave him height. When he trotted over to Brebix and the men they were obliged to squint up at him, screwing their eyes against the glare of the sky.

'We follow the line of the aqueduct towards Vesuvius,' he said. 'And no dawdling. I want us to get there before dark.'

'Get where?' asked Brebix.

'I don't know exactly. It should be obvious when we see it.'

His vagueness provoked an uneasy stir among the men—and who could blame them? He would have liked to know where he was going himself. He turned his mount towards the open country. He raised himself from the saddle so he could see the course of the road beyond the necropolis. It ran straight towards the mountain through neat, rectangular fields of olive trees and corn, separated by low stone walls and ditches—centuriated land, awarded to demobbed legionaries decades ago. There was not much traffic on the paved highway—a cart or two, a few pedestrians. No sign of any plume of dust that might be thrown up by a galloping horseman.

He passed along the avenue between the tombs. He did not look back. The men would follow, he was fairly sure.

At the edge of the cemetery he drew on the reins and waited until he heard the creak of the wagons trundling over the stones. First the oxen passed him, heads down, each team led by a man with a stick, and then the lumbering carts and finally the rest of the work gang. Beside the road, the marker stones of the aqueduct, one every 100 paces, dwindled into the distance. Neatly spaced between them were the round stone inspection covers that gave access to the tunnel. The regularity and precision of it gave the engineer a fleeting sense of confidence. If nothing else, he knew how this worked.

He spurred his horse.

An hour later, with the afternoon sun dipping towards the bay, they were halfway across the plain—the parched and narrow fields spread out all around them, the ochre-coloured walls and watch-towers of Pompeii dissolving into the dust at their backs, the line of the aqueduct leading them remorselessly onwards, towards the blue-grey pyramid of Vesuvius, looming ever more massively ahead.

Hora Duodecima — 18:47 hours

Pliny had been monitoring the frequency of the trembling throughout the day—or, more accurately, his secretary, Alexion, had been doing it, seated at the table in the admiral's library, with a water clock on one side of him and a wine bowl on the other.

The fact that it was a public holiday made no difference to the admiral's routine. He worked whatever day it was. He had broken off from his reading and dictation only once, in midmorning, to bid goodbye to his guests, and had insisted on accompanying them down to the harbour to see them aboard their boats. Lucius Pomponianus and his wife Livia were bound for Stabiae, on the far side of the bay, and it had been arranged that they would take Rectina with them in their modest cruiser, as far as the Villa Calpurnia in Herculaneum. Pedius Cascus, without his wife, would take his own fully manned liburnian to Rome for a council meeting with the emperor. Old, dear friends! He had embraced them warmly. Pomponianus could play the fool, it was true, but his father, the great Pomponius Secundus, had been Pliny's patron, and he felt a debt of honour to the family. And as for Pedius and Rectina—their generosity to him had been without limit. It would have been hard for him to finish the *Natural History*, living outside Rome, without the use of their library.

The number of 'harmonic episodes', as he had decided to call the tremors, had increased steadily. Five in the first hour, seven in the second, eight in the third, and so on. More striking still had been their lengthening duration. Too small to measure at the beginning of the day, as the afternoon went on, Alexion had been able to use the water clock to estimate them—first at one-tenth part of the hour, and then one-fifth, until finally, for the whole eleventh hour, he had recorded one tremor only. The vibration of the wine was continuous.

And increasing in proportion with the movement of the earth, as if Man and Nature were bound by some invisible link, came reports of agitation in the town—a fight at the public fountains when the first hour's discharge had ended and not everyone had filled their pots; a riot outside the public baths when they had failed to open; a woman stabbed to death for the sake of two amphorae of water—water!—by a drunk outside the Temple of Augustus; now it was said that armed gangs were hanging round the fountains, waiting for a fight.

Pliny decreed that the evening's sacrifice to Vulcan should be cancelled and that the bonfire in the Forum must be dismantled at once. A large public gathering at night was a recipe for trouble. It was unsafe, in any case, to light a fire of such a size in the centre of the town when the pipes and fountains were dry and the drought had rendered the houses as flammable as kindling.

'The priests won't like that,' said Antius.

The flagship captain had joined the admiral in the library. The admiral's sister, Julia, who kept house for him, was also in the room, holding a tray of oysters and a jug of wine for his supper.

'Tell the priests we have no choice.' Pliny massaged his arm irritably. It felt numb. 'Have the men, apart from the sentry patrols, confined to barracks from dusk. In fact, I want a curfew imposed across the whole of Misenum from vespera until dawn. Anyone found on the streets is to be imprisoned and fined. Understood?'

'Yes, Admiral.'

'Have we opened the sluices in the reservoir yet?'

'It should be happening now, Admiral.'

Pliny brooded. They could not afford another such day. Everything depended on how long the water would last. He made up his mind. 'I'm going to take a look.'

'Is that wise, Brother?' Julia asked. 'You ought to eat and rest.'

'Don't nag, woman!' Her face crumpled and he regretted his tone at once. Life had knocked her about enough as it was—she was widowed with a boy to bring up. That gave him an idea. 'Gaius,' he said in a gentler voice. 'Forgive me, Julia. I spoke too sharply. I'll take Gaius with me, if that will make you happier.'

PLINY HAD GROWN too fat for a litter. He travelled instead by carriage, a two-seater, with his nephew Gaius wedged in next to him.

An escort of helmeted marines trotted on foot on either side of the carriage, clearing a path for them through the narrow streets. A couple of people jeered. Someone spat.

'What about our water, then?'

'Look at that fat bastard! I bet you he's not going thirsty!'

Gaius said, 'Shall I close the curtains, Uncle?'

'No, boy. Never let them see that you're afraid.'

Pliny knew there would be a lot of angry people on the streets tonight. Not just here, but in Neapolis and Nola and all the other towns, especially on a public festival.

They passed along the harbour front. An immense line of people had formed, queuing for the drinking fountain. Each had been allowed to bring one receptacle only and it was obvious to Pliny that an hour was never going to be sufficient for them all to receive their measure. Those who had been at the head of the line already had their ration and were hurrying away, cradling their pots and pans as if carrying gold. 'We shall have to extend the flow tonight,' he said, 'and trust that young aquarius to carry out the repairs as promised.'

Jolting around in the back of the carriage Pliny nodded off, and the next thing he knew they were drawing into the courtyard of the reservoir, past the flushed faces of half a dozen marines. He returned their salute and descended, unsteadily, on Gaius's arm.

He insisted on going down the steps into the reservoir unaided. The light was fading and a slave went on ahead with a torch. It was years since he had last been down here. Then, the pillars had been mostly submerged, and the crashing of the Augusta had drowned out any attempt at conversation. Now it echoed like a tomb. The size of it was astonishing. The level of the water had fallen so far beneath his feet he could barely make it out, until the slave held his torch over the mirrored surface, and then he saw his own face staring back at him—querulous, broken. The reservoir was also vibrating slightly, he realised, just like the wine.

'How deep is it?'

'Fifteen feet, Admiral,' said the slave.

'Allow half the water to drain away tonight. We shall let the rest go in the morning.'

IN POMPEII, the fire for Vulcan was to be lit as soon as it was dark. Before that, there was to be entertainment in the forum, supposedly paid for by Popidius, but in reality funded by Ampliatus—a bull-fight, three pairs of skirmishing gladiators, some boxers in the Greek style. Nothing elaborate, just an hour or so of diversion for the voters while they waited for night to arrive, the sort of spectacle an aedile was expected to lay on in return for the privilege of office.

Corelia feigned sickness. She lay on her bed thinking about the conversation she had overheard, and about the engineer, Attilius. She had noticed the way he looked at her, both in Misenum yesterday, and this morning, when she was bathing. Lover, avenger, rescuer, tragic victim—in her imagination she pictured him in all these parts, but always the fantasy dissolved into the same brutal coupling of facts: she had brought him into the orbit of her father and now her father was planning to kill him. His death would be her fault.

She listened to the sounds of the others preparing to leave. She heard her mother calling for her, and then her footsteps on the stairs. Quickly she felt for the feather she had hidden under her pillow. She opened her mouth and tickled the back of her throat, vomited noisily, and when Celsia appeared she wiped her lips and gestured weakly to the contents of the bowl.

Her mother sat on the edge of the mattress and put her hand on Corelia's brow. 'Oh, my poor child. I should send for the doctor.'

'No, sleep is all I need. It was that endless, awful meal.'

'But my dear, you hardly ate a thing!'

'That's not true—'

'Hush!' Her mother held up a warning finger. Someone else was mounting the steps, with a heavier tread, and Corelia braced herself for a confrontation with her father. He would not be so easy to fool. But it was only her brother, in his long white robes as a priest of Isis.

Once, the three of them had formed an alliance: had laughed about Ampliatus behind his back—his moods, his rages, his obsessions. But lately that had stopped. Their domestic triumvirate had broken apart under his relentless fury. Individual strategies for survival had been adopted. Corelia had observed her mother become the perfect Roman matron, while her brother had subsumed himself in his Egyptian cult. And she? What was she supposed to do? Marry Popidius and take a second master? Become more of a slave in the household than Ampliatus had ever been? She was too much her father's daughter not to fight.

'Run along, both of you,' she said, bitterly. 'I'm not going to his stupid spectacle.' She rolled onto her side and faced the wall.

IT WAS EXACTLY as the engineer had suspected. Having led them almost directly north towards the summit for a couple of miles, the aqueduct spur suddenly swung eastwards, just as the ground began to rise towards Vesuvius. The road turned with it and for the first time they had their backs to the sea and were pointing inland, towards the distant foothills of the Appenninus.

They had passed through the gridwork of centuriated fields and were entering the wine-growing country, owned by the big estates. The ramshackle huts of the smallholders on the plain, with their tethered goats and their hens pecking in the dust, had given way to handsome farmhouses with red-tiled roofs that dotted the lower slopes of the mountain. They came to a large villa looking out across the plain to the bay and Brebix asked if they could stop for a rest.

'All right. But not for long.'

Attilius dismounted and stretched his legs. Polites had bought a couple of loaves and some greasy sausages and Attilius ate hungrily. Astonishing, always, the effects of a bit of food in an empty stomach. He felt his spirits lift with each mouthful. This was always where he preferred to be—not in some filthy town, but out in the country, beneath an honest sky. He noticed Brebix sitting alone and went over and offered him some bread and a couple of sausages.

Brebix nodded and took the food. He was naked to the waist, his sweating torso crisscrossed with scars.

'What class of fighter were you?'

'Guess.'

'Not a retiarius,' Attilius said. 'I don't see you dancing around with a net and a trident.'

'You're right there.'

'So, a thrax, then. Or a murmillo, perhaps.' A thrax carried a small shield and a short, curved sword; a murmillo was a heavier fighter, armed like an infantryman, with a gladius and a full rectangular shield. The muscles of Brebix's left arm—his shield arm, more likely than not—bulged as powerfully as his right. 'I'd say a murmillo.' Brebix nodded. 'How many fights?'

'Thirty.'

Attilius was impressed. Not many men survived thirty fights. That was eight or ten years of appearances in the arena. 'Whose troop were you with?'

'Alleius Nigidius. I fought all around the bay. Pompeii, mostly. Nuceria. Nola. After I won my freedom I went to Ampliatus.'

'You didn't turn trainer?'

Brebix said quietly, 'I've seen enough killing, Aquarius. Thanks for the bread.' He got to his feet lightly, in a single, fluid motion, and went over to the others.

The engineer took a drink. He could see straight across the bay to the rocky islands off Misenum—little Prochyta and the high mountain of Aenaria—and for the first time he noticed that there was a swell on the water. Flecks of white foam had appeared among the tiny ships that were strewn like filings across the glaring, metallic sea. But none had hoisted a sail. And that was strange, he thought—that was odd—but it was a fact: *there was no wind.* Waves but no wind.

Another trick of nature for the admiral to ponder.

The sun was just beginning to dip behind Vesuvius. A hare eagle—small, black, powerful, famed for never emitting a cry—wheeled and soared in silence above the thick forest. They would soon be heading into shadow. Which was good, he thought, because it would be cooler, and also bad, because it meant there was not long till dusk.

He finished his water and called to the men to move on.

SHE COULD ALWAYS TELL when her father had gone. The whole place seemed to let out its breath. She slipped her cloak round her shoulders and opened the shutters. Her room faced west. On the other side of the courtyard the sky was as red as the terracotta roof, the garden beneath her balcony in shadow. A sheet still lay across the top of the aviary and she pulled it back, to give the birds some air, and then—on impulse: it had never occurred to her before—she released the catch and opened the door at the side of the cage.

It took a while for the goldfinches to sense their opportunity. Eventually, one bird, bolder than the rest, hopped onto the bottom of the door frame. It cocked its red-and-black-capped head at her, then launched itself into the air. It swooped across the garden and came to rest on the ridge tiles opposite. Another bird fluttered to the door and took off, and then another. She would have liked to stay and watch them all escape but instead she closed the shutters.

The passage outside her room was deserted, as were the stairs, as was the garden. She crossed it quickly, keeping close to the pillars in case she encountered anyone. She passed through into the atrium of their old house and turned towards the tablinum. This was where her father conducted his business affairs. It was a symbol of his power that the room contained not the usual one but three strongboxes, attached by iron rods to the stone floor.

Corelia knew where the keys were kept because in happier days she had been allowed to creep in and sit at his feet while he was working. She opened the drawer of the small desk, and there they were.

The document case was in the second strongbox. She did not bother to unroll the small papyri, but simply stuffed them into the pockets of her cloak, then locked the safe and replaced the key. She walked across the courtyard and down the staircase, past the swimming pool and the dining room, moving swiftly around the colonnade towards the drawing room of the Popidii.

A slave was lighting one of the brass candelabra but drew back respectfully against the wall to let her pass. Through a curtain. Another, narrower flight of stairs. And suddenly she was down into a different world—low ceilings, roughly plastered walls, a smell of sweat: the slaves' quarters. She could hear men talking somewhere and a clang of iron pots and then the whinny of a horse.

The stables were at the end of the corridor and, as she had thought, her father had decided to take his guests by litter to the forum, leaving the horses behind. She stroked the nose of her favourite, a bay mare. Saddling her was a job for the slaves but she had watched them often enough to know how to do it.

The stable door opened directly onto the side street. Every sound seemed absurdly loud to her—the bang of the iron bar as she lifted it, the creak of the hinges, the clatter of the mare's hoofs as she led her out into the road. From the direction of the forum came the noise of music and then a low roar, like the breaking of a wave.

She swung herself up onto the horse, sitting astride it like a man. She pressed her knees into the horse's flanks and pulled hard left on the reins, heading away from the forum. She stuck to the empty backstreets and only when she judged she was far enough away from the house to be unlikely to meet anyone she knew did she join the main road. Another wave of applause carried from the forum.

Up the hill she went, past the castellum aquae and under the arch of the city gate. She bowed her head as she passed the customs post, pulling the hood of her cloak low, and then she was out of Pompeii and on the road to Vesuvius.

Vespera — 20:00 hours

Attilius and his expedition reached the matrix of the Aqua Augusta just as the day was ending. One moment the engineer was watching the sun vanish behind the mountain, and the next it had gone. Looking ahead he saw, rising out of the darkening plain, what appeared to be gleaming heaps of pale sand. He squinted at them, then spurred his horse and galloped ahead of the wagons.

Four pyramids of gravel were grouped around a roofless, circular brick wall, about the height of a man's waist. It was a settling tank. He knew there would be at least a dozen of these along the length of the Augusta—one every three or four miles was Vitruvius's recommendation—places where the water was deliberately slowed to collect impurities as they sank to the bottom. Masses of tiny pebbles, worn perfectly smooth as they were washed along the matrix, had to be dug out every few weeks and piled beside the aqueduct to be carted away and either dumped or used for road-building.

A settling tank had always been a favourite place from which to run off a secondary line and as Attilius dismounted and strode across to it he saw that this was indeed the case here. The ground beneath his feet was spongy, the vegetation greener and more luxuriant, the soil singing with saturation. Water was bubbling over the carapace of the tank at every point, washing the brickwork with a shimmering, translucent film.

He rested his hands on the lip and peered over the side. It was twenty feet across and, he would guess, at least fifteen deep. With the sun gone it was too dark to see all the way to the gravel floor of the tank, but he knew there would be three tunnel mouths down there—one where the Augusta flowed in, one where it flowed out, and a third connecting Pompeii to the system. Water surged between his fingers. He wondered if Corvinus and Becco had shut off the sluices at Abellinum. If so, the flow should be starting to ease very soon. He heard feet squelching over the ground behind him. Brebix and a couple of the other men were walking across from the wagons.

'So is this the place, Aquarius?'

'No, Brebix. Not yet. But not far now. You see that? The way the water is gushing from below? That's because the main line is blocked somewhere farther down its course. We need to get moving again.'

It was not a popular decision. Attilius hitched his horse to the back of one of the wagons and when Brebix asked him what he was doing he said, 'I'll walk with the rest of you.' He took the halter of the nearest ox and tugged it forwards. At first nobody moved but then, grudgingly, they set off after him.

They were crossing a narrow plain. Vesuvius was to their left; to their right, the edge of the Appenninus rose like a wall. The road had parted company with the aqueduct and they were following a track, plodding along beside the Augusta—marker stone, manhole, marker stone, manhole, on and on—through ancient groves of olives and lemons, as pools of darkness began to gather beneath the trees. There was little to hear above the rumble of the wheels except the occasional sound of goats' bells in the dusk.

Attilius kept glancing off to the line of the aqueduct. Water was bubbling round the edges of some of the manholes, and that was ominous. The aqueduct tunnel was six feet high. If the force of the water was sufficient to dislodge the heavy inspection covers, then the pressure must be immense, which in turn suggested that the obstruction in the matrix must be equally massive, otherwise it would have been swept away. Where were Corax and Musa?

An immense crash, like a peal of thunder, sounded away to their left. It echoed off the rock face with a flat boom. The ground heaved and the oxen shied, turning from the noise, dragging him with them. He dug his heels into the track and had just about managed to bring them to a halt when one of the men shrieked and pointed. 'Giants!' Huge white creatures, ghostly in the twilight, seemed to be issuing from beneath the earth ahead of them, as if the roof of Hades had split apart and the spirits of the dead were flying into the sky. Even Attilius felt the hair stiffen on the back of his neck and it was Brebix in the end who laughed and said, 'They're only birds, you fools! Look!'

Birds—immense birds: flamingos, were they?—hundreds of them. They rose like some great white sheet that fluttered and dipped and then settled out of sight again. Flamingos, thought Attilius: water birds. In the distance he saw two men, waving.

NERO HIMSELF, if he had spent a year on the task, could not have wished for a finer artificial lake than that which the Augusta had created in barely a day and a half. A shallow depression to the north of the matrix had filled to a depth of three or four feet. The surface was softly luminous in the dusk, broken here and there by clumpy islands formed by the dark foliage of half-submerged olive trees. Water fowl scudded between them; flamingos lined the distant edge.

The men of Attilius's work gang tore off their tunics and ran naked towards it. Whoops and splashes carried to where Attilius stood with Musa and Corvinus. He made no attempt to stop them. He had a fresh mystery to contend with: Corax was missing.

According to Musa, he and the overseer had discovered the lake less than two hours after leaving Pompeii—around noon it must have been—and it was exactly as Attilius had predicted: how could anyone miss a flood of this size? After a brief inspection of the damage, Corax had remounted his horse and set off back to Pompeii to report on the scale of the problem, exactly as agreed.

Attilius's jaw was set in a grim line. 'But that must have been seven or eight hours ago. Come on, Musa—what really happened?'

'I'm telling you the truth, Aquarius. I swear it!' Musa's eyes were wide with alarm. 'Something must have happened to him!'

Beside the open manhole, Musa and Corvinus had lit a fire, not to keep themselves warm—the air was still sultry—but to ward off evil.

'Perhaps we missed him on the road somehow.' But even as he said it Attilius knew that it could not be right. Attilius peered into the encroaching gloom. 'This makes no sense. Besides, I thought I made it clear that you were to bring us the message, not Corax.'

'He insisted on going to fetch you.'

He has run away, thought Attilius. It had to be the likeliest explanation. He and his friend, Exomnius, together—they had fled.

'This place,' said Musa, looking around. 'I'll be honest with you, it gives me the creeps. That noise just now—did you hear it?'

'Of course we heard it. They must have heard it in Neapolis.'

'And just you wait till you see what's happened to the matrix.'

Attilius went to the wagons and collected a torch. He returned and thrust it into the flames. It ignited immediately. The three of them gathered round the opening in the earth, and once again he caught the whiff of sulphur rising from the darkness. 'Fetch me some rope,' he said to Musa. 'It's with the tools.' He glanced at Corvinus. 'And how did it go with you? Did you close the sluices?'

'Yes, Aquarius. We had to argue with the priest but convinced him.'

'What time did you shut it off?'

'The seventh hour.'

Attilius massaged his temples, trying to work it out. The level of water in the flooded tunnel would start to drop in a couple of hours. But unless he sent Corvinus back to Abellinum almost immediately, Becco would follow his instruction, wait twelve hours, and reopen the sluices during the sixth watch. It was all desperately tight.

When Musa came back Attilius handed him the torch. He tied one end of the rope round his waist and sat on the edge of the open manhole. 'Make sure you don't let go of the other end.'

Three feet of earth, thought Attilius, then two of masonry and then six of nothing from the top of the tunnel roof to the floor. Eleven feet in all. I had better land well. He turned and lowered himself into the narrow shaft, his fingers holding tight to the lip of the manhole, and let himself drop, bending his knees as he landed to absorb the shock. He crouched there for a moment, recovering his balance, the stink of sulphur in his nostrils, then cautiously felt outwards with his hands.

The tunnel was only three feet wide. Dry cement beneath his fingers. Darkness. He stood, squeezed himself back a pace and shouted up to Musa, 'Throw down the torch!'

The flame guttered as it fell and for a moment he feared it had gone out, but when he bent to take the handle it flared again, lighting the walls. The lower part was encrusted with lime deposited by the water over the years. Its roughened, bulging surface looked more like the wall of a cave than anything man-made.

He turned awkwardly in the confined space, holding the torch in front of him, and strained his eyes into the darkness. He could see nothing. He began to walk, counting each pace, and when he reached eighteen he gave a murmur of surprise. It was not simply that the tunnel was entirely blocked—he had expected that—but rather it seemed as if the floor had been driven upwards, pushed from below by some irresistible force. The thick concrete bed on which the channel rested had been sheared and a section of it sloped towards the roof. He heard Musa shout behind him, 'Can you see it?'

'Yes, I see it!'

The tunnel narrowed dramatically. He had to get down on his knees and shuffle forwards. The fracturing of the base had buckled the walls and collapsed the roof. Water was seeping through a mass of bricks and earth and lumps of concrete. He scraped at it with his free hand, but the stench of sulphur was strongest here and the flames of his torch began to dwindle. He backed away, reversing all the way to the shaft of the manhole. Looking up he could just make out the faces of Musa and Corvinus framed by the evening sky. He leaned his torch against the tunnel wall.

'Hold the rope fast. I'm coming out.' He untied it from round his waist and gave it a sharp pull. 'Ready?'

'Yes!'

He grasped the rope and hauled himself up into the fresh night air. A full moon was rising.

'Well?' said Musa. 'What did you make of it?'

The engineer shook his head. 'I've never seen anything like it. I've seen roof falls and I've seen landslips on the sides of mountains. But this? This looks as though an entire section of the floor has just been shifted upwards. That's new to me.'

'Corax said exactly the same.'

Attilius got to his feet and peered down the shaft. 'This land,' he said bitterly. 'It looks solid enough. But it's no more firm than water.' He started walking, retracing his steps along the course of the Augusta. He counted off eighteen paces and stopped. Now that he studied the ground more closely he saw that it was bulging slightly. He scraped a mark with the edge of his foot and walked on, counting again. The swollen section did not seem very wide. Six yards, perhaps, or eight. He made another mark.

He experienced a sudden rush of optimism. Actually, it wasn't too big, this blockage. The more he pondered it, the less likely it seemed to him to have been the work of an earthquake, which could easily have shaken the roof down along an entire section—now *that* would have been a disaster. But this was much more localised: more as if the land had risen a yard or two along a narrow line.

He turned in a full circle. Yes, he could see it now. The ground had heaved. The matrix had been obstructed. At the same time the pressure of the movement had opened a crack in the tunnel wall. The water had escaped into the depression and formed a lake. But if they could clear the blockage and let the Augusta drain . . .

He decided at that moment that he would not send Corvinus back to Abellinum. He would try to fix the Augusta overnight. He cupped his hands to his mouth and shouted to the men. 'All right, gentlemen! The baths are closing! Let's get to work!'

WOMEN DID NOT OFTEN travel alone along the public highways of Campania and as Corelia passed peasants working in the fields they turned to stare at her. Even some brawny farmer's wife, as broad as she was tall and armed with a stout hoe, might have hesitated to venture out unprotected at vespera. But an obviously rich young woman? On a fine-looking horse? How juicy a prize was that? Twice men stepped out into the road and attempted to block her path, but each time she spurred her mount onwards and after a few hundred paces they gave up trying to chase her.

She knew the route the aquarius had taken from her eavesdropping that afternoon. But what had sounded a simple enough journey in a sunlit garden—following the line of the Pompeii aqueduct to the point where it joined the Augusta—was a terrifying undertaking when actually attempted at dusk, and by the time she reached the vineyards on the foothills of Vesuvius she was wishing she had never come. But it was too late to turn back now.

Work was ending for the day and lines of exhausted, silent slaves, shackled together at the ankles, were shuffling beside the road in the twilight. The clank of their chains against the stones and the flick of the overseer's whip across their backs were the only sounds. She had heard about such wretches, crammed into the prison blocks attached to the larger farms and worked to death within a year or two: she had never actually seen them close-up. Occasionally a slave found the energy to raise his eyes from the dirt and meet her glance; it was like staring through a hole into hell.

And yet she would not give in, even as nightfall emptied the road of traffic and the line of the aqueduct became harder to follow. Her horse slowed to a walk and she swayed in time with its plodding motion.

It was hot. She was thirsty. (Naturally, she had forgotten to bring any water: that was something the slaves always carried for her.) She was sore where her clothes chafed against her sweating skin. Only the thought of the aquarius and the danger he was in kept her moving. She was just beginning to wonder whether she would ever catch up with him when the heavy air seemed to turn solid and to hum around her, and an instant later, from deep inside the mountain to her left, came a loud crack. Her horse reared, pitching her backwards, and she was almost thrown, the reins snapping through her fingers. When it plunged forwards again and set off at a gallop she only saved herself by wrapping her fingers in its mane and clinging for her life.

It must have charged for a mile or more and when at last it began to slow and she was able to raise her head she found that they had left the road and were cantering over open ground. She could hear water somewhere near and the horse must have heard it, too, or smelled it, because it turned and began walking towards the sound. She could make out white heaps of stone and a low wall that seemed to enclose an enormous well. The horse bent to drink. She whispered to it, and gently dismounted. She was trembling with shock. Her feet sank into mud. In the distance she could see campfires.

ATTILIUS'S FIRST OBJECTIVE was to remove the debris from underground: no easy task. The tunnel was only wide enough for one man at a time to confront the obstruction, to swing a pickaxe and dig with a shovel, and once a basket was filled it had to be passed along the matrix from hand to hand until it reached the bottom of the inspection shaft, then attached to a rope and hauled to the surface, emptied, and sent back again, by which time a second basket had already been loaded and dispatched on its way.

Attilius, in his usual manner, had taken the first turn with the pick.

He tore a strip from his tunic and tied it round his mouth and nose to try to reduce the smell of the sulphur. Hacking away at the brick and earth and then shovelling it into the basket was bad enough. But trying to wield the axe in the cramped space and still find the force to smash the concrete into manageable lumps was a labour fit for Hercules. Before long he had scraped his elbows raw against the walls of the tunnel. As for the heat, compounded by the sweltering night, the sweating bodies and the burning torches—that was worse than he imagined it could be even in the gold mines of Hispania. But still, Attilius had a sense of progress, and that gave him extra strength. He had found the spot where the Augusta was choked. All his problems would be overcome if he could clear these few narrow yards.

After a while, Brebix tapped him on the shoulder and offered to take over. Attilius gratefully handed him the pick and watched in awe as the big man swung it as easily as if it were a toy. The engineer moved back along the line and the others shifted to make room for him. They were working as a team now, like a single body: the Roman way. And whether it was the restorative effects of their bathe, or relief at having a specific task to occupy their thoughts, the mood of the men appeared transformed. He began to think that perhaps they were not such bad fellows after all. You could say what you liked about Ampliatus: at least he knew how to train a slave gang.

Gradually he lost track of time, his world restricted to this narrow few feet of tunnel, his sensations to the ache of his arms and back, the pain of his skinned elbows, the suffocating heat. He was so absorbed that at first he did not hear Brebix shouting to him.

'Aquarius! *Aquarius!*'

'Yes?' He squeezed past the men, aware for the first time that the water in the tunnel was up to his ankles. 'What is it?'

'Look for yourself.'

Attilius took a torch from the man behind him and held it up close to the compacted mass of bricks, concrete and earth. At first glance it looked solid enough, but then he saw that it was seeping water everywhere. Tiny rivulets were running down the oozing bulk, as if it had broken into a sweat. Brebix prodded it with the axe. 'If this lot goes, we'll be drowned like rats in a sewer.'

Attilius was aware of the silence behind him. The slaves had all stopped work and were listening. Looking back he saw that they had already cleared four or five yards of debris. So what was left to hold back the weight of the Augusta? A few feet? He did not want to stop.

But he did not want to kill them all, either.

'All right,' he said, reluctantly. 'Clear the tunnel.'

They needed no second telling, and by the time Attilius and Brebix reached the manhole they were the only ones left below ground.

Brebix offered him the rope. Attilius hesitated. 'No. You go. I'll stay down and see what else can be done.' Brebix looked at him as if he were mad. 'I'll fasten the rope round me for safety. When you get to the top, untie it from the wagon and pay out enough for me to reach the end of the tunnel. Keep a firm hold.'

Brebix ascended the rope, and then Attilius was alone. As he knotted the rope round his waist for a second time he thought that perhaps he was mad, but there seemed no alternative, for until the tunnel was drained they could not repair it. He tugged on the rope. 'All right, Brebix?'

'Ready!'

He picked up his torch and began moving back along the tunnel, the water above his ankles now. He moved slowly, so that Brebix could pay out the rope, and by the time he reached the debris he was sweating, from nerves as much as from the heat. He could sense the weight of the Augusta behind it. He transferred the torch into his left hand and with his right began pulling at the exposed end of a brick that was level with his face, working it up and down and from side to side. A small gap was what he needed: a controlled release of pressure from near the top of the obstruction. At first the brick wouldn't budge. Then water started to bubble around it and suddenly it shot through his fingers, propelled by a jet that fired it past his head, so close that it grazed his ear.

He cried out and backed away as the area around the leak bulged then sprang apart, peeling outwards and downwards in a V before a wall of water descended over him, smashing him backwards, knocking the torch out of his hand and submerging him in darkness. He hurtled under water very fast—on his back, headfirst—swept along the tunnel, scrabbling for a purchase on the smooth cement render of the matrix, but there was nothing he could grip. The surging current rolled him, flipped him over onto his stomach, and he felt a flash of pain as the rope snapped tight beneath his ribs, folding him and jerking him upwards, grazing his back against the roof. For a moment he thought he was saved, only for the rope to go slack again and for him to plunge to the bottom of the tunnel, the current sweeping him on—on like a leaf in a gutter—on into the darkness.

Nocte Concubia — 22:07 hours

Ampliatus had never cared for Vulcanalia. The festival marked that point in the calendar when nights fell noticeably earlier and mornings had to start by candlelight: the end of summer and the start of the long, melancholy decline into winter. And the ceremony itself was distasteful. Vulcan dwelt in a cave beneath a mountain and spread devouring fire across the earth. All creatures went in fear of him, except for fish, and so—on the principle that gods, like humans, desire most that which is least attainable—he had to be appeased by a sacrifice of fish thrown live onto a burning pyre.

It was not that Ampliatus was entirely lacking in religious feeling. He liked to see a good-looking animal slaughtered—the placid manner of a bull, say, as it plodded towards the altar, and the way it stared at the priest so bemusedly; then the stunning and unexpected blow from the assistant's hammer and the flash of the knife as its throat was cut. Now *that* was religious. But to see hundreds of small fish tossed into the flames: there was nothing noble in it as far as he was concerned.

And it was particularly tedious this year because of the record numbers who wished to offer a sacrifice. The endless drought, the failure of springs and the drying of wells, the shaking of the ground—all this was held to be the work of Vulcan, and there was much apprehension in the town.

He did not have a very good position. The rulers of the town, as tradition demanded, were gathered on the steps of the Temple of Jupiter—the magistrates and the priests at the front, the members of the Ordo, including his own son, grouped behind, whereas Ampliatus, as a freed slave, with no official recognition, was invariably banished by protocol to the back. He left before the end.

He decided he would walk rather than ride in his litter. He was not afraid of Pompeii after dark. He knew every stone of the town, every hump and hollow in the road, every storefront, every drain. Besides, the full moon and the occasional streetlight—another of his innovations—showed him the way home clearly enough.

He turned down the hill towards his house—his *houses*, he should say—and stopped for a moment to savour the night air. He loved this town. True, when it was hot and listless, as it was tonight, the grander people complained that the town stank. But he almost preferred it when the air was heavier—the dung of the horses in the streets, the urine in the laundries, the fish-sauce factories down in the harbour, the sweat of twenty thousand human bodies. To Ampliatus this was the smell of life: of activity, money, profit.

He resumed his walk and when he reached his front door he stood beneath the lantern and knocked loudly. It was still a pleasure for him to come in through the entrance he had not been permitted to use as a slave and he rewarded the porter with a smile.

As he passed the swimming pool, lit by torches, he paused to study the fountain. It seemed that it was beginning to lose its strength, and he thought of the solemn young aquarius, out in the darkness somewhere, trying to repair the aqueduct. He would not be coming back. It was a pity. They might have done business together. But he was honest, and Ampliatus's motto was always 'May the gods protect us from an honest man'. He might even be dead by now.

TWICE AFTER THE ROPE gave way Attilius managed to jam his knees and elbows against the narrow walls of the matrix in an effort to wedge himself fast and he succeeded only to be pummelled loose by the pressure of the water and propelled farther along the tunnel. Limbs weakening, lungs bursting, he sensed he had one last chance and tried again, and this time he stuck, spread like a starfish. His head broke the surface and he choked and spluttered, gasping for breath.

In the darkness he had no idea how far he had been carried. He could see and hear nothing, feel nothing except the cement against his hands and knees and the pressure of the water up to his neck, hammering against his body. He had no idea how long he clung there but gradually the pressure slackened and the level of the water fell. When he felt the air on his shoulders he knew the worst was over. Soon after that his chest was clear of the surface. Cautiously he let go of the walls and stood. He swayed backwards in the current and then came upright again, like a tree that had survived a flash flood.

The backed-up waters were draining away, he realised, and because the sluices had been closed in Abellinum twelve hours earlier there was nothing left to replenish them. What remained was being tamed and reduced by the gradient of the aqueduct. He felt something tug at his waist. The rope was streaming out behind him. He fumbled for it in the darkness and hauled it in, coiling it round his arm. When he reached the end he ran his fingers over it. Smooth.

Not frayed or hacked. Brebix must simply have let go. Suddenly he was panicking, frantic to escape. He leaned forwards and began to wade but it was like a nightmare—his hands stretched out invisible in front of him feeling along the walls into the infinite dark. He felt himself doubly imprisoned, by the earth pressing in all around him, by the weight of the water ahead. His ribs ached. His shoulder felt as if it had been branded by fire.

He heard a splash and then in the distance a pinprick of yellow light dropped like a falling star. He stopped wading and listened, breathing hard. More shouts, followed by a second splash, and then another torch appeared. They were searching for him. He heard a faint shout—'Aquarius!'—and tried to decide whether he should reply. He was scaring himself with shadows, surely? The wall of debris had given way so abruptly and with such force that no normal man would have had the strength to hold him. But Brebix was not a man of normal strength and what had happened was not unexpected: the gladiator was supposed to have been braced against it.

He hesitated. There was no other way out of the tunnel. He would have to go and face them. But his instinct told him to keep his suspicions to himself. He shouted back, 'I'm here!' and splashed on through the dwindling water towards the waving lights.

They greeted him with a mixture of wonder and respect—Brebix, Musa and young Polites all crowding round to meet him—for it had seemed to them, they said, that nothing could have survived the flood. Brebix insisted that the rope had shot through his hands like a serpent and as proof he showed his palms. In the torchlight each was crossed by a vivid burn mark. Perhaps he was telling the truth, thought Attilius. He sounded contrite enough. But then any assassin would look shamefaced if his victim came back to life.

'You're favoured by the gods, Aquarius,' declared Musa. 'They have some destiny in mind for you.'

'My destiny,' said Attilius, 'is to repair this aqueduct and get back to Misenum.' He unfastened the rope from round his waist, took Polites's torch and shone the light along the tunnel.

How quickly the water was draining! It was already below his knees, on its way to Nola and the other towns. Soon this section would be drained entirely. There would be nothing more than puddles on the floor.

The point where the tunnel had been blocked was still a mess but the force of the flood had done most of their work for them. Now it was a matter of clearing out the rest of the earth and rubble, smoothing the floor and walls, putting down a bed of concrete and a fresh lining of bricks, then a render of cement—nothing fancy: just temporary repairs until they could get back to do a proper job in the autumn. It was still a lot of work to get through in a night, before the first tongues of fresh water reached them from Abellinum, after Becco had reopened the sluices. He told them what he wanted.

Brebix said, 'At least the stink has gone.'

Attilius had not noticed it before. He sniffed the air. It was true. The pervasive stench of sulphur seemed to have been washed away.

He heard his name being called and he kicked his way back through the water to the inspection shaft. It was Corvinus's voice. 'Aquarius! I think you ought to come and see.'

Attilius took the rope and started climbing. In his bruised and exhausted state it was harder work than before.

There was quite an operation in progress on the surface by now: the heaps of spoil excavated from the tunnel, a couple of big bonfires spitting sparks at the harvest moon, torches planted in the ground to provide additional light. The slaves of Ampliatus's work gang were leaning against the carts, waiting for orders. They watched him with curiosity as he hauled himself to his feet. He must look a sight, he realised, drenched and dirty. He saw Corvinus, who was about thirty paces away, close to the oxen, with his back to the manhole. Attilius shouted to him impatiently. 'Well?'

Corvinus turned and by way of explanation stepped aside revealing behind him a figure in a hooded cloak. Attilius set off towards them and it was only as he came closer and the stranger pulled back the hood that he recognised her. He could not have been more startled if Egeria herself, the goddess of the water spring, had suddenly materialised in the moonlight.

'Corelia—what is this?'

As Corvinus slouched away, Attilius examined her more closely. Cheeks smudged, hair dishevelled, cloak and dress spattered with mud. But it was her eyes, unnaturally wide and bright, that were most disturbing. He took her hand. 'This is no place for you,' he said gently.

'I wanted to bring you these,' she whispered, and from the folds of her cloak she began producing small cylinders of papyri.

The documents were of different ages and conditions. Six in total and small enough to fit into the cradle of one arm. Attilius took a torch and with Corelia beside him moved away from the activity around the aqueduct to a private spot behind one of the wagons.

He took her cloak from her shoulders and spread it out for her to sit on. Then he jammed the handle of the torch into the earth, squatted and unrolled the oldest of the documents. It was a plan of one section of the Augusta—this very section: Pompeii, Nola and Vesuvius were all marked in ink that had faded from black to pale grey. A surveyor's drawing, he thought. Drafted more than a century ago. Such a document could only have come from one of two places: the archive of the Curator Aquarum in Rome, or the Piscina Mirabilis in Misenum.

The next three papyri consisted of columns of numerals and it took him a while to make sense of them. One was headed *Colonia Veneria Pompeianorum* and was divided into years—DCCCXIV, DCCCXV and so on—going back nearly two decades, with further subdivisions of figures and totals. The quantities increased annually, until by the year ended last December, Rome's eight hundred and thirty-third, they had doubled. The second document seemed at first glance to be identical until he studied it more closely and saw that the figures throughout were roughly half as large as in the first. For example, for the last year, the grand total of 352,000 recorded in the first papyri had been reduced in the second to 178,000.

The third document was less formal. It looked like the record of a man's income. Again there were almost two decades' worth of figures and again the sums gradually mounted until they had almost doubled. And a good income it was—perhaps 50,000 sesterces in the last year alone, maybe a third of a million overall.

Corelia was sitting with her knees drawn up, watching him. 'Well? What do they mean?'

'These look like the actual figures for the amount of water consumed in Pompeii.' He showed her the first papyrus. 'Three hundred and fifty thousand quinariae last year—that would be about right for a town of Pompeii's size. And this second set of records I presume is the one that my predecessor, Exomnius, officially submitted to Rome. They wouldn't know the difference. And this'—he did not try to hide his contempt as he flourished the third document—'is what your father paid him to keep his mouth shut.' She looked at him, bewildered. 'Water is expensive,' he explained, 'especially if you are rebuilding half a town. "At least as valuable as money"—that's what your father said to me.' No doubt it would have made the difference between profit and loss. *Salve lucrum!*

He rolled up the papyri. They must have been stolen from

Exomnius's squalid room, he thought. That would explain why it had been searched so thoroughly. He wondered briefly why Exomnius would have run the risk of keeping such an incriminating record. But then he supposed that they would have given him a powerful hold over Ampliatus: *Don't ever think of trying to move against me—because if I am ruined, I can ruin you with me.*

The final pair of documents were so different from the others it was as if they did not belong with them. They were much newer, and instead of figures were covered in writing. The first was in Greek.

> *The summit itself is mostly flat, and entirely barren. The soil looks like ash, and there are cave-like pits of blackened rock, looking gnawed by fire. This area appears to have been on fire in the past and to have had craters of flame which were subsequently extinguished by a lack of fuel. No doubt this is the reason for the fertility of the surrounding area, as at Caetana, where they say that soil filled with the ash thrown up by Etna's flames makes the land particularly good for vines. The enriched soil contains both material that burns and material that fosters production. When it is overcharged with the enriching substance it is ready to burn, as is the case with all sulphurous substances, but when this has been exuded and the fire extinguished the soil becomes ash-like and suitable for produce.*

Attilius had to read it through twice before he was sure he had the sense of it. He passed it to Corelia. *The summit?* The summit of what? Of Vesuvius, presumably—that was the only summit round here. But had Exomnius—lazy, hard-drinking, whore-loving Exomnius—really found the energy to climb to the top of Vesuvius, in a drought, to record his impressions in Greek? It defied belief. And the language was too literary, not at all the sort of phrases that would come naturally to a man like Exomnius, who was surely no more fluent in the tongue of the Hellenes than Attilius was himself. He must have copied it from somewhere. Or had it copied for him. By one of the scribes in the public library on the forum, perhaps.

The final papyrus was in Latin. But the content was equally strange:

> *Lucilius, my friend, I have just heard that Pompeii, the famous city in Campania, has been laid low by an earthquake which also disturbed all the adjacent districts. Also, part of the town of Herculaneum is in ruins. Neapolis also lost many dwellings. To these calamities others were added: they say that hundreds of*

sheep were killed, and some people were deranged and afterwards wandered about unable to help themselves.

I have said that a flock of hundreds of sheep were killed in the Pompeiian district. There is no reason you should think this happened to those sheep because of fear. For they say that a plague usually occurs after a great earthquake, and this is not surprising. For many death-carrying elements lie hidden in the depths. The very atmosphere there is harmful to those breathing it. I am not surprised that sheep have been infected—sheep which have a delicate constitution—the closer they carried their heads to the ground, since they received the afflatus of the tainted air near to the ground itself. If the air had come out in greater quantity it would have harmed people too; but the abundance of pure air extinguished it before it rose high enough to be breathed by people.

Again, the language seemed too flowery to be the work of Exomnius, thc script too professional. In any case, why would Exomnius have claimed to have *just heard* about an earthquake that had happened seventeen years earlier? And who was Lucilius? Corelia had leaned across to read the document over his shoulder. He could smell her perfume, feel her breath on his cheek, her breast pressed against his arm. He said, 'And you are sure these were with the other papyri? They could not have come from somewhere else?'

'They were in the same box. What do they mean?'

'And you didn't see the man who brought the box to your father?'

Corelia shook her head. 'I could only hear him. They talked about you. What they said made me decide to find you. My father said he didn't want you to come back from this expedition alive.'

He tried to sound unconcerned. 'And what did the other man say?'

'He said that it would not be a problem.'

Silence. He felt her hand touch his—her cool fingers on his raw cuts and scratches—and then she rested her head against his chest. For a moment, for the first time in three years, he savoured the sensation of a having woman's body close to his.

After a while she fell asleep. Carefully, so as not to wake her, he disengaged his arm. He left her and walked back over to the aqueduct.

The slaves had stopped bringing debris up out of the tunnel and had started lowering bricks down into it. Attilius warily approached Brebix and Musa, who were standing talking together.

His mind was in a turmoil. That Exomnius was corrupt was no

surprise—he had been resigned to that. And he had assumed his dishonesty explained his disappearance. But these other documents, this piece of Greek and this extract from a letter, these cast the mystery in a different light entirely. Now it seemed that Exomnius had been worried about the soil through which the Augusta passed—the sulphurous, tainted soil—at least three weeks before the aqueduct had been contaminated. Worried enough to look out a set of the original plans and to go researching in Pompeii's public library.

Attilius stared distractedly down into the depths of the matrix. He was remembering his exchange with Corax in the Piscina Mirabilis the previous evening: Corax's sneer—'*He knew this water better than any man alive. He would have seen this coming*'—and his own, unthinking retort—'*Perhaps he did, and that was why he ran away.*' For the first time he had a presentiment of something terrible. Too much was out of the ordinary—the failure of the matrix, the trembling of the ground, springs running backwards into the earth, sulphur poisoning . . . Exomnius had sensed it, too.

'Musa?'

'Yes, Aquarius?'

'Where was Exomnius from? Which part of Sicily exactly?'

'I think the east.' Musa frowned. 'Caetana. Why?'

But the engineer, gazing across the narrow moonlit plain towards the shadowy mass of Vesuvius, did not reply.

JUPITER

August 24: The day of the eruption

Hora Prima — 06:20 hours

He kept his increasing anxiety to himself all through the sweltering night, as they worked by torchlight to repair the matrix. By the time the sky above the manhole was turning grey he knew that they had done enough to bring the Augusta back into service. He would have to return to repair her properly. But for now, with luck, she would hold.

The breaking day showed that they had pitched their camp in rough pasture, littered with rock, flanked by mountains. To the east were the steep cliffs of the Appenninus, with a town—Nola, presumably—just becoming visible in the dawn light about five or six miles away. But the shock was to discover how close they were to Vesuvius. It lay directly to the west and the land started to rise almost immediately, within a few hundred paces of the aqueduct. And what was most unsettling, now that the shadows were lifting, were the streaks of greyish-white beginning to appear across one of its flanks. They stood out clearly against the surrounding forest, shaped like arrow-heads, pointing towards the summit. If it had not been August he would have sworn that they were made of snow.

'Ice?' said Brebix, gawping at the mountain. 'Ice in August?'

Attilius was thinking of the description in the Greek papyri: '*the ash thrown up by Etna's flames makes the land particularly good for vines*'. 'Could it,' he said almost to himself, 'could it perhaps be *ash*?'

'But how can there be ash without fire?' objected Musa. 'And if there had been a fire that size in the darkness we would have seen it.'

'That's true.' Attilius glanced around at their exhausted, fearful faces. The lake had gone, and with it, he noticed, the birds. Along the mountain ridge opposite Vesuvius the sun was beginning to appear. There was a strange stillness in the air. No birdsong of any sort. No dawn chorus. That would send the augurs into a frenzy. 'And you're sure it was not there yesterday, when you arrived with Corax?'

'No.' Musa was staring at Vesuvius transfixed. He wiped his hands uneasily on his filthy tunic. 'It must have happened last night. That crash that shook the ground, remember? That must have been it. The mountain has cracked and spewed.'

There was a general muttering of uneasiness among the men.

Attilius wiped the sweat from his eyes. It was starting to feel hot already. Another scorching day in prospect. And something more than heat—a tautness, like a drumskin stretched too far. Was it his mind playing tricks, or did the ground seem to be vibrating slightly? A prickle of fear stirred the hair on the back of his scalp.

'All right,' he said. 'Let's get away from this place.' He set off towards Corelia. 'We've finished here.'

She was still asleep, or at least he thought she was. She was lying beside the more distant of the two wagons, curled up on her side. He stood looking down at her for a moment, marvelling at the incongruity of her beauty in this desolate spot.

'I've been awake for hours.' She rolled onto her back and opened her eyes. 'Is the work finished?'

'Finished enough.' He knelt and began collecting together the papyri. 'The men are going back to Pompeii. I want you to go on ahead of them. I'll send an escort with you.'

She sat up quickly. 'No!'

He knew how she would react, just as he knew he had no choice. 'You must return those documents to where you found them. If you set off now you should be back in Pompeii well before midday. With luck, he need never know you took them, or brought them to me.'

'But they are the proof of his corruption—'

'No.' He held up his hand to quiet her. 'No, they're not. On their own, they mean nothing. Proof would be Exomnius giving testimony before a magistrate. But I don't have him. I don't have the money your father paid him or even a single piece of evidence he spent any of it. He's been very careful. Besides, this isn't as important as getting you away from here. Something's happening to the mountain. Exomnius suspected it weeks ago. It's as if—' He didn't know how to put it into words. 'As if it's—*coming alive.* You'll be safer in Pompeii.'

She was shaking her head. 'And what will you do?'

'Return to Misenum. Report to the admiral. If anyone can make sense of what is happening, he can.'

'Once you're alone they'll try to kill you.'

'I don't think so. If anything, I'll be safer. I have a horse. They're on foot. They couldn't catch me even if they tried.'

'I also have a horse. Take me with you.'

For a moment he played with the image of the two of them turning up in Misenum together. The daughter of the owner of the Villa Hortensia sharing his cramped quarters at the Piscina Mirabilis. How long would they get away with it? A day, two. And then what? The laws of society were as inflexible as the laws of engineering.

'Corelia, listen.' He took her hands. 'If I could do anything to help you, I would. But this is madness, to defy your father.'

'You don't understand.' Her grip on his fingers was ferocious. 'I can't go back. Don't make me go back. I can't bear to see him again, or to marry that man—'

'But you know the law. When it comes to marriage, you're as much your father's property as any one of those slaves over there.' What could he say? He hated the words even as he uttered them. 'It may not turn out to be as bad as you fear.' She groaned, pulled away her hands and buried her face. He blundered on. 'We can't escape our destiny. And, believe me, there are worse ones than marrying a rich man. You could be working in the fields and dead at twenty. Or a child whore in the back streets of Pompeii. Accept what has to happen. Live with it. You'll survive. You'll see.'

She gave him a long, slow look—contempt, was it, or hatred? 'I swear to you, I sooner would be a whore.'

'And I swear you would not.' He spoke more sharply. 'You're young. What do you know of how people live?'

'I know I could not be married to someone I despised. Could you?' She glared at him. 'Perhaps you could.'

He turned away. 'Leave it, Corelia.'

'Are you married?'

'No.'

'But you *were* married?'

'Yes,' he said quietly, 'I was married. My wife is dead.'

That shut her up for a moment. 'How did she die?'

He did not ever talk of it. But she had got under his skin. To his astonishment, he found himself telling her.

'We were married three years. She was in childbirth. But it came from the womb feet first. I was sure it was a boy. But the day went on—it was June in Rome, and hot: almost as hot as down here—and even with a doctor and two women in attendance, the baby would not move. And then she began to bleed.' He closed his eyes.

'We lost the child, but Sabina's bleeding didn't stop, and the next morning she also died.'

HE SENT HER BACK to Pompeii with Polites. Not because the Greek slave was the strongest escort available but because he was the only one Attilius trusted. He gave him Corvinus's mount and told him not to let her out of his sight until she was home.

She went meekly in the end, with barely another word. She swept her cloak around her and flung her head back, flicking her long dark hair over her collar, and there was something impressive in the gesture: she would do as he asked but she would not accept that he was right. Never a glance in his direction as she swung herself easily into the saddle. She made a clicking sound with her tongue and tugged the reins and set off down the track behind Polites.

It took all his self-control not to run after her. A poor reward, he thought, for all the risks she ran for me. But what else did she expect of him? He believed in fate. One was shackled to it from birth as to a moving wagon. The destination of the journey could not be altered, only the manner in which one approached it—whether one chose to walk erect or to be dragged complaining through the dust.

Still, he felt sick as he watched her go, the sun brightening the landscape as the distance between them increased, so that he was able to watch her for a long time, until at last the horses passed behind a clump of olive trees, and she was gone.

IN MISENUM, the admiral was lying on his mattress in his windowless bedroom, remembering the flat, muddy forests of Upper Germany, and the great oak trees that grew along the shore of the northern sea—and the way that in a storm the trees, with a terrible splintering, would sometimes detach themselves from the bank, vast islands of soil trapped within their roots, and drift upright, their foliage spread like rigging, bearing down on the fragile Roman galleys—

He shuddered and opened his eyes to the dim light, hauled himself up, and demanded to know where he was. His secretary, sitting beside the couch, his stylus poised, looked down at his wax tablet.

'We were with Domitius Corbulo, Admiral,' said Alexion, 'when you were in the cavalry, fighting the Chauci, in eight hundred.'

'Ah, yes. Just so. The Chauci. I remember—'

But what did he remember? The admiral had been trying for months to write his memoirs—his final book, he was sure—and it was a welcome distraction from the crisis on the aqueduct to return to it. But what he had seen and done and what he had read or been told seemed nowadays to run together, in a kind of seamless dream.

The door opened, admitting a shaft of brilliant light. So it was morning already. A slave tiptoed across to the secretary and whispered into his ear. Pliny rolled his fat body over onto one side to get a better view. 'What time is it?'

'The end of the first hour, Admiral.'

'Have the sluices been opened at the reservoir?'

'Yes, Admiral. We have a message that the water has drained away.'

Pliny groaned and flopped back onto his pillow.

'And it seems, sir, that a most remarkable discovery has been made.'

THE OTHERS HAD LEFT about a half-hour after Corelia. There were no elaborate farewells: the contagion of fear had spread throughout the work gang and all were eager to get back to the safety of Pompeii. Even Brebix, the former gladiator, kept turning his small, dark eyes nervously towards Vesuvius. They flung the tools, the unused bricks and the empty amphorae onto the backs of the wagons. Finally, a couple of the slaves shovelled earth across the remains of the night's fires and buried the grey scars left by the cement.

Attilius stood warily beside the inspection shaft with his arms folded and watched them prepare to leave.

Musa was the only one apart from himself with a horse, and once he was in the saddle he called down to Attilius. 'Are you coming?'

'Not yet. I'll catch up with you later.'

'Why not come now?'

'Because I'm going to go up onto the mountain.'

'Why?'

The engineer shrugged. 'Curiosity. Go safely, Musa. I'll see you soon. Either in Pompeii or Misenum.'

Musa gave him a look and seemed about to say something, but changed his mind. He wheeled away and set off after the carts and Attilius was alone. Again, he was struck by the peculiar stillness of the day, as if Nature were holding her breath. The noise of the heavy wooden wheels slowly faded into the distance and all he could hear was the occasional tinkle of a goat's bell and the ubiquitous chafing of the cicadas. The sun was quite high now. He glanced around at the empty countryside, and then lay on his stomach and peered into the matrix. His eye was caught by something—by a glint of reflected light in the darkness. He drew his head back slightly to let the sun shine directly along the shaft and he saw very faintly that the floor of the aqueduct was glistening. Even as he watched the quality of the light seemed to change and become more substantial, rippling and widening as the tunnel began to fill with water.

He whispered to himself, 'She runs!'

Satisfied that the Augusta had indeed begun to flow again, he rolled the manhole cover across the shaft. With a thud the tunnel was sealed.

He untethered his horse and climbed into the saddle. He pulled on the reins and turned away from the Augusta to face Vesuvius. He spurred the horse and they moved off along the track, walking at first but quickening to a trot as the ground began to rise.

AT THE PISCINA MIRABILIS the last of the water had drained away and the great reservoir was empty—a rare sight. It had last been allowed to happen a decade ago and that had been for maintenance, so that the slaves could shovel out the sediment and check the walls for signs of cracking. The admiral listened attentively as the slave explained the workings of the system.

'And how often is this supposed to be done?'

'Every ten years would be customary, Admiral.'

'So this was going to be done again soon?'

'Yes, Admiral.'

They were standing on the steps of the reservoir—Pliny, Gaius, Alexion, and the water slave, Dromo. Pliny had ordered that nothing was to be disturbed until he arrived and a marine guard had been posted at the door to prevent unauthorised access.

The floor of the Piscina looked like a muddy beach after the tide had gone out. There were little pools here and there, where the sediment was slightly hollowed, and a litter of objects—rusted tools, stones, shoes—that had fallen into the water over the years and had sunk to the bottom. The rowing boat was grounded. Several sets of footprints led out from the bottom of the steps towards the centre of the reservoir, where a larger object lay, and then returned. Dromo asked if the admiral would like him to fetch it.

'No,' said Pliny, 'I want to see it where it lies for myself. Oblige me, would you, Gaius.' He pointed to his shoes and his nephew knelt and unbuckled them while the admiral leaned on Alexion for support. He felt an almost childish anticipation and the sensation intensified as he descended the last of the steps and cautiously lowered his feet into the sediment. Black slime oozed between his toes, deliciously cool. He hoisted the folds of his toga and began stepping gingerly across the surface, his feet sinking deep into the mud, which made a delightful sucking noise each time he lifted them. He kept away from the tracks the others had made: it was more enjoyable to rupture the crust of mud where it was still fresh and just beginning to harden in the warm air. The others followed at a respectful distance.

By the time he reached the centre of the reservoir he was breathless with the effort of repeatedly hoisting his feet out of the clinging sediment. He propped himself against a pillar as Gaius came up beside him. But he was glad that he had made the effort. The water slave had been wise to send for him. This was something to see, right enough: a mystery of Nature had become also a mystery of Man.

The object in the mud was an amphora used for storing quicklime. It was wedged almost upright, the bottom part buried in the soft bed of the reservoir. A long, thin rope had been attached to its handles and this lay in a tangle around it. The lid, which had been sealed with wax, had been prised off. Scattered, gleaming in the mud, were perhaps 100 small silver coins.

'Nothing has been removed, Admiral,' said Dromo anxiously. 'I told them to leave it exactly as they found it.'

Pliny blew out his cheeks. 'How much is there, would you say?'

His nephew buried both hands into the amphora, cupped them, and showed them to the admiral. They brimmed with silver denarii. 'A fortune, Uncle.'

'And an illegal one, we may be sure.' Neither the earthenware vessel nor the rope had much of a coating of sediment, which meant, thought Pliny, that it could not have lain on the reservoir floor for long—a month at most. He glanced up towards the vaulted ceiling. 'Someone must have rowed out,' he said, 'and lowered it over the side.'

'And then let go of the rope?' Gaius looked at him in wonder. 'But who would have done such a thing? How could he have hoped to retrieve it? No diver could swim down this deep!'

Pliny dipped his own hand into the coins and examined them in his plump palm, stroking them apart with his thumb. Vespasian's familiar, scowling profile decorated one side; the sacred implements of the augur, the other. They had been minted during the Emperor's third consulship, eight years earlier. 'Then we must assume he didn't plan to retrieve it by diving, Gaius, but by draining the reservoir. And the only man with the power to empty the Piscina whenever he desired was our missing aquarius, Exomnius.'

Hora Quarta — 10:37 hours

The *quattuorviri*—the Board of Four: the elected magistrates of Pompeii—were meeting in an emergency session in the drawing room of Lucius Popidius. The slaves had carried in a chair for each of them, and a small table, around which they sat. Ampliatus, out of deference to the fact that he was not a magistrate, reclined on a couch in the corner, eating a fig. Through the open door he could see the swimming pool and its silent fountain, and also, in a corner of the tiled garden, a cat playing with a little bird.

The noise of his slurping made Popidius wince. 'I must say, you seem supremely confident, Ampliatus.'

'I am supremely confident. You should relax.'

'That's easy enough for you to say,' Popidius replied. 'Your name is not on fifty notices spread around the city assuring everyone that the water will be flowing again by midday.'

'Have faith in Roman engineering, Your Honours. All will be well.'

It was four hours since Pompeii had woken to another hot and cloudless day and to the discovery of the failure of its water supply. Placards, signed by L. Popidius Secundus, posted in the forum and on the larger fountains, announced that repairs were being carried out on the aqueduct and that the supply would resume by the seventh hour. But it was not much reassurance for those who remembered the terrible earthquake of seventeen years ago—the water had failed on that occasion, too—and all morning there had been uneasiness across the town. Some shops had failed to open. A few people had left, with their possessions piled on carts, loudly proclaiming that Vulcan was about to destroy Pompeii for a second time. And now word had got out that the *quattuorviri* were meeting at the House of Popidius. A crowd had gathered in the street outside.

Ampliatus thought he heard something. He rose from the couch and walked out into the sunshine of the garden. The fountain that fed the swimming pool was in the form of a nymph tipping a jug. As he came closer he heard it again, a faint gurgling, and then water began to trickle from the vessel's lip. The flow stuttered, spurted, seemed to stop, but then it began to run more strongly. He beckoned to the others to come and look. 'You see. I told you. Now, Popidius, shall I give the mob the news or will you?'

'You tell them, Ampliatus. I need a drink.'

Ampliatus swept across the atrium towards the great front door. He gestured to Massavo to open it and stepped out onto the threshold. Perhaps 100 people—his people was how he liked to think of them—were crowded into the street. He held up his arms for silence. 'You all know who I am,' he shouted, when the murmur of voices had died away, 'and you all know you can trust me!'

'Why should we?' someone shouted from the back.

Ampliatus ignored him. 'The water is running again! If you don't believe me—like that insolent fellow there—go and look at the fountains and see for yourselves. The aqueduct is repaired! It will take more than a few trembles in the ground and one hot summer to frighten the colony of Pompeii!'

A few people cheered. Ampliatus beamed and waved. 'Good day to you all, citizens! Let's get back to business. *Salve lucrum!*'

He headed back towards the atrium, rubbing his hands with delight. The disappearance of Exomnius had jolted his equanimity, he would not deny it, but he had dealt with the problem, the fountain was running strongly, and if the young aquarius was not dead yet he would be soon. From the drawing room came the sound of laughter and the clink of crystal glass. He was about to walk round the pool to join them when, at his feet, he noticed the body of the bird he had watched being killed. He prodded it with his toe then stooped to pick it up. A red cap, white cheeks, black and yellow wings.

A goldfinch. He weighed it in his hand for a moment, some dark thought moving in the back of his mind, then let it drop and quickly mounted the steps into the garden of his old house. His eyes were fixed on the empty cage on Corelia's balcony and the darkened, shuttered windows of her room. He bellowed, 'Celsia!' and his wife came running. 'Where's Corelia?'

'She was ill. I let her sleep—'

'Get her! Now!' He hurried towards his study. *It was not possible. She would not dare—*

When he opened the strongbox and took out the document case there were no papyri. He tipped up the empty *capsa*, then ran out into the courtyard. His wife had opened Corelia's shutters and was standing on the balcony, her hands pressed to her face.

CORELIA CAME THROUGH the Vesuvius Gate and into the square beside the castellum aquae. She had taken her time on the journey home, never once spurring her horse above walking pace as she skirted Vesuvius and crossed the plain. As she descended the hill towards the big crossroads, Polites plodding faithfully behind her, the blank walls of the houses seemed to rise on either side to enclose her like a prison. She noticed the angry, frustrated faces of the people at the fountains, jostling to jam their pots beneath the dribble of water, and she thought again of the aquarius.

She knew that he was right. Her fate was inescapable. She felt neither angry nor afraid as she neared her father's house, merely dead to it all—exhausted, filthy, thirsty.

She led the way round to the back of the house, towards the stables, and at the sound of the hoofs on the cobbles an elderly groom came out. He looked wide-eyed with surprise at her appearance, but she took no notice. She jumped down from the saddle and handed him the reins. 'Thank you,' she said to Polites and then, to the groom, 'See that this man is given food and drink.'

She passed out of the glare of the street and into the gloom of the house, climbing the stairs from the slaves' quarters. As she walked she drew the rolls of papyri from beneath her cloak. The aquarius had told her to replace them in her father's study and hope their removal had not been noticed. But she would not do that. She would give them to him herself. Even better, she would tell him where she had been. He would know that she had discovered the truth and then he could do to her what he pleased. She did not care. What could be worse than the fate he had already planned? You cannot punish the dead.

She emerged through the curtain into the House of Popidius and walked towards the swimming pool that formed the heart of the villa. She heard voices to her right and saw in the drawing room her future husband and the magistrates of Pompeii. They turned to look at her at exactly the moment that her father appeared on the steps leading to their old home. Ampliatus saw what she was carrying, shouted at her—'Corelia!'—and started towards her but she swerved away and ran into the drawing room, scattering his secrets across the table and over the carpet before he had a chance to stop her.

IT SEEMED to the engineer that Vesuvius was playing a game with him, never coming any closer however hard he rode towards her. Only when he looked back, did he realise how high he was climbing. Soon he had a clear view of Nola. The irrigated fields around it were like a clear green square, no larger than a doll's handkerchief lying on the brown Campanian plain.

He had aimed for the edge of the nearest white-grey streak and he reached it soon after midmorning, at the point where the pasture-land on the lower slopes ended and the forest began. He passed no living creature, neither man nor animal. The occasional farmhouse beside the track was deserted. He guessed everyone must have fled, either in the night when they heard the explosion or at first light, when they woke to this ghostly shrouding of ash. It lay across the ground, like powdery snow, quite still, for there was not a breath of wind to disturb it. When he jumped down from his horse he raised a cloud that clung to his sweating legs. He scooped up a handful. It was odourless, fine-grained, warm from the sun. In the trees it covered the foliage exactly as would a light fall of snow.

He put a little in his pocket, to take back to show the admiral, and drank some water, swilling the dry taste of the dust from his mouth. Looking down the slope he could see another rider, perhaps a mile away, also making steady progress towards this same spot, presumably led by a similar curiosity to discover what had happened. Attilius considered waiting for him, to exchange opinions, but decided against it. He wanted to press on. He remounted, and rejoined the track that led into the forest.

It took him perhaps another hour to pass through the forest. The air was hot, fragrant with the scent of dried pine and herbs. Once he thought he heard a larger animal moving along the track behind him but when he stopped to listen the sound had gone. Soon afterwards the forest began to thin. He came to a clearing.

And now it was as if Vesuvius had decided to play a different game. Having for hours never seemed to come any closer, suddenly the peak rose directly in front of him—a few hundred feet high, a much steeper incline, mostly of rock, without sufficient soil to support much in the way of vegetation except for straggly bushes and plants with small yellow flowers. And it was exactly as the Greek writer had described: a black cap, as if the land had been recently scorched by fire. In places, the rock bulged outwards, almost as if it were being pushed out from beneath, sending small flurries of stones rattling down the slope. Farther along the ridge, larger landslips had occurred. Huge boulders, the size of a man, had been sent crashing into the trees—and recently, by the look of it.

It was too steep a climb for his horse. He dismounted and found a shady spot where he could tie its reins to a tree. He scouted around for a stick and selected one half as thick as his wrist—smooth, grey, long-dead—and with that to support him he began his final ascent.

The sun up here was merciless. He moved from rock to cindery rock in the suffocating heat and the air itself seemed to burn his lungs, a dry heat, like a blade withdrawn from a fire. He could feel the heat through the soles of his shoes. He forced himself to press on, without looking back, until the ground ceased to rise and what was ahead of him was no longer black rock but blue sky. He clambered over the ridge and peered across the roof of the world.

The summit of Vesuvius was not the sharp peak that it had appeared from the base but a rough and circular plain, perhaps 200 paces in diameter, a wilderness of black rock, with a few brownish patches of sickly vegetation that merely emphasised its deadness. Not only did it look to have been on fire in the past, as the Greek papyri had said, but to be burning now. In at least three places thin columns of grey vapour were rising, fluttering and hissing in the silence. There was the same sour stench of sulphur that there had been in the pipes of the Villa Hortensia. Attilius shuddered.

He kept close to the edge of the summit and began working his way round it, mesmerised to begin with by the sulphurous clouds that were whispering from the ground and then by the astonishing panoramas beyond the rim. It seemed to Attilius that the whole of Italy was spread beneath him. As he moved from north to west the Bay of Neapolis came into view. A breeze was beginning to get up. He could feel it on his cheek: the one they called Caurus, blowing from the north west, towards Pompeii, which appeared at his feet as no more than a sandy smudge set back from the coast.

It made him feel light-headed simply to look at it, and he began to pick his way directly across the summit towards the other side, back to where he had started, keeping clear of the plumes of sulphur that seemed to be all around him. The ground was shaking, bulging. He wanted to get away now, as fast as he could. But the terrain was rough, with deep depressions on either side of his path—'*cave-like pits of blackened rock*', as the Greek writer had said—and he had to watch where he put his feet. And it was because of this—because he had his head down—that he smelled the body before he saw it.

The stench was emanating from the large dust bowl straight ahead of him. It was perhaps six feet deep and thirty across, simmering like a cauldron in the haze of heat, and what was most awful, when he peered over the side, was that everything in it was dead: not just the man, who wore a white tunic and whose limbs were so purplish-black Attilius thought at first he was a Nubian, but other creatures—a snake, a large bird, a litter of small animals—all scattered in this pit of death. Even the vegetation was bleached and poisoned.

The corpse was lying at the bottom, on its side, with its arms flung out, a water gourd and a straw hat just beyond its reach, as if it had died straining for them. It must have lain out here for at least two weeks, putrefying in the heat. Yet the wonder was how much of it remained. It had not been attacked by insects, or picked to the bone by birds and animals. No clouds of blowflies swarmed across its half-baked meat. Rather, its burnt flesh appeared to have poisoned anything that had tried to feast on it.

He was sure it must be Exomnius. He had been gone two weeks or more, and who else would have ventured up here in August? But how could he be sure? He had never met the man. Yet he was reluctant to venture down onto that carpet of death. He forced himself to squat close to the lip of the pit and squinted at the body. There was no sign of any wound. What could have killed him? Attilius leaned down and tried to poke at it with his stick and immediately felt himself begin to faint. Bright lights danced before him and he almost toppled forwards. He scrabbled with his hands in the dust and just managed to push himself back, gasping for breath.

'The afflatus of the tainted air near to the ground itself . . .'

His head was pounding. He threw up—bitter, vile-tasting fluid—and was still choking and spitting mucus when he heard, in front of him, the crack of dry vegetation being broken by a step. He looked up groggily. On the other side of the pit, no more than fifty paces away, a man was moving across the summit towards him. He thought at first it must be part of the visions induced by the tainted air and he stood with an effort, swaying drunkenly, blinking the sweat out of his eyes, trying to focus, but still the figure came on, framed by the hissing jets of sulphur, with the glint in his hand of a knife. It was Corax.

Attilius was in no condition to fight. He would have run. But he could barely raise his feet.

The overseer approached the pit cautiously—crouched low, his arms spread wide, shifting lightly from foot to foot, reluctant to take his eyes off the engineer, as if he suspected a trick. He darted a quick glance at the body, frowned at Attilius, then looked back down again. He said softly, 'So what's all this then, pretty boy?'

Attilius tried to speak. His voice was thick and slurred. He wanted to say that Exomnius had not been wrong, that there was terrible danger here, but he could not pronounce the words. Corax was scowling at the corpse and shaking his head. 'The stupid old bastard, climbing up here at his age! Worrying about the mountain. And for what? For nothing! Nothing—except landing us with you.' He returned his attention to Attilius. 'Some pretty boy from Rome, come to teach us all our jobs. Still fancy your chances? Nothing to say now, I notice. Well, why don't I cut you another mouth and we'll see what comes out of that?'

He hunched forwards, tossing his knife from hand to hand, his face set and ready for the kill. He began to circle the pit and it was all Attilius could do to stumble in the opposite direction. When the overseer stopped, Attilius stopped, and when he reversed his steps and started prowling the other way, Attilius followed suit. This went on for a while, but the tactic enraged Corax—'Fuck this,' he yelled, 'I'm not playing your stupid games!'—and suddenly he made a rush at his prey. Red-faced and panting for breath in the heat he ran down the side of the hollow and across it and had just reached the other slope when he stopped. He glanced down at his legs with surprise. With a terrible slowness he tried to wade forwards, opening and shutting his mouth like a fish. He sank to his knees, batting feebly at the air in front of him, then crashed forwards onto his face.

There was nothing Attilius could do except watch him drown in the dry heat. Corax made a couple of feeble attempts to move, then he gave up and quietly lay on his side. His breathing became more shallow then stopped, but long before it ceased Attilius had left him—stumbling across the bulging, trembling summit of the mountain, through the thickening plumes of sulphur, now flattened by the gathering breeze and pointing in the direction of Pompeii.

DOWN IN THE TOWN, the light wind, arriving during the hottest part of the day, had come as a welcome relief. The Caurus raised swirls of dust along the streets as they emptied for the siesta. In the House of Popidius one of the papyri lying on the carpet was caught by the gust and rolled towards the table.

Holconius put out his foot to stop it. 'What's all this?' he asked.

Ampliatus knew that there were times when secrets, carefully revealed, could act like hoops of steel, binding others to you. In a flash of inspiration he saw that this was one of those occasions.

'Read them,' he said. 'I have nothing to hide from my friends.' He stooped and collected the papyri and piled them on the table. 'They come from the room of Exomnius. It's time you knew. Help yourself to more wine. I shall only be a moment. Corelia, you will come with me.' He seized her by the elbow and steered her towards the steps. She dragged her feet but he was too strong for her. He was vaguely aware of his wife and son following.

When they were out of sight, round the corner, in the pillared garden of their old house, he twisted her flesh between his fingers. 'Did you really think,' he hissed, 'that you could hurt me?'

'No,' she said, wincing and wriggling to escape. 'But at least I thought I could try.'

'Oh? And how did you propose to do that?'

'By showing the documents to the aquarius. By showing them to everyone. So that they could all see you for what you are.'

'And what is that?' Her face was very close to his.

'A thief. A murderer. Lower than a *slave*.' She spat out the last word and he drew back his hand and would have hit her but Celsinus grabbed his wrist from behind.

'No, Father,' he said. 'We'll have no more of that.'

For a moment, Ampliatus was too astonished to speak. 'You?' he said. 'You as well?' He shook his hand free and glared at his son. 'Don't you have some religious rite to go to? Get out of my way.'

He dragged Corelia along the path towards the staircase. The other two did not move. He turned and pushed her up the steps, along the passage, and into her room. She fell backwards onto her bed. 'Treacherous, ungrateful child!'

He looked around for something with which to punish her but all he could see were feeble, feminine possessions, neatly arranged—an ivory comb, a silk shawl, a parasol, strings of beads—and a few old toys. Propped in a corner was a wooden doll with movable limbs he had bought her for her birthday years ago and the sight of it jolted him. What had happened to her? He had loved her so much—his little girl!—how had it come to hatred? He stood panting, defeated, as she glared at him from the bed. He did not know what to say. 'You'll stay in here,' he finished lamely, 'until I have decided what should be done with you.' He went out, locking the door behind him.

In the drawing room the magistrates were leaning forwards across the table, muttering. They fell silent as he approached and turned to watch him as he headed towards the sideboard and poured himself some wine. The lip of the decanter rattled against the glass. Was his hand shaking? He examined it, front and back. This was not like him: it looked steady enough. He felt better after draining the glass. He poured himself another, fixed a smile and faced the magistrates. 'Well?'

It was Holconius who spoke first. 'Where did you get these?'

'Corax, the overseer on the Augusta, brought them round to me yesterday afternoon. He found them in Exomnius's room.'

'This should have been brought to our attention immediately.'

'And why's that, Your Honours?'

'Isn't it obvious?' cut in Popidius excitedly. 'Exomnius believed there was about to be another great earthquake!'

'Calm yourself, Popidius. You've been whining about earthquakes for seventeen years. I wouldn't take all that stuff seriously.'

'Exomnius took it seriously.'

'Exomnius!' Ampliatus looked at him with contempt. 'Exomnius always was a bag of nerves.'

'Maybe so. But why was he having documents copied? What do you think he wanted with this?' He waved one of the papyri.

Ampliatus glanced at it. 'It's in Greek. I don't read Greek. You forget, Popidius: I haven't had the benefit of your education.'

'Well, I do read Greek, and I believe I recognise this. I think this is the work of Strabo, the geographer, who travelled these parts in the time of Augustus. He writes here of a summit that is flat and barren and has been on fire in the past. Surely that must be Vesuvius? He says the fertile soil around Pompeii reminds him of Caetana, where the land is covered with ash thrown up by the flames of Etna.'

'So what?'

'Wasn't Exomnius a Sicilian?' demanded Holconius. 'What town was he from?'

Ampliatus waved his glass dismissively. 'I believe Caetana. But what of it?'

'As for this Latin document—this I certainly recognise,' continued Popidius. 'It's part of a book and I know both the man who wrote it and the man to whom the passage it is addressed. It's from Annaeus Seneca—Nero's mentor. Surely even *you* must have heard of him?'

Ampliatus flushed. 'My business is building, not letter-writing.'

'The Lucilius to whom he sent the letter is Lucilius Junior, a native of this city. He was a procurator overseas—in Sicily, as I remember it. Seneca is describing the great Campanian earthquake. It is from his book *Natural Questions*. I believe there is even a copy in our own library. It lays out the foundations of the Stoic philosophy.'

'"The Stoic philosophy!"' mocked Ampliatus. 'And what would Exomnius have been doing with "the Stoic philosophy"?'

'Again,' repeated Popidius, 'isn't it obvious?' He laid the two documents side by side. 'Exomnius believed there was a link, you see?' He gestured from one to the other. 'Etna and Vesuvius. The fertility of the land around Caetana and the land around Pompeii. The terrible omens of seventeen years ago—the poisoning of the sheep—and the omens all around us this summer. He was from Sicily. He saw signs of danger. *And now he's disappeared.*'

'What does this add up to? So Exomnius was worried about earth tremors? So Campania has ashy soil like Sicily, and stinking fumaroles? So? Fumaroles have been part of life on the bay since the days of Romulus.' Ampliatus could see his words were striking home. 'Besides, this isn't the real problem.'

Holconius said, 'And what is the real problem?'

'The other documents—the ones that show how much Exomnius was paid to give this town cheap water.'

Holconius said quickly, 'Have a care, Ampliatus. Your little arrangements are no concern of ours.'

'*My* little arrangements!' Ampliatus laughed. 'That's a good one! Come now, Your Honours, don't pretend you didn't know! How do you think this town revived so quickly after the earthquake? I've saved you a fortune by my "little arrangements". Yes, and helped make myself one into the bargain—I don't deny it. But you wouldn't be here without me! Your precious baths, Popidius, how much do you pay for them? Nothing! And you, Cuspius, with your fountains. And you, Holconius, with your pool. And all the private baths and the watered gardens and the big public pool in the palaestra and the pipes in the new apartments! This town has been kept afloat for more than a decade by my "little arrangement" with Exomnius. And now some nosy bastard of an aquarius from Rome has got to hear about it. That's the real problem.'

Cuspius said, 'But surely we can just cut a deal with this new aquarius, like the one you had with the other fellow?'

'It seems not. I dropped a hint yesterday but all he did was look at me as if I'd just put my hand on his cock. No, I'm afraid I recognise his type. He'll take this up in Rome, they'll check the accounts and we'll have an imperial commission down here before the year's end.'

'Then what are we to do?' said Popidius. 'If this comes out, it will look bad for all of us.'

Ampliatus smiled at him. 'Don't worry. I've taken care of it.'

'How?'

'Popidius!' said Holconius, quickly. 'Take care.'

Ampliatus paused. They did not want to know. They were the magistrates of the town, after all. The innocence of ignorance—that was what they craved. But why should they have peace of mind? He would dip their hands in the blood along with his own.

'He'll be killed.' He looked around. 'Before he gets back to Misenum. An accident out in the countryside. Does anyone disagree? Speak up if you do. Popidius? Holconius? Brittius? Cuspius?' He waited. It was all a charade. The aquarius would be dead by now, whatever they said: Corax had been itching to slit his throat. 'I'll take that as a unanimous endorsement. Shall we drink to it?'

He reached for the decanter but stopped, his hand poised in mid-air. The heavy crystal glass was not merely shaking now: it was moving sideways along the polished wooden surface. He frowned at it stupidly. That could not be right. Even so, it reached the end of the sideboard and crashed to the floor. There was a vibration beneath his feet. It gradually built in strength and then a gust of hot air passed through the house, powerful enough to bang the shutters. An instant later, far away—but very distinctly, unlike anything that he, or anyone else, had ever heard—came the sound of a double boom.

Hora Septa — 13:07 hours

A hundred and twenty miles away in Rome it was heard as a thud, as if a heavy statue or a tree had toppled. Those who escaped from Pompeii, which was five miles downwind, swore they had heard two sharp bangs, whereas in Capua, some twenty miles distant, the noise from the start was a continuous, tearing crack of thunder. But in Misenum, which was closer than Capua, there was no sound at all, only the sudden appearance of a narrow column of brown debris fountaining silently into the cloudless sky.

For Attilius, the effect was like a great, dry wave that came crashing over his head. He was roughly two miles clear of the summit, descending fast on horseback along the mountain's western flank, following an old hunting trail through the forest. His plan was to pick up the coastal road at Herculaneum and ride directly to Misenum to warn the admiral of what he was sure was coming. He reckoned he would be there by midafternoon. The effects of the poisoning had shrunk to a small fist of pain hammering behind his eyes and in place of the drowsiness everything seemed oddly sharpened.

The shock of the blast struck him from behind and knocked him forward. Hot air, like the opening of a furnace door. Then something seemed to pop in his ears and the world became a soundless place of bending trees and whirling leaves. His horse stumbled and almost fell and he clung to its neck as they plunged down the path, riding the crest of the scalding wave, and then, abruptly, it was gone. The trees sprang upright, the debris settled, the air became breathable again. He tried to talk to the horse but he had no voice and when he looked back towards the top of the mountain he saw that it had vanished and in its place a boiling stem of rock and earth was shooting upwards.

From Pompeii it looked as if a great brown arm had punched through the peak and was aiming to smash a hole in the roof of the sky—bang, bang: that double crack—and then a hard-edged rumble, unlike any other sound in Nature, that came rolling across the plain. Ampliatus ran outside with the magistrates. From the bakery next door and all the way up the street people were emerging to stare at Vesuvius, shielding their eyes, their faces turned towards this new dark sun rising in the north on its thundering plinth of rock.

It would stop at any moment, Ampliatus thought. Let it subside now, and the situation will still be controllable. He had the nerve, the force of character, he could handle even this. But the thing did not stop. Up and up it went. A thousand heads tilted backwards as one to follow its trajectory and gradually the isolated screams became more widespread. The pillar was starting to broaden as it rose, its apex flattening out across the sky. Someone shouted that the wind was carrying it their way.

Ampliatus stepped into the centre of the street and held his arms out wide. 'Wait!' he shouted. 'Cuspius, Brittius—all of you—link hands with me. Set them an example!'

The cowards did not even look at him. Holconius broke first, jamming his bony elbows into the press of bodies to force his way down the hill. Brittius followed, and then Cuspius. Popidius turned tail and darted back inside the house. Up ahead, the crowd had become a solid mass as people streamed from the side streets to join it. Its back was to the mountain, its face was to the sea, its single impulse: flight.

Ampliatus was engulfed by the stampeding crowd, thrown sideways, and would have disappeared beneath their feet if Massavo had not seen him fall and scooped him up to safety on the step. He saw a mother drop her baby and heard its screams as it was trampled, saw an elderly matron slammed headfirst against the opposite wall then slip, unconscious, out of sight, as the mob swept on regardless. Some screamed. Some sobbed. Most were tight-mouthed, intent on saving their strength for the battle at the bottom of the hill, where they would have to fight their way through the Stabian Gate.

Ampliatus looked above the heads of the crowd towards the mountain but already it had mostly disappeared. A vast black wall of cloud was advancing towards the city, as dark as a storm. But it was not a storm or a cloud, he realised; it was a thundering waterfall of rock. He looked in the other direction. He still had his cruiser moored in the harbour. They could put to sea, try to head to the villa in Misenum. But the cram of bodies in the street leading to the gate stretched back up the hill. He would never reach the port. And even if he did, the crew would be scrambling to save themselves.

His decision was made for him. And so be it, he thought. This was how it had been seventeen years ago. The cowards had fled, he had stayed, and then they had all come crawling back again! He felt his old energy and confidence returning. Once more the former slave would give his masters a lesson in Roman courage. He gave a final, contemptuous glance to the river of panic streaming past him, stepped back and ordered Massavo to close the door. Close it and bolt it. They would stay, and they would endure.

IN MISENUM it looked like smoke. Pliny's sister, Julia, strolling on the terrace with her parasol, picking bougainvillea for the dinner table, assumed it must be another of the hillside fires that had plagued the bay all summer. But the height of the cloud, its bulk and the speed of its ascent were like nothing she had ever seen. She decided she had better wake her brother, who was dozing in the garden below.

Even in the heavy shade of the tree his face was as scarlet as the flowers in her basket. She stroked his hair and whispered, 'Brother, wake up. There is something you will want to see.'

He opened his eyes at once. 'The water—is it flowing?'

'No. Not the water. It looks like a great fire on the bay, coming from Vesuvius.'

'Vesuvius?' He blinked at her then shouted to a nearby slave, 'My shoes! Quickly!'

He lumbered across the dry grass towards the terrace. By the time he reached it most of the household slaves were lining the balustrade, looking east across the bay towards what looked like a gigantic umbrella pine made of smoke growing over the coast. A thick brown trunk, with black and white blotches, was rolling miles into the air, sprouting at its crown a clump of feathery branches. These broad leaves seemed in turn to be dissolving along their lower edges, beginning to rain a fine, sand-coloured mist back down to earth.

It was an axiom of the admiral's that the more he observed Nature, the less prone he was to consider any statement about her to be impossible. But surely this *was* impossible. Nothing he had read of came close to matching this spectacle. Perhaps Nature was granting him the privilege of witnessing something never before recorded in history? Those long years of accumulating facts, the prayer with which he had ended the *Natural History*—'Hail Nature, mother of all creation, and mindful that I alone of the men of Rome have praised thee in all thy manifestations, be gracious towards me'—was it all being rewarded at last? If he had not been so fat he would have fallen to his knees. 'Thank you,' he whispered. 'Thank you.'

He must start work at once. *Umbrella pine . . . tall stem . . . feathery branches . . .* He needed to get all this down for posterity, while the images were still fresh in his head. He shouted to Alexion to collect pen and paper and to Julia to fetch Gaius.

'He's inside, working on the translation you set him.'

'Well, tell him to come out here at once. He won't want to miss this.'

He beckoned to one of the slaves. 'Go down to the naval school and find the flagship captain. Tell him I want a liburnian made ready and put at my disposal.'

CORELIA HAD THROWN open her shutters and was standing on the balcony. To her right, above the flat roof of the atrium, a gigantic cloud was advancing, as black as ink, like a heavy curtain being drawn across the sky. The air was shaking with thunder. She could hear screams from the street. In the courtyard garden slaves ran back and forth, to no apparent purpose. She shouted down—'What's happening?'—but nobody paid her any attention.

The drumming of the cloud was getting louder. She ran to the door and tried to open it but the lock was too strong. She ran back onto the balcony but it was too high to jump. Below, and to the left, she saw Popidius coming up the steps from his part of the house, shepherding his elderly mother, Taedia, before him. She screamed—'Popidius!'—and he stopped and glanced around. She waved to him. 'Help me! He's locked me in!'

He shook his head in despair. 'He's trying to lock us all in! He's gone mad!'

'Please—come up and open the door!'

As he took half a pace towards her something hit the tiled roof behind him and bounced off into the garden. A light stone, the size of a child's fist. Another struck the pergola. And suddenly it was dusk and the air was full of missiles. He was being hit repeatedly on the head and shoulders. Frothy rocks, they looked to be: a whitish, petrified sponge. They weren't heavy but they stung. It was like being caught in a hailstorm—a warm hailstone, if such a thing were imaginable. He ran for the cover of the atrium, ignoring Corelia's cries, pushing his mother in front of him. The door ahead—Ampliatus's old entrance—was hanging open and he stumbled out into the street.

Corelia ducked back into her room to escape the bombardment. She had one last impression of the world outside, shadowy in the dust, and then all light was extinguished and there was nothing in the pitch darkness, not even a scream, only the roaring waterfall of rock.

IN HERCULANEUM life was peculiarly normal. The sun was shining, the sky and sea were a brilliant blue. As Attilius reached the coastal road he could even see fishermen out in their boats casting their nets. Even the noise from the mountain seemed unthreatening—a background rumble, drifting with the veil of debris towards the peninsula of Surrentum.

Outside the town gates a small crowd had gathered to watch the proceedings, and a couple of enterprising traders were setting up stalls to sell pastries and wine. A line of dusty travellers was already plodding down the road, mostly on foot and carrying luggage, some with carts piled high with their belongings. A man sitting on a milestone called out to ask what it was like back there.

'As black as midnight in Oplontis,' someone replied, 'and Pompeii must be even worse.'

'Pompeii?' said Attilius sharply. 'What's happening in Pompeii?'

The traveller shook his head, drawing his finger across his throat, and Attilius recoiled, remembering Corelia. When he had forced her to leave the aqueduct he had thought he was sending her out of harm's way. But now, as his eye followed the curve of the road towards Pompeii, to the point where it disappeared into the murk, he realised he had done the opposite. The outpouring of Vesuvius, caught by the wind, was blowing directly over the town.

'Don't go that way, citizen,' warned the man, 'there's no way through.' But Attilius was already turning his horse to face the stream of refugees.

THE FARTHER HE WENT the more clogged the road became, and the more pitiful the state of the fleeing population. Most were coated in a thick grey dust, their hair frosted, their faces like death masks, spattered with blood. Some carried torches, still lit: a defeated army of whitened old men, of ghosts, unable even to speak. Their animals—oxen, asses, horses, dogs and cats—resembled alabaster figures come creakingly to life. Behind them on the highway they left a trail of ashy wheel marks and footprints.

On one side of him, isolated crashes came from the olive groves. On the other, the sea seemed to be coming to the boil in a myriad of tiny fountains. There was a clatter of stones on the road ahead. His horse stopped, put its head down and refused to move. Suddenly the edge of the cloud, which had seemed to be almost half a mile away, came rushing towards them. The sky was dark and whirling with tiny projectiles and in an instant the day passed from afternoon sun to twilight and he was under a bombardment. Not hard stones but white clinker, small clumps of solidified ash, falling from some tremendous height. Women screamed. Torches dimmed in the darkness. His horse shied and turned. Attilius ceased to be a rescuer and became just another part of the panicking stream of refugees, frantically trying to outrun the storm of debris. His horse slipped down the side of the road into the ditch and cantered along it. Then the air lightened and they burst back into the sunshine.

Everyone was hurrying now, galvanised by the threat at their backs. Not only was the road to Pompeii impassable, Attilius realised, but a slight shift in the wind was spreading the danger westwards round the bay towards Herculaneum.

The shifting position of the wall of falling rock had been noticed at the city gates and by the time he reached them the traders were hastily packing away their goods. The crowd was breaking up, some heading for shelter in the town, others pouring out of it to join the exodus on the road. And still, amid all this, Attilius could see across the red-tiled roofs the normality of the fishermen on the bay. *The sea*, he thought: if he could somehow launch a boat, it might just be possible to skirt the downpour of stones and approach Pompeii from the south—*by sea*. He guessed it would be useless to try to fight his way down to the waterfront in Herculaneum, but the great villa just outside it—the home of the senator, Pedius Cascus, with his troop of philosophers—perhaps they might have a vessel he could use.

He rode until he came to a high pair of gateposts that he judged must belong to the Villa Calpurnia. He tied his horse to a railing in the courtyard and walked through the open door into the grand atrium. A slave appeared round a corner pushing a wheelbarrow stacked high with rolls of papyri.

'Where's the senator?'

'He's in Rome.' The slave was young, terrified, sweating.

'Your mistress?'

'Beside the pool.'

Attilius ran out into the sun. Beneath the terrace was the huge pool he had seen from the liburnian on his voyage to Pompeii and all around it people: dozens of slaves and white-robed scholars hurrying back and forth ferrying armfuls of papyri, stacking them into boxes at the water's edge, while a group of women stood to one side, staring along the coast towards the distant storm, which looked from here like an immense brown sea fog. The craft offshore from Herculaneum were fragile twigs against it. The fishing had stopped. The waves were getting up. Some of the women were wailing, but the elderly matron in the centre of the group, in a dark blue dress, seemed calm as he approached her. He remembered her—the woman with the necklace of giant pearls.

'Are you the wife of Pedius Cascus?'

She nodded.

'Marcus Attilius. Imperial engineer. I met your husband two nights ago, at the admiral's villa.'

She looked at him eagerly. 'Has Pliny sent you?'

'No. I came to beg a favour. To ask for a boat.'

Her face fell. 'Do you think if I had a boat I would be standing here? My husband took it yesterday to Rome.'

Attilius turned to go.

'Wait!' She called after him. 'You must help us.'

'There's nothing I can do. You'll have to take your chance on the road with the rest.'

'I'm not afraid for myself. But we must rescue the library.'

'My concern is for people, not books.' He began climbing the path back up towards the house.

'Wait!' She ran after him. 'Where are you going?'

'To find a boat.'

'Pliny has boats. Pliny has the greatest fleet in the world at his command. Come with me!'

He would say this for her: she had the will-power of any man. He followed her up a flight of steps and into a library. Most of the compartments had been stripped bare.

'This was where we kept the volumes that my ancestors brought back from Greece. One hundred and twenty plays by Sophocles alone. The works of Aristotle, some in his own hand. We have never allowed them to be copied.' She gripped his arm. 'Men are born and die by the thousand every hour. What do we matter? These great works are all that will be left of us. Pliny will understand.' She sat at the small table, took up a pen and dipped it in a brass inkstand. A red candle flickered beside her. 'Take him this letter. He knows this library. Tell him Rectina pleads with him for rescue.'

She rolled the letter and sealed it with the dripping candle, pressing her ring into the soft wax. 'You have a horse?'

'I'd go faster with a fresh one.'

'You'll have it.' She called to one of the slaves. 'Take Marcus Attilius to the stables and saddle the swiftest horse we have.'

Hora Nona — 15:32 hours

It took Attilius two hours to reach Misenum. The road wound along the coastline, sometimes running directly beside the water's edge, sometimes climbing higher inland. He mostly had his back to the mountain, but when he rounded the northern edge of the bay and began to descend towards Neapolis, he could see it again, away to his left—a thing of extraordinary beauty now. A veil of white mist had draped itself round the central column, rising for mile after mile in a perfect translucent cylinder, reaching up to brush the lower edge of the mushroom-shaped cloud that was toppling over the bay.

There was no sense of panic in Neapolis. He had outpaced the refugees emerging from beneath the hail of rock and no word of the catastrophe enveloping Pompeii had yet reached the city. In the hills behind the town he could see the red-brick arcade of the Aqua Augusta where she ran above the surface. He wondered if the water was flowing yet. He wondered what had happened to his men. But the image of which he could not rid himself was Corelia—the way she had swept back her hair as she mounted her horse, and the way she had dwindled into the distance, following the road he had set for her—to the fate that he, and not Destiny, had decreed.

PLINY'S GREATEST CONCERN was that it might all be over before he got there. Every so often he would come waddling out of his library to check on the progress of the column—'the manifestation', as he had decided to call it. If anything, it seemed to be growing.

In order to make his observations as accurate as possible he had ordered that his water clock should be carried down to the harbour and set up on the poop deck of the liburnian. While this was being done and the ship made ready he searched his library for references to Vesuvius. He had never paid much attention to the mountain before, preferring instead to concentrate on Nature's more esoteric aspects. But the first work he consulted, Strabo's *Geographica*, brought him up short. 'This area appears to have been on fire in the past and to have had craters of flame . . .' Why had he never noticed it before? He called in Gaius to take a look.

'You see here? He compares the mountain to Etna. Yet how can that be? Etna has a crater two miles across. I have seen it with my own eyes, glowing across the sea at night. No one has ever reported embers on Vesuvius.'

'He says the craters of flame "were subsequently extinguished by a lack of fuel",' Gaius pointed out. 'Perhaps that means some fresh source of fuel has now been tapped by the mountain, and brought it back to life.' His nephew looked up excitedly. 'Could that explain the arrival of the sulphur in the water of the aqueduct?'

Pliny regarded him with fresh respect. Yes. The lad was right. That must be it. Sulphur was the universal fuel of all these phenomena.

He pushed himself to his feet. 'I must get down to my ship. Alexion!' he shouted for his slave. 'Gaius, return to your studies.'

Leaning on the arm of his secretary, and without a backward glance, the admiral shuffled out of his library.

ATTILIUS HAD RIDDEN past the Piscina Mirabilis, over the causeway into the port, and was beginning his ascent of the steep road to the admiral's villa, when he saw a detachment of marines ahead clearing a path for Pliny's carriage. He just had time to dismount and step into the street before the procession reached him.

'Admiral!'

Pliny saw a figure he did not recognise, covered in dust, his tunic torn, his face, arms and legs streaked with dried blood. The apparition spoke again. 'Admiral! It's Marcus Attilius!'

'Engineer?' Pliny signalled for the carriage to stop.

'It's a catastrophe, Admiral. The mountain is exploding—raining rocks—' He licked his cracked lips. 'Oplontis and Pompeii are being buried. I've ridden from Herculaneum. I have a message for you'—he searched in his pocket—'from the wife of Pedius Cascus.'

'Rectina?' Pliny took the letter from his hands and broke the seal. He read it twice, his expression clouding, and suddenly he looked ill.

'This is really true?' he asked. 'The Villa Calpurnia is threatened?'

'The entire coast is threatened, Admiral. The danger follows the wind. It swings like a weather vane.'

Pliny beckoned to his secretary who had been running with the marines beside the carriage. 'Where is Antius?'

'At the quayside, Admiral.'

'We need to move quickly. Climb in next to me, Attilius.' He rapped his ring on the side of the carriage. 'Forward!' Attilius squeezed in beside him as the carriage lurched down the hill. 'Now tell me everything you've seen.'

Attilius tried to order his thoughts, but it was hard to speak coherently. Still, he tried to convey the power of what he had witnessed. The roof of the mountain had lifted off. And the blasting of the summit, he said, was merely the culmination of a host of other phenomena—the sulphur in the soil, the pools of noxious gas, the earth tremors, the swelling of the land that had severed the matrix of the aqueduct, the disappearance of the local springs. All these things were interconnected.

'And none of us recognised it,' said Pliny, with a shake of his head.

'That's not quite true, Admiral. One man recognised it—a native of the land near Etna: my predecessor, Exomnius.'

'Exomnius?' said Pliny, sharply. 'Who hid a quarter of a million sesterces at the bottom of his own reservoir?' He noticed the bafflement on the engineer's face. 'It was discovered this morning when the last of the water had drained away. Do you know how he came by it?'

They were entering the docks. Attilius could see a familiar sight—the *Minerva* lying alongside the quay, ready to sail—and he tried to think how best he could describe the chain of events to the admiral. But he had barely started before Pliny waved him to stop.

'The pettiness and avarice of man!' he said impatiently. 'It would make a book in itself. What does any of it matter now? Put it in a report and have it ready on my return. And the aqueduct?'

'Repaired, Admiral. Or she was when I left her this morning.'

'Then you have done good work, Engineer. And it will be made known in Rome, I promise you. Now go to your quarters and rest.'

Torquatus stood by the *Minerva*'s aft gangplank talking to the flagship commander, Antius, and a group of seven officers. They came to attention as Pliny's carriage approached.

'Admiral, with your permission, I would rather sail with you.'

Pliny looked at him in surprise, then grinned and clapped his podgy hand on Attilius's knee. 'A scientist! You're just like me! I knew it the moment I saw you! We shall do great things this day, Marcus Attilius.' He was wheezing out his orders even as his secretary helped him from the carriage. 'Torquatus—we sail immediately. Antius—sound the general alarm. Have a signal flashed to Rome in my name: "Vesuvius exploded at the seventh hour. The population of the bay is threatened. I am putting the entire fleet to sea to evacuate survivors."'

Antius stared at him. 'The *entire* fleet, Admiral?'

'Everything that floats. Come on, Antius! You were complaining the other night that we had the mightiest fleet in the world but it never saw action. Well, here is action for you.'

'But action requires an enemy, Admiral.'

'There's your enemy.' He pointed to the dark pall spreading in the distance. 'A greater enemy than any force Caesar ever faced.'

For a moment Antius did not move, and Attilius wondered if he might even be considering disobeying, but then a gleam came into his eyes, and he turned to the officers. 'You heard your orders. Signal the Emperor and sound the general muster. And let it be known that I'll cut the balls off any captain who isn't at sea within half an hour.'

IT WAS at the midpoint of the ninth hour, according to the admiral's waterclock, that the *Minerva* was pushed away from the quayside.

'Note the time,' commanded Pliny, and Alexion, squatting beside him, dipped his pen into his ink and scratched down a numeral.

A comfortable chair with a high back had been set up for the admiral on the small deck and from this elevated position he surveyed the scene. Antius had promised him he would have twenty ships operational immediately. That was 4,000 men—a legion!

The *Minerva* threaded between the anchored warships, and then passed along the natural rock wall of the harbour. For the first time they had a clear view of what was happening across the bay.

Pliny gripped the arms of his chair. For a few moments he was too overcome to speak, but then he remembered his duty to science. 'Beyond the promontory of Pausilypon,' he dictated hesitantly, 'the whole of Vesuvius and the surrounding coast are masked by a drifting cloud, whitish-grey in colour, and streaked with black. Thrusting above this, bulging and uncoiling, as if the hot entrails of the earth are being drawn out and dragged towards the heavens, rises the central column of the manifestation. It grows as if supported by a continual blast. But at its uppermost reaches, the weight of the exuded material becomes too great, and in pressing down spreads sideways. Wouldn't you agree, Engineer?' he called. 'It is the weight that is spreading it sideways?'

'The weight, Admiral,' Attilius shouted back. 'Or the wind.'

'Yes, a good point. Add that to the record, Alexion. The wind appears stronger at the higher altitude, and accordingly topples the manifestation to the south east.' He gestured to Torquatus. 'We should take advantage of this wind, Captain! Make full sail!'

Torquatus shouted to his officers: 'Raise the mainsail!'

The transverse pole that supported the sail was hauled up the mast. The sail filled immediately, tautening with the force of the wind. The *Minerva* picked up speed, scudding through the waves, raising curls of white foam on either side of her sharp prow.

Pliny felt his spirits lift with the sail. He pointed to the left. 'There's our destination, Captain. Herculaneum! Steer straight towards the shore—to the Villa Calpurnia!'

'Yes, Admiral! Helmsman—take us east!'

The sail cracked and the ship banked. A wave of spray drenched Attilius—a glorious sensation. He rubbed the dust from his face and ran his hands through his filthy hair.

'Observations at the tenth hour,' said Pliny. 'Are you ready, Alexion?' He placed his fingertips together and frowned. 'Drawing closer,' he began, 'the manifestation appears as a gigantic, heavy rain cloud, increasingly black. As with a storm viewed from a distance of several miles, it is possible to see individual plumes of rain, drifting like smoke across the dark surface. And yet, according to the engineer, Marcus Attilius, these are falls not of rain but of rock.' He pointed to the deck beside him. 'Come up here, Engineer. Describe to us again what you saw. For the record.'

Attilius climbed the short ladder to the poop deck. He started to give his account once more and then a bolt of lightning arced across the roiling mass of cloud—not white, but a brilliant, jagged streak of red. It hung in the air, like a vivid vein of blood.

'Add that to the list of phenomena,' said Pliny. 'Lightning.'

Torquatus shouted, 'We're sailing too close!'

Beyond the admiral's shoulder, Attilius could see the quadriremes of the Misene fleet, still in sunlight, streaming out of harbour. But then he became aware that the sky was darkening. A barrage of falling stones was exploding on the surface of the sea to their right, creeping rapidly closer. The quadriremes blurred, dissolved to ghost-ships, as the air was filled with whirling rock.

IN THE PANDEMONIUM, Torquatus was everywhere, bellowing orders. Men ran along the deck in the half-light. The sail was lowered. The helmsman swung hard left. An instant later a ball of lightning came hurtling from the sky, touched the top of the mast, travelled down it and then along the yard arm. The fireball shot off the edge of the pole and plunged into the sea, trailing fumes of sulphur. Attilius could feel the drumming of the stones on his shoulders, hear them rattling across the deck. The *Minerva* must be brushing along the edge of the cloud, he realised, and Torquatus was trying to row them out from beneath it—and abruptly he succeeded. There was a final lash of missiles and they burst back out into the sunshine.

He heard Pliny coughing and opened his eyes to see the admiral standing, brushing the debris from the folds of his toga. He had held on to a handful of stones and as he flopped back into his chair he examined them in his palm. All along the length of the ship, men were shaking their clothes and feeling their flesh for cuts. The *Minerva* was still steering directly towards Herculaneum, now less than a mile distant and clearly visible, but the wind was getting up, and the sea with it, the helmsman straining to keep them to their course as the waves crashed against the left side of the ship.

'Encounter with the manifestation,' said Pliny, calmly. 'Are you taking this down? What time is it?'

Alexion leaned towards the clock. 'The mechanism is broken, Admiral.' His voice was trembling. He was almost in tears.

'Well, no matter. Let's say the eleventh hour.' Pliny held up one of the stones and peered at it closely. 'The material is a frothy, bubbled pumice. Greyish-white. As light as ash, which falls in fragments no larger than a man's thumb.'

Torquatus stumbled towards them. 'Admiral—this wind will run us straight into the storm—we must turn back!'

Pliny ignored him. 'The pumice is less like rock, than airy fragments of a frozen cloud.' He craned his neck to stare over the side of the ship. 'It floats on the surface of the sea like lumps of ice. Do you see? Extraordinary!'

Attilius had not noticed it before. The water was covered in a carpet of stone. The oars brushed it aside with every stroke but more floated in immediately to replace it.

For a short while longer they managed to plough on, but the pace of the oars was weakening, defeated not by the wind or the waves but by the clogging weight of pumice on the water. It deepened as they neared the coast, two or three feet thick—a broad expanse of rustling dry surf. The blades of the oars flailed helplessly across it, unable to bring any pressure to bear, and the ship began to drift with the wind towards the waterfall of rock. The Villa Calpurnia was tantalisingly close. Attilius could see figures running along the shore, the piles of books, the white robes of the Epicurean philosophers.

The rest of the fleet was beginning to scatter as each of the ships battled to save themselves. And then it was dusk again and the familiar thunder of pumice hammering drowned out every other sound. Torquatus shouted, 'We've lost control of the ship! Everybody—below decks. Engineer—help me lift him down from here.'

'My records!' protested Pliny.

'Alexion has your records, Admiral.' Attilius had him by one arm and the captain by the other. They lugged him along the deck towards the open trap door that led down to the rowing stations as the air turned to rock. 'Make way for the admiral!' panted Torquatus and they almost threw him down the ladder. Alexion went next with the precious papers, then Attilius jumped down in a shower of pumice, and finally Torquatus, slamming the trap behind them.

Vespera — 20:02 hours

In the stifling heat and the near darkness beneath the *Minerva*'s decks they crouched and listened to the drumming of the stones above them. The air was rank with the sweat and breath of 200 sailors. Occasionally, a foreign voice would cry out in some unrecognisable tongue only to be silenced by a harsh shout from one of the officers. The ship was rocking violently but none of the oars was moving. There was no purpose to any activity: they had no idea of the direction in which they were pointing. There was nothing to do but endure, each man huddled in his own thoughts.

How long this went on, Attilius could not calculate. Perhaps one hour; perhaps two. He could hear Pliny wheezing somewhere close,

Alexion snuffling like a child. The incessant hammering of the pumice fall, sharp to begin with as it rattled on the timber of the deck, gradually became more muffled, as pumice fell on pumice, sealing them off from the world. He wondered how long the joists of the deck would hold, or whether the sheer weight of what was above them would push them beneath the waves. He tried to console himself with the thought that pumice was light: the engineers in Rome, when constructing a great dome, sometimes mixed it into the cement in place of rock and fragments of brick. Nevertheless he gradually became aware that the ship was starting to list and soon after that a cry of panic went up from some of the sailors to his right that water was pouring through the oar-holes.

Torquatus shouted at them to be quiet then called to Pliny that he needed to take a party of men above decks to try to shovel off the rockfall. 'Engineer, will you help me?' He had mounted the short ladder to the trap door and was trying to push it open but the weight of the pumice made it hard to lift. Attilius joined him on the ladder, holding on to it with one hand, heaving with the other at the wooden panel above his head. Together they raised it slowly, releasing a cascade of debris that bounced off their heads and clattered onto the timbers below. 'I need twenty men!' ordered Torquatus. 'You five banks of oars—follow me.'

Attilius climbed out after him into the whirl of flying pumice. There was a strange almost brownish light, as in a sandstorm, and as he straightened Torquatus grabbed his arm and pointed. It took Attilius a moment to see what he meant, but then he glimpsed a row of winking yellow lights, showing faintly through the murk.

'We've drifted through the worst of it and come in close to the coast!' shouted the captain. 'We'll try to run her aground! Help me at the helm!' He turned and pushed the nearest of the oarsmen back towards the trap door. 'Get back below and tell the others to row—to row for their lives! The rest of you—hoist the sail!'

He ran towards the stern and Attilius followed, his head lowered, his feet sinking into the heavy blanket of white pumice that covered the deck like snow. They were so low in the water he felt he could almost have stepped down onto the carpet of rock and walked ashore. He clambered up onto the poop deck and with Torquatus he seized the great oar that steered the liburnian. But even with two men swinging on it the blade wouldn't move against the weight.

Dimly, he could see the shape of the sail beginning to rise before them. He heard the crack as it started to fill, and at the same time there was a ripple of movement along the banks of oars. The helm shuddered slightly beneath his hands. Torquatus pushed and he heaved. Slowly he felt the wooden shaft begin to move. For a while the liburnian seemed to list, motionless, and then a gust of wind propelled them forwards. He heard the drum beating again below, the oars settling into a steady rhythm, and from the gloom ahead the shape of the coast began to emerge.

Suddenly the rudder jumped and moved so freely he thought it must have snapped and Torquatus swung it hard, aiming them towards the beach. They had broken clear of the clinging pumice, the force of the sea and the wind propelling them directly at the shore. Torquatus cried out, 'Brace yourselves!' and an instant later the hull scraped rock and Attilius went flying down onto the deck, his landing cushioned by the foot-thick mattress of stone.

He lay there for a moment, winded, his cheek pressed to the warm, dry pumice, as the ship rolled beneath him. He heard the shouts of the sailors coming up from below decks, and the splashes as they jumped into the surf. He raised himself and saw the sail being lowered, the anchor flung over the side. Men with ropes were running up the beach, trying to find places to secure the ship. It was twilight—not the twilight thrown out by the eruption but the natural dusk of early evening. The shower of stones was light and the noise as they scattered over the deck and plopped into the sea was lost in the boom of the surf and the roar of the wind. Pliny had emerged from the trap door and was stepping carefully through the pumice, supported by Alexion. As Attilius approached he raised his arm.

'Well, this is a piece of good fortune, Engineer. Do you see where we are? I know this place well. This is Stabiae—a most pleasant town in which to spend an evening. Torquatus!' He beckoned to the captain. 'I suggest we stay here for the night.'

Torquatus regarded him as if he were mad. 'We have no choice about it, Admiral. No ship can be launched against this wind.'

Pliny gazed across the surf at the lights of the little town. It was separated from the beach by the coast road that ran all round the bay. The highway was clogged with refugees. On the shore itself, perhaps 100 people had congregated with their possessions, hoping to escape by sea, but unable to do more than gaze hopelessly at the crashing waves. One fat and elderly man stood apart, surrounded by his household, and Attilius felt a stir of recognition. Pliny had noticed him, too. 'That's my friend, Pomponianus,' he said. 'A nervous fellow at the best of times. He'll need our comfort. We must wear our bravest faces. Assist me to the shore.'

Attilius jumped down into the sea, followed by Torquatus. The water was up to their waists at one moment, at the next it was swirling round their necks. It was no easy task to take off a man of the admiral's weight and condition. With Alexion's help Pliny finally got down onto his backside and shuffled forwards and as they took his arms he slipped into the water. They managed to keep his head above the surface, and then, in an impressive show of self-control, he shrugged off their support and waded ashore unaided.

'A stubborn old fool,' said Torquatus, as they watched him march up the beach and embrace Pomponianus. 'A magnificent, courageous, stubborn old fool.'

Attilius glanced along the coast towards Vesuvius but he could not see much in the gathering darkness. He said, 'How far are we from Pompeii?'

'Three miles,' answered Torquatus. 'Perhaps less. It looks like they're taking the worst of it, poor wretches.'

He began wading towards the shore leaving Attilius alone.

If Stabiae was three miles downwind of Pompeii, and Vesuvius lay five miles the other side of the city, then this monstrous cloud must be eight miles long. Eight miles long, and—what?—at least five miles wide, given how far it reached out into the sea. Unless Corelia had fled very early she would have had no chance of escape.

POMPONIANUS HAD a villa on the seafront only a short walk along the road and Pliny was suggesting they should all return to it. Attilius could hear them arguing as he approached. Pomponianus, panicky, was objecting that if they left the beach they would lose their chance of a place in a boat. But Pliny waved that away. 'No sense in waiting here,' he said. 'Besides, you can always sail with us when the wind and sea are more favourable.' His voice was urgent. 'Come, Livia—take my arm.' And with Pomponianus's wife on one side and Alexion on the other, he led them up onto the road.

Just as they reached the gates of the villa it came on them again like a summer storm—first a few heavy drops, as a warning, and then the air exploded over the myrtle bushes and the cobbled courtyard. Attilius could feel someone's body pressing into his from behind, he pushed into the man in front and together they tumbled through the door and into the darkened, deserted villa. People were wailing, knocking blindly into the furniture. He heard a woman's scream and a crash. The disembodied face of a slave appeared, illuminated from below by an oil lamp, and then the face vanished and he heard the familiar *wumph* as a torch was lit. They huddled in the comfort of the light, masters and slaves alike, as the pumice clattered onto the terracotta roof of the villa and smashed into the gardens outside.

Someone went off with the oil lamp to fetch more torches, and some candles, and the slaves went on lighting them long after there was sufficient light, as if somehow the brighter the scene, the safer they would be. The crowded hall soon had an almost festive feel to it, and that was when Pliny declared that he would like to eat.

The admiral put on a display of bravery over the next few hours which none who survived the evening would afterwards forget. Five of them sat down to dinner—Pliny, Pomponianus, Livia, Torquatus and Attilius—not an ideal number from the point of etiquette, and the din of the pumice on the roof made conversation difficult. The table and the couches had been carried in from the dining room and set up in the sparkling hall. And if the food was not up to much—the fires were out and the best the kitchens could come up with were cold cuts of meat, fowl and fish—then Pomponianus, at Pliny's gentle prompting, had at least made up for it with the wine. He produced a Falernian, 200 years old, a vintage from the consulship of Lucius Opimius. It was his final jar ('Not much point in hanging on to it now,' he observed, gloomily).

When the admiral announced that he was going to bed he could see that the others assumed he must be joking. But no, he assured them, he was serious. He had trained himself to fall asleep at will—even upright, in a saddle, in a freezing German forest. This? This was nothing! 'Your arm, Engineer, if you will be so kind.' He wished them all good night.

Attilius held a torch aloft in one hand and with the other he supported the admiral. Together they went out into the central courtyard. The garden was in pitch darkness, trembling with the roar of falling stone. Pumice was strewn across the covered walkway and the clouds of dust from the dry and brittle rock set off Pliny's wheezing. He stopped outside the door of his usual room and waited for Attilius to clear a space so that he could pull open the door. He shuffled into the windowless room, leaving Attilius to close the door behind him.

The engineer stayed where he was, leaning against the wall, watching the rain of pumice. He detected a different, harsher sound to the dropping rock, and the ground beneath his feet was trembling. He ventured out from beneath the canopy, holding his torch towards the ground, and immediately he was struck hard on his arm. He almost dropped the torch. He grabbed a lump of the freshly fallen rock. Pressing himself against the wall he examined it in the light.

It was greyer than the earlier pumice—denser, larger, as if several pieces had been welded together—and it was hitting the ground with greater force. The shower of frothy white rock had been unpleasant and frightening but not especially painful. To be struck by a piece of this would be enough to knock a man unconscious.

He carried it into the hall and gave it to Torquatus. 'It's getting worse,' he said. 'The stones have been getting heavier.' Then, to Pomponianus, 'What sort of roofs do you have here, sir? Flat or pitched?'

'Flat,' said Pomponianus. 'They form terraces. You know—for the views across the bay.'

'And how old is the house?'

'It's been in my family for generations,' said Pomponianus. 'Why?'

'It isn't safe. With that weight of rock falling on old timber, sooner or later the joists will give way. We need to go outside.'

Torquatus hefted the rock in his hand. 'Outside? Into this?'

'We have cushions, don't we?' said Pomponianus's wife, Livia. 'And pillows and sheets? We can protect ourselves from rocks.'

Torquatus said, 'Then let's return to the beach.'

Livia was shouting to the slaves to fetch pillows and linen as Attilius hurried back into the courtyard. He could hear Pliny's snores. He banged on the door and tried to open it but even in the short time he had been away the path had filled again with debris. He had to kneel to clear it, then dragged open the door and ran in with his torch. He hooked his elbow under Pliny's armpit and hauled him to his feet. Staggering under the weight, he pushed the admiral towards the door and they were barely across the threshold when he heard one of the ceiling beams crack behind them and part of the roof came crashing to the floor.

They put the pillows on their heads crossways, so that the ends covered their ears, and tied them in place with strips torn from the sheets, knotting them tightly under their chins. Then each collected a torch or a lamp and with one hand on the shoulder of the person in front—apart from Torquatus, who took the lead and was wearing his helmet rather than a pillow—they set off to walk the gauntlet down to the beach.

All around them was a fury of noise—the heaving sea, the blizzard of rock, the boom of roofs giving way. Occasionally, Attilius felt the muffled thump of a missile striking his skull and his ears rang. They edged forwards slowly, sinking up to their knees in the loose pumice, unable to move any faster than the admiral, whose wheezing seemed to worsen each time he stumbled forwards. He was holding on to Alexion and being held on to by Attilius; behind the engineer came Livia and, behind her, Pomponianus, with the slaves at the back.

The force of the bombardment had cleared the road of refugees but down on the beach there was a light, and it was towards this that Torquatus led them. A few of the citizens of Stabiae and some of the men of the *Minerva* had broken up one of the useless ships and set it on fire. With ropes, the heavy sail from the liburnian and a dozen oars they had built themselves a large shelter beside the blaze. People who had been fleeing along the coast had come down from the road, begging for protection, and a crowd of several hundred was jostling for cover. They did not want to let the newcomers share their makeshift tent, and there was some jeering and scuffling round the entrance until Torquatus shouted that he had Admiral Pliny with him and would crucify any marine who refused to obey his orders.

Grudgingly, room was made, and Alexion and Attilius lowered Pliny to the sand just inside the entrance. He asked weakly for some water and Alexion took a gourd from a slave and held it to his lips. He swallowed a little, coughed and lay down on his side. Alexion gently untied the pillow and placed it under his head. He glanced up at Attilius. The engineer shrugged. He did not know what to say. It seemed unlikely that the old man could survive much more of this.

Attilius peered into the interior of the shelter. People were wedged together, barely able to move. The weight of the pumice was causing the roof to dip and from time to time a couple of the sailors cleared it by lifting it with the ends of their oars, tipping the stones away. Children were crying. Otherwise nobody spoke or shouted. He wondered how long they could endure.

He tugged the pillow from his sweating head and as his face was uncovered he heard someone croak his name. In the crowded near darkness he could not make out who it was at first. Only when the man spoke—'It's me, Lucius Popidius'—did he realise that it was one of the aediles of Pompeii.

Attilius seized his arm. 'Corelia? Is she with you?'

'I tried to bring her. But that madman had locked her in her room.'

'So you abandoned her?'

'What else could I do? He wanted to imprison us all!' He clutched at Attilius's tunic. 'Take me with you. That's Pliny over there, isn't it? You've got a ship—'

Attilius pushed him away and stumbled towards the entrance of the tent. The bonfire had been crushed to extinction by the rain of rocks and now that it had gone out the darkness on the beach was not even the darkness of night but of a closed room.

He heard a woman scream and raised his eyes. Faint and miraculous, far in the distance and yet growing in intensity, he saw a corona of fire in the sky.

VENUS

August 25: The final day of the eruption

Inclinatio — 00:12 hours

The light travelled slowly downwards from right to left. A sickle of luminous cloud—that was how Pliny described it—*a sickle of luminous cloud* sweeping down the western slope of Vesuvius leaving in its wake a patchwork of fires. Some were winking, isolated pinpricks—farmhouses and villas that had been set alight. But elsewhere whole swaths of the forest were blazing. Vivid, leaping sheets of red and orange flame tore jagged holes in the darkness. The scythe moved on, implacably, for at least as long as it would have taken to count to 100, flared briefly, and vanished.

'It's hard to tell from here,' Torquatus said, 'but I reckon that cloud of flame may just have rolled over Herculaneum.'

'And yet it doesn't seem to be on fire,' replied Attilius. 'That part of the coast looks entirely dark. It's as if the town had vanished—'

They looked towards the base of the burning mountain, searching for some point of light, but there was nothing.

On the beach at Stabiae they could smell the fires on the wind at once, a pungent, acrid taste of sulphur and cinders. Then one of the sailors who had been prodding the roof with his oar exclaimed that the heavy linen was no longer sagging.

Attilius cautiously stretched out his arm beyond the shelter of the tent, his palm held upwards, as if checking for rain. The marine was right. The air was still full of small missiles but the storm was not as violent as before. It was as if the mountain had found a different outlet for its malevolent energy, in the rushing avalanche of fire rather than in the steady bombardment of rock. In that moment he made up his mind. Better to die doing something than to cower beneath this flimsy shelter. He reached for his discarded pillow and planted it firmly on his head. Torquatus asked him quietly what he was doing.

'Leaving.'

'Leaving?' Pliny looked up sharply. 'You'll do no such thing. I absolutely refuse you permission to go.'

'With the greatest respect, Admiral, I take my orders from Rome, not from you.'

Torquatus took off his helmet. 'Take this,' he said. 'Metal is better protection than feathers.' Attilius started to protest but Torquatus thrust it into his hands. 'Take it—and good luck.'

'Thank you.' Attilius grasped his hand. 'May luck go with you, too.'

It fitted him well enough. He stood and picked up a torch. He felt like a gladiator about to enter the arena.

'But where will you go?' protested Pliny.

Attilius stepped into the storm. The light stones pinged off the helmet. It was utterly dark apart from the few torches planted into the sand round the perimeter of the shelter and the distant, glowing pyre of Vesuvius.

'Pompeii.'

TORQUATUS HAD ESTIMATED the distance between Stabiae and Pompeii at three miles—an hour's walk along a good road on a fine day. But the mountain had changed the laws of time and space and for a long while Attilius seemed to make no progress at all.

He managed to get off the beach and onto the road without too much difficulty and he was lucky that the view of Vesuvius was uninterrupted because the fires gave him an aiming-point. He knew that as long as he walked straight towards them he must come to Pompeii eventually. But he was pushing into the wind, so that even though he kept his head hunched, the rain of pumice stung his face and clogged his mouth and nostrils with dust. With each step he sank up to his knees in pumice and the effect was like trying to climb a hill of gravel. Every few hundred paces he swayed to a stop and somehow, holding the torch, he had to drag first one foot and then the other out of the clinging pumice and pick the stones out of his shoes.

The temptation to lie down and rest was overwhelming and yet it had to be resisted, he knew, because sometimes he stumbled into the bodies of those who had given up already. His torch showed soft forms, mere outlines of humanity, with occasionally a protruding foot, or a hand clawing at the air. Sometimes the living as well as the dead emerged fleetingly out of the darkness—a man carrying a cat; a young woman, naked and deranged; another couple carrying a brass candelabrum across their shoulders. They were heading in the opposite direction to him. From either side came isolated, barely human cries and moans, such as he imagined might be heard on a battlefield after the fighting was done. All this lasted for several hours.

At some point the crescent of light appeared again at the summit of Vesuvius, sweeping down, following more or less the same trajectory as before. It was followed by the same easing in the fall of rock. But this time on the slopes of the mountain it seemed to extinguish the fires rather than rekindle them.

Soon afterwards his torch began to stutter. Most of the pitch had burned away. He pushed on with renewed energy because he knew that when it died he would be left helpless in the darkness. And when that moment came it was indeed terrible. He could see nothing, not even if he brought his hand right up to his eyes.

The fires on the side of Vesuvius had also dwindled to an occasional tiny fountain of orange sparks. More red lightning gave a pinkish glow to the underside of the black cloud. He was no longer sure in which direction he was facing. He was disembodied, utterly alone, buried almost to his thighs in stone, the earth whirling and thundering around him. He flung away his torch and let himself sink forwards. He stretched out his hands and lay there, feeling the mantle of pumice slowly accumulating around his shoulders, and it was peculiarly comforting, like being tucked up in bed at night as a child. He laid his cheek to the warm rock and felt himself relax. A sense of tranquillity suffused him. If this was death then it was not too bad: he could accept this—welcome it, even, as one might a well-earned rest at the end of a hard day's work out on the aqueducts.

HE WAS WOKEN by heat, and by the smell of burning.

He did not know how long he had slept. Long enough to be almost entirely buried. He was in his grave. Panicking, he pushed with his forearms and slowly he felt the weight on his shoulders yield and split, heard the rustle of stones as they tumbled off him. He raised himself and shook his head, spitting the dust from his mouth, blinking his eyes, still buried below the waist.

The rain of pumice had mostly stopped and in the distance, immediately before him, he saw again the familiar scythe of glowing cloud. Except that this time, instead of moving like a comet from right to left it was descending fast and spreading laterally, coming his way. Immediately behind it was an interval of darkness that sprang into fire a few moments later as the heat found fresh fuel on the southern flank of the mountain. Before it, carried on the furnace-wind, came a rolling boom of noise, such that if he had been Pliny he would have varied his metaphor and described it not as a cloud but as a wave—a boiling wave of red-hot vapour that scorched his cheeks and watered his eyes. He could smell his hair singeing.

He writhed to free himself from the grip of the pumice as the sulphurous dawn raced across the sky towards him. Something dark seemed to be growing in the centre of it and he realised that the crimson light was silhouetting a town less than half a mile away. He picked out city walls and watchtowers, a row of windows—and *people*, the shadows of *people*, running along the lines of the ramparts. The spectacle was sharp for only a little while, just long enough for him to recognise it as Pompeii, and then the glow behind it slowly faded, taking the city with it, back into the darkness.

Diluculum — 06:00 hours

He pulled off his helmet and used it as a bucket, digging the lip of the metal into the pumice and emptying it over his shoulder. Gradually as he worked he became aware of the pale white shapes of his arms. Such a trivial matter, to be able to see one's hands, and yet he could have cried with relief. The morning was coming. A new day was struggling to be born. He was still alive.

He finished digging, wrestled his legs loose and hauled himself to his feet. The freshly ignited crop of fires high up on Vesuvius had restored his sense of direction. He even thought he could see the shadow of the city. He set off towards Pompeii, wading up to his knees again, sweating, thirsty, dirty, with the acrid stench of burning in his nose and throat. Through the dust he had a vague impression of low walls on either side of him and as he stumbled forwards he realised that these weren't fences but buried buildings, and that he was labouring along a street at roof level. The pumice must be seven or eight feet deep at least.

Impossible to believe that people could have lived through such a bombardment. And yet they had. Not only had he seen them moving on the city's ramparts, he could see them now, emerging from holes in the ground, from beneath the tombs of their houses. They stood around in the grainy brown half-light, brushing the dust from their clothes, gazing at the sky.

Apart from an occasional scattering of missiles the fall of rock had ceased. But it would come again, Attilius was certain. There was a pattern. The greater the surge of burning air down the slopes of the mountain, the more energy it seemed to suck from the storm and the longer the lull before it started anew. There was no doubt, either, that the surges were growing in strength. The first appeared to have hit Herculaneum; the second to have travelled beyond it, out to sea; the third to have reached almost as far as Pompeii itself. The next might easily sweep across the entire town. He did not have much time.

The harbour had entirely vanished, a few masts poking out of the sea of pumice the only clues it had ever existed. He could hear the sea, but it sounded a long way off. Occasionally, the ground shook and then would come the distant crash of walls and timbers giving way, roofs collapsing. It became harder to make progress. He sensed that he was wading up a slope and he tried to visualise how the port had looked, the ramped roads leading up from the wharves and quaysides to the city gates.

He reached the top of the ramp. He groped through the dusty twilight until he found a corner of heavy masonry and felt his way round it, into the low tunnel that was all that remained of the Stabian Gate, the great entrance to the town.

He waded on up the hill. He was sure this was the way to the Vesuvius Gate—he could see the orange fringes of fire working their way across the mountain far ahead—which meant he could not be far from the House of the Popidii, it should be on this very street.

People were digging frantically, some with planks of wood, a few with their bare hands. Others were calling out names, dragging out boxes, carpets, pieces of broken furniture. An old woman screaming hysterically. Two men fighting over something—he could not see what—another trying to run with a marble bust cradled in his arms.

He saw a team of horses, frozen in mid-gallop, swooping out of the gloom above his head, and he stared at them stupidly for a moment until he realised it was the equestrian monument at the big crossroads. He went back down the hill again, past what he remembered was a bakery and at last, very faintly on a wall, at knee-height, he found an inscription: HIS NEIGHBOURS URGE THE ELECTION OF LUCIUS POPIDIUS SECUNDUS AS AEDILE.

He managed to squeeze through a window on one of the side streets and picked his way among the rubble, calling her name. There was no sign of life.

It was still possible to work out the arrangement of the two houses by the walls of the upper storeys. The roof of the atrium had collapsed, but the flat space next to it must have been where the swimming pool was. He poked his head into some of the rooms of what had once been the upper floor. Dimly he could make out broken pieces of furniture, smashed crockery, scraps of hanging drapery. Drifts of pumice were mixed with terracotta tiles, bricks, splintered beams. He found an empty birdcage on what must have been a balcony and stepped through into an abandoned bedroom, open to the sky. It had obviously been a young woman's room. Abandoned jewellery. A comb. A broken mirror. A doll. He lifted what he thought was a blanket from the bed and saw that it was a cloak. He tried the door—locked—and then sat on the bed and examined the cloak more closely.

He had never had much of an eye for what women wore. But this, he was sure, was Corelia's. Popidius had said she had been locked in her room and this was a woman's bedroom. There was no sign of a body, either here or outside. For the first time he dared to hope she had escaped. But when? And to where?

He turned the cloak over in his hands and tried to think what Ampliatus would have done. 'He wanted to imprison us all'—Popidius's phrase. Presumably he had blocked all the exits and ordered everyone to sit it out. But there must have come a moment, as the roofs began to collapse, when even Ampliatus would have recognised that the old house was a deathtrap. He would not have fled the city, though: that would not have been in character, and besides, by then it would have been impossible to travel very far. No: he would have tried to lead his family to a safe location.

Where was safe? He tried to think as an engineer. What kind of roof was strong enough to withstand the stresses imposed by eight feet of pumice? Nothing flat, that was for sure. Something built with modern methods. A dome would be ideal.

He dropped the cloak and stumbled back onto the balcony.

HUNDREDS OF PEOPLE were out in the streets now, milling around in the semidarkness. Some were aimless—lost, bewildered, demented with grief. Others appeared purposeful, pursuing their own private schemes of search or escape. Worst of all were the names called plaintively in the darkness. Had anyone seen Felicio or Pherusa, or Appuleia—the wife of Narcissus?—or Specula or the lawyer, Terentius Neo? Parents had become separated from their children. Children stood screaming outside the ruins of houses. Torches flared towards Attilius in the hope that he might be someone else—a father, a husband, a brother. He waved them away, shrugging off their questions, intent on counting off the city blocks as he climbed the hill north towards the Vesuvius Gate.

At the corner of the fourth block he found the row of shops, three-quarters buried, and scrambled up the slope of pumice onto the low roof. He crouched just behind the ridge. Its outline was sharp. There must be fires beyond it. Slowly he raised his head. Across the flat surface of the buried builder's yard were the nine high windows of Ampliatus's baths, each one brilliantly, defiantly, lit by torches and scores of oil lamps. He could see figures moving.

Attilius slithered down into the enclosed space and set off across it. As he came closer he saw that the figures were slaves and that they were clearing the drifts of pumice where they had been blown into the three big chambers—the changing room, the tepidarium and the caldarium—digging it out like snow with wooden shovels where it was deepest, or elsewhere merely sweeping it away with brooms. Patrolling behind them was Ampliatus, shouting that they should work harder. Attilius stood watching for a few moments, hidden in the darkness, and then cautiously began to climb towards the middle room—the tepidarium—at the back of which he could see the entrance to the domed sweating chamber.

There was no chance he could enter without being seen so in the end he simply walked in through the open window, the slaves staring at him in amazement. He was halfway to the sweating room when Ampliatus saw him—'Aquarius!'—and hurried to intercept him. He was smiling, his palms spread wide.

He had a cut on his temple and the hair on the left side of his scalp was stiff with blood. The mouth was turned up at the corners: a mask of comedy. Before Attilius could say anything he started talking again. 'We must get the aqueduct running immediately. Everything is ready, you see. Nothing is damaged. We could open for business tomorrow, if only we could connect the water.' He was talking very quickly. 'People will need one place in the town that works. They'll need to bathe—it'll be dirty work, getting everything back in order. But it's not just that. It'll be a symbol around which they can gather. If they see the baths are working, it will give them confidence. Confidence is the key to everything. The key to confidence is water. Water is everything. I need you, Aquarius. Fifty-fifty. What do you say?'

'Where's Corelia?'

'Corelia?' Ampliatus's eyes were alert for a potential deal. 'You want Corelia? In exchange for the water?'

'Perhaps.'

'A marriage? I'm willing to consider it.' He jerked his thumb. 'She's in there. But I'll want my lawyers to draw up the terms.'

Attilius turned away and strode through the narrow entrance into the laconium. Seated on the stone benches around the small domed sweating room, lit by the torches in their iron holders on the wall, were Corelia, her mother and her brother. Opposite them were the steward, Scutarius, and the giant gatekeeper, Massavo. A second exit led to the caldarium. As the engineer came in, Corelia looked up.

'We need to leave,' he said. 'Hurry. Everyone.'

Ampliatus, at his back, blocked the door. 'Oh no,' he said. 'Nobody leaves. We've endured the worst. This isn't the time to run.'

Attilius directed his words to Corelia. 'Listen. The falling rock is not the main danger. It's when the fall stops that winds of fire travel down the mountain. Everything in their path is destroyed.'

'No, no. We're safer here than anywhere,' insisted Ampliatus. 'Believe me. The walls are three feet thick.'

'Safe from heat in a sweating room?' Attilius appealed to them all. 'Don't listen to him. If the hot cloud comes, this place will cook you like an oven. Corelia.' He held out his hand to her. She glanced quickly towards Massavo. They were under guard, Attilius realised.

'Nobody is leaving,' repeated Ampliatus. 'Massavo!'

Attilius seized Corelia's wrist and tried to drag her towards the caldarium before Massavo had time to stop him, but the big man was too fast. He sprang to cover the exit and when Attilius tried to shoulder him aside Massavo grabbed him by the throat with his forearm and dragged him back into the room. Attilius let go of Corelia and tried to prise away the grip from his windpipe.

He heard Ampliatus order Massavo to break his neck and then there was a whoosh of flame close to his ear and a scream of pain from Massavo. The arm released him. He saw Corelia with a torch clenched in both hands and Massavo on his knees. Ampliatus called out her name, and there was something almost pleading in the way he said it, stretching out his hands to her. She whirled round and hurled the torch at her father, and then she was through the door and into the caldarium, shouting to Attilius to follow.

He blundered after her, down the tunnel and into the brightness of the hot room, across the immaculately cleaned floor, past the slaves, out through the window, into the darkness, sinking into the stones. When they were halfway across the yard he looked back and he thought perhaps that Ampliatus had given up—he could see no signs of pursuit at first—but of course, in his madness, he had not. Massavo appeared in the window with his master beside him and the light of the window quickly fragmented as torches were passed out to the slaves. A dozen men armed with brooms and shovels jumped out of the caldarium and began fanning out across the ground.

It seemed to take an age of slipping and sliding to clamber back up onto the perimeter roof and drop down into the street. For an instant they must have been dimly visible on the roof—long enough, at least, for one of the slaves to see them and shout a warning. Attilius felt a sharp pain in his ankle as he landed. He took Corelia's arm and limped a little way farther up the hill and then they both drew back into the shadow of the wall as the torches of Ampliatus's men appeared in the road behind them. Their line of escape to the Stabian Gate was cut off.

He thought then that it was hopeless. They were trapped between the flames of the torches and the flames on Vesuvius, and even as he looked from one to the other he detected a faint gleam beginning to form in the same place high up on the mountain as before, where the surges had been born. An idea came to him in his desperation—

absurd: he dismissed it—but it would not go away, and suddenly he wondered if it had not been in the back of his mind all along. Perhaps it had been waiting for him from the start: his destiny.

He peered towards the mountain. No doubt about it. The worm of light was growing. He whispered to Corelia, 'Can you run?'

'Yes.'

'Then run as you've never run before.'

They edged out from the cover of the wall. Ampliatus's men had their backs to them and were staring into the murk towards the Stabian Gate. He heard Ampliatus issuing more orders—'You two take the side street, you three down the hill'—and then there was nothing for it but to start thrashing their way through the pumice again. He had to grind his teeth against the agony in his leg and she was quicker than he was. He stumbled after her, aware of fresh shouting from Ampliatus—'There they go! Follow me!'—but when they reached the end of the block and he risked a glance over his shoulder he could see only one torch swaying after them. 'Cowards!' Ampliatus was shrieking. 'What are you afraid of?'

But it was obvious what had made them mutiny. The wave of fire was unmistakably sweeping down Vesuvius, growing by the instant, not in height but in breadth—roiling, gaseous, hotter than flame: white-hot—only a madman would run towards it. Even Massavo would not follow his master now. Attilius felt the heat on his face. The scorching wind raised whirls of ash and debris. Corelia looked back at him but he urged her forwards. They had passed another city block and there was only one more to go. Ahead of them the glowing sky outlined the Vesuvius Gate and beside it he could see the squat cube of the castellum aquae.

'Wait!' Ampliatus shouted. 'Corelia!' But his voice was fainter, he was falling behind.

Attilius reached the corner of the castellum aquae and pulled Corelia after him, down the narrow alley. Pumice had almost completely buried the door. Only a narrow triangle of wood was showing. He kicked it, the lock gave way and pumice poured through the opening. He pushed her in and slid down after her into the pitch darkness. He could hear the water, groped towards it, felt the edge of the tank and clambered over it, up to his waist in water, pulled her after him, and fumbled round the edges of the mesh screen for the fastenings, found them, lifted away the grille. He steered Corelia into the mouth of the tunnel and squeezed in after her.

'Move. As far as you can go.'

A roaring, like an avalanche. She scrambled forwards. He followed, putting his hands on her waist and pressing her down to her knees, so that as much of her body should be immersed as possible. He threw himself upon her. They clung to one another in the water. And then there was only scalding heat and the stench of sulphur in the darkness of the aqueduct, directly beneath the city walls.

Hora Altera — 07:57 hours

An incandescent sandstorm raced down the hill towards Ampliatus. Exposed walls sheared, roofs exploded, tiles and bricks, beams and stones and bodies flew at him and yet so slowly, as it seemed to him in that long moment before his death, that he could see them turning against the brilliance. And then the blast hit him, burst his eardrums, ignited his hair, blew his clothes and shoes off, and whirled him upside-down, slamming him against the side of a building.

He died in the instant it took the surge to reach the baths and shoot through the open windows, choking his wife who, obeying orders to the last, had remained in her place in the sweating room. It caught his son, who was trying to reach the Temple of Isis. It overwhelmed the steward and the porter, Massavo, who were running down the street towards the Stabian Gate. It passed over the brothel, where the owner, Africanus, had returned to retrieve his takings, and where Zmyrina was hiding under Exomnius's bed. It killed Brebix, who had gone to the gladiators' school at the start of the eruption to be with his former comrades, and Musa and Corvinus, who had decided to stay with him. It even killed the faithful Polites who had been sheltering in the harbour and went back into the town to see if he could help Corelia. It killed more than 2000 in less than half a minute and it left their bodies arranged in a series of grotesque tableaux for posterity to gawp at.

For although their hair and clothes burned briefly, these fires were quickly snuffed out by the lack of oxygen, and instead a muffling, six-foot tide of fine ash, travelling in the wake of the surge, flowed over the city, shrouding the landscape and moulding every detail of its fallen victims. This ash hardened. More pumice fell. In their snug cavities the bodies rotted, and with them, as the centuries passed, the memory that there had even been a city on this spot. Pompeii became a town of perfectly shaped hollow citizens—huddled together or lonely, their clothes blown off or lifted over their heads, grasping hopelessly for their favourite possessions or clutching nothing—vacuums suspended in midair at the level of their roofs.

AT STABIAE, the wind from the surge caught the makeshift shelter of the *Minerva*'s sail and lifted it clear of the beach. The people, exposed, could see the glowing cloud rolling over Pompeii and heading straight towards them.

Everyone ran, Pomponianus and Popidius in the lead.

They would have taken Pliny with them. Torquatus and Alexion had him by the arms and had raised him to his feet. But the admiral was finished with moving and when he told them, brusquely, to leave him and to save themselves, they knew he meant it. Alexion gathered up his notes and repeated his promise to deliver them to the old man's nephew. Torquatus saluted. And then Pliny was alone.

He had done all he could. He had timed the manifestation in all its stages. He had described its phases—column, cloud, storm, fire—and had exhausted his vocabulary in the process. He had lived a long life, had seen many things and now Nature had granted him this last insight into her power. In these closing moments of his existence he continued to observe as keenly as he had when young—and what greater blessing could a man ask for than that?

The line of light was very bright and yet filled with flickering shadows. What did they mean? He was still curious.

It was hard to breathe, or even to stand in the wind. The air was full of ash and grit and a terrible brilliance. He was choking, the pain across his chest was an iron band. He staggered backwards.

The tide engulfed him.

FOR THE REST of the day, the eruption continued, with fresh surges and loud explosions that rocked the ground. Towards the evening its force subsided and it started to rain. The water put out the fires and washed the ash from the air and drenched the drifting grey landscape of low dunes and hollows that had obliterated the fertile Pompeiian plain and the beautiful coast from Herculaneum to Stabiae. It filled the wells and replenished the springs and created the lines of new streams, meandering down towards the sea. The river Sarnus took a different course entirely.

As the air cleared, Vesuvius reappeared, but its shape was completely altered. It no longer rose to a peak but to a hollow, as if a giant bite had been taken from its summit. A huge moon, reddened by dust, rose over an altered world.

Pliny's body was recovered from the beach—'he looked more asleep than dead,' according to his nephew—and carried back to Misenum, along with his observations. These subsequently proved so accurate that a new word entered the language of science: 'Plinian', to describe 'a volcanic eruption in which a narrow blast of gas is ejected with great violence from a central vent to a height of several miles before it expands sideways'.

The Aqua Augusta continued to flow, as she would for centuries to come.

People who had fled from their homes on the eastern edges of the mountain began to make a cautious return before nightfall and many were the stories and rumours that circulated in the days that followed. Miraculous were the tales of survival. A man was said to have buried himself inside the belly of a dead horse on the highway to Stabiae, and in that way had escaped the heat and the rocks. Two beautiful, blond children—twins—were found wandering, unharmed, in robes of gold, without a graze on their bodies, and yet unable to speak: they were sent to Rome and taken into the household of the Emperor.

Most persistent of all was the legend of a man and a woman who had emerged out of the earth itself at dusk on the day the eruption ended. They had tunnelled underground like moles, it was said, for several miles, all the way from Pompeii, and had come up where the ground was clear, drenched in the life-giving waters of a subterranean river, which had given them its sacred protection. They were reported to have been seen walking together in the direction of the coast as the sun fell over the shattered outline of Vesuvius. But this particular story was generally considered far-fetched and was dismissed as a superstition by all sensible people.

ROBERT HARRIS

Robert Harris was planning to write a novel about modern day America—'the Walt Disney company takes over the world', being his theme—when he read an article about Pompeii in the *Daily Telegraph*. New information had come to light, which challenged the familiar story he had been taught at school, that everyone in Pompeii had died instantly when Vesuvius erupted in AD 79. In reality, the disaster was much more drawn out and complex, the article claimed, and Harris immediately saw the potential for an interesting novel set at the time of the world's *first* superpower—the Roman Empire.

'The eruption started at one o'clock in the afternoon, but no one died for eighteen hours,' Harris explains. 'There was a great shower of ash and rock falling, and by the following morning there were two or three thousand people walking around Pompeii at roof level because the streets were filled with pumice stone. It was only then that they were hit by a terrible, searing cloud of gas that ran at enormous speed down the side of the mountain and asphyxiated them. Because it didn't all end instantly, there were choices to be made—people could stay in the city, or leave and then come back because they though it was all over. When you consider that the eruption was a hundred thousand times the power of Hiroshima, one comes away with a healthy respect for the powers of Nature.'

Robert Harris started his career as a reporter for the BBC, working on programmes such as *Newsnight* and *Panorama* before becoming political editor of the *Observer* and an award-winning columnist for the *Sunday Times*. As well as three best-selling thrillers—*Fatherland*, *Enigma* and *Archangel*—he has written five nonfiction books including *Selling Hitler,* a fascinating account of the infamous attempt to sell forgeries of Hitler's diaries to the *Sunday Times*. His novels are often referred to as intelligent thrillers, a description he would probably be happy with. 'Of course you want to make people think, but my books are always written to entertain,' he says. 'Even as an adolescent I never wrote for myself, to work things out about "my own troubled life". I've always been an extrovert writer.'

shutter island

DENNIS LEHANE

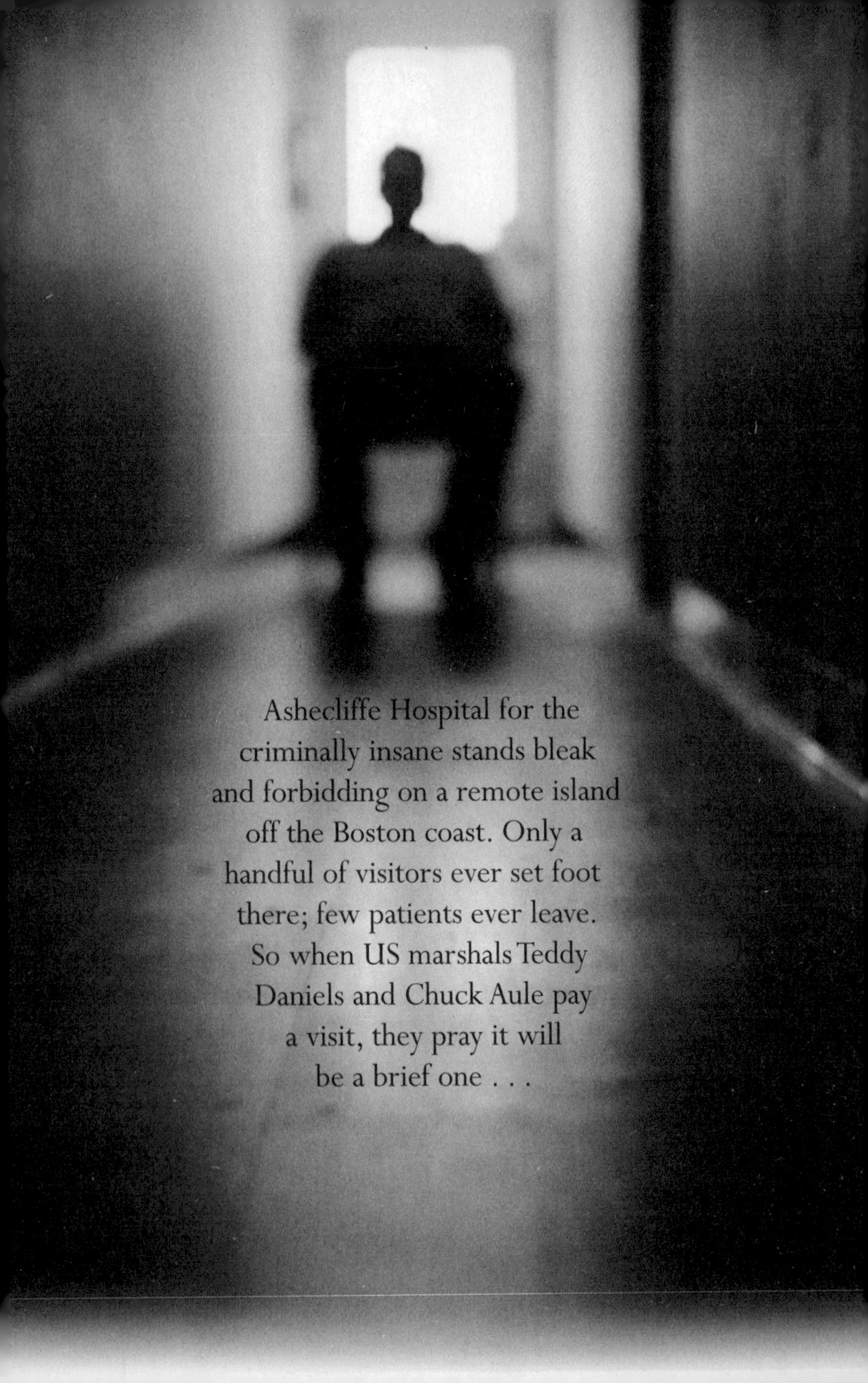

Ashecliffe Hospital for the criminally insane stands bleak and forbidding on a remote island off the Boston coast. Only a handful of visitors ever set foot there; few patients ever leave. So when US marshals Teddy Daniels and Chuck Aule pay a visit, they pray it will be a brief one . . .

PROLOGUE
FROM THE JOURNALS OF DR LESTER SHEEHAN, MAY 3, 1993

I haven't laid eyes on the island in several years. The last time was from a friend's boat that ventured into the outer harbour, and I could see it off in the distance, shrouded in the summer haze, a careless smudge of paint against the sky.

I haven't stepped foot on it in more than two decades, but my wife says (sometimes joking, sometimes not) that she's not sure I ever left. She said once that time is nothing to me but a series of bookmarks that I use to jump back and forth through the text of my life. If she is right, then I feel as if someone has shaken the book and those yellowed slips of paper, torn matchbook covers and flattened coffee stirrers have fallen to the floor, and the dogeared flaps have been pressed smooth. I misplace things far too often these days, my glasses, my car keys. I enter stores and forget what I've come for.

I want to write these things down. Not to alter the text so that I fall under a more favourable light. No, no. I want only to preserve the text, to transfer it from its current storage facility to these pages.

Ashecliffe Hospital sat benignly on the island's northwestern side. It looked nothing like a hospital for the criminally insane and even less like the military barracks it had been before that. Its appearance reminded me of a boarding school. Just outside the main compound, a mansarded Victorian housed the warden, and a Tudor minicastle, which had once housed the Union commander of the northeastern shoreline, served as the quarters of our chief of staff. Inside the wall were the staff quarters—quaint clapboard cottages for the clinicians, three low-slung cinder-block dormitories for the orderlies, guards and nurses. And in the centre of the compound, twin redbrick colonials on either side of the hospital itself, a structure of large, charcoal-coloured stones and handsome granite. Beyond were the bluffs and the tidal marsh and a long valley, where the night winds often came howling in off the ocean. And the fort, of course, which stood long before the first hospital staff arrived, and the lighthouse beyond, out of service since before the Civil War, rendered obsolete by the beam of Boston Light.

From the sea, it didn't look like much. You have to picture it the way Teddy Daniels saw it on that calm morning in September of 1954. Barely an island, you'd think, so much as the idea of one.

Rats were the most voluminous of our animal life. They scrabbled in the brush, formed lines along the shore at night, clambered over wet rock. In the years following those four strange days, I took to studying the rats from a hill overlooking the northern shore. I was fascinated to discover that sometimes, when the current reached its lowest ebb, they would try to swim for Paddock Island, little more than a rock in a cupful of sand that remained submerged twenty-two hours out of every day. They were always driven back by the rip tide.

I say always, but I saw one make it. The night of the harvest moon in October '56, I saw its black moccasin of a body dart across the pearl-grey sand that was already beginning to drown again as the current returned to swallow Paddock Island, and swallow that rat, I assume, for I never saw it swim back.

In that moment, as I watched it scurry up the shore, I thought of Teddy. I thought of Teddy and his poor dead wife, Dolores Chanal, and those twin terrors, Rachel Solando and Andrew Laeddis, the havoc they wreaked on us all. I thought that if Teddy were sitting with me, he would have seen that rat too.

And I'll tell you something else. Teddy would have clapped.

DAY ONE—RACHEL

1

Teddy Daniels's father had been a fisherman. He lost his boat to the bank when Teddy was eleven, spent the rest of his life hiring onto other boats when they had the work, unloading freight along the docks when they didn't, going long stretches when he was back at the house by ten in the morning, sitting in an armchair, whispering to himself, his eyes gone wide and dark.

He'd taken Teddy out to the islands when Teddy was still a small boy, too young to be much help on the boat. All he'd been able to do was untangle the lines and tie off the hooks.

They'd left in the dark, and when the sun appeared it was a cold ivory that pushed up from the edge of the sea, and the islands appeared out of the fading dusk, huddled together, as if they'd been caught at something. Teddy's father pointed out the prison on Deer Island and the stately fort on George's. On Thompson, the high trees were filled with birds.

Out past them all, the one they called Shutter lay like something tossed from a Spanish galleon. Back then, in the spring of '28, it had been left to itself in a riot of its own vegetation, strangled in vines and topped with great clouds of moss.

'Why Shutter?' Teddy asked.

His father shrugged. 'Some places just get a name and it sticks. Pirates probably.'

'Pirates?' Teddy liked the sound of that. He could see them—big men with eye patches and tall boots, gleaming swords.

His father said, 'This is where they hid in the old days.' His arm swept the horizon and the islands. 'Hid themselves. Hid their gold.'

Teddy imagined chests of it, the coins spilling down the sides.

Later he got sick, repeatedly and violently, over the side of the boat. His father was surprised because Teddy hadn't begun to vomit until hours into the trip, when the ocean was flat and quiet.

His father said, 'It's OK. It's your first time. Nothing to be ashamed of. Sometimes there's motion, and you can't even feel it until it climbs up inside you.'

Teddy nodded, wiped his mouth with a cloth, unable to tell his father that it wasn't motion that had turned his stomach. It was all that water. Stretched out around them until it was all that was left of the world. Until that moment, he'd never known they were this alone.

He looked up at his father, his eyes red, and his father said, 'You'll be OK,' and Teddy tried to smile.

His father went out on a Boston whaler ten years later and never came back. The next spring, pieces of the boat—a strip of keel, a hot plate with the captain's name etched in the base—washed up on Nantasket Beach in the town of Hull, where Teddy grew up.

They held the funeral for the four fishermen in St Theresa's

Church, its back pressed hard against the same sea that had claimed so many of its parishioners, and Teddy stood with his mother and heard testimonials to the dead men.

Standing in that church, Teddy remembered that day on his father's boat because they'd never gone out again. His father kept saying they would, but Teddy understood that he said this only so his son could hold on to some pride. His father never acknowledged what had happened that day, but a look had passed between them as they headed home, back through the string of islands.

'It's the sea,' his father said, a hand rubbing Teddy's back as they leaned against the stern. 'Some men take to it. Some men it takes.'

And Teddy knew which he'd probably grow up to be.

To get to Shutter Island in '54, Teddy and his new partner, Chuck Aule, took the ferry from Boston. Teddy started the trip down on his knees in front of the toilet, heaving into the bowl as the ferry's engine chugged and clacked and his nasal passages filled with the oily smells of gasoline and the late-summer sea.

The final heave seemed to carry a piece of his chest with it, and as Teddy sat back on the metal floor and wiped his face with his handkerchief, he thought that this wasn't the way you wanted to start a new partnership.

He could just imagine Chuck telling his wife back home—if he had a wife; Teddy didn't even know that much about him yet—about his first encounter with the legendary Teddy Daniels. 'Guy liked me so much, honey, he threw up.'

Since that trip as a boy, Teddy had never enjoyed being out on the water. Even in the war, it wasn't the storming of the beaches he feared so much as those last few yards from the boats to the shore, legs slogging through the depths, strange creatures slithering over your boots. He'd prefer to be out on deck, facing it in the fresh air, rather than back here, sickly warm, lurching.

When he was sure it had passed, his stomach no longer bubbling, his head no longer swimming, he washed his hands and face, checked his appearance in a small mirror mounted over the sink. Teddy was still a relatively young man with a government-issue crew cut. But his face was lined with evidence of the war, his penchant for pursuit and violence living in eyes that Dolores had once called 'dog-sad'.

I'm too young, Teddy thought, to look this hard.

He adjusted his belt around his waist so the gun and holster rested on his hip. He took his hat from the top of the toilet and put it back on, adjusted the brim until it tilted just slightly to the right. He tightened the knot in his tie. It was one of those loud floral ties that had been going out of style for about a year, but he wore it because she had given it to him one birthday. Pressing her lips to his. Sliding into his lap, removing the tie, Teddy keeping his eyes closed. Just to smell her. To imagine her. To create her in his mind and hold her there.

He could still do it—close his eyes and see her. But lately, white smudges would blur parts of her—an ear lobe, her eyelashes, the contours of her hair—and Teddy feared time was taking her from him, grinding away at the pictures in his head.

'I miss you,' he said, and went out through the galley to the foredeck.

It was warm and clear out there, but the water was threaded with dark glints of rust and an overall pallor of grey, a suggestion of something growing dark in the depths, massing.

'You OK?' Chuck asked. 'You look pale.'

Teddy shrugged it off. 'I'm fine. Just finding my sea legs.'

They stood in silence for a bit, the sea undulating all around them, pockets of it as dark and silken as velvet.

'You know it used to be a POW camp?' Teddy said.

Chuck said, 'The island?'

Teddy nodded. 'Back in the Civil War. They built a fort there, barracks.'

'What do they use it for now?'

Teddy shrugged. 'Couldn't tell you. The institution use the old troop quarters as accommodation.'

Chuck said, 'Be like going back to basic, huh?'

'Don't wish that on us.' Teddy turned on the rail. 'So what's your story, Chuck?'

Chuck smiled. He was a bit stockier and a bit shorter than Teddy, and he had a head of tight, curly black hair, olive skin and slim, delicate hands that seemed incongruous, as if he'd borrowed them until his real ones came back from the shop. His left cheek bore a small scythe of a scar, and he tapped it with his index finger. 'I always start with the scar,' he said. 'People usually ask sooner or later.'

'OK.'

'Wasn't from the war,' Chuck said. 'My girlfriend says I should just say it was, be done with it, but . . .' He shrugged. 'It was from *playing* war, though. When I was a kid. Me and this other kid shooting slingshots at each other in the woods. My friend's rock just misses me, so

I'm OK, right?' He shook his head. 'His rock hit a tree, sent a piece of bark into my cheek. Hence the scar.'

Teddy nodded. 'You transferred from Oregon?' he asked.

'Seattle. Came in last week.'

Teddy waited, but Chuck didn't offer any further explanation.

Teddy said, 'How long you been with the marshals?'

'Four years.'

'So you know how small it is.'

'Sure. Everyone knows everyone in the service. So eventually, there'll be—what do they call it?—scuttlebutt.'

'That's a word for it.'

Chuck nodded and spat over the rail. 'My girlfriend's Japanese. Well, born here, but you know . . . Grew up in a camp. There's still a lot of tension out there—Portland, Seattle, Tacoma. No one likes me being with her.'

'So they transferred you.'

Chuck nodded, spat again, watched it fall into the churning foam. 'They say it's going to be big,' he said.

Teddy lifted his elbows off the rail and straightened. He patted the pockets of his overcoat, looking for his Chesterfields. 'Who's "they"? What's "it"?'

'They. The papers,' Chuck said. 'The storm. Big one, they say. Huge.' He waved his arm at the pale sky, as pale as the foam churning against the bow. But there, along its southern edge, a thin line of purple cotton swabs grew like inkblots.

Teddy sniffed the air. 'You remember the war, don't you, Chuck?'

Chuck smiled in such a way that Teddy suspected they were already tuning in to each other's rhythms, learning how to work with each other.

'A bit,' Chuck said. 'I seem to remember rubble. Lots of rubble. People denigrate rubble, but I say it has its place, its own aesthetic beauty. I say it's all in the eye of the beholder.'

'You talk like a dime novel. Has anyone else told you that?'

'It's come up.' Chuck gave the sea another of his small smiles.

Teddy patted his trouser pockets, searched the inside pockets of his suit jacket. 'You remember how often the deployments were dependent on weather reports.'

Chuck rubbed the stubble on his chin. 'Oh, I do, yes.'

'Do you remember how often those weather reports proved correct?'

Chuck furrowed his brow, wanting Teddy to know he was giving this due and proper consideration. Then he smacked his lips and said, 'About thirty per cent of the time, I'd venture.'

'At best.'

Chuck nodded. 'At best.'

'And so now, back in the world as we are . . .'

'Oh, back we are,' Chuck said. 'Ensconced, one could even say.'

Teddy suppressed a laugh, liking this guy a lot now. 'Ensconced,' he agreed. 'Why would you put any more credence in the weather reports now than you did then?'

'Well,' Chuck said as the sagging tip of a small triangle peeked above the horizon line, 'I'm not sure my credence can be measured in terms of less or more. Do you want a cigarette?'

Teddy stopped in the middle of a second round of pocket pats. 'I had them when I boarded.'

Chuck looked back over his shoulder. 'Government employees. Rob you blind.' He shook a cigarette free of his pack of Luckies, handed one to Teddy, and lit it for him with his brass Zippo, the stench of the kerosene climbing over the salt air and finding the back of Teddy's throat. Chuck snapped the lighter closed, then flicked it back open with a snap of his wrist and lit his own.

Teddy exhaled, and the triangle tip of the island disappeared for a moment in the plume of smoke.

'You got a girl, Teddy? Married?' Chuck said.

'Was,' Teddy said, picturing Dolores, a look she gave him once on their honeymoon, turning her head, her chin almost touching her bare shoulder. 'She died.'

Chuck came off the rail, his neck turning pink. 'Oh, Jesus.'

'It's OK,' Teddy said.

'No, no.' Chuck held his palm up by Teddy's chest. 'It's . . . I'd heard that. I don't know how I could've forgotten. A couple of years ago, wasn't it?'

Teddy nodded. He heard the whine of the engine change pitch behind them and felt the ferry give a small lurch underfoot. He could make out the hard, jutting angles of an old fort atop the southern cliff face as they came around towards the western side of the island. The cannons were gone, but Teddy could make out the turrets easily enough. He figured Ashecliffe Hospital sat somewhere beyond, overlooking the western shore.

Chuck was saying, 'I feel like an idiot. Really. I'm so sorry.'

Teddy saw her again, her back to him as she walked down the

apartment hallway, wearing one of his old uniform shirts, and a familiar weariness invaded his bones. He would prefer to do just about anything rather than speak of Dolores, of the facts of her being on this earth for thirty-one years and then ceasing to be. But it was like Chuck's scar, he supposed—the story that had to be dispensed with before they could move on, or otherwise it would always be between them. The hows. The wheres. The whys. Dolores had been dead for two years, but she came to life in his dreams, and he sometimes went full minutes into a new morning thinking she was out in the kitchen or taking her coffee on the front stoop of their apartment on Buttonwood.

'There was a fire in our apartment building. I was working. Four people died. She was one of them. The smoke got her, Chuck, not the fire. So she didn't die in pain. That's important.'

Chuck brought out a flask, took a sip from it and offered it to Teddy.

Teddy shook his head. 'I quit. After the fire. She used to worry about it, you know? Said all of us soldiers and cops drank too much. So . . .' He could feel Chuck beside him, sinking in embarrassment. 'You learn how to carry something like that, Chuck. You got no choice. Like all the shit you saw in the war. Remember?'

Chuck nodded, his eyes going small with memory for a moment. 'Sure,' he said eventually, his face still flushed.

The dock appeared, as if by trick of light, stretching out from the sand, a stick of chewing gum from this distance, insubstantial and grey.

Teddy felt dehydrated from his time at the toilet and maybe a bit exhausted from the last couple of minutes; no matter how much he'd learned to carry it, carry her, the weight could still wear him down. A dull ache settled into the left side of his head, just behind his eye. It was too early to tell if it were merely a minor side effect of the dehydration, the beginnings of a common headache, or the first hint of something worse—the migraines that had plagued him since adolescence. Migraines, his anyway, never visited during times of pressure or work, only afterwards, when all had quieted down. The trick, he had learned, was to stay busy and stay focused. They couldn't catch you if you didn't stop running.

He said to Chuck, 'Heard much about this place?'

'A mental hospital, that's about all I know.'

'For the criminally insane,' Teddy said.

'Well, we wouldn't be here if it weren't,' Chuck said.

Teddy caught him smiling that dry grin again. 'You never know, Chuck. You don't look a hundred per cent stable to me.'

'Maybe I'll put a deposit down on a bed while we're here, make sure they hold a place for me.'

'Not a bad idea,' Teddy said as the engines cut out for a moment, and the bow swung starboard as they turned with the current. Then the engines kicked in again and the ferry backed towards the dock.

'And this woman who escaped?'

Teddy said, 'She slipped out last night is all I know. I figure they'll tell us everything else.'

Chuck looked around at the water. 'Where's she going to go? She's going to swim home?'

Teddy shrugged. 'The patients here, apparently, suffer a variety of delusions. You won't find your everyday lunatics, guys who're afraid of sidewalk cracks. Far as I could tell from the file, everyone here is, you know, *really* crazy.'

Chuck said, 'How many you think are faking it, though? I've always wondered that. You remember all the Section Eights you met in the war? How many, really, did you think were nuts?'

'I served with a guy in the Ardennes; he woke up one day speaking backwards. He'd say, "Sarge, today here blood much too is there." By late afternoon, we found him hitting his own head with a rock. Over and over. We were so rattled that it took us a minute to realise he'd scratched out his own eyes. I heard from a guy a few years later who ran across the blind guy in a vet hospital in San Diego. Still talking backwards, and he had some sort of paralysis, sat in a wheel-chair by the window all day, kept talking about having to get to his crops. Thing was, the guy grew up in Brooklyn.'

'Well, guy from Brooklyn thinks he's a farmer, I guess he is Section Eight.'

'That's one tip-off, sure.'

DEPUTY WARDEN McPherson met them at the dock. He was young for a man of his rank, his blond hair was cut a bit longer than the norm, and he had a kind of lanky grace to his movements.

He was flanked by orderlies, mostly Negroes, who wore white shirts and white trousers and moved in a pack. They barely glanced at Teddy and Chuck, just moved down the dock to the ferry and waited for it to unload its cargo.

Teddy and Chuck produced their badges upon request and

McPherson took his time studying them, looking up from the ID cards to their faces, squinting. 'I'm not sure I've ever seen a US marshal's badge before,' he said.

'And now you've seen two,' Chuck said. 'A big day.'

McPherson gave Chuck a lazy grin and flipped the badge back at him, while the orderlies loaded the mail and the medical cases onto handcarts. McPherson signed for the items on a clipboard and handed it back to one of the ferry guards, who said, 'We'll be off, then.'

'We'll contact the station when we need a pick-up,' Teddy said.

The guard nodded. The only regular runs were the supply runs on Tuesdays and Saturdays.

McPherson led them up a path that rose gently through a stand of trees. When they'd cleared the trees, they crossed a paved road. Off to the left Teddy could see a mansarded Victorian house with black trim and small windows. The building to the right was a Tudor-style house that commanded its small rise like a castle.

They continued on, climbing a slope that was steep and wild with seagrass before the land levelled out to a more traditional lawn, which spread for several hundred yards before coming to a stop at a long wall of orange brick that seemed to curve away the length of the island. It was ten feet tall and topped with a single strip of wire, and something about the sight of the wire got to Teddy. He felt a sudden pity for all those people on the other side who must realise just how badly the world wanted to keep them in. Several men in dark blue uniforms stood outside the wall.

Chuck said, 'Correctional guards at a mental institution. Weird sight, if you don't mind me saying, Mr McPherson.'

'This is a maximum security institution,' McPherson said. 'We operate under dual charters—one from the Massachusetts Department of Mental Health, the other from the Federal Department of Prisons.'

'I understand that,' Chuck said. 'I've always wondered, though—you guys have much to talk about round the dinner table?'

McPherson smiled and gave a tiny shake of his head.

Teddy saw a man with black hair who wore the same uniform as the rest of the guards, but his was accented by yellow epaulettes and a standing collar, and his badge was gold. He walked with his head held up, one hand pressed behind his back as he strode among the men, and the stride reminded Teddy of full colonels he'd met in the war, men for whom command was a necessary burden, not simply of the military but of God. The man nodded in their direction and walked down the slope from which they'd come.

'The warden,' McPherson said. 'You'll meet him later.'

Teddy nodded, wondering why they didn't meet now, and the warden disappeared on the other side of the rise.

One of the orderlies used a key to open the gate in the centre of the wall. The gate swung wide, and, after the orderlies had pushed their carts through, two guards approached McPherson and came to a stop on either side of him.

McPherson straightened to his full height, all business now, and said, 'I've got to give you gentlemen the basic lay of the land. You will be accorded all the courtesies we have to offer, all the help we can give. During your stay, however short that may be, you will obey protocol. I have to stress that unmonitored contact with patients of this institution is forbidden. Is that understood?'

Chuck nodded, and Teddy almost said, Yes, sir, as if he were back in basic, but he stopped short with a simple 'Yes.'

'Ward A of this institution is the building behind me to my right, the male ward. Ward B, the female ward, is to my left. Ward C is beyond those bluffs directly behind this compound and the staff quarters, housed in what was once Fort Walton. Admittance to Ward C is forbidden without the written consent and physical presence of both the warden and Dr Cawley. Understood?'

Another set of nods.

McPherson held out one massive palm. 'You are hereby requested to surrender your firearms.'

Chuck looked at Teddy. Teddy shook his head. 'Mr McPherson, we are federal marshals. We are required by government order to carry our firearms at all times.'

McPherson's voice hit the air like steel cable. 'Executive Order 391 of the Federal Code of Penitentiaries and Institutions for the Criminally Insane states that the peace officer's requirement to bear arms is superseded only by the direct order of his immediate superiors or that of persons entrusted with the care and protection of penal or mental health facilities. Gentlemen, you find yourself under the aegis of that exception. You will not be allowed to pass through this gate with your firearms.'

Teddy looked at Chuck. Chuck tilted his head at McPherson's extended palm and shrugged.

Teddy said, 'We'd like our exceptions noted for the record.'

McPherson said, 'Guard, please note the exceptions of Marshals Daniels and Aule.'

'Noted, sir.'

Teddy pulled back his overcoat and removed the service revolver from his holster. He snapped the cylinder open with a flick of his wrist and placed the gun in McPherson's hand. McPherson handed it to a guard, who placed it in a leather pouch. Chuck was a little slower with his weapon, fumbling with the holster snap, but McPherson showed no impatience, just waited until Chuck placed the gun awkwardly in his hand.

McPherson handed the gun to the guard, and the guard added it to the pouch and stepped through the gate.

'Your weapons will be checked into the property room,' McPherson said softly, his words rustling like leaves, 'which is in the main hospital building. You will pick them up on the day of your departure.' McPherson's grin returned. 'Well, that about does it for the official stuff for now. What do you say we go see Dr Cawley?'

And he turned and led the way through the gate, which was closed behind them.

Inside the main compound, gardeners with manacled ankles tended the grass and flowerbeds, flanked by orderlies. Teddy saw other patients in manacles walking the grounds with odd, ducklike steps. Most were men, a few were women.

To the right and left of the hospital stood two identical redbrick colonials with white trim, barred windows and panes yellowed by salt and sea wash. The hospital itself was charcoal-coloured, the stone surface rubbed smooth by the sea, and it rose six storeys to dormer windows that stared down at them.

Teddy noticed a tower he'd seen from the ferry. The tip of it peeked just above the tree line on the far side of the island.

'What's the tower?'

'An old lighthouse,' McPherson said. 'Hasn't been used as such since the early 1800s. The Union army posted lookout sentries there, or so I've heard, but now it's a sewage treatment facility.'

'Fascinating,' Chuck said. He lit a cigarette, taking it from his mouth to suppress a soft yawn as he blinked in the sun.

'Beyond the wall, that way'—McPherson pointed past Ward B—'is the original commander's quarters. You probably saw it on the walk up. Cost a fortune to build at the time, and the commander was relieved of his duties when Uncle Sam got the bill. You should see the place.'

'Who lives there now?' Teddy said.

'Dr Cawley,' McPherson said. 'None of this would exist if it weren't for Dr Cawley. And the warden, of course. They created something really unique here.'

They'd looped around the back of the compound, passed more manacled gardeners and orderlies, many hoeing a dark loam against the rear wall.

'Cawley's a legend in his field,' McPherson was saying as they passed back around towards the front of the hospital. 'Top of his class at both Johns Hopkins and Harvard, published his first paper on delusional pathologies at the age of twenty. Has been consulted numerous times by Scotland Yard, MI5 and the OSS.'

'The Office of Strategic Services? Why would they consult a psychiatrist?' Teddy asked.

'War work,' McPherson said.

'Right,' Teddy said slowly. 'What kind, though?'

McPherson paused in front of the hospital. He seemed at a loss. 'Well, I guess you can ask him,' he said at last.

They followed McPherson up the steps and in through a marble foyer, the ceiling arching into a coffered dome above them. A gate buzzed open as they approached it, and they passed on into a large anteroom where an orderly sat at a desk. They produced their badges again and McPherson signed their three names to a clipboard as the orderly checked their IDs and handed them back. Behind the orderly was a cage, and Teddy could see a man in there wearing a uniform, keys hanging from their rings on a wall behind him.

They climbed a staircase to the first floor and turned into a corridor that smelt of wood soap, the oak floor gleaming underfoot and bathed in a white light from the large window at the far end.

'Lot of security,' Teddy said.

McPherson said, 'We take every precaution.'

Chuck said, 'To the thanks of a grateful public, Mr McPherson, I'm sure.'

'You have to understand,' McPherson said, turning back to Teddy as they walked past several closed doors bearing the names of doctors on small silver plates, 'that there is no other facility like this in the United States. We take only the most damaged patients, the ones no other facility can manage.'

'Gryce is here, right?' Teddy said.

McPherson nodded. 'Vincent Gryce, yes. In Ward C.'

Chuck said to Teddy, 'Gryce was the one . . .?'

Teddy nodded. 'Killed all his relatives, scalped them, made hats.'

'And wore them into town, right?'

'According to the papers.'

They had stopped outside a set of double doors. A plate affixed to the right door read CHIEF OF STAFF, DR J. CAWLEY.

McPherson turned to them, one hand on the doorknob. 'In a less enlightened age,' he said, 'a patient like Gryce would have been put to death. But here they can study him, define a pathology, maybe isolate the abnormality in his brain that caused him to disengage so completely from acceptable patterns of behaviour. If they can do that, maybe we can root that kind of disengagement out of society entirely.'

He seemed to be waiting for a response.

'It's good to have dreams,' Chuck said. 'Don't you think?'

2

Dr Cawley was thin to the point of emaciation. His small dark eyes sat far back in their sockets, and the shadows that leaked from them bled across his sunken cheeks. What remained of his hair was as dark as his eyes and the shadows underneath.

He had an explosive smile, however, bright and bulging with a confidence that lightened his irises, and he used it now as he came round the desk to greet them, his hand outstretched. 'Marshal Daniels and Marshal Aule, glad you could come so quickly.'

His hand was dry and smooth in Teddy's, and his grip was a shocker, squeezing the bones until Teddy could feel the press of it up his forearm. Cawley moved on to Chuck and shook his hand with a 'Pleased to meet you, sir,' and then the smile shot off his face and he said to McPherson, 'That'll be all for now, Deputy Warden. Thank you.'

McPherson said, 'Yes, sir. A pleasure, gentlemen,' and backed out of the room.

Cawley's smile returned, but it was a more viscous version. 'He's a good man, McPherson. Eager.'

'For?' Teddy said, taking a seat in front of the desk.

Cawley's smile morphed again, curling up one side of his face and freezing there for a moment. 'I'm sorry?'

'He's eager,' Teddy said. 'But for what?'

Cawley sat behind the teak desk, spread his arms. 'For the work. A fusion between law and order and clinical care. Just half a century ago, the thinking on the kind of patients we deal with here was that they should be shackled and left in their own filth. They were systematically beaten, as if that could drive the psychosis out. We demonised them. We drove screws into their brains.'

'And now?' Chuck said.

'Now we treat them. We try to heal, to cure. And if that fails, we at least provide them with a measure of calm in their lives.' He raised his eyebrows. 'Now, did the senator explain the situation?'

Teddy and Chuck shot each other glances as they sat.

Teddy said, 'We were assigned by the state field office, Doctor.'

Cawley propped his elbows on a green desk blotter, rested his chin on top of his hands, and stared at them over the rim of his glasses. 'My mistake, then. So what have you been told?'

'We know a female prisoner is missing.' Teddy placed his notebook on his knee, flipped the pages. 'A Rachel Solando.'

'Patient.' Cawley gave them a dead smile.

'Patient,' Teddy said. 'I apologise. We understand she escaped within the last twenty-four hours.'

Cawley nodded. 'Last night. Between ten and midnight.'

'Is Miss Solando considered dangerous?' Chuck asked.

'All our patients have shown a proclivity for violence. It's why they're here. Rachel Solando was a war widow. She drowned her three children in the lake behind her house. Took them out there one by one and held their heads under until they died. Then she brought them back into the house and arranged them round the kitchen table and ate a meal there before a neighbour dropped by. He called the police. Rachel still believes the children are alive, waiting for her. It might explain why she's tried to escape.'

'To return home,' Teddy said.

Cawley nodded.

'And where's that?' Chuck asked.

'A small town in the Berkshires. Roughly a hundred fifty miles from here.' With a tilt of his head, Cawley indicated the window behind him. 'Swim that way and you don't reach land for eleven miles. Swim north and you don't reach land until Newfoundland.'

Teddy said, 'And you've searched the grounds.'

'The warden and his men and a detail of orderlies spent the night and a good part of the morning scouring the island and every building in the institution. Not a trace. What's even more disturbing is that we can't tell how she got out of her room. It was locked from the outside and its sole window was barred.' Cawley's eyes were shiny and distant. 'It's as if she evaporated straight through the walls.'

'Are you sure that she *was* in that room at lights out?' Teddy asked.

'Positive.'

'How so?'

Cawley pressed the call button on his intercom. 'Nurse Marino? Please tell Mr Ganton to come in.'

'Right away, Doctor.'

There was a small table near the window with a pitcher of water and four glasses on top. Cawley went to it and filled three of the glasses. He placed one in front of Teddy and one in front of Chuck, took his own back behind the desk with him.

Teddy said, 'You wouldn't have some aspirin, would you?'

Cawley gave him a small smile. 'I think we could scare some up.' He rummaged in his desk drawer, came out with a bottle and handed it across the desk.

Teddy tossed a couple of tablets in his mouth, chased them with the water.

'Prone to headaches, Marshal?'

Teddy said, 'Prone to seasickness, unfortunately.'

Cawley nodded. 'Ah. Dehydrated.'

Teddy nodded and Cawley opened a walnut cigarette box, held it open to Teddy and Chuck. Teddy took one. Chuck shook his head and produced his own pack, and all three of them lit up.

Then Cawley handed a photograph across the desk—a young dark-haired woman, beautiful, her face blemished by dark rings under the eyes. The eyes themselves were too wide, as if something hot were prodding them from inside her head.

Chuck unleashed a low whistle. 'My God.'

Cawley took a drag on his cigarette. 'Are you reacting to her beauty or her apparent madness?'

'Both,' Chuck said.

Those eyes, Teddy thought. Even frozen in time, they howled. You wanted to climb inside the picture and say, 'No, no, no. It's OK. Sssh. Everything will be all right.'

The office door opened and a tall Negro with thick flecks of grey in his hair entered. He was wearing the white uniform of an orderly.

'Mr Ganton,' Cawley said, 'these are the gentlemen I told you about—Marshals Aule and Daniels.'

Teddy and Chuck stood and shook Ganton's hand, Teddy getting a strong whiff of fear from the man, as if he wasn't quite comfortable shaking hands with the law.

'Mr Ganton is the head orderly here. It was he who escorted Rachel to her room last night. Mr Ganton?'

Ganton sat on a spare chair, placed his hands on his knees, and hunched forward a bit. 'There was group at nine o'clock. Then—'

Cawley said, 'That's a group therapy session led by Dr Sheehan.'

Ganton waited until he was sure Cawley had finished before he began again. 'So, yeah. They was in group, and it ended round ten. I escorted Miss Rachel up to her room. She went inside. I locked up from the outside. We do checks every two hours during lights out. I go back at midnight. I look in, and her bed's empty. I figure maybe she's sleeping on the floor. They do that a lot here. I open up and go in. Miss Rachel ain't nowhere to be found. I shut the door and check the window and the bars. They locked tight too.' He shrugged. 'I call the warden.' He looked up at Cawley, and Cawley gave him a soft, paternal nod.

'Any questions, gentlemen?'

Teddy said, 'Mr Ganton, you said you entered the room and ascertained that the patient wasn't there. What did this entail?'

'Sir?'

Teddy said, 'Is there a closet? Space beneath the bed?'

'Both.'

'And you checked those places while the door was still open.'

'Sir?'

'You said that you entered the room and looked around and couldn't find the patient. *Then* you shut the door behind you.'

'No, I . . . Well . . .'

Teddy waited, took another hit off the cigarette Cawley had given him. The smell of the smoke was almost sweet.

'It took all of five seconds, sir. No door on the closet. I look there, I look under the bed, and I shut the door. No place she could have been hiding. Room's small,' Ganton said.

'Against the wall?' Teddy said. 'To the right or the left of the door?'

'Nah.' Ganton shook his head, and Teddy thought he glimpsed anger, a sense of resentment behind the 'Yes, sirs' and 'No, sirs'.

'It's unlikely,' Cawley said to Teddy. 'Once you see the room, you'll understand that Mr Ganton would have been hard-pressed to miss the patient if she were standing *anywhere* within its four walls.'

'That's right,' Ganton said, staring furiously at Teddy now.

'Thank you, Mr Ganton,' Cawley said. 'That'll be all for now.'

Ganton rose, his eyes lingering on Teddy for another few seconds, and then he said, 'Thank you, Doctor,' and left the room.

They were quiet for a moment and then Chuck said, 'I think we should see the room now, Doctor.'

'Of course.' Cawley came out from behind his desk, a large ring of keys in his hand. 'Follow me.'

IT WAS A TINY ROOM with the steel door opening inwards and to the right. To their left was a short length of wall and then a small wooden closet with a few smocks and drawstring trousers hanging on plastic hangers. A small dresser sat against the right wall.

'There goes that theory,' Teddy admitted.

Cawley nodded. 'There would have been no place for her to hide.'

He closed the door behind them and Teddy felt an immediate sense of imprisonment. With three of them in the room, there was barely space to move without bumping limbs.

Teddy said, 'Who else would have access to the room?'

'The orderlies, of course.'

'Doctors?' Chuck said.

'The doctors have keys to the room,' Cawley said with just a hint of annoyance. 'But by ten o'clock, they've signed out for the night.'

'And turned in their keys?'

'Yes.'

'Could we check last night's sign-in log?' Teddy said.

'Yes, yes. Of course.'

'And the personnel files of the medical staff and the orderlies and the guards. We'll need access to those.'

Cawley peered at him as if Teddy's face were sprouting blackflies. 'Why?'

'A woman disappears from a locked room, Doctor. I have to at least consider that she had help.'

'I'll have to speak with the warden and some of the other staff,' Cawley said. 'We'll make a determination of your request—'

'Doctor,' Teddy said, 'it wasn't a request. We're here by order of the government. If you refuse to aid two US marshals in the apprehension of a dangerous patient you are obstructing justice.'

'Yes, well,' Cawley said, his voice stripped of life, 'all I can say is that I will do what I can to accommodate your request.'

Teddy and Chuck exchanged a small glance, went back to looking round the bare room. Teddy went to look in the tiny closet, saw two pairs of white shoes. 'How many shoes are the patients given?'

'Two pairs.'

'She left this room barefoot?'

'Yes.' Cawley pointed at a sheet of paper lying on the bed. 'We found that behind the dresser. We don't know what it means. We were hoping someone could tell us.'

Teddy lifted the sheet of paper and held it up for Chuck to see:

THE LAW OF 4
I AM 47
THEY WERE 80
+YOU ARE 3
WE ARE 4
BUT
WHO IS 67?

Cawley stepped up beside them. 'Rachel is quite brilliant in her games,' he said. 'To sustain her delusions—particularly the one that allows her to believe her three children are alive—she has conceived an elaborate narrative thread to her life that is completely fictitious.'

Chuck turned his head slowly, looked at Cawley. 'I'd need a degree to understand that, Doctor.'

Cawley chuckled. 'Think of the lies you tell your parents as a child. How elaborate they are. Instead of keeping them simple to explain why you missed school or forgot your chores, you embellish, you make them fantastical. Yes?'

Chuck thought about it and nodded.

Teddy said, 'Sure. Criminals do the same thing.'

'Exactly. The idea is to confuse the listener until they believe out of exhaustion more than any sense of truth. Now imagine those lies being told to yourself. That's what Rachel does. In four years she has never so much as acknowledged that she is in an institution. As far as she is concerned, she is back home in the Berkshires in her house, and we are delivery men, milkmen, postal workers, just passing by. She uses sheer force of will to make her illusions stronger.'

'But how does the truth never get through?' Teddy said. 'I mean, she's in a mental institution. Doesn't she ever notice that?'

'Ah,' Cawley said, 'now we're getting into the true horrible beauty of the full-blown schizophrenic's paranoid structure. If you believe, gentlemen, that you are the sole holder of truth, then everyone else must be lying.'

'Which means that any truth they say,' Chuck said, 'must be a lie.'

Cawley cocked his thumb and pointed his finger at him like a gun. 'You're getting it.'

Teddy said, 'And that somehow plays into these numbers?'

'It must. They have to represent something. With Rachel, no thought is idle or ancillary. I sincerely believe that this'—he tapped the sheet of paper—'will tell us where she's gone.'

For just a moment, Teddy thought it was speaking to him, becoming clearer. It was the first two numbers—the '47' and the '80'—he could feel something about them scratching at his brain like the melody of a song he was trying to remember while the radio played a completely different tune. The '47' was the easiest clue. It was right in front of him. It was so simple. It was . . .

And then any possible bridges of logic collapsed, and Teddy felt his mind go white, and knew the connection was in flight. He placed the page down on the bed again.

'Insane,' Chuck said.

'What's that?' Cawley said.

'Where she's gone,' Chuck said. 'In my opinion.'

'Well, certainly,' Cawley said. 'I think we can take that as a given.'

THEY STOOD OUTSIDE the room. The corridor led off in both directions from a staircase in the centre. Rachel's door was to the left of the stairs, halfway down on the right-hand side.

'This is the only way off this floor?' Teddy said.

Cawley nodded. 'And all the rooms were checked immediately. As soon as she was discovered missing.'

Teddy pointed at the orderly who sat by a small card table in front of the stairs. 'Someone's there twenty-four hours?'

'Yes. Orderly Ganton was on duty there last night, actually.'

They walked to the staircase and Chuck said, 'So, Miss Solando gets out of her locked room into this corridor, goes down these steps.' They went down the steps themselves and Chuck jerked a thumb at the orderly waiting for them by the first-floor landing. 'She gets past another orderly here, we don't know how, makes herself invisible or something, goes down this next flight, and comes out into . . .'

They turned down the last flight and were facing a large open room with several couches pressed against the wall, a large folding table in the centre, bay windows saturating the space with light.

'The main living area,' Cawley said. 'Where most patients spend their evenings. The nurses' station is just through that portico there. After lights out, the orderlies congregate here. They're supposed to be cleaning and such, but often we catch them here, playing cards.'

'And last night?'

'According to those who were on duty, the card game was in full swing. Seven men, playing stud poker, right here.'

Chuck put his hands on his hips, let out a long breath through his mouth. 'She does the invisible thing again, apparently.'

'The only doors to the outside are on the other side of the living area, or back down the corridor behind the staircase. Both had men at their stations last night.' Cawley glanced at his watch. 'Gentlemen, I have a meeting. If you have any questions, please feel free to ask any of the staff or visit McPherson. He's handled the search thus far. Staff eat at six sharp in the mess hall. After that, we'll assemble here in the staff lounge and you can speak to anyone who was working during last night's incident.'

He hurried out of the front door, and they watched him until he disappeared.

Teddy said, 'Is there anything about this that *doesn't* feel like an inside job?'

'I'm kind of fond of my invisible theory. In fact, she could be watching us right now, Teddy.' Chuck looked over his shoulder quickly, then back at Teddy. 'Something to think about.'

IN THE AFTERNOON they joined the search party and moved inland as the breeze grew swollen, warmer. So much of the island was overgrown, clogged with weeds and tall grass threaded with tendrils of ancient oak and green vines, that in most places human passage was impossible, even with the machetes some of the guards carried.

The search struck Teddy as desultory, as if no one but he and Chuck truly had their heart in it. The men wound their way along the inner ring above the shoreline with downcast eyes and sullen steps. At one point they rounded a bend on a shelf of black rocks and faced a jagged cliff. Teddy could see oblong holes in the side of the cliff.

'You check the caves?' he asked McPherson.

McPherson sighed. 'She had two pairs of shoes, Marshal. Both found back in her room. How's she going to get through what we just came through, cross over these rocks, and scale that cliff?'

Teddy turned inland, pointed to some low hills that rose steadily beyond a small glade. 'She takes the long way, works her way up from the west?'

McPherson placed his own finger beside Teddy's. 'See where the glade drops off? That's marshland right there at the tip of your finger, and the base of those hills is covered in poison ivy and plants with thorns. No, gentlemen. She would've had no choice but to stick hard to the shoreline, and halfway round in either direction she would've run out of beach and met that cliff.'

NO ONE CAME to their table at dinner. They sat alone, damp from careless spits of rain that had been carried on the warm breeze. Outside, the island had begun to rattle in the dark, the breeze turning into a wind.

'A locked room,' Chuck said.

'Barefoot,' Teddy said.

'Past three interior checkpoints.'

'A roomful of orderlies.'

Teddy stirred his food, some kind of shepherd's pie, the meat stringy. 'Over a wall with electric security wire.'

'Or through a manned gate.'

'Out into that.' The wind shaking the building, shaking the dark.

Chuck pushed his tray away. 'Who we speaking to after this?'

'The staff.'

'You think they'll be helpful?'

'Don't you?'

Chuck grinned. He lit a cigarette, his eyes on Teddy, his grin turning into a soft laugh, the smoke chugging out in rhythm with it.

TEDDY STOOD in the centre of the room, the staff in a circle around him. He rested his hands on a metal chair. Chuck slouched against a beam beside him, hands in his pockets.

'I assume everyone knows why we're all here,' Teddy said. 'You had an escape last night. Far as we can tell, the patient vanished. We have no evidence that would allow us to believe the patient left this institution without help. Deputy Warden McPherson, would you agree?'

'Yup. I'd say that's a reasonable assessment at this time.'

'And you and your men have searched the grounds.'

'Sure did.' McPherson stretched in his chair. 'We found no evidence to suggest a woman in flight. No shreds of torn clothing, no footprints, no bent vegetation. The current was strong last night, the tide pushing in. A swim would have been out of the question.'

'But she could have tried.' This from the nurse, Kerry Marino, a slim woman with a bundle of loose red hair that she'd unclipped as soon as she'd walked into the room. Her cap sat in her lap, and she finger-combed her hair in a lazy way that suggested weariness.

McPherson said, 'What was that?'

Marino dropped her fingers to her lap. 'How do we know she didn't try to swim, end up drowning?'

'She would have washed ashore by now.' Cawley yawned into his fist. 'Marshal, ask your questions, please. It's been a long day.'

Teddy glanced at Chuck and Chuck gave him a small tilt of the eyes back. A missing woman with a history of violence at large on a small island and everyone seemed to just want to get to bed.

Teddy said, 'Mr Ganton has already told us he checked on Miss Solando at midnight and discovered her missing. The locks to the window grate in her room and the door were not tampered with. Mr Ganton, was there ever a point last night where you didn't have a view of the second-floor corridor?'

Several heads turned to look at Ganton, and Teddy was confused to see amusement in some of the faces, as if Teddy were the third-grade teacher who'd asked a question of the hippest kid in class.

Ganton spoke to his own feet. 'Only time my eyes weren't on that corridor was when I entered her room, found her gone.'

'And you never left your post? Get a cup of coffee, nothing?'

Ganton shook his head. 'No, sir.'

'All right, people,' Chuck said, straightening. 'I have to make a huge leap here. For the sake of argument, let's play with the idea that somehow Miss Solando crawled across the ceiling or something.'

Several members of the group chuckled.

'And she gets to the staircase leading down to the first floor. Who's she gotta pass?'

A milk-white orderly with orange hair raised his hand.

'And your name?' Teddy said.

'Glen. Glen Miga.'

'OK, Glen. Were you at your post all night?'

'Uh, yeah.'

Teddy said, 'Glen.'

'Yeah?' He looked up from the hangnail he'd been picking.

'Come on. The truth.'

Glen looked over at Cawley, then back at Teddy. 'I went to the bathroom,' he said.

Cawley leaned forward. 'Who stepped in as your relief?'

'It was a quick piss,' Glen said. 'A minute. Tops. Sorry, sir.'

'You breached protocol,' Cawley said. 'Christ.'

'Sir, I know. I—'

'What time was this?' Teddy said.

'Eleven thirty. Thereabouts.' Glen's fear of Cawley was turning into hate for Teddy. A few more questions, he'd get hostile.

'Thanks, Glen,' Teddy said, and tilted his head at Chuck.

'At eleven thirty,' Chuck said, 'or thereabouts, was the poker game still in full swing?'

Several heads turned towards one another and back to Chuck, and then one Negro nodded, followed by the rest of the orderlies.

'Who was still sitting in at that point?'

Four Negroes and one white orderly raised their hands.

Chuck zeroed in on the ringleader, the first guy to raise his hand. A round, fleshy guy, his head shaved and shiny under the light.

'Name?'

'Trey, sir. Trey Washington.'

'Trey, you were all sitting where?'

Trey pointed at the floor. 'Right about here. Centre of the room. Looking right at that staircase. Had an eye on the front door, one on the back.'

Chuck walked over by him. 'Good position,' he said.

Trey lowered his voice. 'Ain't just about the patients, sir. We ain't supposed to be playing cards. Gotta be able to see who's coming, grab us a mop right quick.'

Chuck smiled. 'Bet you move fast too.'

'You ever seen lightning in August? Slow compared to me getting on that mop.'

Nurse Marino was unable to suppress a smile. And Teddy knew then that, for the duration of their stay, Chuck would play Good Cop. He had a knack with people. Teddy wondered how the Seattle office could have let him go, Jap girlfriend or not.

He envied Chuck, his ability to believe in the words he spoke. In silly flirtations. In his easy-GI's penchant for quick, meaningless word play. But most of all for the weightlessness of his charm.

Charm had never come easily to Teddy. After the war, it had come harder still. After Dolores, not at all.

Charm was the luxury of those who still believed in the essential rightness of things. In purity and picket fences.

'OK, OK.' Chuck held up a hand to quiet the laughter, still grinning himself. 'So, Trey, when did you know something was wrong?'

'When Ike—ah, Mr Ganton, I mean—he start shouting down, "Call the warden. We got us a break."'

'And what time was that?'

'Twelve-oh-two and thirty-nine seconds.'

Chuck raised his eyebrows. 'You a clock?'

'No, sir, but I trained to look at one the first sign of trouble. If anything might be what you call an "incident", we all going to have to fill out an IR, an "incident re-port". First thing you get asked on an IR is the time the incident began. You do enough IRs, gets to be second nature to look at a clock the first hint of trouble.'

Several of the orderlies were nodding as he spoke, a few 'Uh-huhs' and 'That's rights' tumbling out of their mouths as if they were at a church revival.

'Warden arrives on scene when?' Teddy said.

Trey said, 'Hicksville—he one o' the guards—he's first through the door. Was working the gate, I think. He come through at twelve-oh-six. The warden, he come four minutes after that with six men.'

Teddy turned to Nurse Marino. 'You hear all the commotion and you . . .'

'I lock the nurses' station. I come out into the rec hall at about the same time Hicksville was coming through the front door.'

'And nobody could have gotten by you in the nurses' station.'

'Gotten by me to where? Hydrotherapy? You go in there, you're locked in a cement box with a lot of tubs, a few small pools.'

'Nurse Marino,' Teddy said, 'you were part of the group therapy session last night.'

'Yes.'

'Anything unusual occur?'

'This is a mental institution, Marshal. For the criminally insane. "Usual" isn't a big part of our day.'

Teddy gave her a sheepish smile. 'Let me rephrase. Anything occur in group last night that was more memorable than, um . . .?'

'Normal?' she said.

That drew a smile from Cawley, a few stray laughs.

Teddy nodded.

She thought about it for a minute, then, 'No. Sorry.'

'And did Miss Solando speak last night?'

Marino looked over at Cawley.

He said, 'We're waiving patient confidentiality for now.'

She nodded. 'Rachel spoke a couple of times, yes. We were discussing anger management, appropriate and inappropriate ways to display anxiety or displeasure.'

'Has Miss Solando had any anger issues of late?'

'Rachel? No. Rachel only became agitated when it rained. That was her contribution to group last night. "I hear rain. I hear rain. It's not here, but it's coming."'

'And there was a Dr Sheehan here last night. He ran the group. Is he here?'

No one spoke.

Eventually, Cawley said, 'Dr Sheehan left on the morning ferry. The one you took on the return trip.'

'Why?'

'He'd been scheduled for a vacation for some time.'

'But we need to talk to him.'

Cawley said, 'I have all his notes on the group session. His vacation was long overdue and we saw no reason to keep him here.'

Teddy looked to McPherson. 'You approved this?'

McPherson nodded.

'It's a state of lockdown,' Teddy said. 'A patient has escaped. How do you allow anyone to leave?'

'He's a *doctor*,' Cawley said, before the deputy warden could speak.

'Jesus,' Teddy said softly. Biggest breach in standard operating procedure he'd ever encountered at any penal institution and everyone was acting like it was no big deal. 'Where's he gone to?'

Cawley looked up at the ceiling, trying to recall. 'New York, I believe. It's where his family is from.'

'I'll need a phone number,' Teddy said.

'I don't see why—'

'Doctor,' Teddy said. 'I'll need a phone number.'

'We'll get that to you, Marshal.' Cawley kept his eyes on the ceiling. 'Anything else?'

'You bet,' Teddy said.

Cawley's chin came down and he looked across at Teddy.

'I need a phone,' Teddy said.

THE PHONE in the nurses' station gave off nothing but a white hiss of air, so Teddy and Dr Cawley walked over to the central switchboard in the main hospital building. The operator looked up as they came through the door, a set of headphones looped round his neck.

'Sir,' he said, 'we're down. Even radio communication.'

Cawley said, 'It's not all that bad out.'

The operator shrugged. 'It's not so much what it's doing here. It's what kinda weather they're having back on the other side.'

'Keep trying,' Cawley said. 'You get it up and running, you get word to me. This man needs to make a pretty important call.'

The operator nodded and put the headphones back on.

Outside, the air felt like trapped breath.

Cawley said, 'I'll be having drinks and a cigar or two at my house later. Nine o'clock, if you and your partner feel like dropping by.'

'Oh,' Teddy said. 'Can we talk then?'

Cawley stopped, looked back at him. The dark trees on the other side of the wall had begun to sway and whisper.

'We've been talking, Marshal.'

CHUCK AND TEDDY walked the dark grounds, feeling the storm swelling hot in the air around them.

'This is bullshit,' Teddy said.

'Yup. You call the field office?'

Teddy shook his head. 'The switchboard's down.' He raised his hand. 'The storm, you know.'

Chuck spat tobacco off his tongue. 'Storm? Where?'

'You can feel it coming.' Teddy looked at the dark sky. 'It's taken out their radio too.'

'Their *radio*, boss?' Chuck's eyes bloomed wide.

Teddy nodded. 'Pretty bleak, yeah. They got us locked down on an island looking for a woman who escaped from a locked room . . .'

'Past four manned checkpoints.'

'Scaled a ten-foot brick wall with electric wire up top.'

'Swam eleven miles against an irate current. Teddy, this whole thing, you know?'

'And the missing Dr Sheehan.'

Chuck said, 'Struck you as odd too, huh? I've been thinking, boss. What if we're the cover story here? What if we were brought here to help them cross t's and dot i's?'

'Clarity, Watson.'

Chuck smiled. 'All right, boss, try and keep up. Let's say a certain doctor has an infatuation with a certain patient.'

'Miss Solando.'

'You saw the picture.'

'She is attractive.'

'Teddy, she's a pin-up in a GI's locker. So she works our boy, Sheehan . . . You seeing it now?'

Teddy flicked his cigarette into the wind, watching the ash ignite in the breeze, then streak back past him and Chuck. 'And Sheehan gets hooked, decides he can't live without her.'

'So they scram. Off the island.'

Teddy stopped at the far end of the staff dormitories, faced the orange wall. 'But why *not* call in the dogs?'

'Well, they did,' Chuck said. 'Protocol. They had to bring in someone, and in the case of an escape from a place like this, they call us in. But if they're covering up staff involvement, then we're just here to substantiate their story—that they did everything by the book.'

'OK,' Teddy said. 'But why cover for Sheehan?'

Chuck lit a cigarette. 'I don't know. Haven't thought that through.'

'And why those codes in Rachel Solando's room?'

'Well, she *is* crazy.'

'Why show them to us, though? I mean, if this is a cover-up, why not make it easier for us to sign off on the reports and go home?'

'Maybe they were lonely. All of them. Needed some company.'

'Sure. Made up a story so they could bring us here? Have something new to chat about? I'll buy that.'

Chuck turned and looked back at Ashecliffe. 'Joking aside . . . I'm starting to get nervous here, Teddy.'

3

'The original owner, Colonel Spivey, called it the Great Room,' Cawley said as he led them through his foyer to two oak doors with brass knobs the size of pineapples. He yanked back on one of them and the door opened.

Chuck let loose a low whistle. The floor was marble, covered here and there by dark Oriental rugs. The fireplace was taller than most men. The drapes alone—three yards of dark purple velvet per window and there were nine windows—had to cost more than a US marshal made in a year. A billiards table took up one corner under oil paintings of a man in Union army formal blue and a woman in a frilly white dress.

'The colonel?' Teddy said.

Cawley followed his gaze, nodded. 'Relieved of his command shortly after those paintings were finished.'

As Cawley led them towards the fireplace, Teddy realised there was another man in the room. He sat with his back to them in a high-back wing chair facing the fireplace, an open book on his knee.

Cawley crossed to a liquor cabinet. 'Your poison, gentlemen?'

Chuck said, 'Rye, if you got it.'

'I think I can scare some up. Marshal Daniels?'

'Soda water and some ice.'

The stranger looked up at them. 'You don't indulge in alcohol?'

Teddy looked down at the guy. A small red head perched like a cherry on top of a chunky body.

'And you are?' Teddy said.

'My colleague,' Cawley said. 'Dr Jeremiah Naehring.'

The man blinked in acknowledgment but didn't offer his hand.

'I'm curious,' he said as Teddy and Chuck took the two seats on his left side. 'Isn't it common for men in your profession to imbibe?'

Cawley handed him his drink and Teddy stood and crossed to the bookshelves to the right of the hearth. 'Common enough,' he said. 'And your profession. It's overrun with boozers, isn't it?'

'Not that I've noticed.'

'Haven't looked too hard, then, huh?'

'I'm not sure I follow.'

'That's, what, cold tea in your glass?'

Naehring glanced at his glass, a silkworm of a smile twitching his soft mouth. 'Excellent, Marshal. You possess outstanding defence mechanisms. I assume you're quite adept at interrogation.'

Teddy shook his head, noticing that Cawley kept little in the way of medical texts, at least in this room. 'I'm a federal marshal,' he said. 'We bring them in. That's it. Others handle the interviewing.'

'I called it "interrogation", you called it "interviewing". Yes, Marshal, you do have astonishing defence capabilities.' He clicked the bottom of his Scotch glass on the table several times as if in applause. 'Men of violence fascinate me.'

'Men of what?' Teddy strolled over to Naehring's chair, looked down at the little man and rattled the ice in his glass.

Naehring tilted his head back, took a sip of Scotch. 'Violence.'

'Hell of an assumption to make, Doc.' This from Chuck, looking as openly annoyed as Teddy had ever seen him.

Teddy gave his glass one more rattle before he drained it. 'I'd have to agree with my partner,' he said and took his seat.

'No.' Naehring turned one syllable into three. I said you were men of violence. That's not the same as accusing you of being violent men.'

Teddy gave him a smile, rested his elbows on his knees. 'Edify us.'

'Since the school yard,' Naehring said, 'I would bet neither of you has ever walked away from physical conflict. That's not to suggest you enjoyed it, only that retreat wasn't an option. Yes?'

Teddy looked over at Chuck. Chuck gave him a small smile, slightly abashed, then said, 'Wasn't raised to run, Doc.'

'Ah, yes—raised. And who did raise you?'

'Bears,' Teddy said.

Naehring didn't seem appreciative of the humour. 'Believe in God?'

Teddy laughed. 'Ever seen a death camp, Doctor?'

Naehring shook his head.

'You go see a death camp someday, then get back to me with your feelings about God.'

Naehring slowly closed and reopened his eyelids and then he turned his gaze on Chuck. 'And you? Do you believe in God?'

Chuck shrugged. 'Haven't given him a lot of thought, one way or the other, in a long time.'

'Since your father died, yes?'

Chuck leaned forward now, too, stared at the fat little man.

'Your father is dead, yes? And yours as well, Marshal Daniels? In fact, I'll wager that both of you lost the dominant male figure in your lives before your fifteenth birthdays.'

'Five of diamonds,' Teddy said.

'I'm sorry?'

'Is that your next parlour trick?' Teddy said. 'You tell me what card I'm holding. Or, no, wait—you cut a nurse in half, pull a rabbit from Dr Cawley's head.'

'These are not parlour tricks.'

'How about this?' Teddy said. 'You teach a woman how to walk through walls, levitate over a building full of orderlies and penal staff, and float across the sea.'

Chuck said, 'That's a good one.'

Naehring gave a slow blink. 'Again, your defence mechanisms are impressive, Marshal. But the issue at hand—'

'The issue at hand,' Teddy said, 'is that this facility suffered about nine flagrant security breaches last night. You've got a missing woman and no one's looking for—'

'We're looking.' Naehring glanced over at Cawley in such a way that Teddy wondered which of them was really in charge.

Cawley caught Teddy's look and his jaw turned slightly pink. 'Dr Naehring serves as chief liaison to our board of overseers. I asked him here in that capacity tonight to address your earlier requests.'

'Which requests were those?'

Naehring stoked his pipe back to life with a cupped match. 'We will not release personnel files of our clinical staff.'

'Sheehan,' Teddy said.

'Anyone.'

'You're blocking us, essentially.'

'Marshal, we'll help your investigation where we can, but—'

'No.'

'Excuse me?' Cawley leaning forward now, all four of them with hunched shoulders and extended heads.

'No,' Teddy repeated. 'This investigation is over. We'll return to the city on the first ferry. We'll file our reports and the matter will be turned over, I assume, to Hoover's boys. But we're out of this.'

Naehring's pipe hovered in his hand. Cawley took a pull on his drink, then placed the empty glass on the table beside his chair.

'As you wish, Marshal.'

It was pouring when they left Cawley's house, and by the time they arrived at the orderlies' dormitory they were drenched.

They shared a room with Trey Washington and another orderly named Bibby Luce. The room was a good size, with two sets of bunk beds and a small sitting area where Trey and Bibby were playing cards. Teddy and Chuck pulled up chairs and joined the game.

Trey and Bibby played penny-ante, and cigarettes were deemed an acceptable substitute if anyone ran short of coins. Teddy strung all three of them along on a hand of seven-card, came away with five bucks and eighteen cigarettes on a club flush, pocketed the cigarettes, and played conservative from that point on.

Chuck turned out to be the real player, though, jovial as ever, impossible to read, amassing coins, cigarettes and eventually dollar bills and glancing down at the end of it all as if surprised at how such a fat pile got in front of him.

Trey said, 'You got yourself some of them X-ray eyes, Marshal?'

'Lucky, I guess.'

'Booshit. You got some voodoo working.'

Chuck said, 'You tug your ear lobe, Mr Washington. Every time you got less than a full house.' He pointed at Bibby. 'And he gets all squirrelly-eyed, looks at everybody's chips before he bluffs. When he's got a hot hand, though, he gets all serene and inward-looking.'

Trey ripped the air with a loud guffaw and slapped the table. 'What about Marshall Daniels? How's he give himself away?'

Chuck grinned. 'I'm going to rat on my partner? No, no, no.'

'SO WHAT GAVE me away?' Teddy asked Chuck late that night as they lay in the dark. Across the room, Trey and Bibby were locked in a snoring competition. In the last half an hour the rain had gone soft as if it were catching its breath, awaiting reinforcements.

'At cards?' Chuck said from the lower bunk. 'Forget it.'

'No, I want to know.'

'You thought you were pretty good up till now, didn't you? Admit it.'

'I didn't think I was *bad*, but you cleaned my clock.'

'I won a few bucks.'

'Your daddy was a gambler, that it?'

'My daddy was a prick.'

'Oh, sorry.'

'Not your fault. Yours?'

Teddy tried to picture his father in the dark, could only see his hands, welted with scars. 'He was a stranger,' Teddy said. 'To everyone. Even my mother. Hell, I doubt *he* knew who he was. He was his boat. When he lost the boat, he just drifted away.'

Chuck didn't say anything and after a while Teddy figured he'd fallen asleep.

'Hey, boss.'

'You still awake?'

'We really going to pack it in?' Chuck asked.

'Yeah. You surprised?'

'I dunno . . . I just never quit anything before.'

Teddy lay quiet for a bit. Finally, he said, 'We haven't heard the truth once. We got no way through to it and we got nothing to fall back on, nothing to make these people talk.'

'I know, I know,' Chuck said. 'I never quit anything before is all.'

'Rachel Solando didn't slip barefoot out of a locked room without help. A lot of help. The whole institution's help. My experience? You can't break a whole society that doesn't want to hear what you have to say. But maybe the threat worked and Cawley's sitting in his mansion right now, rethinking his attitude. Maybe in the morning . . .'

They lay in silence, and Teddy listened to the ocean for a while.

'You purse your lips,' Chuck said, his voice beginning to garble with sleep.

'What?'

'When you're holding a good hand. You only do it for a second, but you always do it.'

'Oh.'

''Night, boss.'

''Night.'

DOLORES COMES TOWARDS HIM down the long hallway of their apartment on Buttonwood, anger in her eyes. She says, 'Jesus, Teddy.' She's holding an empty bottle of JTS Brown in her hand, and Teddy realises she's found one of his stashes. 'Are you ever sober any more?'

But Teddy can't speak. He's not even sure where his body is. There's a mirror at the other end of the hall behind Dolores, and he's not reflected in it.

She turns left into the living room and the back of her is charred, smouldering a bit. The bottle is no longer in her hand, and small ribbons of smoke unwind from her hair.

She stops at a window. 'Oh, look. They're so pretty like that. Floating.'

Teddy is beside her at the window, and she's no longer burnt, she's soaking wet, and he can see his hand as he places it on her shoulder, and she turns her head and gives his fingers a quick kiss.

'Baby, why you all wet?' he says, but isn't surprised when she doesn't answer.

He looks out of the window. There's a small pond out there with small logs floating in it, and Teddy notices how smooth they are, turning almost imperceptibly.

'She's here,' Dolores says.

'Rachel?'

Dolores nods. 'She never left. You almost saw it. You almost did.'

'The Law of Four.'

'It's code.'

'Sure, but for what?'

'She's here. You can't leave.'

He wraps his arms round her, buries his face in the side of her neck. 'I'm not going to leave. I love you. I love you so much.'

Her belly springs a leak and the liquid flows through his hands.

'I'm bones in a box, Teddy. You have to wake up.'

'You're here.'

'I'm not. You have to face that. She's here. You're here. He's here too. Count the beds. He's here.'

'Who?'

'Laeddis.'

The name crawls through his flesh and climbs over his bones. 'No.'

'Yes.' She bends her head back, looks up at him. 'Laeddis is here. You can't leave.' Then: 'I need to go.'

'No.' Teddy is crying. 'No. Stay.' His tears spill down. 'I need to hold you just a little longer. Please.'

She lets loose a small bubble of a sound—half sigh, half howl, so torn and beautiful in its anguish—and she kisses his knuckles. 'OK. Hold tight. Tight as you can.'

And he holds his wife. He holds her and holds her.

AT FIVE O'CLOCK in the morning, Teddy climbed off the top bunk and took his notebook from his jacket. He sat at the table and opened the notebook to the page where he'd transcribed Rachel Solando's Law of 4.

It was simple once you knew how to read it. A child's code, really. It was still code, though, and it took Teddy until six to break it.

He looked up, saw Chuck watching him from the lower bunk, his chin propped up on his fist. 'We leaving, boss?' he asked.

Teddy shook his head.

'Ain't nobody leaving in this shit,' Trey said, climbing out of his bunk, pulling up the window shade on a drowning landscape.

The dream was harder to hold suddenly, the smell of her evaporating with the ascent of the shade, a dry cough from Bibby, Trey stretching with a loud, long yawn. Teddy wondered, and not for the first time, if this was the day that missing her would finally be too much for him. As the years passed, he missed her more, not less, and his need for her became a cut that would not scar over.

We were supposed to grow old together, Dolores. Have kids. I wanted to watch the lines etch themselves into your flesh and know when each and every one of them appeared. Die together.

Not this. Not this.

Chuck was staring at him, waiting.

Teddy said, 'I broke Rachel's code.'

'Oh,' Chuck said, 'is that all?'

DAY TWO—LAEDDIS

4

Cawley met them in the foyer of Ward B. He was drenched, and looked like a man who'd spent the night on a bus-stop bench.

Chuck said, 'The trick, Doctor, is to sleep when you lie down.'

Cawley wiped his wet face with a handkerchief. 'Oh, I knew I was forgetting something. Sleep, you say. Right.'

They climbed the yellowed staircase, nodded at the orderly posted at the first landing.

'And how was Dr Naehring this morning?' Teddy asked.

Cawley gave him a weary look. 'I apologise for that. Jeremiah is a genius, but he could use some social polishing.'

'You guys do that a lot? Sit around over drinks, probing people?'

'Occupational hazard, I guess. How many psychiatrists does it take to screw in a light bulb?'

'I don't know. How many?'

'Eight.'

'Why?'

'Oh, stop overanalysing it.'

Teddy caught Chuck's eyes and they both laughed.

'Shrink humour,' Chuck said. 'Who would've guessed?'

'You know what the state of the mental health field is these days, gentlemen?'

'Not a clue,' Teddy said.

'Warfare,' Cawley said. 'Ideological, philosophical and yes, even psychological warfare.'

'You're doctors,' Chuck said. 'You're supposed to play nice, share your toys.'

Cawley smiled as they passed the orderly on the first-floor landing. 'The old school,' he said, 'believes in shock therapy, partial lobotomies, spa treatments for the most docile patients. Psychosurgery is what we call it. The new school is enamoured of psychopharmacology. It's the future, they say. Maybe it is. I don't know.'

He paused midway between the first floor and the second, and Teddy could sense his exhaustion.

'How does psychopharmacology apply?' Chuck asked.

Cawley said, 'A drug has just been approved—lithium is its name—that relaxes psychotic patients, tames them. Manacles, bars even, will become a thing of the past, or so the optimists say. The new school will be stronger, I think, and it will have money behind it.'

'Money from where?'

'Pharmaceutical companies, of course. Buy stock now, gentlemen, and you'll be able to retire to your own island. New schools, old schools. My God, I do rant sometimes.'

'Which school are you?' Teddy asked gently.

'Believe it or not, Marshal, I believe in talk therapy, basic interpersonal skills. I have this radical idea that if you treat a patient with respect, listen to what he's trying to tell you, you just might reach him.'

'But *these* patients?' Teddy said.

Cawley smiled. 'Well, yes, many of these patients need to be medicated and some need to be manacled. No argument. But it's a slippery slope. Once you introduce the poison into the well, how do you ever get it out of the water?'

'You don't,' Teddy said.

He nodded. 'That's right. What should be the last resort gradually becomes standard response. Sleep,' he said to Chuck wearily. 'Right. I'll try that next time.'

'I've heard it works wonders,' Chuck said, and they headed up the final flight.

In Rachel's room, Cawley sat heavily on the edge of her bed and Chuck leaned against the door. He said, 'Hey. How many surrealists does it take to screw in a light bulb?'

Cawley looked over at him. 'I'll bite. How many?'

'Fish,' Chuck said and let loose a bright bark of a laugh.

'You'll grow up someday, Marshal,' Cawley said. 'Won't you?'

'I've got my doubts.'

Teddy held the sheet of paper in front of his chest and tapped it to get their attention. 'Take another look.'

THE LAW OF 4
I AM 47
THEY WERE 80
+YOU ARE 3
WE ARE 4
BUT
WHO IS 67?

After a minute, Cawley said, 'I'm too tired, Marshal. It's all gibberish to me right now. Sorry.'

Teddy looked at Chuck. Chuck shook his head.

Teddy said, 'It was the plus sign that got me going, made me look at it again. Look at the line under "They were eighty".We're supposed to add the two lines above it together. What do you get?'

'A hundred and twenty-seven.'

'One, two and seven,' Teddy said. 'Right. Now you add three. But it's separated. She wants us to keep the integers apart. So you have one plus two plus seven plus three. What's that give you?'

'Thirteen.' Cawley sat up on the bed a bit.

'Does thirteen have any particular relevance to Rachel Solando? Was she born on the thirteenth? Married on it?'

'I'd have to check,' Cawley said. 'But thirteen is often a significant number to schizophrenics. Most schizophrenics live in a state of fear. And most are also deeply superstitious. Thirteen plays into that.'

'That makes sense, then,' Teddy said. 'Look at the next number. Four. One plus three is four. But one and three on their own is thirteen.'

'And the last number,' Cawley said. 'Sixty-seven. Six and seven equals thirteen.'

Teddy nodded. 'It's not the "law of four". It's the law of thirteen. There are thirteen letters in the name Rachel Solando.'

Teddy watched both Cawley and Chuck count it up in their heads.

Cawley said, 'Go on.'

'Once we've accepted that, Rachel leaves a whole lot of breadcrumbs. The code follows the rudimentary principle of number-to-letter assignation. One equals *A*. Two equals *B*. You with me?'

Cawley nodded, followed by Chuck a few seconds later.

'The first letter of her name is *R*. Numerical assignation of *R* is eighteen. *A* is one. *C* is three. *H* is eight. *E* is five. *L* is twelve. Eighteen, one, three, eight, five and twelve. Add 'em up, guys, and what do you get?'

'Jesus,' Cawley said softly.

'Forty-seven,' Chuck said, his eyes gone wide, staring at the sheet of paper over Teddy's chest.

'That's the "I",' Cawley said. 'Her first name. I get that now. But what about "they"?'

'Her last name,' Teddy said. 'It's theirs. Her husband's family and their ancestors. Solando. Take the letters and add up their numerical assignations and, yeah, trust me, you come up with eighty.'

Cawley came off the bed, and both he and Chuck stood in front of Teddy to look at the code draped over his chest.

Chuck looked up after a while, into Teddy's eyes. 'What're you—Einstein?'

'Have you broken code before, Marshal?' Cawley said, eyes still on the sheet of paper. 'In the war?'

'No.'

'So how did you . . .?' Chuck said.

Teddy placed the sheet on the bed. 'I don't know. I do a lot of crosswords. I like puzzles.'

Cawley said, 'But you were Army Intelligence overseas, right?'

Teddy shook his head. 'Regular army. You, though, were OSS?'

Cawley said, 'No. I did some consulting.'

'What kind of consulting?'

Cawley gave him that sliding smile of his, gone almost as soon as it appeared. 'The never-talk-about-it kind.'

'But this code,' Teddy said, 'it's pretty simple.'

'Simple?' Chuck said. 'You explained it, and my head still hurts.'

'But for you, Doctor?'

Cawley shrugged. 'I wasn't a code breaker.' He turned his attention back to the code. 'So we've figured out—well, you have, Marshal—the forty-seven and the eighty. What about the three?'

Teddy said, 'It either refers to us, in which case she's clairvoyant—'

'Not likely.'

'Or it refers to her children.'

'I'll buy that.'

'Add Rachel to the three . . .'

'And you get the next line,' Cawley said. '"We are four."'

'So who's sixty-seven?'

Cawley looked at him. 'You have no theories?'

Teddy said, 'It's the one I can't break. Whatever it refers to isn't anything I'm familiar with, which makes me think it's something on this island. You have any theories, Doctor?'

'None. I wouldn't have gotten past the first line.'

'You said that, yeah. Tired and all.'

'Very tired, Marshal.' He said it with his gaze fixed on Teddy's face, and then he crossed to the window, watched the rain sluice down it in thick sheets. 'You said last night that you'd be leaving.'

'First ferry out,' Teddy said.

'There won't be one today. I'm pretty sure of that.'

'So tomorrow, then. Or the next day. You still think she's out there? In this?'

'No,' Cawley said. 'I don't.'

'So where?'

He sighed. 'I don't know, Marshal. It's not my specialty.'

Teddy gestured at the sheet of paper. 'This is a template. A guide for deciphering future codes. I'd bet a month's salary on it.'

'And if it is?'

'Then she's not trying to escape, Doctor. She brought us here.'

'She *brought* you here?' Cawley said. 'To what end?'

'You tell me.'

Cawley closed his eyes and stayed silent for so long that Teddy began to wonder if he'd fallen asleep.

He opened his eyes again, looked at both of them. 'I've got a full day. I've got staff meetings, budget meetings, emergency maintenance meetings in case this storm really hits us. I've scheduled interviews for you with all the patients who were in group therapy with Miss Solando the night she disappeared, beginning in fifteen minutes. Gentlemen, I appreciate you being here. I do. I'm jumping through as many hoops as I can, whether it appears so or not.'

'Then give me Dr Sheehan's personnel file.'

'I can't do that.' He leaned his head back against the wall. 'Marshal, I've got the switchboard operator trying his number on a regular basis. But we can't reach anyone right now. For all we know, the whole eastern seaboard is under water. Patience, gentlemen. That's all I'm asking. We'll find Rachel, or we'll find out what happened to her.' He looked at his watch. 'I'm late. Is there anything else?'

THEY STOOD under an awning outside the hospital, the rain sweeping across their field of vision in sheets.

'You think he knows what sixty-seven means?' Chuck said.

'Yup.'

'You think he broke the code before you did?'

'I think he was OSS. I think he's got a gift or two in that department.'

Chuck wiped his face, flicked his fingers towards the ground. 'How many patients they got here?'

'It's small,' Teddy said. 'Maybe twenty women, thirty guys?'

'Not quite sixty-seven anyway.'

Teddy turned, looked at him. 'But . . .' he said.

'Yeah,' Chuck said. 'But.'

And they looked off at the tree line and beyond, at the top of the fort, indistinct like a charcoal sketch in a smoky room.

Teddy remembered what Dolores had said in the dream—Count the beds. 'How many they got up *there*, you think?' he said.

'I don't know,' Chuck said. 'We'll have to ask the helpful doctor.'

'Oh, yeah, he just screams "helpful", don't he?'

'Hey, boss. How many do you think these buildings could hold? A couple hundred more?'

'At least.'

'And the staff-to-patient ratio. It's like two-to-one favouring staff. You ever seen anything like that?'

'I gotta say no to that one.'

'What *is* this place?' Chuck said.

THEY HELD THE INTERVIEWS in the cafeteria, Chuck and Teddy sitting at a table in the rear. Two orderlies sat within shouting distance. The first was a stubbled wreck of tics and eye blinks. He sat hunched into himself like a horseshoe crab, scratching his arms, and refused to meet their eyes.

Teddy looked down at the top page in the file Cawley had provided—just thumbnail sketches from Cawley's own memory, not the actual patient files. The guy's name was Ken Gage and he was in here because he'd attacked a stranger in a corner grocery store, beat the victim on the head with a can of peas, all the time saying, 'Stop reading my mail.'

'So, Ken,' Chuck said, 'how you doing?'

'I got a cold. I got a cold in my feet.'

'Sorry to hear that.'

'It hurts to walk, yeah.' Ken scratched around the edges of a scab on his arm.

'Were you in group therapy the night before last?'

'I got a cold in my feet and it hurts to walk.'

'You want some socks?' Teddy tried. He noticed the two orderlies looking over at them, snickering.

'Yeah, I want some socks.' Whispering it, head down.

'Well, we'll get you some in a minute. We just need to know if—'

'It's just so cold. In my feet? It's cold and it hurts to walk.'

Teddy looked over at Chuck. Chuck smiled at the orderlies as the sound of their giggles floated to the table.

'Ken,' Chuck said. 'Ken, can you look at me?'

Ken kept his head down. 'It shouldn't hurt. It shouldn't. But they want it to. They fill the air with cold. They fill my kneecaps.'

Both orderlies stood and crossed to the table. The white one said, 'You guys about done, or you want to hear more about his feet?'

'My feet are cold.'

The black orderly raised an eyebrow. 'It's OK, Kenny. We'll take you to Hydro, warm you right up.'

The white one said, 'I been here five years. Topic don't change.'

'Ever?' Teddy said.

'Ever.'

THE NEXT ONE, Peter Breene, was twenty-six, blond and pudgy. A knuckle-cracker and a nail-biter.

'What are you here for, Peter?' Chuck asked.

Peter looked across the table at Teddy and Chuck with eyes that seemed permanently damp. 'I'm scared all the time.'

'Of what?'

'Things.'

'OK.'

Peter propped his left ankle up on his right knee, gripped the ankle, and leaned forward. 'It sounds stupid, but I'm afraid of watches. The ticking. It gets in your head. Rats terrify me.'

'Me too,' Chuck said. 'I get the shivers just looking at one.'

'Don't go out past the wall at night, then,' Peter said. 'They're everywhere.'

'Good to know. Thanks.'

'I'm afraid of you.'

'Me?' Chuck asked.

'No,' Peter said, pointing his chin at Teddy. 'Him.'

'Why?' Teddy asked.

He shrugged. 'You're big. Mean-looking crew cut. You can handle yourself. Your knuckles are scarred. My father was like that. Mean-looking. My brothers too. They used to beat me up.'

'I'm not going to beat you up,' Teddy said.

'But you could. Don't you see? You have that power. And I don't. And that makes me vulnerable. Being vulnerable makes me scared.'

'And when you get scared?'

Peter rocked back and forth. 'She was nice. I didn't mean anything. But she scared me, the way she moved in that white dress, coming to our house every day. And she had so much sexual knowledge. It was apparent in her eyes.'

Teddy tilted the file so Chuck could see Cawley's notes:

```
Patient assaulted his father's nurse with a broken
glass. Victim critically injured, permanently scarred.
Patient in denial over his responsibility for the act.
```

'It's only because she scared me,' Peter said. 'She wanted me to pull out my thing so she could laugh at it. Tell me how I'd never be a man? Because, otherwise, you can see it in my face—I wouldn't hurt a fly. It's not in me. But when I'm scared? Oh, the mind.'

'Your mind?' Chuck's voice was soothing.

'*The* mind,' he said. 'Mine, yours, anyone's. It's an engine essentially. That's what it is. And it's got all these pieces, all these gears and bolts and hinges. And if just one gear slips, just *one*, the whole system goes haywire. Can you live knowing that?' He tapped his temple. 'That it's all trapped in here and you can't *get to it* and you don't really control it. But it controls you, doesn't it? And if it decides one day that it doesn't feel like coming to work?' He leaned forward, and they could see tendons straining in his neck. 'Well, then you're pretty much fucked, aren't you?'

'Interesting perspective,' Chuck said.

Peter leaned back, suddenly listless. 'That's what scares me most.'

Teddy, whose migraines gave him a bit of insight into the lack of control one had over one's mind, would cede a point to Peter on the general concept, but mostly he just wanted to pick him up by his throat, slam him against the wall, and ask him about that poor nurse, ask him if he even remembered her name. What do you think she feared, Pete? Huh? *You*. That's what.

Instead, Teddy closed the file and said, 'You were in group therapy the night before last with Rachel Solando. Correct?'

'Yes, I sure was, sir.'

'You see her go up to her room?'

'No. The men left first. She was still sitting there with Bridget Kearns and Leonora Grant and that nurse.'

'That nurse?'

Peter nodded. 'The redhead. Sometimes I like her. She seems genuine. But other times, you know?'

'No,' Teddy said, keeping his voice as smooth as Chuck's had been, 'I don't.'

'Well, you've *seen* her, right? She's trash. Dirty, dirty, dirty.'

'Peter?'

Peter looked up at Teddy.

'Did anything unusual happen in group that night? Did Rachel Solando say or do anything out of the ordinary?'

'She didn't say a word. She's a mouse. She just sat there. She killed her kids, you know. Three of them. You believe that? What kind of person does that sort of thing?'

'People have problems,' Chuck said. 'Some are deeper than others. They need help.'

'They need gas,' Peter said. 'Gas the bitch.'

They sat silent, Peter glowing as if he'd illuminated the world.

After a while, Teddy broke the silence. 'Do you know a patient, Peter, by the name of Andrew Laeddis?'

'No.'

'No one here by that name?'

Peter shrugged. 'Not in Ward A. He could be in C. We don't mingle with them. They're nuts.'

AFTER PETER BREENE, they interviewed Leonora Grant. Leonora was convinced that she was Mary Pickford and Chuck was Douglas Fairbanks and Teddy was Charlie Chaplin. She thought she was in an office on Sunset Boulevard and they were there to discuss a public stock offering in United Artists. She kept caressing the back of Chuck's hand and asking who was going to record the minutes.

In the end, the orderlies had to pull her hand from Chuck's wrist.

'*Adieu, mon chéri. Adieu,*' Leonora cried as she was led away across the cafeteria.

After that, they met Arthur Toomey, who kept insisting they call him Joe. Joe had slept through group therapy that night. Joe, it turned out, was a narcoleptic. He fell asleep twice on them.

Teddy was feeling the place in the back of his skull by that point. It was making his hair itch, and while he felt sympathy for all the patients, except for Breene, he couldn't help wonder how anyone could stand working here.

Next came a small woman with blonde hair and a face shaped like a pendant. Her eyes pulsed with clarity. And not the clarity of the insane, but the everyday clarity of an intelligent woman. She smiled and gave them each a small, shy wave as she sat.

Teddy checked Cawley's notes—Bridget Kearns.

'I'll never get out of here,' she said after they'd been sitting there for a few minutes. She smoked her cigarettes only halfway before stubbing them out, she had a soft, confident voice, and a little over a decade ago she'd killed her husband with an axe. 'I'm not sure I should,' she added.

'Why's that?' Chuck said. 'Excuse me for saying it, Miss Kearns—'

'Mrs.'

'Mrs Kearns. Excuse me, but you seem, well, normal to me.'

She leaned back in her chair, as at ease as anyone they'd met in this place, and gave a soft chuckle. 'I suppose. I doubt I'd go out and kill someone again, but you can never tell.' She pointed the tip of her cigarette in their direction. 'I think if a man beats you and fucks half the women he sees and no one will help you, axing him isn't the least understandable thing you can do.'

She met Teddy's eyes and something in her pupils—a schoolgirl's shy giddiness, perhaps—made him laugh.

'Maybe you *shouldn't* get out,' he said.

'You say that because you're a man,' she said, laughing with him. 'And I don't blame you.'

It was a relief to laugh after Peter Breene, and Teddy wondered if he was actually flirting a bit too. With a mental patient. An axe murderer. *This is what it's come to, Dolores.* But he didn't feel altogether bad about it, as if after these two long dark years of mourning he was maybe entitled to a little harmless repartee.

'Can you tell us about Rachel Solando?' Chuck asked.

Bridget paused, and Teddy watched her eyes turn up slightly, as if she were searching her brain for the right file. Her words came more carefully and smelt of rote. 'Rachel is nice enough. She keeps to herself. She talks about rain a lot, but mostly she doesn't talk at all. She believes her kids are alive. She believes she's still living in the Berkshires and that we're all neighbours and postmen, delivery men, milkmen. She's hard to get to know.' She spoke with her head down, and when she finished, she couldn't meet Teddy's eyes. Her glance bounced off his face, and she lit another cigarette.

Teddy thought about what she'd just said, realised the description of Rachel's delusions was almost word for word what Cawley had said to them yesterday. He scribbled '*lies*' in his notebook.

'Anything unusual happen the last time you saw her?'

'No.'

'That was in group therapy, the night before last.'

'Yeah, yeah.' She nodded several times.

'And then you all went up to your rooms together.'

'With Mr Ganton, yes.'

'What was Dr Sheehan like that night?'

She looked up, and Teddy saw confusion and maybe some terror in her face. 'I don't know what you mean.'

'Was Dr Sheehan there that night?'

She looked at Chuck, then over at Teddy, sucked her upper lip against her teeth. 'Yeah. He was there.'

'What's he like?'

'He's OK. He's nice. Handsome.'

'Did he ever flirt with you? Come on to you?'

'No, no, no. Dr Sheehan's a good doctor.'

'And that night?'

'That night?' She gave it some thought. 'Nothing unusual happened that night. We spoke about, um, anger management? And Rachel complained about the rain. And Dr Sheehan left just before the group broke up, and Mr Ganton led us up to our rooms, and we went to bed, and that was it.'

In his notebook, Teddy wrote '*coached*' underneath '*lies*' and closed the cover. 'That was it?'

'Yes. And the next morning Rachel was gone.'

'But that night? Around midnight—you heard the commotion, right? When she was discovered missing. There was shouting, guards running everywhere, alarms sounding.'

'No. I . . . I thought it was a dream.'

'A dream?'

She nodded fast. 'Sure. A nightmare.' She looked at Chuck. 'Could I have a glass of water?'

'You bet.' Chuck stood and looked around, saw a stack of glasses in the rear of the cafeteria beside a steel dispenser.

One of the orderlies half rose from his seat. 'Marshal?'

'Just getting some water. It's OK.'

As Chuck crossed to the machine, Bridget Kearns grabbed Teddy's notebook and pen. She looked at him, holding him with her eyes, and flipped to a clean page, scribbled something on it, then flipped the cover closed and slid the notebook and pen back to him.

Teddy gave her a quizzical look, but she dropped her eyes.

Chuck brought the water back and sat down.

They watched Bridget drain half the glass and then say, 'Thank you. Do you have any more questions? I'm kind of tired.'

'You ever meet a patient named Andrew Laeddis?' Teddy asked.

Her face showed no expression. None whatsoever. It was as if it had turned to alabaster. Her hands stayed flat on the tabletop, as if removing them would cause the table to float to the ceiling. 'No,' she said. 'Never heard of him.'

'YOU THINK she was coached?' Chuck said.

'Don't you?'

'OK, it sounded a little forced.'

They were on the walkway outside the hospital, impervious to the rain now.

'A little? She used the exact same words Cawley used in some cases. When we asked what the topic was about in group, she paused and then she said "anger management?". Like she wasn't sure. Like she was taking a quiz and she'd spent last night cramming.'

'So what's that mean?'

'I don't know,' Teddy said. 'All I got are questions.'

'Hey, here's a question for you—who's Andrew Laeddis?'

'You caught that, huh?' Teddy lit a cigarette.

'You asked nearly every patient we talked to.'

'True.'

'I'm your partner, boss.'

Teddy turned his head, looked at Chuck. 'We just met,' he said.

'Oh, you don't trust me.'

'I trust you, Chuck. I do. But I'm breaking the rules here. I asked for this case specifically. The moment it came over the wire.'

'So?'

'So my motives aren't exactly impartial.'

Chuck nodded, took some time to think about it, then said, 'You gotta tell me why we're here, Teddy. I'm your partner. Who the hell is Andrew Laeddis?'

Teddy dropped the butt of his cigarette to the stone walk and ground it out with his heel.

Dolores, he thought, I've got to tell him. I can't do this alone. I want to atone for my sins—all my drinking, all the times I left you alone for too long, let you down, broke your heart. This might be the last opportunity I'll have. You, of all people, would understand that.

'Andrew Laeddis,' he said to Chuck, and the words clogged in his dry throat. He swallowed, tried again . . . 'Andrew Laeddis,' he said, 'was the maintenance man in the apartment building where my wife and I lived.'

'OK.'

'He was also an arsonist.'

Chuck took that in, studied Teddy's face. 'So . . .'

'Andrew Laeddis,' Teddy said, 'lit the match that caused the fire—that killed my wife.'

TEDDY AND CHUCK pressed close to the wall to avoid the rain.

'Laeddis,' Chuck said.

'Killed my wife.'

'You said that. How?'

'Laeddis was the maintenance man in our apartment building. Got in a fight with the owner. The owner fired him. At the time, all we knew was that the fire was arson. *Someone* had set it. Laeddis was on a list of suspects, but it took them a while to find him, and once they did, he'd shored up an alibi. Hell, I wasn't even sure it was him.'

'What changed your mind?'

'A year ago, I open the paper and there he is. Burned down a schoolhouse where he'd been working. Same story—they fired him and he came back, primed the boiler so it would explode. Exact same MO. Identical. Laeddis went to trial, claimed he heard voices, what have you, and they committed him to Shattuck. Something happened there—I don't know what—but he was transferred here six months ago.'

'But no one's seen him.'

'No one in Ward A or B.'

'Which suggests he's in C.'

'Yup.'

'If you find him, Teddy, what are you going to do?'

'I don't know.'

'Don't bullshit me, boss.'

'You know, the last morning I was with my wife, she spoke about the Cocoanut Grove fire. That's where we met. The Grove. She had this rich roommate and I was let in because they gave a serviceman's discount. It was just before I shipped out. Danced with her all night. Even the foxtrot.'

Chuck craned his neck out from the wall, looked into Teddy's face. 'You doing the foxtrot? I'm trying to picture it, but . . .'

'If you'd seen my wife that night, you'd have hopped around the floor like a bunny if she asked.'

'So you met her at the Cocoanut Grove.'

Teddy nodded. 'And then it burned down while I was in—Italy? Yeah, I was in Italy then—and she found that fact, I dunno, meaningful, I guess. She was terrified of fire.'

'But she died in a fire,' Chuck said softly.

'Beats all, don't it?' Teddy bit back against an image of her from that last morning.

'Teddy?'

Teddy looked at him.

Chuck spread his hands. 'I'll back you on this. No matter what. You want to find Laeddis and kill him? That's jake with me.'

'Jake.' Teddy smiled. 'I haven't heard that since—'

'But, boss? I need to know what to expect. I'm serious. I think you know about this place. I think you know stuff you haven't told me. I think you came here to do damage.'

Teddy fluttered a hand over his heart.

'I'm serious, boss.'

Teddy said, 'We're wet.'

'So?'

'My point. Care if we get wetter?'

THEY LEFT THROUGH the gate and walked the shore. The rain blanketed everything. Waves the size of houses hit the rocks.

'I don't want to kill him,' Teddy shouted over the roar.

'Not sure I believe you.'

Teddy shrugged. 'I'm tired of killing. In the war? I lost track. How's that possible, Chuck? But I did.'

'Still. Your wife, Teddy. And anyway, don't you think Cawley knows why you're really here?'

'I'm *really* here for Rachel Solando.'

'But if the guy who killed your wife was committed here, then—'

'He wasn't *convicted* for it. There's nothing to tie me and him to each other. Nothing.'

Chuck sat down on a stone, lowered his head to the rain. 'The guy might even be dead. Why don't we see if we can find the graveyard, now that we're out here? There must be one. We see a "Laeddis" headstone, we know half the battle's over.'

Teddy looked off at the dark ring of trees beyond. 'Fine.'

Chuck stood. 'What did she say to you, by the way?'

'Who?'

'The patient.' Chuck snapped his fingers. 'Bridget. She sent me for water. She said something to you, I know it.'

'She didn't.'

'She didn't? You're lying. I know she—'

'She wrote it,' Teddy said and found his notebook in the pocket of his trench coat, turned it so that Chuck could see the page, the single word written there, tightly scrawled and already beginning to bleed in the rain: *run*.

5

They found the stones about half a mile inland as the sky rushed towards darkness under slate-bottomed clouds. They came over soggy bluffs where the seagrass was lank and slick with rain, and they were both covered in mud from clawing and stumbling their way up.

A field lay below them, as flat as the undersides of the clouds, bald except for a multitude of small stones that Teddy initially assumed had ridden down on the wind. He paused halfway down the far side of the bluff, though, gave them another look.

They were spread across the field in small, tight piles, about six inches apart. Teddy put his hand on Chuck's shoulder and pointed.

'How many piles do you count?'

'What?' Chuck gave him a look, then turned his attention to the field. After a minute, he said, 'I count ten.'

'Me too.'

The mud gave way under Chuck's foot and he slipped, flailed back with an arm that Teddy caught and held until Chuck righted himself.

'Can we go down?' Chuck said, with a mild grimace of annoyance.

They worked their way down and Teddy went to the stone piles and saw that they formed two lines, one above the other. He walked between the two lines and then stopped and looked over at Chuck.

'We miscounted.'

'How?'

'Between these two piles here?' Teddy waited for Chuck to join him. 'That's one stone right there. Its own single pile. And in the next row, the same thing occurs again twice. Single stones.'

'So?'

'So, there're thirteen piles of rock, Chuck.'

'You think *she* left this. You really do.'

'I think someone did. It's another code.'

Teddy squatted by the rocks, pulling his trench coat over his head and extending the flaps to protect his notebook from the rain. He moved sideways like a crab and paused at each pile to count the number of stones and write it down. When he was finished, he had thirteen numbers: 18–1–4–9–5–4–19–1–12–4–23–14–5.

'Maybe it's a combination,' Chuck said, 'for the world's biggest padlock.'

Teddy closed the notebook and placed it in his pocket. 'Good one.'

'Thank you, thank you,' Chuck said. 'I'll be appearing twice nightly in the Catskills.'

They walked on, northwards, with the cliffs off to the right and Ashecliffe to their left, shrouded somewhere in the smash of wind and rain. They had to press their shoulders together in order to hear each other talk.

Chuck said, 'Cawley asked you if you were Army Intelligence. Did you lie to him?'

'I did and I didn't. I received my discharge from the regular army.'

'How'd you enter, though?'

'Out of basic, I was sent to radio school. From there a crash course at War College and then, yeah, Intel.'

'So how'd you end up in regulation brown?'

'I fucked up.' Teddy had to shout against the wind, which was growing worse. 'I blew a decoding. Enemy position coordinates.'

'How bad?'

'About half a battalion. Served 'em up like meat loaf.'

There was nothing but the gale in Teddy's ears for a minute, and then Chuck yelled, 'I'm sorry. That's horrible.'

They crested a knoll and the wind up top nearly blew them back off it, but Teddy gripped Chuck's elbow and they surged forward, bowing their heads and bodies into the wind. They didn't even notice the headstones at first. They kept trudging along with the rain filling their eyes, and then Teddy bumped into a slate stone that had been wrenched from its hole by the wind and lay flat on its back:

JACOB PLUGH
BOSUN'S MATE
1832–1858

A tree broke to their left, and the crack of it sounded like an axe through a tin roof. Parts of it were picked up by the wind and shot past their eyes. They moved into the graveyard with their arms up around their faces and the dirt and leaves and pieces of trees gone alive and electric, and they fell several times, almost blinded by it, and Teddy saw a fat charcoal shape ahead and pointed.

A mausoleum. The door was steel but broken at the hinges. Teddy pulled the door back and the wind tore into him, banged him to his left with the door. He fell to the ground and the door rose off its broken lower hinge and slammed back against the wall. Teddy rose to his feet, then plunged forward into the black doorway.

'You ever see anything like this?' Chuck said as they stood inside and watched the island whirl itself into a rage.

'Never,' Teddy said.

Chuck found a pack of matches that was still dry in the inside pocket of his coat and he lit three at once and tried to block the wind with his body. They saw that the concrete slab in the centre of the room was empty of a coffin. A stone bench was built into the wall on the other side of the slab, and they walked to it as the matches went out. They sat down, and the wind continued to hammer the door against the wall.

'Guess we should have stayed closer to home base,' Chuck said. 'We might have to ride this out here.'

Teddy nodded. 'I don't know enough about hurricanes, but I get the feeling it's just warming up.'

'It was so *fast.* One second it was just heavy rain, the next second we're Dorothy heading to Oz.'

'That was a tornado.'

'Oh.'

The squealing rose in pitch and Teddy could hear the wind find the thick stone wall behind him, pounding on it like fists.

'Just warming up,' he repeated.

They sat silent for a while and each had a cigarette.

'I was in North Africa in '42,' Chuck said eventually. 'Went through a couple of sandstorms. Nothing like this, though.'

'I can take this,' Teddy said. 'I mean, I wouldn't start strolling around out there, but it beats the cold. The Ardennes, Jesus, your breath froze coming out of your mouth. To this day, I can feel it.'

'North Africa, we had the heat. Guys just standing there one minute, on the deck the next. Guys had coronaries from it. I shot this guy and his skin was so soft from the heat, he actually turned and watched the bullet fly out the other side of his body.'

'Only guy you ever killed?'

'Up close. You?'

'I was the opposite. Killed a lot, saw most of them.' Teddy leaned his head back against the wall, looked up at the ceiling. 'If I ever had a son, I don't know if I'd let him go to war. I'm not sure that should be asked of anyone.'

'What?'

'Killing.'

Chuck raised a knee to his chest. 'My parents, my girlfriend, friends who couldn't pass the physical, they all ask, what was it *like*? That's what they want to know. And you want to say, "I don't know what it was like. It happened to someone else. I was just watching it from above or something."' He held out his hands. 'I can't explain it any better. Did that make a bit of sense?'

Teddy said, 'At Dachau, the SS guards surrendered to us. We executed every one of them. Machine-gunned over three hundred at one time. Walked down the line putting bullets into the head of anyone still breathing. A war crime if ever there was one. Right? But, Chuck, that was the *least* we could have done. It was homicide. And yet they deserved so much worse. So, fine—but how do you live with that? How do you tell the wife and the parents and the kids that you've executed unarmed people? You've killed boys? Boys with guns and uniforms, but boys just the same? Answer is—You can't tell 'em. They'll never understand. Because what you did was for the right reason. But what you *did* was also wrong.'

After a while, Chuck said, 'At least it was for the right reason. We stopped Adolf. We saved millions of lives. Right? We did something.'

'Yeah, we did,' Teddy admitted. 'Sometimes that's enough.'

An entire tree swept past the door, upside-down, its roots sprouting upwards like horns. 'You see that?'

'Yeah. It's gonna wake up in the middle of the ocean, say, "Wait a *second.* This isn't right."'

'"I'm supposed to be over there."'

'"Took me years to get that hill looking the way I wanted it."'

They laughed softly in the dark and watched the island race by like a fever dream.

'So how much do you really know about this place, boss?'

Teddy shrugged. 'Enough to scare me.'

'Oh, great. What's a normal mortal supposed to feel, then?'

Teddy smiled. 'Abject terror?'

'OK. Consider me terrified.'

'It's known as an experimental facility. I told you—radical therapy. Its funding comes partially from the Bureau of Federal Penitentiaries, but mostly from a fund set up by the House Un-American Activities Committee in '51.'

'Oh,' Chuck said. 'Terrific. Fighting the Commies from an island in Boston Harbor. How *does* one go about doing that?'

'They experiment on the mind. That's my guess. Write down what they know, turn it over to Cawley's old OSS buddies who are CIA now. Maybe. I dunno. You ever heard of phencyclidine?'

Chuck shook his head.

'LSD? Mescaline?'

'Nope and nope.'

'They're drugs that cause you to hallucinate. In even minimal doses, strictly sane people—you or I—would start seeing things.'

'Upside-down trees flying past our door?'

'Ah, but if we're both seeing it, it's not a hallucination. Everyone sees different things. Say you looked down right now and your arms had turned to cobras and the cobras were rising up, opening their jaws to eat your head?'

'I'd say that would be a hell of a bad day. But, hey, you're saying a drug could make you think stuff like that was really happening?'

'Not just "could". Will. The effect of these drugs is supposedly identical to what it's like to be a severe schizophrenic. They see things that aren't there, hear voices no one else hears, jump from perfectly sound roofs because they think the building's on fire, and on and on. And what do you think would happen if you gave hallucinogens to people with extreme schizophrenia?'

'No one would do that.'

'They do it, and it's legal. Only humans get schizophrenia. So how are you going to test cures for it?'

'On humans.'

'Give that man a cigar.'

Chuck stood and placed his hands on the stone slab, looked out at the storm. 'So they're giving schizophrenics drugs that make them even more schizophrenic?'

'That's one test group.'

'What's another?'

'People who don't have schizophrenia are given hallucinogens to see how their brains react.'

'Bullshit.'

'This is a matter of public record, buddy. Attend a psychiatrists' convention someday. I have.'

'But you said it's legal. If it's legal, we can't do anything about it.'

Teddy leaned into the slab. 'No argument. I'm not here to arrest anyone just yet. I was sent to gather information. That's all.'

'Wait a minute—sent? How deep are we here?'

Teddy sighed, looked over at him. 'Deep.'

'Back up.' Chuck held up a hand. 'From the top. How'd you get involved in all this?'

'It started with Laeddis. A year ago, I went to Shattuck with a story about how a known associate of his was wanted on a federal warrant and I thought Laeddis could shed some light on his whereabouts. Thing was, Laeddis had been transferred to Ashecliffe. I call over here, but they claim to have no record of him. That gets me curious. I make some phone calls to some of the psych hospitals in town but no one wants to talk about Ashecliffe. Then I talk to the warden at Renton Hospital for the Criminally Insane. I'd met him a couple of times, and I say, "Bobby, what's the big deal? It's a hospital and it's a prison, no different from your place." He shakes his head and says, "Teddy, that place is something else entirely. Something classified." '

'So you've just been waiting for an excuse to come out here?'

'Pretty much,' Teddy said. 'And, hell, I couldn't bet it would ever happen. I mean, even if there was a patient break, I didn't know if I'd be in town when it happened. Or if someone else would be assigned to it. Or, hell, a million ifs. I got lucky.'

'Lucky? It's not luck, boss. Luck doesn't work that way. You think you just *happened* to get assigned to this detail?'

'Sure. Sounds a little crazy, but—'

'When you first called here about Laeddis, did you ID yourself?'

'Of course. But, Chuck, it was a full year ago.'

'So? You don't think they keep tabs? Particularly in the case of a patient they claim to have no record of?' Chuck lowered his voice. 'Let's say they are doing some bad shit here. What if they've been onto you since before you ever stepped foot on this island? What if *they* brought *you* here?'

'Oh, bullshit.'

'Bullshit? Where's Rachel Solando? Where's one shred of evidence that she ever existed? We've been shown a picture of *a* woman and a file anyone could have fabricated.'

'But even if they staged this whole thing, there's still no way they could have predicted that I would be assigned to the case.'

'You've made enquiries about this place, Teddy. They got under a hundred patients in a facility that could hold three hundred. They got a ward inside a fort. This place is scary, Teddy. You got a chief of staff with OSS ties, funding from a slush fund created by HUAC. Everything about this place screams "government ops". And you're surprised by the possibility that instead of you looking at them for the past year, they've been looking at you?'

'How many times do I have to say it, Chuck: how could they know I'd be assigned to Rachel Solando's case?'

'They knew you'd jump at an excuse to come here. Your wife's killer is here. All they had to do was pretend someone escaped. They knew you'd pole-vault your way across that harbour if you had to.'

The door ripped free of its sole hinge and they watched it hammer the stone wall, then lift into the air above the graveyard and disappear in the sky.

Both of them stared at the doorway, and then Chuck said, 'We *both* saw that, right?'

'They're using human beings as guinea pigs,' Teddy said. 'Doesn't that bother you?'

'It terrifies me, Teddy. But how do you know this? You say you were sent to gather information. Who sent you?'

'In our first meeting with Cawley, you heard him ask about the senator?'

'Yeah.'

'Senator Hurly, Democrat, New Hampshire. Heads up a subcommittee on public funding for mental health affairs. He saw what kind of money was being funnelled to this place, and he didn't like it. Now, I'd come across a guy named George Noyce. Noyce spent time here. In Ward C. He was off the island two weeks when he walked into a bar in Attleboro and began stabbing people. Strangers. His lawyer wants to claim insanity. If ever there was a case for it, it's this guy. He's bonkers. But Noyce fires his lawyer, goes in front of the judge and pleads guilty, pretty much begs to be sent to a prison, any prison, just not a hospital. Takes him about a year in prison, but his mind starts coming back, and eventually he starts telling stories about Ashecliffe. Stories that sound crazy, but the senator thinks they're maybe not as crazy as everyone else assumes.'

Chuck sat up on the slab and lit a cigarette, smoked it for a bit as he considered Teddy. 'But how'd the senator know to find you and how'd you both manage to find Noyce?' he asked.

For a moment, Teddy thought he saw lights arcing through the eruptions outside. 'It was the other way around. Noyce found me and I found the senator. Bobby Farris, the warden at Renton, called me one morning and asked if I was still interested in Ashecliffe. I said sure, and he told me about this convict down in Dedham who was making all this noise about Ashecliffe. So I go to Dedham, talk to Noyce. Noyce says when he was in college he got a bit tense one year around exam time. Shouted at a teacher, put his fist through a window. He ends up talking to somebody in the psych department. Next thing you know, he agrees to be part of a test so he can make a little pocket change. A year later, he's a fully fledged schizophrenic, raving on street corners, seeing things, the whole nine yards.'

Teddy saw lights again flaring through the storm and he walked nearer to the door, stared out. 'This is a kid who started out normal as pecan pie. Maybe had some—what do they call it here?—"anger management issues", but all in all, perfectly sane. A year later, he's out of his mind. Sees this guy in Park Square one day, thinks it's the professor in the psych department. It ain't, but Noyce beats him up pretty bad. Gets sent to Ashecliffe. Ward C. They fill him up with hallucinogens and watch as the dragons come to eat him and he goes crazy. In the end, just to calm him down, they performed surgery.'

'Surgery,' Chuck said.

Teddy nodded. 'A transorbital lobotomy. Those are fun, Chuck. They zap you with electroshock and then they go in through your eye with, get this, an ice pick. I'm not kidding. No anaesthesia. They poke around here and there and take a few nerve fibres out of your brain, and then that's it, it's over. Piece of cake.'

Chuck said, 'The Nuremberg Code prohibits—'

'—experimenting on humans purely in the interest of science, yes. I thought we had a case based on Nuremberg too. No go.

Experimentation is allowable if it's used to directly attack a patient's malady. So as long as a doctor can say, "Hey, we're just trying to help the poor bastard, see if these drugs can induce schizophrenia and these drugs over here can stop it"—then they're in the clear.'

'Wait a second,' Chuck said. 'If this Noyce had a trans, um—'

'A transorbital lobotomy, yeah.'

'If the point of that, however medieval, is to calm someone down, how's he manage to go stab some people in a bar in Attleboro?'

'Obviously, it didn't take.'

'Is that common?'

Teddy saw the arcing lights again, and this time he was pretty sure he could hear the whine of an engine behind all that squealing.

'Marshals!' The voice was weak on the wind, but they both heard it.

Chuck jumped off the slab and joined Teddy at the doorway. They could see headlights at the far end of the cemetery and they heard the squawk of a megaphone: 'Marshals! If you are out here, please signal us. This is Deputy Warden McPherson. Marshals!'

Teddy said, 'How about that? They found us.'

'It's an island, boss. They'll always find us.'

Teddy met Chuck's eyes and nodded. For the first time since they'd met, he could see fear in Chuck's eyes.

'It's going to be OK, partner.'

Chuck said, 'I don't know.'

'I do,' Teddy said, though he didn't. 'Stick with me. We're walking out of this place, Chuck. Make no mistake about it.'

And they stepped out of the doorway and into the cemetery. The wind hit their bodies like a team of linemen but they stayed on their feet, locking arms as they stumbled towards the light.

6

'Are you crazy?' This from McPherson, shouting into the wind, as the Jeep hurtled down a makeshift trail along the western edge of the cemetery.

He was in the passenger seat, looking back at them with red eyes, all vestiges of charm washed away in the storm. The driver was a young, lean-faced kid who drove like a professional, tearing through scrub brush and storm debris like it wasn't even there.

'This has just been upgraded from a tropical storm to a hurricane. By midnight, the winds are expected to hit a hundred fifty. And you guys go strolling off in it?'

'How do you know it was upgraded?' Teddy said.

'Ham radio. We expect to lose that within a couple of hours too.'

'Of course,' Teddy said.

'We could have been shoring up the compound right now, but instead we were looking for you. Dr Cawley just can't wait to talk to you guys.' He slapped the back of his seat, then turned forwards, done with them.

THEY SHOWERED in the basement of the staff dormitory and were given white shirts and trousers from the orderlies' stockpile. Their own clothes were sent to the hospital laundry.

Trey Washington stuck his head in the bathroom. He seemed to be biting back on a smile as he appraised their new clothes and said, 'I'm to bring you to Dr Cawley.'

'How much trouble we in?'

'Oh, a bit, I'd expect.'

'GENTLEMEN,' CAWLEY SAID as they entered a boardroom on the top floor of the hospital. 'Good to see you.'

The room was filled with doctors, some in white lab coats, some in suits, all sitting round a long teak table. Naehring sat at the head of the table.

'Doctors, these are the federal marshals we discussed, Marshals Daniels and Aule,' Cawley said. The chief of staff seemed in a magnanimous mood, his eyes bright.

'Where are your clothes?' one man asked.

'We were out in the storm,' Teddy said.

'Out in that?' The doctor pointed at the tall windows. They'd been crisscrossed with heavy tape and the panes drummed with fingertips of rain. The entire building creaked under the press of wind.

'Afraid so,' Chuck said.

'Please take a seat, gentlemen,' Naehring said.

While they found two seats at the end of the table, Cawley went and fixed a cup of coffee for himself at the sideboard.

'Rumour has it you were both found in a mausoleum,' he said, and there were soft chuckles from around the table.

'You know a better place to sit out a hurricane?' Chuck said.

Cawley said, 'Here. Preferably in the basement.'

'We hear it may hit land at a hundred fifty miles an hour.'

Cawley nodded, his back to the room. 'This morning, Newport, Rhode Island, lost thirty per cent of its homes.'

'Worst storm to hit the eastern seaboard in thirty years,' one of the doctors said.

'Turns the air to pure static electricity,' Cawley added. 'That's why the switchboard went to hell last night. If it gives us a direct hit, I don't know what's going to be left standing.'

'Which is why,' Naehring said, addressing his colleagues now, 'I repeat my insistence that all Blue Zone patients be placed in manual restraints.'

'Blue Zone?' Teddy said.

'Ward C,' Cawley said. 'Patients who have been deemed a danger to themselves, and the public at large.' He turned to Naehring. 'We can't do that. If that facility floods, they'll drown.'

'It would take a lot of flooding.'

'We're in the ocean. About to get hit with hurricane winds of a hundred fifty miles per hour. A "lot of flooding" seems distinctly possible. They're already locked down in cells, for Christ's sake.'

'It's a gamble, John.' This was said quietly by a brown-haired man in the middle of the table. 'If the power fails, those cells will open.'

'It's an island,' Cawley said. 'Where's anyone going to go? It's not like they can catch a ferry, scoot over to Boston.' He looked up and down the table, and Teddy suddenly felt a compassion coming from him that he'd barely sensed before. He had no idea why Cawley had allowed them into this meeting, but it seemed the man didn't have many friends in the room.

'Doctor,' Teddy said, 'I don't mean to interrupt.'

'Not at all, Marshal. We brought you here.'

'When we spoke this morning about Rachel Solando's code—'

'Everyone's familiar with what the marshal's talking about?'

'The Law of Four,' one of the doctors said with a smile that Teddy wanted to take a pair of pliers to. 'I just love that.'

Teddy said, 'When we talked this morning you said you had no theories about the final clue.'

'"Who is sixty-seven?"' Naehring said. 'Yes?'

Teddy nodded and then leaned back in his chair, waiting. But everyone looked back down the table at him, baffled.

'You have sixty-six patients here,' he said.

They stared back at him like birthday-party children waiting for the clown's next bouquet.

'Forty-two patients, combined, in Wards A and B. Twenty-four in Ward C. That's sixty-six.'

Teddy could see the realisation dawn on a few faces, but the majority still looked dumbfounded.

'That suggests that the answer to "Who is sixty-seven?" is that there's a sixty-seventh patient here,' Teddy said. 'That's what Rachel Solando was suggesting.'

'But there isn't,' Cawley said. 'It's a great idea, Marshal, and it would certainly crack the code if it were true. But there are only sixty-six patients on the island. If this hurricane weren't going on we would have received two new patients this morning, making our total sixty-eight. The total number of patients can change week by week.'

'But,' Teddy said, 'on the night Miss Solando wrote her code . . .'

'There were sixty-six here, including her, I'll grant you that, Marshal. But there's no sixty-seventh patient here.'

'Would you permit my partner and me to go through the patient files?'

That brought frowns and offended looks from the table.

'Absolutely not,' Naehring said.

'We can't do that, Marshal. I'm sorry,' Cawley said.

Teddy lowered his head for a minute, looked at his silly white shirt and matching trousers. He looked like a soda jerk. 'We can't access your staff files. We can't access your patient files. How are we supposed to find your missing patient, gentlemen?'

Naehring leaned back in his chair, cocked his head.

Cawley's arm froze, a cigarette half lifted to his lips. 'The warden didn't tell you?' he said.

Several of the doctors whispered to one another.

'We've never spoken to the warden. McPherson picked us up.'

'Oh,' Cawley said, 'my goodness.' He looked around at the other doctors, his eyes wide.

'What?'

'We found her.'

'You what?'

Cawley nodded and took a drag off his cigarette. 'Rachel Solando. We found her this afternoon. She's here, gentlemen. Just down the hall. Your quest is over.'

CAWLEY AND NAEHRING led them down a black-and-white-tiled corridor and through a set of double doors into the main hospital ward. They passed a nurses' station on their left and turned right into a large room, and there she was, sitting up on a bed in a pale green smock that ended just above her knees, her dark hair freshly washed and combed back off her forehead. There wasn't a mark on her. Her face and arms and legs were unblemished. Her feet were bare, and the skin was untouched by branches or thorns or rocks.

'Rachel,' Cawley said, 'we've dropped by with some friends. I hope you don't mind.'

She smoothed the hem of the smock under her thighs and looked at Teddy and Chuck with a child's air of expectation. 'How can I help you?' she asked Teddy.

'Miss Solando, we came here to—'

'You're not here to sell something, I hope. I don't want to be rude, but my husband makes all those decisions.'

'No, ma'am. We're not here to sell anything.'

'Well, that's fine, then. What can I do for you?'

'Could you tell me where you were yesterday?'

'I was here, at home.' She looked at Cawley. 'Who are these men?'

Cawley said, 'They're police officers, Rachel.'

'Did something happen to Jim? Or the children?' She looked around. 'They didn't get into any mischief, did they?'

Teddy said, 'Miss Solando, no. Your children aren't in any trouble. Your husband's fine.' He caught Cawley's eye and Cawley nodded in approval. 'We just, um, we heard there was a known subversive in your street yesterday. He was seen passing out Communist literature.'

'Oh, dear Lord, no. On this street?

'I'm afraid so, ma'am. I was hoping you could account for your whereabouts so we'd know if you ever crossed paths with the gentleman in question.'

'Are you accusing me of being a Communist?' Her back came off the pillows and she bunched the sheet in her fists.

Cawley gave Teddy a look that said: You dug the hole. You dig your way out.

'A Communist, ma'am? You? What man in his right mind would think that? You're as American as Betty Grable. But it's important we know every move this subversive made yesterday. Now you might not have even seen him. He's a sneaky one. So we need to know what *you* did so that we can match that against what we know about where he was, so we can see if you two may have ever passed each other.'

'Like ships in the night?' She unclenched her hands from the sheet and sat up on the bed, tucking her legs underneath her. Teddy felt her movements in his stomach and groin.

'So if you could walk me through your day,' he said.

'Well, let's see. I made Jim and the children their breakfast and then I packed Jim's lunch and Jim left, and then I sent the children off to school and then I decided to take a long swim in the lake.'

'You do that often?'

'No,' she said, laughing, as if he'd made a pass at her. 'I just, I don't know, I felt a little kooky. You know how you do sometimes?'

'Sure.'

'So I took off all my clothes and swam in the lake until my arms and legs were heavy, and then I came out and dried off and put my clothes right back on and took a walk along the shore. And I skipped some stones and built several small sandcastles.'

'You remember how many?' Teddy asked.

She thought about it, eyes tilted towards the ceiling. 'I do. Thirteen.'

'And then what did you do?'

'I thought about you,' she said.

Teddy saw Naehring's surprised glance over at Cawley from the other side of the bed.

'Why me?' Teddy said.

Her smile exposed white teeth. 'Because you're my Jim, silly. You're my soldier.' She rose on her knees and reached out and took Teddy's hand in hers, caressed it. 'I miss you, Jim. You're never home.'

'I work a lot,' Teddy said.

'Sit.' She tugged his arm.

Cawley nudged him forward with a glance, so Teddy allowed himself to be led to the bed. He sat beside her. Whatever had caused that howl in her eyes in the photograph had fled from her, at least temporarily, and it was impossible, sitting this close, not to be fully aware of how beautiful she was.

'You work too much,' she said and ran her fingers over the space just below his throat, as if smoothing a kink in the knot of his tie.

'Gotta bring home the bacon,' Teddy said.

'Oh, we're fine,' she said. 'We've got enough to get by.'

'For now,' Teddy said. 'I'm thinking about the future.'

'My poppa always used to say, "Future's something you put on layaway. I pay cash."' She gave him a soft giggle and leaned in so close that he could feel her breasts against the back of his shoulder. 'No, baby, we've got to live for today. The here and now.'

It was something Dolores used to say. And the lips and hair were both similar, enough so that if Rachel's face got much closer, he could be forgiven for thinking he was talking to Dolores. They even had the same tremulous sensuality.

Teddy tried to remember what he was supposed to ask her. He knew he was supposed to get her back on track. Have her tell him about her day yesterday, that was it, what happened after she walked the shore and built the castles.

'What did you do after you walked the lake?' he said.

'You know what I did.'

'I don't.'

She leaned in so that her face was slightly below his, those dark eyes staring up to his. 'You don't remember? If you forgot that, James Solando, you are in for some trouble.'

'So, tell me,' Teddy whispered.

She ran her palm down his cheekbone and her voice was thicker when she spoke. 'I came back still wet from the lake and you licked me dry.'

Teddy placed his hands on her face before she could close the distance between them. He looked into her eyes. 'Tell me what else you did yesterday,' he whispered, and he saw something fighting against the water-clarity in her eyes. Fear, he was pretty sure. And then he could feel tremors in her flesh.

She searched his face and her eyes widened and flicked from side to side. 'I buried you,' she said.

'No, I'm right here.'

'I buried you. In an empty casket because your body was blown all over the North Atlantic. I buried your dog tags because that's all they could find. Your beautiful body was burned up and eaten by sharks.'

'No, that wasn't me.'

'They killed Jim. My Jim's dead. So who are you?' She wrenched from his grip and crawled up the bed to the wall and then turned to look back at him. 'Who is that?' She pointed at Teddy.

He couldn't move. He stared at her, at the rage filling her eyes.

'You get the hell out of here! You rapist! Where are my babies? You give me back my babies! My husband will come and cut your head off and we'll drink the blood!' She lunged at him.

Teddy jumped from the bed, and two orderlies swooped past him with thick leather belts and caught Rachel under the arms and flipped her back onto the bed. As one orderly lay across her chest and the other one grasped her ankles in a massive hand they slid the belts through metal slots in the bed rails and crossed them over Rachel's chest and ankles and pulled them through slots on the other side, snapped them shut.

She let loose a scream that rode up Teddy's spine like a bullet.

Cawley said, 'We'll come check on you later, Rachel.'

He nodded at Teddy and Chuck and started walking and they fell into step behind him, Teddy looking back over his shoulder to see Rachel looking him right in the eye as she arched her shoulders off the mattress and the cords in her neck bulged. She shrieked at him, shrieked like she'd seen all the century's dead climb through her window and walk towards her bed.

CAWLEY HAD A BAR in his office, and he went to it as soon as they entered, crossing to the right, and that's where Teddy lost him for a moment. He vanished behind a film of white gauze. Teddy thought: No, not now. Not now, for Christ's sake.

'Where'd you find her?' he asked.

'On the beach near the lighthouse. Skipping stones into the ocean.'

Cawley reappeared, but only because Teddy shifted his head to the left as Cawley continued on to the right. As Teddy turned his head, the gauze covered a built-in bookcase and then the window. Then he felt it along the left side of his head—the pain erupted like a dozen dagger points pushed slowly into his cranium. He winced and raised his fingers to his temple, rubbed hard.

'Marshal?'

He looked up to see Cawley on the other side of his desk, a ghostly blur to his left.

'You OK, boss?' Chuck was beside him suddenly.

'Fine,' Teddy managed, and Cawley placed his Scotch glass down on the desk, and the sound of it was like a shotgun report.

'Migraine?' Cawley asked, leaning against the desk.

Teddy looked up at the blur of him. 'Yeah,' he managed.

'I could tell by the way you're rubbing your temple. You get them often?'

'Half-dozen'—Teddy's mouth dried up and he took a few seconds to work some moisture back into his tongue—'times a year.'

'You're lucky,' Cawley said. 'A lot of migraine sufferers get cluster migraines once a week or so.' Teddy heard him unlock a drawer in his desk. 'All the centuries we've studied the brain, and we know no more about the cause or long-term effects of migraine than we do about how to stop the common cold. Can you believe that? We know migraines usually attack the parietal lobe, and cause a clotting of the blood. It's infinitesimal as these things go, but have it occur in something as delicate and small as the brain, and you will get explosions.'

Cawley handed him a glass of water and put two yellow pills in his hand. 'These should do the trick. Knock you out for an hour or two, but when you come to, you should be fine. Clear as a bell.'

Teddy looked down at the yellow pills, the glass of water that hung in a precarious grip.

Whatever you do, a voice started to say in his head . . . then fingernails prised open the left side of his skull and poured a shaker of thumbtacks in there, and Teddy sucked in his breath.

'Boss, boss. You OK.'

'He'll be fine, Marshal.'

The voice tried again: *Whatever you do, Teddy* . . . Someone hammered a steel rod through the field of thumbtacks, and his stomach lurched. . . . *don't take those pills*. His stomach went fully south, sliding across into his right hip as flames licked the sides of the fissure in his head. He vomited onto the floor.

'My, my,' Cawley said. 'You do get it bad.'

Teddy raised his head. *Don't take those fucking pills*, the voice screamed. Someone had inserted a blade lengthwise into the burning canyon now. The blade had begun to saw back and forth. He had to bite down against a scream and he heard Rachel's screams in there too, and he saw her looking into his eyes and felt her breath on his lips and felt her face in his hands as his thumbs caressed her temples and that saw went back and forth through his head—and he slapped his palm up to his mouth and felt the pills fly back in there and he chased them with water and swallowed.

'You're going to thank me, Marshal,' Cawley said.

Chuck was beside him again and he handed Teddy a handkerchief and Teddy wiped his mouth with it and dropped it to the floor.

They turned Teddy so he could see a black door in front of him. 'Don't tell anyone,' Cawley said, 'but there's a room through there where I steal a nap sometimes. We're going to put you in there, and you'll sleep this off. Two hours from now, you'll be fit as a fiddle.'

Teddy saw his hands draping off their shoulders. They looked funny—his hands hanging like that. And the thumbs, they both had something odd on them. What was it? Cawley was opening the door now, and Teddy took one last look at the smudges on both thumbs. Black smudges.

Shoe polish, he thought as they led him into the dark room. How the hell did I get shoe polish on my thumbs?

7

They were the worst dreams Teddy had ever had.

They began with him walking through the streets of Hull, streets he had walked countless times from childhood. But no one was there. The entire town was empty. And dead quiet. He couldn't even hear the ocean, and you could always hear the ocean in Hull.

It was terrible—his town, and everyone gone. He sat down on the sea wall and searched the empty beach, and he sat and waited but no one came. They were all dead, he realised, long dead and long gone. He was a ghost, come back through the centuries to his ghost town.

He found himself in a great marble hall next, and it was filled with people and gurneys and he immediately felt better. No matter where this was, he wasn't alone. Three children—two boys and a girl—crossed in front of him. All three wore hospital smocks. The girl was afraid. She clutched her brothers' hands and said, 'She's here. She'll find us.'

Andrew Laeddis leaned in and lit Teddy's cigarette. 'Hey, no hard feelings, right, buddy?'

Laeddis was a grim specimen of humanity—a gnarled cord of a body, a gangly head with a jutting chin, misshapen teeth, sprouts of blond hair on a pink skull—but Teddy was glad to see him. He was the only one he knew in the room.

'Got me a bottle,' Laeddis said, 'if you want to have a toot later.' He winked at Teddy and clapped his back and turned into Chuck and that seemed perfectly normal.

'We've gotta go,' Chuck said. 'Clock's ticking away here.'

Teddy said, 'My town's empty. Not a soul.'

And he broke into a run because there she was, Rachel Solando, shrieking as she ran through the ballroom with a cleaver. Before Teddy could reach her, she'd tackled the three children, and the cleaver went up and down, and Teddy froze, knowing that there was nothing he could do, that those kids were dead.

Rachel looked up at him, her face and neck speckled with blood. She said, 'Give me a hand.'

Teddy said, 'What? I could get in trouble.'

She said, 'Give me a hand and I'll be Dolores. I'll be your wife. She'll come back to you.'

So he said, 'Sure, you bet,' and helped her. They lifted all three children at once somehow and carried them out through the back door and down to the lake. Gently they laid them on the water and the children sank.

They stood on the shore and watched and she put her arm round Teddy's waist and said, 'You'll be my Jim. I'll be your Dolores. We'll make new babies.'

That seemed a perfectly just solution, and Teddy wondered why he'd never thought of it before.

He followed her back into Ashecliffe and they met up with Chuck and the three of them walked down a long corridor. Teddy told Chuck, 'She's taking me to Dolores. I'm going home, buddy.'

'That's great!' Chuck said. 'I'm glad. I'm never getting off this island. But it's OK, boss. It really is. I belong here. This is my home.'

'I'm glad you're home.'

'Thanks, boss.' He slapped his back and turned into Cawley and Rachel had somehow got far ahead of them.

Cawley said, 'You can't love a woman who killed her children.'

'I can,' Teddy said, walking faster. 'We've got a deal. She'll be my Dolores. I'll be her Jim. It's a good deal.'

'Uh-oh,' Cawley said.

The three children came running back down the corridor towards them then. They were soaking wet and they were screaming.

'What kind of mother kills her kids?' Cawley said.

Teddy watched the children run past him and Cawley, and then the air changed or something because they ran and ran but never moved forwards.

'She didn't mean to,' Teddy said. 'She's just scared.'

The little girl said, 'She's coming. You must help us.'

'I'm not your daddy. It's not my place.'

'I'm going to call you Daddy.'

'Fine,' Teddy said with a sigh and took her hand.

They walked the cliffs overlooking the Shutter Island shore and then they wandered into the cemetery and Teddy found a loaf of bread and some peanut butter and jelly and made them sandwiches in the mausoleum, and the little girl was so happy, sitting on his lap, eating her sandwich, and Teddy took her out with him into the graveyard and pointed out his own headstone:

EDWARD DANIELS
BAD SAILOR
1920–1957

'Why are you a bad sailor?' the girl asked.

'I don't like water.'

'I don't like water, either. That makes us friends.'

'I guess it does.'

'You're already dead. You got a whatchamacallit.'

'A headstone.'

'Yeah. I'm dead too, you know.'

'I know. I'm sorry about that.'

'You didn't stop her.'

'What could I do? By the time I reached her, she'd already . . .'

'Oh, boy.'

'What?'

'Here she comes.'

And there was Rachel walking into the graveyard. She took her time. She was so beautiful, her hair wet and dripping from the rain, and she'd traded in the cleaver for an axe with a long handle and she dragged it beside her and said, 'Teddy, come on. They're mine.'

'I know. I can't give them to you, though.'

'It'll be different this time. I got my head right now.'

Teddy wept. 'I love you so much.'

'And I love you, baby. I do.' She came up and kissed him, really kissed him, her hands on his face and her tongue sliding over his.

'Now give me the girl,' she said.

He handed the girl to her and she held her in one arm and picked up the axe in the other and said, 'I'll be right back. OK?'

'Sure,' Teddy said.

He waved to the girl, knowing she didn't understand. But it was for her own good. You had to make tough decisions when you were an adult, decisions children couldn't possibly understand. But you made them for the children. He kept waving, even though the girl wouldn't wave back as her mother carried her towards the mausoleum. She stared at Teddy, her eyes beyond hope for rescue, resigned to this sacrifice, her mouth still smeared with peanut butter and jelly.

TEDDY SAT UP. He was crying. He felt he'd wrenched himself awake, torn his brain into consciousness just to get out of that dream.

'How are you, Marshal?'

He blinked several times into the darkness. 'Who's there?'

Cawley turned on a small lamp that stood beside his chair in the corner of the room. 'Sorry. Didn't mean to startle you.'

Teddy sat up on the bed. 'How long have I been here?'

Cawley gave him a smile of apology. 'The pills were a little stronger than I thought. You've been out for four hours.'

'Shit.' Teddy rubbed his eyes with the heels of his hands.

'You were having nightmares, Marshal. Serious nightmares.'

'I'm in a mental institution on an island in a hurricane.'

'Touché,' Cawley said. 'I was here a month before I had a decent night's sleep. Who's Dolores?'

Teddy swung his legs off the side of the bed. 'My mouth is dry.'

Cawley nodded, and lifted a glass of water from the table beside him. He handed it to Teddy. 'A side effect, I'm afraid. Here.'

Teddy took the glass and drained it in a few gulps.

'How's the head?'

Teddy remembered why he was in the room in the first place and took a few moments to take stock. Vision clear. No more thumbtacks in his head, just a mild ache in the right side.

'I'm OK,' he said. 'Those were some pills.'

'We aim to please. So who's Dolores? You kept saying her name.'

'My wife,' Teddy said. 'She's dead. And, yes, Doctor, I'm still coming to terms with it. Is that OK?'

'It's fine, Marshal. And I'm sorry for your loss. She died suddenly?'

Teddy looked at him and laughed. 'I'm really not in the mood to be psychoanalysed, Doc.'

Cawley crossed his legs at the ankles and lit a cigarette. 'And I'm not trying to mess with your head, Marshal. Believe it or not. But something happened in that room tonight with Rachel. I'd be negligent in my duties as her therapist if I didn't wonder what kind of demons you're carrying around.'

'I was just playing the part she wanted me to,' Teddy said. 'I'm an officer of the law, Doctor. Whatever you think you saw, you didn't.'

Cawley held up a hand. 'Fine. As you say.' Silent and watchful he sat back and smoked and considered Teddy.

Teddy could hear the storm outside, could feel it pressing against the walls. Finally he said, 'She died in a fire. I miss her like . . . If I was under water, I wouldn't miss oxygen that much.' He raised his eyebrows at Cawley. 'Satisfied?'

Cawley leaned forward and handed Teddy a cigarette and lit it for him. 'I'm good at what I do, Marshal. Ever since I was a boy, I could read people. Better than anyone. I say what I'm about to say meaning no offence, but have you considered that you're suicidal?'

'Well,' Teddy said, 'I'm glad you didn't mean to offend me.'

'But have you considered it?'

'Yeah. It's why I don't drink any more, Doctor. I'd have eaten my gun a long time ago, if I did.'

Cawley nodded. 'At least you're not deluding yourself.'

'Yeah, at least I got that going for me.'

'When you leave here,' Cawley said, 'I can give you some names. Damn good doctors. They could help you.'

Teddy shook his head. 'US marshals don't go to head doctors. Sorry. If it ever leaked, I'd be pensioned out.'

'OK, OK. Fair enough. But if you keep steering your current course, Marshal, I'd say it's not a matter of if. It's a matter of when.'

'You don't know that.'

'Yes. Yes, I do. I specialise in grief trauma and survivor's guilt. I saw you look into Rachel Solando's eyes a few hours ago and I saw a man who wants to die. Your boss, the agent in charge at the field office? He told me you came back from the Ardennes with enough medals to fill a chest. True?'

Teddy shrugged.

'Said you were part of the liberating force at Dachau.'

Another shrug.

'And then your wife is killed? How much violence, Marshal, do you think a man can carry before it breaks him?'

Teddy said, 'Don't know, Doc. Kind of wondering, myself.'

Cawley leaned across and clapped Teddy on the knee. 'Take those names from me before you leave. OK? I'd like to be sitting here five years from now, Marshal, and know you're still in the world.'

Teddy looked down at the hand on his knee. Looked up at Cawley. 'I would too,' he said softly.

8

He met back up with Chuck in the basement of the men's dormitory, where they'd assembled cots for everyone while they rode out the storm. To get here, Teddy had come through a series of underground corridors that connected all the buildings in the compound. He'd been led by an orderly named Ben, a hulking mountain of white flesh, through four locked gates and three manned checkpoints. The corridors were long and dimly lit, and Teddy wasn't all that fond of how similar they were to the corridor in his dream.

He felt embarrassed to see Chuck. He'd never had a migraine attack that severe in public before, and it filled him with shame to remember vomiting on the floor.

But as Chuck called, 'Hey, boss!' from the other side of the room, it surprised Teddy to realise what a relief it was to be reunited with him. He was glad not to be alone.

They shook hands and he remembered what Chuck had said to him in the dream—'I'm never getting off this island'—and Teddy felt a sparrow's ghost pass through the centre of his chest and flap its wings.

'How you doing, boss?' Chuck clapped his shoulder.

Teddy gave him a sheepish grin. 'A little shaky, but all in all, OK.'

Chuck lowered his voice. 'You had me scared, boss. I thought you were having a heart attack or a stroke or something.'

'Just a migraine.'

'Just,' Chuck said. He lowered his voice even further and they walked to the wall on the south side of the room, away from the other men. 'I thought you were faking it at first, you know, like you had some plan to get to the files or something.'

'I wish I was that smart.'

Chuck looked in Teddy's eyes, his own glimmering. 'It got me thinking, though.'

'You didn't.'

'I did. I told Cawley I'd sit with you. And after a while he got a call and he left the office . . .'

'You went after his files?'

Chuck nodded. 'The filing cabinets were locked. But I did get into his desk. Crazy, huh? You can slap my wrist later.'

'Slap your wrist? Give you a medal.'

'No medal. I didn't find much, boss. Just his calendar. Here's the thing, though—yesterday, today, tomorrow and the next day were all blocked off, bordered in black. And he'd written across the four boxes. You know what I mean? Like you'd write "Vacation on Cape Cod". Following me?'

Teddy said, 'Sure. So the words on the calendar didn't say "Vacation on Cape Cod", I presume. What'd they say?'

' "Patient sixty-seven".'

'That's it?'

'That's it.'

'That's enough, though, huh?'

'Oh, yeah. I'd say so.'

HE COULDN'T SLEEP. He listened to the men snore and huff and inhale and exhale, and after a while the noise achieved a kind of comfortable rhythm that reminded Teddy of a muffled hymn.

The outside was muffled too, but Teddy could hear the storm scrabble along the ground and thump against the foundation, and he wished there were windows down here so he could see the flash of it, the weird light it must be painting on the sky. He thought about what Cawley had said to him. *It's not a matter of if. It's a matter of when.*

Was he suicidal? He supposed he was. He couldn't remember a day since Dolores's death when he hadn't thought of joining her, and it sometimes went further than that. Sometimes he felt as if continuing to live was an act of cowardice. What was the point of buying groceries, of filling the Chrysler tank, of shaving, standing in yet another line, reading the paper, eating—alone, always alone—or going to a movie, if none of it brought him closer to her?

He knew he was supposed to move on. Recover. Put it behind him. But to do that, he'd have to find a way to put Dolores on a shelf, let her gather enough dust to soften his memory of her. Mute her image. Until one day she'd be less a person who had lived and more the dream of one . . .

He wished he'd never taken those pills. He was wide awake at three in the morning. Wide awake and hearing her and seeing her . . .

That night he'd met her at the Cocoanut Grove. The band had been playing a big, brassy set and the air was silver with smoke and everyone was dressed to the nines. Teddy was there with Frankie Gordon, another sergeant from Intel, and a few other guys, all of them shipping out in a week, but he dumped Frankie the moment he saw her. He walked down to the dance floor, lost her for a minute in the throng between them, then caught the flash of her violet dress again.

It was a beautiful dress and the colour had been the first thing to catch his eye. But there were a lot of beautiful dresses there that night, too many to count, so it wasn't the dress that held his attention but the way she wore it. Nervously. Self-consciously. She'd never worn a dress like that before. It terrified her.

She'd caught Teddy watching as she fidgeted with the strap. She dropped her eyes, the colour rushing up from her throat, and then looked back up and Teddy held her eyes and smiled and thought, I feel stupid in this get-up too. Willing that thought across the floor. And maybe it worked, because she smiled back, less a flirtatious smile than a grateful one, and Teddy set off through the sweaty siege of dancers. What was he going to say to her? Nice dress? Can I buy you a drink? You have beautiful eyes?

She said, 'Lost?'

His turn to spin. He found himself looking down at her. She was a small woman, no more than five four in heels. Outrageously pretty. Not in a tidy way, like so many of the other women in there with perfect noses and hair and lips. There was something unkempt about her face, eyes maybe a bit too far apart, lips that were so wide they seemed messy on her small face, a chin that was uncertain.

'A bit,' he said.

'Well, what are you looking for?'

He said it before he could think to stop himself: 'You.'

Her eyes widened and he noticed a flaw, a speckle of bronze, in the left iris, and he felt horror sweep through his body as he realised he'd blown it, come off as a Romeo, too smooth, too full of himself.

'Well,' she said, 'at least you didn't have to walk far.'

He felt a goofy grin break across his face. 'No, miss, I guess I didn't.'

'My God,' she said, leaning back to look at him, her martini glass pressed to her upper chest. 'You're as out of place here as I am, aren't you, soldier?'

LEANING IN THROUGH the cab window as she sat in the back with her friend, Teddy said, 'Dolores.'

'Edward.'

He laughed. 'No one calls me Edward but my mother.'

'Teddy, then.'

He loved hearing her say the word.

'Teddy,' she said again, trying it out.

'Hey. What's your last name?' he said.

'Chanal.'

Teddy cocked an eyebrow at that.

She said, 'I know. It doesn't go with the rest of me at all. Sounds so highfalutin.'

'Can I call you?'

'Winter Hill six-four-three-four-six,' she said.

He'd stood on the sidewalk as the cab pulled away, and the memory of her face just an inch from his—on the dance floor—nearly short-circuited his brain, almost drove her name and number right out of there.

He thought: So this is what it feels like to love. No logic to it—he barely knew her. But there it was just the same. He'd just met the woman he'd known, somehow, since before he was born. The measure of every dream he'd never dared indulge.

Dolores.

Everything he'd ever needed, and now it had a name.

TEDDY TURNED OVER on his cot and reached down to the floor, searched around until he found his notebook and a box of matches. He lit a first match, held it above the page he'd scribbled on in the storm. He went through four matches before he'd ascribed the appropriate letters to the numbers:

18–1–4–9–5–4–19–1–12–4–23–14–5
R–A–D–I–E–D–S–A–L–D–W–N–E

It didn't take long, though, to unscramble the code. Another two matches, and Teddy was staring at the name as the flame winnowed its way down towards his fingers: Andrew Laeddis.

As the match grew hotter, he looked over at Chuck, sleeping two cots over, and he hoped his career wouldn't suffer. It shouldn't. Teddy would take all the blame. Chuck should be fine. He had that aura about him—no matter what happened, he would emerge unscathed.

Teddy looked back at the page, got one last glimpse before the match blew itself out.

Going to find you today, Andrew. If I don't owe Dolores my life, I owe her that much, at least. Going to find you.

Going to kill you dead.

DAY THREE—PATIENT SIXTY-SEVEN

9

The two homes outside the wall—the warden's and Cawley's—took direct hits. Half of Cawley's roof was gone, the tiles flung all over the hospital grounds like a lesson in humility. A tree had gone through the warden's living-room window, roots and all.

The compound was strewn with tree branches and was under an inch and a half of water. The foundation of the main hospital building looked like someone had taken a jackhammer to it, and Ward A had lost four windows. Two of the staff cottages had been turned into sticks, and a few others lay on their sides. The staff dormitories had lost several windows and suffered some water damage between them. All over the island, Teddy could see trees with their tops snapped off, the naked wood pointing up like spears.

Teddy and Chuck watched McPherson and a guard jump in a Jeep and roar out through the gates and up the incline towards Ward C.

Cawley walked into the compound, paused to pick up a piece of his roof and stare at it before dropping it back to the watery ground. His gaze swept past Teddy and Chuck twice before he recognised them in their white orderly clothing and their black slickers and black ranger's hats. He seemed about to approach them when a doctor with a stethoscope round his neck ran up to him.

'Number two's gone. We can't get it back up. We've got those two criticals. They'll die, John.'

'Where's Harry?'

'Harry's working on the back-up, but he can't get a charge.'

'All right. Let's get in there.'

They strode off into the hospital, and Teddy said, 'Their back-up generator failed?'

Chuck said, 'These things will happen in a hurricane, apparently.'

'You think the whole electrical system is fried?'

Chuck said, 'Good possibility.'

'That would mean all electronic security. Fences. Gates. Doors.'

'Oh, dear God, help us.' Chuck turned to Teddy. 'You want to go into that fort, don't you?'

Teddy tilted his face into the soft rain. 'Perfect day for it.'

The warden made an appearance then, driving into the compound with three guards in a Jeep. The warden noticed Chuck and Teddy standing idly in the yard, and it seemed to annoy him. He had taken them for orderlies, Teddy realised, just as Cawley had. He drove past, though, his head snapping forwards, on to more important things.

'Probably should get going, then,' Chuck said. 'This won't hold for ever.'

They started walking towards the gate.

Chuck said, 'I'd whistle, but my mouth's too dry.'

The guard at the gate had a little boy's face and cruel eyes. He said, 'All orderlies are to report to the admin office. You guys are on cleanup detail.'

Teddy flashed his badge at the guard. 'Our clothes are still in the laundry.'

The guard glanced at the badge, then looked at Chuck, waiting.

Chuck sighed and removed his wallet, flipped it open under the guard's nose.

The guard said, 'What's your business outside the wall? The missing patient was found.'

Any explanation, Teddy decided, would make them look weak and place the balance of power firmly in this little shit's hand. Teddy had met little shits like this in his company during the war, and he had learned that you couldn't teach them anything. The only thing they respected was power.

Teddy stepped up to the guy, searched his face, a small smile tugging the corner of his lips, waiting until the guy met his eyes and held them. 'We're going on a stroll,' he said.

'You don't have authorisation.'

'Yes, we do.' Teddy stepped closer so the boy had to tilt his eyes up. 'We're federal marshals on a federal facility. That's the authorisation of God himself. We could choose to shoot you, boy, and there's not a court in the country that would even hear the case. So open the gate.'

The kid tried to hold Teddy's stare. He swallowed.

Teddy said, 'I repeat: Open that—'

'OK.'

'I didn't hear you,' Teddy said.

'Yes, sir.'

The kid turned his key in the lock and swung back the gate, and Teddy walked through without a look back.

They turned right and walked along the outside of the wall for a bit before Chuck said, 'You were a ballbuster overseas, weren't you?'

'I was a battalion sergeant with a bunch of kids under my command. You don't "nice" your way to respect, you scare it into 'em.'

'Yes, Sergeant. Damn straight.' Chuck snapped a salute at him. 'Even with the power out, you recall that this is a fort we're trying to infiltrate, don't you?'

'It did not slip my mind, no.'

'Any ideas?'

'Nope.'

'You think they have a moat? That'd be something.'

'Maybe some vats of hot oil up on the battlements.'

'Archers,' Chuck said. 'If they have archers, Teddy . . .'

'And us without our chain mail.'

They stepped over a fallen tree, the ground soggy and slick with wet leaves. Through the shredded vegetation ahead of them, they could see the fort's great grey walls, and the tracks from the Jeeps that had been going back and forth all morning.

'That guard had a point,' Chuck said. 'Now that Rachel's been found, our authority here is pretty much non-existent.'

Teddy felt exhausted, hazy. Four hours of drug-induced, nightmare-ridden sleep was all he'd had last night. The drizzle pattered the top of his hat, collected in the brim. His brain buzzed, almost imperceptibly, but constantly. If the ferry came today—and he doubted it would—one part of him wanted to just hop on it and go. Get off this rock. But without something to show for this trip, whether that was evidence for Senator Hurly or Laeddis's death certificate, he'd be returning a failure. Still borderline-suicidal, and with the added weight on his conscience that he'd done nothing.

He flipped open his notebook. 'Those rock piles Rachel left us yesterday. This is the broken code.' He handed the notebook to Chuck.

Chuck cupped a hand around it, close to his chest. 'So, he's here. Patient sixty-seven, you think?'

'Be my guess.' Teddy stopped in the middle of a muddy slope. 'You can go back, Chuck. You don't have to be involved in this.'

Chuck looked up at him. 'We're marshals, Teddy. What do marshals always do?'

Teddy smiled. 'We go through the doors.'

'First,' Chuck said. 'We go through the doors first. We don't wait for some city doughnut cops to back us up if time's a-wasting.'

He handed the notebook back to Teddy, and they continued towards the fort.

One look at it up close, nothing separating them but a stand of trees and a short field, and Chuck said what Teddy was thinking: 'We're fucked.'

The Cyclone fence that normally surrounded the fort had been blown out of the ground in sections, and the rest sagged in various states of uselessness. Armed guards roamed the perimeter, several of them doing steady circuits in Jeeps. A contingent of orderlies was picking up the debris around the exterior and another group had set to work on a thick tree that had downed itself against the wall. There was no moat, but there was only one door, a small red one of dimpled iron set in the centre of the wall. Guards stood sentry up on the battlements, rifles held to their shoulders and chests.

'There's got to be a duct of some sort, right?' Chuck said. 'Maybe to dump water or waste out into the sea? We could go in that way.'

Teddy shook his head. 'We're just going to walk right in.'

Chuck frowned at him. 'Oh, like Rachel walked out of Ward B? I get it. Take some of that invisible powder she had. Good idea.'

Teddy touched the collar of his rain slicker. 'We're not dressed like marshals, Chuck. Know what I mean?'

Chuck looked back at the orderlies working the perimeter and watched one come out through the iron door with a cup of coffee in his hand. 'Amen,' he said. 'Amen, brother.'

'Where's the mop detail?' Chuck said to a guard lounging against the wall by the door.

He jerked his thumb and opened the door and they passed through into the receiving hall.

'I don't want to appear ungrateful,' Chuck whispered, 'but that was too easy.'

Teddy said, 'Sometimes you get lucky.'

The first thing that hit Teddy was the smells. An aroma of industrial-strength disinfectant doing its level best to disguise the reek of vomit, faeces, sweat and urine.

Then the noise billowed down from the upper floors: the rumble of running feet, shouts echoing off thick walls, sudden high-pitched yelps and the pervasive yammering of several voices talking at once.

Someone shouted, 'You can't do that! You hear me? You can't. Get away . . .' And the words trailed off.

A guard sat at a card table at the base of the staircase, looking at them, smiling. 'First time, huh?'

Teddy looked over at him. 'Yeah. Heard stories, but . . .'

'You get used to it,' the guard said. 'You get used to anything.'

'Ain't that the truth.'

He said, 'If you guys are working inside, you can hang your coats and hats in the room behind me.'

'They told us we're on the roof,' Teddy said. 'Something about a tree up there.'

The guard pointed. 'Just follow those stairs. We got most of the inmates locked down to their beds now, but a few are running free. You see one, you shout, all right? Whatever you do, don't try to restrain him yourself. Clear?'

'Clear.'

They climbed the stairs, and at the first landing they paused. Facing them was a gate, and through it they could see a great, empty hall with an arched ceiling of hammered copper, a dark floor polished to mirror gloss. The gate had been left ajar. Teddy felt mice scurry along his ribs as he stepped into the room because it reminded him of the room in his dream, the one where Rachel had slaughtered her children.

Chuck clapped a hand on his shoulder. 'I repeat,' he whispered, 'this is too easy. Where's the guard? Why isn't the gate locked?'

Teddy could see Rachel, wild-haired and shrieking, as she ran through the room with a cleaver. He felt beads of sweat pop out along his neck. 'I don't know,' he said.

Chuck leaned in and hissed in his ear. 'This is a set-up, boss.'

Teddy began to cross the room. His head hurt from the lack of sleep. From the rain. From the shouting and running feet above him. They flashed before his eyes: two boys and a little girl, holding hands, looking over their shoulders, trembling.

'We need to go right back out, Teddy. We need to leave. This is bad. You can feel it, I can feel it.'

They reached the end of the hall and were met with a wide stone landing and a stairwell that curved down steeply into darkness, another that rose towards shouting and the snaps of metal and chains.

A voice came from the top of the stairwell: 'Somebody give me a hand here!'

Teddy and Chuck looked up and saw two men rolling down the stairs in a ball. One wore guard blues, the other patient whites, and they slammed to a stop at the curve in the staircase, on the widest step. The patient got a hand free and dug it into the guard's face just below his left eye. The guard screamed and wrenched his head back.

Teddy and Chuck ran up the steps. The patient's hand plunged forward again, but Chuck grabbed it at the wrist.

The guard wiped at his eye and all four of them took breaths. Teddy saw the guy under him rear up with his mouth wide open, and he said, 'Chuck, watch it,' and slammed the heel of his hand into the patient's forehead before he could take a bite out of Chuck's wrist.

'You got to get off him,' he said to the guard. 'Come on. Get off.'

The guard freed himself of the patient's legs and scrambled back up two steps. Teddy clamped down hard on the patient's shoulder, pinning it to the stone. As he looked over his shoulder at Chuck, a baton sliced between them, cutting the air with a hiss before it broke the patient's nose.

Teddy felt the body underneath him go slack and Chuck said, 'Jesus Christ!'

The guard swung again and Teddy turned and blocked the man's arm with his elbow. 'Hey! Hey! He's out cold. Hey!'

The guard cocked the baton again.

Chuck said, 'Look at me! Look at me!'

The guard's eyes jerked to Chuck's face.

'You stand down, you hear me? You stand *down.* This patient is subdued.' Chuck let go of the patient's wrist and his arm flopped to his chest. He sat back against the wall, kept his stare locked on the guard. 'Do you hear me?' he said softly.

The guard lowered the baton. 'He tore my face open.'

Teddy leaned in, took a look at the wound. He'd seen a lot worse; the kid wouldn't die from it or anything. He said, 'You'll be fine. Couple of stitches.'

Above them they could hear the crash of bodies and furniture.

'You got a riot on your hands?' Chuck said.

'Close to.'

Chuck pulled a handkerchief from his pocket, handed it to the kid. The kid nodded his thanks and pressed it to his face.

Chuck lifted the patient's wrist again, and Teddy watched him feel for a pulse. He dropped the wrist and pushed back one of the man's eyelids. He looked at Teddy. 'He'll live.'

'Let's get him up,' Teddy said.

They slung the patient's arms round their shoulders and followed the guard up the steps. When they reached the top, the guard turned.

'You're the marshals,' he said.

'What's that?'

He nodded. 'You are. I saw you when you arrived.' He gave Chuck a small smile. 'That scar on your face, you know?'

Chuck sighed.

'What are you doing in here?' the kid said.

'Saving your face,' Teddy said.

The kid took the handkerchief from his wound, looked at it, and pressed it back there again. 'Guy you're holding there?' he said. 'Paul Vingis. Killed his brother's wife and two daughters while the brother was serving in Korea. Left them to rot in a basement.'

Teddy resisted the urge to let Vingis drop back down the stairs.

'Truth is,' the kid said, and cleared his throat. 'Truth is, he had me.'

'What's your name?'

'Baker. Fred Baker.'

Teddy shook his hand. 'Look, Fred? Hey, we're glad we could help.'

Baker looked at the spots of blood on his shoes. 'Again: what are you doing here?'

'Taking a look around,' Teddy said. 'A couple of minutes, and we'll be gone.'

The kid took some time considering that, and Teddy could feel the previous two years of his life—losing Dolores, homing in on Laeddis, finding out about this place, stumbling across George Noyce and his stories of drug and lobotomy experiments, making contact with Senator Hurly, waiting for the right moment to cross the harbour—all of it hanging in the balance of this kid's pause.

'I've worked a few rough places,' Baker said. 'Jails, a max prison, a hospital for the criminally insane. But this place?' He gave each of them a long, level gaze. 'They wrote their own playbook here.'

He stared at Teddy, and Teddy tried to read the answer in the kid's eyes, but the stare was of the thousand-yards variety, flat, ancient.

'A couple of minutes?' Baker nodded to himself. 'All right. You take your couple minutes and then get out, OK?'

'Sure,' Chuck said.

'And, hey.' Baker gave them a small smile as he reached for the door. 'Try not to die in those few minutes, OK? I'd appreciate that.'

THEY WENT THROUGH the door and entered a granite cell block that ran the length of the fort under archways ten feet wide and fourteen feet tall. Tall windows at either end of the floor provided the only light, and the ceiling dripped water.

Baker said, 'Our main generator blew at around four this morning. The locks on the cells are controlled electronically. Great idea, huh? So all the cells opened at four. Luckily we can still work those locks manually, so we got most of the patients back inside and locked them in, but we think some prick got hold of a key.'

He led them to the third cell on the right and opened it. 'Toss him in there.'

He clicked on a flashlight and shone the beam inside and they laid Vingis on the bed and he moaned.

'I need to get some back-up,' Baker said as they left the cell. 'The basement's where we keep the guys we don't even feed unless there's six guards in the room. If they get out . . .'

'You get medical assistance for him first,' Chuck said.

Baker looked in through the bars at Vingis. 'Yeah. All right. I'll find a doctor. And you two? In and out in record time, right?'

'Right.'

Baker locked the cell door, then jogged down the cell block, side-stepping three guards dragging a bearded giant towards his cell.

'What do you think?' Teddy said. His eyes were beginning to adjust to the pewter light in the main room, but the cells remained black.

'There has to be a set of files here somewhere,' Chuck said. 'If only for reference purposes. You look for Laeddis, I look for files?'

'Where do you figure those files are?'

'By the sounds of it, it gets less dangerous the higher you go. I figure their admin has gotta be up.'

'OK. Where and when do we meet?'

'Fifteen minutes?'

Some of the men moaned in their cells, moans so deep and abandoned they could have come from a battlefield.

Teddy nodded. 'Fifteen sounds right. Meet back in that big hall?'

'Sure.' They shook hands and Chuck's was damp. 'You watch your ass, Teddy.'

A patient banged through the door behind them and ran past, barefoot, into the ward. He ran like he was training for a prize fight—fluid strides working in tandem with shadow-boxing arms.

'See what I can do.' Teddy gave Chuck a smile.

Chuck walked to the door, and as he opened it two orderlies came through from the stairs. Chuck turned the corner and disappeared.

One of the orderlies said to Teddy, 'You see the Great White Hope come through here?'

Teddy looked through the archway, saw the patient dancing in place on his heels, punching the air with combinations.

He pointed and the three of them fell into step.

'He was a boxer?' Teddy said.

The guy on his left, a tall, older black guy, said, 'Oh, you come up from the vacation wards, huh? Yeah, well, Willy there, he think he training for a bout at Madison Square with Joe Louis.'

They were nearing the guy, and Teddy watched his fists shred the air. 'It's going to take more than three of us,' he said.

The older orderly chuckled. 'Won't take but one. I'm his manager. You didn't know?' He called out, 'Yo, Willy. Gotta get you a massage, my man. Ain't but an hour till the fight.'

'Don't want no massage.' Willy started jabbing the air.

'Can't have my meal ticket cramping up on me in the big fight,' the orderly said. 'Training room's right over here.' The orderly swept his arm out to the left with a flourish.

Willy walked towards the cell. 'Just don't touch me. I don't like to be touched before a fight. You know that.'

'Oh, I know, killer.' He opened up the cell. 'Come on now.'

Teddy and the other orderly kept walking, the orderly holding out a brown hand. 'I'm Al.'

Teddy shook the hand. 'Teddy, Al. Nice to meet you.'

'Why you all got up for the outside, Teddy?'

Teddy looked at his slicker. 'Roof detail. Saw a patient on the stairs, though, and chased him in here.'

Al said, 'You see your guy yet?'

Teddy shook his head. 'No, I—'

'Aww, shit,' Al said. 'I see mine.'

He was coming right at them, soaking wet, and Teddy saw the guards with a hose behind him, giving chase. A small guy with red hair, a face like a swarm of bees, covered in blackheads, red eyes that matched his hair. He broke right at the last second, and slid on his knees, rolled under Al's arms, and then scrambled up.

Al broke into a run after him, then the guards rushed past Teddy, batons held over their heads, as they gave chase. Teddy had started to step into the chase, from instinct, when he heard the whisper.

'Laeddis.'

He stood in the centre of the room, waiting to hear it again. Nothing. The collective moaning, momentarily stopped by the pursuit of the little redhead, began to well up again.

'Laed. Dis.'

He turned and faced the three cells to his right. All dark. Teddy waited, wondering if the speaker could be Laeddis himself.

'You were supposed to save me.'

It seemed to come from the one in the centre. Not Laeddis's voice. Definitely not. But one that was familiar just the same.

Teddy approached the bars. He fished in his pockets, found a box of matches, pulled it out. He struck the match and the flame flared high over his finger. He held it to the bars and stared in.

The man sitting on the bed in the left corner had his head down, his face pressed between his knees, his arms wrapped round his calves. He was bald up the middle, pepper-and-salt on the sides. He was naked except for a pair of white boxer shorts.

Teddy licked his lips. He stared over the match and said, 'Hello?'

'You failed me. You told me I'd be free of this place. But they took me back. They say I'm home now.'

'Could you raise your head? I can't see your face.'

'They say I'll never leave.'

'Let me see your face.'

'You don't recognise my voice? All the conversations we had? I used to like to think it became more than strictly professional. That we became friends of a sort.'

Teddy stared at the swath of bald skin. 'I'm telling you, buddy—'

'Telling me what? What can you tell me? More lies, that's what.'

'I don't—' The flame burned the tip of his index finger and the side of his thumb and he dropped the match.

The cell vanished. He could hear the bed springs wheeze, a coarse whisper of fabric against stone. He heard the name again: 'Laeddis.'

He struck another match.

The bed was empty. He moved his hand to the right and saw the man standing in the corner, his back to him.

'This was never about the truth. Was it?'

'What?' Teddy said.

'This is about you. And Laeddis. This is all it's ever been about. I was incidental. I was a way in.'

The man spun round. His face was a swollen mess of purple, black and cherry red, the nose broken and covered in white tape.

'Jesus,' Teddy said. 'Who did this?'

'You did this.'

'How the hell could I have—?'

George Noyce stepped closer to the bars, his lips black with sutures. 'All your talk and I'm back in here. Because of you.'

Teddy remembered the last time he'd seen Noyce in the visiting room at the prison in Dedham. He'd looked healthy, vibrant.

'Look at me,' George Noyce said. 'Don't look away. You never wanted to expose this place.'

'George,' Teddy said, keeping his voice low, calm, 'that's not true. I've spent the last year of my life planning for this. Now. Right here.'

'Fuck you!' Teddy felt the scream hit his face. 'You spent the last year of your life planning to kill. That's all. Kill Laeddis. And look where it got *me.* Back here. I can't take this horror house. Not again.'

'George, listen. How did they get to you? There have to be transfer orders. Psychiatric consultations. Files, paperwork.'

Noyce laughed. 'You want to hear a secret? You know what dear Dr Cawley's specialty is?'

Teddy ran a palm over his forehead. 'Survivor guilt, grief trauma.'

'Noooo.' The word left George's mouth in a dry chuckle. 'Violence. In the male of the species, specifically. He's doing a study.'

'No. That's Naehring.'

'Cawley,' Noyce said. 'All Cawley. They get the most violent patients and felons shipped here from all over the country. Why do you think the patient base here is so small? And do you honestly think that anyone is going to look closely at the transfer paperwork of someone with a history of psychological issues and violence?'

Teddy fired up another match.

'I got away once,' Noyce said. 'Not twice. Never twice.'

Teddy said, 'Calm down, calm down. How did they get to you?'

'They *knew.* Don't you get it? Everything you were up to. Your whole plan. This is a game. A handsomely mounted stage play. All this'—his arm swept the air above him—'is for you.'

Teddy smiled. 'They threw in a hurricane just for me, huh? Neat trick. I don't think so. Let's relax with the paranoia. OK?'

'Been alone much?' Noyce said, staring through the bars at him. You *ever* been alone since this whole thing started?'

Teddy said, 'All the time.'

Noyce cocked one eyebrow. '*Completely* alone?'

'Well, with my partner.'

'And who's your partner?'

'His name's Chuck. He's—'

'Let me guess. You've never worked with him before, have you?'

Teddy felt the cell block around him. The bones in his upper arms were cold. For a moment he could not speak.

Then he said, 'He's a US marshal from the Seattle—'

'You've *never worked with him before*, have you?'

Teddy said, 'That's irrelevant. I know this guy. I trust him.'

'Based on what?'

There was no simple answer for that. How did anyone know how faith developed? Teddy had known men he'd trust with his life on a battlefield and yet never with his wallet once they were off it. He'd known men he'd trust with his wallet *and* his wife but never to watch his back in a fight. Chuck could have refused to accompany him, could have stayed back in the men's dormitory, waiting for word of the ferry. Their job was done—Rachel Solando had been found—and yet he was here, following Teddy on his search for Laeddis, his quest to prove that Ashecliffe made a mockery of the Hippocratic oath.

'I trust him,' Teddy repeated. 'That's the only way I can put it.'

Noyce looked at him sadly through the steel bars. 'Then they've already won.'

Teddy pushed open the matchbox and found the last match.

'Please,' Noyce whispered, and Teddy knew he was weeping. 'Please don't let me die here.'

'You won't die here.'

'They're going to take me to the lighthouse. You know that. They're going to cut out my brain.'

Teddy lit the match, saw Noyce in the sudden flare grip the bars and shake them, the tears falling down his swollen face.

'They're not going to—'

'You go there. See for yourself what they do there.' Noyce pressed his bare scalp to the bars and wept silently.

'George, look at me.'

Noyce raised his head.

'I'm going to get you out of here. Don't do anything you can't come back from. You hear me? I'll come back for you.'

George Noyce smiled and shook his head very slowly. 'You can't kill Laeddis and expose the truth at the same time. You have to make a choice. You understand that, don't you?'

'Where is he?'

'Tell me you understand.'

'I understand. I won't kill anyone. George? I won't.'

And looking at Noyce, he felt this to be true. If that's what it took to get this poor wreck home, then he would bury his vendetta. Save it for another time. And hope Dolores understood.

'I won't kill anyone,' he repeated.

'She's dead. Let her go.' He pressed his smiling, weeping face between the bars and held Teddy with his soft swollen eyes.

Teddy could see her sitting in that dark orange light a city gets on summer nights just after sundown, looking up as he pulled to the kerb and the kids returned to their ball game in the middle of the street, and the laundry flapped overhead, and she watched him approach with her chin propped on the heel of her hand, and he'd brought flowers for once, and she was so simply his love, his girl.

Let her go, Noyce had said.

'I can't,' Teddy said, and the words came out cracked and too high and he could feel screams welling in the centre of his chest.

Noyce leaned back as far as he could and still maintain his grip on the bars. 'Then you'll never leave this island,' he said.

Teddy said nothing.

Noyce sighed as if what he was about to say bored him to the point of falling asleep on his feet. 'He was transferred out of Ward C. If he's not in Ward A, there's only one place he can be.'

He waited until Teddy got it. 'The lighthouse?'

Noyce nodded, and the final match went out.

For a full minute Teddy stood there, staring into the dark, and then he heard the bed springs again as Noyce lay down.

He turned to go.

'Hey.'

He stopped, his back to the bars, and waited.

'God help you.'

10

Walking back through the cell block, he could hear Noyce asking if he'd ever been alone. He thought back through his three days here, tried to find a single instance in which he'd been entirely alone. Even using the bathroom, he was using staff facilities, a man at the next stall or waiting just outside the door. But, no, he and Chuck had gone out on the island alone several times . . .

He and Chuck. What exactly did he know about Chuck? He pictured his face for a moment, could see him on the ferry, looking off at the ocean . . . Great guy, instantly likable, had a natural ease with people, the kind of guy you wanted to be around. From Seattle. Recently transferred. Hell of a poker player. Hated his father—the one thing that didn't seem to jibe with the rest of him. There was something else off, too, something buried in the back of Teddy's brain . . . What was it?

Awkward. That was the word. But, no, there was nothing remotely awkward about the man. But hadn't there been one blip in time when Chuck had been clumsy in his movements? Yes. Teddy was sure of it. But he couldn't remember the specifics . . . And, anyway, he trusted Chuck. Chuck had broken into Cawley's desk, after all.

Did you see him do it?

Chuck, right now, was risking his career to get to Laeddis's file.

How do you know?

He'd reached the door now and he turned the knob. There were no orderlies or guards waiting on the landing. He was completely alone. He let the door close behind him and turned to go down the stairs and saw Chuck standing at the curve where they'd run into Baker and Vingis. His partner looked up at him as he came down the steps, and turned and started moving fast.

'I thought we were meeting in the hall.'

'They're here,' Chuck said as Teddy caught up to him and they turned into the vast hall.

'Who?'

'The warden and Cawley. Just keep moving. We gotta fly.'

'They see you?'

'I don't know. I was coming out of the records room two floors up. I see them down the other end of the hall. Cawley's head turns and I go right through the exit door into the stairwell.'

'So, they probably didn't give it a second thought.'

'An orderly in a rain slicker and a ranger's hat coming out of the records room on the admin floor? Oh, I'm sure we're fine.'

The lights went on above them in a series of liquid cracks that were followed by an explosion of yells and catcalls. Alarm bells pealed throughout the stone floors and walls.

'Power's back. How nice,' Chuck said, and turned into the stairwell.

They went down the stairs as four guards came running up, and they shouldered the wall to let them pass.

The guard at the card table was still there, on the phone, looking up with glazed eyes as they descended, and then his eyes cleared and he said, 'Wait a sec,' into the phone, and then to them as they cleared the last step, 'Hey, you two, hold on a minute.'

A crowd was milling around in the foyer—orderlies, guards, two manacled patients—and Teddy and Chuck moved right into them.

And the guard said, 'Hey! You two! Hey!'

They didn't break stride and Teddy saw faces looking around, wondering who the guard was calling to.

'I said, "Hold up!"' he called again.

Teddy hit the door chest high with his hand. It didn't budge.

'Hey! I need to talk to you!'

Teddy turned the knob and pushed the door open and two guards were coming up the steps. Teddy pivoted and held the door open as Chuck passed through and the guard on the left gave him a nod of thanks. He and his partner passed through and Teddy let go of the door and they walked down the steps.

He saw a group of identically dressed men to their left, standing around smoking cigarettes and drinking coffee in the faint drizzle. He and Chuck crossed the distance to them, waiting for the sound of the door opening behind them, a fresh round of calls.

'You find Laeddis?' Chuck said.

'Nope. Found Noyce, though.'

'What?'

'You heard me.'

They nodded at the group as they reached them. Smiles and waves and Teddy got a light off one of the guys and then they kept walking along the wall, kept walking as what could have been shouts in their direction hit the air, kept walking as they looked at the rifle shafts peeking over the battlements fifty feet above them.

They reached the end of the wall and turned left into a soggy field and saw that sections of the fence had been replaced there, groups of men filling the post holes with liquid cement, and they could see it stretching all the way round. There was no way out.

They turned back.

'We're going to gut it out, aren't we, boss?'

'Damn straight.'

The same guard was waiting for them, and Teddy said to Chuck, 'Let's not even slow down.'

'Deal.'

Teddy tried to read the guy's face. It was dead flat and he wondered whether it was because he was steeling himself for conflict.

Teddy waved as he passed, and the guard said, 'They got trucks to take you guys back now. You want to wait, one just left about five minutes ago. Should be back any time.'

'Nah. Need the exercise.'

For a moment, something flickered in the guard's face. Maybe it was just Teddy's imagination or maybe the guard knew a whiff of bullshit when he smelt it.

'Take care now.' Teddy turned his back, and he and Chuck walked towards the trees and he could feel the guard watching, could feel the whole fort watching. But no one shouted, no one fired a warning shot, and they vanished into the stand of thick trunks and leaves.

'Jesus,' Chuck said.

Teddy sat down on a boulder and felt the sweat saturating his body. He felt exhilarated. This was, outside of love, the greatest feeling in the world. To have escaped. He looked at Chuck and held his eyes and they both laughed.

'I turned that corner and saw that fence back in place,' Chuck said, 'and oh *shit*, Teddy, I thought that was it.'

Teddy lay back against the rock, feeling free in a way he'd only felt as a child. He watched the sky begin to appear behind smoky clouds and he felt the air on his skin. He wanted to close his eyes and wake up back on the other side of the harbour, in Boston, in his bed.

He almost nodded off, and that reminded him of how tired he was. He sat up and fished a cigarette from his shirt pocket and bummed a light off Chuck. 'We have to assume that they'll find out we were inside. That's if they don't know already.'

Chuck nodded. 'Baker, for sure, will fold under questioning.'

The foghorn of Boston Light moaned across the harbour, a sound Teddy had heard every night of his childhood in Hull. The loneliest sound he knew.

'Noyce,' Chuck said. 'He's really here.'

'Yeah.'

Chuck said, 'For Christ's sake, Teddy, how'd he get here?'

And Teddy told him about Noyce, about the beating he'd taken, his fear, his weeping. He told Chuck everything except what Noyce had suggested about Chuck. And Chuck listened, watching Teddy the way a child watches a camp counsellor round the fire as the late-night boogieman story unfolds.

And what was all this, Teddy was beginning to wonder, if not that?

Afterwards Chuck said, 'You believe him? After all, he could have had a psychological breakdown. I mean, an actual one. This could all be legitimate. He cracks up in prison and they say, "Hey, this guy was once a patient at Ashecliffe. Let's send him back."'

'It's possible,' Teddy said. 'But the last time I saw him, he looked pretty damn sane to me.'

'And what about the lighthouse?' Chuck said. 'You believe there's a bunch of mad scientists in there, implanting antennas into Laeddis's skull as we speak?'

'I don't think it's just a sewage treatment facility.'

Chuck nodded. 'But it's all a bit Grand Guignol, isn't it?'

Teddy frowned. 'Gron-gee-what?'

'Grand Guignol,' Chuck said. 'It's French. Forgive me. Horrific, in a fairy-tale, *boo-ga-boo-ga-boo-ga* way.'

Teddy watched Chuck trying to smile his way through it, probably thinking of a way to change the subject.

Teddy said, 'You study a lot of French growing up in Portland?'

'Seattle.'

'Right. Forgive *me*.'

'I like the theatre, OK?' Chuck said. 'It's a theatrical term.'

'You know, I knew a guy worked in the Seattle office,' Teddy said. 'You probably knew him too.'

'Probably,' Chuck said, patting his pockets, distracted. 'You want to see what I got from the Laeddis file?'

'His name was Joe. Joe . . .' Teddy snapped his fingers, looked at Chuck. 'Help me out here. Joe, um, Joe . . .'

'There's a lot of Joes,' Chuck said, reaching for his back pocket.

'I thought it was a small office.'

'Here it is.' Chuck's hand jerked up from his back pocket and his hand was empty.

Teddy could see the folded square of paper that had slipped from his grasp still sticking out of the pocket.

'Joe Fairfield,' Teddy said, thinking back at the way Chuck's hand had jerked out of that pocket. Awkwardly. 'You know him?'

Chuck reached back again. 'Name doesn't ring a bell.'

'Or maybe it was Portland. I get them mixed up.'

Chuck pulled the paper free and Teddy could see him the day of their arrival handing over his gun to the guard in a fumble of motion, having trouble with the holster snap. Not something your average marshal had trouble with. Kind of thing, in fact, that got you killed on the job.

Chuck held out the piece of paper. 'It's his intake form. Laeddis's. That and his medical records were all I could find. No incident reports, no session notes, no picture. It was weird.'

'Weird,' Teddy said. 'Sure.'

Chuck's hand was still extended, the piece of folded paper drooping off his fingers. 'Take it,' he said.

'Nah,' Teddy said. 'I'll look at it later.'

He looked at his partner. He let the silence grow.

'What?' Chuck said finally. 'I don't know who Joe is, so now you're looking at me funny?'

'I'm not looking at you funny, Chuck. Like I said, I get Portland and Seattle mixed up a lot. Let's keep walking.'

Teddy stood. Chuck sat there for a few seconds, looking at the piece of paper still dangling from his hand.

The foghorn sounded again.

Chuck stood and returned the piece of paper to his back pocket. He said, 'OK. Fine. By all means, lead the way.'

Teddy started walking east through the woods.

'Where you going?' Chuck said. 'Ashecliffe's the other way.'

Teddy looked back at him. 'I'm not going to Ashecliffe.'

Chuck looked annoyed. 'Then where are we going, Teddy?'

Teddy smiled. 'The lighthouse.'

'WHERE ARE WE?' Chuck said.

'Lost.'

They'd come out of the woods and instead of facing the lighthouse, they'd somehow managed to move well north of it. Teddy had known they'd be off course by a bit, because they'd been forced off the path by a number of downed trees, but judging by his latest calculations, they'd meandered their way almost as far as the cemetery.

He could see the lighthouse peeking out from behind some trees on a long rise, but directly beyond the patch of field where they stood was a long tidal marsh, and beyond that, jagged black rocks formed a natural barrier to the tree-covered slope. They would have to go back through the woods and hope to find the place where they'd taken the wrong turn. He said as much to Chuck.

Chuck used a stick to swipe at his trouser legs, free them of burs. 'Or we could loop around, come at it from the east. That's got to be the cemetery over that hill there. We could work our way around?'

'Better than what we just came through.'

'Oh, you didn't like that?' Chuck ran a palm across the back of his neck. 'Me, I love mosquitoes. Fact, I think I have one or two spots left on my face that they didn't get to.'

It was the first conversation they'd had in over an hour, and Teddy could feel both of them trying to reach past the bubble of tension that had grown between them.

But the moment passed when Teddy remained silent too long, and Chuck set off along the edge of the field, moving more or less northwest towards the shore.

Teddy watched Chuck's back as they walked some more. His partner, he'd told Noyce. He trusted him, he said. But why? Because he'd had to. Because no man could be expected to go up against this alone. If he disappeared, if he never returned from this island, Senator Hurly was a good friend to have. No question. His enquiries would be heard. But in the current political climate, would the voice of a relatively unknown Democrat be loud enough? The marshals would certainly send men. But the question was one of time. Would they get there before Ashecliffe and its doctors had altered Teddy irreparably, turned him into Noyce? Or worse.

Teddy hoped so, because the more he found himself looking at Chuck's back, the more certain he grew that he was now alone in this. Completely alone.

'MORE ROCKS,' Chuck said. 'Jesus, boss.'

They were on a narrow promontory with the sea a straight drop down on their right and an acre of scrub plain below them to the left.

The rock piles were spaced out on the scrub plain. Nine of them in three rows of three.

Teddy said, 'What, we ignore it?'

Chuck raised a hand to the sky. 'We're going to lose the sun in a couple of hours. We're not at the lighthouse, in case you haven't noticed. We're not even sure we can get there from here. And you want to climb all the way down there and look at rocks.'

'Hey, if it's code . . .'

'What does it matter now? We have proof that Laeddis is here. You saw Noyce. All we have to do is head back home with that information, that proof. And we've done your job.'

He was right. Teddy knew that.

Right, however, only if they were still working on the same side. If they weren't, and this was a code Chuck didn't want him to see . . .

'Ten minutes down, ten minutes to get back up,' Teddy said.

Chuck sat down wearily on the dark rock face, pulled a cigarette from his jacket. 'Fine. But I'm sitting this one out. Try not to break your neck.'

Teddy made it down in seven minutes, three less than his estimate, because the ground was loose and sandy and he slid several times. He wished he'd had more than coffee this morning because his stomach was yowling from its emptiness, and the lack of sugar in his blood combined with lack of sleep had produced eddies in his head, stray, floating specks in front of his eyes.

He counted the rocks in each pile and wrote them in his notebook with their alphabetical assignations beside them:

13(M)–21(U)–25(Y)–18(R)–1(A)–5(E)–8(H)–15(O)–9(I)

He closed the notebook, placed it in his front pocket, and began the climb back up the sandy slope, taking whole clumps of seagrass with him as he slipped and slid. It took him twenty-five minutes to get back up and the sky had turned a dark bronze and he knew that Chuck had been right, whatever side he was on: they were losing the day fast and this had been a waste of time.

Even if they could reach the lighthouse, what then? If Chuck was working with them, then Teddy going with him to the lighthouse was like a bird flying towards a mirror.

Teddy saw the top of the hill and the edge of the promontory and the bronze sky arched above it all and he thought, This may have to be it, Dolores. This may be the best I can offer for now. Laeddis will live. Ashecliffe will go on. But we'll content ourselves knowing we've begun a process, a process that could, ultimately, bring the whole thing tumbling down.

He reached the top of the hill, and pushed himself up onto the promontory. Then he lay on his side, looking out at the sea. So blue at this time of day, so vibrant as the afternoon died around it. He felt the breeze on his face and the sea spreading out for ever under the darkening sky and he felt so small, so utterly human, but it wasn't a debilitating feeling. It was an oddly proud one. To be a part of this. A speck, yes. But part of it, one with it. Breathing.

He looked across the dark, flat stone, one cheek pressed to it, and only then did it occur to him that Chuck wasn't with him.

11

Chuck's body lay at the bottom of the cliff, the water lapping over him.

Teddy slid forwards over the lip of the promontory, legs first, searched the black rocks with the soles of his shoes until he was almost sure they'd take his weight. He let out a breath he hadn't even known he'd been holding, slid his elbows off the lip and felt his feet sink onto the rocks.

He turned his body round so that he was pressed like a crab to the rocks, and began to climb down. There was no fast way to do it. Some rocks were wedged hard into the cliff, as secure as bolts in a battleship; others weren't held by anything but the ones below them. You couldn't tell which one was until you placed your weight on it.

After about ten minutes he saw one of Chuck's Luckies, half smoked, the tip gone black and pointed like a carpenter's pencil.

What had caused the fall? The breeze had picked up, but it wasn't strong enough to knock a man off a flat ledge.

Perhaps he'd dropped something and followed it down. Perhaps, like Teddy now, he'd tried to work his way down the cliff, grasping and toeing stones that might not hold.

Teddy paused for breath, the sweat dripping off his face. It was then he saw the piece of paper wedged between a rock and a brown tendril of roots. He pinched the paper between his fingers and he didn't have to unfold it to know what it was.

Laeddis's intake form.

He slid it into his back pocket. He knew now why Chuck had come down here. For this piece of paper.

For Teddy.

THE LAST TWENTY feet of cliff face was comprised of giant boulders covered in kelp, and Teddy turned when he reached them, turned so that his arms were behind him and the heels of his hands supported his weight, and worked his way across and down them, past rats hiding in their crevices.

When he reached the shore, he spied Chuck's body and walked over to it and realised it wasn't a body at all. Just another rock, bleached by the sun and covered in thick black ropes of seaweed.

Thank . . . something. Chuck was not dead.

Teddy cupped his hands around his mouth and called Chuck's name. Called and called and heard it bounce off the rocks and carry out to sea on the breeze.

He stopped and waited to hear Chuck call back to him. It was growing too dark to see up to the top of the cliff. Teddy heard the rats in the crevices of the boulders. He heard a gull caw. The ocean lap. A few minutes later, he heard the foghorn from Boston Light again.

His vision adjusted to the dark and he saw eyes watching him. Dozens of them. The rats lounged on the boulders and stared at him, unafraid. This was their beach at night, not his.

He started walking slowly along the shore and he saw that there were hundreds of them, taking to the rocks in the moonlight like seals to the sun.

He looked up at the cliff, thankful for the moon, which was near full, and the stars, which were bright and countless. And then he saw a colour that didn't make any sense at all.

Orange. Midway up the black cliff face. At dusk.

Teddy stared at it and watched as it flickered, subsided, then flared and subsided and flared. Like flame.

A cave, he realised. Or at least a sizable crevice. And someone was in there. Chuck. It had to be. Maybe he had chased that paper down off the promontory. Maybe he'd got hurt and had ended up working his way across instead of down.

Teddy took off his ranger cap and approached the nearest boulder. A half-dozen pairs of eyes considered him and he whacked at them with the hat and they jerked and twisted and flung their bodies off the boulder and Teddy stepped up there fast and kicked at a few on the next boulder and they went over the side. He ran up the boulders then, jumping from one to the next, and then he was climbing the cliff face, his hands still bleeding from the descent.

It took him an hour and a half in the moonlight, and he climbed with the stars studying him much the way the rats had, and he lost Dolores as he climbed, couldn't picture her, couldn't see her face. He felt her gone from him as he'd never felt since she died, and he knew it was all the physical exertion and lack of sleep and lack of food, but she was gone. Gone as he climbed under the moon.

But he could hear her in his brain, and she was saying, *Go on, Teddy. Go on. You can live again.*

Was that all there was to it? After these two years of walking under water, of staring at his gun on the end table in the living room as he sat in the dark listening to Duke Ellington, of being certain that he couldn't possibly take one more day of this shithole of a life—after all that, could this honestly be the moment when he put her away?

The orange light was flickering just above him. He placed his hand on a ledge, pulled himself up and forwards onto his elbows, saw the orange light reflecting off craggy walls. He stood. He found the opening of the cave and saw that the light came from a pile of wood in a small hole dug into the cave floor and a woman stood on the other side of the fire with her hands behind her back.

'Who are you?'

'Teddy Daniels.'

The woman had long hair streaked with grey and wore a patient's light pink shirt and drawstring trousers and slippers.

'That's your name,' she said. 'But what do you do?'

'I'm a cop.'

She tilted her head. 'You're the marshal.'

Teddy nodded. 'Could you take your hands from behind your back?'

'Why?' she said.

'Because I'd like to know what you're holding.'

'Why?'

'Because I'd like to know if it could hurt me.'

She gave a small smile. 'I suppose that's fair.' She removed her hands from behind her back, and she was holding a long, thin surgical scalpel. 'I'll hold on to it, if you don't mind.'

Teddy held up his hands. 'Fine with me.'

'Do you know who I am?'

Teddy said, 'A patient from Ashecliffe.'

She touched her smock. 'My. What gave me away? Are all US marshals so astute?'

'I haven't eaten in a while. I'm a little slower than usual.'

She hiked up her trousers at the knees and sat on the floor, beckoned him to do the same.

Teddy sat and stared at her over the fire. 'You're Rachel Solando,' he said. 'The real one.'

She shrugged.

'You kill your children?' he said.

She poked a log with the scalpel. 'I never had children.'

'No?'

'No. I was never married. I was, you'll be surprised to realise, more than just a patient here.'

'How can you be more than just a patient?'

'I was staff,' she said. 'Since just after the war.'

'You were a nurse?'

She looked over the fire at him. 'I was a doctor, Marshal. The first female doctor on staff here at Ashecliffe. A genuine pioneer.'

Or a delusional mental patient, Teddy thought.

He looked up and found her eyes on him, and hers were kind and wary and knowing. She said, 'You think I'm crazy. What else would you think of a woman who hides in a cave?'

'I've considered that there might be another reason.'

She smiled darkly and shook her head. 'I'm not crazy. I'm not. Of course, what else would a crazy person claim? That's the Kafkaesque genius of it all. If you're not crazy but people have told the world you are, then all your protests to the contrary just underscore their point. Do you see what I'm saying?'

'Sort of,' Teddy said.

'Look at it as a syllogism. Let's say the syllogism begins with this principle: "Insane men deny that they are insane." You follow?'

'Sure,' Teddy said.

'OK, part two: "Bob denies he is insane." Part three: "Ergo—Bob is insane."' She placed the scalpel on the ground by her knee and stoked the fire with a stick. 'If you are deemed insane, then all your actions are an insane person's actions. Your sound protests constitute *denial.* Your valid fears are deemed *paranoia.* Your survival instincts are labelled *defence mechanisms.* It's a no-win situation. Once you're here, you're not getting out. No one leaves Ward C. No one. Well, a few have, I'll grant you. But they've had surgery. On the brain. It's barbaric, unconscionable, and I told them that. I fought them. I wrote letters. And they could've removed me, you know? They could've fired me or dismissed me, let me practise out of state, but no. They couldn't let me leave. No, no, no.'

She'd grown more and more agitated as she spoke, stabbing the fire with her stick, talking more to her knees than to Teddy.

'You really were a doctor?' Teddy said.

'Oh, yes. I began to ask about large shipments of Sodium Amytal and opium-based hallucinogens. I began to wonder—aloud unfortunately—about highly experimental surgical procedures.'

'What are they up to here?' Teddy said.

She gave him a grin. 'You have no idea?'

'I know they're performing radical treatments.'

'Radical, yes. Treatments, no. There is no treating going on here, Marshal. You know where the funding for this hospital comes from?'

Teddy nodded. 'HUAC.'

'Not to mention slush funds,' she said. 'Money flows into here. Now, the brain controls pain, it controls fear, sleep, empathy, hunger. Everything.' Her eyes shone in the firelight. 'Imagine if you could control it? Re-create a man so that he doesn't need sleep, doesn't feel pain. Or love. Or sympathy. A man who can't be interrogated because his memory banks are wiped clean.' She stoked the fire and looked up at him. 'They're creating ghosts here, Marshal. Ghosts to go out into the world and do ghostly work.'

'But that kind of knowledge is—'

'Years off,' she agreed. 'Oh, yes. It's a decades-long process. Where they've begun is much the same place the Soviets have—brainwashing. Deprivation experiments. Much like the Nazis experimented on Jews to see the effect of hot and cold extremes and apply those results to help the soldiers of the Reich. But don't you see, a half-century from now, people will look back and say this is where it all began. The Nazis used Jews. The Soviets used prisoners in the gulags. Here, in America, we tested patients on Shutter Island.'

Teddy said nothing.

She looked back at the fire. 'They can't let you leave. You know that, don't you?'

'I'm a federal marshal,' Teddy said. 'How can they stop me?'

That elicited a gleeful grin and a clap of her hands. 'I was an esteemed psychiatrist from a respected family. That wasn't enough. Let me ask you—any past traumas in your life?'

'Who doesn't have those?'

'Ah, yes. But we're not taking about generalities. We're talking about you. Is there an event or events in your past that could be considered predicating factors to your losing your sanity? So that when they commit you here, and they will, your friends and colleagues will say, "Of course. He cracked. Finally. And who wouldn't? It was the war that did it to him. And losing his mother—or what have you—like that." Hmm?'

Teddy said, 'That could be said about anyone.'

'That's the point. It could be said about anyone, but they're going to say it about you. How's your head? Any funny dreams lately?'

'Sure.'

'Headaches?'

'I'm prone to migraines.'

'Have you taken pills since you've come here, even aspirin?'

'Yes.'

'Feeling just a bit off, maybe? No big deal, you say. Maybe your brain isn't making connections *quite* as fast as normal. But you haven't been sleeping well, you say: a strange bed, a strange place, a storm. You say these things to yourself. Yes?'

Teddy nodded.

'And you've eaten in the cafeteria, I assume. Tell me, at least, that you've been smoking your own cigarettes.'

Teddy could feel the cigarettes he'd won at poker that night nestled in his shirt pocket. He remembered smoking one of Cawley's the day they'd arrived, how it had tasted sweeter than most tobaccos.

She could see the answer in his face.

'It takes an average of three to four days for neuroleptic narcotics to reach workable levels in the bloodstream. During that time, you'd barely notice their effects. Sometimes, patients have seizures. Seizures can often be dismissed as migraines, particularly if the patient has a migraine history.'

'How much damage could already be done?'

She pulled her hair back off her face and twisted it into a knot behind her head. 'A lot, I'm afraid.'

'Let's say I can't get off this island until tomorrow. Let's say the drugs have begun to take effect. How will I know?'

'The most obvious indicators will be a dry mouth, and palsy. Small tremors. And you'll stutter more.'

He nodded, listening to the ocean smashing against the rocks. 'What goes on in the lighthouse?' he said eventually.

She hugged herself and leaned towards the fire. 'Surgery. Not the "Let's-open-the-skull-and-fix-that" kind. No. The "Let's-open-the-skull-and-see-what-happens-if-we-pull-on-this" kind. The illegal kind, Marshal. That's where they try to build their ghosts.'

'Who knows about this? On the island, I mean?'

'Everyone.'

'Come on. The orderlies, the nurses?'

She held Teddy's eyes through the flame, and hers were steady and clear. 'Everyone,' she repeated.

HE DIDN'T REMEMBER falling asleep, but he must have, because she was shaking him.

'I'm sorry,' she said. 'But you have to go. They think I'm dead, drowned. If they come looking for you, they could find me.'

He stood and rubbed his cheeks just below his eyes.

'There's a road,' she said. 'Just east of the top of this cliff. Follow it and it'll take you out behind the old commander's mansion.'

'Are you Rachel Solando? I know the one I met was a fake.'

'How do you know?'

Teddy thought back to his thumbs the night before, when they put him to bed. Shoe polish, he'd thought, but then he remembered touching her face . . .

'Her hair was dyed. Recently,' he said.

'You need to go.' She turned him gently towards the opening.

'I'll come back and get you, take you off here,' he said.

She gave him a sad smile and brushed the hair back along his temples. 'You haven't heard a word I've said, have you? You'll never get off here. You're one of us now.' She pressed her fingers to his shoulder, nudged him towards the opening.

Teddy stopped at the ledge, looked back at her. 'I had a friend. He was with me tonight and we got separated. Have you seen him?'

She gave him the same sad smile. 'Marshal,' she said, 'you have no friends.'

BY THE TIME he reached Cawley's house, he could barely walk.

He started up the road to the main gate, feeling as if the distance had quadrupled since this morning, and a man came out of the dark on the road beside him and slid his arm under Teddy's and said, 'We've been wondering when you'd show up.'

The warden.

His skin was the white of candle wax, as smooth as if it were lacquered, and his eyes were silken blue, filled with a strange wonderment. The eyes of a baby.

'Nice to finally meet you, Warden. How are you?'

'Oh,' the man said, 'I'm tiptop. Yourself?'

'Never better.'

'Good to hear. Taking a leisurely stroll, were we?'

'Well, now that the patient's been found, I thought I'd tour the island.'

'Wonderful. Did you come across our natives?'

It took Teddy a minute. His head was buzzing constantly now. 'Oh, the rats,' he said.

The warden clapped his back. 'The rats, yes! There's something strangely regal about them, don't you think?'

Teddy looked into the man's eyes and said, 'They're rats.'

'Vermin, yes. I understand. But the way they sit on their haunches and stare at you if they believe they're at a safe distance . . .' He looked up at the stars. 'Well, maybe *regal* is the wrong word. How about *utile*? They're exceptionally utile creatures.'

They'd reached the main gate and the warden kept his grip on Teddy's arm and turned him so that they were looking back at Cawley's house and the sea beyond.

'Did you enjoy God's latest gift?' the warden said.

Teddy looked at the man and sensed disease in those perfect eyes. 'I'm sorry?'

'God's gift,' the warden said, and his arm swept the torn grounds. 'His violence. When I first saw the tree in my living room, it reached towards me like a divine hand. Not literally, of course. But figuratively. God loves violence. You understand that, don't you?'

'No,' Teddy said, 'I don't.'

The warden walked a few steps forwards and turned to face Teddy. 'Why else would there be so much of it? God gives us earthquakes, hurricanes, tornadoes. He gives us mountains that spew fire onto our heads. Oceans that swallow ships. He gives us nature, and nature is a smiling killer. We wage war in His honour. To show Him that we've learned from His example. There is no moral order as pure as this storm we've just seen. There is no moral order at all. There is only this—can my violence conquer yours?'

Teddy said, 'I'm not sure I—'

'Can it?' The warden stepped in close, and Teddy could smell his stale breath.

'I'm not violent.'

The warden spat on the ground. 'You're as violent as they come. I know, because I'm as violent as they come. Don't embarrass yourself by denying your own blood lust, son. If the constraints of society were removed, and I was all that stood between you and a meal, you'd crack my skull with a rock.' He leaned in. 'If my teeth sank into your eye right now, could you stop me before I blinded you?'

Teddy saw glee in his baby eyes. 'Give it a try,' he said.

'That's the spirit,' the warden whispered.

Teddy smiled. 'They really broke the mould with you, didn't they, Warden?'

A thin smile to match Teddy's own. 'He thinks it's OK.'

'What's OK?'

'You. Your little endgame. He thinks it's harmless. But I don't.'

'No, huh?'

'No.' The warden crossed his hands behind his back and set his feet apart in the military fashion. He stared at Teddy. 'You say you were out for a stroll, but I know better. I know you, son.'

'We just met,' Teddy said.

The warden shook his head. 'Our kind have known each other for centuries. I know you to your core. And I know you're dangerous.'

'Every man has a right to his opinion,' Teddy said.

The warden's face darkened. 'No, he doesn't. Men are foolish. They eat and drink and fornicate and procreate, and this last is particularly unfortunate, because the world would be a much better place with far fewer of us in it. Retards and lunatics and people of low moral character—that's what we produce. That's what we spoil this earth with. In the South now, they're trying to keep their niggers in line. But I'll tell you something, they're all niggers down there, son. White niggers, black niggers, women niggers. You're a nigger, son. You're of low fibre. I can smell it in you.'

His voice was surprisingly light, almost feminine.

'Well,' Teddy said, 'you won't have to worry about me after this, will you, Warden?'

The warden smiled. 'No, I won't, son.'

'I'll be out of your hair and off your island.'

The warden's smile dissolved. He held Teddy in his gaze. 'You're not going anywhere, son.'

'I beg to differ.'

'Beg all you want.' And he turned and walked up the road towards his house.

THE MEN'S DORMITORY was abandoned. Not a soul there. Teddy went up to his room and hung his slicker in the closet and looked for any evidence that Chuck had returned, but there was none.

He thought of sitting on the bed, but he knew if he did he'd pass out and probably not wake until morning, so he went down to the bathroom and splashed cold water on his face and went outside into the main compound.

There was a guard on the gate, but otherwise the place was empty.

The air was actually warming up, growing humid and sticky. Teddy made his way over to the hospital and went up the steps and pulled on the door only to find it locked. He heard a squeak of hinges and looked out to see that the guard had opened the gate and gone out to join his comrade on the other side, and then closed the gate again.

He sat on the steps for a minute. So much for Noyce's theory. Teddy was now, beyond any doubt, completely alone. Locked in, yes. But unwatched, as far as he could tell.

He walked round to the back of the hospital and saw an orderly sitting there, smoking.

Teddy approached, and the kid, a slim black kid, looked up. Teddy pulled a cigarette from his pocket and said, 'Got a light?'

'Sure do.'

Teddy leaned in as the kid lit his cigarette, smiled his thanks as he leaned back and remembered what the woman had told him about smoking their cigarettes, and let the smoke flow slowly out of his mouth without inhaling. 'Where is everyone tonight?'

The kid jerked his thumb behind him. 'In there. Some big meeting. All the doctors and nurses and some of the patients too. Most of us orderlies. I got stuck with this here door 'cause the latch don't work real good. Otherwise, though, yeah. Everyone in there.'

Teddy wondered if he should just bluff his way in, hope the kid took him for another orderly, one from Ward C maybe.

Then he saw through the window behind the kid that the hallway was filling and people were heading for the front door.

He thanked the kid for the light and walked around out front, was met with a crowd of people milling there, talking, lighting cigarettes. He saw Nurse Marino laughing with Trey Washington, and he started to walk over to them.

Then he heard Cawley call to him from the stairs. 'Marshal!'

Teddy turned and Cawley came down the stairs towards him, touched Teddy's elbow, and began walking towards the wall.

'Where've you been?' Cawley said.

'Wandering. Looking at your island.'

'Really? Find anything amusing?'

'Rats.'

'Well, sure, we have plenty of those.'

'How's the roof repair coming?' Teddy said.

Cawley sighed. 'I have buckets all over my house catching water.

The attic is wrecked. So's the floor in the guest bedroom. My wife's going to be beside herself. Her wedding gown was in that attic.'

'Where is your wife?' Teddy said.

'Boston,' Cawley said. 'We keep an apartment there. She and the kids needed a break from this place, so they took a week's vacation. It gets to you sometimes.'

'I've been here three days, Doctor, and it gets to me.'

Cawley nodded with a soft smile. 'But you'll be going now that Rachel's been found, I guess. The ferry usually gets here before eleven in the morning. Have you back in Boston by noon, I'd expect.'

'Won't that be nice.'

'Yes, won't it?' Cawley ran a hand over his head, looking as tired in his wrinkled lab coat and loosened tie as Teddy felt. Eventually he said, 'There was a rumour going around Ward C this afternoon that an unidentified man in orderly's clothes was on the main floor.'

'How about that.'

'Said stranger apparently had some experience subduing dangerous men.'

'You don't say. What else did Said Stranger get up to?'

'Well.' Cawley stretched his shoulders back and removed his lab coat, draped it over his arm. 'Said Stranger allegedly—and I can't confirm this, mind you—had a long conversation with a known paranoid schizophrenic named George Noyce.'

'Hmm,' Teddy said. 'So this, um . . .'

'Noyce,' Cawley said.

'Noyce,' Teddy repeated. 'Yeah, that guy—he's delusional, huh?'

'To the extreme,' Cawley said. 'He spins tall tales and he gets everyone agitated. Two weeks ago, in fact, he got people so cross that a patient beat him up.'

'Imagine that.'

Cawley shrugged. 'It happens.'

'So, what kind of yarns?' Teddy asked. 'What kind of tales?'

Cawley waved at the air. 'The usual paranoid delusions. The whole world being out to get him and such.' He looked at Teddy. 'So, you'll be leaving.'

'The first ferry.' Teddy gave him a frosty smile. 'As long as someone wakes us up.'

Cawley returned the smile. 'I think we can handle that.'

Teddy said, 'Ever have a patient here named Andrew Laeddis?'

'Doesn't ring a bell. Should it?'

Teddy shook his head. 'He was a guy I knew. He—'

'How did you know him?'

'In the war,' Teddy said.

'Oh.'

'Anyway, I'd heard he went a little crazy, got sent here.'

'You heard wrong,' Cawley said.

'Apparently.'

'Hey, it happens. I thought you said "us" a minute ago.'

'What?'

'I thought you said, "As long as someone wakes *us* up."'

'Well, I did. Of course. Have you seen him by the way?'

Cawley raised his eyebrows. 'Who?'

Teddy said, 'Come on. Is he here?'

Cawley laughed, looked at him. 'Is this some weird joke of yours, Marshal?'

'What joke?' Teddy said. 'I just want to know if he's here.'

'Who?' Cawley said, a hint of exasperation in his voice.

'Chuck.'

'Chuck?' Cawley said slowly.

'My partner,' Teddy said. 'Chuck.'

Cawley straightened. 'You don't have a partner, Marshal. You came here alone.'

12

Teddy said, 'Wait a minute . . .'

Cawley was closer now, peering at him. His gaze was the coldest thing Teddy had ever seen. Probing, intelligent and fiercely bland.

Teddy closed his mouth, felt the summer night find his eyelids.

Cawley said, 'Tell me again. About your partner.'

It was the gaze of a straight man in a vaudeville revue, pretending not to know where the punch line would come from. And Teddy was a buffoon with loose suspenders. The last one in on the joke.

If Teddy protested, if he demanded to know where Chuck was, if he even argued that there *was* a Chuck, he played into their hands.

Teddy met Cawley's eyes and he saw the laughter in them. 'Insane men deny they're insane,' he said.

'Excuse me?'

'Bob denies he's insane. Ergo, Bob is insane.'

Cawley leaned back on his heels, and now the smile found his face.

Teddy met it with one of his own.

They stood there like that for some time, the night breeze moving through the trees above the wall with a soft flutter.

'You know,' Cawley said, toeing the grass at his feet, head down, 'I've built something valuable here. But valuable things also have a way of being misunderstood in their own time. Patience and forbearance become the first casualties of progress. It's always been so.' He raised his head. 'So I have many powerful enemies. People who would wrest what I've built from my control. I can't allow that without a fight. You understand?'

Teddy said, 'Oh, I understand, Doctor.'

'Good.' Cawley folded his arms. 'And this partner of yours?'

Teddy said, 'What partner?'

TREY WASHINGTON was in the room when Teddy got back, lying on the bed reading an old issue of *Life*.

Teddy looked at Chuck's bunk. The bed had been remade so that you'd never know someone had slept there two nights before.

Teddy's jacket, shirt, tie and trousers had been returned from the laundry and hung in the closet, and he changed into them.

Trey flipped the pages of the magazine. 'How you doing, Marshal?'

'Doing OK.'

'That's good, that's good.'

He noticed that Trey wouldn't look at him, kept his eyes on that magazine, turning the pages over and over.

Teddy transferred the contents of his pockets, placing Laeddis's intake form in his inside jacket pocket along with his notebook. He sat on Chuck's bunk and tied his tie, then sat there quietly.

Trey turned another page. 'Going to be hot tomorrow.'

'Really?'

'Yup. Patients don't like the heat. No, sir. Make 'em all itchy and whatnot. All we need.'

'How long you been here, Mr Washington?'

'Oh, long time now. Since I got out of the army in '46.'

'You were in the army?'

'Yes, I was. Came there for a gun, they gave me a pot. Fought the Germans with bad cooking. And you was in all sorts of places, huh?'

'Yeah, I was. Saw the world.'

'Uh-huh?'

'You know what the warden called me tonight, Mr Washington?'

'What's that, Marshal?'

'A nigger.'

Trey looked up from the magazine. 'He what?'

Teddy nodded. 'Said there were too many people in this world who were of low fibre. Niggers. Retards. Said I was just a nigger to him.'

'You didn't like that, did you?' Trey chuckled, and the sound died as it left his mouth. 'You don't know what it is to be a nigger, though.'

'I'm aware of that, Trey. This man is your boss, though.'

'Ain't my boss. I work for the hospital end of things. The White Devil? He on the prison side.'

'Still your boss.'

'No, he ain't, you hear?' Trey swung his legs over the bed and sat up. 'You trying to make me mad, sir?'

Teddy shook his head.

'So then why don't you agree with me when I tell you I don't work for that white son of a bitch?'

Teddy shrugged. 'In a pinch, if it came down to it and he started giving orders? You'd hop to just like a bunny.'

Trey considered Teddy with a hard grin of disbelief.

'I don't mean any offence,' Teddy said. 'It's just I've noticed that people on this island have a way of creating their own truth. Figure they say it's so enough times, then it must be so.'

'I don't work for that man.'

'Yeah, that's the island truth I know and love.'

Trey looked ready to hit him.

'See,' Teddy said, 'they held a meeting tonight. And afterwards, Dr Cawley comes up and tells me I never had a partner. And if I ask you, you'll say the same thing. You'll deny that you sat and played poker with the man and laughed with the man. You'll deny he ever slept right here in this bed. Won't you, Mr Washington?'

Trey looked down at the floor. 'Don't know what you're talking about, Marshal.'

'Oh, I know, I know. I never had a partner. That's the truth now. I never had a partner and he's not somewhere out on this island hurt. Or dead. Or locked up in the lighthouse. Come on. Try it.'

Trey looked up. 'You never had a partner.'

Teddy said, 'And you don't work for the warden.'

Trey clasped his hands on his knees. He looked at Teddy and Teddy could see that this was eating him. His chin trembled. 'You need to get out of here,' he whispered.

'I'm aware of that.'

'No.' Trey shook his head several times. 'You don't have any idea what's really going on here. And there ain't no coming back from what they going to do to you. No coming back no how.'

'Tell me,' Teddy said. 'Tell me what's going on here.'

But Trey was shaking his head again. 'I can't do that. I can't.' His eyes widened. 'You on your own. You gotta watch out for yourself. And I wouldn't be waiting on no ferry.'

Teddy chuckled. 'I can't even get out of this compound, Trey. I'm locked in.'

Trey stood and went to the window, looked out into the dark. 'You can't ever tell no one I told you anything.' He looked back over his shoulder at Teddy. 'Ferry be here tomorrow at ten. Leave for Boston at eleven sharp. A man was to stow away on that boat, he might just make it across the harbour. Otherwise, a man would have to wait two or three more days and a fishing trawler, name of *Betsy Ross*, she pull up real close to the southern coast, drop a few things off the side. Kinda things men ain't supposed to have on this island.'

'I can't do three days on this island,' Teddy said. 'I don't know the terrain. The warden and his men will find me.'

'Then it's the ferry,' Trey said eventually.

'It's the ferry. But how do I get out of the compound?'

'You might not buy this, but it *is* your lucky day. Storm fucked up the electrical systems. Now we repaired most of the wires on the wall. But right in the southwest corner, those two sections are dead. The rest of them will fry you like chicken. Hear?'

'I hear.'

'Then I'd suggest you git. Time's wasting.'

Teddy stood. 'Chuck,' he said.

Trey scowled. 'You get back to the world, you talk about Chuck all you like, all right? But here? The man never happened.'

IT OCCURRED TO TEDDY as he faced the southwest corner of the wall that Trey could be lying. If Teddy put a hand to those wires, got a good grip, and they were live, they'd find his body in the morning at the foot of the wall, as black as last month's steak. Problem solved. Trey gets employee of the year, maybe a nice gold watch.

He searched around until he found a long twig, and then he leapt up and slapped the twig down on the wire. Nothing.

There was a metal post atop the section where the walls met, and Teddy took three runs at the wall before he got a grip. He held tight and climbed up to the top and his knees and forearms hit the wire, and each time, he thought he was dead.

He wasn't. And once he'd reached the top, there wasn't much to do but lower himself down to the other side.

He stood in the leaves and looked back at Ashecliffe. He'd come here for the truth, and hadn't found it. He'd come here for Laeddis, and hadn't found him either. Along the way, he'd lost Chuck.

He'd have time to regret all that back in Boston. Time to feel guilt and shame then. Time to consult with Senator Hurly and come up with subpoenas and federal search warrants.

Now, though, he was just relieved to be alive and on the other side of this wall.

Relieved. And scared.

IT TOOK HIM an hour and a half to get back to the cave. The woman had left. Her fire had burned down to a few embers, and Teddy sat by it even though the air outside was unseasonably warm.

He waited for her, hoping she'd just gone out for more wood, but he knew, in his heart, that she wasn't going to return. Maybe she believed he'd already been caught and was, at this moment, telling the warden and Cawley about her hiding place.

When the fire went out, Teddy took off his suit jacket and draped it over his chest and shoulders and placed his head back against the wall. Just as he had the night before, the last thing he noticed before he passed out were his thumbs.

They'd begun to twitch.

DAY FOUR—THE BAD SAILOR

13

'You see him, you shoot first.'

Teddy threw his coat off his chest and crawled to the edge of the cave. The warden and his men were up on the ridge above him. The sun was up. Teddy looked at his watch: 8 a.m.

'You do not take chances,' the warden said. 'This man is combat-trained and combat-hardened. He killed two men in Sicily with his bare hands.'

That information was in his personnel file, Teddy knew. But how did they get his personnel file?

Three guards came down the side of the cliff face on ropes and Teddy moved away from the ledge and watched them work their way down to the beach. A few minutes later, they climbed back up and Teddy heard one of them say, 'He's not down there, sir.'

He listened for a while as they searched up near the promontory and the road, and then they moved off and Teddy waited a full hour before leaving the cave. It was twenty past nine by the time he reached the road, and he followed it back towards the west, trying to maintain a fast pace but still listen for men moving either ahead or behind him.

Trey had been right in his weather prediction. It was hot as hell. Teddy removed his jacket and folded it over his arm. His mouth was as dry as rock salt.

If the plan was for Teddy to be driven insane, then it couldn't be the same for Chuck. Nobody would believe two marshals had lost their minds in the same four-day span. They would have to make it look as if Chuck had met with an accident. If they were really smart—and it seemed they were—then maybe Chuck's death would be represented as the event that had tipped Teddy past the point of no return.

There was an undeniable symmetry to the idea.

But if Teddy didn't make it off this island, the field office would never accept the story without sending other marshals out here to see for themselves. And what would they find?

Teddy looked down at the tremors in his wrists and thumbs. They were getting worse. And his brain felt no fresher for a night's sleep. If the drugs had taken over by the time the field office got men out here, they'd probably find Teddy drooling into his bathrobe. And the Ashecliffe version of the truth would be validated.

He heard the ferry blow its horn and came up on a rise in time to see it finish its turn in the harbour and steam towards the dock. He picked up his pace, and ten minutes later he could see Cawley's Tudor through the woods.

He turned off the road into the cover of the trees and saw several orderlies down on the dock, unloading the ferry, the two pilots leaning back against the stern. He saw guards, lots of guards, rifle butts resting on hips, scanning the trees and the grounds that led up to Ashecliffe, and Teddy knew then that their only job this morning was to make damn sure he didn't reach that boat.

He crept on through the woods and came out by Cawley's house. In the carport on the western side of the house he found a '47 Buick Roadmaster. Maroon with white leather interior. Waxed and shiny the day after a hurricane. A beloved vehicle.

Teddy opened the driver's door and he could smell the leather, as if it were a day old. He opened the glove compartment and found several packs of matches, and he took them all.

He pulled his tie from his pocket, found a small stone on the ground and knotted the narrow end of the tie round it. He unscrewed the gas tank cap, and then he threaded the tie and the stone down the pipe and into the tank until all that hung out of the pipe was the fat, floral front of the tie, as if it hung from a man's neck.

He used one match to light the entire book and then used the book to light the tie.

And then he ran like hell.

He was halfway through the woods when the car exploded. He heard men yell and he looked back, and through the trees he could see the flames vaulting upwards, and then there was a set of smaller explosions, like firecrackers, as the windows blew out.

As he reached the edge of the woods he saw the guards and the ferrymen running up the path towards Cawley's house, and he knew that if he was going to do this he had to do it right now.

He ran out of the woods and along the shore, and just before he reached the dock he cut hard to his left and ran into the water.

Teddy had hoped the heat of the day might have warmed it up a bit, but the icy cold tore up through his body and punched the air out of his chest. He kept ploughing forwards, trying not to think about what was in that water—eels, jellyfish, crabs and sharks too, maybe. Hearing shouts coming from up by Cawley's house, he ignored the sledgehammer strokes of his heart and dived under the surface.

He saw Dolores, from his dreams, floating just below him, her eyes open and resigned. He shook his head and she vanished and he could see the keel ahead of him, a thick black stripe that undulated in the green water, and he swam to it and got his hands on it. He moved along it to the front and came round the other side, and forced himself to come up out of the water slowly, just his head. He felt the sun on his face as he exhaled and then sucked in oxygen and tried to ignore a vision of his legs dangling down there in the depths and some creature swimming along and coming close for a sniff . . .

The ladder was where he remembered it. Right in front of him, and he got a hand on the third rung and hung there. He could hear the men running back to the dock now, hear their heavy footsteps on the planks, and then he heard the warden: 'Search that boat.'

'Sir, we were only gone—'

'You left your post, and now you wish to argue?'

'No, sir. Sorry, sir.'

The ladder dipped in his hand as several men placed their weight on the ferry, and Teddy heard them going through the boat, heard doors opening and furniture shifting.

Something slid between his thighs like a hand, and he gritted his teeth. Whatever it was kept moving, and Teddy let out a breath.

'My car. He blew up my car.' Cawley, sounding ragged and out of breath.

The warden said, 'This has gone far enough, Doctor.'

'We agreed that it's my decision to make.'

'If that man gets off this island, we'll be destroyed.'

Cawley's voice rose. 'He's not going to get off the island!'

Neither spoke for a full minute. Teddy could hear their weight shifting on the dock.

'Fine, Doctor. But that ferry stays. It does not leave this dock until that man is found.'

Teddy hung there, the cold finding his feet and burning them. He closed his mouth before his teeth could chatter.

Footsteps on the stern.

'He's not in there, sir. We checked everywhere.'

'So where did he go?' the warden said. 'Anyone?'

'Shit!'

'Yes, Doctor?'

'He's headed for the lighthouse.'

'That thought did occur to me.'

'I'll handle it.'

'Take some men.'

'I said I'll handle it. We've got men there.'

Teddy heard Cawley's shoes bang their way back up the dock and get softer as they hit the sand.

'Lighthouse or no lighthouse,' the warden said to his men, 'this boat goes nowhere. Get the keys from the pilot and bring them to me.'

HE DROPPED AWAY from the ferry and swam towards shore until he was close enough to the sandy bottom to use it, clawing along until he'd gone far enough to raise his head from the water and risk a glance back. He'd covered a few hundred yards and he could see the guards forming a ring round the dock.

He slipped back under the water and continued clawing, unable to risk the splashing that even doggy-paddling would cause, and after a while he came to the bend in the shoreline and made his way round it and walked up onto the sand and shook from the cold.

He walked as much of the shore as he could before he ran into a set of outcroppings that pushed him back into the water, and he tied his shoes together and hung them round his neck and went for another swim, envisioning his father's bones somewhere on this same ocean floor, sharks and barracuda with rows of white teeth, and he knew that the only way to conquer fear was to face it—he'd learned that in the war enough—but even so, if he could manage it, he would never, ever, get in the ocean again.

At about one o'clock he saw the lighthouse. He couldn't be sure because his watch was back in his jacket, which he'd hidden near the dock before he'd gone for his swim, but the sun was in roughly the right place. He came ashore just below the bluff on which it stood and he lay against a rock and took the sun on his body until the shakes stopped and his skin grew less blue.

If Chuck was up there, no matter his condition, Teddy was bringing him out. Dead or alive, he wouldn't leave him behind.

You'll die then.

It was Dolores's voice, and he knew she was right. If he had to wait two days for the arrival of the *Betsy Ross*, and he had anything but a fully alert, fully functional Chuck with him, they'd never make it. They'd be hunted down . . .

I can't leave him, he told Dolores. Can't do it. If I can't find him, that's one thing. But he's my partner. I have to bring him out.

Even if you die?

Even if I die.

Then I hope he's not in there.

As he followed a path of sand and shells that curled round the seagrass, it occurred to him that what Cawley had thought suicidal in him wasn't that. It was more a death wish. For years he couldn't think of a good reason to live, true. But he couldn't think of a good reason to die, either. By his own hand? Even in his most desolate nights, that had seemed such a puny, pathetic option. But to—

The guard was suddenly standing there, as surprised by Teddy's appearance as Teddy was by his. He started to reach for the rifle slung behind his back, then changed his mind, but by then Teddy had driven the heel of his hand into his Adam's apple. He grabbed his throat, and Teddy dropped to a crouch and swung his leg into the back of the guard's and the guard flipped over on his back. Teddy straightened up and kicked him hard in the right ear and the guard's eyes rolled back in his head and his mouth flopped open.

Teddy bent down by him and slid the rifle strap off his shoulder and pulled the rifle out from under him. Now he had a gun.

He used it on the next guard, the one in front of the fence. He disarmed him, a kid, a baby, really, and the guard said, 'You going to kill me?'

'Hell, no,' Teddy said and snapped the rifle butt into the kid's temple.

THERE WAS A SMALL bunkhouse inside the fence perimeter, and Teddy checked that first, found a few cots and girlie magazines, a pot of old coffee, a couple of guard uniforms hanging from a hook on the door.

He went back out and crossed to the lighthouse and used the rifle to push open the door and found nothing on the ground floor but a dank concrete room, empty of anything but mould on the walls, and a spiral staircase made from the same stone as the walls.

He followed that up to a second room, as empty as the first. He heard a scraping sound above him and he went back out to the stairs and followed them up another flight and came to a heavy iron door. He pressed the tip of the rifle barrel to it and felt it give a bit.

He heard that scraping sound again and he could smell cigarette smoke and hear the ocean and feel the wind up here, and he knew that if the warden had been smart enough to place guards on the other side of this door, then Teddy was dead as soon as he opened it.

Run, baby.

Can't.

Why not?

Because it all comes to this.

What does?

All of it. You. Me. Laeddis. Chuck. Noyce, that poor kid. It all comes to this. Either it stops now. Or I stop now.

It was his hands. Chuck's hands. Don't you see? They didn't fit him.

Teddy knew what she meant. He knew something about Chuck's

hands was important, but not so important he could waste any more time in this stairwell thinking about it.

Teddy crouched to the left of the door and kicked out with his left foot. The door swung wide and he dropped to his knee and placed the rifle to his shoulder and sighted down the barrel.

At Cawley. Sitting behind a table, his back to a small square window, the ocean spread blue and silver behind him, the smell of it filling the room.

Cawley didn't look startled. He tapped his cigarette against the side of the ashtray in front of him and said, 'Why you all wet, baby?'

14

The walls behind Cawley were covered in pink bed sheets, their corners fastened by wrinkled strips of tape. On the table in front of him were several papers, a military-issue field radio, a reel-to-reel recorder, a small microphone sitting on top, and Teddy's notebook and jacket.

Teddy brought the rifle down from his shoulder but kept it pointed at Cawley and entered the room. 'What did you say?'

'You know exactly what I said.' Cawley started scribbling in a black, leather-bound notebook. 'The rifle's empty, by the way. It doesn't have any bullets in it. Given all your experience with firearms, how could you fail to notice that?'

Teddy pulled back the breech and checked the chamber. Empty.

'Just put it in the corner and sit down,' Cawley said.

Teddy laid the rifle on the floor and pulled the chair out from the table but didn't sit in it. 'What's under the sheets?'

'We'll get to that. Sit down. Here.' Cawley reached down to the floor, came back up with a heavy towel and tossed it across the table to Teddy. 'Dry yourself off a bit. You'll catch cold.'

Teddy dried his hair then stripped off his shirt and dried his upper body. When he finished, he took his jacket from the table. 'You mind?'

Cawley looked up. 'No, no. Help yourself.'

Teddy put the jacket on and sat in the chair.

Cawley wrote a bit more, the pen scratching the paper. 'How badly did you hurt the guards?'

'Not too,' Teddy said.

Cawley nodded, dropped his pen and cranked up the field radio. He flicked the transmit switch and spoke into the receiver. 'Yeah, he's here. Have Dr Sheehan take a look at your men before you send him up.'

'The elusive Dr Sheehan,' Teddy said as Cawley hung up. 'Let me guess—he arrived on the morning ferry.'

Cawley shook his head. 'He's been on the island the whole time.'

'Hiding in plain sight,' Teddy said.

Cawley held out his hands and gave a small shrug. 'He's a brilliant young psychiatrist. This was our plan, his and mine.'

Teddy felt a throb in his neck just below his left ear. 'How's it working out for you so far?'

'Not so well. I'd had higher hopes.'

He looked across at Teddy and Teddy could see in his face what he'd seen in the staff meeting just before the storm, and it didn't fit with this terrible game they were playing. Compassion. If he didn't know any better, he'd swear that was what it was.

Teddy looked away from Cawley's face, looked around at the small room, those sheets on the walls. 'So this is it?'

'This is it,' Cawley agreed. 'This is the lighthouse. The Holy Grail. The great truth you've been seeking. Is it everything you hoped for?'

'I haven't seen the basement.'

'There is no basement. It's a lighthouse.'

Teddy looked at his notebook lying on the table between them.

Cawley said, 'Your case notes, yes. We found them with your jacket in the woods near my house. You blew up my car.'

Teddy shrugged. 'Sorry.'

Cawley shook his head. 'Did you think for one second that we'd let you get to that ferry? Even if you'd blown up the whole island as a diversion, what did you think would happen?'

Teddy shrugged. 'It was the only way off. I had to try.'

Cawley stared at him, and muttered, 'I loved that car.'

Teddy said, 'You got any water?'

Cawley considered the request for a while and then turned his chair to reveal a pitcher and two glasses on the windowsill. He poured each of them a glass and handed one to Teddy.

Teddy drained the entire glass in one long swallow.

'Dry mouth, huh?' Cawley said. He slid the pitcher across the table and watched as Teddy refilled his glass. 'Tremors in your hands. Those are getting pretty bad. How's your headache?'

And as he said it, Teddy felt a hot wire of pain behind his left eye that extended out to his temple and then down south to his jaw. 'Not bad,' he said.

'It'll get worse.'

Teddy drank some more. 'I'm sure. That woman told me as much.'

Cawley sat back with a smile. 'Who's this now?'

'Didn't get her name,' Teddy said, 'but she used to work with you.'

'Oh. And she told you what exactly?'

'She told me the neuroleptics took four days to build up workable levels in the bloodstream. She predicted the dry mouth, the headaches, the shakes.'

'It's not from neuroleptics.'

'No?'

'No. It's from withdrawal.'

'Withdrawal from what?'

Another smile and then Cawley's gaze grew distant, and he flipped open Teddy's notebook to the last page he'd written, pushed it across the table to him. 'That's your handwriting, correct?'

Teddy glanced down at it. 'Yeah.'

'You didn't break the code yet?'

'I didn't have the chance. Things got a bit hectic, in case you didn't notice.'

'Sure, sure.' Cawley tapped the page. 'Care to break it now?'

Teddy looked down at the nine numbers and letters:

13(M)–21(U)–25(Y)–18(R)–1(A)–5(E)–8(H)–15(O)–9(I)

He could feel the wire poking his left eye. 'I'm not really feeling my best at the moment.'

'But it's simple,' Cawley said. 'Nine letters.'

'Withdrawal from what?' Teddy said. 'What did you give me?'

Cawley leaned back into his chair with a shuddering yawn. 'Chlorpromazine. It has its downsides. Many, I'm afraid. I'm not too fond of it. I'd hoped to start you on imipramine before this latest series of incidents, but that won't happen now.'

'Chlorpro . . .'

'. . . mazine.' Cawley nodded. 'Chlorpromazine. That's what you're on now. What you're withdrawing from. The same thing we've been giving you for the last two years.'

Teddy said, 'The last what?'

'Two years.'

Teddy chuckled. 'Look, I know you guys are powerful. You don't have to oversell your case, though.'

'I'm not overselling anything.'

'You've been drugging me for two years?'

'I prefer the term "medicating".'

'And, what, you had a guy working in the US marshals' office in Boston? Guy's job was to spike my coffee every morning?'

'Not in Boston,' Cawley said quietly. 'Here.'

'Here?'

He nodded. 'Here. You've been a patient here for two years.'

Teddy could hear the tide coming in now, angry, hurling itself against the base of the bluff. He clasped his hands together to quiet the tremors and tried to ignore the pulsing behind his eye, growing more insistent. 'I'm a US marshal,' he said.

'*Were* a US marshal,' Cawley said.

'Am,' Teddy said. 'I am a federal marshal and left Boston on Monday morning, September the 22nd, 1954.'

'Really? Tell me how you got to the ferry.'

'I took the subway.'

'The subway doesn't go out that far.'

'Transferred to a bus.'

'Why didn't you drive?'

'Car's in the shop.'

'Oh. And Sunday, what is your recollection of Sunday? Can you tell me what you did? Can you honestly tell me anything about your day before you woke up in the bathroom of the ferry?'

Teddy could. Well, he would have been able to, but the wire in his head was digging through the back of his eye now.

All right. Remember. Tell him what you did Sunday. You came home from work. You went to your apartment on Buttonwood. No, no. Not Buttonwood. Buttonwood burned to the ground when Laeddis set it on fire. No, no. Where do you live? He could see the place. Right. The place on . . . Castlemont. That's it. Castlemont Avenue.

OK, OK. Relax. You came back to the place on Castlemont and you ate dinner and drank some milk and went to bed. Right? Right.

Cawley said, 'What about this? Did you get a chance to look at this?' He pushed Laeddis's intake form across the table.

'No.'

'No?' He whistled. 'You came here for it. If you got that piece of paper back to Senator Hurly—proof of a sixty-seventh patient we claim to have no record of—you could have blown the lid off this place.'

'True.'

'And you couldn't find time to give it a glance?'

'Again, things were a bit—'

'Hectic, yes. I understand. Well, take a look at it now.'

Teddy glanced down at it, saw the pertinent name, age, date of intake info for Laeddis. In the comments section, he read:

```
Patient is highly intelligent and delusional. Known
proclivity for violence. Shows no remorse for his crime
because he denies that any such crime ever took place.
```

The signature below read *Dr L. Sheehan.*

Teddy said, 'Sounds about right.'

'In regards to whom?'

'Laeddis.'

Cawley stood. He walked over to the wall and pulled down one of the sheets. Four names were written there in block letters:

EDWARD DANIELS—ANDREW LAEDDIS
RACHEL SOLANDO—DOLORES CHANAL

Teddy waited, but Cawley seemed to be waiting too, neither of them saying a word for a full minute.

Eventually Teddy said, 'You have a point, I'm guessing.'

'Look at the names. Your name, Patient Sixty-seven's name, the missing patient's name and your wife's name.'

'Uh-huh. I'm not blind.'

'There's your rule of four,' Cawley said.

'How so?' Teddy rubbed his temple hard, trying to massage that wire out of there.

'Well, you're the genius with code. You tell me.'

'Tell you what?'

'What the names Edward Daniels and Andrew Laeddis have in common.'

Teddy looked at his own name and Laeddis's for a moment. 'They both have thirteen letters.'

'Yes, they do,' Cawley said. 'Yes, they do. Anything else?'

Teddy tried to concentrate, already tiring of this parlour game. 'I can't see anything. Just thirteen letters.'

Cawley whacked the names with the back of his hand. 'Come on!'

Teddy shook his head and felt nauseated. The letters jumped.

'Concentrate.'

'I am concentrating.'

'What do those letters have in common?' Cawley said.

Teddy peered at the letters until they blurred. 'Nothing. What do you want me to say?'

Cawley shouted it: 'They're the same letters! The names are anagrams for each other.'

'No. They can't be.'

'They are. Open your eyes. Look at them.'

Teddy opened his eyes but continued to shake his head, tried to get the letters to stop quivering.

Cawley slapped the next line with the back of his hand. 'Try this, then. Dolores Chanal and Rachel Solando. Both thirteen letters. You want to tell me what *they* have in common?'

Teddy knew what he was seeing, but he also knew it wasn't possible. 'It can't be.'

'It is,' Cawley said. 'The same letters again. Anagrams for each other. You came here for the truth? Here's your truth, Andrew.'

'Teddy,' Teddy said.

Cawley stared down at him, his face once again filling with lies of empathy. 'Your name is Andrew Laeddis,' Cawley said. 'The sixty-seventh patient at Ashecliffe Hospital? He's you, Andrew.'

'Bullshit!' Teddy screamed it and the scream rocketed through his head.

'Your name is Andrew Laeddis,' Cawley repeated. 'You were committed here by court order twenty-two months ago.'

Teddy threw his hand at that. 'This is below even you guys.'

'Please, Andrew. Look at the evidence. You came here two years ago because you committed a terrible crime. One that society can't forgive, but I can. Look at me.'

Teddy's eyes rose from the hand Cawley had extended, and into his face, the man's eyes brimming now with that false compassion.

'My name is Edward Daniels.'

'No.' Cawley shook his head with an air of weary defeat. 'Your name is Andrew Laeddis. You did a terrible thing, and you can't forgive yourself, no matter what, so you play-act. You convince yourself you're still a US marshal and you're here on a case. And you've uncovered a conspiracy, which means that anything we tell you to the contrary plays into your fantasy that we're conspiring against you. And maybe we could let that go, let you live in your fantasy world. I'd like that. If you were harmless, I'd like that a lot. But you're violent, you're very violent. And because of your military and law-enforcement training, you're too good at it. You're the most dangerous patient we have here. We can't contain you. It's been decided—look at me.'

Teddy looked up, saw Cawley half stretching across the table, his eyes pleading.

'It's been decided that if we can't bring you back to sanity—now, right now—permanent measures will be taken to ensure you never hurt anyone again. Do you understand what I'm saying to you?'

For a moment—a tenth of a moment—Teddy almost believed him.

Then Teddy smiled. 'It's a nice act you've got going, Doc. Who's the bad cop—Sheehan?'

'Look at me,' Cawley said. 'Look into my eyes.'

Teddy did. They were red and swimming from lack of sleep.

'Listen,' Cawley said, 'I'm all you've got. I've been hearing this fantasy for two years now. I know every detail, every wrinkle—the codes, the missing partner, the storm, the woman in the cave, the evil experiments. I know about Noyce and the fictitious Senator Hurly. I know you dream of Dolores all the time and she's soaking with water. I know about the logs.'

'You're full of shit,' Teddy said. He ticked off the evidence on his trembling fingers: 'I've been eating your food, drinking your coffee, smoking your cigarettes. Hell, I took three "aspirin" from you the morning I arrived. Then you drugged me the other night. You were sitting there when I woke up. I haven't been the same since.'

Cawley leaned back and grimaced. 'I'm running out of time,' he whispered. 'I was given four days. I'm almost out.'

'So let me go. I'll file a complaint with the marshals' office, but with all your powerful friends I'm sure it won't amount to much.'

Cawley said, 'No, Andrew. I'm almost out of friends. I've been fighting a battle here for eight years and the scales have tipped in the other side's favour. I'm going to lose my funding. I swore before the entire board of overseers that I could construct the most extravagant role-playing experiment psychiatry has ever seen and it would save you. It would bring you back. But if I was wrong?' His eyes widened and he looked across the table at Teddy. 'Don't you understand, Andrew? If I fail, it's all over.'

'Gee,' Teddy said, 'that's too bad.'

Outside, some gulls cawed. Cawley said, 'Let's try this another way—do you think it's a coincidence that Rachel Solando, a figment of your own imagination by the way, would have the same letters in her name as your dead wife, the same history of killing her children?'

Teddy stood and the shakes rocked his arms from the shoulders on down. 'My wife did not kill her kids. We never had kids.'

'You never had kids? OK.' Cawley walked over to the wall and pulled down another sheet. Behind it—a crime-scene diagram, photographs of three dead children. And then the names, written in the same block letters:

EDWARD LAEDDIS
DANIEL LAEDDIS
RACHEL LAEDDIS

Teddy dropped his eyes and stared at his hands; they jumped as if they were no longer attached to him.

'Your children, Andrew. Are you going to deny they ever lived?'

Teddy pointed across the room at him with his jerking hand. 'Those are Rachel Solando's children. That is the crime-scene diagram of Rachel Solando's lake house.'

'That's your house. You went there because the doctors suggested it for your wife. You remember? After she *accidentally* set your previous apartment on fire. Get her out of the city, they said, give her a more bucolic setting. Maybe she would get better.'

'She wasn't ill.'

'She was insane, Andrew.'

'Stop calling me that! She was not insane.'

'Your wife was clinically depressed. She was diagnosed as manic-depressive. She was—'

'She was not,' Teddy said.

'She was suicidal. She hurt the children. You refused to see it. You thought she was weak. All she had to do was remember her *responsibilities.* To you. To the children. You drank, and your drinking got worse. You floated into your own shell. You stayed away from home. You ignored all the signs.'

'My wife was not insane!'

'The only reason she ever saw a psychiatrist was because she tried to commit suicide and ended up in the hospital. And they told you she was a danger to herself. They told you—'

'We never saw any psychiatrists!'

'—she was a danger to the children. You were warned.'

'We never had children. She couldn't get pregnant.' His head felt like someone was beating glass into it with a rolling pin.

'Come over here,' Cawley said. 'Really. Come and look at these crime-scene photos. You'll be interested to know—'

'You can fake those. You can make up your own.'

'You dream. You can't stop dreaming, Andrew. You've told me about them. Have you had any lately with the two boys and the little girl? Huh? Has the little girl taken you to your headstone? You're a "bad sailor", Andrew. Know what that means? It means you're a bad father. You didn't navigate for them. You didn't save them. You want to talk about the logs? Huh? Come over here and look at them. Tell me they're not the children from your dreams.'

'Bullshit.'

'Then look. Come here and *look*.'

'You drug me, you kill my partner, you say he never existed. You're going to lock me up here because I know what you're doing. I know about the experiments. I know what you're giving schizophrenics, your liberal use of lobotomies, your utter disregard for the Nuremberg Code. I am *onto you*, Doctor.'

'You are?' Cawley leaned against the wall and folded his arms. 'Please, educate me. You've had the run of the place the last four days. Where are the Nazi doctors? Where are the satanic operating rooms?' He walked back to the table, consulted his notes for a moment. 'Do you still believe we're brainwashing patients, Andrew? Implementing some decades-long experiment to create—what did you call them once? Oh, here it is—ghost soldiers? Assassins?' He chuckled. 'I mean, I have to give you credit, Andrew—even in these days of rampant paranoia, your fantasies take the cake. Show me one piece of evidence that your theory can hold water. Just one.'

Teddy said nothing.

'And to all the evidence that *I've* presented, you have refused to respond.'

'That's because it's not evidence at all. It's fabricated.'

Cawley pressed his hands together and raised them as if in prayer.

'Let me off this island,' Teddy said. 'As a federally appointed officer of the law, I demand that you let me leave.'

Cawley closed his eyes for a moment. When he opened them, they were clearer and harder. 'OK, OK. You got me, Marshal. Here, I'll make it easy on you.' He pulled a soft leather briefcase off the floor and undid the buckles and opened it and tossed Teddy's gun onto the table. 'That's your gun, right?'

Teddy stared at it.

'Those are your initials engraved on the handle, correct?'

Teddy could see the dent in the barrel from the day when Phillip Stacks took a shot at him and hit the gun instead and Stacks ended up shot from the ricochet of his own bullet. He could see the initials E.D. engraved on the handle, a gift from the field office after he ended up shooting it out with Breck in Maine.

'Is that your gun, Marshal?'

'Yeah.'

'Pick it up, Marshal. Make sure it's loaded.'

Teddy lifted the gun from the table and it shook in his hand.

'Is it loaded?' Cawley asked.

'Yes. I can feel the weight.'

Cawley nodded. 'Then blast away. Because that's the only way you're ever getting off this island.'

Teddy tried to steady his arm with his other hand, but that was shaking too. He took several breaths, exhaling them slowly, sighting down the barrel through the sweat in his eyes and the tremors in his body, but he was listing up and down and side to side as if they both stood on a boat in the high seas.

'You have five seconds, Marshal.'

Cawley lifted the phone out of the radio pack and cranked the handle, and Teddy watched him place the phone to his mouth. 'Three seconds now.'

Teddy could feel the weight of the gun. He still had a chance if he took it now. Killed Cawley, killed whoever was waiting outside.

Cawley said, 'Warden, you can send him up.'

And Teddy's vision cleared and he looked down the barrel as Cawley put the phone back in the pack.

Cawley got a curious look on his face, as if only now did it occur to him that Teddy might have the faculties left to pull this off. He held up a hand, and said, 'OK, OK.'

And Teddy shot him dead centre in the chest.

Then he raised his hands a half an inch and shot Cawley in the face. With water.

Cawley took a handkerchief from his pocket.

The door opened behind Teddy, and he spun in his chair and took aim as a man entered the room.

'Don't shoot,' Chuck said. 'I forgot to wear my raincoat.'

Cawley wiped his face with the handkerchief and Chuck came

round the table to Cawley's side and Teddy turned the gun in his palm and stared down at it. He looked across the table as Chuck took his seat, and Teddy noticed he was wearing a lab coat.

'I thought you were dead,' Teddy said.

'Nope,' Chuck said.

It was suddenly hard to get words out. He felt the inclination to stutter, just as the woman doctor had predicted. 'I . . . I . . . was . . . I was willing to die to bring you out of here. I . . .' He felt all strength drain from his body. He fell into his chair.

'I'm genuinely sorry about that,' Chuck said. 'We agonised for weeks before we put this into play. I never wanted to cause you undue anguish. But we were certain we had no alternative.'

'There's a bit of a clock ticking on this one,' Cawley said. 'This was our last-ditch effort to bring you back, Andrew.'

Teddy wiped at the sweat in his eyes, ended up smearing it there. He looked through the blur at Chuck. 'Who are you?' he said.

Chuck stretched a hand across the table. 'Dr Lester Sheehan.'

Teddy left the hand hanging in the air and Sheehan eventually withdrew it.

'So,' Teddy said, 'you let me go on about how we needed to find Sheehan when you . . . you *were* Sheehan.'

Sheehan nodded.

'Called me "boss". Told me jokes. Kept me entertained.'

Sheehan dropped his gaze to his tie. 'I had to keep an eye on you, make sure you were safe.'

'Safe,' Teddy said. 'So that made everything OK. Moral.'

'I've been your primary psychiatrist for two years, Andrew. Look at me. Don't you even recognise me?'

Teddy used the cuff of his jacket to wipe the sweat from his eyes, and this time they cleared, and he looked across the table at Chuck. Good ol' Chuck with his awkwardness around firearms and those hands that didn't fit his job description because they weren't the hands of a cop. They were the hands of a doctor.

'You were my friend,' Teddy said. 'I trusted you. I climbed down a cliff looking for you. Were you watching me then? Keeping me safe then? You were my friend, Chuck. Oh, I'm sorry. Lester.'

Lester lit a cigarette and Teddy was pleased to see that his hands shook too. Not as badly as Teddy's, but still . . . I hope you've got it too, Teddy thought. Whatever this is.

'Yeah,' Sheehan said, 'I was keeping you safe. My disappearance was, yes, part of your fantasy. But you were supposed to see Laeddis's intake form on the road, not down the cliff. I dropped it off the promontory by mistake. Just pulling it out of my back pocket, and it blew away. I went down after it, because I knew if I didn't, *you* would. And I froze. Right under the lip. Twenty minutes later, you drop down right in front of me. I mean, a foot away. I almost reached out and grabbed you.'

Cawley cleared his throat. 'We almost called it off when we saw you were going to go down that cliff. Maybe we should have.'

'Called it off.' Teddy suppressed a giggle into his fist.

'Yes,' Cawley said. 'Called it off. This was a pageant, Andrew. A—'

'My name's Teddy.'

'—play. You wrote it. We helped you stage it. But the play wouldn't work without an ending, and the ending was always your reaching this lighthouse.'

'Convenient,' Teddy said and looked around at the walls.

'You've been telling this story to us for almost two years now. How you came here to find a missing patient and stumbled onto our Third Reich-inspired surgical experiments. How the patient Rachel Solando had killed her children in much the same way your wife killed yours. How just when you got close, your partner—and don't you love the name you gave him? Chuck Aule. I mean, Jesus, say it a couple of times fast. It's just another of your jokes, Andrew—your partner was taken and you were left to fend for yourself, but we got to you. We drugged you. And you were committed before you could get the story back to your imaginary Senator Hurly.'

'You faked all this?' Teddy said.

'Yes.'

Teddy laughed. He laughed as hard as he'd laughed since before Dolores had died. 'How do you fake a hurricane?' he said and slapped the table. 'Tell me that, Doctor.'

'You can't fake a hurricane,' Cawley said.

'No,' Teddy said, 'you can't.' And he slapped the table again.

Cawley looked at his hand, then up into his eyes. 'But you can predict one from time to time, Andrew. Particularly on an island.'

Teddy shook his head, felt a grin still plastered to his face, even as the warmth of it died. 'You guys never give up.'

'A storm was essential to your fantasy,' Cawley said. 'We waited for one.'

Teddy said, 'Lies.'

'Lies? Explain the anagrams. Explain how the children in those pictures—children you've never seen if they belonged to Rachel Solando—are the same children in your dreams. Explain, Andrew, how I knew to say to you when you walked through this door, "Why you all wet, baby?" Do you think I'm a mind-reader?'

'No,' Teddy said. 'I think I was wet.'

Cawley took a long breath, and leaned into the table. 'Your codes? They're showing, Andrew. You're playing jokes on yourself. Look at the one in your notebook. The last one. Look at it. Nine letters. Three words. Should be a piece of cake to break. Look at it.'

Teddy looked down at the page:

13(M)–21(U)–25(Y)–18(R)–1(A)–5(E)–8(H)–15(O)–9(I)

'We're running out of time,' Lester Sheehan said. 'Please understand, it's all changing. Psychiatry. It's had its own war going on for some time, and we're losing.'

'Yeah?' Teddy said absently. 'And who's "we"?'

Cawley said, 'Men who believe that the way to the mind is not by way of ice picks through the brain or large dosages of dangerous medicine but through an honest reckoning of the self.'

'If we fail here,' Sheehan said, 'we've lost. Not just with you. Right now, the balance of power is in the hands of the surgeons, but that's changing. The pharmacists will take over, and it won't be any less barbaric. The zombiefication will continue, but under a more palatable veneer. It comes down to you, Andrew.'

'My name is Teddy. Teddy Daniels.'

Cawley nodded. 'We had four days on this. If we fail, you go into surgery.'

'Surgery for what?'

Cawley looked at Sheehan.

Sheehan studied his cigarette. 'A transorbital lobotomy.'

Teddy blinked at that and looked back at his page. He guessed the first word was probably 'you', the second 'are'. He looked up. 'Just like Noyce,' he said. 'I suppose you'll tell me he's not here, either.'

'He's here,' Cawley said. 'And a lot of the story you told Dr Sheehan about him is true, Andrew. But he never came back to Boston. You never met him in a jail. He's been here since August 1950. He did get to the point where he transferred out of Ward C and was trusted enough to live in Ward A. But then two weeks ago you assaulted him. Damn near killed him.'

'Why would I do that?'

Cawley looked over at Sheehan.

'Because he called you Laeddis,' Sheehan said.

'No, he didn't. I saw him yesterday and he—'

'He what?'

'He didn't call me Laeddis, that's for damn sure.'

'No?' Cawley flipped open his notebook. 'I have read the transcript of your conversation. The tapes are back in my office, but for now let's go with the transcripts. Tell me if this sounds familiar.' He adjusted his glasses, head bent to the page. 'I'm quoting here—"This is about you. And, Laeddis, this is all it's ever been about. I was incidental. I was a way in."'

Teddy shook his head. 'He's not calling me Laeddis. You switched the emphasis. He was saying "this is about you"—meaning me—*and* Laeddis.'

Cawley chuckled. 'You really are something.'

Teddy smiled. 'I was thinking the same thing about you.'

Cawley looked down at the transcript. 'How about this—Do you remember asking Noyce what happened to his face?'

'Sure. I asked him who was responsible.'

'And Noyce replied—again I'm quoting here—"You did this."'

Teddy said, 'Right, but . . . He was speaking like . . .' Teddy was having trouble getting words to connect, to follow in line like boxcars. 'He was saying'—he spoke slowly, deliberately—'that my failure to keep him from getting transported back here led, in an indirect way, to his getting beaten up. He wasn't saying I beat him.'

Cawley turned a page. 'How about this, then? Noyce speaking again—"They *knew.* Don't you get it? Everything you were up to. Your whole plan. This is a game. A handsomely mounted stage play. All this is for you."'

Teddy sat back. 'All these patients, all these people I've supposedly known for two years, and none of them said a word to me while I was performing my, um, masquerade the last four days?'

Cawley closed the notebook. 'They're used to it. You've been flashing that plastic badge for a year now. Go on. Open your wallet. Tell me if it's plastic or not, Andrew.'

'Let me finish the code.'

'You're almost done. Three letters to go. Want help, Andrew?'

'Teddy.'

Cawley shook his head. 'Andrew. Andrew Laeddis.' He watched

him arrange the letters on the page. 'What's it say?'

Teddy laughed, then shook his head. 'You did this. You left those codes. You created the name Rachel Solando using my wife's name. This is all you.'

Cawley spoke slowly, precisely. 'What does the last code say?'

Teddy turned the notebook so they could see it:

you are him

'Satisfied?' he said.

Cawley stood. He looked exhausted. Stretched to the end of his rope. He spoke with an air of desolation Teddy hadn't heard before. 'We hoped. We hoped we could save you. We stuck our reputations on the line. And now word will get out that we allowed a patient to play-act his grandest delusion and all we got for it were a couple of injured guards and a burnt car. Since you've been here, you've injured eight guards, not including the two today, four patients and five orderlies. Dr Sheehan and I have fought for you as long and as hard as we've been able. But most of the staff are demanding we show results or else we incapacitate you.' He leaned across the table and fixed Teddy in his sad, dark gaze. 'This was our last gasp, Andrew. If you don't accept who you are and what you did, if you don't make an effort to swim towards sanity, we can't save you.' He held out his hand. 'Take it,' he said, and his voice was hoarse. 'Please. Andrew? Help me save you.'

Teddy smiled and shook the hand. He gave Cawley his most forthright grip, his most forthright gaze. 'Stop calling me Andrew.'

THEY LED HIM to Ward C in shackles, took him to the basement.

While he remained manacled, a guard standing on either side of him, a nurse entered the cell and injected something into his arm. She had strawberry hair and smelt of soap and Teddy caught a whiff of her breath as she leaned in to deliver the shot, and he knew her.

'You pretended to be Rachel,' he said. 'It was you. With dye in your hair. You're Rachel.'

She said, 'Don't flinch,' and sank the needle into his arm.

He caught her eye. 'You're an excellent actress. I mean, you really had me, all that stuff about your dear, dead Jim. Very convincing, Rachel.'

She dropped her eyes from his. 'I'm Emily,' she said and pulled the needle out. 'You sleep now.'

'Please,' Teddy said.

She paused at the cell door and looked back at him.

'It was you,' he said.

The nod didn't come from her chin. It came from her eyes, a tiny, downward flick of them, and then she gave him a smile so bereft he wanted to kiss her hair. 'Good night,' she said.

He never felt the guards remove the manacles, never heard them leave. The sounds from the other cells died and he felt as if he were lying on his back in the centre of a wet cloud. And he dreamed. And in his dreams he and Dolores lived in a house by a lake. Because they'd had to leave the city. Because the city was mean and violent. Because she'd lit their apartment on Buttonwood on fire. Trying to rid it of ghosts.

And his Rachel said to him one night when he was drunk, but not so drunk that he hadn't managed to read her a bedtime story, his Rachel said, 'Daddy?'

He said, 'What, sweetie?'

'Mommy looks at me funny sometimes.'

'Funny how?'

'Like I make her really sad.'

And he tucked her in and kissed her good night and nuzzled her neck with his nose and told her she didn't make anyone sad. Wouldn't, couldn't. Ever.

HE WOULD SAY to her: 'What's wrong? What don't I do? What don't I give you? How can I make you happy?'

And she'd say, 'I'm happy.'

'No, you're not. Tell me what I need to do. I'll do it.'

'I'm fine.'

'You're not fine. You get so angry. And if you're not angry, you're too happy, bouncing off the walls. It scares the kids, scares me.'

'I'm fine.'

'You're sad all the time.'

'No,' she'd say. 'That's you.'

HE TALKED to the priest and the priest made a visit or two. He talked to her sisters, and the older one, Delilah, came up from Virginia for a week once, and that seemed to help for a while.

They both avoided any suggestion of doctors. Doctors were for crazy people. Dolores wasn't crazy. She was just tense.

Tense and sad.

HE DREAMED he came home to the house by the lake.

He'd been in Oklahoma. Spent two weeks chasing a guy from the South Boston docks to Tulsa with about ten stops in between, Teddy always half a step behind until he literally bumped into the guy as he was coming out of a gas station men's room.

He walked back in the house at eleven in the morning, grateful that the boys were in school, and he could feel the road in his bones and a crushing desire for his own pillow. He walked into the house and called out to Dolores as he poured himself a Scotch and she came in from the back yard and said, 'There wasn't enough.'

He turned with his drink in hand and said, 'What's that, hon?' and noticed that she was wet, as if she'd just stepped from the shower, except she wore an old dress with a faded floral print. She was barefoot and the water dripped off her hair and dripped off her dress.

'Baby,' he said, 'why you all wet?'

She said, 'There wasn't enough,' and placed a bottle down on the counter. 'I'm still awake.'

And she walked back outside.

Teddy saw her walk towards the gazebo, taking long, meandering steps, swaying. And he put his drink down on the counter and picked up the bottle and saw that it was the laudanum the doctor had prescribed after her hospital stay. If Teddy had to go on a trip, he portioned out the number of teaspoonfuls he figured she'd need while he was gone, and decanted them to a small bottle in her medicine cabinet. Then he took this bottle and locked it up in the cellar.

There were six months of doses in this bottle and she'd drunk it dry.

He saw her stumble up the gazebo stairs, fall to her knees, and get back up again.

How had she managed to get to the bottle? Teddy had the only key to the lock on the cellar cabinet.

He watched her sit in the porch swing in the centre of the gazebo and he looked at the bottle. He remembered standing right here the night he left, adding the teaspoons to the medicine cabinet bottle, having a belt or two of rye for himself, looking out at the lake, putting the smaller bottle in the medicine cabinet, going upstairs to say goodbye to the kids, coming back down as the phone rang, and he'd taken the call from the field office, grabbed his overnight bag and kissed Dolores at the door and headed to his car . . . leaving the bigger bottle behind on the kitchen counter.

Now he went outside and crossed the lawn to the gazebo and

walked up the steps and she watched him come, soaking wet, one leg dangling as she pushed the swing back and forth in a lazy tilt.

He said, 'Honey, when did you drink all this?'

'This morning.' She gave him a dreamy smile. 'Not enough, though. Can't sleep. Just want to sleep. Too tired.'

He saw the logs floating in the lake behind her and he knew they weren't logs, but he looked away, back at his wife. 'Why are you tired?'

She shrugged, flopping her hands out by her side. 'Tired of all this. So tired. Just want to go home.'

'You are home.'

She pointed at the curved ceiling. 'Home-home,' she said.

Teddy looked out at those logs again, turning gently in the water. 'Where's Rachel?'

'School.'

'She's too young for school, honey.'

'Not my school,' his wife said and showed him her teeth.

And Teddy screamed. He screamed so loudly that Dolores fell out of the swing and he jumped over her and jumped over the railing at the back of the gazebo and ran screaming, screaming no, screaming God, screaming please, screaming not my babies . . . And he plunged into the water. He stumbled and fell forwards on his face and went under and the water covered him like oil and he swam forwards and came up in the centre of them. The three logs. His babies.

Edward and Daniel were face down, but Rachel was on her back, her eyes open and looking up at the sky, her mother's desolation imprinted in her pupils, her gaze searching the clouds.

He carried them out one by one and laid them carefully on the shore. He caressed their cheeks. He caressed their shoulders and their rib cages and their legs and their feet. He kissed them many times.

He dropped to his knees and vomited until his chest burned and his stomach was stripped.

He went back and crossed their arms over their chests, and he noticed that Daniel and Rachel had rope burns on their wrists, and he knew that Edward had been the first to die. The other two had waited, knowing she'd be coming back for them.

He kissed each of his children again on both cheeks and their foreheads and he closed Rachel's eyes.

Had they kicked in her arms as she carried them to the water? Had they screamed? Or had they gone soft and moaning, resigned to it?

He saw his wife in her violet dress the night he'd met her at the

Cocoanut Grove and saw the look in her face that first moment of seeing her, that look he'd fallen in love with. He'd thought it had just been the dress, her insecurity about wearing such a fine dress in a fine club. But that wasn't it. It was terror, barely suppressed, and it was always there. It was terror of the outside—of trains, bombs, rattling streetcars and dark avenues and Russians and submarines and taverns filled with angry men. She was afraid of all that and so much more, but what terrified her most was inside her, an insect of unnatural intelligence who'd been living in her brain her entire life, playing with it, clicking across it, wrenching loose its cables on a whim.

Teddy left his children and sat on the gazebo floor for a long time, watching her sway, and the worst of it all was how much he loved her. If he could sacrifice his own mind to restore hers, he would. Sell his limbs? Fine. She had been all the love he'd ever known for so long. She had been what carried him through the war, through this awful world. He loved her more than his life, more than his soul.

But he'd failed her. Failed his children. Failed the life they'd built together because he'd refused to see Dolores, really *see* her, see that her insanity was not her fault, not some proof of moral weakness.

He'd refused to see it because if she actually were his true love, his immortal other self, then what did that say about his brain, his sanity, his moral weakness?

And so, he'd hidden from it. He'd left her alone, his one love, and let her mind consume itself.

He watched her sway. Oh, how he loved her.

Teddy sat on the floor of the gazebo and wept. He wasn't sure for how long. He wept and he saw Dolores looking back over her shoulder at him on their honeymoon and Dolores in her violet dress and pregnant with Edward and curled in his arms as she gave his hand a peck and smiling her Sunday-morning smiles and staring at him as the rest of her face broke around those big eyes and she looked so scared and so alone, always, some part of her, so alone . . .

He stood and took a seat beside his wife and she said, 'You're my good man.'

'No,' he said. 'I'm not.'

'You are.' She took his hand. 'You love me. I know that. I know you're not perfect.'

What had they thought—Daniel and Rachel—when they woke to their mother tying rope round their wrists?

'Oh, baby,' he said, 'please don't say any more.'

And Edward. Edward would have run. She would have had to chase him through the house.

She was bright now, happy. 'Let's put them in the kitchen,' she said. 'Let's sit them at the table, Andrew.'

He held her to him and wept into her shoulder.

She said, 'They'll be our living dolls. We'll dry them off.'

'*What?*' His voice muffled in her shoulder.

'We'll change their clothes.' She whispered it in his ear.

He couldn't see her in a box, a white rubber box with a small viewing window in the door.

'We'll let them sleep in our bed tonight.'

'Please stop talking.'

'And then tomorrow we can take them on a picnic.'

'If you ever loved me . . .' Teddy could see them lying on the shore.

'I always loved you, baby.'

'If you ever loved me, please stop talking,' Teddy said.

He wanted to go to his children, to bring them alive, to take them away from here, away from her.

Dolores placed her hand on his gun.

He clamped his hand over hers.

'I need you to love me,' she said. 'I need you to free me.'

She pulled at his gun, but he removed her hand. He looked in her eyes. They were so bright they hurt. They were not the eyes of a human. A dog maybe. A wolf, possibly.

After the war, after Dachau, he'd sworn he would never kill again unless he had no choice. Unless the other man's gun was already pointed at him. Only then.

He couldn't take one more death. He couldn't.

She tugged at his gun, her eyes growing even brighter, and he removed her hand again.

He looked out at the shore and saw them neatly lined up, shoulder to shoulder.

He pulled his gun free of its holster. He showed it to her.

She bit her lip, weeping, and nodded. She said, 'We'll pretend they're with us. We'll give them baths, Andrew.'

And he placed the gun to her belly and his hand trembled and his lips trembled and he said, 'I love you, Dolores.'

And even then, with his gun to her body, he was sure he couldn't do it.

She looked down as if surprised that she was still there, that he was still below her. 'I love you, too. I love you so much. I love you like—'

And he pulled the trigger. And she placed her hand over the hole and looked at him, her other hand gripping his hair.

And as it spilled out of her, he pulled her to him and she went soft against his body and he wept his terrible love into her faded dress.

HE SAT UP in the dark and smelt the cigarette smoke before he saw Sheehan taking a drag on the cigarette, watching him. He sat on the bed and wept. He couldn't stop weeping.

'Rachel, Rachel, Rachel,' he said, over and over. And he saw her eyes watching the clouds and her hair floating out around her.

When the convulsions stopped, when the tears dried, Sheehan said, 'Rachel who?'

'Rachel Laeddis,' he said.

'And you are?'

'Andrew,' he said. 'My name is Andrew Laeddis.'

Sheehan turned on a small light and revealed Cawley and a guard on the other side of the bars, staring in.

'Why are you here?' Cawley asked.

He took the handkerchief Sheehan offered and wiped his face. 'Because I murdered my wife.'

'And why did you do that?'

'Because she murdered our children and she needed peace.'

'Are you a US marshal?' Sheehan said.

'No. I was once. Not any more.'

'How long have you been here?'

'Since May the 3rd, 1952.'

'Who was Rachel Laeddis?'

'My daughter. She was four.'

'Who is Rachel Solando?'

'She doesn't exist. I made her up.'

'Why?' Cawley said.

Teddy shook his head. 'I don't know, I don't know . . .'

'Yes, you do, Andrew. Tell me why.'

Teddy grabbed his head and rocked in place. 'Don't make me say it. Please? Please, Doctor?'

Cawley gripped the bars. 'I need to hear it, Andrew.'

He looked through the bars at him. 'Because,' he said and stopped. He cleared his throat, spat on the floor. 'Because I can't take knowing that I let my wife kill my babies. I ignored all the signs. I tried to wish it away. I killed them because I didn't get her some help. And knowing that is too much. I can't live with it.'

'But you have to. You realise that.'

He nodded. He pulled his knees to his chest.

Sheehan looked back over his shoulder at Cawley.

Cawley stared in through the bars. He lit a cigarette, watched Teddy steadily. 'Here's my fear, Andrew. We've been here before. We had this exact same break nine months ago. And then you regressed. Rapidly.'

'I'm sorry.'

'I appreciate that,' Cawley said, 'but I can't use an apology right now. I need to know that you've accepted reality. None of us can afford another regression.'

Teddy looked at Cawley, this too-thin man with great pools of shadow under his eyes. This man who'd come to save him. This man who might be the only true friend he'd ever had.

'I won't regress,' he said. 'My name is Andrew Laeddis. I murdered my wife, Dolores, in the spring of '52 . . .'

15

The sun was in the room when he woke.

He sat up and looked towards the bars, but the bars weren't there. Just a window, lower than it should have been until he realised he was on the top bunk in the room he'd shared with Trey and Bibby.

It was empty. He hopped off the bunk and opened the closet and saw his clothes there, fresh from the laundry, and he put them on. He walked to the window and placed a foot up on the ledge to tie his shoe and looked out at the compound and saw patients and orderlies and guards in equal number, some milling in front of the hospital, others continuing the cleanup, some tending the rosebushes.

When he'd tied the second shoe he left the room and walked down the stairs and out into the compound. He passed Nurse Marino and she gave him a smile and said, 'Morning.'

'Beautiful one,' he said.

'Gorgeous. I think that storm blew summer out for good.'

He looked at a sky the colour of baby-blue eyes and he could smell a freshness in the air that had been missing since June.

'Enjoy the day,' Nurse Marino said, and he watched her as she walked away, felt it was maybe a sign of health that he enjoyed the sway of her hips.

He walked into the compound and passed some orderlies on their day off tossing a ball back and forth and they waved and said, 'Good morning,' and he waved and said 'Good morning' back.

He heard the sound of the ferry horn as it neared the dock, and he saw Cawley and the warden talking on the lawn in front of the hospital and they nodded in acknowledgment and he nodded back.

He sat down on the corner of the hospital steps and looked out at all of it and felt as good as he'd felt in a long time.

'Here.'

He took the cigarette and put it in his mouth, leaned in towards the flame and smelt that kerosene stench of the Zippo before it was snapped closed.

'How we doing this morning?'

'Good. You?' He sucked the smoke back into his lungs.

'Can't complain.'

'So what's our next move?' he said.

'You tell me, boss.'

He smiled at Chuck. The two of them sitting in the morning sunlight, taking their ease, acting as if all was just fine with the world.

'Gotta find a way off this rock,' Teddy said. 'Get our asses home.'

Chuck nodded. 'I figured you'd say something like that.'

'Any ideas?'

Chuck said, 'Give me a minute.'

Teddy nodded and leaned back against the steps. He had a minute. Maybe even a few minutes. He watched Chuck raise his hand and shake his head at the same time and he saw Cawley nod in acknowledgment and then Cawley said something to the warden and they crossed the lawn towards Teddy with four orderlies falling into step behind them, one of them holding a white bundle, some sort of fabric, Teddy thinking he might have spied some metal on it as the orderly unrolled it and it caught the sun.

Teddy said, 'I don't know, Chuck. You think they're onto us?'

'Nah.' Chuck tilted his head back, squinting a bit in the sun, and he smiled at Teddy. 'We're too smart for that.'

'Yeah,' Teddy said. 'We are, aren't we?'

DENNIS LEHANE

Part psychological drama, part thriller, *Shutter Island* is a new departure for this Irish-American author who has built his reputation with a string of six crime novels starring the detective duo Patrick Kenzie and Angie Gennaro. Lehane wanted to give those characters a rest, plus he'd been inspired by an idea that came to him out of the blue: 'What if a guy showed up on an island, during the Cold War, to investigate a disappearance?' That starting point, combined with an irresistibly gothic setting, resulted in the gripping and thought-provoking *Shutter Island*.

Lehane was first published almost by accident. In his mid-twenties he had dropped out of two colleges and was doing a variety of jobs. He'd always written short stories and loved writing, but his life seemed to be going nowhere. The turning point came when he won a fellowship for a graduate writing programme in Miami. A professor and good friend asked to see the draft of a novel that Lehane had knocked out in three weeks 'as something to do', and suggested it was redrafted and sent to an agent. That book, *A Drink Before the War*, won a Shamus Award in 1994 and transformed Lehane's life.

Since then, with films of both *Prayers for Rain* and *Mystic River* in the making (the latter to be directed by Clint Eastwood), Lehane has gone from strength to strength, forging his talent on the old maxim that character should drive plot. 'That's the fun of writing,' he says. 'That moment when, all of a sudden, your character does something that you didn't intend him to do and you realise it had been oddly inevitable since the first time you introduced him. That's why I write. That's the high.'

Lehane, who was raised on Boston's rough south side, still lives near the city. He reckons himself to be 'a boring guy' who relaxes by playing poor tennis, watching movies with his wife Sheila and messing around with his two English bulldogs. 'Outside of a serious addiction to watching football during the autumn, that's about it.'

THE
RUNNER

PETER MAY

Beijing is in the icy grip of winter, the gusting snow and freezing winds whipping the gridlocked cars and skidding cyclists. But the weather is not what's troubling Detective Li Yan. His plans to marry have put his career in jeopardy, and now a government official is asking him to cover up the truth.

Prologue

The swimmers come in by the south gate, off Chengfu Lu. A dozen of them, balancing carefully in the early evening dark as plummeting temperatures turn the snow-melt to ice under the slithering tyres of their bicycles. The only thing that can dampen their spirits ahead of tomorrow's competition is the death that lies in silent wait for them, just minutes away.

But for now, their only focus is the warm chlorine-filled air, water slipping easily over sleek, toned muscles, the rasp of lungs pumping air in the vast echoing chamber of the pool. A final training session before confrontation tomorrow with the Americans. A flutter of fear in the stomach, a rush of adrenaline that accompanies the thought. So much riding on them. The aspirations of a nation. China. More than a billion people investing their hopes in the efforts of this chosen few.

They wave at the guard, who glares sullenly at them as they cycle past. He stamps frozen feet and hugs his fur-lined grey coat tighter for warmth, icy breath clouding round his head like smoke.

Turning right, by pink accommodation blocks, the swimmers shout their exuberance into the night, the foggy vapour of their breath clearing in their wake like the pollution the authorities have promised to sweep from Beijing's summer skies before the world finally descends for the Greatest Show on Earth. The vast, sprawling campus of Qinghua University is laid out before them, delineated in the dark by light reflecting off piles of swept snow. It is here that John Ma inspired the rebirth of Chinese sport more than seventy years ago, building the first modern sports complex in China. Snow rests now on the head and shoulders of his stone-cold statue by a frozen lake somewhere.

But they are not even aware of this nugget of history, of the statue, of the old pool where Mao used to swim in splendid isolation while the building was ringed by armed guards. They are interested only in the lights, beyond the gymnasium and the running track, of the natatorium. For it is here they have spent these last weeks, burning muscles, pushing themselves to the limits of pain and endurance, urged on by the relentless barking of their coach.

The swimmers park up among the hundreds of bicycles stacked in rows beneath the student apartments. They trot across the concourse, swinging arms to keep warm, and push open the double doors of the east entrance, warm air stinging cold skin. Down deserted corridors to the locker room that has become so familiar.

It is only as they strip and drag on costumes that they notice he is missing.

'Hey, where's Sui Mingshan?'

'Said he'd meet us here,' someone replies. 'You see him when we came in?'

No one has seen him. He isn't here. Which is unusual. Because if anything, Sui Mingshan is the keenest of them. Certainly the most likely to beat the Americans. The best prospect for the Olympics.

'He probably got held up by the weather.'

They pass through the disinfectant foot bath and climb steps leading up to the pool, excited voices echoing between the rows of empty blue seats in the auditorium, wet feet slapping on dry tiles.

When they first see him, they are slow to understand. A moment of incomprehension, a silly joke, and then silence as they realise, finally, what it is they are witnessing.

Sui Mingshan is naked, his long, finely sculpted body turning slowly in a movement forced by air conditioning. He dangles almost midway between the highest of the diving platforms above and the still waters of the diving pool below. He has fine, broad shoulders tapering to a slim waist. His thighs are curved and powerful, built to propel him through water faster than any other living human. Except that he is no longer living. His head is twisted at an unnatural angle where the rope that broke his fall has snapped his neck.

It takes the swimmers several moments to realise who he is. For his head of thick black hair has been shaved to the scalp, and in death he looks oddly unfamiliar.

Chapter One

Margaret tried to ignore the ache in her lower back that had begun to trouble her over the last couple of weeks. She sat with her back straight and stretched her legs out in front of her, then slowly bent her knees, bringing the soles of her feet together and pulling them towards her. She always found this exercise difficult.

Now in her mid-thirties, she was ten years older than most of the other women here, and her joints and muscles would not twist and stretch as they had once done. She looked at the women laid out on the floor around her. Most were lying on their sides with pillows beneath their heads. Expectant fathers squatted beside them, their eyes closed, breathing as one with the mothers of their unborn children. It was the new Friendly to Family Policy in practice. Where once men had been banned from the maternity wards of Chinese hospitals, their presence was now encouraged.

Margaret felt a pang of jealousy. She knew that there would be a good reason for Li Yan's failure to turn up. There always was. An armed robbery. A murder. A rape. A meeting he could not escape. And she could not blame him for it. But she felt deprived of him; frustrated that she was the only one among twenty whose partner regularly failed to attend; anxious that, in her third trimester, she was the only one in her antenatal class who was not married. While attitudes in the West might have changed, single mothers in China were still frowned upon. She stood out from the crowd in every way, and not just because of her Celtic blue eyes and fair hair.

From across the room she caught Jon Macken looking at her. He grinned and winked. She forced a smile. An American freelance photographer, Macken had come to China five years earlier on an assignment and fallen in love with his translator. He was somewhere in his middle sixties, and Yixuan was four years younger than Margaret. The couple had not wanted to leave China, and Macken had established himself in Beijing as the photographer of choice when it came to snapping visiting dignitaries, or shooting glossies for the latest joint venture.

When Li had not been at their first antenatal class, Yixuan had appointed herself unofficial translator for a bewildered Margaret.

The two of them had become friends, but, like Margaret, Yixuan was a loner, and so their friendship was conducted at a distance—unobtrusive, and therefore tolerable.

As the class broke up, Yixuan waddled across the room to Margaret. She smiled sympathetically. 'Still the police widow?'

Margaret shrugged, struggling to her feet. 'I knew it went with the territory. So I can't complain.' She placed the flats of her hands on the joints above her buttocks and arched her back. 'God . . .' she sighed. 'I don't know if I can take it for another whole month.'

Yixuan found a slip of paper in her bag and began scribbling on it in spidery Chinese characters. She said, without looking up, 'A journey of a thousand miles begins with a single step, Margaret. You have only a few more left to take.'

'Yeah, but they're the hardest,' Margaret complained. 'The first one was easy. It involved sex.'

'Did I hear someone mention my favourite subject?' Macken shuffled over to join them. With his cropped grey hair and patchy white beard, he cut an oddly scrawny figure in his jeans and T-shirt.

Yixuan thrust her scribbled note into his hand. 'If you take this down to the store on the corner,' she said, 'they'll box the stuff for you. I'll get a taxi and meet you there in about ten minutes.'

Macken glanced at the note and grinned. 'You know, that's what I love about China,' he said to Margaret. 'It makes me feel young again. I mean, who can remember the last time they were sent down to the grocery store with a note they couldn't read?' He turned his grin on Yixuan and pecked her affectionately on the cheek. 'I'll catch up with you later, hon.' He patted her belly. 'Both of you.'

Margaret and Yixuan made their way carefully downstairs together, wrapped up warm to meet the blast of cold night air that would greet them as they stepped out into the car park. Yixuan waited while Margaret searched for her bike, identifying it from dozens of others parked in the cycle racks by the scrap of pink ribbon tied to the basket on the handlebars.

'You should not still be riding that thing,' Yixuan said.

Margaret laughed. 'You're just jealous because Jon won't let you ride yours.' She would be in more danger, she figured, in the crowded buses and overfull subway carriages than on her bike.

Yixuan squeezed her arm. 'Take care. I'll see you Wednesday.' And she watched as Margaret slipped onto her saddle and pulled out into the stream of bicycles heading west in the cycle lane.

Margaret's scarf muffled her nose and mouth against the biting cold of the Beijing night. Her woollen hat, pulled down over her forehead, kept her head cosy and warm. But nothing could stop her eyes from watering. The forecasters had been predicting –20°C, and it felt like they were right.

She kept her head down, ignoring the roar of traffic on the main carriageway. On the other side of the road, beyond the high walls of Zhongnanhai, the leaders of this vast land were safe and warm in the centrally heated villas that lined the frozen lakes of Zhonghai and Nanhai. In the real world outside, people swaddled themselves in layers of clothes and burned coal briquettes in tiny stoves.

Not for the first time, Margaret found herself wondering what the hell she was doing here. An on-off relationship with a Beijing cop, a child conceived in error and then miscarried in tears. A decision that needed to be taken, a commitment that had to be made. Or not. And then a second conception. Although not entirely unplanned, it had made the decision for her. And so here she was. A highly paid job in Texas abandoned for a poorly remunerated lectureship at the University of Public Security in Beijing, training future Chinese cops in the techniques of modern forensic pathology. Not that they would let her teach any more. Maternity leave was enforced. She felt as if everything she had worked to become had been stripped away, leaving her naked and exposed as a woman and mother-to-be. And soon-to-be wife, with the wedding just a week away. They were not roles she had ever seen herself playing.

She waved to the security guard at the gate of the university compound and he called a greeting. It was a long ride from the hospital to the twenty-storey white tower block in Muxidi that housed the University of Public Security's 1,000 staff, and Margaret was exhausted. She would make something simple for herself to eat and have an early night. Her tiny two-roomed apartment on the eleventh floor felt like a prison cell, a lonely place that she was not allowed, officially, to share with Li. Even after the wedding, they would have to continue their separate lives until such time as the Ministry allocated Li a married officer's apartment.

The elevator climbed slowly through eleven floors, the thickly padded female attendant studiously ignoring her. The air was dense with the smell of stale smoke and squashed cigarette ends. Margaret tried to hold her breath until she could step out into the hallway and, with some relief, slip the key in the door of number 1123.

Inside, the reflected lights of the city below crept in through her kitchen window, enough for her to see to put on a kettle without resorting to the harsh overhead bulb, which was unshaded and cheerless. But she didn't see the shadow that crossed the hall behind her. The darting silhouette of a tall figure that moved silently through the doorway. His hand, slipping round to cover her mouth, prevented a scream from reaching her lips, and then immediately she relaxed as she felt his other hand slide gently across the swell of her belly, his lips nuzzling her ear.

'You bastard,' she whispered when he took his hand from her mouth and turned her to face him. 'You're not supposed to give me frights like that.'

He cocked an eyebrow. 'Who else would be interested in molesting some ugly fat foreigner?'

'Bastard!' she hissed again, and then reached on tiptoe to take his lower lip between her front teeth and hold it there until he forced them apart with his tongue.

When they broke apart, she looked up into his coal-dark eyes and asked, 'Where were you?'

'Margaret . . .' He sounded weary.

'I know,' she said quickly. 'Forget I asked.' Then, 'But I do miss you, Li Yan. I'm scared of going through this alone.'

He drew her to him, and pressed her head into his chest, his large hand cradling her skull. Li was a big man for a Chinese, powerfully built, more than six foot tall below his flat-top crew cut, and when he held her like this it made her feel small, like a child. But she hated feeling dependent.

'When will you hear about the apartment?'

She felt him tense. 'I don't know,' he said, and he moved away from her as the kettle boiled. She stood for a moment, watching him in the dark. Lately she had sensed his reluctance to discuss the subject.

'Well, have you asked?'

'Sure.'

'And what did they say?'

She sensed rather than saw him shrug. 'They haven't decided yet.'

'Haven't decided what? What apartment we're going to get? Or whether they're going to give us one at all?'

'Margaret, you know that it is a problem. A senior police officer having a relationship with a foreign national . . . there is no precedent.'

Margaret glared at him, and although he could not see her eyes, he could feel them burning into him. 'We're not having a *relationship*, Li Yan. I'm having your baby. We're getting married next week. And I'm sick and tired of spending lonely nights in this cold apartment.'

To her annoyance she felt tears welling in her eyes, and she fought to control herself. Li, she knew, was as helpless in this situation as she was. The authorities frowned upon their relationship. Nights together in her apartment or his were stolen, furtive affairs, unsanctioned and, in the case of her staying over with him, illegal. Li's position as the head of Beijing's Serious Crime Squad made them subject to rules that almost no one else bothered about these days. It was hard to take, and they had both hoped that their decision to marry would change it. But as yet, they had not received the blessing from above.

He moved closer to take her in his arms again. 'I can stay over.'

'You'd better,' she said, and turned away from him to pour hot water over green tea leaves in two glass mugs. She felt the heat of his body as he pressed himself into her back and she shivered as his hands slipped around her. She abandoned the green tea and turned to seek his mouth with hers, wanting to devour him, consume him.

The depressingly familiar ring-tone of Li's cellphone resonated in the dark.

'Don't answer,' she whispered.

For a moment she actually thought he wouldn't, as his hands drew her against him. But the shrill warble of the phone was relentless and finally he gave in, breaking away, flushed and breathless.

'I've got to,' he said and, heavy with disappointment, he unclipped the phone from his belt and lifted it to his ear. '*Wei?*'

Margaret, still shaking and aroused, turned back to her green tea, knowing that the moment had passed. Angry with him, but knowing that it was not his fault. His work intruded on their lives all the time. She had known it would. And there was even a time when she could have shared in it. But it was months since she had last worked on a case, performed an autopsy. Li had forbidden it, fearing that there could be health risks for the baby, and she had not resisted.

He clipped his phone back on his belt. 'I have to go,' he said.

'Of course you do,' she said in a flat tone. She reached over to switch on the overhead light and turned to blink at him in the sudden brightness. 'What is it this time? Another murder?'

'No,' Li said. 'At least, it doesn't appear that way.' Although he smiled, he was perplexed. 'Death by sex, apparently.' He stooped to kiss her on the lips. 'Perhaps we had a narrow escape.'

LI'S BIKE RATTLED in the back of his Jeep. The Chrysler four-wheel drive, built in the city by a Chinese-American joint venture, was affectionately known as the Beijing Jeep, much loved by the municipal police. The vehicle allocated to Li as section chief was an unmarked dark green with smoked-glass windows. Normally he left it at Section One and cycled home, because that was often faster than trying to negotiate the capital's increasingly frequent gridlocks, but it was a long way across the city in the bitter cold to Margaret's apartment, so tonight he had used the Jeep and bundled his bike in the back..

West Chang'an Avenue, the brightly lit arterial route that dissected the city east to west, was free of ice and the traffic was light. Hotels and ministry buildings were all floodlit, and Li could see the lights of Christmas trees twinkling in hotel forecourts. Christmas in Beijing, just two weeks away, was primarily for the tourists.

Li took a left into Nanchang Jie and saw the long, narrow, tree-lined street stretching in front of him in the darkness. Beyond the Xihuamen intersection it became Beichang Jie—North Chang Street—and on his right, a high grey wall hid from sight the restored homes of mandarins and Party cadres that lined this ancient road along the banks of the moat surrounding the Forbidden City. Up ahead, pulled up near a pair of tall electronic gates, were two patrol cars, a Section One Jeep and a couple of unmarked vans from the forensics section in Pao Jü Hutong. A uniformed officer stood by the gates, huddled in his black, fur-collared coat, stamping his feet.

Detective Wu's call to Li's cellphone had been cryptic. He had no reason to believe this was a crime scene. It was a delicate matter, perhaps political, and he had no idea how to deal with it.

Li was curious. Wu was a brash, self-confident detective of some fifteen years' experience. Delicacy was not something one normally associated with him. All that he had felt able to tell Section Chief Li on the phone was that there was a fatality, and that it was of a sexual nature. But as soon as he had given the address, Li had known this was no normal call-out. This was a street inhabited by the powerful and the privileged—people of influence. They would be required to tread carefully.

The officer at the gates recognised Li immediately, and saluted as he got out of the Jeep. The gates were open and a couple of saloon cars, a BMW and a Mercedes, sat in the courtyard beyond, beneath a jumble of grey slate roofs.

'Who lives here?' Li asked him.

'No idea, Section Chief.'

'Where's Detective Wu?'

'Inside.' He jerked a thumb towards the courtyard.

Li crossed the cobbled yard and entered the sprawling, single-storey house through double glass doors leading into a sun lounge. Three uniformed officers stood among expensive cane furnishings, engaged in hushed conversation with Wu and several forensics officers. Wu's leather jacket hung open, the collar still up, his cream silk scarf dangling from his neck. He was pulling nervously at his feeble attempt at a moustache with nicotine-stained fingers. His face lit up when he saw Li.

'Hey, Chief. Glad you're here. This one's a real bummer.' He steered Li quickly out into a narrow hallway. From somewhere in the house came the sound of a woman sobbing.

'What the hell's going on here, Wu?'

Wu's voice was low and tense. 'Local Public Security boys got a call an hour ago from the maid. She was hysterical. They couldn't get much sense out of her, except that somebody was dead.'

'So who is it?'

'Guy called Jia Jing. Chinese weightlifting champion.'

'How did he die?'

'Doc thinks it's natural causes.' He nodded his head towards the end of the hall. 'He's still in there.'

Li was perplexed. 'So what's the deal?'

'The deal is,' Wu said, 'we're in the home of a high-ranking member of the Beijing Organising Committee of the Olympic Games. He's in Greece right now. His wife's hysterical in their bedroom with a three-hundred-pound weightlifter lying dead on top of her.' He couldn't resist a smirk. 'Seems like his heart gave out just when things were getting interesting.'

'In the name of the sky, Wu!' Li felt the first flush of anger. 'You mean you just left him like that? For more than an hour?'

'Hey, Chief.' Wu held his hands up. 'We didn't have any choice. Have you ever tried moving three hundred pounds of dead meat? It's going to take everyone here to lift him off.'

Li raised his eyes to the heavens and took a deep breath. The implications were scandalous, not criminal, and his immediate inclination was to wash the section's hands of it as quickly as possible. 'Wipe that smile off your face!' he said quietly, and the smirk vanished instantly. 'A man is dead here, and a woman is seriously distressed.' He took another deep breath. 'You'd better show me.'

Wu led him through into a bedroom of extraordinary opulence and bad taste. A thick-piled red carpet, walls lined with crimson silk, black lacquer screens inlaid with mother of pearl set round a huge bed dressed in peach and cream satin. The room's incongruous focal point comprised the large, flaccid buttocks of the 300-pound weightlifting champion of China. His thighs and calves were enormous below a thick waist and deeply muscled back and shoulders. By contrast, the legs he lay between were absurdly fragile.

The woman was sobbing more quietly now, her eyes clouded and staring off into the distance. Dr Wang Xing, duty pathologist from the Centre of Criminal Technological Determination, was sitting in a chair by the bedside holding her hand.

He cocked an eyebrow in Li's direction. 'It might be worth trying to get him off her now.'

It took eight of them to lift Jia Jing clear of his lover long enough for Dr Wang to pull her free and get her into a chair. It seemed incredible that she had not been crushed by this monster of a man. Li tossed a silk dressing gown over her nakedness and cleared the room.

'So you think it was a heart attack?' Li asked Wang.

'That's how it looks. But I won't know until I get him on the slab.'

'And the woman?'

'She'll be OK, Chief.

Li knelt down beside her and took her hand. Her chin was slumped on her chest. He lifted it up with thumb and forefinger, turning her head slightly to look at him. 'Is there someone who can come and spend the night with you? A friend maybe?' Her eyes were glazed. 'Do you understand what I'm saying?'

There was no response. Li looked at Wang.

Suddenly she clutched his wrist, her eyes dark and frightened. 'He doesn't have to know, does he?' Li didn't have to ask who. 'Please . . .' she begged. 'Please tell me you won't tell him.'

DONGZHIMENNEI STREET was a blaze of light and animation as Li nursed his Jeep west towards Section One of the Criminal Investigation Department of the Beijing Municipal Police. Hundreds of red lanterns outside dozens of restaurants danced in the icy wind. Ghost Street, they called this road. While most of the city slept, the young and wealthy would haunt the restaurants and bars until three in the morning, or later.

Li took a left and saw the lights of Section One above the roof of the food market. He turned left again and parked under the trees. Then he got out of the Jeep, slipped in the side entrance of the four-storey building and climbed the stairs to the top floor. The detectives' office was buzzing with activity when he poked his head in. It was often busier at night than during the day.

Wu was already at his desk, blowing cigarette smoke thoughtfully at his computer screen. He looked up when Li appeared. 'How do you want me to play this, Chief?'

'Dead straight,' Li said. He was only too well aware of the possible repercussions of what they had witnessed that night. Members of the Beijing Organising Committee of the Olympic Games were political appointees and their president was the city's mayor. China regarded the success of the forthcoming Games as vital to its standing in the world, and a scandal involving one of the committee's senior members would send shock waves rippling through the corridors of power.

Li glanced towards the office of his deputy. The door was ajar, and the office beyond it in darkness. He had not expected to find Tao Heng at his desk at this hour and was relieved not to have to discuss this with him. He made his way down the corridor to his own office, flicked on his desk lamp and sat down, tilting back in his chair so that his head was beyond the ring of light it cast. He closed his eyes and wished fervently that he could have a cigarette. But he had told Margaret that he would give up, for the baby's sake, and he was not about to break his promise.

A knock on his door brought him sharply back from his tobacco reverie and he tipped forward again in his chair. 'Come in.'

Sun Xi stepped in from the corridor. 'Do you have a minute, Chief?'

He was a young man, not yet thirty, who had recently transferred to Beijing from Canton. As Li had once been, he was now the youngest detective in Section One, which specialised in solving Beijing's most serious crimes. And, like Li before him, he had already tied up an impressive number of cases in just a few short months in the section. Li had immediately spotted his potential and taken him under his wing. Sun dressed smartly, his white shirts always neatly pressed, pleated slacks folding onto polished black shoes. His hair was cut short above the ears, but grew longer on top, parted in the centre and falling down either side of his forehead above dark eyebrows and black, mischievous eyes. He was a good-looking man and all the girls in the office were anxious to catch his eye, despite the fact that he was already spoken for.

'Pull up a chair,' Li said, glad of the diversion. And as Sun slipped into the seat opposite, he asked, 'How's Wen settling in?'

Sun shrugged. 'You know how it is, Chief,' he said. 'Provincial girl in the big city. It's blowing her mind. And the little one's started kicking hell out of her.' Like Li, Sun was anticipating fatherhood in a little over a month. Unlike Li, Sun had been allocated a married officer's apartment, and his wife had just arrived from Canton.

Li smiled. 'Margaret's been going to the antenatal classes at the maternity hospital for several months. Maybe she could give Wen some advice on where to go, who to see.'

'I'm sure Wen would appreciate that,' Sun said.

Li said, 'I'll speak to her.' Then he sat back. 'What's on your mind?'

Sun took out a packet of cigarettes. 'Is it OK?'

'Sure,' Li said reluctantly, and he watched enviously as Sun lit up and pulled a lungful of smoke out of his cigarette.

'I got called out to a suspicious death earlier this evening, Chief. Not long after you left. At the natatorium at Qinghua University.' He grinned. 'That's a swimming pool to you and me.' He pulled again on his cigarette and his smile faded. 'Apparent suicide. Champion swimmer. He was supposed to take part in a training session at the pool with the national squad ahead of tomorrow's two-nation challenge with the Americans.' He paused and looked at Li. 'Do you follow sport?'

Li shook his head. 'Not really.'

'Well, they got this challenge thing this week with the US. Two days of swimming events and three days of indoor track and field. First ever between China and America.'

Li had been aware of it. Vaguely. There had been a considerable build-up in the media, but he hadn't paid much attention.

'Anyway,' Sun said, 'this guy's been breaking world records, expected to beat the Americans hands down. He turns up for tonight's training session before the rest of them. The security man on the door claims he never even saw him go in. The swimmer goes into the locker room and drinks half a bottle of brandy before he undresses and hangs all his stuff neatly in his locker. Then he takes a five-metre length of rope and goes up to the pool wearing nothing but his birthday suit. He climbs to the highest diving platform, ten metres up. Ties one end of the rope to the rail, loops the other round his neck and jumps off.' Sun made a cracking sound with his tongue. 'Neck snaps, clean as you like. Dead in an instant.'

Li felt an icy sensation spreading in his stomach. 'Weren't there three members of the national athletics team killed in a car crash in Xuanwu District last month?'

Sun was surprised. 'Yeah . . . that's right. Members of the sprint relay team.' He frowned. 'I don't see the connection.'

Li held up a hand, his brain sifting information that he had absorbed and filed under *Of No Apparent Importance But Worth Retaining. Maybe.* He found what he was searching for.

'There was a cyclist . . . I can't remember his name . . . He came second or third in the Tour de France last summer. Best ever performance by a Chinese. Drowned in a freak swimming accident a couple of weeks ago.'

Sun nodded, frowning again.

'And I've just come from a house where a weightlifter collapsed and died tonight during intercourse. A heart attack. Apparently.'

Sun chuckled. 'So you figure the Americans are bumping off our top athletes so they'll get more medals?'

But Li wasn't smiling. 'I'm not figuring anything,' he said. 'I'm laying some facts on the table. Perhaps we should look at them.' He paused. 'You said *apparent* suicide.'

Sun leaned into the light of Li's desk lamp. Cigarette smoke wreathed around his head. 'I don't think it was, Chief.'

The ringing of Li's telephone crashed into the room like an uninvited guest. Li snatched the receiver irritably. '*Wei?*'

'Section Chief, this is Procurator General Meng Yongji.'

Li's lungs seized mid-breath. The Procurator General was the highest ranking law officer in Beijing, and it was a moment before Li could draw in enough air to say, 'Yes, Procurator General.'

'I received a call several minutes ago from the executive assistant to the Minister of Public Security.' Meng did not sound too pleased about it. 'It seems the Minister would like to speak to you, Section Chief. In his home. Tonight. There is a car on its way to pick you up. What have you been up to, Li?'

'Nothing, Procurator General. Not that I know of.'

'Keep me informed.'

A click and the line went dead.

Li held the receiver halfway between his ear and the phone for several moments before finally hanging up. To be summoned to the home of the Minister of Public Security at ten thirty on a cold December night could only be bad news.

THE BLACK BMW felt as if it were gliding on air as it sped past the north gate of the Forbidden City and turned south into the street where Li had attended the death of Jia Jing only two hours earlier. The street was deserted now as they passed through the tunnel of trees that arched across the road, before turning west at the Xihuamen intersection. High walls rose up before them. When the car stopped at a gate, Li's electronic window wound down and he showed his maroon Public Security ID to the armed guard. The car was waved through and Li was within the walls of Zhongnanhai for the first time in his life. The car whisked them along a dark road before emerging into the glare of moonlight shining on frozen water. Zhonghai Lake. Here, on the shores of the lake, his country's leaders and high officials lived in luxury and seclusion.

The driver pulled up outside an impressive villa built on two levels in the traditional Chinese style, pillars the colour of dried blood supporting the sloping roof of a verandah.

Inside, the driver left Li standing nervously in a dark hallway before a woman in a black suit appeared and asked him to follow her up thickly carpeted stairs. He was shown into a small room where the Minister was sitting on a black two-seater sofa. He was wearing soft, corduroy trousers, an open-necked shirt and carpet slippers. A pair of half-moon glasses balanced on the end of his nose.

He waved Li to a well-worn leather armchair opposite. 'Sit down, Li.'

Feeling stiff and awkward in his uniform, Li perched uncomfortably on the edge of the seat.

The Minister appeared to be lost in reflection, as if unsure where to begin. At last he said, 'A certain wife of a certain member of a certain committee made a telephone call tonight after you left her home.'

Li remained impassive. He should have realised that a woman in her position would know someone of influence.

'The recipient of that call made another call, and then my telephone rang.' The Minister smiled. 'You see how connections are made?'

Li saw only too well.

The Minister removed his glasses and fidgeted with them as he spoke. 'As far as we are aware, no crime was committed tonight. Correct?'

Li nodded.

'Then it is perfectly possible that a certain weightlifter arrived at the home of a certain committee member to make representations on behalf of his sport to that committee member who, unfortunately, was out of the country. But, then, we'll never know, will we?

Since the poor chap collapsed and died. Heart attack, is that right?'

'We'll know for sure after the autopsy.'

'And that, of course, will all be reflected in the official report?'

Li hesitated for a long moment. He despised the thought of being involved in any way in a cover-up. If he had thought there was anything more to it than sparing the blushes of a few officials, he might have fought against it. But in the circumstances it hardly seemed worth it. He could almost hear his Uncle Yifu referring him to Sunzi's *Art of War* and the advice offered by that most famous military strategist: *He who knows when to fight and when not to fight will always win*. And there were other, more important battles, he knew, that lay ahead. 'I'll see that it does, Minister,' he said.

The Minister smiled and appeared to relax. 'I'm glad. It would be a great pity, damaging even, if certain people were embarrassed by certain unwarranted speculation.'

'It certainly would,' Li said, unable to keep an edge of sarcasm out of his voice.

The Minister glanced at him sharply, his smile dissolving. 'However,' he said, 'there are other, more consequential issues raised by the death of Jia Jing tonight. You may not be aware of it, Li, but he is the fifth senior Chinese sportsman to die within the last month. All, apparently, from natural or accidental causes.'

'Three sprinters,' Li said. 'A cyclist, a weightlifter.'

The Minister looked at him thoughtfully and raised an eyebrow.

'But you're going to have to revise that figure, Minister,' Li continued, 'the number is now up to six.'

The Minister appeared suddenly to age ten years. 'Tell me.'

'I don't have all the details yet. It appears to have been a suicide. A member of the swimming team. He was found hanging from the diving platform in the training pool at Qinghua.'

'Who was it?'

'His name was Sui Mingshan.'

The name had meant nothing to Li, but the Minister knew immediately who he was. 'In the name of the sky, Li! Sui was our best prospect of Olympic gold. He should have been swimming against the Americans tomorrow.' He sighed and rose from the sofa. 'It can't be coincidence can it? Six of our leading athletes dead within a month?'

'On the balance of probability, Minister, it seems unlikely,' Li said.

'Well, you'd better find out, pretty damned fast. And I don't want to read about this in the foreign press, do you understand? It will be difficult enough to explain the absence of such athletes from this event with the Americans, but with the Olympics coming to Beijing in 2008, we cannot afford even the whiff of a scandal.'

Li stood up, holding his black peaked cap with its silver braiding and shiny badge. 'The investigation is already under way, Minister.'

The Minister scrutinised Li thoughtfully. 'We can't afford to lose officers of your calibre, Section Chief,' he said. 'This . . . this personal problem that you have. How can it be resolved?'

Li's heart sank. 'With all due respect, Minister, I don't believe that I am the one with the problem. There is no legal requirement—'

The Minister cut him off. 'Damn it, Li. It's not law; it's policy.'

'Then you could make an exception.'

'No.' His response was immediate. 'No exceptions. You make one, others follow. And when many people pass one way, a road is made.'

'Then I may have to pass on the baton before the case is resolved.'

The Minister glared at him. 'You're stubborn, Li. Just like your Uncle Yifu.'

'I'll take that as a compliment.'

'He was a foxy old bastard, Yifu. Good policeman, though.' The Minister stared intently at Li for several long moments, then finally turned away. 'Just keep me informed.'

And Li realised he was dismissed.

WU'S REPORT WAS WAITING for him on his desk when he got back to Section One. It was nearly midnight. He slumped into his seat wearily to read it. Then he got up again, crossed to the door and shouted down the corridor. 'Wu!'

After a moment, Wu appeared. 'Chief?'

Li beckoned him up the corridor and went back to his desk. When Wu came in he chucked his report back at him.

'Do it again.'

Wu frowned.

'Only this time, leave out the stuff in the bedroom. Our weightlifter arrived looking for our committee member, but before he could say why, he collapsed and died. OK?'

'But . . .' Wu looked at him curiously. 'That's not like you, boss.'

'No, it's not. Just do it.'

Wu shrugged and headed for the door.

Li called after him, 'And tell Sun I want to talk to him.'

When Sun came in Li motioned him to take a seat. Li's eyes were stinging and gritty. It had been a long day. 'Tell me why you think this swimmer didn't kill himself,' he said.

Sun described how he and Qian Yi, one of the section's older detectives, had arrived at the natatorium shortly after seven thirty. 'What made us suspicious initially was the security man on the door saying he didn't see Sui going in. So I asked if there was any other way in. Turns out there are half a dozen emergency exits that you can only open from the inside. We looked at them all. One of them was not properly shut, which had to be how Sui got in.'

Li thought about it for a moment. 'Why would he have to sneak in the emergency exit? And how did he open it from the outside?'

'I asked myself the same questions,' Sun said. 'The only thing I could think was that he wasn't on his own.'

Li frowned. 'What do you mean?'

'I mean that he didn't go there of his own free will, Chief. That he was taken, against his will, by people who had already got him drunk. People who had arranged to have that fire door left unlocked.'

Li raised a sceptical eyebrow. 'And all this speculation because the security man didn't see him going in? Maybe he was reading and didn't notice Sui going past.'

'And the fire door?'

Li shrugged. 'Doors get left open.'

Sun seemed slightly crestfallen.

Li said, 'Tell me you're basing your doubts on more than a security man and a fire door.'

Sun shook his head, exasperated by his boss's scepticism. 'Chief, I don't know what to say. It just didn't *feel* right. Everything about it. His teammates said he never touched alcohol. Yet he was stinking of drink and there was a half-empty bottle of brandy in his locker. Would he have been in any state to fold up his clothes and leave them hanging in his locker? And why would he shave his head?'

Li sat forward. This was new information. 'He'd shaved his head?'

'Yeah. There were fresh nick marks on his scalp, dried blood, and he had a full head of hair the last time anyone saw him.'

Li puzzled over this. 'Was there a pathologist in attendance?'

'Doc Zhu, one of Wang's deputies from Pao Jü Hutong.'

Li knew him. He was young, inexperienced. 'What did Zhu say?'

'Not a lot, Chief. Just that there were no external signs of a struggle, and that death appeared to have been caused by a broken neck. Of course, he couldn't commit to that until after he does the autopsy.'

'Put a stop on that. I don't want anyone with his lack of experience touching the body.'

Sun was taken aback, and for a moment didn't know how to respond. Was this vindication? 'You mean you think I might be right? That this isn't just a straightforward suicide?'

Li pondered his response briefly. 'While accepting that our assumptions are speculative, Sun, I think they are not unreasonable. For two reasons. One, we have got to look at this in the context of six top athletes dead in a month. It stretches the theory of coincidence just a little far. And two, there's the hair thing.'

Sun looked puzzled. 'How do you mean?'

'You asked why Sui would have shaved his head. My understanding is that it's not unusual for swimmers to shave off their hair in order to create less resistance in the water.'

Sun nodded. 'And . . . ?'

Li said, 'Well, if you were planning to kill yourself, why would you shave your head to make yourself faster for a race in which you had no intention of taking part?' He saw the light of realisation dawning in Sun's eyes, and added, 'But that leaves us with an even more implausible question. Why would somebody else do it?'

THE NEARLY FULL MOON was bathing Margaret's bedroom in a bright silver light, keeping her awake. In just over a week she would be married. And yet the thought of the ordeals of the next few days filled her with dread. A belated betrothal meeting. The reunion with her mother. The first meeting with Li's father. And then what? What would be different? Until Li was allocated an apartment for married officers they would still be forced to spend much of their lives apart. And when the baby came . . . She closed her eyes. It was a thought she did not want to face. She found pain hard enough to cope with when it was other people's. Her own scared her to death.

She pulled the covers up over her head, determined to try to sleep, and heard a key scraping in the latch. She sat bolt upright and glanced at the bedside clock. It was 1.14 a.m. Surely he hadn't come back at this time of night? 'Li Yan?' she called.

Her bedroom door swung open and he stood there in the moonlight in his uniform and his cap, his coat slung over his shoulder. 'I didn't mean to wake you,' he said.

She tutted her disbelief. 'Of course you did. You're sex obsessed. Why else are you here?'

But he didn't smile. 'I've got a couple of favours to ask.'

'Oh, yes?'

He moved into the room with an easy, powerful grace, and started to undress. She felt the rekindling of her earlier frustrated desires as he slipped out of his trousers and stood three-quarters silhouetted against the window.

'There's a young guy in the section,' he said. 'I've talked to you about him. Sun. He came up from Canton three months ago, and they've just allocated him married quarters.'

'Oh, I see,' she said, stung. 'So the junior detective gets an apartment, but his boss has to wait.'

'That's just an administrative thing,' Li said quickly, not wanting to get involved in a discussion about apartments. 'The point is, his wife's just arrived. She doesn't know anybody here, and she's due about the same time as you are. I thought . . . well, I wondered, if maybe you could show her the ropes, so to speak.'

Margaret snorted. 'You didn't come here at one o'clock in the morning just to ask me that?'

'Well,' Li said. 'There was something else. I want you to do an autopsy.'

'I thought I was banned,' she said quietly. 'You thought there could be health risks for the baby. What's changed?'

'I wouldn't ask if I didn't think it was important.' He paused. 'And I won't ask if you think there *is* the slightest risk.'

She knew that if there was no risk to her there was no risk to the baby. 'What's the case?' She could barely keep the excitement out of her voice. It was a chance to take her life back, to put all these other personas—wife, mother, daughter—on the back burner.

He sat on the edge of the bed and took her through the events of the evening.

She lay thinking about it for a long time. 'Who's doing the autopsy on the weightlifter?'

'Wang.'

She nodded. Wang was OK. She had worked with him before. 'What about the others? The road accident victims, the guy who drowned. Can I see their autopsy reports?'

Li shook his head. 'We don't autopsy every accidental death, Margaret. Only if there are suspicious circumstances, or cause of death is not apparent. We don't have enough pathologists.'

'I don't suppose we can dig them up?'

Li sighed, realising himself just how little they were going to have to go on. 'I'm pretty sure they'll all have been cremated.'

'You're not making this very easy for us, are you?'

Li said, 'The more I think about it, the more it seems to me like someone else has been trying to make it that way. Will you do the autopsy on the swimmer?'

'Try stopping me.' She grabbed his arm. 'Although, right now I'm hoping we can get to the third reason you came back.'

'There was a third reason?' he asked innocently.

'There had better be.' And she pulled him into her bed.

Chapter Two

She was late, but Margaret knew that to hurry could be dangerous. She pumped her pedals at a slow and even rate, keeping pace with the flow of cyclists heading east along Chang'an Avenue.

When she had woken, Li was gone, but his warmth and the smell of him lingered on the sheets and pillow beside her. She had rolled over and breathed him in, remembering how good it had been just a few hours before when he had made slow and careful love to her, and she had lost herself in all his soft, gentle goodness. And then she had seen the clock, and knew that Mei Yuan would be waiting for her.

The sky was light in the east, pale gold rising to the deepest blue, but the sun had not yet found its way between the skyscrapers. It was so cold her muscles had nearly seized solid.

Up ahead, traffic had been halted at Tiananmen Square to allow the dawn ritual of the raising of the flag. She dismounted to guide her bike between stationary vehicles to the other side of the avenue. Then she cycled to the arched Gate of Heavenly Peace and parked the bike, before hurrying into the entrance hall with its crimson pillars and hanging lanterns, and paying her two-yuan entrance fee.

She found Mei Yuan in a courtyard in front of the Yu Yuan Pavilion. Along with half a dozen others, Mei Yuan moved in slow, controlled exercises to traditional Chinese music playing gently from someone's ghetto blaster. Tai chi looked easy, but its leisurely control demanded something of nearly every muscle. It was a wonderful way of maintaining fitness, particularly for the elderly. Or the pregnant.

When she saw Margaret, Mei Yuan broke off to give her a hug. She looked forty but was nearer sixty. Her smooth moon face beneath a soft white ski hat creased in a smile around her beautifully slanted almond eyes. She was shorter than Margaret, stocky, and wrapped in layers of clothes below a quilted green jacket. 'Have you eaten?' she asked in *putonghua* Chinese. It was the traditional Beijing greeting, born of a time when food was scarce and hunger a way of life.

'Yes, I have eaten,' Margaret replied, also in *putonghua*. 'I can't stay this morning. Li Yan has asked me to do an autopsy.'

Mei Yuan said nothing. But Margaret saw her disapproval clearly in her face. They walked through Zhongshan Park together, the sunlight slanting through the naked branches of ancient trees.

Mei Yuan was the closest thing to a mother-figure in Li's life—Li's mother had died in the Cultural Revolution—and Margaret, too, had become very fond of her. She thought of her as her 'Chinese' mother and wondered how her real mother would get on with Mei Yuan when she arrived. Li had asked Mei Yuan to make the arrangements for a traditional Chinese wedding, and Margaret had been happy to leave everything to someone else. She was only half listening to Mei Yuan now, for the wedding still seemed distant and remote.

'I have reserved a room for the wedding ceremony, and I have ordered the flowers for the altars,' Mei Yuan was saying.

She had already explained to Margaret that there were no formal wedding vows in Chinese culture. The couple simply interlinked arms and drank from cups joined by red string, a symbol of their binding commitment. This was performed in front of two altars to honour the ancestors of each family. It had already been decided that this would not take place at Li's home, as was traditional, since the apartment was too small.

'Now, it is usual to place a rice bowl and chopsticks on one of the altars if there has been a recent bereavement in either of the families,' Mei Yuan went on.

'Perhaps Li will want to make the gesture in memory of his uncle,' Margaret said.

'It is some years since Yifu died.'

'Yes, but his death still casts a shadow over the family. I know that not a day goes by when Li doesn't think about him. I'll ask him.'

Mei Yuan nodded. 'I have spoken to Ma Yun, and she will be happy to cater for the wedding banquet. Her price is far too high, but we can negotiate her down. However, there are certain items that *must* appear on the menu, and they will be expensive.'

'Oh?' Margaret was not too concerned. Her definition of expensive and Mei Yuan's were rather different. Mei Yuan earned her living selling fast-food Beijing pancakes called *jian bing* from a street stall. She was lucky if she made seventy dollars a month.

'There must be fish, roast suckling pig, pigeon, chicken cooked in red oil, lobster, dessert bun stuffed with lotus seeds . . .'

'Sounds good,' Margaret said. 'But why?'

'Ah,' Mei Yuan said, 'because every item of food has a symbolic meaning. We must have fish, because in Chinese the word for fish is pronounced the same as *abundance*, which means the newlyweds will have plentiful wealth. Lobster is literally called *dragon shrimp* in Chinese, and having lobster and chicken together indicates that the dragon and phoenix are in harmony and that the Yin and Yang elements of the union are balanced. The roast suckling pig is served whole as a symbol of the bride's virginity.' She stopped suddenly, realising what she'd said, and the colour rose on her cheeks as her eyes strayed to Margaret's bump.

Margaret grinned. 'Maybe we'd better skip the suckling pig.'

They passed the studded red gates of the Beijing Centre of Communication and Education for Family Planning, and Margaret was reminded that, in a country where birth had been controlled for decades by the One Child Policy, her baby was a precious thing.

At the Gate of Heavenly Peace she retrieved her bicycle and said, 'Say hi to Li for me. You'll probably see him before I do.'

Mei Yuan's stall was on a street corner not far from Section One. It was where Li had first met her, and he still had *jian bing* for breakfast most mornings.

Mei Yuan opened her satchel, brought out a small, square parcel and handed it to Margaret. 'A gift,' she said, 'for your wedding day.'

Margaret took it, embarrassed. 'Oh, you shouldn't go buying me things.' But she knew she could not turn it down. She carefully opened the soft parcel to reveal a large, red, silk and lace square. 'It's beautiful,' she said. She realised it had probably cost Mei Yuan half a week's earnings.

'It's a veil,' Mei Yuan said. 'To be draped over the head during the ceremony. Red, because that is the symbolic colour of happiness.'

Margaret's eyes filled. She hugged Mei Yuan. 'Then, of course, I will wear it,' she said. 'And wish for all the happiness in the world.'

SMOKE MADE IT nearly impossible to see from one side of the meeting room to the other. It was too cold to open a window, and almost the only person in the room without a cigarette was Li. He wondered why he had bothered giving up.

There were more than twenty detectives in the room, each with his own mug or insulated tankard of piping hot green tea. Everyone knew now why they were there, that this was a priority investigation.

The tone of the meeting was set from the start by a clash between Li and his deputy, Tao Heng. Tao was a man in his fifties with thinning dark hair scraped back across a mottled scalp, his bulging eyes magnified behind thick-rimmed glasses. Nobody liked him.

'I'd appreciate,' Tao said, 'being told why the autopsy of last night's suicide victim was cancelled.' He looked around the room.

'The autopsy has not been cancelled, Deputy Section Chief,' Li said evenly. 'Merely reassigned to the American pathologist, Margaret Campbell.'

'Ah,' Tao said. 'Keeping it in the family, then?'

There was a collective intake of breath around the room. Nepotism was considered a form of corruption, and in the present political climate, police corruption was very much under the microscope.

Li said coldly, 'Dr Campbell is the most experienced forensic pathologist available to us. If you have a problem with that, Tao, you can raise it with me after the meeting.'

Relations between Li and his deputy were strained at best. When Li had left the section to work as criminal liaison at the Chinese Embassy in Washington, DC, Tao had succeeded him as deputy section chief, coming from the Criminal Investigation Department in Hong Kong. He had known there was no way he could try to follow in the footsteps of the most popular deputy anyone in Section One could remember, so from the start he had done things his own way. He believed in a dress code, which was unpopular, and fined detectives for the use of foul language in the office. If anyone crossed him they could expect to get the worst assignments on the section.

When Section Chief Chen Anming had retired earlier that year, Tao was expected to succeed him. But Chen's retirement coincided with Li's return from America and Li was appointed over Tao's head, colouring their relationship from the start.

Tao resumed his silent sulking, and they listened as Wu gave his account of Jia Jing's adulterous misadventure the previous evening. The official report, for reasons they did not need to know, reflected less than the full story, Li told them. Then Sun went over his report on the 'suicide' of the swimmer, Sui Mingshan. He had altered it to take account of Li's thoughts on the shaven head.

Li took over, flipping through the folder in front of him. 'You all have the report on the accident that killed three members of the sprint relay team last month.' There had been no reason then for anyone to think it was anything other than an accident. Three young men travelling too fast in a car late at night, losing control on black ice and wrapping their vehicle round a lamppost. 'And the cyclist who was killed in a freak accident in a private pool. Three witnesses saw him slip on the diving board and crack his skull as he fell in.' Li took a deep breath. 'We have no autopsy reports. No bodies. But in light of last night's fatalities, we have no choice but to go back over all these deaths in the minutest detail. I doubt if there's anyone in this room who would think the deaths of six athletes in little over four weeks worthy of anything other than our undivided attention.'

There was nobody in the room who did.

'So let's kick it around,' Li said. 'Anyone got any thoughts?'

Wu had the report on the cyclist open in front of him. 'These three witnesses all have addresses in Taiwan. Are they still going to be around for further questioning?'

'Why don't you make it your personal responsibility to find out?'

Wu pulled a face, and there was a sprinkling of laughter.

'Talk to the attending officers,' Li went on. 'Get them to go over it all again, in the smallest detail.' He turned to the detective next to him. 'And Qian, why don't you talk to the officers who attended the car crash? Same thing.'

'Sure, Chief.' Qian was about ten years older than Li. He would never be management material, but he was steady and reliable.

'Shouldn't we talk to the relatives, too?' This came from Zhao, one of the youngest detectives in the section, an intelligent investigator.

'Absolutely,' Li said, 'and the coaches, other athletes, and as many friends as we can track down. We need to look at financial records, any remaining personal belongings.'

'What about drugs?' asked Sang. He was another of the section's younger detectives. 'If we're looking for a motive—'

'We're not looking for a motive, Detective.' Tao cut him off sharply, and the earlier tension returned to the room. 'We're looking for evidence. Only then will we see the bigger picture.'

It was the traditional Chinese approach to criminal investigation.

Accumulate enough evidence and you will solve the crime. Unlike in the West, motive was regarded as being of secondary importance.

Li said, 'Deputy Tao clearly thinks you've been reading too many American detective novels, Sang.' This provoked some laughter and softened the tension. 'But I agree with him. It's too early to be looking at motive. We don't even know if there has been a crime.'

As the meeting broke up and Li gathered his papers, he became aware of Tao hanging back to speak to him, and he sighed inwardly.

Tao kept his peace until they were on their own. Then he crossed the room to drop his copy of Wu's report on the death of Jia Jing in front of Li. 'Why was I not consulted about this?'

'You weren't here last night, Tao. And this morning there was no time for protocol. I'm sorry if you feel slighted.'

Tao stood his ground. 'I want to put on record my strongest objections that this report has been doctored.' He tapped his forefinger on the file.

Li was losing patience. 'Are you objecting to the doctoring of the report or the fact that you weren't consulted about it?' They each knew it was the latter.

'Both,' Tao said defiantly. 'As far as I am aware it is not the practice of this section to file inaccurate reports.'

'You're right,' Li said. 'It's not. But this case is an exception. And if you have a problem with that then I suggest you take it up with the Minister of Public Security.'

Tao drew his lips into a thin, tight line. 'And is the Minister also responsible for reassigning the autopsy on Sui Mingshan?'

'I've already told you the reason for that.'

'Ah, yes,' Tao said. 'Dr Campbell is the "best available". You seem to be of the opinion that anything American is better than everything Chinese.' He paused. 'Perhaps you should have stayed there.'

Li glared back at him. 'Your trouble, Tao, is that you spent too long under the British in Hong Kong learning how to be arrogant and superior. Perhaps you should have stayed there.' He brushed past his deputy, leaving Tao silently fuming in the cold, empty room.

LI AND WU ARRIVED at the forensic laboratories at Pao Jü Hutong as the autopsy was nearing its completion. Jia Jing lay on the stainless-steel autopsy table, his chest cavity cut open and prised wide like a carcass in a butcher's shop. Dr Wang was swaddled in layers of protective clothing, eyes darting behind his goggles.

'Never seen muscles like these,' he was saying. 'A man of this size, you'd expect a lot of fat. There's hardly an ounce of it. But all the weight he was carrying, and all the weight he was lifting, will have contributed in no small way to his death.' He crossed to the table where the sections of Jia Jang's heart lay at an angle, piled one on top of the other, like thick slices of bread. 'In this case'—he picked up a slice of heart—'the left anterior descending coronary artery was clogged, causing it simply to erupt. Probably congenital.' Holding up the cross-section of the artery, he added, 'You can see here that the artery is about seventy-five per cent blocked. And if you look closely'—Li made a face, but moved closer to see—'there's a thin layer of red. Blood. Under pressure from the artery it has dissected into and under the atherosclerotic plaque, stopping blood flow to the portion of the heart that the artery serves. Effectively, he had a massive heart attack.'

'Way to go,' Wu said.

'Is there any way you can tell if he'd been taking steroids?' Li asked. He smelt a scandal. Some high-profile Chinese weightlifters and swimmers had tested positive for drug-taking in the nineties and been banned from national and international sport.

'I've asked specifically for hormone screening. If he took any during the last month it'll show up in tox. Of course, there can be behavioural changes with steroid abuse. Users can become moody, aggressive. Talk to people who knew him.'

Li walked over to a side table against the wall, where Jia Jing's clothes were laid out along with the contents of his pockets and a small shoulder bag he had had with him.

There was a leather purse with some coins; a wallet with several 100-yuan notes; a couple of credit cards; a small, gold-coloured aerosol breath freshener. Li sprayed a tiny puff of it into the air, sniffed and recoiled from its pungent menthol sharpness. He picked up a dog-eared photograph. The picture was a little fuzzy, but Li recognised Jia immediately. There was a gold medal on a blue ribbon round his neck and Jia was holding it up for emphasis. He was flanked on one side by a small elderly man with thinning grey hair, and on the other by an even smaller woman. Li turned the picture over: *With Mum and Dad, June 2000.* Li looked at Mum and Dad again, saw the pride in their smiles, and for a moment felt their pain.

He turned briskly to Wang. 'You'll let me have your report?'

'Of course.'

Li said to Wu, 'You might as well stay with it. I'm heading out to Qinghua University with Sun to talk to Sui Mingshan's teammates. Keep me up-to-date with any developments.'

He hurried out, feeling oddly squeamish. Death was never easy, but Jia Jing had been only twenty-three years old.

SUN STEERED LI'S JEEP carefully through the bike and tricycle carts that thronged the narrow Dongzhimen Beixiao Street, taking them down from Section One onto Ghost Street. Li sat in the passenger seat, huddled in his woollen coat, a red scarf tied at the neck, his gloved hands resting in his lap. He gazed out at the featureless wasteland on their left. The streets and courtyards, the jumble of roofs that had once stretched away to the distant trees beyond, were all gone, soon to be replaced by tower blocks and shops.

Li told Sun to pull in at the corner where a woman was cooking *jian bing* in a pitched-roof glass shelter mounted on the back of an extended tricycle. She wore blue protective sleeves over a white jacket, and a long black and white chequered apron. A round white hat was pulled down over her eyes, and there was a red and white silk scarf round her neck. For years Mei Yuan had occupied the space on the southeast corner of the intersection. Now she had been forced to the opposite side of the road.

Li gave her a hug. 'My stomach has been grumbling all morning.'

'Well, we can put that right straight away,' she said, brown eyes shining with fondness. She glanced at Sun. 'One? Two?'

Li turned to Sun. 'Have you tried a *jian bing* yet?'

Sun shook his head. 'I've driven past often enough,' he said, 'but I never stopped to try one.' He did not sound very enthusiastic.

'Well, now's your chance,' Li said, turning to Mei Yuan. 'Two.'

They watched as she poured a scoop of batter mix onto a large hot plate. She dragged it into a perfect circle before breaking an egg onto it and smearing it over the pancake. She sprinkled it with seeds and then flipped it over, steam rising from it all the while.

She smeared the pancake with hoisin and chilli and other spices, before throwing on a couple of handfuls of chopped spring onion. Finally she placed a square of deep-fried whipped egg white in its centre, folded the pancake in four and scooped it up in a paper bag.

Li handed it to Sun, who looked apprehensive. 'Try it,' he said.

Reluctantly, Sun bit into the soft pancake, which dissolved almost immediately in his mouth. He smiled his surprise. 'Wow,' he said, 'this is good.' And he took another mouthful, and another.

Li grinned. Mei Yuan had already started on his. He reached over and pulled out a book stuffed down behind her saddle. It was where she always kept the book she was currently reading in snatches between the cooking of pancakes.

'*Bon-a-part-e*,' he read, ignorance furrowing his brow. 'What is it?'

Her face lit up. 'Ah,' she said, 'the life of Napoleon Bonaparte. He was a dictator in nineteenth-century France who conquered nearly all of Europe. He died in lonely exile, banished to a tiny island in the South Atlantic. Some people even think he was murdered there. It is a fascinating story.'

'You speak English?' Sun asked. He was clearly astonished at the idea that some peasant woman selling snacks on a street corner could speak a foreign language. Then suddenly he realised how he must have sounded. 'I'm sorry, I didn't mean . . .'

'Do *you* speak English?' Mei Yuan asked.

He shrugged, embarrassed now. 'A little,' he said. 'Not very well.'

Li grinned. 'Mei Yuan graduated in art and literature.'

'But life does not always follow the path we plan for it,' she said quickly, turning to Sun. 'Do you have any English books? My passion is reading.'

'I'm afraid not,' Sun said, clearly disappointed that he could not oblige. Then suddenly he said, 'But I have a friend whose English is excellent. He has many books. I'm sure he would be happy to lend you some. I'll see what he has.'

When Li had finished his *jian bing*, he wiped his mouth with the back of his hand, licking his lips. 'Did you see Margaret this morning?' he asked Mei Yuan.

'Yes.' She smiled ruefully. 'I am doing my best, Li Yan, to educate her in the niceties of the traditional Chinese wedding. But she seems a little . . . distracted.' She paused. 'She said to say hi, I'm not sure why, because she'll see you at the autopsy.'

Li knew immediately from her tone that she disapproved. 'I'll see you tomorrow, Mei Yuan,' he said pointedly, drawing a line that he did not want her to cross. He dropped a ten yuan note in her tin.

'And your young friend?'

'Try keeping me away,' Sun grinned. 'You don't mind if I bring my wife sometime? She always complains I keep her tied to the kitchen and never take her out for a meal.'

Li cuffed him playfully around the head. 'Cheapskate,' he said.

WHEN THEY GOT onto the ring road heading north, Sun said, 'So you're going ahead with the wedding, then?'

Li looked at him, but Sun kept his eyes on the road. He guessed that everyone in the section must know by now. No doubt Tao was waiting in the wings to fill his shoes. 'Yes,' he said simply.

Sun refrained from comment. Instead, he asked, 'When do your parents arrive for it?'

'My father gets here from Sichuan tomorrow,' Li said. 'Margaret's mother flies in from America the day after.' He grimaced and blew air through clenched teeth. 'I'm not looking forward to it. Thank heaven we have Mei Yuan to bridge the gap.' He turned to Sun, a sudden recollection returning. 'Who do you know in Beijing who has English books?'

Sun shrugged. 'No one,' he said. 'I thought maybe I could buy her some books at the English Language Bookstore. She wouldn't ever have to know, would she?'

Li was moved by his thoughtfulness. 'No,' he said. 'She wouldn't.'

Chapter Three

Li and Sun sat in the tiered rows of blue seats with a grandstand view of the Olympic-sized swimming pool. The air was warm and damp and both men had unbuttoned their coats, Li also loosening the scarf at his neck. Away to their right, forensics officers had taped off the diving area and were painstakingly searching every square inch of tile. So far all their efforts had been unrewarded.

The national swimming team coach, Zhang, could not sit still. He was a small man in his fifties, wiry and nervous, with close-cropped hair and darting black eyes. 'It's outrageous,' he said. 'My team are in competition this afternoon and they have nowhere to warm up.'

Li said, 'You seem more concerned about training facilities than the death of your star swimmer.'

Zhang flicked him a wounded look. 'Of course, I am shocked by Sui's death,' he said. 'But we still have to compete. Your people won't even allow us to say why Sui's name has been withdrawn.'

Li had no reply to that. Instead, he asked about Sui. 'When was the last time you saw him?'

'At training, the night before last.'

'Did he discuss with you the idea of shaving his head?'

Zhang frowned. 'No. No, he didn't. But it doesn't surprise me. Sui was a very single-minded young man. He had a bout of flu about ten days ago. Knocked the stuffing out of him. We thought he wasn't going to be able to compete this week. But he worked so hard in training . . .' Zhang lost himself for a moment in some distant, private thought. 'I just can't believe he committed suicide.'

Nor could his teammates. Li and Sun found them gathered in one of the changing rooms downstairs, sitting on slatted benches. Their mood was sombre and silent. None of them had had contact with Sui on the day of his death, so nobody had seen his shaven head until they found him dangling above the diving pool.

'What was he like, I mean as a person?' Li asked.

'He used to be a lot more fun,' one of them said. 'But lately he started taking it all much more seriously.'

'How lately?'

'About six months ago, when he started winning big time.'

'He was a pain in the ass,' someone else said. 'He'd bite the head off you if you looked at him the wrong way.'

Li remembered Wang's words at Jia Jing's autopsy. *There can be behavioural changes with steroid abuse. Users can become moody, aggressive.* He said, 'Is there any chance he was taking drugs?'

'No way!' said a broad-shouldered boy, and there was a murmur of agreement from around the changing room. 'He treated his body like a temple, with his diet, his training.'

'And yet,' Li said, 'if appearances are to be believed, he drank a half bottle of brandy and then hanged himself. Hardly the actions of someone who treated his body like a temple.'

None of them had anything to say to that.

SUI MINGSHAN had rented an apartment in one of the city's most up-market new housing complexes, above Beijing New World Taihua Plaza on Chongwenmenwai Street. Three shining new interlinked towers formed a triangle containing eighteen storeys of luxury apartments for the wealthy of the new China.

Sun parked in a side street and they entered the apartment block on the northwest corner. Marble stairs led them to chrome and glass doors. Sun showed the security man his ID.

'You'll have come to see Sui Mingshan's place on the fifteenth floor. Some of your people are already there,' the man said. 'I'll show you up, if you like.' He rode with them in the elevator.

'How long was Sui living here?' Li asked.

The man sucked air through his teeth. 'About five months.'

Sun asked, 'Did he have many visitors?'

'In all the time I've been on duty, not one,' said the security man. 'Which makes him just about unique in this place.'

The door of Sui's apartment was lying open. They ducked under the yellow and black crime-scene tape and stepped into another world, feet sinking into a deep-pile fawn carpet laid throughout the flat. The walls were painted in pastel peach and cream. Expensive black lacquered furniture was arranged in a seating area around a window giving onto a panoramic view of Beijing.

There were voices coming from the kitchen. Li called out, and after a moment Fu Qiwei pushed his head round the door. He was the chief forensics officer from Pao Jü Hutong, a small, wizened man with tiny coal-black eyes and an acerbic sense of humour.

'Oh, hi, Chief,' he said. 'Welcome to paradise.'

'Do we need to get suited-up, Fu?' Li asked.

Fu shook his head. 'We're just about finished here. Not that we found anything worth a damn. He left no traces of himself.'

'How do you mean?' Li was curious.

'Just look at the place.' Fu led them into the bedroom. 'It's like a hotel room. When we got here the bed was made up like it had never been slept in.' He slid open the mirrored doors of a built-in wardrobe. Rows of clothes, immaculately laundered and ironed, hung neatly on the rail. 'And I'm thinking, this guy's what—nineteen? You ever been in a teenager's bedroom that looked like this?'

He took them through to the kitchen. Every surface was polished to a shine. The hob looked as though it had never been used. The refrigerator was virtually empty and the larder was sparsely stocked.

'If I didn't know the kid lived here,' Fu said, 'I'd have said it was a showhouse, you know, to show potential customers. Totally soulless.'

They followed him through into a small study, where they saw for the first time the only evidence that Sui had lived here at all. The walls were covered with framed winner's medals, newspaper articles extolling Sui's victories, photographs of Sui on the winner's podium. Almost like a shrine. And his teammate's words came back to Li. *He treated his body like a temple.*

The bathroom, like the rest of the apartment, was unnervingly immaculate. The cabinet revealed a spare box of toothpaste, two packs of soap, an unopened box of aspirin, a jar of cotton pads. Sun said, 'Well, if he was taking steroids, or any other kind of performance enhancers, he didn't keep them here.'

On the shelf above the basin there was a razor and a box of four heads. There were also two bottles of Chanel aerosol aftershave. Li frowned. It was an unexpected character clue. A young man who liked his scents. He picked up one of the bottles, sprayed it into the air and sniffed, his nose wrinkling at the bitter orange scent.

'Wouldn't catch me wearing that,' he said.

Sun lifted the box of razor heads. 'None of them have been used.' Then he picked up a small, gold-coloured aerosol. 'What's this?'

Li took it from him and frowned. 'It's a breath freshener.' It was exactly the same as the one found among Jia Jing's belongings. He sprayed a tiny puff of it into the air, as he had done a couple of hours earlier in the autopsy room. The same sharp menthol smell.

Sun sniffed and screwed up his face. 'I'd rather have bad breath.'

In the living room, Li looked out on the sun slanting between the skyscrapers of the Beijing skyline and wondered what kind of boy Sui had been to have lived such an ascetic existence. He turned to Sun. 'I don't think this boy had any kind of life outside the pool, Sun. No reason for living except winning. If he killed himself it was because someone took that reason away.'

'Do you think he did?'

Li checked his watch. 'Margaret will be starting the autopsy shortly. Let's find out.'

AT THE CENTRE of Material Evidence Determination, Margaret had donned a plastic gown over green surgeon's pyjamas, plastic shoe covers, a plastic shower cap, goggles, latex gloves and a white mask. She was examining a section of Sui Mingshan's heart when her concentration was broken by the sound of voices in the corridor. She looked up as Li and Sun came in, pulling on aprons and shower caps.

'You're a little late,' she said caustically. 'I've finished. The services of the assistants were only available to me for a short time, and I didn't think I was in any condition to go heaving a body around on my own.'

'No, of course not,' Li said quickly. He half turned towards Sun. 'You've met Sun, haven't you?'

'I don't think so,' Margaret said. 'But I feel as if I have, the amount of talking you've done about him. You didn't tell me he was such a good-looking boy. Afraid I might make a pass at him?'

Li grinned. 'I wouldn't wish that on my worst enemy.' He looked at Sun, who was blushing. 'Are you following any of this?'

'A little,' Sun said.

'Ignore her. She loves to embarrass people.'

'Well, anyway,' Margaret said, 'it doesn't matter that you're late. You've missed all the boring bits. We can get straight to the point.'

'Which is?' Li asked.

She crossed to the table where Sui Mingshan lay, cold and inanimate, devoid of organs, brain removed. Even in death he was a splendid specimen. Broad shoulders, beautifully developed pectorals, lithe, powerful legs.

Margaret pointed to the muscles of the neck. 'The hyoid bone, just above the Adam's apple, is broken, and the neck dislocated between the second and third cervical vertebrae, as you can see, cleanly severing the spinal cord.' She turned the head each way to show them the deep abrasions under the jaw bone where the rope had burned his neck. 'Most suicidal hangings don't involve such a drop, so the neck isn't usually broken. Effectively they are strangled by the rope, and there would be evidence of pinpoint haemorrhages where tiny blood vessels had burst round the face, eyes, neck. We know that he was alive when he made the drop, because the abrasions made by the rope on his neck are red and bloody. There is no doubt that death was caused by a dislocation of the vertebrae of the neck severing the spinal cord. A broken neck to you.'

'So . . . you think he kill himself?' Sun ventured in English.

Margaret pursed her lips behind her mask. 'Not a chance.'

Li looked at her. 'How can you be so sure?'

'The amount of alcohol in his stomach.'

'Half bottle brandy,' Sun said.

'Oh, much more than that,' Margaret replied brightly.

'But he didn't drink,' Li said. 'His teammates were quite definite.'

'Well, then, I'm surprised it wasn't the alcohol that killed him. From the smell alone, I'd say we were looking at enough to seriously disable, or even kill, the untrained drinker. Maybe somebody encouraged him to drink the first few. Perhaps with a gun at his head. And if he wasn't used to alcohol, then it probably wasn't long before they were able to pour it down his throat.'

'How do you know he didn't drink it himself?' Li persisted.

'Well, maybe he did.' Margaret removed her mask and goggles, and Li saw the perspiration beaded across her brow. 'But with that much alcohol coursing through his veins, he wouldn't have been able to stand up, let alone climb ten metres to the top ramp of a diving pool, tie one end of the rope round the rail, the other around his neck and then jump off. Someone got him very drunk, took him up there, placed the noose around his neck and pushed him over.'

They heard the hum of the air conditioning in the silence that followed, before Li said stupidly, 'So somebody killed him.'

'When you push someone off a thirty-foot ramp with a rope around their neck, they usually call it murder.' Margaret returned her attention to the body. 'Has the question of drug-taking arisen?'

Li frowned. 'Why? Was he taking drugs?'

'I have no idea. I've sent several samples down to toxicology.'

'You *think* he was, then?'

She shrugged noncommittally and ran her fingers across the tops of Sui's shoulders and upper back. The whole area was covered with acne spots and scars. 'Acne is quite a common side effect of steroids. On the other hand boys of his age can suffer like this.'

'Toxicology should tell us, though?'

Margaret peeled off her latex gloves. 'Actually, probably not. He was due to swim in competition today, right?'

Li nodded.

'So there would be a high risk of testing. If he *was* taking steroids he'd have stopped long enough ago that it wouldn't show up.'

ONCE OUTSIDE, Sun lit up a cigarette as Li dialled Section One on his cellphone. He was put through to the detectives' room.

'Qian? It's Li. Tell the boys it's official. Sui was murdered.' He watched Sun drawing on his cigarette and envied him every mouthful. 'Check when any of these athletes was last tested for drugs.'

'You think it is drug-related, then?' Qian asked.

'No, I don't think anything,' Li said. 'I just want every little piece of information we can get.' He couldn't stand it any longer. He put his hand over the mouthpiece and said to Sun, 'Give me one of those.' And he held his hand out for a cigarette.

Sun looked surprised, then took out a cigarette and handed it to him. Li stuck it in his mouth and said to Qian, 'This indoor athletics competition with the Americans, it starts today, right?'

'Yes, Chief.'

'OK, get me a couple of tickets for tonight.'

'I didn't know you were a sports fan, Chief.'

'I'm not,' Li said, and disconnected.

Sun flicked open his lighter. Li leaned forward to light his cigarette then saw, over Sun's shoulder, Margaret coming down the steps behind him. He quickly coughed into his hand, snatching the cigarette from his mouth and crumpling it in his fist. Sun was left holding his lighter in midair. He looked perplexed.

'Put that thing away!' Li hissed.

Sun recoiled as if he had been slapped, slipping the lighter quickly back in his pocket. Then he saw Margaret approaching and a slow smile of realisation crossed his face. Li met his eyes and blushed.

As she joined them, Margaret said, 'Where are you off to now?'

'We're going to have a look at the weightlifter's place.'

'I thought Wang said it was natural causes?'

'He did,' Li said. 'I just don't like coincidences.'

Margaret's hair was held back by a band, and she had not a trace of make-up on her face. But she looked lovely, her skin clear and soft and brushed pink by pregnancy. 'I'm going back to the apartment,' she said, 'to shower and change. Will I see you later?'

'I'm getting a couple of tickets for the indoor athletics tonight. I thought you might like to come along and watch?'

'Sure.'

And then he remembered. 'Oh, and I thought we might have lunch tomorrow, with Sun Xi and his wife, Wen. Maybe you could take her up to the hospital tomorrow afternoon. Get her sorted out.'

There was murder in Margaret's eyes, but she kept a smile fixed on her face. 'Maybe that wouldn't be convenient for Detective Sun,' she said through slightly clenched teeth.

Sun was oblivious. 'No,' he said in all innocence. 'Tomorrow will be good. I very grateful to you Misses, eh . . . Miss . . .'

'Doctor,' Margaret said, flicking Li a look that might have dropped a lesser man. 'But you can call me Margaret. And it's my pleasure.' She turned and headed off into the afternoon sunshine towards the white apartment block at the north end of the campus.

JIA JING HAD LIVED in another of Beijing's new luxury apartment complexes, this time at the east end of Jianguomenwai Avenue. After taking the elevator up to the twelfth floor, Li and Sun let themselves in with a key the security man on the desk had given them. It was a large apartment, with a rectangular living and dining area with three bedrooms off it. It was filled with hard surfaces, unrelenting, austere.

The floors were polished wood, reflecting cold, blue light from the windows. The furniture was antique, purchased for its value rather than its comfort. There were lacquered wooden chairs and an unforgiving settee, and a magnificent mirrored darkwood cabinet inlaid with beech. The walls were hung with traditional Chinese scrolls.

One of the bedrooms was empty. In another, a large rug on the wall above Jia's antique bed was woven with a strange modern design. Facing the bed, a huge television sat on an antique dresser.

'I'm surprised it's not an antique television as well,' Sun said.

The bathroom was spartan and functional, with cold white tiles on the floor. In a wall cabinet above the basin, they found two bottles of aerosol aftershave, identical to those they had found in Sui Mingshan's bathroom. The same brand. Chanel.

'You think maybe the whole Chinese team got a job lot?' Sun said, smiling. 'Maybe Chanel is sponsoring our Olympic effort. We could be the best-smelling team at the Games.'

But Li wasn't smiling. There were warning bells ringing in his head. He knew there was something wrong here. He picked up one of the bottles and fired a burst of aerosolised perfume into the air. They both sniffed and recoiled in unison. It was a strange, musky smell, like almonds and vanilla, with a bitter edge to it.

Li sprayed a tiny puff from the other bottle onto his wrist and smelt a familiar bitter orange scent. He held his wrist out for Sun to sniff.

Sun wrinkled his nose. 'Same as the one at Sui Mingshan's place.'

Li nodded. 'Let's get out of here.' The smell was making Li feel a little queasy. 'I don't like breathing this stuff.'

WHEN LI AND SUN got back to Section One, they found most of the officers in the detectives' office crowded around a portable television. The excited voices of a couple of commentators soared above the roar of the crowd belting out of the set's tiny speakers.

'What the hell's going on?' Li barked. And they all turned guiltily towards the door, like naughty children caught in an illicit act. Someone hurriedly turned the set off.

Wu said, 'Professional interest, Chief. They've already had the four-hundred-metres freestyle and they've got the breast stroke and the crawl to come. We figured we should take it in.'

'Oh, did you? And what does Deputy Tao think?'

'He told us to turn it off,' Sang said.

'And you ignored him?' Li was incredulous.

'Not while he was here,' Wu said. 'But he went out about half an hour ago. He didn't say we had to keep it switched off.'

Li cast a disapproving glare around the faces turned towards him. 'You guys are fools. You didn't even put a look-out on the stairs.'

And they all burst out laughing.

But Li's face never cracked. 'I suggest you get back to your work. We've got a murder inquiry in progress here.'

He turned back to the door and was halfway down the corridor when Qian caught up with him. He was clutching a sheaf of notes.

'Couple of things, Chief.' He followed Li into his office. 'You asked about dope-testing.'

Li was surprised. 'You've got that already?'

'It's a matter of record, Chief. Same with all the sports authorities. Seems that nowadays they all do out-of-competition testing, to discourage athletes and other sportsmen from using drugs to enhance their training. They're given twenty-four hours' notice, and then it's mandatory to provide the required urine samples.'

'Couldn't they just turn in clean samples? Someone else's urine?'

'Not these days,' Qian said. 'The guy I spoke with at the Chinese authority said the athlete being tested is assigned a chaperone of the same sex. He or she stays with the athlete the whole time.'

'So what about the people we're interested in?'

'Sui was tested two weeks ago. Clean. Two of the three killed in the car crash were tested a week before the accident. Also clean. The cyclist hasn't been tested since he was last in competition. It's normal to test first, second and third in any competition, and then they pick someone else at random. He came third in his last event and was clean then. Jia Jing was tested six weeks ago. Also clean.'

Li sat down thoughtfully. 'Almost too good to be true.' He looked up at Qian. 'You said, a couple of things.'

'That's right, Chief. The officer who attended the car crash that killed those three athletes? He's downstairs.'

THE TRAFFIC COP sat in an interview room on the second floor, his white-topped peaked cap on the table in front of him. He stood up immediately when Li and Qian came in, clearly ill at ease at finding himself on the wrong side of a Section One interrogation.

'Sit down,' Li told him, and he and Qian sat down to face him. 'We have the report you filed on the fatal car crash you attended in Xuanwu District on November the 10th. Three members of the Chinese hundred-metres sprint relay team were found dead inside the wreck of their car.' Li dropped the report on the table. 'I want to know what's not here. What you felt, what you thought.'

'The car must have been doing over a hundred kph,' the officer began. 'It was a hell of a mess. So were the guys inside. Three of them. Two in the front, one in the back—at least, that's where they started off. They weren't wearing seat belts.' He grimaced, recalling the scene. 'It's bad enough when you don't know them, but when it's people you've seen on television, you know, big-time sports stars . . .'

'You recognised them, then?'

'Well, two of them, yeah. I mean, they always wore their hair short anyway, so they didn't look that different with their heads shaved.'

Li felt as if the room around them had faded to black. 'Their heads were shaved?' he said slowly.

The cop shrugged. 'Well, it's a bit of a fashion these days, isn't it?'

'So you didn't think it was odd?'

'Not in those two, no. It was the other one that kind of shocked me. Xing Da. He always wore his hair shoulder length. You always knew it was him on the track, all that hair flying out behind him.'

'And his head was shaved, too?' Li asked.

'All gone,' the traffic cop said. 'It looked really weird on him.'

AS THEY CLIMBED the stairs back to the top floor, Li asked Qian, 'What about the doctor's report?'

'Got it upstairs, Chief. But all he did was sign off the death certificates. Death caused by multiple injuries suffered in a car accident.'

Li cursed roundly. A staged suicide in which the victim's head had been shaved. Three deaths in what appeared at the time to have been an accident. All with their heads shaved. And all four, members of the Chinese Olympic team. The trouble was, the evidence from the crash—the vehicle and the bodies—was long gone.

Wu intercepted them on the top corridor. 'Those tickets you ordered for tonight arrived, Chief. I put them on your desk.'

'Fine.' Li brushed past, his mind on other things.

Wu called after him. 'Something else, Chief . . .'

Li turned and barked, 'What?'

'Those three athletes in the car crash?'

He had Li's attention now. 'What about them?'

'Only two of them were cremated, Chief. The parents of the other one live out in a village near the Ming tombs. Seems they buried him in their orchard.'

Li wanted to punch the air. But all he said was, 'Which one?'

'Xing Da.'

THE VILLAGE OF DALINGJIANG lay fifty kilometres northwest of Beijing in the shadow of the Tianshou Mountains, a stone's throw from the last resting place of thirteen of the sixteen Ming emperors. Li and Sun had headed out of the city on the Badaling Expressway, past countless developments of pastel-painted luxury apartments with security-gated compounds and private pools.

It was twilight as they drove into Dalingjiang. The village square was a dusty, open piece of broken ground where several village elders were gathered in the dying light, indulging in desultory conversation. They watched in curious silence as the Jeep rumbled past.

Sun pulled up at the village shop, a single-storey brick building with a dilapidated roof and ill-fitting windows. The door rattled and complained as Li pushed it open. A middle-aged woman behind two glass counters smiled at him. 'Can I help you?' she asked.

'I'm looking for the home of Lao Da,' Sun replied. 'Do you know him?'

'Of course,' said the woman. 'But you won't be able to drive there. You'll have to park at the end of the road and walk.'

She gave him instructions and they parked the Jeep further up the dirt road and turned off through a maze of frozen rutted tracks between the walls of the villagers' courtyard homes. They found Xing Da's parents' house next to a derelict cottage. Sun followed Li into the courtyard, and Li knocked on the door. A wizened old man opened it, too old to be Xing Da's father. Li told him who he was and who he was looking for, and the old man beckoned them in.

He was Xing's grandfather, it turned out. He called through to the bedroom and Lao Da emerged, peering at Li and Sun with suspicious eyes. Although *lao* meant old, Lao Da was only in his forties. He glanced beyond them to the kitchen doorway where his wife had appeared, holding aside the ragged curtain that hung from it.

'It's the police,' he said to her. And then to Li, 'What do you want?'

'It's about your son,' Li said. 'We have reason to believe that the crash he was involved in might not have been an accident.'

A frown of confusion spread over Lao Da's face.

'We'd like to perform an autopsy,' Li said.

'But we buried him,' his mother said, in a small voice that betrayed her fear of what was coming next. 'Out there, in the orchard.'

'If you'd agree to it, I'd like to have him exhumed.'

'You mean you want to dig him up?' his father said.

Li nodded.

Lao Da glanced towards his wife. Then he looked again at Li. 'You'll have a job,' he said. 'The ground is frozen out there.'

Li waited until he and Sun were away from the house before he called the exhumation team on his cellphone. They would need pick-axes to break the ground, he told them, perhaps even a pneumatic drill. And lights, for it would be dark.

LI WAS LOST in silent thoughts that Margaret did not want to interrupt. She had agreed to do the autopsy on Xing Da, but Li had refrained from telling her too much, so as not to influence her findings.

He turned in at the entrance to the Chinese Skating Association and showed his ID to the man on the gate, who waved them through. Li parked in front of the hotel where the American athletes were staying, and they walked the rest of the way to the stadium.

'We're not really coming here just to watch the athletics, are we?' Margaret asked as they approached a large ornamental wall carved with figures of ice skaters and the interlinked rings of the Olympics.

Li dragged himself away from his thoughts. 'I want to talk to some of the athletes,' he said. 'And their coach.'

Supervisor Cai Xin turned out to be a tall, lean man with short grey hair and square steel-rimmed glasses. Li had expected to find him in a track suit and trainers. Instead, he wore a dark business suit with polished black shoes. He seemed distracted, and less than pleased to see Li and Margaret, but he led them down a long, brightly lit corridor beneath the main stand, and into a private room with leather settees and windows with a view onto the track.

'How can I help you?' he asked, keeping a constant eye on proceedings outside.

'I want to talk to some of your athletes,' Li told him. 'In particular, members of the men's sprint relay team. But, in general, anyone who knew the three sprinters who died in last month's car crash. I have reason to believe their deaths might not have been accidental.'

Li watched Cai's reaction very carefully. He was clearly searching for a response, but in the end nothing came.

Li said, 'And at some time I would like to speak to colleagues of Jia Jing, his coach, others in his weight class. You know, of course, that Jia was found dead last night?'

Cai said quietly, 'I understood it was a heart attack.'

'It was.'

'Then what's the connection?'

'I don't know that there is one.'

Cai regarded him thoughtfully. 'We seem to be losing most of our best medal hopes,' he said at last. 'But I don't want you speaking to any of my athletes when they are just about to compete. I don't believe my superiors, or yours, would be happy if we were to upset our competitors and lose to the Americans.' He made a tiny nod of acknowledgment towards Margaret. 'With all due respect.'

'With all due respect,' Li said, 'I won't speak to anyone until after they have competed. Do we have any of the sprint events tonight?'

Cai said grudgingly, 'The men's and women's sixty metres, the four hundred and the eight hundred.'

'Then I'll be able to speak to some of them later,' Li said.

Cai glanced at his watch. 'Is that all?'

'Actually, no,' Li said. 'I'd like you to tell me what you know about doping. What are the more commonly used substances?'

Cai's face clouded and a frown gathered round his eyes. 'Anabolic steroids,' he said. 'They increase muscle strength by encouraging new muscle growth. They help the athlete to train harder and longer. But usually an athlete stops taking them at least a month in advance of competition, because they are so easily detectable. They're used mainly by swimmers and sprinters.'

'And weightlifters?' Li asked.

Cai flicked him a look. 'Yes,' he confirmed. 'Although generally human growth hormone would be the drug of choice for weightlifters. Being a naturally produced hormone it is very difficult to detect. It is excellent for building muscles and muscle strength.'

Margaret said, 'And it can cause heart and thyroid disease.'

Li looked at her and raised an eyebrow.

'As well as enlargement and thickening of the hands and face.'

It seemed inconceivable to Li that people would voluntarily submit themselves to such horrors. 'So what else do they take?' he asked.

'There are plenty of other drugs,' Cai said. 'Diuretics, amphetamines, beta blockers, narcotics. Which is why supplying banned drugs to athletes was made a criminal offence in China in 1995.

Unlike the United States, where most of them can be bought freely on the Internet.'

'Why don't we keep our point-scoring to the track and field,' Li said pointedly.

Cai glared at Li. 'I really cannot spare any more time, Section Chief. Are you finished, do you think?'

'For the moment,' Li said.

THEY TOOK THEIR SEATS high up in the main stand where they had a superb view of the track and the field events within it. A giant television screen also kept them apprised of what was happening, and a constantly changing scoreboard flashed digital figures in red, green and yellow. The stadium was filled with the buzz of anticipation.

A giant of an American with blond hair tied back in a ponytail threw his shot-put more than twenty-three metres sixty, taking the lead in the competition, to a groan of disappointment from the crowd. The Americans had already won the pole vault.

'I don't understand,' Li said to Margaret, 'why an athlete would risk so much just to stand on the winner's podium. I mean, it's not just the risk of being caught and branded a cheat. It's what they're doing to their bodies.'

'The pressure to win must be enormous,' Margaret said. 'And there are the rewards, of course. Big prize money, sponsorship, the fame and the glory. One minute you're nobody, the next you're a star.' She thought about it for a moment. 'And then there's national prestige. Just look at the lengths East Germany went to so that their athletes would bring home gold medals.'

Li shook his head. He knew nothing about East German athletes. 'I've never really followed sport, Margaret.'

'Sport?' She laughed. 'It was never about sport, Li Yan. The East German state seemed to think that if their athletes brought home more gold medals than anyone else, it would somehow endorse a whole political system. So they took their most promising young athletes away from their parents, many of them still children, and systematically pumped them full of drugs.'

'And the kids just took the stuff, without question?'

Margaret shook her head. 'They didn't know. They were twelve-, thirteen-year-old kids, subjected to the most ferocious training regimes and given little pills they were told were vitamins, but which were, in fact, state-produced steroids.'

Li looked at her quizzically. 'You seem to know a lot about this.'

She smiled. 'I don't know much about drug-taking these days, but back in the nineties I came face to face with it on the autopsy table. A former East German swimmer, Gertrude Klimt, who emigrated to the United States.' She could still see the pale, bloodless flesh of the young woman lying on her table. 'She was only in her early thirties. Died from tumours on the kidneys. Prosecutors in Berlin paid for me to go to Germany to give evidence in court against former East German coaches. A lot of former athletes were giving evidence. Some had tumours, some of the women had had children with horrific birth defects, one had even been pumped full of so much testosterone she had changed sex.'

Li shook his head in wonder. 'I never knew anything about this.'

Margaret cocked an eyebrow. 'Call me cynical, Li Yan, but I doubt very much if anyone in China heard much about it. And the Chinese were having their own drug-taking problems in the nineties, weren't they? I seem to recall something like thirty-plus Chinese athletes testing positive at the World Championships.'

Li sighed, embarrassed by his country's record in international competition. 'In the late nineties Cai coached a team of athletes from one of the western provinces. Several of them scored big successes. At home and abroad. Gold medals, world records. Then one by one they started turning up positive in dope tests. They were almost all discredited, and so was Cai.'

Margaret looked at him in amazement. 'So he was made Supervisor of Coaching?'

Li said, 'He was in the wilderness for years. He always claimed he had no idea his athletes were taking drugs—there was never any proof against him. And there was no denying his talents. I guess he must have friends in high places who believe his talents can't be overlooked.'

The crack of the starting pistol cut across their conversation, and they turned to see six women flying from their blocks, legs and arms pumping with powerful intensity.

MARGARET STOOD in the foyer, drawing looks from competitors and officials alike. They all knew she wasn't an athlete because of her distended belly. Li was in the dressing rooms talking to athletes.

It was hot and airless, a sour smell of body odour hanging in what air there was. She was beginning to feel a little faint and for a moment closed her eyes and became aware of herself swaying.

She felt a hand on her arm and a girl's voice said, 'Are you OK?'

Margaret opened her eyes, startled, and found herself looking into the concerned face of a young woman with an ugly purple birthmark covering most of one cheek. 'Yes. Thank you.'

The girl was nervous. 'My name Dai Lili. Everyone call me Lili.' A smile flitted briefly across her face.

'Are you an athlete?' Margaret asked.

'Sure. I run in three-thousand-metre heats tomorrow.' She hesitated. 'You lady pathologist, yes? With Chinese policeman?'

Margaret was taken aback. 'How do you know that?'

'Everyone talking about it in dressing room. Supervising Coach Cai, he say no one to talk to you.'

Margaret felt her hackles rising. 'Did he now?' She looked at the girl. 'But *you're* talking to me.'

'Yes,' she said. 'I wanna speak to you, lady. I must speak to you. Ve-err important. Don't know who else to talk to.' Her eyes darted down the corridor to the dressing rooms. 'Not now. Later, OK?'

And she hurried away down the corridor, eyes to the floor, brushing past Supervising Coach Cai as he emerged into the foyer. He glanced after the girl and then looked over at Margaret, clearly wondering if there had been some kind of exchange.

Margaret forced a smile. 'Congratulations, Supervisor Cai,' she said. 'The Americans will have to do better tomorrow.'

He inclined his head in the minutest acknowledgment, but his face never cracked. He turned and strode off.

When Li emerged from the dressing rooms fifteen minutes later, his mood was black. 'A complete waste of time,' he told Margaret as he led her out into the cold night. 'Like trying to get blood from a stone.'

'Perhaps that's because Cai warned them all not to talk to you.'

He stopped and looked at her. 'How do you know that?'

'Because a young female athlete told me. She's running in the heats of the three thousand metres tomorrow. She said she needed to speak to me urgently about something very important, and that Supervisor Cai had told all the athletes not to talk to us.'

Li was seething. 'What does that bastard think he's playing at?'

'What's more interesting is why that girl wanted to speak to me,' said Margaret.

'She didn't tell you?'

Margaret shook her head. 'She saw Cai coming and scuttled off.' She slipped her arm through his. 'So they didn't tell you *anything*?'

Li shrugged. 'Just confirmed what I already knew.' He held up his arms in frustration. 'I don't know what to think. I really don't.' He checked his watch. 'But right now I'd better get you home. I have to get back to the station.'

Chapter Four

The next morning, when Li arrived at the autopsy room, Margaret raised her eyes behind her goggles and froze in mid-cut. 'You're late. Again.'

Li shifted uncomfortably and glanced at Sun who stood on the opposite side of the body from Margaret, wearing a green apron and shower cap. 'Have I missed anything?' he asked, ignoring the barb.

Margaret turned her attentions back to the recently exhumed Xing Da. His body was just a shell now, ribs cut through and prised apart. 'He was a mess,' she said. 'You could almost choose from half a dozen different injuries as being the cause of death, although in fact it was none of them.'

'So what did kill him?' Li asked, intrigued.

'I have no idea. Yet. But I can tell you what didn't kill him—the car crash. He was dead before the car hit the lamppost. And since he was driving, and we all know that dead men can't drive, one has to wonder how the car came to be travelling at a hundred kilometres an hour down a Beijing street at eleven o'clock at night.'

'How can you tell he was dead before the crash?'

'Detective Sun will tell you,' Margaret said airily. 'Since he was here on time, he's already had that described for him. Meantime, I'm going to prepare sections of the heart for microscopic examination.' She walked away to another table.

Li looked at Sun. 'Well?'

'Hey, Chief,' he said, 'my English isn't that great. I think I understood, but . . .' With some distaste, Sun indicated Xing Da's injuries about his head, chest and stomach. 'Dr Campbell says if this guy had been alive when he picked up these injuries, they would look quite different. They should be kind of red, or purple. Apparently you don't bleed too well if you're dead—injuries like these would be kind of tough, golden, parchment-like.' Which they were. Sun took a deep breath. 'Same with the internal stuff. His liver was pretty much crushed. According to the Doc there should have been at least a couple of litres of blood as a result. There was virtually none.'

Li looked at the body of the athlete thoughtfully. If he was dead before the crash, then it seemed improbable that the others in the car had been alive.

He crossed to the other table and watched as Margaret prepared a section of heart tissue and looked at it under a microscope. After a moment she straightened up, pressing both her hands into her lumbar region. She appeared to be looking at Li, but he saw that her eyes were glazed. She was looking through him at something that existed only in her mind.

'What is it?' he said.

Her focus returned. 'I'm not sure I've seen anything like it in a healthy young male before,' she said, and shook her head. 'There are big coronary arteries on the surface of the heart that we all seem to manage to clog up as we age. It's the most common cause of a heart attack.' She paused. 'But there are also tiny arteries that run through the muscle of the heart. Microvasculature we call them. It's possible for these to clog and thicken. But the thing is,' she said, frustrated in her attempt to describe what she had seen, 'Xing's are not really clogged *with* anything. It's like they closed themselves up, causing a massive coronary. If I had to guess, and that's all it would be, I'd say it looked like they had been attacked by some kind of virus.'

Sun had followed Li over to the table, listening intently, concentrating hard to understand everything. But the technical vocabulary had been beyond him. 'So how he die?' he asked Margaret.

'At this stage it's just a theory,' Margaret said. 'And if you quote me I'll deny it. But in layman's terms, it looks like he had a heart attack brought on—maybe—by a virus.'

Li's head was filled with a single, perplexing question. He gave it voice. 'Why would you take someone who had died of natural causes and try to make it appear they had been killed in a car crash?'

Margaret waggled a finger. 'I can't answer that one for you, Li Yan. But I have another question that we can answer very quickly: Were our suicide–murder and our weightlifter also suffering from a thickening of the microvasculature?'

Li looked nonplussed. 'Were they?'

Margaret laughed. 'I don't know. We'll have to look.' She pushed her goggles back. 'I prepared sections of Sui Mingshan's heart for storage. I assume Dr Wang will have done the same with Jia Jing's. Why don't you phone him and ask him to look at them under the microscope while I dig out the ones I prepared yesterday?'

When Li returned from telephoning Wang, Margaret had dug out the slides from the previous day's autopsy and was slipping the first one under the microscope. She set her eyes to the lens and adjusted the focus. After a moment she looked up at Li.

'Well, well,' she said. 'If someone hadn't strung our boy up from a diving platform his heart would have seized up on him sooner rather than later. Same as our friend on the table: he had pronounced thickening of the microvasculature.'

There was nothing to discuss. The facts spoke for themselves, but made absolutely no sense. And Li was reluctant to jump to conclusions before they had heard from Dr Wang. So Margaret had the results of the toxicology report on Sui's samples sent up from the lab. She sat on a desk in the pathologists' office and read through the results while Li and Sun watched in expectant silence.

She shrugged. 'As I predicted, blood alcohol level almost zero-point-four per cent. Apart from that, nothing unusual.'

The phone rang, and Li snatched the receiver from its cradle. It was Wang. He listened for almost two minutes without comment, and then thanked the doctor and hung up. He said, 'Jia also had marked thickening of the microvasculature. But Wang says it was the narrowing of the main coronary artery that killed him.'

Margaret said, 'Yes, but the thickening of the arterioles would have done the job eventually, even if his artery hadn't burst on him.'

Li nodded. 'That's pretty much what Wang said. Oh, and toxicology also confirmed, no steroids.'

Sun had again been concentrating on following the English. And now he turned to Li and said, 'So if Jia Jing hadn't died of a heart attack, he would probably have turned up dead in an accident somewhere, or "committed suicide".'

Li nodded thoughtfully. 'Probably. And he'd probably have had that long pony tail of his shaved off.' He frowned. 'But why?'

THE BRIEFING WAS SHORT and to the point. The meeting room was filled with detectives and smoke. Nearly every officer in the section was there, and there were not enough chairs for them all. Deputy Section Chief Tao Heng sat listening resentfully, nursing his grudges to keep them warm in this cold, crowded room.

Delivering the preliminary autopsy reports to the section had helped Li clarify things in his own head, to assemble the facts in some kind of order. 'What is clear,' he told them, 'is that we have one murder and at least three suspicious deaths. There is little doubt, from the findings of the autopsy, that the swimmer Sui Mingshan did not commit suicide. He was murdered. Xing Da, who was driving the car in which the three athletes died, was dead before it crashed, so the accident was staged. And although we don't have their bodies for confirmation, I think we have to assume that the other two were also dead prior to the crash. But what's bizarre is that Xing seems to have died from natural causes—possibly a virus which attacked the microscopic arteries of the heart.'

He looked around the faces in the room. 'Stranger still, Sui Mingshan and Jia Jing were also suffering from hypertrophy—thickening—of the microvasculature. Both would have died from it sooner or later if fate had not intervened. But perhaps the strangest thing of all is that each of them had had his head shaved. With the exception, of course, of Jia.'

Wu cut in. 'Could that be because he was the only one who really did die a natural death? Before anyone could mess with him?'

One of the other detectives said, 'But why was anybody messing with any of them anyway, if it was some virus that was killing them?'

'I'd have thought that was pretty obvious,' Wu said. 'Obviously someone didn't want anyone to know about the virus.'

'And the shaven heads?'

Wu shrugged. 'Jia's head wasn't shaved. There's also the cyclist. We don't know that his head was shaved.'

'We don't know that he's involved at all,' Li said.

'Actually, I think we do, Chief.' This from Qian.

'What do you mean?' Li asked.

Qian said, 'I spoke to the doctor who signed the death certificate. He remembered quite distinctly that the deceased's head had been shaved. Recently, he thought. There were several nick marks on the scalp.' There was an extended period of silence around the room, before he added, 'And there's something else.' He waited.

'Well?' Deputy Tao said impatiently.

'The three "friends" who were with him when he fell into the pool? They've all gone back to Taiwan. None is available for further questioning.' Qian paused. 'All three are known to the police in Taipei. All suspected members of a Hong Kong-based gang of Triads.'

More silence around the room, and then Li said, 'So somebody brought them here to be witnesses to an "accident".'

'And got them out again pretty bloody fast,' Wu said. He screwed up his eyes as he realised what he had said, and his hand shot up. 'Sorry, boss. Ten yuan in the swear box.'

There was laughter. But Li was not smiling. The more they knew, the denser the mist of obfuscation surrounding this case became.

DEPUTY SECTION CHIEF TAO pursued Li down the corridor after the meeting. 'We need to talk, Chief,' he said.

'Not now.'

'It's important.'

Li stopped and turned and found the older man regarding him with a mixture of frustration and dislike. 'What is it?'

'Not something I think we should discuss in the corridor.'

Li waved his hand dismissively. 'I don't have time just now. I have a lunch appointment.' And he turned and headed towards the stairs where Sun was waiting for him.

Tao watched him go with deep resentment burning in his heart.

LI AND SUN had picked up Sun's wife from the police apartments in Zhengyi Road before heading to the Old Beijing Noodle King restaurant. Margaret was there waiting for them and introductions were made on the steps outside. Wen was in her early twenties, a slight, pretty girl on whom the swelling of her baby seemed unnaturally large. She shook Margaret's hand coyly.

'Verr pleased meet you,' she said, blushing.

'Hi, I'm Margaret.'

With difficulty, Wen got her tongue part of the way around this strange, foreign name. 'Maggot,' she said.

Margaret glanced in Li's direction and saw him smirking. She got *Maggot* a lot. 'You can call me Maggie,' she said to Wen.

'Maggee,' Wen said, and smiled, pleased with herself. And Margaret knew they were never going to be soul mates.

Inside, rows of square lacquered tables stretched out before them, to a wall covered in framed inscriptions and a panoramic window opening onto the street. White-jacketed chefs worked feverishly behind long counters, while each table was attended by a waiter wearing the traditional blue jacket with white turned-up cuffs. Li led them to a table near the back and Sun and Wen looked around, wide-eyed. The Beijing Noodle King was a new experience for them.

'Shall I order?' Li asked, and they nodded. Li took the menu and looked at it only briefly. He knew what was good. His Uncle Yifu had brought him here often.

A waiter scrawled their order and hurried off.

'So,' Wen said, and she patted her stomach, 'how long?'

'Me?' Margaret asked. Wen nodded. 'A month.'

Wen frowned. 'No possible. You too big.'

For a moment Margaret was perplexed, then the light dawned. 'No, not one month pregnant. One month to go.'

Wen clearly did not understand, and Li explained. Then she smiled. 'Me, too. Another four week.' She reached out and put her hand over Margaret's. 'Girl? Boy?'

'I don't know,' Margaret said. 'I don't want to know.'

Wen's eyebrows shot up in astonishment. How could anyone not want to know? 'I got boy,' she said proudly.

'Good for you.' Margaret's cheeks were aching from her fixed smile. She turned it on Li, and he saw it for the grimace it really was.

As two beers and two glasses of water arrived at the table, Li said to Wen in English, 'Margaret could take you to her antenatal class this afternoon.' He looked at Margaret. 'You could get her enrolled.'

'Sure,' Margaret said. Once she got there, she knew she could dump responsibility onto Jon Macken's wife, Yixuan, who could deal with Wen in Chinese. 'They encourage husbands to go, too.' She turned to Sun. 'You'll want to go, Detective Sun, won't you?'

Sun looked a little bemused. He came from a world where men and women led separate lives. He looked to Li for guidance.

Li said, 'Sure he will. But not this afternoon. He'll be too busy.'

'And I suppose that applies to his boss, too,' Margaret said.

'I'm picking up my father at the station, remember?' Li replied.

Reality came flooding back. For two days Margaret had been able to return to her former self, focused on her work. Now, suddenly, she was back in the role of expectant mother and bride-to-be. Li's father arrived today, her own mother tomorrow. The betrothal meeting was the day after. The wedding next week. She groaned inwardly.

The food arrived. Fried aubergine dumplings, mashed aubergine with sesame paste, sliced beef and tofu. They ate in silence for several minutes, then Wen said to Margaret, 'You must have big apartment, Maggee, married to senior officer.'

Margaret shook her head. 'We're not married. Yet.' Wen looked shocked, and Margaret realised that it was not something Sun had discussed with her. 'But we get married next week,' she added for clarification. 'And, yes, we will have a big apartment. I hope.'

Li was aware of Sun glancing in his direction, but he kept his eyes fixed on his food. And then the noodles arrived. Four steaming bowls on a tray, each one surrounded by six small dishes containing beanpaste sauce, coriander, chopped radish, chickpeas and spring onions. Four waiters surrounded the holder of the tray, and called out the name of each dish as it was emptied over the noodles.

'This is one hell of a noisy restaurant,' Margaret said as she mixed her noodles with their added ingredients. 'But the food's good.'

When they finished eating, Li said to Margaret, 'Why don't you and Wen get a taxi up to the hospital? I'll take your bike in the back of the Jeep, and you can get a taxi home. I'll bring it back tonight.'

'What about your father?'

Li smiled. 'He goes to bed early.' He paused. 'And your mother arrives tomorrow.'

'Don't remind me,' she said. But she had not missed his point. It would be their last chance to be alone together before the wedding.

Li asked for the bill, and Wen and Margaret went to the ladies' room.

Sun looked at Li. 'Chief? She doesn't know, does she?'

And all the light went out of Li's eyes. Nobody had ever raised it with him directly before. 'No,' he said. 'And I don't want her to.'

WHEN THE TAXI dropped Margaret and Wen outside the First Teaching Hospital of Beijing Medical University, a girl came down the steps towards them, her gloved hands tucked up under her arms to keep them warm, her eyes watering and her nose bright red. She stepped in front of them to halt their progress, but it wasn't until she turned to glance behind her that Margaret saw the purple birthmark on her left cheek and remembered.

'Lili,' she said.

Behind the tears of cold there was fear in the girl's eyes. 'I told you, I need to talk to you, lady.'

'Aren't you supposed to be running today?'

'I already run in heats. First place. I get in final tomorrow.'

'Congratulations.' Margaret frowned. 'How did you know to find me here?'

Lili almost smiled and lowered her eyes towards Margaret's bump. 'I phone hospital to ask times of classes for antenatal.'

'And how did you know it was this hospital?'

'Best maternity hospital in Beijing for foreigner. I take chance.'

Margaret was intrigued. 'I can give you a few minutes.'

'No.' The girl looked around suddenly, as if she thought someone might be watching. 'Not here. I come to your home.'

For the first time, Margaret became wary. 'Not if you won't tell me what it is you want to talk to me about.'

'Please, lady. I can't say.' She glanced at Wen, who was looking at her wide-eyed. 'Please, lady, please. You give me address.'

There was such pleading in her eyes that Margaret, although reluctant, could not resist. 'Hold on,' she said, and she fumbled in her bag for a business card. It had her home address and number on the back. 'Here.' She held it out and the girl took it. 'When will you come?'

'I don't know. Tonight, maybe. You be in?'

'I'm in most nights.'

Lili tucked the card carefully in her pocket and wiped her watering eyes. 'Thank you, lady. Thank you,' she said. And she made a tiny bow and then pushed past them, disappearing into the crowd.

Wen turned excitedly to Margaret. 'You know who that is? That Dai Lili. She verr famous Chinese runner.'

LI SAT ON THE WALL outside the subway, watching crowds of travellers streaming out from the arrivals gate at Beijing railway station. He had butterflies in his stomach and his mouth was dry. He had not set eyes on his father for nearly five years, a state of affairs for which, he knew, his father blamed him. Not without cause. For in all the years since Li had left his home in Sichuan Province to attend the University of Public Security in Beijing, he had returned on only a handful of occasions. And although he had been too young to be a participant in the Cultural Revolution, Li felt that his father blamed him for the death of his mother during that time of madness. A time that had left his father diminished, robbed of hope and ambition. And love.

They had not spoken since the funeral of Li's Uncle Yifu, his father's brother. It had been a painful, sterile affair at a city crematorium, attended mostly by fellow police officers who had served under Yifu during his years as one of Beijing's top cops, or alongside him in the early days. Old friends had travelled all the way from Tibet, where Yifu had been sent in the fifties by the Communists, who had decided that this particular intellectual would be less of a danger to them a long way from the capital. Later, during the Cultural Revolution, he had been thrown in prison, an experience that might have broken a lesser man but from which he drew only strength.

Li saw his father emerging from the gates, dragging a small suitcase on wheels behind him. He was a sad, shuffling figure in a long, shabby duffle coat, with a fez-like fur hat over his thinning hair.

Li made his way through the crowds to greet him with a heart like lead. When he got close up, his father seemed very small, as if he had shrunk, and Li had a sudden impulse to hug him. But it was an impulse he restrained, holding out his hand instead.

'Hi, Dad.'

His father did not smile. 'Are you going to take my case?' he asked.

'Of course.'

Li took the handle from him, and steered him towards the Jeep. He put the case in the back and opened the passenger door to help his father in. But the old man pushed away his hand.

'I don't need your help,' he said. 'I have lived for sixty-seven years without any help from you.'

They drove in silence from the station to Zhengyi Road, where the armed guard at the back entrance to the Ministry of State and Public Security glanced in the window, saw Li, and waved them through.

Li pulled up outside his apartment block, and he and his father rode up in the elevator together to the fourth floor. Still they had not spoken since getting into the Jeep.

The apartment was small. One bedroom, a living room, a tiny kitchen, a bathroom and a long, narrow hallway. Li would sleep on the settee while his father was there. He showed the old man to his room and left him to unpack. He went to the refrigerator, took out a beer, popped the cap and moved through to the living room, which opened onto a terrace. He drained nearly half the bottle in one long pull, then turned at the sound of the door opening behind him.

Divested of his coat and hat, his father seemed even smaller. His hair was very thin, wisps of it swept back over his skull. He looked at the bottle in his son's hand. 'Are you not going to offer me a drink?'

'Of course,' Li said. 'I'll show you where I keep the beer. You can help yourself any time.' He got another bottle from the refrigerator and opened it for his father, pouring the contents into a long glass.

They went back through to the living room, their awkwardness like a third presence. They sat down and drank in further silence until finally the old man said, 'So when do I get to meet her?'

'The day after tomorrow. At the betrothal meeting.'

His father stared at him for a long time before shaking his head. 'Why an American?' he asked. 'Are Chinese girls not good enough?'

'Of course,' Li said. 'But I never fell in love with one.'

'Love!' His father was dismissive, almost contemptuous.

'Didn't you love my mother?' Li asked.

'Of course.'

'Then you know how it feels to be in love with someone, to feel about them the way you've never felt about anyone else.'

'I know how it feels to lose someone you feel that way about.' And the old man's eyes were lost in reflected light as they filled with tears.

'I lost her, too,' Li said.

And suddenly there was fire in his father's voice. 'You didn't know your mother. You were too young.'

'I needed my mother.'

'And I needed a son!' And there it was, the accusation he had never put into words before. That he had been abandoned while Li selfishly pursued a career in Beijing. In the traditional Chinese family, the son remained at the home of his parents. But Li had left, and Xiao Ling, his sister, had gone shortly after to live with her husband's parents. Their father had been left on his own to brood upon the death, at the hands of Mao's Red Guards, of the woman he loved.

'You never lost your son,' Li said

'Maybe I wish I'd never had one,' his father fired back. 'Your mother only incurred the wrath of the Red Guards because she wanted to protect you from their indoctrination.' Finally, he had given voice to his deepest resentment of all, that if it wasn't for Li his mother might still be alive. 'And maybe my brother would still have been alive today if it hadn't been for the carelessness of my *son*!'

Li's tears were blinding him. He had always known that some twisted logic had led his father to blame him for his mother's death. But to blame him for the death of his uncle? This was new and much more painful. He stood up, determined that his father should not see his tears. But it was too late. They were streaming down his face.

'I have to go,' he said. 'I have a murder inquiry.' And as he turned towards the door, he saw the bewildered look on his father's face, as if for the first time in his life it might have occurred to the old man that other people hurt, too.

'Li Yan,' his father called after him, but he didn't stop until he had closed the door behind him, and stood shaking and fighting to contain the howl of anguish that was struggling to escape from within.

MARGARET HAD WAITED up as long as she could. As she undressed for bed, moonlight poured in through her window. She saw her silhouette on the wall, and wondered what kind of child she and Li were going to have. Would it be dark or fair, have brown eyes or blue? Would it have her fiery temper, or Li's infuriating calm? As she slipped between the sheets, she smiled to herself, and knew that however their genes had combined, it would be their child and she would love it.

Her thoughts were interrupted by the sound of a key in the lock, and her heart leapt. Li had come after all. She glanced at the clock. It was nearly eleven. Better late than never. But as soon as he opened the bedroom door she could see there was something wrong.

She knew better than to ask, and said simply, 'Come to bed.'

He undressed quickly and slipped in beside her. He had brought with him the cold of the night outside, and she wrapped her arms round him. They lay folded around each other for a long time without saying anything. In the world outside, he always towered over her, dominant and strong. But here, lying side by side, she was his equal, or greater, and could lay his head on her shoulder and mother him as if he were a little boy. And tonight she sensed that somehow that was what he needed more than anything. She spoke to him then, out of a need to say something. Something normal. Something that carried no weight to burden him.

'Jon Macken didn't turn up today at the antenatal class. Turned out his studio was broken into last night. He had an alarm system and everything installed. So it must have been professionals.'

Li grunted. The first sign of interest.

'Anyway, the weird thing is, they didn't really take much. Trashed the place and took some prints or something, and that was it. He says the police were useless. I told Yixuan you'd ask about it.'

'What the hell did you tell her that for?'

'Because she's my friend. And what's the point in getting married to one of Beijing's top cops if you can't pull a few strings?'

His silence then surprised her. She had thought she was drawing him out and had no idea that she had touched a raw nerve. So she was even more surprised when he said, 'I'll ask about it tomorrow.'

Finally she drew herself up and said, 'What's wrong?'

'Nothing that a family transplant wouldn't cure.'

'Your father,' she said flatly.

'According to *Dad*, not only did I abandon him, but I was responsible for the death of my mother, as well as . . .' He broke off.

Margaret felt a surge of anger at his father's cruelty. How could Li possibly be responsible for his mother's death? 'As well as what?' she asked softly.

'Yifu.'

She heard the way his throat constricted and choked off his voice, and she wanted just to hold him for ever and take away all his pain. She knew how he felt about Yifu, how the guilt had consumed him in the years since his uncle's death. She felt the tears wet on his cheeks and said, 'Li Yan, it was not your fault.' But she knew she would never convince him. And so she held him tighter and willed her love to him through every point of contact between them.

He lay in her arms for what felt like an eternity. And then, 'I love you,' Margaret said quietly.

'I know.' His voice whispered back to her in the dark.

She kissed his forehead and his eyes, and ran her hands across his chest. It was their last night together before her mother's arrival, and she wanted to make the most of it, to give herself to Li completely.

The knocking on the door crashed over them like a bucket of ice cold water. She sat up, heart pounding. 'Who the hell's that?'

Li said, 'Stay in bed. I'll go see.' He got up and pulled on his trousers and shirt, and left the bedroom as the knocking came again.

At the end of the hall he opened the door to find himself looking into the face of a skinny girl with straggling shoulder-length hair. She looked alarmed to find herself confronted by Li.

'What do you want? Who are you looking for?' he demanded.

'No one,' she said in a tremulous voice. 'I'm sorry.' And she turned and hurried away towards the stairwell, retracing her steps down the eleven flights she must have climbed to get here, for the lift did not operate at this time of night.

'Who was it?'Margaret asked. She was sitting up.

'I don't know. Some girl. She must have got the wrong apartment, because she took off pretty fast when she saw me.'

Margaret's heart was pounding. 'Did she have a large purple birthmark on her face?'

Li was surprised. 'Yes,' he said. 'You know her?'

'Her name is Dai Lili. She is the athlete who said she wanted to speak to me last night at the stadium.'

Now Li was astonished. 'How did she find out where you live?'

'I gave her my card.'

'Are you mad? When?'

'She tracked me down to the maternity hospital this afternoon. She was scared, Li Yan. She said she had to speak to me and asked if she could come here. What else could I say?'

Li cursed softly under his breath with the realisation that he had just been face to face with the only person in this case who was prepared to talk—even if not to him. 'I could still catch her.' He pulled on his shoes and ran to the door.

'You need a coat,' Margaret called after him. 'It's freezing out there.'

The only response was the sound of the apartment door slamming.

By the time Li got to the ground floor and out through the glass doors he knew she was gone. Even if he had known which way, he could never catch her. She was a runner, after all, at the peak of her fitness. He stood gasping for a moment, perspiration turning to ice on his skin, before facing the long climb back up.

Chapter Five

Li pulled up on the stretch of waste ground opposite the food market and walked back to Mei Yuan's stall on the corner.

He had slept like a log in Margaret's arms, but had woken early, enveloped still by the fog of depression his father had brought with him from Sichuan. He had returned to his apartment before his father woke, to prepare him breakfast, then had left him with a spare key and fled to the safety of his work.

'I missed you yesterday.' Mei Yuan had seen him coming and had already poured the pancake mix onto the hot plate.

'I am in the middle of a murder investigation, and my father arrived from Sichuan.' He was aware of her eyes flickering briefly away from her hot plate in his direction and then back again. She knew that relations between them were difficult.

'And how is he?'

'Oh,' Li said airily, 'much the same as usual. Nothing wrong with him that a touch of murder wouldn't cure.'

'I hope that's not the investigation you're conducting.'

'I wish,' Li said. 'It would be an easy one to break. Only one suspect, with both motive and opportunity.' Flippancy was an easy way to hide your emotions, but he knew she wasn't fooled.

Mei Yuan finished his *jian bing* and handed it to him wrapped in brown paper. 'If you have read the teachings of Lao Tzu in the *Tao Te Ching*,' she said, 'then you know that the Tao teaches, be good to people who are good. To those who are not good be also good. Thus goodness is achieved.'

Li bit into his *jian bing* and felt its soft, savoury hotness suffuse his mouth with flavour. He laughed and said, 'You certainly achieved goodness with this, Mei Yuan.' He tossed some coins into her tin. 'I will see you tomorrow night.'

As he turned to head back to the Jeep, she said, 'Your young friend came yesterday.' He stopped, and she drew a book out of her bag. 'He brought me this.'

It was a copy of the Scott Fitzgerald classic, *The Great Gatsby*.

'You haven't read it, have you?' Li asked.

'No,' Mei Yuan replied. 'But neither has anyone else.' She paused. 'He said his friend gave it to him to lend to me. But this is a brand new book.'

Li smiled. 'He means well.'

'Yes,' she said. 'But he lies too easily. I would prefer his honesty.'

LI STOPPED at the door of the detectives' office. 'Qian?'

The detective looked up from his computer keyboard.

'I want you to look into a burglary for me. It's probably being handled by the local public security bureau. An American photographer called Jon Macken. He had a studio down on Xidan. It was broken into the night before last.'

Qian frowned. 'What interest do we have in it, Chief?'

Li said. 'None that I know of. Just take a look for me, would you?'

'Sure.'

He was about to go when Qian stopped him. 'Chief, I left a note on your desk.' He hesitated, and Li had the distinct impression that everyone in the room was listening, even though they appeared still to be working. 'Commissioner Hu Yisheng's office called. The Commissioner wants to see you straight away.' Several heads lifted to see his reaction. Now he knew they'd been listening. And why.

THE NOISE OF DIGGERS and demolition resounded in the narrow Dong Jiaminxiang Lane as Li picked his way past heavy machinery to the redbrick building that housed the headquarters of the Criminal Investigation Department. In the outer office, a secretary called the Commissioner to let him know that Li had arrived. A short while later, he emerged from his office, pulling on his jacket.

He nodded towards Li. 'Section Chief.' He turned to the secretary, 'Can't think with this noise. If anyone wants me, we'll be next door.'

They swung past the workmen and Li followed the Commissioner up the steps of the old CID headquarters, now a police museum.

'I used to have my office on the top floor here,' the Commissioner said, as they passed through its arched entrance.

They climbed up several flights, past exhibits that illustrated the history of the police and fire departments. The top floor was a celebration of the modern force, but it was dominated by a huge curved stone wall, the Martyrs' Wall, which was a monument to all the police officers of Beijing who had died on active duty since the creation of the People's Republic in 1949. Li stood staring up at the wall. It was the first time he had visited the museum.

'Impressive, isn't it?' Commissioner Hu said. 'You know your uncle is listed among the martyrs?'

Li was shocked. It was the first he had heard of it. 'But he did not die on active duty,' he said. 'He was retired.'

'He was murdered by the subject of an active investigation. And in the light of his outstanding record as a police officer, it was decided that his name should be included in the roll of honour.'

Li found this unexpectedly comforting. His uncle had been given a kind of immortality, a place among heroes, which is what he had been.

The Commissioner was watching him closely. He said, 'There are two matters I want to discuss with you, Section Chief. I received a call last night from the Procurator General regarding the official report into the death of the weightlifter, Jia Jing. It had been drawn to his attention that the report was not entirely accurate. He also discovered that since you attended the incident you must have known this to be the case. And yet you signed off the report as being accurate. The Procurator General is furious. And frankly, so am I.'

Li said, 'And who was it who drew the Procurator General's attention to this alleged inaccuracy?'

The Commissioner took Li firmly by the arm and steered him closer to the wall. 'Don't play games with me, Li. I think you know who it was. I hear that all is far from well between you and another senior member of your section.' He let go of Li's arm and took a deep breath. 'Are you going to tell me why this report was doctored?'

Li said quietly, 'Perhaps you should ask the Minister.'

Hu narrowed his eyes. 'Are you telling me the Minister asked you to alter an official report?'

Li nodded.

'And do you think for one minute he would admit to that?'

And Li saw for the first time just what kind of trouble he could be in. He said, 'One or two minor facts were omitted purely to save embarrassment for the people involved. That's all. The Minister—'

Hu cut him off. 'The Minister will not back you up or bail you out on this, Li. Take my word for it. Get the officer concerned to issue a full and accurate report, and we will withdraw the current report.'

Li was kicking himself. He knew he should never have agreed to the cover-up. 'The investigation into the death of Jia and other leading athletes looks like turning into a murder investigation that will shake Chinese athletics to the core, Commissioner.'

The Commissioner was clearly shocked. At length he said, 'Take no action for the moment, Section Chief. I will speak to the Procurator General and let you know my decision.'

Li nodded again. 'You said *two* things, Commissioner.'

'What?'

'You wanted to speak to me about *two* things.'

'Ah . . . yes.' And for the first time Commissioner Hu avoided his eyes. 'It is a matter I had intended to raise with you anyway.'

'To tell me I had been allocated a married officer's apartment?'

Anger flashed quickly in Hu's eyes and he snapped, 'You know perfectly well there's no question of you getting an apartment!'

Li felt the resentment that had been simmering inside him for weeks now start bubbling to the surface. 'Really? That's the first time anybody has conveyed that particular piece of information to me. So I don't know how I would know it, perfectly well, or otherwise.'

For a moment he thought the Commissioner was going to strike him. 'You really are hell-bent on ending your career, aren't you?'

'I wasn't aware I had much of a choice, Commissioner.'

'So you're still intent on marrying her?'

'Next week.'

The Commissioner took a very deep breath. 'You really are a fool, Li, aren't you? You *know* that it is Public Security policy that none of its officers may marry a foreign national.' He sighed his frustration. 'In the name of the sky, why do you have to *marry* her? We've turned a blind eye to your relationship up until now.'

'Because I love her, and she's carrying my baby. If marrying her is such a threat to national security, I'd have thought conducting an illicit affair was an even greater one. And if you're prepared to turn a blind eye to that, then aren't you just being hypocritical?'

The Commissioner shook his head in despair. 'I don't know what your uncle would have thought of you.'

'My uncle always told me to be true to myself, and that the universe is ruled by letting things take their course, not by interfering.'

'Then I will expect your resignation on my desk by next week.'

'No, I am not going to resign.'

The Commissioner looked astonished. 'If you insist on following this course, then I *will* remove you from the force. You will lose your apartment, and your pension, all medical rights and rights to social security. And who will employ a disgraced former police officer?' He paused to let his words sink in. 'Have you really thought this through?'

Li stood rock still, keeping his emotions on a tight rein.

'For heaven's sake, Li, you are the youngest section chief in the history of the department. You are one of the most highly regarded police officers in China. It is just a shame that your uncle is not here to talk some sense into your bone head. You can expect notice to clear your desk in a matter of days.'

HEADS LIFTED in only semi-disguised curiosity as Li strode into the detectives' office. Tao was standing by Wu's desk reading through a sheaf of forensic reports. Li looked at him very directly.

'A word, please, Deputy Section Chief.' And he walked into Tao's office leaving his deputy to follow him in. Li closed the door behind them and turned to face Tao, his voice low and controlled. 'You went behind my back on the Jia Jing report.'

Tao shook his head. 'No,' he said. 'I tried to speak to you about it the other day, but you were "too busy". A lunch appointment, I think.' He hesitated, as if waiting for Li to say something.

'Go on.'

'I had a call from Procurator General Meng yesterday morning asking me to verify the details contained in Wu's report.'

'Why did he call you and not me?'

'I would have thought that since you had signed off the report and he was seeking verification, that was obvious.'

'So you told him I'd had it doctored.'

'No. I had Wu come into my office and tell me what happened that night. I passed that information on to the Procurator General as requested. I play things by the book, Section Chief Li. I always have.'

His supercilious smile betrayed just how safe he thought he was, with Li's expulsion from the force only a matter of days away. It was clearly an open secret now. For Li, what made it even worse, the salt in the wound, was the knowledge that Tao would probably succeed him as section chief. It was almost more than he could bear.

MARGARET SIGHED and tried to calm herself. But the imminent arrival of her mother was making her tense beyond her control. She had put off even thinking about it until the very last minute—almost until the taxi had dropped her off at the airport.

The first passengers came through the gate in ones and twos, dragging cases or pushing trolleys, and then slowly it turned into a flood. Margaret scoured the faces, watching nervously for her mother. Finally she saw her, pale and anxious among a sea of Chinese faces, tall, slim, lipstick freshly applied, her coiffured grey-streaked hair immaculate. She was wearing a dark green suit with a cream blouse and was carrying a camel-hair coat. She looked for all the world like a model in a clothes catalogue for the elderly. She had three large suitcases piled on a trolley.

Margaret hurried to intercept her. 'Mom,' she called and waved.

Her mother turned as she approached and smiled coolly. 'Margaret.'

They exchanged a perfunctory hug and peck on the cheek, before her mother cast a disapproving eye over the swelling that bulged beneath her smock. 'Look at you! I can't *believe* you went and got yourself pregnant to that Chinaman.'

Margaret said patiently. 'He's not a Chinaman, Mom. He's Chinese. And he's the man I love.'

Whatever went through her mother's mind, she thought better of expressing it. Instead, as Margaret steered her towards the taxi queue, she said, 'It was a dreadful flight. Full of . . . Chinese.' She said the word as if it left a nasty taste in her mouth. Her mother thought of anyone who was not white, anglo-saxon, as being barely human. 'They ate and snorted and snored and sneezed through fifteen hours of hell,' she said. 'And the smell of garlic . . . You needn't think that I'll be a regular visitor.'

'Well, there's a blessing,' Margaret said, drawing a look from her mother. She smiled. 'Only kidding. Come on, let's get a taxi.'

Once they were outside the building, the wind destroyed in fifteen seconds the coiffure that had survived fifteen hours of air travel.

Her mother slipped her arms into her coat and shivered. 'My God, Margaret, it's colder than Chicago!'

'Yes, Mom, and it's bigger and dirtier and noisier. Get used to it, because that's how it's going to be for the next week.'

As they sped into the city on the freeway, Margaret's mother stared in silence from the window of their taxi. Margaret tried to imagine seeing it all again through new eyes. But even in the few years since her first trip, Beijing had changed beyond recognition. The number of bicycles was diminishing in relation to the increase in the number of motor vehicles. New high-rise buildings were altering the skyline almost daily, and electronic advertising hoardings blazed the same logos as you might expect to find in any American city.

As they hit the Third Ring Road, looping round to the south side of the city, her mother said, 'I'd no idea it would be like this.'

'What did you think it would be like?'

'I don't know. Like in the tourist brochures. Chinese lanterns and curling roofs, and streets filled with people in blue Mao suits.'

'Well, some of these things still survive,' Margaret said. 'But really Beijing is just a big modern city.'

It took nearly an hour to get to Margaret's apartment block. Her mother cast a sharp eye over her surroundings—looking for fault, Margaret thought—while their taxi driver carried the cases into the lobby and stacked them in the elevator before taking his leave. There was no sign of the sullen operator, so Margaret ushered her mother into the lift and stabbed the button for the eleventh floor. The stale smell of cigarette smoke surrounded them as they travelled upwards in silence. On reaching the eleventh floor, they dragged the heavy cases from the elevator into the tiny hallway of Margaret's apartment.

'Your bedroom's this way.' Margaret led her mother up the hall.

Mrs Campbell stopped to take everything in. She looked into the bedroom, where the double bed nearly filled the room. 'You *live* here?' She was incredulous. She marched back down the hall and cast an eye over the tiny kitchen before turning into the living room. There was no disguising the horror on her face. 'I hope you're not expecting me to share a bed with you?'

'No, Mom. I'll be sleeping on the settee.'

Mrs Campbell looked earnestly at her daughter. 'Margaret, what have you been reduced to in this godforsaken country?'

'I'm perfectly happy here,' Margaret said, lying. 'I have everything I need. Anyway, after the wedding Li and I will be moving into family accommodation provided by the police. They're big apartments.'

It took nearly an hour for them to unpack and find places for all of her mother's clothes. And for the first time, Margaret realised just how limited her space really was. Her mother was clearly having doubts about whether she could last out until the wedding.

'Is it really a week till you get married?'

'Six days,' Margaret said. 'But we have the betrothal meeting tomorrow night.'

'What on earth is that?'

'It's kind of where Li Yan officially asks me to marry him. In front of both families.'

'You mean I'm going to have to meet his people tomorrow?'

'Just his father. His mother died in prison during the Cultural Revolution.'

Mrs Campbell looked shocked.

'But Li's sister and his niece will be there. We've rented a private room in a restaurant, and we'll have a traditional meal. And before the meal we'll have an exchange of gifts. Between the families.'

'But I haven't brought anything.'

'Don't worry, we'll get what we need tomorrow.'

'Such as?'

'Well, an easy one is money. Just a token amount. Usually ninety-nine yuan, or even nine hundred and ninety-nine. Nine is a very lucky number in China, because it is three times three, and three is the luckiest number of all. Other gifts are things like tea, dragon and phoenix cake, a pair of male and female poultry—'

'I have no intention of giving or receiving hens,' Mrs Campbell said firmly, rising up on her dignity.

Margaret couldn't contain her smile. 'People in the city don't exchange real poultry, Mom. Just symbols. Usually china ornaments, or paper cut-outs.'

'And what would we do with a picture of a hen?'

Margaret shook her head and pressed on. 'Tea is important, too, because, traditionally, both families want the couple to provide them with as many descendants as there are tea leaves.'

Mrs Campbell cocked an eyebrow. 'That would be difficult in a country that only allows couples to have one child, would it not?'

For a dreadful moment, Margaret saw and heard herself in her mother. The tone. The withering sarcasm.

Her mother went on, 'I'm not sure I approve of any of it. And

God knows what the wedding itself will be like.' She headed back down the hall to the living room.

Margaret sighed and followed, and found her looking round the tiny room, shaking her head.

'And if you think I'm going to spend the next six days sitting around in this pokey little place, you're very much mistaken.' She delved into her bag and pulled out a brochure. 'My travel agent told me if there's one thing worth seeing while I'm here, it's the Forbidden City.' She glanced at her watch. 'And no time like the present.'

LI HAD ALL THE REPORTS in front of him. Autopsy, forensic, toxicology. Reports from officers on every case under investigation. He had read through everything. Twice. Still nothing made any sense to him. None of the athletes, it seemed, had been taking drugs. The random urine tests, and the results from toxicology, bore each other out.

And why would anyone fake the deaths of people who had already died, apparently from natural causes? The odd thing here was that in the case of the three relay sprinters, none of them had even consulted a doctor in the recent past, so clearly they had no idea they were unwell. But where had they been when they died, prior to being bundled into their ill-fated car and sent speeding into a lamppost? And had they all died at the same time? Li found it baffling.

They had no evidence whatsoever that the cyclist had been the victim of foul play. But the witnesses to his 'accidental' death were, very conveniently, unavailable, and distinctly unreliable.

And the cyclist, too, had had his head shaved.

Li felt that somehow the shaving of the heads had to be the key to the whole sordid mystery. Was it some kind of ritual? A punishment? And this mystery virus that would probably have killed them all. Where had it come from? Who wanted to cover it up, and why? No matter how many times Li turned these things over in his mind, it brought him no nearer to enlightenment.

There was a knock on the door. Li called irritably, 'Come in.'

It was Qian. 'Sorry to disturb you, Chief. I got the information you asked for on the break-in at that photographer's studio.'

Li frowned, for a moment wondering what Qian was talking about. Then he remembered. The American married to Margaret's Chinese friend at the antenatal classes. He waved Quian into a seat. 'Anything interesting?'

Qian shrugged. 'Not really, Chief.' He sat down and opened a folder containing a one-page report. 'Just a break-in. The photographer's name is Jon Macken. An American. He's worked in Beijing for more than five years. Married to a local girl.'

'Yeah, yeah, I know,' Li said impatiently. 'What did they take?'

'Well, that's the only strange thing about it, Chief. A roll of film. That was it.'

'Are we investigating petty robberies now?' Tao's voice startled them both. He was standing in the open doorway.

Li said, 'I asked Qian to look into this one for me.'

Tao glanced at the folder in Li's lap. 'What's our interest?'

'I don't know,' Li said. 'Maybe none. Why don't you draw up a chair, Deputy Section Chief, and listen in?'

Tao hesitated, but Li knew he would take up the offer. Tao was hungry for Li's job, and here was a titbit to whet his appetite. He brought a chair to the desk and sat down. Qian recapped for him.

'So why would someone go to the trouble of breaking into a studio with an alarm system just to steal a roll of film?' Li asked.

'It was a used roll,' Qian said. 'I mean, Macken had already taken a whole bunch of pictures with it and developed them.'

'So it was the negatives that were taken?' Tao said.

'That's right.'

'And what was on the film?' Li asked.

'Nothing of much interest,' Qian said. 'Macken's been commissioned to take pictures for a glossy brochure advertising a new club. He'd been there on a recce the day before, and taken a few pictures. Nothing that you would think anyone would want to steal.'

'Well, that's something we'll never know,' said Tao, 'since he no longer has them.'

'Oh, but he has,' Qian said. 'Apparently he'd already taken a set of contact prints. He's still got those. He told me he'd looked very carefully, but can't find a single reason why anyone would want them.'

'This place that he's been commissioned to photograph. What is it, a nightclub?' Li asked.

'No, nothing like that, Chief.' Qian's eyes widened. 'Actually, it sounds like a really amazing place. Macken told me all about it. It's some kind of investment club for the very rich. It costs you a million yuan just to join, Chief. A million!' He repeated the word with a sense of awe. 'And that then entitles you to five million in credit.'

'Credit for what?' Tao asked.

'Investment. This place is plumbed into stock exchanges around the world. If you're a member you can buy and sell stocks and shares anywhere at the touch of a button. Macken says it's got about thirty private rooms with TV and lounge chairs, two restaurants, four conference rooms, a sauna, swimming pool . . . you name it.'

'A high-class gambling den, in other words,' Tao said with a hint of disapproval.

Li shook his head in wonder. 'I had no idea places like that existed.'

Qian shrugged. 'It's all change these days. It's hard to keep up.'

Tao stood up. 'Well, it doesn't sound like there's much there to interest us,' he said.

Li said, 'I agree. I think we'll leave it to the locals.'

Qian closed his folder and got to his feet. 'There was just one other thing,' he said. 'Macken got the job because he and his wife are friends with the PA of the club's chief executive. The PA recommended him.' He hesitated. 'Well, apparently, she's disappeared.'

Li scowled. 'What do you mean, disappeared?'

'Well, there's not necessarily anything sinister about it,' Qian said quickly. 'It's just, you know, she's a young girl, early twenties. Lives on her own and, well, nobody seems to know where she is.'

THE WIND ALMOST BLEW them over as they emerged from the escalators at Tiananmen West subway station. Margaret took her mother's arm and hurried her along the sidewalk, past the white marble bridges that spanned the moat to the Gate of Heavenly Peace, red flags whipping in the wind around Mao's portrait.

Mrs Campbell turned and followed Mao's gaze south. 'Where's the square?' she said.

'You're looking at it.'

Mrs Campbell's eyes widened. '*That's* the square? It's *huge*.' On this dull winter's afternoon, she could not even see its southern end.

Margaret said, 'We can walk across it afterwards.' And she steered her mother through the arched tunnel that took them under the Gate of Heavenly Peace and into the long concourse that led to the Meridian Gate and the entrance to the Forbidden City itself.

They arrived at the ticket office outside the gate only to find chains fencing it off, and a large sign in Chinese erected outside.

'You want buy book?' a voice at Margaret's elbow said.

She turned to the owner of the voice, an old peasant woman, and said, 'What does the sign say?'

'Close,' the old lady said.

'Closed?' Margaret was incredulous. 'It can't be.'

'Big work inside. They fix.'

'Renovation?'

The old lady nodded vigorously. 'Yeah, yeah, yeah. Renovation. You can still see. Buy book.'

'I don't believe it,' Margaret's mother said. 'What do I tell the folks back home? I went to China, and it was shut?'

TIANANMEN SQUARE was busy, perhaps because the Forbidden City was closed, and the queues at Mao's mausoleum seemed longer than usual. Margaret's mother declined to join the line.

'I'm getting tired, Margaret. Perhaps we should go home.' Words Margaret was relieved to hear.

They went through the pedestrian subway and up the stairs to the north side of Chang'an Avenue, where they could get the underground train home. As they emerged again into the icy blast, Mrs Campbell stumbled and fell with a shriek of alarm. She sprawled full length, with one knee taking the brunt of her weight.

Margaret crouched immediately beside her. 'Mom, are you OK?'

'I'm fine, I'm fine.' But there were tears smearing her mother's eyes, and, as she tried to get up, Margaret saw blood running down her shin from a gash on her knee.

'Don't move. You're bleeding. I'll need to bandage your knee.'

As she fumbled in her bag, Margaret became aware of a crowd gathering around them. The Chinese were inveterate busybodies. They always had to know what was going on, and to see for themselves. A woman picked up Mrs Campbell's bag and handed it to her. Another knelt down and held her hand. Margaret found a packet of antiseptic wipes and started cleaning the wound. Then she pulled out a hanky and tied it round the knee.

'It's OK, Mom, it's just a graze. You can try and get up now.'

As she took her mother's arm, there was an immediate gasp from the crowd, and several pairs of hands drew Margaret away. One woman issued a stream of rapid-fire Mandarin into her face. Margaret had the distinct impression she was being lectured for some misdemeanour, and then she realised that's exactly what was happening. She was pregnant. She should not even be attempting to help her mother up.

To Mrs Campbell's extreme embarrassment, she was lifted vertical by many hands and put back on her feet.

'We'll need to get a taxi,' Margaret said.

A small man in blue cotton trousers and an overcoat several sizes too large raised his voice above the other onlookers and, as the crowd parted, stepped forward to take charge of Margaret's mother. He led her, hobbling, through the crowd to his trishaw and eased her up onto the padded seat mounted over the rear axle. Margaret climbed up beside her and told the driver their address. He strained sinewy old legs to get the pedals turning, and then they bumped down into the cycle lane heading west. Mrs Campbell, pale and drawn, sat clutching her daughter's arm. Her eyes brimmed with tears.

'I wish I'd never come,' she said. 'I knew I shouldn't have come.'

Chapter Six

Li cycled up Chaoyangmen Nanxiaojie Street as the first light broke in a leaden sky. He had taken his father out for a meal the night before, and they had sat in silence as they ate. For all the hurt and misunderstanding that lay between them, they had nothing to say to each other. Li had gone to bed early, and risen early to be free of the atmosphere that his father had brought to the apartment. He wasn't sure when he would get away from the office, so his sister had agreed to collect the old man from Li's apartment and take him to the Imperial Restaurant on Tiananmen Square, where they had booked the room for the betrothal meeting. Li was dreading it.

The narrow street was busy with traffic and bicycles. Braziers flared and spat sparks as hawkers cooked breakfast in great stacks of bamboo steamers for workers on the early shift. Lights flooded out from the offices of Section One into the dark, tree-lined street as Li chained his bicycle to the railing at the side entrance.

Wu was at his desk when Li popped his head round the door of the detectives' room. The television was on and he was watching an early news bulletin. He jumped when Li spoke. 'Anything new?'

'Oh, it's you, Chief.' He hurriedly turned the sound down on the television. 'We got beat in the swimming. And didn't do too well in the track and field either. We might just have pinched it, only the women's three-thousand-metres champion failed to turn up.'

Li sighed. 'I was talking about the investigation, Wu.'

'Sorry, Chief. A lot of legwork, but nothing really.'

The door of Tao's office opened, and Qian emerged from it clutching an armful of folders. 'Morning, Chief.'

'Qian. I thought it was a bit early for the deputy section chief.'

Qian grinned and dumped the folders on his desk. Li was halfway up the corridor before Qian caught up with him. 'Chief, there was another break-in at that photographer's studio last night. Only this time Macken was there and they gave him a bit of a going over.'

Li stopped. 'Is he all right?' He had a picture in his memory of Macken as a small, fragile man.

'Just cuts and bruises, I think. The thing is, Chief, it was something specific they were after.' He paused, knowing he had Li's interest.

'What?' Li said.

'The contact prints he made from those negatives.'

Li scowled. He was more than interested now. 'How the hell did they know he'd taken contact prints?'

Qian shrugged. 'That's what I wondered, Chief. Outside of the local bureau, and the three of us, who even knew he'd made them?'

Li glanced at his watch and made a decision. 'Let's go see him.'

MACKEN AND YIXUAN lived in a small two-bedroomed apartment on the tenth floor of a new tower block in Chaoyang District. Yixuan was not at home when they arrived, and Macken showed them into his small, untidy study. The walls were covered with prints, and a Macintosh computer on his desk was almost submerged beneath drifts of paper and stacks of photography books.

''Scuse the mess, folks,' Macken said. 'I'm gonna have to get this place cleared out before the baby arrives. It's gonna be the nursery.' He had a bruise beneath his left eye and a nasty graze on his forehead and cheek. He caught Li looking. 'They threatened to do a lot worse. And, hey, I'm no hero. So I gave 'em the contacts.' His smile faded. 'What I can't figure is how the hell they knew I had them.'

'Who else knew?' Li asked.

'Outside of me, Yixuan, and the officers from the bureau, no one. Except you guys, I guess.' He paused. 'So when the officers from the bureau came the second time, I didn't tell them I still had a copy. I suppose it's safe enough to tell you.'

'You made two contact sheets?' Li said.

'No. After the negatives got taken the other night I scanned the contacts into the computer.' He searched about through the mess of papers on his desk and found a disk. He held it up. 'Brought 'em home with me, too. Wanna take a look?'

Li nodded, and as Macken loaded the file into his computer, glanced at Qian. Qian's English was limited, and Macken spoke fast. Li wondered how much he understood. 'You following this?'

Qian shrugged. 'Just about. His wife translated for us yesterday.'

Macken took them through each of the photographs, one by one. Shots of comfortable lounge seats arranged round giant TV screens, massage rooms, the sauna, a restaurant, the communications centre with young women wearing headsets sitting at banks of computers. In a shot of the main entrance, light falling through twenty-foot windows onto polished marble, there were five figures. Three of them, in lounge suits, looked like management types. A fourth was a big man who wore a track suit and had long hair tied back in a ponytail. A fifth, unexpectedly, was white, European or American. He looked to be a man in his sixties, abundant silver hair smoothed back from a tanned face against which his neatly cropped silver beard was starkly contrasted. He looked paunchy and well fed, but unlike the others was dressed casually, in a corduroy jacket and slacks.

Li asked him to hold that one. 'Do you know these people?'

Macken said, 'The one on the left is the CEO. The bigwig. The other two suits, I dunno. The guy in the track suit is a personal trainer; they got a gym downstairs. The guy in the beard, no idea.'

'Can you give me a print-out of that one?'

'Sure. I can print them all off if you want.'

'That would be good.'

Macken resumed their journey through the remaining contacts. The gym was well equipped with every mechanical aid to muscle-building you could imagine, plus some. There was a shot of the toilets, marble and mirrors in abundance, then they came to a picture of a large office with a chequerboard wall at one end. Opposite was a huge horseshoe desk and a glass meeting table with five chairs around it. One wall was also completely glass. An armed security guard stood by the door, a young woman in black by the desk. Her hair was drawn back from an attractive, finely featured face.

'That's JoJo,' Macken said, and he turned to Qian. 'You know, the one I told you about yesterday.'

Qian nodded, and Li said, 'The one you thought was missing.'

'I don't just think it,' Macken said, frowning. 'She *is* missing. After I spoke to you people yesterday I made a real effort to track her down. No one knows where she is.' He half smiled. 'My reasons for wanting to find her ain't entirely altruistic. She set this job up, but I ain't signed a contract, and without a contract there ain't no money.'

'When did you take the pictures?' Li asked.

'Day before yesterday.'

'So she's only really been "missing" for two days?'

Macken thought about it and shrugged. 'I guess. Seems longer.'

Li nodded towards the screen. 'Why the armed guard?'

'Oh, they got this big collection of priceless artefacts in the boss's office.' He pointed at a door beyond the desk. 'Worth a fortune.'

'Do you have a picture of it?'

'Nah. Asked, you know. But they wouldn't let me in there.'

Li turned to Qian. 'I think we'd better pay this place a visit.'

THE BEIJING ONECHINA Recreation Club was in the heart of a redeveloped area of Xicheng District on the west side of the city. Li had called ahead, and they were expected.

Two girls in shimmering gold *qipaos* bowed to them in greeting as they entered, and a tall young man in a dark suit asked them to follow him. He led them through hushed corridors, walls lined with pale hessian, past polished beechwood doors and unexpected groupings of sofas and lounge chairs in private corners. They took an elevator up two floors to the administration level and came out into the office where JoJo had stood by her desk watching Macken take his photographs. Thick-piled carpets deadened their footsteps as the flunky led them past an armed guard at the entrance. He knocked on the door behind JoJo's empty desk and waited until a voice invited them to enter, then he opened the door and let Li and Qian in.

Li recognised the CEO from the photograph. He was young, perhaps only thirty, with the square-jawed, round-eyed good looks of a Hong Kong film actor.

'I'm very pleased to meet you, Section Chief Li,' he said. 'Your reputation goes before you. I'm Fan Zhilong, chief executive of the company, and the club. Come in. Come in.'

They crossed an acre of cream carpet to a boomerang-shaped black lacquer desk. Fan urged them to be seated while he rounded the desk, then he handed each of them a business card and sat back in his chair.

Li glanced at the card. Fan Zhilong was CEO of OneChina Holdings Limited, a company listed on the Hong Kong stock exchange, who were owners of the Beijing OneChina Recreation Club. He looked up to find Fan regarding him thoughtfully.

'What can I help you with, Section Chief?'

'I am hoping that I can, perhaps, be of assistance to you,' Li said. And as he spoke, he noticed the large alcove beyond the desk. The priceless artefacts of which Macken had spoken were arranged on black shelves, each with its own spotlight. Plates, vases, daggers, tiny figurines. 'We are investigating a break-in at the studio of the photographer you commissioned for your publicity brochure.'

'Ah, yes. Mr Macken. The American. Of course, the job has not exactly been promised to him.' Fan paused. 'A break-in?'

'Yes,' Li said. 'What's odd is that the only thing stolen were the negatives of the film he shot here in your club.'

Fan looked suitably perplexed. 'Why would anyone want to steal them? Are you sure that's what they were after?'

'They came back the following night when they learned he had taken contact prints and demanded that he hand them over, too.'

Fan frowned. 'Well, it's all very puzzling, but I don't really see what it has to do with us.'

'Perhaps nothing at all,' Li said. 'But it turned out that Macken had copied his contact prints into his computer.' He lifted a large envelope. 'In fact he was able to run off prints for us.'

'May I see?' Fan reached out, and Li handed him the envelope. The CEO drew out the prints to look at them.

'It was while he was showing them to me that Mr Macken told me about the items you have on display here in your office, explaining that was why you have an armed guard on the door.' Li paused. 'That's when it occurred to me that these people may well have been after these prints in preparation for a robbery.'

Fan glanced up at him. 'You think so?'

'It's possible, Mr Fan. Just what kind of price would you put on your'—he nodded towards the alcove—'collection?'

'The insurance company valued it at around five million yuan, Section Chief. They would only insure it if we provided armed security, so we're pretty well prepared for any eventuality.'

'That's reassuring to hear, Mr Fan.' Li held out his hand for the photographs, which Fan had slipped back in the envelope. 'But I thought it worth making you aware of what had happened. I'll not waste any more of your time.' He stood up. 'It's quite a place you have here. Do you have many members?'

'Oh, yes, we've done brisk business since we opened six months ago. However, it was a massive investment, you understand. So we are always anxious to attract new members.'

'Hence the brochure.'

'Exactly. And, of course, the photographs will also be going onto our Internet site. So they're hardly a state secret. Would you like to have a look around? We do have special introductory rates for VIPs such as yourself. We already count several senior figures in the Beijing municipal administration among our members, as well as a number of elected representatives of the National People's Congress, and even some members of the Central Committee of the CCP.'

Li bridled—this sounded like both a bribe and a threat. A cheap membership on offer as well as a warning that Fan was not without influence in high places. Why on earth would he feel the need to make either? 'Is membership exclusively for Chinese?' Li asked.

'Not *exclusively*,' Fan said. 'Although, as it happens, all of our members are.'

'Oh?' Li pulled out the prints again. He held up the photograph of the four Chinese and the Westerner for Fan to see. 'Who's this, then?'

Fan squinted at the picture and shrugged. 'I don't know. I expect he was a guest of one of the members.' He held out his hand towards a door opposite his desk. 'If you'd like to follow me, gentlemen . . .'

He led them into a private lounge and on through double doors to the swimming pool they had seen in Macken's photographs. From there he took them on a tour of the club, through a labyrinth of rooms and corridors, finally coming to a halt in the entrance hall.

Fan looked at Li. 'Give you a taste for the good life, Section Chief?'

'I'm quite happy with my life the way it is, thank you, Mr Fan,' Li said. He glanced at a plaque on the wall beside tall double doors, which read: THE EVENT HALL. 'What's an event hall?'

'Just what it says, Section Chief,' Fan said. 'A place where we hold major events. Concerts, ceremonies, seminars. I'd let you see it, but it's being refurbished at the moment.'

Fan opened the front door. 'I appreciate your visit and your concern, Section Chief. And I will review our security.'

Li turned to leave, then paused. 'By the way,' he said, 'Mr Macken seemed concerned about the whereabouts of your PA, JoJo.'

Fan raised an eyebrow. 'Did he?'

'Perhaps we could have a word with her before we go?'

'Sadly, that's not possible, Section Chief. I fired her.' Fan sighed.

'JoJo had one of our apartments upstairs. It went with the job. I discovered she was "entertaining" members up there after hours.'

'Which means you threw her out of her apartment as well?'

'She was asked to leave immediately, and I put a stop on her cellphone account, which was also provided by the company.'

'Have you any idea where she went?'

'None at all. I do know she had a boyfriend in Shanghai at one time. Perhaps she's gone off there to lick her wounds.'

When they were out on the street again, Qian turned to Li. 'What do you think, Chief?' he asked.

'Hmmm.' Li was thoughtful for a moment. 'I think we've probably been wasting our time on this, Qian. Better get back to the section.'

A DOZEN DETECTIVES were gathered round the TV set at Section One and a few faces turned towards the door as Li and Qian came in.

Sun waved Li over. 'Chief, this could be important.'

There was a news bulletin on air, reporting on the failure of the Chinese distance runner, Dai Lili, to turn up for her race the previous evening. She had been favourite to win the 3,000 metres, which would have tipped the overall points balance in China's favour. So there were a lot of unhappy people around. In the background an American reporter was speaking to camera. 'The failure of Chinese champion Dai Lili to turn up for the event comes on top of a disastrous month for Chinese athletics in which up to six of the country's top athletes have died in unusual circumstances . . .' So the genie was out of the bottle. And there would be no way now to get it back in.

Wu was saying, 'She lives on her own in an apartment on the north side, Chief, but apparently there's nobody home.' Then an image of her face on the screen caught his eye. 'That's her.'

Li looked at the face and felt the skin prickling all over his head. He had seen her for only a few moments in poor lighting on the landing of Margaret's apartment, but the birthmark was unmistakable. She had wanted to speak to Margaret. Given the fate met by six of her fellow athletes, it was all just too close to home for comfort.

He said to Sun, 'Get your coat. We're going to the stadium.'

LI AND SUN had to elbow their way through the crowds of reporters and cameramen gathered outside the stadium entrance. The light snow that had fallen earlier in the day had given way to big flakes. Li rapped on the glass and showed his ID to an armed guard inside.

Supervisor of Coaching Cai Xin was not pleased to see them. 'I have better things to do with my time, Section Chief, than to waste it on fruitless police interviews.'

Li said evenly, 'I can arrange, Supervisor Cai, to have you taken to Section Six for interrogation by professionals, if you'd prefer.'

Cai looked at Li appraisingly, wondering if this was a hollow threat. 'I don't see what possible interest the police could have in any of this.'

'We have six dead athletes,' Li said. 'And now a seventh has gone missing. So don't mess with me, Cai. Where can we talk?'

Cai took a deep breath and led them to his private room, where he had spoken to Li and Margaret three nights earlier.

'Why didn't Dai Lili turn up last night?' Li asked.

'You tell me. She seemed very cosy with your American friend.'

'What makes you think that?'

'I saw them talking out there in the lobby the other night.'

'After you'd given your athletes strict instructions not to speak to either of us,' Li said, and Cai immediately flushed.

'I don't know anything about that,' he said.

'She was very keen to speak to Dr Campbell about something. She never got the chance because she ran off scared when she saw you. I don't suppose you'd know what she wanted to tell her so urgently?'

'No, I wouldn't. And I resent being questioned like this, Section Chief. I resent your tone and I resent your attitude.'

'Well, you know what, Supervisor Cai? My investigation into your dead athletes has turned into a murder inquiry. And there's a young girl out there somewhere who could be in grave danger. So I don't particularly care if you don't like my tone. Because right now yours is the only name on a suspect list of one.'

Cai blanched. 'You're not serious?'

'You'll find out just how serious I am, Supervisor Cai, if I don't get your full cooperation. I want her parents' address and any other information that you have on her. And I want it now.'

As they left the stadium, Sun turned to Li. 'You were a bit hard on him, Chief,' he said. 'You don't really consider him a suspect, do you?'

'He's the best we've got. He's the only common factor. He was known to all of the victims and he has a very dodgy track record on the subject of doping. He saw Dai Lili speaking to Margaret. Suddenly Dai Lili goes missing. Big coincidence.'

'What *did* she want to speak to Dr Campbell about?'

Li shook his head in frustration. 'I wish I knew.'

DAI LILI'S PARENTS lived in a quarter of the city just west of Qianmen and south of the old city wall. The entrance to their courtyard home was through a small red doorway in a grey brick wall. Li asked an old woman where he could find the Dais, and she pointed him to an open doorway with a curtain hanging in it.

Li pulled the curtain aside. 'Hello? Anybody home?' he called.

A young man emerged from the gloom, scowling and aggressive. 'What do you want?' His white T-shirt was stretched over a well-sculpted body. A tattoo of a snake wound around his right arm, its head and forked tongue etched into the back of his right hand.

'Police,' Li said. 'We're looking for the parents of Dai Lili.'

The young man regarded them sullenly for a moment then flicked aside another curtain and led them into a tiny room with a large bed, a two-seater settee and a huge television on an old dresser. A man in his fifties sat huddled in a padded jacket, watching the flickering screen. A woman was squatting on the bed, dozens of photographs spread out in front of her. 'Police,' the young man said.

Li glanced at the photographs that the woman was looking at. They were pictures, taken trackside, of Dai Lili bursting the tape, or sprinting the last hundred metres, or arms raised in victory salute. Dozens of them.

'Do you know where she is?' he asked.

The woman looked at him with dull eyes. 'I thought maybe you were coming to tell us.'

'Why?' Sun asked. 'Do you think something has happened to her?'

The man turned to look at them. 'If something had not happened to her, she would have been there to run the race.'

'When was the last time you saw her?'

'About two weeks ago.'

'How did she seem?'

Her father dragged his attention away from the screen again. 'Difficult,' he said. 'Argumentative. Like she's been for months.'

'Things haven't been easy for her,' her mother said quickly in mitigation. 'Her sister has been going downhill fast.'

'Her sister?' Sun asked.

'Ten years ago she was the Chinese ten-thousand-metres champion,' the old woman said. 'Now she is a cripple. Multiple sclerosis.'

'Lili's done everything for Lijia!' Li and Sun were startled by the voice of the young man in the doorway. 'That's all that ever drove her to win. To get money to pay for the care of her sister.'

Sun said, 'Where is Lijia?'

'She is in a clinic in Hong Kong,' her father said. 'We have not seen her for nearly two years. They say she is dying now.'

'Could Lili have gone to see her?' Li asked.

The mother shook her head. 'She never goes to see her. She couldn't bear to look at her, to see her wasting like that.'

Li said to the father, 'You said Lili was argumentative?'

'She never used to be,' her mother said quickly.

'Until she started winning all those big races,' her father said, 'and making all that money. It was like she felt guilty for being able to run like that while her sister was withering to a shadow.'

'If anything made her feel guilty it was you.' There was unexpected bitterness in the voice of Dai Lili's brother. 'You resented it, didn't you? That she was the only one who could do anything to help Lijia.'

'Do you have a key for her apartment?' Li asked.

THE SNOW WAS TREACHEROUS UNDERFOOT now and there was very little light left in the sky, helping to deepen the depression that Li carried with him from the house. He handed Sun the keys of the Jeep.

'You'd better take it,' he said. 'You'll be late for your antenatal class.'

'I don't care about the class, Chief,' Sun said. 'It's Wen having the baby, not me. I'll go to the girl's apartment with you.'

Li shook his head. 'I'll get a taxi. And then I'm going straight on to the betrothal meeting.' He summoned a smile from somewhere. 'Go on. Go to the hospital. It's your baby, too. Wen'll appreciate it.'

Chapter Seven

Margaret's taxi dropped them on the east side of Tiananmen Square outside the Imperial Restaurant, which stood behind stark winter trees hung with coloured Christmas lights. Mrs Campbell's knee, bandaged and heavily strapped, had stiffened up so that she could hardly bend it, and Margaret, to her mother's indignation, had borrowed a walking cane from an elderly neighbour.

Margaret helped her up the steps and they were greeted inside the restaurant by two girls in imperial costume—embroidered silk gowns and tall, winged black hats with red pompoms. A manageress, all in black, led them past the main restaurant and into the royal corridor. There were private banqueting rooms to the left and right.

Li had booked the Emperor's Room, and Margaret's mother's jaw dropped in astonishment as she hobbled in ahead of her daughter. A four-lamp lantern with dozens of red tassels was suspended over a huge circular banqueting table. Each of seven place settings had three gold goblets, a rice bowl, spoon, knife and chopstick rest, also in gold, and lacquered chopsticks. At one end of the room, on a raised dais, were two replica thrones. At the other, cushioned benches and seats were gathered around a low table on which all the presents from each family were carefully arranged.

Earlier in the day, Margaret had taken gifts from the Campbell family to Mei Yuan's home. Acting as Li's proxy, Mei Yuan had selected the gifts from the Li family and arrived early at the restaurant to set out the offerings and await the guests. She stood up, tense, smiling. Margaret looked at her in wonder. She wore a turquoise-blue embroidered silk jacket over a cream blouse and a full-length black dress. There was a touch of brown around her eyes, and red on her lips. Margaret had never seen her dressed up, or wearing make-up. The small peasant woman was transformed, dignified, almost beautiful.

'Mom, I'd like you to meet Mei Yuan, my best friend in China.'

Mrs Campbell shook Mei Yuan's hand warily, but was scrupulously polite. 'How do you do, Mrs Yuan?'

Margaret laughed. 'No, Mom, if it's Mrs anything, its Mrs Mei.'

Her mother looked confused.

Mei Yuan explained. 'In China, the family name always comes first. I am happy for you simply to call me Mei Yuan.' She smiled. 'I am very pleased to meet you, Mrs Campbell.'

There was an awkward exchange of pleasantries before the conversation began to run dry. Then they all took their seats as a girl in a red tunic and black trousers poured them jasmine tea. Mei Yuan broke the silence. 'Li Yan did not come for his breakfast this morning.'

Mrs Campbell said, 'Margaret's fiancé takes his breakfast at your house?'

'No, Mom. Mei Yuan has a stall on a corner near Li Yan's office. She makes kind of hot, savoury Beijing pancakes called *jian bing*.'

Mrs Campbell could barely conceal her surprise, or her horror. 'You sell pancakes on a street corner?'

'I make them fresh on a hot plate,' Mei Yuan said. 'But really only to feed my passion in life.'

Margaret's mother was almost afraid to ask. 'And what's that?'

'Reading. I love books, Mrs Campbell.'

'Do you? My husband lectured in modern American literature. But I don't suppose that's the kind of reading you're used to.'

'I am a great admirer of Ernest Hemingway,' Mei Yuan said. 'And I am just now reading *The Great Gatsby* by Scott Fitzgerald.'

Mrs Campbell looked at her appraisingly. But they had no opportunity to pursue their conversation further, interrupted then by the arrival of Li's sister, Xiao Ling, and her daughter, Xinxin, with Li's father. Xinxin rushed to Margaret and threw her arms round her.

'Careful, careful,' Mei Yuan cautioned. 'Remember the baby.'

Xinxin stood back for a moment and looked at the swelling of Margaret's belly with a kind of wonder. She grinned, and then noticed Mrs Campbell. 'Who's this?'

'This is my mommy,' Margaret said.

Xinxin looked at her in astonishment. 'You are Magret's mommy?'

'Yes,' Mrs Campbell said, and Margaret saw that her eyes were alive for the first time since she had arrived. 'What's your name?'

'My name's Xinxin and I'm eight years old.' She turned to Xiao Ling. 'And this is *my* mommy, Xiao Ling. She doesn't speak English.'

Mei Yuan took over then and made all the introductions in Chinese and English. Mrs Campbell remained seated after Margaret had explained that her mother had injured her knee in a fall. The last to be introduced were Margaret and Li's father. Margaret shook the hand that he offered limply, and searched for some sign of Li in his eyes. But she saw nothing there. His face was a blank.

Xinxin was oblivious to any of the tensions that underlay relations among this odd gathering of strangers and said to Mrs Campbell, 'What's your name, Magret's mommy?'

'Mrs Campbell.'

Xinxin laughed and laughed. 'No, no,' she said. 'Your *real* name.'

Mrs Campbell seemed faintly embarrassed. 'Actually, it's Jean.'

'Jean,' Xinxin repeated. 'Can I sit beside you, Jean?'

The elderly American flushed with unexpected pleasure. 'Of course, Xinxin,' she said, trying to pronounce the name correctly.

And Xinxin climbed onto the bench beside her and sat down. She took Mrs Campbell's hand quite unselfconsciously and said, 'I like Magret's mommy.' And in Chinese to Li's father, 'Do you like Jean, too, Granddad?'

And Margaret saw him smile for the first time, although she had no idea what was said in the exchange between grandfather and grandchild. 'Sure I do, little one. Sure I do.'

Margaret glanced at her watch. 'Well, the only thing missing is Li Yan. As usual. I hope he's not too late.'

THE TAXI DROPPED LI on the edge of a wide slash of waste ground. There were no lights, the road was pitted and broken, and the driver refused to take his car any further. Somehow, somewhere, he had taken a wrong turn. Li could see the lights of the tower blocks where Dai Lili lived, but they were on the other side of this bleak, open stretch of ground. It was easier to walk across it than have the driver go round again to try to find the right road.

He watched the taillights of the taxi recede, and pulled up his collar against the snow and wind to make his way across the wasteland that stretched in darkness before him. He knew that he was already late for the betrothal. Once he got to the apartment he would call on his cellphone to say he would be another hour.

A voice came out of the darkness to his left, low, sing-song and sinister. 'What do we have here?'

'Someone's lost his way.' Another voice from behind.

'Lost your way, big man?' Yet another voice, off to his right this time. 'We'll set you on your way. For a price.'

'Better hope you got a nice fat wallet, big man. Or you could be a big dead man.' The first voice again.

Li froze and peered into the darkness, and gradually he saw the shadows of three figures emerging from the driving snow, converging on him. He saw the glint of a blade. He fumbled quickly in his pocket for his penlight, and turned its pencil-thin beam on the face of the nearest figure. It was a young man, only seventeen or eighteen, and he raised a hand instinctively to cover his face.

'You boys had better hope you can run fast,' Li said, surprised by the strength of his own voice. 'I'm a cop, and if I catch you you're going to spend the next fifteen years re-educating yourself through labour.

'Yeah, sure.'

Li pulled out his ID, holding it up and turning the penlight to illuminate it. 'You want to come closer for a better look?'

There was a long, silent stand-off in which some unspoken message must have passed between the muggers, because almost without Li realising it they were gone, slipping off into the night as anonymously as they had arrived.

He peered through the driving snow but could see nothing, and he felt the tension in his chest subsiding. God only knew how close he had been to a knife between the ribs. Nice place to live, he thought.

DAI LILI'S APARTMENT was on the seventh floor. The elevator was not working, every landing was piled with garbage and the smell of urine permeated the building. Li could not help but make a comparison with the upmarket homes of the other athletes he had visited.

When, finally, he got to Dai Lili's apartment and unlocked the door, he stepped into another world. The foul odours that had accompanied him on his climb were absent from the cool, sterile atmosphere of the apartment. He hurriedly closed the door to keep the foul stuff out, and found the light switch. The apartment was small. Two rooms, a tiny kitchen, and an even smaller toilet. The walls were painted cream and there was little or no furniture. A bed and a small desk in one room. Nothing in the other except for a padded grey exercise mat on the floor.

He went back into the bedroom, where sliding doors revealed a built-in closet. Track suits and T-shirts and shorts. Nothing for dressing up. On the desk, there was a comb, a tub of facial cleanser, unscented. No make-up. This girl was obsessive. There was room for only two things in her mind, in her life: her fitness and her running.

In the kitchen there were fresh vegetables and fruit, packets of brown rice and dried lentils. In the tiny refrigerator there was tofu and fruit juice and yoghurt. No meat anywhere. No comfort food.

The toilet was spotlessly clean. There was anti-bacterial soap and a bottle of unperfumed hypo-allergenic shampoo. Li opened a small wall cabinet above the basin and felt the hair stand up on his neck. This girl, who wore no make-up, who used unscented soap and shampoo, who cleaned her face with unperfumed cleanser, had two bottles of Chanel sitting in her bathroom cabinet. The same brand as the aftershave he had found in the homes of Sui and Jia Jing. He sprayed each in turn into the air and sniffed. One he did not recognise. It had a harsh, lemon smell, faintly acidic. The other he knew immediately was the same as the aftershave he had breathed in at Jia Jing's apartment. Strange, musky, bitter, like almonds and vanilla.

It was a coincidence too far, bizarre and unfathomable. He slipped one of the bottles into his pocket, then went through the apartment again. In the bedroom, he checked inside every shoe and went through the pockets of the jogpants. Nothing. He was about to leave when something lying on the floor beneath the desk caught his eye. Something small and gold-coloured that was catching the light. He went down on his knees to retrieve it, knowing that he had found what he was looking for. He was holding a little cylindrical aerosol breath freshener, and suspected that when he finally found this girl she was going to be long dead.

In the hallway outside her apartment, he locked the door then remembered that he had meant to call the restaurant to tell them he would be late for the betrothal. He cursed under his breath and fumbled to switch on his phone in the dark.

The slightest of sounds made him lift his head in time to see a fist, illuminated by the light of his phone, in the moment before it smashed into his face. He staggered backwards, dropping the phone, gasping and gagging on the blood that filled his airways. Someone behind him struck him very hard on the back of the neck and his legs buckled. He heard his own breath gurgling in his lungs before a blackness descended on him.

PLATES OF FOOD sat piled on the revolving centre of the banqueting table. Everything hot had long since gone cold. Nothing had been touched. The gifts in front of them remained unopened.

Margaret was angry and worried at the same time. It was more than an hour since Mei Yuan had called Section One to find out what had happened to Li. Nobody knew. And there was no response from his cellphone. Xinxin was fast asleep with her head on Mrs Campbell's lap, the only one of them unconcerned by the fact that her uncle was more than two hours late.

Suddenly, the manageress entered with a harrassed-looking Qian in tow. His cheeks were flushed beneath wide eyes that betrayed his concern. He spoke breathlessly in Chinese.

Margaret was on her feet immediately. 'What is it?'

Mei Yuan looked at Margaret and said in a small voice, 'Li Yan has been attacked. He is in the hospital.'

LI HAD BEEN DRIFTING in and out of consciousness for some time, aware of a dazzle of overhead light and a pain that was wrapped round his chest like a vice. His head throbbed and his face felt swollen. To close his eyes and slip away was a blissful escape.

A shadow fell over his eyes and he opened them to see Margaret's worried face looking at him. He tried to smile, but his mouth hurt.

'Sorry I was late for the betrothal,' he said.

She shook her head. 'The lengths you'll go to just to get out of marrying me, Li Yan.'

Her words brought a dark cloud of recollection—his meeting with the Commissioner. Had it really only been yesterday morning?

'The doctor says nothing's broken.'

'Oh, good,' Li said. 'For a moment there I thought it was serious.'

Margaret's hand felt cool on his skin as she laid it gently on his cheek. 'Who did this to you, Li Yan?'

'Some punk kids.' He cursed his carelessness. They must have followed him and waited in the dark for him to come back out. 'They threatened me outside and I scared them off.' They had taken his wallet, his cellphone, the keys of the apartment, his ID card.

'Not far enough,' Margaret said.

He raised himself up on one elbow and groaned with the pain.

'What are you doing?' she asked, concerned.

'The plastic bag on that chair,' he said with difficulty. 'You'll find my jacket inside.' He found it hard to believe now that he had had the presence of mind to get the first officer on the scene to strip it off him and bag it. He had become conscious when Dai Lili's neighbour from the end of the hallway had nearly fallen over him in the dark. Almost his first thought had been the bottle in his pocket. His fingers had found broken glass as they felt for it in the dark, the strange musky-smelling liquid soaking into the fabric. 'There's a bottle of perfume in one of the pockets. Broken. Only, I don't think it's perfume that was inside it. I'm hoping there's enough of it soaked into the fabric of the jacket for you still to be able to analyse it.'

Margaret left him briefly to look inside the bag. She recoiled from the smell. 'Jesus, who would wear perfume like that?'

'Athletes,' Li said. 'Dead athletes. I found it in the apartment of the girl who was so keen to talk to you.'

Margaret was shocked. 'Is she dead?'

'I'm not confident of finding her alive. In one of the other pockets you'll find an aerosol breath freshener. I'd like to know what's in it.'

'We're not going to know any of that till tomorrow,' Margaret said, 'so there's no point worrying about it till then. OK?'

His attempt at a smile turned into a wince. 'I guess.' He paused. 'So what did you make of my father?'

Margaret thought about how his father had barely looked at her during their two-hour wait in the restaurant. 'It's difficult to know,' she said tactfully, 'when someone doesn't speak your language.'

Li frowned. 'He speaks English as well as Yifu.'

Margaret felt anger welling suddenly inside her. 'Well, if he does, he didn't speak a word of it to me.'

Li closed his eyes. 'He *is* an old bastard,' he said. 'He disapproves of me marrying outside of my race.'

'Snap,' Margaret said. 'My mother's exactly the same. If only she'd known he spoke English they could have passed the time exchanging disapproval.' She squeezed his hand. 'Oh, Li Yan, why did we bother with any of them?' She sighed. 'What are we going to do?'

'I'll re-book the restaurant. We'll do it tomorrow night.'

'You're in no fit state,' she protested. 'You're concussed.'

'I'm out of here first thing tomorrow,' Li said. 'Whether I'm concussed or not. That girl's missing. If there's the least chance that she's still alive, then I'm not going to lie here feeling sorry for myself when somebody out there might be trying to kill her.'

SUN PULLED INTO THE KERB outside the Beijing New World Taihua Plaza and slithered round to the passenger side to help Li out. About three inches of snow had fallen overnight and Beijing had ground to a halt. There were no ploughs or gritters and it was only the Jeep's four-wheel drive that had kept them on the road.

Li pushed Sun aside irritably and eased himself out onto the street. The strapping on his chest helped support him, but it still hurt like hell if he bent or twisted. His face was swollen, black under each eye, and it was still painful to eat or smile. Not that he was much inclined to smile today. Sun reached in beyond him to retrieve the rubber-tipped walking stick that Wu had brought into the section that morning. What irked Li was that he found it nearly impossible to get around without it. Especially in the snow. He snatched it from Sun and hobbled to the entrance of Sui's apartment.

The security man remembered them. He couldn't take his eyes off Li as he rode up with them in the elevator to the fifteenth floor. 'Fall in the snow?' he ventured.

'No. Hazards of the job,' Li growled.

The man opened the door to the apartment and Li tore off the crime-scene tape rather than trying to duck under it. They went straight to the bathroom. The razor and the box of four heads were still on the shelf above the basin. But the two bottles of Chanel after-shave and the gold-coloured breath freshener were gone.

Li turned angrily to the security man. 'Who the hell's been in here?'

'No one,' he answered, shaken. 'Just cops and forensics. You people.'

Sun's cellphone rang. He answered, then held the phone out to Li. 'Wu,' he said. Li had sent Wu over to Jia Jing's apartment to get the aftershave from the bathroom there.

'Chief,' Wu's voice crackled in his ear. 'I can't find any aftershave. Are you sure it was in the bathroom cabinet?'

Li had also sent Qian over to Dai Lili's apartment to get the bottle of perfume he had left behind, but now he knew that too would be gone. And he began to wonder if his attackers had, after all, been the muggers he had taken them for. He told Wu to go back to the section and handed the phone back to Sun.

'What's happened?' Sun asked.

Li shook his head. 'The aftershave's gone there, too.'

Sun's cellphone rang again. Sun answered. '*Wei?*' He listened intently for a few moments. Then he snapped his phone shut. 'They found a body in Jingshan Park,' he said. 'A young woman.'

JINGSHAN PARK WAS SITUATED at the north end of the Forbidden City, on an artificial hill constructed with earth excavated from the moat around the Imperial Palace. Five pavilions sited round the hill represented the five directions of Buddha—north, south, east, west and centre. Each had commanding views of the city. The police had closed the park, and a crowd had gathered outside the south gate. Li and Sun had to push their way through.

Detective Sang hurried across to them from the path that led up the hill. 'She's at the Jifangting Pavilion. Be careful on these steps, Chief. They're lethal in the snow.'

Li's eyes panned west, but the green-glazed tiles of the pavilion's two-tiered roof were obscured by trees. They began the long climb.

'One of the park attendants found her about an hour after they opened up this morning, Chief,' Sang told them on the way up. 'The weather meant there weren't too many people around, or she'd probably have been found earlier. Poor guy's been treated for shock.'

'The attendant?'

'Yeah. It's pretty messy up there, Chief. Blood everywhere. She must have been brought here during the night and butchered. She was left lying on this kind of stone dais thing under the roof.'

It took nearly fifteen minutes to climb the serpentine path up the side of the hill to where the track divided, heading east to the summit and west down to Jifangting, the Fragrance Pavilion. Through the trees below them, Li saw its snow-covered roof and the crowd of uniformed and plain-clothes officers around it. He and Sun made their way carefully down the path in Sang's wake.

'In the name of the sky, Li, can you not keep these moron detectives off my snow!'

Li turned to find himself looking into the coal-black eyes of Chief Forensics Officer Fu Qiwei. They opened wide when he saw Li's face.

'What happened to you?'

'Collision with a fist and a foot. Surely you can't make any sense of these tracks now, Fu?'

'Weather centre says it stopped snowing sometime during the night. Killers' tracks could be frozen under the second fall. If you can keep your flatfoots from trampling all over it, we might be able to brush the snow back down to the frozen stuff.'

'All right,' Li shouted. 'Anyone not essential get back up the hill now!'

Detectives and uniformed officers moved away in quiet acquiescence, leaving Fu's team nearly invisible in their white suits. Dr Wang and his photographer from pathology stood shivering under the roof. The body had been covered with a white sheet. Normally, by now, blood would have soaked through it. But the blood, like the body beneath it, was frozen solid. And it was everywhere, in icy pools and rivulets around the central dais.

A grim-faced Wang approached him. 'I never really understood what bloodlust meant until today, Section Chief. These bastards must have gorged themselves on it.'

'More than one?'

'At least half a dozen, judging by the footprints in the blood.' He sighed. 'I counted more than eighty stab wounds, Chief. These guys brought her up here, stripped her naked, and just kept stabbing her and stabbing her.' He shook his head. 'Never seen anything like it. You want to take a look? We've still got to do the pics.'

Li had no real desire to see what lay beneath the sheet. He pictured her as he had seen her outside Margaret's apartment. She had been so young and timid. 'Let's do it,' he said.

They stepped carefully up to the dais and Wang pulled back the sheet. She looked as if she were covered in large black insects, but Li quickly saw that they were the wounds left in her flesh by the knives. She was covered in blood, and her flesh was blue-tinged. Her black hair was fanned out on the stone. Longer than Li remembered it. He frowned. The birthmark was gone. He stood staring at her in confusion before the mist cleared and he realised it was not who he had expected to see. It was not the runner, Dai Lili. It was Jon Macken's missing friend, JoJo.

MARGARET SIGHED. She had asked Mei Yuan to look after her mother today so that she could check out the lab results on Li's perfume and breath freshener. But Mrs Campbell wasn't pleased. 'I don't need a baby sitter,' she had said.

The taxi drew up outside Mei Yuan's home and Margaret asked the driver to wait. She helped her mother out of the car and supported her left arm as she hobbled through the red gateway into the courtyard beyond. Mrs Campbell looked around with some distaste.

Mei Yuan greeted them at the door. 'Good morning, Mrs Campbell.'

Margaret's mother put on a brave face. 'Mei Yuan,' she said, her pronunciation still less than perfect.

'I thought today I might teach you how to make *jian bing*.' Mei Yuan smiled mischievously.

'Jan beeng?' Mrs Campbell frowned.

'Yes, you remember, Mom, I told you. That's the Beijing pancakes that Mei Yuan makes at her stall.'

Her mother looked horrified, but Mei Yuan took her hand to lead her into the house. 'Don't worry, I'm sure I can find you some heavy clothes to keep you warm.'

Margaret said quickly, 'Got to go. Have a good day. I'll catch up with you later.' And before her mother could object she was gone, and the taxi went slithering off down the lakeside road.

THE CORRIDOR on the top floor of Section One was deserted. Margaret looked into the detectives' room, but it, too, was empty. She walked on down the corridor and heard raised voices coming from the big meeting room at the end. And then one voice silencing the others, grave and authoritative. She recognised it immediately. Li. She smiled to herself and went into his office to wait for him.

She sat in his seat and saw Macken's prints strewn across the desk beneath an open folder. She moved the folder aside and began idling through the photographs. She had no idea what they were. Grainy colour prints of some very upmarket sort of establishment. She stopped for a moment and looked at a picture of a girl standing by a desk. She dropped it and moved on, stopping again at a picture of three young men in dark suits, a fourth, bigger man in a track suit, and a Westerner. A man perhaps in his middle sixties, with a head of well-groomed silver hair and a close-cropped silver beard. The odd thing was that he seemed vaguely familiar. Margaret struggled to try to find a context, but infuriatingly nothing would come.

It was then that she noticed another pile of photographs. She could see they were taken at a crime scene. A body lying in blood. She pulled them across to take a look and was shocked by the number of stab wounds puncturing the naked body. There was something almost regular about them. It smacked of ritual. And then she looked at the face and realised it was the girl standing by the desk in the photograph she had looked at just moments earlier.

THE DETECTIVES in the room listened in silence as Li took them through the events of the preceding day, when he and Qian had followed up what had initially seemed like a minor break-in at a photographer's studio. A sequence of events that had led them to an instant recognition of the girl in the park, and the thought that perhaps in some way the break-in and the murder might be connected.

'It's as if her killers were making a statement of some kind,' Li said. 'And the fact there were half a dozen or more of them involved means there was collusion. Planning.' He shook his head. 'Like some kind of ritual, or sacrifice.' Unknowingly, he had touched on the same thought as Margaret, although for different reasons.

Li was both horrified and intrigued, but also acutely aware that time was running out. This case was a distraction, a side show at the main event. His announcement that he was putting Sun in charge of it was met with silence. Most of the officers in the room were more senior than Sun, but Li needed them focused on the dead athletes. He snatched a glance at Tao sitting at the other end of the table, and saw the animosity in his eyes. The most natural thing would have been for him to delegate the JoJo murder to his deputy. But he was unwilling to place too much trust in Tao. He looked away. There were bigger issues than office politics.

'I don't want us losing our focus on the athletics case,' he said, 'because the events of the last twenty-four hours are starting to raise some serious issues, not least for our own investigation.' He paused. 'Someone with inside knowledge has been tampering with evidence.' This time the silence around the table was positively tangible. 'After I took one of the Chanel bottles from Dai's apartment last night, all the other bottles disappeared from the other apartments.'

Qian said, 'How do you know they weren't taken before that?'

'I don't,' Li said. 'But I suspect now that the attack on me was not, after all, unrelated to the case. The very fact that I had taken the bottle clearly alerted someone to the fact that I suspected a significance. And so all the bottles in the other apartments had to go.'

'Are you suggesting that someone within the section is responsible?' Tao asked, and there was no mistaking the hostility in his voice.

'No,' Li said. 'I'm not. But somebody is watching us very carefully. Somebody seems to know enough about what we're doing to stay one step ahead of us.' He took a long, slow breath. 'I thought, last night, that the breath freshener I took from Dai Lili's apartment was still in my jacket pocket. But when I got back here this morning, I got a call from the lab to tell me they couldn't find it. Last night, Dr Campbell took my jacket from the hospital to the lab, sealed in an evidence bag. It was locked in the repository overnight until the technicians came in this morning. No breath freshener. It may be that it wasn't there in the first place, or that my attackers took it last night. Or it may be that someone removed it during the night. Either way, apparently they didn't know we already had another one.'

'That's right,' Wu said suddenly, remembering. 'Jia Jing had one on him. We found it when we went through his stuff at the autopsy.'

Li nodded. 'So we still have something to analyse. And what the stealers of the perfume didn't realise either, is that there was enough of it soaked into my jacket for us to analyse that, too.'

'What about the girl?' Sang said. 'The runner, Dai Lili. What do you think has happened to her?'

'I have no idea,' Li said. 'But I have no doubt that her disappearance is related to all the other cases. We've got to move this case forward as fast as we possibly can, so who's got anything fresh?'

Qian raised a finger. 'I dug up some interesting financial facts and figures, Chief.' He flipped through his notebook. 'Seems like all these athletes had pretty extravagant lifestyles and were living way beyond their officially declared earnings. And they paid the monthly rental on those expensive apartments with cash, big wads of notes.'

'So somebody was paying them in cash,' one of the detectives said.

'What for?' Wu asked.

Qian shrugged. 'Who knows? It certainly wasn't for throwing races. I mean, they were all winning big time.'

The room fell silent again. Then Wu cleared his throat noisily. 'I came across something interesting. I noticed from a couple of the statements that some of the deceased had been suffering from flu not long before they died.'

Li remembered the words of Sui's coach: *He had a bout of flu about ten days ago*, he had said of Sui. *Knocked the stuffing out of him.*

'So I checked,' Wu went on. 'Turns out that every one of them, including our weightlifter, who we know died of natural causes, suffered from the flu within six weeks of their death. Which seems pretty strange to me.'

TAO'S EYES WERE ABLAZE with anger. 'He's a puppy!' he spluttered. 'The newest kid on the block, still wet behind the ears. You can't put him in charge of a serious investigation like this.'

There were just Li and Tao left in the room after the meeting. Li had known he would have to face the storm.

'He may be the newest kid on the block, but he's also one of the brightest,' he said. 'Anyway, I need everyone else on the other case.'

Tao squinted at him. 'Do you really think you're going to crack this one before they kick your ass into touch next week? I mean, that's what this is all about, isn't it?' The gloves were off now. He was no longer making any attempt to disguise his contempt for his boss.

'If you were less fixated on rank and position, Tao, and more concerned with getting the job done, you wouldn't see it that way. But if you think that making detectives wear suits and fining them for swearing constitutes "good disciplined police work", then God help this section when I'm gone.' Li turned and marched out of the room.

MARGARET LOOKED UP as Li banged into his office and dropped his files on the desk.

'What are you doing here?' he snapped.

'I came along to see if I could help make sense of the tests they're doing for you at the pathology centre.' She stood up. 'But if you're going to be like that, I'll just go home again.'

'I'm sorry,' he said quickly. 'It hasn't been a good morning.'

'What's happened?'

He told her. About the other bottles of perfume and aftershave going missing. The breath freshener disappearing from his pocket. 'You didn't look in the pockets, did you?'

She shook her head.

And then he told her about the girl in the park.

She lifted up the photographs from the desk. 'This her?'

He nodded.

'Who is she?'

She was shocked to learn that JoJo was a friend of Macken. 'What happened about the break-in at his studio?'

He shrugged. 'We don't know.'

The phone rang. He snatched the receiver and conducted several quick-fire exchanges, then he listened for a long while, and finally he hung up. 'That was Chief Forensics Officer Fu at Pao Jü Hutong. He has the results of the analysis.'

'And?'

'The perfume's alcohol-based. The scent is a mix of almond and vanilla. Not very pleasant, but not very sinister either. And the breath freshener is apparently just breath freshener. Active ingredient Xylitol.' Li ran his hands back over his finely stubbled head. 'I don't understand. I really thought this was going to be a breakthrough.'

'In what way?' Margaret asked.

'I don't know. I just thought it was too much of a coincidence.' But he was still hanging on to one last hope. 'Fu said there was something else. He said it would be easier to show me than tell me.'

Margaret came round the desk. 'Well, let's go see.'

FU GREETED THEM enthusiastically when they arrived at the Pao Jü laboratories of forensic pathology, which were housed in a multi-storey building about ten minutes' drive from Section One. 'We got some good footprints frozen under the snow at Jingshan,' he told Li. 'We've now got seven quite distinctly different treads.'

Li said impatiently, 'I thought you were going to show me something to do with the perfume.'

'Not the perfume,' Fu said. 'The bottle.'

He took them through glass doors into a lab. On a table sat the Chanel bottle partially reconstructed from the pieces found in Li's pocket. Beside it was the label. Cream lettering on black. Chanel No. 23. It was torn and creased, and the black ink had turned brown.

'Cheap crap,' Fu said in English.

'Chanel is hardly cheap, or crap,' Margaret said.

'Chanel, no,' Fu said grinning. 'But this no Chanel.'

'What do you mean?' Li asked.

Fu reverted to Chinese. 'I went to the expense of buying a bottle of Chanel,' he said. And he took another bottle from a drawer and placed it on the table beside the broken one and its damaged label. 'It was the cheap ink that made me wonder,' he said.

Margaret picked up the new bottle and looked very carefully at the lettering. There were subtle but distinct differences, and the black was deeper, sharper. She looked at the label recovered from Li's bottle. 'It's a fake,' she said.

'Yeah, it a fake,' Fu confirmed. 'We phoned Chanel. They don't make number twenty-three.'

'IT JUST DOESN'T make any sense.' Li's mood had not been improved by their visit to Pao Jü Hutong. They had made the short trip back to Section One in silence and these were the first words he had spoken, standing on the third-floor landing one floor down from his office, trying to catch his breath. His beating last night had taken more out of him than he would care to admit.

Margaret said, 'Almost every label on every market stall is fake.'

'Yes, I know. But why would these athletes all go out and buy the same fake Chanel? And why were they all using breath freshener?'

'There's a lot of garlic in Chinese food,' Margaret said. Her flippancy turned his glare in her direction. 'Sorry.'

They carried on up to the top floor and Li went into the detectives' room. Margaret headed on down the corridor to his office. She would call a taxi and then pick up her mother from Mei Yuan's stall and retreat to her apartment.

There was a man standing staring out of the window in Li's office when she walked in. He turned expectantly at the sound of the door opening, and she recognised him immediately as Li's deputy, Tao Heng. A man, she knew, whom Li detested.

'Oh,' he said. 'I'm sorry. I was waiting for the section chief.'

'He'll be along in a moment,' Margaret said.

'I'll not wait,' Tao said, and he walked briskly to the door, avoiding her eye. He stopped in the doorway, hesitated a moment and then said, 'I suppose it'll be a relief to you, not to have him coming home every night railing about his deputy.'

In fact, Li hardly ever talked about Tao, although his deputy clearly thought he did. Margaret was startled. 'I'm sorry, I don't know what you're talking about.'

'What are you going to do? Take him back to America? I suppose there are many agencies over there who would consider it a feather in their cap to have an ex-Chinese cop of Li's standing on their books.'

Bizarrely, Margaret wondered for a moment at the quality of Tao's English, before remembering that he had worked for years with the British in Hong Kong. And then she replayed his words and felt the cold chill of a dreadful misgiving.

'Ex-Chinese cop?'

Tao looked at her blankly, and then a mist cleared from his eyes. 'You don't know, do you?' A smile that Margaret could have sworn was almost gleeful spread across his face. 'He hasn't told you.'

Margaret's shock reduced her voice to a whisper. 'Told me what?'

Tao became suddenly reticent. 'It's not for me to say.'

'You've started,' Margaret said, now angry. 'You'd better finish.'

'It's policy,' he said. 'Just policy. I can't believe you don't know.'

'What policy?'Margaret demanded.

He took a deep breath and looked her straight in the eye. She felt suddenly disconcerted by him, afraid. 'It is impossible for a Chinese police officer to marry a foreign national and remain in the force. When Li marries you, his career will be over.'

WHEN LI GOT BACK to his office he was surprised not to find Margaret there. He called the switchboard and asked if anyone had ordered a taxi for her. No one had. Then he looked out of the window and saw Margaret on the street below, walking towards the red lanterns of the restaurant on the corner, and then turning south towards Ghost Street. He was puzzled only for a moment, before turning his mind to other things.

TEARS BLURRED Margaret's vision, making her unaware of the looks she was drawing from curious Chinese. She cut an odd figure here in northwest Beijing, her long coat pushed out by her bulging belly, golden curls flying out behind her, tears staining pale skin.

How could he not have told her? But she knew the answer. Because she would not have married him if he had. His work was his life. How could she have asked him to give it all up? Of course, he knew that, which is why he had decided to deceive her.

But you can't build a relationship on lies, she thought. He had been stalling her for weeks on the issue of the apartment for married officers. And how stupid was she that she hadn't suspected? That it had never occurred to her that there would be a price for getting married? And how had he been going to tell her after the deed had been done? What did he imagine she would think, or say, or do?

The thoughts were flashing through her mind with dizzying speed. She wiped her eyes and took deep breaths, trying to steady herself.

The snow, which had earlier retreated into the leaden sky, started to fall again with renewed vigour. Suddenly Beijing no longer felt like home. It was big and cold and alien, and she felt lost in it. The irony was that, 100 metres down the road, Mei Yuan would be turning out *jian bing* in the lunchtime rush, and Margaret's mother would be with her. There was no chance to be alone, to come to terms with all this before she had to face Li again. She knew her mother would be expecting her, and there was no way she could abandon her 10,000 miles from home.

Margaret dried her remaining tears and headed off towards the corner where Mei Yuan plied her trade. As she approached it, she saw a large queue. Mei Yuan hardly ever did this kind of business. And then Margaret saw why.

Mei Yuan was standing a pace or two back from the hot plate, supervising, as Mrs Campbell made the *jian bing* with an expertise Margaret found hard to believe. Even harder to believe was the sight of her mother in a blue jacket and trousers beneath a large chequered apron, with a scarf tied round her head.

Mrs Campbell caught sight of Margaret as she handed a *jian bing* to a smiling Chinese. 'You'll have to take your place in the line,' she said. And her face broke into a wide grin. 'Mei Yuan says we're doing ten times her normal business.' She looked at the next in line, a middle-aged woman. '*Ni hau*,' she said. '*Yi?*'

'*Yi*,' the woman said timidly, holding up one finger.

Margaret turned to a smiling Mei Yuan. 'When did my mother learn to speak Chinese?' she asked.

'Oh, we had a small lesson this morning,' Mei Yuan said. 'She can say hello, goodbye, thank you, and count from one to ten. She also makes very good *jian bing*.' Then a slight frown of concern clouded her face, and she peered at Margaret. 'Are you all right?'

'Yes, I'm fine,' Margaret said quickly, remembering that she wasn't. 'I was just coming to collect my mother to take her home.'

'I'll get a taxi back later,' Mrs Campbell said without looking up from her *jian bing*. 'Must make hay while the sun shines.'

Mei Yuan was still looking at Margaret. 'Are you sure you're OK?'

'Of course,' Margaret said, self-consciously. 'Look, I have to go. I'll see you later, Mom.'

She knew she should be happy at this unexpected change in her mother, a woman freed somehow from the constraints of her own self-image. And free, for the first time that Margaret could remember, to be unreservedly happy.

But Margaret was unable to break free from the constraints of her own unhappiness, and as she slipped into the back seat of a taxi on Ghost Street, she was overwhelmed again by self-pity.

THE APARTMENT was strangely empty without her mother. Margaret shrugged off her coat, kicked off her boots and eased herself onto the sofa. She felt her baby kicking inside her, and it set her heart fluttering with both fear and anticipation of a future that had been thrown into confusion in the space of a couple of hours.

She stretched out and closed her eyes, and suddenly saw the face of the bearded Westerner in the photograph on Li's desk, followed immediately by a certain knowledge of who he was. She sat bolt upright, heart pounding. Dr Hans Fleischer. Shit!

Immediately, she crossed to her little gate-leg table, set her laptop on it and plugged it in. She drew in a chair, dialled up her Internet server and accessed a search engine.

She had first heard of Dr Fleischer during a trip to Germany in the late nineties to give evidence on behalf of a dead client, the athlete, Gertrude Klimt. The prosecutors had brought charges against many of the doctors in the former East German state who had been responsible for feeding drugs to young athletes. But the one they most wanted, the biggest fish of all, had somehow swum through their net. Fleischer had disappeared.

Margaret tapped in 'Hans Fleischer' and hit the return key. After a few seconds her screen was filled with links to dozens of pieces of information from around the Internet. She scrolled through the list until she came to a piece carried by *Time* magazine in 1998. The photographs that went with it confirmed Margaret's identification.

The article traced Fleischer's career from a brilliant double degree in sports medicine and genetics at the University of Potsdam to his meteoric rise through the ranks at the state-owned pharmaceutical giant, Nitsche Laboratories, to become its head of research, aged only twenty-six. The next five years were something of a mystery, but there was speculation that he had spent those missing years in the Soviet Union. Then, in 1970, he had turned up again in the unlikely role of senior physician with the East German Sport Club, SC Dynamo Berlin. At this point, the *Time* piece fast-forwarded to the demise of the German Democratic Republic, when the true role of Dr Fleischer was revealed for the first time. An agent of the East German secret police, the Stasi, he had been instrumental in establishing and controlling the systematic state-sponsored doping of GDR athletes for nearly two decades.

Pioneering the use of state-developed steroids, his initial success in developing a new breed of super athletes was startling. From a medal count of twenty at the 1972 Olympics, East German competitors doubled their medal tally to forty in just four years.

Most of the athletes had come to him as children, taken from their parents and trained and educated in a strictly controlled environment, which included administering little blue and pink pills on a daily basis. By the time they were old enough to realise that the pills were more than just vitamins, the damage had been done, both to their psyches and their bodies. Many of them, like Gertrude Klimt, would later die of cancer or endure other kinds of living hell.

The *Time* article quoted sources saying that Fleischer had left SC Dynamo Berlin in the late eighties and returned to work for Nitsche. There he was reported to have been involved in the development of a new method of stimulating natural hormone production. He had disappeared from Nitsche's employment records in 1989.

Margaret looked at an on-screen photograph of Fleischer smiling into the camera. There was something sinister in his cold, unsmiling eyes. Something ugly. He was here, this man. In Beijing. And Olympic athletes were dying for no apparent reason. And yet there was nothing to connect him to them. A chance snapshot taken at a club for wealthy businessmen. That was all.

Chapter Eight

Li knew there was something wrong the moment he arrived at the restaurant. 'Oh, you made it tonight?' Margaret said with an acid tone. 'My mother was thinking perhaps you had gone and got yourself beaten up again just so you wouldn't have to meet her.'

'I did not!' Mrs Campbell was horrified.

Margaret ignored her. 'Mom, this is Li Yan. Honest, upstanding officer of the Beijing Municipal Police. He's not always this ugly. But almost. Apparently some unsavoury members of the Beijing underworld rearranged his features last night. At least, that was his excuse for failing to come and ask me to marry him.'

Li was embarrassed, and blushed as he shook her mother's hand. 'I'm pleased to meet you, Mrs Campbell.'

'Uncle Yan, what happened to your face?' Xinxin asked, concerned.

Li stooped tentatively to give her a hug, and winced as she squeezed his ribs. 'Just an accident, little one,' he said.

Xiao Ling gave him a kiss and ran her fingers lightly over her brother's face, concern in her eyes. 'You sure you're OK?' she asked.

He nodded. 'Sure.'

Mei Yuan quickly took over. 'Now we're all here tonight, because Li Yan and Margaret have announced their intention to get married,' she said. 'And in China that means a joining together not only of two people, but of two families.' And she turned to the presents, which she had set out on the lacquer table for the second night running.

When, finally, a tin of green tea was presented to Mrs Campbell she said, 'Ah, yes, to encourage as many little Lis and Campbells as possible.' She looked pointedly at Margaret's bump. 'It's just a pity they didn't wait.' She paused a moment before she smiled, and then everyone else burst out laughing, a release of tension.

Margaret's smile was fixed and false. She said, 'I see Mr Li is having no trouble with his English tonight.'

The smile faded on the old man's face, and he glanced at Li, who could only shrug, bewildered and angered by Margaret's behaviour. But the moment was broken by the arrival of the manageress, who announced that food would now be served.

As everyone rose to cross the room, Mrs Campbell grabbed her daughter's arm and hissed, 'What on earth's got into you?'

'Nothing,' Margaret said. She pulled free of her mother's grasp and took her seat. She knew she was behaving badly, but she could not help herself. It was all a charade. A farce.

Mei Yuan made the first toast, to the health and prosperity of the bride and groom to be, then Mrs Campbell raised her goblet to toast the generosity of her Chinese hosts. When they had all sipped their wine, she cleared her throat and said, 'And who is it, exactly, who is going to pay for the wedding?'

Li glanced at Margaret, embarrassed. 'Well, it's not going to be a big wedding, so, well . . . we thought we'd pay for it ourselves.'

'Nonsense!' Mrs Campbell said loudly, startling them. 'It may be a

Chinese wedding, but my daughter is an American. And in America it is the tradition that the bride's family pays for the wedding. And that's what I intend to do.'

'I don't think I could allow you to do that, Mrs Campbell,' Li's father said suddenly, to everyone's surprise.

But Margaret's mother put her hand over his. 'Do not argue with an American lady on her high horse, Mr Li.'

'Mrs Campbell, I do not know much about Americans. But I know plenty about women. And I know just how dangerous it is to argue with one, regardless of her nationality.'

That produced a laugh around the table.

'Good,' Mrs Campbell said. 'We understand one another perfectly.'

Margaret felt an anger growing inside her. 'Oh, spare me!' Everyone turned at the sound of her breaking voice, and were shocked to see the tears brimming in her eyes.

Her mother said, 'Margaret, what on earth—?'

But Margaret wasn't listening. 'How long is it, Mr Li? Two days, three, since I wasn't good enough to marry your son because I wasn't Chinese?' She turned her tears on her mother. 'And you were affronted that your daughter should be marrying one.'

'Magret, Magret, what's wrong, Magret?' Xinxin ran round the table to clutch Margaret's arm, distressed by her tears.

'I'm sorry, little one,' Margaret said, and she ran a hand through the child's hair. 'It's just, it seemed like no one wanted your Uncle Yan and me to get married.' She looked at the faces around the table. 'And that's the irony of it. Just when you all decide you're going to be such big pals, there isn't going to be a wedding after all.'

She tossed her napkin on the table before hurrying out of the Emperor's Room and running blindly down the royal corridor.

For a moment, they all sat in stunned silence. Then Li stood up. 'Excuse me,' he said, and went out after her.

Margaret was out in the street before she realised that she had no coat. The snow was nearly ankle-deep and the wind cut through her like a blade. Her tears turned icy on her cheeks as they fell, and she hugged her arms round herself for warmth, staring wildly about, confused and uncertain of what to do now.

'Come back in, Margaret.' Li's breath was warm on her cheek.

She felt him slip his jacket round her shoulders and steer her towards the steps, where the girls with the tall black hats and the red pompoms stared at her in wide-eyed wonder.

Li led her back into the restaurant. 'Is there somewhere private we can go?' he asked.

One of the girls nodded towards a room beyond the main restaurant, and Li hurried Margaret past the gaze of curious diners and into a large, semidarkened room filled with empty banqueting tables.

He wiped the tears from her eyes, but she wouldn't look at him. He wrapped his arms round her to warm her and stop her from shivering.

'What is it, Margaret? What have I done?'

'It's what you didn't do,' she said.

'What? What didn't I do?'

'You didn't tell me you would lose your job if we got married.'

And the bottom fell out of a fragile world he had only just been managing to hold together. She felt him go limp.

'Why *didn't* you tell me?' She broke free of him and looked into his eyes for the first time, seeing all the pain that was there, and knowing the answer to her question before he even opened his mouth.

'You know why.' He paused. 'I want to marry you, Margaret.'

'I want to marry you, too, Li Yan. But not if it's going to make you unhappy.'

'It won't.'

'Of course it will! For God's sake, being a cop is all you've ever wanted. And you're good at it. I can't take that away from you.'

They stood for a long time before he said, 'What would we do?'

She gave a shrug. 'I don't know.' And she put her arms round him and pushed her cheek into his chest. He grunted involuntarily from the pain of it. She immediately pulled away. 'I'm sorry. I forgot.'

'How did you know?' he asked.

'Your deputy told me. Tao Heng.'

Anger bubbled up inside him. 'That bastard! I'll kill him!'

'No, you won't. It's the message that matters. Not the messenger.'

'And the message is what?'

'That it's over, Li Yan. The dream. Whatever it is we were stupid enough to think the future might hold for us. It's out of our hands.'

He wanted to tell her she was wrong, that their destiny was their own to make. But the words would have rung hollow, even to him. And if he could not convince himself, how would he ever persuade her? His life, his career, his future, were all spiralling out of control. And he seemed helpless to do anything about it.

He felt the weight of the world descend on him. After a very long silence, he said finally, 'Margaret—' and she cut him off immediately.

'By the way, I forgot to tell you earlier . . .' And he knew from her tone that she was saying she wasn't going to discuss it further.

'Forgot to tell me what?' he said wearily.

'I found a photograph on your desk. One of the ones taken by Jon Macken at the club where that murdered girl worked. It showed a Westerner, with silver hair and a beard. He was with some Chinese.'

Li said, 'What about him?'

'I recognised him. Not right away. But it came to me this afternoon, and I checked him out on the net. He's Dr Hans Fleischer—known as Father Fleischer to the East German athletes he was responsible for doping over nearly twenty years.'

AS THEY DROVE in convoy past the eastern flank of Yuyuantan Park, Li dragged his thoughts away from Margaret. No one had asked why the wedding was being called off, and Li had made no attempt to explain. It was nearly an hour since he had got everyone into taxis, and then taken Margaret home, and he wondered now what he would accomplish by his search of the club. There was, after all, nothing to link Fleischer with the deaths of the athletes. And Margaret herself had conceded that there was nothing to suggest that any of them had been taking drugs. But the coincidence was just too much to ignore.

As if reading Li's thoughts, Sun glanced towards his passenger. 'What do you think we're going to find here, Chief?'

Li shrugged. 'I doubt if this will prove to be anything more than an exercise in harassment. Letting CEO Fan know that we're watching him. After all, if it's true that Fan really doesn't know who Fleischer is, then the link to the club is extremely tenuous.' He slipped the photograph of Fan and Fleischer and the others out of a folder on his knee and squinted at it by the intermittent glow of the streetlights.

'You think there's a connection?'

'I think there could be one between the break-in and the fact that Fleischer features in one of Macken's pictures.' He glanced at Sun and waggled the photograph. 'Think about it. Fleischer is internationally reviled, not the sort of person an apparently respectable businessman like Fan would want people to know he was connected to. So, you're coming out of a room in your private club. You think you're perfectly safe. And flash. A guy with a camera catches the two of you together on film. Maybe you'd want that picture back.'

'But would you kill for it?'

'That might depend on how deep or unsavoury your connection with Fleischer was.' Li sighed. 'On the other hand, I might just be talking through a very big hole in my head.'

The convoy ground to a halt at some traffic lights, and Li peered again at the photograph in his hand. He frowned and switched on the courtesy light and held the print up to it.

'Now, there's something I didn't notice before.' Li stabbed at the image of the plaque on the wall beside the door. 'They're coming out of the Event Hall.'

Sun shrugged. 'Is that significant?'

'Fan Zhilong told me and Qian that it was being refurbished.'

He flicked off the courtesy lamp as the traffic lights turned green, and their wheels spun before catching and propelling them slowly round the corner to the Beijing OneChina Recreation Club.

FAN ZHILONG was less than happy to have his club overrun by a posse of uniformed and plain-clothed officers. 'It's an invasion of privacy,' he railed. 'Having the place raided is going to do nothing for my club's reputation. You could be in trouble for this, Section Chief.'

Li dropped his search warrant on Fan's desk. 'A girl has been stabbed to death, Mr Fan. Your personal assistant.'

'My *ex*-personal assistant,' Fan corrected him.

Li threw the photograph of Fleischer on top of the warrant. 'And a man wanted in the West for serially abusing young athletes with dangerous drugs was photographed on these premises.'

Fan tutted and sighed and raised his eyes towards the ceiling. 'I already told you, Section Chief, I never met him before the day that photograph was taken. I couldn't even tell you his name.'

'What's going on, Mr Fan?' The voice coming from the doorway behind them made Li and Sun turn. It was the track-suited personal trainer, who was also in the Fleischer photograph. 'The members downstairs are packing up and leaving. They're not happy.'

'Neither am I, Hou. But I'm afraid I have very little control over the actions of Section Chief Li and his colleagues.'

Li lifted the photograph from the desk and held it out towards Hou. 'Who's the Westerner in the picture?' he asked.

Hou glanced at his boss, then shook his head. 'No idea. One of the members brought him.'

'Which one?'

'I can't remember.'

'How very convenient. I take it it wasn't one of the other two in the picture?'

Hou shook his head. 'Members of staff.'

'So yourself, and Mr Fan, and two other members of staff were left on your own, by a member whose name you've forgotten, to entertain this Westerner, whose name you don't remember?'

'That's right,' Hou said.

'How very forgetful.'

Qian appeared in the doorway leading to JoJo's office. 'Chief,' he said. 'Remember that Event Hall that was being refurbished? Well, I think you should come and take a look at it.'

THE EVENT HALL was huge: marble walls soaring more than twenty feet, tiled floors stretching off towards distant pillars, a ceiling dotted with tiny lights, like stars in a night sky. Li looked around with a growing sense of unease. Long banners hung from the walls, decorated with Chinese characters that made no sense to him. Several items were laid out on the floor. A large bamboo hoop, with serrated pieces of red paper stuck to it. Pieces of charcoal arranged in a square. Three small circles of paper set out one after the other. Two lengths of string laid side by side.

'What is this?' Li said.

'Nothing really,' Fan said. 'Some ceremonial fun and games we have here for the members.'

'You said it was being refurbished.'

'I probably meant it was being rearranged for the ceremony.'

'And what exactly does this ceremony consist of, Mr Fan?'

Fan smiled and looked faintly embarrassed. 'It makes the members feel like they're part of something exclusive.'

Li nodded and stepped up onto a platform against a curtained wall at the end of the room. A table was strewn with more odd items: a white paper fan, an oil lamp, a white cloth with what looked like red ink stains on it, a short-bladed sword, a writing brush, an ink-stone, five pieces of fruit, and more than a dozen other items.

'What's this stuff?'

'Gifts,' Fan said. 'From members. They have to be unusual.'

'They are certainly that,' Li said. 'What's behind this curtain?'

'Nothing.'

Li stepped forward and drew it aside to reveal a double door. 'I thought you said there was nothing here.'

'It's just a door, Section Chief.'

Li tried the handle and pulled the right-hand door open. There was just marble wall behind it. The door and its façade were false.

Li looked at Fan, who returned his stare uneasily. Then his eyes fell on the club's personal trainer. He noticed that, although his hair was gathered behind his head in a ponytail, it looped down over his ears, hiding them from view. The tip of his right ear was just visible through the hair. But the loop on the left lay flat against his head. It looked odd, somehow. Something came back to Li from his secondment in Hong Kong. Something he had heard, but never seen. He stepped up to Hou and pushed the hair back from the left side of his head to reveal that the left ear was missing, leaving only a half-moon of livid scar tissue around the hole in his head.

'Nasty accident,' he said. 'How did it happen?'

'Like you said, Section Chief, a nasty accident.' Hou flicked his head away from Li's hand.

Li took another long look at Fan, saw defiance in his eyes, and felt a shiver of apprehension. 'I think we've seen enough,' he said. 'Thank you, Mr Fan, we'll not disturb you any longer.' He walked to where his detectives stood waiting. 'We're finished here,' he said to Qian.

Qian nodded, and called the rest of the team to go as they crossed the entrance hall to the tall glass doors.

They pushed out into the icy night, large snowflakes slapping cold on hot faces. Li hobbled round to the passenger side of the Jeep. Inside, Sun started the motor to get the blower going.

He turned to Li. 'So what was going on in there, Chief?'

'These people are Triads,' Li said.

'Triads?'

Li looked at him. 'You know what Triads are, don't you?'

'Sure. Organised crime groups in Hong Kong, or Taiwan. But here? In Beijing?'

Li shook his head sadly. 'There's always a price to pay, isn't there? It seems we haven't only imported Hong Kong's freedoms and economic reforms. We've imported their criminals as well.' He turned to the young police officer. 'Triads are like viruses, Sun. They infect everything they touch.' He nodded towards the club. 'That hall was an initiation chamber. And trainer Hou, with the ponytail? He must have transgressed at some point. He didn't lose his ear by accident. It was cut off. That's how they punish members for misdemeanours.'

'I had no idea, Chief,' Sun said. He lit a cigarette.

Li grabbed the packet from him and took one. 'Give me a light.'

'Are you sure, Chief?'

'Just give me a light.' Li leaned over Sun's lighter and sucked smoke into his lungs for the first time in nearly a year. 'I spent six months in Hong Kong in the nineties,' he said. 'I came across quite a number of Triads then. All that stuff in there, it's a kind of re-creation of a journey made by the five Shaolin monks who supposedly created the first Triad society, or "Hung League", as they called it, set up to try to restore the Ming Dynasty. I never came across anything on this scale, though. These people have serious money. And serious influence.' He shook his head. 'I still can't believe they're here in Beijing.'

LI LIMPED QUICKLY down the corridor on the top floor of Section One, supporting himself on his stick. Thirty hours after his beating outside Dai Lili's apartment, every muscle in his body had stiffened up. But he was a man driven. Sun was struggling to keep up.

'Go home,' Li told him. 'There's nothing more you can do now.'

'You're not sending anyone else home,' Sun protested.

'No one else has a pregnant wife waiting for them.' He spotted Qian taking a call at someone else's desk. 'Qian!'

'*You* do, Chief,' Sun persisted.

Li looked at him. 'She's not my wife,' he said. And he knew that if Margaret had her way now, she never would be.

'Yes, Chief?' Qian had hung up his call.

'Get on to Immigration, Qian. I want everything they've got on Fleischer.' He scanned the desks until he saw the bleary face of Wu at his computer. 'And Wu, run downstairs for me and ask the duty officer in Personnel for the file on Deputy Tao.'

Several heads around the room lifted in surprise, and Wu seemed to wake up. 'They'll not give it to me, Chief. Tao's a senior ranking officer. They'll only release his file to someone more senior.'

Li sighed. 'I was hoping to avoid having to go up and down two flights of stairs.'

'Sorry, Chief.'

Li turned and almost bumped into Sun. 'Are you still here?'

'I'll ask Personnel if you want.'

'Go home!' Li barked at him, and he set off towards the stairs, his mood blackening with every step.

It was after ten by the time Li got back to his office with Tao's employment records from the Royal Hong Kong Police in six box files. He sat and closed his eyes. He really didn't want to think about anything but the investigation, but he could not get Margaret out of his head. He couldn't face going back to confront his father tonight, not after everything that had happened. And he needed to talk to Margaret, to lie with her and put his hand on her belly and to be reassured that they had, at least, some kind of a future.

Li made a decision, and took out a sheet of official Section One stationery. He scrawled a handful of cryptic characters across the crisp page, then signed it. He folded it quickly, slipped it into an envelope and wrote down an address. He got up and hobbled to the door, and hollered for Wu to take a letter down to the mail room.

Once Wu had headed off with the envelope, Li returned to his desk and pulled the telephone directory towards him. He found the number of the Jinglun Hotel and dialled it. The Jinglun was Japanese owned. Neutral territory. The receptionist answered.

'This is Section Chief Li of the Beijing Municipal Police. I need to book a double room for tonight.'

When he'd made the reservation, he dialled again. Margaret answered almost immediately. 'It's me,' he said. She was silent for a long time at the other end of the line. 'Hello, are you still there?'

'I love you,' is all she said. And he heard the catch in her voice.

'I've booked us a room at the Jinglun Hotel on Jianguomenwai. Take a taxi. I'll meet you there in an hour.'

And he hung up. The deed was done, and there would be no going back. He opened the files on Tao.

Much of what was in them he knew already. Tao had been born in Hong Kong. He had joined the Royal Hong Kong Police straight from school, and he had risen to the rank of detective sergeant in the Criminal Investigation Department. The marriage he had entered into in his early twenties had gone wrong after their baby girl died from typhoid. He had never remarried.

He had been involved in several murder investigations, and a huge drugs bust which had netted more than 5 million dollars' worth of heroin. He had also taken part in a major investigation into Triad gangs in the colony, including some undercover work. But despite what appeared to have been a major police effort to crack down on the Triads, success had been limited to a few minor arrests and a handful of prosecutions. Li remembered the persistent rumours of a Triad insider within the force itself, rumours that were never fully investigated, perhaps for fear of what such an investigation might turn up.

Triads had been endemic in Hong Kong since the late nineteenth century. All attempts by the British to stamp them out had failed. Originally it was the Communists who drove the Triads out of mainland China, forcing them to concentrate their efforts in Hong Kong and Taiwan. Now, as freedom of movement and economic reform took hold, the scourge of the Triads was returning to the mainland.

Li closed the files and sighed. Someone close to their investigation had known enough to be one step ahead of them on the bottles of perfume and aftershave. Why not Tao? And someone had told the thieves who broke into Macken's studio that he had made contact prints. Only the investigating officers from the local bureau had known that. And in Section One, only Li and Qian. And Tao.

The trouble was, there was not one single reason for him to connect Tao with either breach. The fact that he disliked the man was no justification. Even for the suspicion.

A GOLDEN CHRISTMAS TREE dotted with lights twinkled opposite the revolving door of the Jinglun Hotel. In the lobby, beneath soaring gold pillars and palm trees, Margaret was sitting on her own. She stood up when she saw Li.

He took her arm. 'Come on, let's go upstairs.'

Their room was on the fifth floor, at the far end of a long corridor. Li did not draw the curtains, and once their eyes had adjusted there was sufficient ambient light from the avenue below by which to see.

A strange urgency overtook them as they undressed and slipped into bed. The warmth of her skin on his immediately stirred his desire. He found her lips, and the sweetness of her tongue, and then he slipped inside her. They moved together in slow rhythmic waves, gripped by their passion, but gentle with the knowledge of their baby lying curled between them.

Afterwards they rested, lying on their backs, listening to snowflakes brush the window like falling feathers.

'You've been smoking,' Margaret said suddenly.

'Just one.' He hesitated for a long time, steeling himself. 'Margaret, we need to talk about the wedding. I still want to marry you.'

'Forget it.' And she tried very hard not to succumb to the self-pity that was welling up inside.

'What are you thinking?'

'I'm thinking about how much I just want to hurt you for lying to me. For deceiving me.' She made a determined effort to force a change of topic. 'So how did it go tonight? Did you find Fleischer?'

Li closed his eyes. He still didn't have the courage to tell her. So he released his thoughts to run over the night's events, and shuddered again at the recollection of what he had uncovered at the club. 'No,' he said. 'But if there's a connection between Fleischer and the dead athletes, then we're up against something much more powerful than I could ever have imagined.'

'What do you mean?'

'The club where Fleischer was photographed is run by Triads.'

She frowned. 'Triads? That's like a kind of Chinese mafia, isn't it?'

'Bigger, more pervasive, steeped in ritual and tradition. The Event Hall at the club is a ceremonial chamber for the induction of new members. Most times I would have walked into it and never have known, but tonight it was all set up for an induction ceremony.'

He described to her the layout of the hall, and the items laid out on the floor, symbolic of a journey made by the founding monks.

'The monks came from a Shaolin monastery in Fujian,' he said. 'They were supposed to have answered a call by the last Ming emperor to save the dynasty and take up arms against the Ch'ing. But one of their number betrayed them, and most were killed when the monastery was set on fire. Five escaped. According to legend they had a series of extraordinary adventures and miraculous escapes. Their numbers grew until they became an army, and they called themselves the "Hung League". But over the years they became fragmented, dividing into hundreds of different gangs, who inducted new members by re-enacting the original legend.' He snorted. 'Of course, they never did restore the Ming Dynasty. They turned to crime instead. I guess they were one of the world's first crime syndicates.'

Margaret listened in fascination. 'What does it all mean, exactly?'

'Everything's related to the original legend,' Li said. 'I don't know all the details. I think the bamboo hoop with the red serrated paper was supposed to represent a hole through which the monks escaped from the burning monastery. And the two lengths of string symbolise a two-planked bridge, which also aided their escape.' He described what he had seen lying on the table on the platform. 'The white cloth with the red stains represents a monk's robe smeared with blood. The sword would be used to execute traitors. The punishment for anyone breaking one of the thirty-six oaths of allegiance is "death by a myriad of swords".'

Margaret felt goosebumps rise up all along her arms. 'That girl you found in the park,' she whispered. 'You said she worked at the club. She died of multiple stab wounds, didn't she? Laid out on a stone slab like a ritual sacrifice. Or execution.'

'My God,' Li said, the thought dawning on him for the first time. '*They* killed her.'

'But why? She wouldn't have been a member, would she?'

'No. It's an all-male preserve. But she must have known something, betrayed a confidence, I don't know . . .' He sat up in bed, all fatigue banished from body and mind. 'They took her up there and stabbed her to death and laid her out for the world to see. Like they were making an example of her. Or issuing a warning.'

'Who to?'

'I don't know. I just don't know.'

And then Li remembered something that had got lost in a day of traumas and revelations. He turned to her.

'Margaret, Wu came up with something at the meeting this morning. It's maybe nothing at all. But it did seem strange.'

'What?'

'All of the athletes, including Jia Jing, had the flu at some point in the five or six weeks before they died.' He paused. 'Could that have been the virus that caused their heart trouble?'

Margaret frowned. 'No,' she said. 'The flu wouldn't do that to them.' She paused. 'But it could have activated a retrovirus.'

Li screwed up his face. 'A what?'

'We've all got them in our DNA. Retroviruses. Organisms that have attacked us at some point in human history, that we've learned to live with because they have become a part of us. Usually harmless. But sometimes, just sometimes, activated by something else that finds its way in there. A virus. Like herpes. Or flu.'

'You think that's what happened to these athletes?'

She shrugged. 'I've no idea. But if they all came down with flu, and that's the only common factor we can find, it's a possibility.'

Li was struggling to understand. 'And how would that help us?'

Margaret shook her head. 'I don't know that it would.'

Li fell back on the pillow. 'I give up.'

She smiled and shook her head. 'I doubt it. You're not the type.'

He closed his eyes and she said, 'So what are *you* thinking?'

He said, 'I'm thinking about how I quit the force tonight.'

Margaret's heart pounded. 'What?'

'I want to marry you, Margaret.' She started to protest, but he forced his voice over hers. 'And if you won't marry me, then I'll have to live with that. But it won't change my mind about quitting.' He turned his head on the pillow to look at her. 'I wrote my resignation letter tonight. It's in the mail. So no going back.'

'Well, you'd better find a way,' Margaret said brutally. 'Because I won't marry you, Li Yan. Not now. I won't have your unhappiness on my conscience for the rest of my life.'

Chapter Nine

Margaret was still asleep when he left. He had no idea when either of them had drifted off, finally, to escape from their stalemate for a few short hours. But he had woken early and lay listening to her slow, steady breathing on the pillow beside him. She had looked so peaceful, so innocent in sleep, this woman he loved. This pig-headed, stubborn, utterly unreasonable woman he loved.

Traffic in the city had already ground to a halt, and there was not even light in the sky yet. Li hobbled past lines of stationary vehicles blocking all six lanes on Jianguomenwai Avenue. A few taxis were making their way gingerly along the cycle lanes, cyclists weaving past them on both sides, leaving drunken tracks in the snow. He would have to take the subway to Section One.

Li limped down the steps of the subway station, and squeezed into a crowded train. At Dongzhimen he struggled painfully to the top of the stairs, emerging once more into the cold, bitter wind that blew the snow in from the Gobi Desert. The sky was filled with a purple-grey light now, and the traffic was grinding slowly in both directions along Ghost Street.

Li was surprised to see Mei Yuan serving customers at her usual corner, steam rising in the cold from her hot plate.

'You're early,' he said to her.

She looked up, surprised. 'So are you.' There was a moment of awkwardness between them. Unfinished business from the betrothal meeting, unspoken exchanges. 'Would you like a *jian bing*?'

He nodded. 'I'm sorry about last night.'

She shrugged. 'Some day, perhaps, you'll tell me about it.'

'Some day,' he said. But he did not want to get into that now. He tried to change the subject. 'Are you enjoying your book?'

'It's not a serious biography on Napoleon,' she said. 'The writer seemed more intent on making a fool of the Frenchman. But there's an element of criminal investigation in it that might interest you.'

Li thought how very soon he would have no interest of any kind in criminal investigation. 'Oh?'

'When the British finally defeated Napoleon,' Mei Yuan said, 'he was banished to St Helena, in the South Atlantic, where he died in 1821. It has long been rumoured that he was actually murdered there to prevent his escape and return to France. It was said that his food was laced with arsenic, and that he died from poisoning.' She reached behind her saddle and pulled out the book. 'But according to this, a medical archaeologist from Canada disproved the murder theory nearly one hundred and eighty years after Napoleon's death.'

In spite of his mood and the cold and the snow, Li found his interest engaged. 'How?'

'Locks of his hair were taken at autopsy and kept for posterity. This medical archaeologist got access to the hair and conducted an analysis of it. Apparently the hair is like a kind of log of chemicals and poisons that pass through our bodies. He contended that if Napoleon had, indeed, been poisoned, there would still be traces of the arsenic that killed him in his hair. He found none.'

But Li was a long way from St Helena and arsenic poisoning. In his mind he was in an autopsy room looking at a young swimmer with a shaven head. To her surprise, he took Mei Yuan's red smiling face in his hands and kissed her. 'Thank you, Mei Yuan. Thank you.'

MARGARET WOKE LATE, disorientated, panicked by unfamiliar surroundings. It was a full five seconds before she remembered where she was, and the blanks in her memory started filling themselves in. Li. Triads. His resignation. Fighting. His words coming back to her. *I wrote my resignation letter tonight.* But she could feel no anger. Only his pain. And she wished that she could make it go away.

She slipped out of bed and took a shower, then dressed and hurried downstairs. The revolving door propelled her out onto the sidewalk and the cold hit her like a physical blow. She stopped for a moment to catch her breath, and saw that the traffic in the avenue was still gridlocked. No chance of a taxi.

It took her an hour to get back to her apartment, trudging the last twenty minutes through snow from the subway station. One side of her was white where the wind had driven the thick, soft flakes against her coat and jeans.

Her face had frozen rigid by the time she stepped into the elevator. Even if she had felt the desire to smile at the sullen operator, her facial muscles would not have obliged. She peeled off her red ski hat and shook out her hair. At least her ears were warm.

'Mom,' she called out as she let herself in. But there were no lights on, and it felt strangely empty. 'Mom?' Then she saw a note on the gate-leg table beside her laptop in the sitting room.

It was written in Mei Yuan's hand: *I have taken your mother to Zhongshan Park to teach her tai chi in the snow.*

Margaret felt hugely relieved. Her mother was the last person she had felt like facing right now. She sat down at the table, turning on her laptop. She connected to the Internet and pulled up the *Time* article on Hans Fleischer. She read it all through again very carefully, and stopped near the end of it. He was said to have been involved 'in the development of a new method of stimulating natural hormone production'.

An idea was taking shape in her mind.

She grabbed her coat from where it was dripping melting snow onto the kitchen floor, and pulled on her ski cap and gloves, a vision of the runner with the purple birthmark filling her mind with a bleak sense of urgency. She had only just stepped into the elevator when the phone rang in her apartment. But the doors closed before she heard it.

LI TAPPED HIS DESK impatiently, listening to the long, single ring of the phone go unanswered at the other end. He waited nearly a minute before he hung up. He had phoned the hotel some time earlier, but she had already left.

There was a knock at the door and Qian poked his head round it. 'Got a moment, Chief?'

Li nodded. 'Sure.' He felt a pang of regret. After today nobody would call him 'Chief' any more.

'I got that information you wanted from Immigration. About Dr Fleischer.' Qian sat down opposite Li and flipped through his notes. 'He was first granted an entry visa into China in 1999. It was a one-year business visa with a work permit allowing him to take up a position with a joint-venture Swiss–Chinese chemical company called the Peking Pharmaceutical Corporation. The visa has been renewed annually but he doesn't seem to be with PPC any more.' He looked up. 'Which is odd. Because there isn't any record of who's employing him now.' He shrugged. 'Anyway, he has two addresses. He rents an apartment near the China World Trade Centre. And he also has a small country cottage just outside the village of Guanling near the Miyun reservoir.'

Li knew the reservoir well. It supplied more than half the city's water. It was a huge lake about sixty-five kilometres northeast of Beijing. He had spent many weekends there during his student days, fishing and swimming.

He wondered what Fleischer was doing with a house out there.

THE SNOW WAS LYING thick on the ground. On a day like this the students were all indoors, and Margaret made the only tracks on the road from the main campus to the Centre of Material Evidence Determination, where she had carried out her autopsies. Inside, the centre was warm and she pulled off her hat and made her way along the first-floor corridor that led to Professor Yang's office.

The professor was a tall, lugubrious man with large, square, rimless glasses and a head of thick, sleekly brushed hair. He was an extremely able forensic pathologist, but it was his political acumen and administrative skills that had propelled him into his current position of power as head of the most advanced forensics facility in China.

He had a soft spot for Margaret. 'What can I do for you, my dear?' His English was almost too perfect, the kind of English no one spoke any more. Even in England.

'Professor, I have a favour to ask,' she said. 'I've been working with Section Chief Li on the dead athletes case.'

'Yes,' he said, 'I've been following it quite closely. Very interesting.'

'I wonder if you might know anyone with a background in genetics. Someone who might be able to do a little blood analysis for me.'

'As it happens,' Professor Yang said, 'my best friend from school is now Professor of Genetics at Beijing University. And there is, my dear, a certain matter of some outstanding *guanxi* between myself and Professor Xu. So, of course, if I ask him, he will do *me* a favour.'

Margaret couldn't resist a smile. Professor Yang took the Chinese system of *guanxi*—a favour given is a debt owed—very literally. 'And then I will owe you,' she said.

He beamed. 'I do so much like having *guanxi* in the bank.'

'I'll need to retrieve some of the heart blood I took from the swimmer, Sui Mingshan. There should be enough left.'

'Well, let us go and see, my dear,' he said, and he stood up and lifted his coat from a stand behind the door. 'And I shall accompany you to the university myself.'

There was still a good fifty millilitres of Sui's blood in the refrigerator available for testing. Margaret drew off most of it into a small glass vial, which she sealed and packed carefully into her bag.

Professor Yang arranged for a car and driver to take them across town to Beijing University. Snowploughs had been out on the ring road and they made slow but steady progress.

Professor Xu's office was on the second floor of the College of Biogenic Science. He could not have been more different from Professor Yang—short, round, balding, with tiny wire-rimmed glasses.

Xu looked at Margaret. 'He always more lucky than me, Lao Yang. Always with pretty girl on his arm. You have blood?'

Margaret took the vial out of her bag. 'I hope it's enough. I took it from a young man who was suffering from an unusual heart condition. I am wondering if his condition might have been brought about by some kind of genetic disorder.'

Xu took the vial. 'Why you think there is genetic element?'

'To be honest,' Margaret said, 'I don't know that there is.' She glanced at Yang. 'I'm making a wild guess, here. This condition has already killed several people and may kill several more. The victims might have been subjected to some kind of genetic modification.'

Yang translated, and Margaret could see that Xu found the suggestion intriguing. He looked at her. 'OK, I give it big priority.'

On the way back in the car, Yang asked Margaret, 'You think someone might have been tampering with the DNA of these athletes?' He, too, was clearly intrigued.

Margaret looked embarrassed. 'I hope I am not wasting your friend's time, Professor. It really is the wildest stab in the dark.'

A POLICE JEEP, windows opaque with condensation, was parked at the front door of the Centre of Material Evidence Determination when Professor Yang's car pulled in. As the professor helped Margaret towards the steps, the doors on each side of the Jeep opened simultaneously, and Li and Sun got out. Margaret watched as Li limped towards her on his stick. At least, she thought, he still appeared to be in a job. She searched his face anxiously as he approached, and saw from his eyes that there had been developments.

'What's happened?' she asked.

He said, 'I know why they shaved the athletes' heads. At least, I think I do. But I need you to prove it.'

Yang said, 'Well, let's not stand here discussing it in the snow, shall we? You had better come along to my office and we'll have some tea.'

Li could barely contain himself on the walk along the hall. His revelation was burning a hole in his brain.

Yang stopped by his secretary and asked her to make them tea, then swept into his office. He hung his coat on the stand and said, 'Well? Are you going to put us out of our misery, Section Chief?'

Li said, 'It's the hair. If they were taking drugs there would be a record of it on their heads. Even if they managed to get the stuff out of their systems there would still be traces of it in their hair.'

'Of course,' Margaret whispered.

Yang said, 'But if all their heads were shaved, how will we know?'

Margaret said, 'But they weren't, were they?' She turned to Li. 'The weightlifter who died from the heart attack. He still had his hair.'

'And plenty of it,' Li said. 'A ponytail halfway down his back.'

Margaret looked troubled. 'The only problem is,' she said, 'I have no expertise in this area.'

Yang's secretary knocked and came in with a tray of tall glasses and a flask of hot tea.

'Ah, good, thank you, my dear,' said Yang, as she set the tray down. 'Ask Dr Pi to step into my office for a few moments, would you?'

She nodded and left. The professor started pouring.

'You know Dr Pi, don't you, Margaret?' he said.

'Head of the forensics laboratory, isn't he?'

Yang nodded. 'Spent some time last year on an exchange trip to the US. I believe he took part in a study to ascertain cocaine abuse by performing hair assays.' He started handing glasses of tea round.

Dr Pi was a tall, good-looking young man with impeccable American English. Yes, he confirmed when he came in, he had taken part in such a study. 'We found we could look at drug exposure months after it had passed out of the urine or the blood. A kind of retrospective window of detection.'

Li said, 'If we could provide you with a hair sample, would you be able to analyse it for us and open up that retrospective window?'

'Sure. I'd need forty to fifty strands of hair cut at scalp level.'

Margaret said to Li, 'Is the weightlifter still at Pao Jü Hutong?'

'In the chiller.'

'Then we'd better get straight over there and give him a haircut.'

THE LIGHT WAS FADING by the time Margaret got back to her apartment. She had cut a lock of Jia Jing's silken black hair and delivered it back to the Centre of Material Evidence Determination.

Her mother had not yet returned, and there was something cheerless about the place. Margaret arched her spine, pressing her palms into her lower back. It had started to ache again. Her antenatal class was due to begin in just over an hour, but she did not feel like going out again into the cold and dark.

A hammering at the door crashed into her thoughts and startled her. Not her mother or Mei Yuan. Not Li, who had a key. She hurried to open the door, but before she did, she put it on its chain. A young man stepped back into the light of the landing, squinting at her between door and jamb. He was rough-looking, with a tattoo of the head of a serpent emerging from the arm of his jacket onto the back of his hand.

'You Doctah Cambo?'

Margaret felt a shiver of apprehension. 'Who wants to know?'

'You come with me.'

'I don't think so.' She tried to close the door, but his foot was preventing her from shutting it. 'I'll scream!' she said shrilly.

'My sister, Dai Lili, wanna talk t'you,' young man said gruffly.

Margaret stepped back from the door as if she had received an electric shock.

The young man fumbled in his jacket pocket and pulled out a dog-eared business card. 'She gimme this to give you.' It was the card she had given Dai Lili that day outside the hospital.

Margaret took a deep, tremulous breath. She knew she probably should not go, but the picture in her mind of the young runner's face, the fear in her eyes, was still very vivid. 'Give me a minute,' she said, closing the door. She went to the kitchen and fetched her coat and hat.

When she opened the door again, the young man seemed startled to see her, as if he had already decided she was not going to reappear.

'Where is she?' Margaret asked.

'You follow me.'

IN THE DETECTIVES' ROOM, Li gasped his frustration. Dr Fleischer, apparently, had disappeared into thin air. They had officers watching his apartment and the club. Enquiries with his previous employer, Peking Pharmaceutical Corporation, revealed that he had been running their highly sophisticated laboratory complex for the last three years, but had left six months ago, just after his work permit and visa had been renewed. Li headed for the door.

'By the way, Chief,' Wu called after him. 'Anything we put in the internal mail last night is history.'

Li stopped in his tracks. 'What do you mean?'

'Motorbike courier was involved in a smash first thing this morning. Mail was all over the road . . . most of it ruined.'

Li lingered in the doorway. Was it fate? Good luck, bad luck? Did it make any difference? He said, 'What about the courier?'

'Broke his wrist. A bit shaken up. OK, though.'

But even if his letter of resignation had failed to reach its destination, it was only a stay of execution. Li shook his head to clear his mind. It was not important now. Other things took precedence. He turned into the corridor and nearly collided with Sun.

'Chief, is it OK if I take a couple of hours to go up to the hospital with Wen? I still haven't made it to one of those antenatal classes yet and she's been giving me hell.'

'Sure,' Li said, distracted.

'I mean, I know it's not the best time just now . . .'

'I said OK,' Li snapped, and he strode off to his office.

Tao was waiting for him, standing staring out of the window into the dark street below. He turned as Li came in.

'What do you want?' Li said.

Tao walked purposefully past him and closed the door. He said, 'You had my personnel file out last night. I want to know why.'

Li sighed. 'I don't have time for this right now, Tao.'

'Well, I suggest you make time.' The low, controlled threat in Tao's voice was clear and unmistakable.

It cut right through Li's preoccupation, and he looked at Tao, surprised. 'I'm not sure I like your tone, Deputy Section Chief.'

'I'm not sure I care,' Tao said. 'After all, you're not going to be around long enough for it to make any difference. Seems to me it's a serious breach of trust when you go and pull my file from Personnel. Makes it look like it's me who's under investigation.'

'Well, maybe it is,' Li snapped. 'You were involved in an investigation by the Hong Kong Police into the activities of the Triad gangs. You got very close to what was happening on the ground. But you didn't make any single arrest of note.'

'No one working on that investigation did.' Tao had gone very pale. 'We never got the break we needed.'

'I remember hearing a rumour that was because the Triads were always one step ahead of the police.'

Tao glared at him. 'The insider theory. You think it was me, don't you? That's why you pulled my file.'

'We've got Triads in Beijing, Tao. Anyone with specialist knowledge could be valuable.'

Tao narrowed his eyes. 'You're trying to smear my name so I won't get your job.' He gave a small, bitter laugh. 'Your parting shot.' He turned on his heels and stormed out, slamming the door behind him.

Li closed his eyes and tried hard to stop himself from shaking.

Chapter Ten

Crowds jammed the Dong'anmen night market, where dozens of stallholders under red-and-white-striped canopies were frying, barbecuing, steaming, grilling. The smell of food rose with the steam and smoke to fill the night air. Chefs in white coats and tall hats kept themselves warm over fiery woks, while hungry customers flitted from stall to stall. No one paid any attention to two figures cycling past, hunched against the cold.

The lights and the sounds and smells of the night market receded, and, to Margaret's surprise, Lili's brother dismounted under the high walls of the Donghua Gate, the east entrance to the Forbidden City.

'You leave bike here,' he said.

They leaned their bikes against the wall and she followed him into the shadowed arch of the great central doorway. He pushed hard against the right-hand door, and it opened just enough to let them slip through. The young man quickly glanced around before he ushered Margaret in and heaved the door closed behind them.

Within its walls the Forbidden City lay brooding silently in the dark, 600 years of history witness to the virgin footsteps Margaret and Lili's brother made in the snow as they followed a path through another gate, and out into a huge cobbled square.

Margaret was breathless already. She grabbed the boy's arm to stop him. 'What in God's name are we doing here?' she demanded.

'I work for'—he searched for the words—'building firm. We do renovation work, Forbidden City. But work no possible with snow.'

He struggled again with the language. 'I hide Lili here. No one come. You follow with me.' And he set off across the vast, ancient square.

Margaret breathed a sigh of despair and set off after him, leaving shadowed tracks in luminous snow.

Slippery steps took them up to the Taihe Hall. Through an open gate, between stout crimson pillars, Margaret could see the next in a series of halls standing up on its marble terrace at the far side of another square, flanked by what had once been the gardens and homes of imperial courtiers. By the time they reached it, Margaret was exhausted, and alarmed by cramps in her stomach. She stopped, gasping for air, and supported herself on a rail surrounding a huge copper pot more than a metre in diameter that had once been used to hold water in case of fire.

'Stop,' she called, and Dai Lili's brother hurried back to see what was wrong. 'For God's sake. I'm pregnant. I can't keep up with you.'

The boy appeared embarrassed. 'You take rest. Not far now.'

Suddenly, and unexpectedly, a tear in the clouds released a flood of silver light from a full moon, and the Forbidden City lit up all around them, eerie in its deserted silence. The falling snow was swept away on an equally sudden breath of wind, leaving the air clear and still for just a moment before it resumed its steady descent. Their footprints in the square below were an alarming betrayal of their passing there.

Margaret looked ahead, through the next gate, and saw yet another hall, on yet another terrace, and regretted her decision to go with the boy. But she had come too far to turn back now.

'OK,' she said. 'Let's go. But not so fast.'

The boy nodded, and they set off again, at a more sedate pace. From the terrace of the Qianqing Palace, Margaret could see beyond the walls of the Forbidden City to the lights of Beijing, where people were going about their normal lives.

Lili's brother took Margaret's arm as they carefully negotiated the steps down into an ancient alleyway, and through a gate to Chu Xiu, the Palace of Gathering Excellence, which was built around a quiet courtyard with tall conifers in each corner. Margaret's legs were turning to jelly as she dragged herself on. She had suffered several cramps now, and her apprehension was starting to turn to fear.

'I can't go any further,' she gasped.

'Lili here,' her brother said. 'No go any further.' And he guided her gently by the arm across the courtyard, past statues of dragons and peacocks, and up steps to the terrace of a long, low pavilion.

He whispered loudly in the darkness and, after a moment, Margaret heard a whispered response from inside the pavilion. There were several more exchanges before the door creaked open a crack, and Margaret saw Lili's frightened face caught in the moonlight, her birthmark like a shadow across her left cheek. She motioned quickly for Margaret to come in.

'I wait out here,' her brother said.

Inside, painted beams, ceramic tiles, an ornamental throne, were brushed in shadow. The only light came from an oil lamp that illuminated a very small circle of Lili's things. A sleeping-bag, a pillow, a holdall spilling clothes, and a small paraffin heater, which made no impression on the bone-jarring cold of this inhospitable place.

Margaret took Lili's hands in hers. 'You've been living here?'

Lili nodded. 'Hiding. They kill me if they find me,' she babbled. 'I know when I hear about Sui that I am next. They did it to me, too. I know I am going to die.' Sobs were breaking her voice.

'Woah,' Margaret said. 'Slow down. Start at the beginning.' She steered her towards a seat and drew the paraffin heater close.

Lili took a deep, trembling breath. 'They came the first time maybe six, seven months ago.'

'Who are "they"?'

'I don't know. Men. Men in suits, men with cars and money. They take me to fancy restaurant and say they can make me big winner. And I make big money.' She looked at Margaret, with a pleading in her eyes for understanding. 'I no greedy girl, lady. I only say yes for my sister. So I can pay for her. Everything.'

Margaret crouched down beside her and squeezed her arm. 'I believe you, Lili. I'm on your side.'

'I say no drug. They say no drug. Minor—physical—adjustment.' She had trouble saying it in English. She clutched Margaret's hand. 'They tell me it is safe. There are others. And they tell me some names. I know them, because they are big names. All winning.'

'Who were the other names?'

'Xing Da. He big hero of me. And Sui Mingshan. They say there are others, but they no tell me.'

'When you agreed to these . . . minor physical adjustments, what happened then?'

Lili shook her head miserably. 'I don't know, lady. They take some blood from me, and then a week later, maybe ten days, they come and take me to apartment downtown. Then foreign man come in.'

'Silver hair? Beard?'

Lili looked at Margaret with astonishment, and then perhaps a little fear. 'How you know this?'

'He's a bad man, Lili.' Margaret paused. 'What did he do to you?'

Lili shrugged. 'He give me jab.' She patted the top of her left arm. 'That's all. Then he say someone else explain, and he leave.'

'Explain what?'

'How it work.' She corrected herself. 'How I make it work.'

They heard a dull thud from out in the courtyard, and they both froze. It sounded to Margaret like snow falling from a roof, but she couldn't be sure. She leaned over and extinguished the oil lamp, and they were plunged into total darkness.

Lili clutched her arm. 'What is it?' she whispered.

'Shhh.'

They waited for several minutes, listening intently. But there was no further sound. A little moonlight started seeping into the pavilion and, slowly, Margaret eased herself up into a standing position and made her way to the door. Lili followed. Margaret pushed the door open a crack and peered out into dazzling moonlight. Finally, the snow had stopped. The courtyard was empty. She saw the footprints she and Lili's brother had left in the snow, tracking across the courtyard to the pavilion. And then his footsteps after Margaret had gone inside and he had wandered back down into the square. They headed off towards the southwest corner, and into the deep shadow cast by the long, low building that bounded the south side.

'Can you see Solo,' Lili whispered.

'Solo?' Margaret glanced at her, confused.

'My brother. Is his nickname.'

'No, he's not there. But I can see his footsteps heading across the courtyard. He must be sheltering in the gallery over there.'

'I'm scared,' Lili whispered.

'Me, too,' Margaret said. 'Let's go find him.' And as the words left her mouth, darkness fell across the courtyard as the sky closed up above them and shut out the moon.

Lili scuttled across the flagstones to retrieve the oil lamp, and as she lit it they both blinked in its sudden brightness. And then a sharp cramp made Margaret gasp.

'What's wrong?' Lili said urgently.

Margaret put a hand to her belly and found herself breathing rapidly. 'Nothing,' she said quickly, as she took the lamp. 'Come on.'

The lamp did not cast its light very far across the courtyard. Lili held Margaret's arm with both hands, and they made their way across the snow, following the footprints that led towards the far side. Suddenly Margaret stopped, and fear touched her like cold hands on hot skin. Two more sets of footprints converged on Solo's, coming from the left. She swung round to her right, and by the light of the lamp they saw Solo lying in the snow, face up, a wide grin across his throat where it had been cut from ear to ear.

Lili screamed then, and the shadows of men came at them out of the darkness. Margaret swung the lamp hard at the leading figure. It appeared to explode against him, oil igniting as it splashed over him through broken glass. In a matter of seconds his whole upper body was alight, his hair, his face. He howled in agony, spiralling away across the courtyard. Two other men froze for a moment in horror as they saw their friend on fire. All thoughts of the women vanished as they dived towards him, knocking him over to roll him in the snow, desperately trying to extinguish the flames.

Margaret grabbed Lili's hand. 'Run!' she hissed, and the two women set off in fear and panic.

Behind them, they heard the voices of men shouting, and Margaret knew she could never outrun them, even if Lili could. The cramps in her stomach were coming frequently. She put a protecting arm around the swelling of her child and feared the worst.

Lili was the stronger, half pulling her up the steps towards the vast open space that lay before the Qianqing Gate. They ran across the terrace, the voices of their pursuers close behind them.

Margaret stopped, doubled up in pain. 'I can't go on,' she gasped.

'We hide,' Lili whispered urgently. 'Quick. In pot.'

Margaret saw that here, too, a huge copper pot flanked each side of the gate. She allowed herself to be dragged towards the fence around the nearer of the pots, and with a great effort she clambered over it. Lili helped her up over the lip of the pot, enormous strength in such small hands, and she dropped down into its echoing darkness. She heard the patter of Lili's feet as she scuttled across the terrace to the other side. Then silence. Except for her breathing, which was hard and fast and painful. But the voices that had pursued them were no longer calling in the dark.

And then she remembered their footprints, almost at the same time as a shadow loomed over the lip of the pot above her and grabbing hands reached in. She heard Lili scream.

LI RODE UP in the elevator to the eleventh floor. He stepped out onto the landing and took a deep breath, preparing to put a positive face on things for Margaret's mother. He had to stop himself using the key, and knocked instead. After a moment, the door flew open and Li found himself confronted by Mrs Campbell.

'What kind of hour do you call this?' she said sharply, and then realised that Li was alone. 'Where is Margaret?'

'She's not here?' Li asked, perplexed.

'Would I be asking you if she was?' Mrs Campbell snapped.

Mei Yuan appeared behind her. 'You'd better come in, Li Yan. We've been waiting for her for more than two hours.'

Mrs Campbell reluctantly stepped aside to let Li into the apartment.

'She had an antenatal class tonight,' he said, and looked at his watch. 'She should have been back ages ago.' He pushed into the sitting room, snatched the phone and dialled the switchboard at Section One. When the operator answered he said, 'It's Section Chief Li. Give me Detective Sun's home number.' He scribbled it on a notepad, hung up and then dialled again. After a few moments a girl's voice answered. 'Wen?' he said.

'Who is this?' Wen asked cautiously.

'It's Chief Li. Wen, was Margaret at the antenatal class tonight?'

'Margaret? No,' Wen said. 'I was there on my own.'

Li frowned. 'On your own? Wasn't Sun Xi with you?'

'No.'

Li was surprised. 'But he asked me if he could have the time off to go with you today.' To his dismay, Wen began sobbing softly at the other end of the phone. 'Wen? Are you all right? What's wrong?'

Her voice was quivering when she said, 'I can't talk about it.' And he heard her crying aloud in the moment before she hung up.

'Well?' Margaret's mother had been watching him critically.

'She didn't go to her antenatal class.' He was alarmed and puzzled by Wen's reaction, and more than a little afraid now for Margaret. 'She didn't leave a note or anything?'

'Nothing,' Mei Yuan said.

'I'm going down to talk to the security guard on the gate,' Li said as he hurried out onto the landing.

The elevator took an eternity to reach the ground floor. Li ran out, down the steps, still limping, and scuffed his way through the snow to the small wooden hut that provided shelter for the security guard.

'You know the American lady?' Li said. 'On the eleventh floor?'

'Sure,' said the guard.

'Did you see her go out tonight?'

'Yeah. She went on her bike.'

'On her bike?' Li could barely believe it. 'Are you sure it was her?'

'Sure I'm sure. The two of them left together. Both on bikes.'

'Two of them?' Li shook his head in consternation. 'What are you talking about?'

The guard was becoming uneasy. 'It was the guy who went up to see her,' he said. 'He stopped here to check that this was the right block. I told him she was on the eleventh floor.'

'Describe him,' Li snapped.

The guard shrugged. 'I don't know. Young, early twenties maybe. Bit scruffy. Looked like a workman.'

'You're going to have to do better than that,' Li said.

The guard made a face. 'I don't know . . .' And then he remembered. 'Oh, yeah. He had a tattoo. On the back of his hand. It was like the head of a snake or something.'

And Li knew straight away that it was Dai Lili's brother. He remembered the sullen-faced boy at Lili's family home, the snake tattoo that twisted round his arm, culminating with the head on the back of his hand. The cellphone on Li's belt rang. He had forgotten it was there. Wu had loaned him his so that he could be contacted at any time. He fumbled to answer it. '*Wei?*'

'Chief?' It was Qian. 'We've got a murder at the Forbidden City. Deputy Tao's on his way.'

'So why are you telling me?' Li was irritated by the interruption. Right now, he was much more concerned about Margaret.

'I thought you'd want to know, Chief. Apparently the whole place has been closed down for renovation work. The company have a night watchman on site. He found the east gate lying open about an hour ago, and half a dozen tracks or more coming in and out. He found the body of a young man with his throat slit in a courtyard outside the Chu Xiu Palace. The night watchman recognised him as one of the workers employed by the company.'

'Why would *I* be interested in this?' Li asked impatiently.

'The dead kid is the brother of the missing athlete, Dai Lili.'

THE DONGHUA GATE was choked with police and forensic vehicles, blue and orange lights strobing in the dark. Several dozen uniformed officers were keeping a growing crowd of curious onlookers at bay.

Li pushed past them and stopped in his tracks. There, leaning against the wall, was Margaret's bicycle, with its distinctive pink ribbon tied to the basket on the handlebars. Another bicycle was propped up a few feet away. Tao and Wu emerged from inside the Forbidden City as he looked up. Tao was surprised to see him.

'What are you doing here, Chief?' he asked coolly.

Li found he could barely speak. He nodded towards the bike with the pink ribbon. 'That's Margaret's bike,' he said. 'Dr Campbell. She left her apartment about two hours ago with Dai Lili's brother.'

'Well, she's not with him now,' Tao said grimly. 'There's just the one body in there.'

'Yeah, but lots of footprints,' Wu said.

'You'd better take a look,' Tao said. His concern appeared genuine.

Li was so shaken he could not even respond. He nodded mutely, and the three men went through the gate into the Forbidden City. The lights had all been turned on, and the roofs and walkways and vast open spaces glowed in the snow.

Fluttering black and yellow tape had been strung between traffic cones to keep investigators from disturbing the tracks left by the players in whatever tragic drama had unfolded here.

Tao said, 'Unfortunately, the night watchman and the security people who originally came in did not take any care over where they put their feet. You can see where their tracks cross the originals. Lucky for us it stopped snowing.'

Li was feeling anything but lucky.

The body of Dai Lili's brother still lay in the courtyard where Margaret and his sister had found it. But the snow had been savagely disturbed. Pathologist Wang stood in hushed conversation with Chief Forensics Officer Fu Qiwei. Wang looked up grimly.

'Multiple stab wounds, Chief. Just like the girl at Jingshan.'

Li glanced at Tao. 'I thought he'd had his throat cut.'

'Oh, sure,' Wang said. 'That's what killed him. The throat was slit left to right. He'd have been dead within two minutes.'

'You said multiple stab wounds,' Li said.

Wang nodded. 'Between thirty and forty of them. You can see where the knives have cut through his clothing. Of course, he was already dead by then, so there was no bleeding from the wounds.'

'Knives?' Li asked. 'Plural?'

'Both from the number of wounds, and the number of prints in the snow, I'd say there were several assailants. At least three.'

'Why would they stab him when he was already dead?' Li said.

'Death by a myriad of swords,' Tao said quietly and Li looked at him. 'Symbolic,' Tao added. 'Like leaving a calling card.'

Li turned to Fu Qiwei. 'What do you think happened here, Fu?'

Fu shrugged. 'It's a matter of interpretation, Chief. It looks like two people arrived here together. One set of prints is smaller than the other. Could be a woman. They went into the palace building there. At least, they stepped up into the shelter of the terrace.'

They followed him into the palace itself, now brightly illuminated. Fu pointed to the packets and tins lying around the floor. 'Someone's been living in here. For several days by the look of it.' He lifted up a pair of track-suit bottoms with his white-gloved hands. 'Probably a woman.' And he retrieved a long black hair as if to prove his point. 'Oddly enough, we also found some of these.' And he took out a plastic evidence bag and held it up to the light so that they could see several long, single, blond hairs. 'So she had company.'

Li's stomach turned over, and he found Tao watching him closely.

'The thing is,' Fu said, 'there's a small heater, but no light.' He paused. 'But we found the remains of a smashed oil lamp on the other side of the square, near the body.' He led them back out onto the steps. 'You can see a single set of footprints heading off across the courtyard here. I figure one of them went inside, the blond, and the other one, the victim, crossed the square where he was jumped by at least three attackers. They cut his throat and, when he was dead, they kneeled round him, stabbing him repeatedly. The two inside heard something, came out with the oil lamp and found the young man lying in the snow. Then they got attacked, too. Now, here's the interesting thing . . .' Li, Tao and Wu followed him across the square. 'There's been a hell of a ruckus here. Broken glass. Melted snow. We found shreds of burned clothing. And this.' He shone his flashlight onto a strange, blackened indentation in the snow. 'Damned if it doesn't look like a face print to me.'

And Li saw, then, the shape of an eye, a mouth, a nose.

'I figure somebody got that lit oil lamp full in the face and got pretty badly burned,' Fu went on. 'Then there was a chase. The three bigger sets of feet running after the two smaller ones, I'd say.'

With a heart like lead, Li followed the forensics man up onto the wide concourse in front of the Qianqing Gate. Tao and Wu walked silently in their wake.

'I guess that the two on the run were probably the women, from the size of their prints. You can clearly see they went first to one of these copper pots, with one set of tracks leading to the other. They must have hidden inside them.'

Li closed his eyes, conjuring a dreadful image of Margaret crouched inside one of these pots in fear and panic.

Fu said, 'With all these lights, we can see their tracks quite clearly. Although it was dark then, I figure their pursuers must have been able to see them, too. The pots were no hiding place at all. You can pick out the other prints that followed them, straight to the pots, and then the scuffles around them where they must have dragged the women out. There's some blood in the snow here.'

Li looked away quickly. 'What happened then?' he whispered.

'They dragged them off,' Fu said. No one had told him that the blonde woman was almost certainly Li's lover. 'Back out to the Donghua Gate. Then probably bundled them into a vehicle.'

Li felt a hand on his arm, and turned to find Tao looking at him, concerned. Li wondered if it was really sympathy he saw in those dark eyes magnified behind thick lenses.

'You OK, Chief?' Tao asked.

Li nodded.

'We'll find her.'

They left Fu and walked back in silence to the Donghua Gate, where Li turned to Wu. 'I want arrest warrants for Fleischer, and Fan Zhilong, the CEO of the OneChina Recreation Club. And also for Coaching Supervisor Cai Xin. I want them held for questioning. Nobody gets to talk to them before me. Understood?'

'You got it, Chief.' Wu hurried off.

Tao walked with Li to his Jeep. He took out a cigarette and offered him one. Li took it without thinking. They stood for nearly a minute, smoking in silence.

'I'm sorry,' Tao said eventually.

'About what?'

'About everything.'

A car pulled in behind Li's Jeep, and the tall, bespectacled figure of Professor Yang stepped out. 'Section Chief?' he called, and as Li and Tao turned, he hurried carefully through the snow towards them. 'I've been trying to reach Margaret for hours. They told me at Section One that you were here. I thought she might be, also.'

Li shook his head.

'Well, then, I should pass the information on to you.'

'I don't really have time just now, Professor.'

'I think it could be important. I know Margaret thought it was.'

It was enough to catch Li's attention. 'What?'

She asked me this morning if I knew anyone who could perform a genetic analysis on a sample of blood that she had taken from the swimmer she autopsied.'

'Sui Mingshan?'

'That's him. Well, I took her up to see my friend at the College of Biogenic Science, Professor Xu. Margaret wanted him to analyse the sample to see if he could find any evidence of genetic disorder. She didn't confide in me, but I know she was hoping for more than that.'

'And what did Professor Xu find?' Li asked.

'Oh, he found something,' Yang said. 'But not a genetic disorder. Genetically modified HERV. Human endogenous retrovirus.'

'Retrovirus. Margaret told me about that. It's in our DNA.'

'Endogenous,' Yang said, 'means it's something produced from within us. These HERV, they're in all of us. The viral remnants of primeval diseases. No longer harmful to us, but although they are dormant, some scientists believe that they can be activated—'

'By a virus,' Li said, remembering Margaret's spoken thoughts.

Yang smiled. 'Yes,' he said. 'Viruses could do it. There could be other factors. But the point is that, once activated, it is possible that they could be responsible for some very dangerous human diseases.'

Li began to see a glimmer of light. 'Like thickening of the microvasculature of the heart?'

'Yes, yes, I suppose so.'

Li said, 'And you're saying someone has . . . genetically modified these HERV?'

'It appears that some of them had been removed from our swimmer, modified in some way, and then put back.'

'Why?'

Yang shrugged his shoulders. 'I have no idea, Section Chief. And neither has Professor Xu.' He raised his eyebrows. 'But I have an idea that Margaret might.'

Li said grimly, 'If I knew where she was I'd ask her.'

Yang frowned, but he had no chance to ask.

'Thank you,' Li said, and he tapped Tao's arm and nodded towards the Jeep. 'Get in.'

Tao looked surprised. 'Where are we going?'

'Detective Sun's apartment.'

THE VAN LURCHED and bounced over a frozen, rutted track. From the rear of it, where Margaret and Lili had been tied hand and foot and forced to sit with their backs to the door, Margaret could see headlights raking a grim winter landscape. She was racked by pain now, and knew she was in serious trouble. She felt blood, hot and wet, between her legs, and every bone-jarring pitch of the van provoked a fresh fork of cramp in her belly. Lili was absolutely silent, but Margaret could feel her fear.

The only sound during their journey was the whimpering of the man Margaret had set on fire. He lay curled up in the back, within touching distance, wrapped in a blanket.

After they had dragged her from the copper pot, they had pushed her to the ground and kicked her until she thought they were going to kill her there and then. She had curled into a foetal position to try to protect her baby. They did not care that she was pregnant. Eventually they had dragged the two women to the Donghua Gate and bundled them into the back of the waiting van. Margaret thought they must have been on the road for more than an hour and a half since then.

Finally the van juddered to a halt and the driver and his passenger opened the doors and jumped down. After a moment the back doors were thrown open, and Margaret and Lili nearly fell out into the snow. Rough hands grabbed them and pulled them out into the freezing night. Margaret was bruised and aching, and the joints in her legs had seized up. She could barely stand. The two men crouched in the snow to untie their feet, and they were led through a gate, along a winding path to the door of a cottage.

The door was unlocked and the two women were pushed through it into a small sitting room. One of the men flicked a switch, and a harsh yellow light flooded the room. Two chairs with woven straw seats were brought in and Margaret and Lili were forced to sit in them, side by side. Their feet were tied again, and their hands untied and then retied to the backs of the chairs.

The men had an urgent conversation in low voices, and one of them went outside to make a call on his cellphone. After a few minutes, he returned and waved his friend to follow him. The second man switched off the light as he left. Margaret and Lili heard the engine of the van coughing into life before driving off.

It was some minutes before Margaret found the ability to speak. 'What did they say?' she asked.

'They take their friend for medical treatment. The one who is burnt. The driver talk to someone on the phone who say they will be here soon.' Lili's voice sounded very small.

The ropes were cutting into Margaret's wrists and ankles, but she knew there was no chance of freeing them. They sat, then, in silence for what seemed like hours but may have been no more than fifteen minutes. And then Lili began sobbing, softly, uncontrollably. Margaret closed her eyes and felt her own tears burn hot tracks down her cheeks. They were more for her lost child than for herself.

After another ten minutes, they heard the distant purr of a motor. As it grew closer, Margaret's fear increased. She tried hard to free her hands, but only succeeded in burning the skin.

They heard three car doors bang shut. Footsteps crunched in the snow, and Margaret turned her head towards the door as it opened.

The overhead light, when it came on, nearly blinded her, and a man she recognised as Dr Hans Fleischer walked in. He beamed at the two women, then focused his gaze on Margaret.

'Dr Campbell, I presume,' he said. 'Welcome to my humble abode.' His English was almost accentless.

Another man came in behind him. Chinese, much younger, immaculately dressed.

'I don't believe you know Mr Fan, my generous benefactor,' Fleischer said. 'But he knows all about you.'

The CEO of the Beijing OneChina Recreation Club smiled, dimpling his cheeks. But he appeared tense and did not speak.

Margaret became aware that a third man had entered. She craned her neck to look at him, and for a moment hope burned in her heart. It was Detective Sun. But the flame quickly died. He could not even meet her eye. And she knew that he was one of the bad guys, too.

Chapter Eleven

An armed guard, fur collar turned up on a long green coat, glanced impassively at Li and Tao as Li turned his Jeep through the back entrance of the Ministry of State and Public Security.

Li took a right along the front of the apartment blocks allocated to junior public security officers and their families, then pulled in outside the third block along. He and Tao got out and took the elevator to the seventh floor. From the window on the landing, Li could see the lights from his apartment in the senior officers' block, and knew that his father was waiting for him there. He had not seen him for forty-eight hours.

Tao knocked loudly on Sun's door, and after a few moments Wen opened it. There were dark rings beneath her eyes and red blotches on pale cheeks. She did not appear surprised to see them.

'He's not here,' she said dully.

'May we come in?' Li asked.

She led them mutely through to a living room with a terrace.

'Where is he?' Li asked.

She shook her head. 'I have no idea.'

He looked at her contemplatively for a moment. 'Why did you start crying when I phoned earlier?'

She sucked in her lower lip and bit down on it. 'I never know where he is,' she said, her voice breaking. 'I've hardly seen him since I got here.' She threw her hand out in a gesture towards the packing cases stacked against one wall. 'I've had to do all this myself. We haven't had a meal together in days. He doesn't get in until two or three in the morning.' And she couldn't stop the sobs from catching in her throat. 'Just like it was in Canton. Nothing's changed.'

'How was it in Canton?'

She brushed aside fresh tears. 'He was always out. More than half the night sometimes.' She breathed deeply to try to control herself. 'He was a gambler, Section Chief. He loved it. Couldn't ever let a bet go.' She paused. 'He ran up terrible debts. We had to sell nearly everything. And then, when he got the job here, I thought maybe it would be a fresh start. He promised me . . . for the baby.' She shook her head helplessly. 'But nothing's changed. He behaves so strangely. I don't know him any more. I'm not sure I ever did.'

Li was both shocked and dismayed by her description of a man he thought he knew, the detective he had been nurturing and encouraging. What shocked him even more was how badly he had misjudged him. He glanced at Tao. Had he also been as wrong about his deputy?

Tao said to Wen, 'You say Sun Xi's been behaving strangely. How?'

She threw her hands up in despair. 'I found a piece of paper in one of his jacket pockets. It had a poem written on it. Some stupid poem that didn't make sense. When I asked him about it he went berserk. He snatched it from me and accused me of spying on him. I found it a couple of days later between the pages of a book on his bedside table.'

'Is it still there?' Li asked.

She nodded. 'I'll get it.'

She returned a few moments later, with a grubby sheet of paper folded into quarters, well rubbed along the folds. She thrust it at Li. He and Tao leaned over it. The poem was written in neat characters and, as Wen had said, appeared to make very little sense.

We walk in the green mountains, small paths, valleys and bays,
The streams from the high hills are heard murmuring. Hundreds of birds keep on singing in the remote mountains.
It is hard for a man to walk ten thousand Li.
You are advised not to be a poor traveller
Who guards Kwan Shan every night, suffering from hunger and cold.
Everyone said he would visit the peak of Wa Shan.
I will travel around all eight mountains of Wa Shan.

Li was completely nonplussed 'It's not much of a poem,' he said.

Tao said quietly, 'None of the Triad poems are.'

Li blinked at him, confused now. 'What do you mean?'

'It's a tradition that has mostly passed from use,' Tao said. 'Members are given personal poems to memorise. They can be interrogated on them to verify their identification. They are supposed to destroy them once they have been memorised.'

Wen was listening to their exchange with growing disbelief. 'What do you mean? Are you telling me Sun Xi is a Triad? I don't believe it.'

Tao looked at Li and shrugged. 'Canton was one of the first areas in mainland China the Triads moved back into after the Hong Kong handover. If Sun had got himself into financial trouble with gambling, he would have been a prime candidate for Triad recruitment. And a feather in their caps, too—a detective in criminal investigation.'

'Even more so now,' Li said. 'Now that he's an elite member of Beijing's Serious Crime Squad.' He felt sick. He had been succouring the cuckoo in the nest, his personal dislike of Tao leading him to look in all the wrong places. He was almost unable to meet his deputy's eye. 'I guess I owe you an apology,' he said.

'What are you talking about!' Wen was nearly hysterical. 'He's not a Triad! He can't be a Triad!'

Tao paid her no attention. He said to Li, 'Apologies are not what's important now, Chief. Finding Dr Campbell is.'

A SMALL LAMP on a table somewhere close by cast the only light in the room. Fleischer had switched off the ceiling light.

Margaret was having trouble concentrating. She was gripped by almost unbearable cramps every few minutes, and feared that she was going to give birth right there, still tied to the chair.

Fleischer was oblivious to her distress, and she had the impression that he was showing off to her, preening himself before someone who might just recognise his genius. He seemed oblivious to the others in the room.

'We selected seven all told,' he was saying, 'making sure we represented the major disciplines: sprinting, distance running, a swimmer, a weightlifter, a cyclist. Each of them was in the top half-dozen in their respective sports, but not necessarily gold medal winners.'

'And what did you do to them?' Margaret said. She pushed her head back and forced herself to focus on him.

'I made them better,' he said proudly. 'I produced the first genetically modified winners in the history of athletics. Human engineering.' He paused, and grinned. 'You want to know how I did it?'

And Margaret did. In spite of her pain and her predicament. But she was damned if she was going to let Fleischer know it.

'Of course you do,' he said. He drew a chair out of the darkness and into the circle of light, turning it round so he could sit astride the seat and lean on its back, watching Margaret closely as he spoke. 'All the drugs that these idiot athletes around the globe are still using to improve their performances are synthetic. All they can ever do is emulate what the body does of its own accord in the world's best natural athletes, using real testosterone and human growth hormone to build muscle and strength, and endogenous erythropoietin—a hormone known as EPO—to feed oxygen to tired muscles. That's what makes winners. That's what makes champions.' He shrugged. 'So I do two things. First, I program the body to produce naturally what it needs. If you run fast I increase the testosterone. If you run long, I increase the EPO. If you lift weights, I increase the growth hormone. And second, in case they want to test you, I program your body to destroy the excess.'

Margaret gasped as another cramp gripped her, and she wondered fleetingly if Fleischer thought she was perhaps gasping in admiration. 'How?' she managed to ask.

'Ah,' Fleischer said. 'The sixty-four thousand dollar question. In this case, perhaps, the sixty-four *million* dollar question.'

Margaret dug her fingernails into her palms to stop herself from passing out. With a great effort she said, 'Well?'

The German chuckled. 'HERV,' he said.

Margaret frowned. 'HERV?

'You know what HERV is?'

'Of course.'

He was positively gleeful. 'It is so deliciously simple, Doctor. Human endogenous retroviruses comprise about one per cent of the human genome. I chose the HERV-K variant, because it is known to carry functional genes. It was an easy enough matter to isolate pieces of HERV-K from blood samples, and then amplify those pieces by cloning them in a bacterium. Are you following me?'

'Just about.' Margaret's voice was no more than a whisper.

'I was then able to modify the cloned HERV, embedding in it genes with a unique promoter that would stimulate hormone production. In some cases the promoter would stimulate the athlete's body to produce increased amounts of testosterone, or human growth hormone. In others it would stimulate increased quantities of EPO.' He leaned further into the light. 'Did you know that EPO can increase performance by up to fourteen per cent? It gives an athlete a phenomenal edge.'

In spite of everything, Margaret found the concept fascinating as well as horrifying. But there were still gaps in her understanding. 'But how? How did you make it work?'

He laughed. 'Also simple. I reinfected them with their own HERV. A straightforward injection, and the modified retrovirus carried the new genes straight into the chromosome.'

Margaret shook her head. 'But if suddenly these athletes are creating excesses of whatever hormone it is you've programmed them to produce, they would OD on it. It would kill them.'

Fleischer was amused by this. 'You must think I am incredibly stupid, Doctor.'

'Stupid is not the word I would have used to describe you,' she said, working hard to maintain eye contact.

His smile faded. 'I'll keep it simple for you,' he snapped. 'The genes can be switched off and on. One chemical activates the gene. Another switches it off. And a second HERV, activated by a third chemical, will literally munch up the excess hormone. It can be activated at a moment's notice so that the presence of increased hormone in the system is undetectable.'

Margaret let another wave of pain wash over her, and then tried to refocus. 'So you engineered these athletes to produce, within themselves, whatever hormone would best enhance their particular discipline. And you also gave them the ability to flush it out of their system at a moment's notice, so they could never be accused of doping.'

'Makes it sound devilishly simple when you put it like that. Don't you want to know how they were able to switch the hormone producing genes off and on?'

'I've already worked that one out,' Margaret said.

'Have you?' Fleischer sounded a little disappointed.

'The bottles of aftershave, and perfume.'

His smile was a little less amused. She had stolen his thunder. 'You're a very clever lady, aren't you, Dr Campbell? Yes, the aerosols act like a gas. The athlete only has to spray and inhale, and the unique chemical content of each scent sends the requisite message to the appropriate gene. Hormone on, hormone off.'

'And the breath freshener?'

'Triggers the destructive protease to chew up the excess hormone.' He straightened up in his seat and beamed at her triumphantly.

From the depths of her misery, Margaret gazed at him with something close to hatred. 'So what went wrong?'

And his face darkened, and all his self-congratulatory preening dissolved in an instant. 'I don't know,' he said. 'Well, not exactly. There was some kind of recombination between the introduced and endogenous HERV. It created a new retrovirus which attacked the microscopic arteries of the heart. Our cyclist dropped dead without warning. The last thing we wanted was anyone performing an autopsy, so we arranged for him to die "by accident". The body was removed from its coffin before it was burned at the crematorium, and then we were free to perform our own examination. We discovered the thickening of the microvasculature.'

'And you *knew* that your retrovirus had caused that?'

'No, not immediately. It wasn't until the three members of the sprint relay team became ill after coming down with the flu, that I began to piece things together. An autopsy on one of them, after he had been "cremated", confirmed all my fears.'

'So you decided to get rid of the rest of your guinea-pigs before someone else started figuring it all out?'

Fan Zhilong moved into the light. 'The risks were too great. We could not afford to have any of our athletes panic and start to talk.'

Margaret looked at him with disgust. 'And you funded all this?' He inclined his head in acknowledgment. 'Why?'

'Why? Because I am a gambler, Dr Campbell. We are all gamblers here. And like all gamblers, we spend our lives in pursuit of the impossible. The sure thing.'

'Only there *is* no such thing as a *sure* thing, is there, Dr Fleischer?' Margaret turned her contempt on the German doctor.

Fleischer gave her a long, sour look, and then he eased himself out of his chair and stood up. 'I'll get it right next time,' he said.

'I'm afraid there won't be a next time,' Fan said. Fleischer turned towards him in surprise as Fan drew a small pistol from inside his jacket and fired point blank into the old man's face.

Lili screamed as Fleischer momentarily staggered backwards. Then he dropped to his knees and fell face forward onto the floor.

Fan stepped back fastidiously to avoid getting Fleischer's blood on his shoes. He looked at Margaret. 'The police are far too close to the truth,' he said. 'We have to remove *all* the evidence.' And he raised his gun towards Margaret and fired again.

Margaret screwed up her face, but felt nothing but the ear-splitting sound of the second shot ringing in the confined space. There was a moment of silence and confusion, and then she opened her eyes in time to see Lili crashing to the floor, still tied to her chair.

Margaret started to lose control. She just wanted it all to be over. But Fan was in no particular hurry.

'I suppose your boyfriend is going to wonder what happened to you,' he said softly. 'Maybe he'll think you just changed your mind about getting married and took off back to America. But he'll never find you. So he'll never know.' He turned to Sun, who was still hovering just beyond the reach of the light. 'You do it.'

Without meeting her eye, Sun slipped a gun from under his leather jacket and raised it unsteadily towards Margaret.

She looked straight at him, the tears running down her face. 'At least have the guts to look me in the eye, Sun Xi,' she said. 'I hope your child, when he is born, will be proud of you.' She gasped, struggling to control herself. 'And I hope every time you look him in the eye you'll see me. And remember my child.'

'Get on with it!' Fan snapped impatiently.

And Sun turned and put a bullet straight through the centre of Fan's forehead. He was dead before he hit the floor.

Sun turned back to Margaret. He shook his head. And through

her own tears, she saw that he was weeping, too. 'I never knew it be like this,' he said pathetically. 'I sorry. I so sorry.' He raised his gun again and Margaret closed her eyes. The roar of the shot filled her head, and when she looked again he was lying on the floor. Four dead people lying all around her, and a pain that gripped her so powerfully that all she wanted to do was join them.

LI WAS EXHAUSTED by the time he and Tao got back to Section One. He was closer to despair than he had ever been in his life. Closer to simply giving up. It all seemed so hopeless. It was two, maybe three hours since Margaret had been taken from the Forbidden City. The chances of her still being alive were so remote he could not even contemplate them. His office felt bleak and empty.

Tao said, 'I'll get some tea and check on developments.' And he left Li to slump into his chair.

On top of his in-tray was a faxed report from Dr Pi. In the sample of Jia Jing's hair, he had found a record of abnormal concentrations of human growth hormone. It was the real thing, produced by Jing's own body. But it hardly mattered now that Li knew why the athletes' heads had been shaved. That somehow they had produced concentrations of endogenous hormone to enhance their performance. And that someone had cut off their hair to hide that fact. Without Margaret, nothing mattered. Li let the report fall back into the tray.

Which was when Li saw the envelope in the internal mail tray, its public security emblem embossed on the flap, and he knew that it came from the Commissioner's office. Wearily he lifted it from the tray and tore it open. It was acknowledgment of receipt of his letter of resignation—so it had reached the Commissioner after all—and confirmation that he was relieved of all duties with immediate effect. Deputy Section Chief Tao was to assume control of the section.

Tao came in, then, with two mugs of steaming hot green tea, and put one of them down in front of Li. His eye fell on the letter, and he glanced at his old boss.

Li shrugged. 'I guess you're the chief now.'

Tao said, 'Apparently the Commissioner's office has been trying to contact me.' He grimaced. 'There was a letter on my desk, too.'

A flushed-looking Qian hurried in. 'Chief, we just got a report from the Public Security Bureau out at Miyun that residents of Guanling reported hearing gunfire from a cottage just outside the village. Guanling is where Fleischer has his holiday cottage.'

Hope and fear filled Li's heart as the implications of Qian's words hit home. He looked at Tao, who sighed, resigned.

'I could say I didn't open the letter till tomorrow,' he said.

Li was on his feet immediately. 'I want every available detective,' he said to Qian. 'Armed. I'll sign out the weapons.'

AS THEY DROVE through the village in convoy, a few shreds of light momentarily illuminated the snow-capped mountains beyond. There were lights in nearly every window, and dozens of villagers were standing out on the frozen track. Through a clutch of evergreens, they saw the blue flashing lights of the local police, who had surrounded the cottage but had been instructed not to enter.

The local bureau chief shook Li's hand when they arrived. 'There hasn't been a sound or a movement from in there since we got here, Chief,' he said in a low voice. He nodded towards a sleek, shiny black Mercedes parked at the gate and took out a notebook. 'I got them to phone in the number. It's registered to'—he found the name—'some guy called Fan Zhilong.'

Li felt a tightness across his chest. He was not surprised, but that did nothing to diminish his sense of dread. He waved Wu and Sang to the far side of the gate. Tao and Qian followed him to the nearside gatepost, and they all took out their weapons. Li started along the path, and signalled the others to follow.

They reached the house, and Li gingerly tried the door handle. It turned easily and the door slipped soundlessly off the latch. He nodded to the others, and after the briefest hesitation, they burst in, gun barrels panning left and right to cover the room. There were four bodies on the floor, and a sickening amount of blood. Sun, Fan and Fleischer, and Dai Lili, still tied to the chair, tipped on her side. It was all Li could do to stop himself from being sick.

His eyes raked across the carnage before coming to rest on a figure slumped in a chair. It was a moment before he realised that it was Margaret. Her face was ghostly pale, her head lying at an angle, mouth gaping. She was soaked in blood from the waist down, and with an awful sense of the inevitable, Li knew that she was dead.

SOMETHING OUT THERE was trying to get in. It was light, and it was pain, all at once. And then it was blinding her, coming from beyond the protective cover of her eyelids as they broke apart to allow the outside in. Still the world was a blur. Only her pain was focused.

Somewhere down there. She made an effort and felt her hand move towards her belly. The swelling was gone. Her baby was no longer there. Only the pain remained. And it bubbled up to explode in her throat, a deep howl of anguish.

Immediately, she felt a hand on her forehead. She turned her head and a shadow fell across her tear-filled eyes. She blinked hard and saw Li's poor, bruised face swim into focus.

'My baby . . .' Her voice tailed away. 'I lost my baby . . .'

'No,' she heard him say, inexplicably, and she fought to make sense of this world that was crashing in on her. She was in a room. Pastel pink. A window. And Li. 'Our child is fine,' he was saying, smiling his reassurance. 'They cut you open. A Caesarian section. It was the only way to save the baby.'

Margaret managed a nod. 'Where is it?'

'Not "it".' He paused for emphasis. '*He*.' And there was no doubting the pride in his smile. 'We have a baby boy, Margaret.'

And from outside the limits of her conscious reach came the tiny sound of a baby crying, and she forced herself to look beyond Li, and saw her mother there with a swaddle of soft wool and cotton in her arms. She leaned over and laid the bundle beside Margaret on the bed. And Margaret turned to see her son for the first time. A pink, wrinkled little face, crying hard to let them know he was alive.

She heard her mother's voice. 'He looks just like his father. But then all babies are ugly.'

And finally Margaret was able to laugh.

Her mother was smiling.

Margaret whispered, 'You don't mind having a Chinese grandson?'

'You know, it's strange,' her mother said. 'I don't see him as Chinese. Just my grandson.'

IT HAD STOPPED SNOWING when Li stepped from the door of the hospital into the deserted car park. The first grey light of dawn smudged the sky in the east and the clouds had lifted. The day seemed less threatening, somehow, less dark. Like life. Li no longer needed his stick. He felt free. Of responsibility, of fear. He was suffused by an overwhelming sense of happiness as he crunched carefully over the frozen snow towards his Jeep. But through all his euphoria, one tiny, nagging doubt came bubbling up from somewhere in the darkness.

A picture started replaying itself in his head. He saw himself sitting in his office with Tao and Qian, discussing the break-in at the studio of the American photographer. Qian was saying, *He'd been there on a recce the day before, and taken a few pictures. Nothing that you would think anyone would want to steal.*

And Tao responded, *Well, that's something we'll never know, since he no longer has them.*

Oh, but he has, Qian came back at him. *Apparently he'd already taken a set of contact prints. He's still got those.*

Li unlocked the Jeep and climbed in. Sun had not been there. So how could he have known about the contact prints?

Suddenly, a hand curled round his forehead and forced it back with a jolt against the headrest, holding it there like a vice. And he felt the sharp blade of a knife piercing the skin of his neck. He froze, knowing that any attempt to free himself would kill him.

He heard the hot breath of Tao's voice in his ear. 'Sooner or later,' Tao said, 'I knew you would figure it out. You arrogant bastard. You thought that Sun was your protégé, your boy. But he was mine. Right from the start. Always.' He issued a small, sour laugh. 'And now we both know it, and you have to die.'

Li sensed the muscles in Tao's arm tensing. He glanced in the rearview mirror, and saw Tao's face, eyes wide behind the dark frames of his glasses. He felt the blade cutting into his flesh. And then a roar that almost deafened him. Glass and smoke and blood filled the air. And Tao was gone. Li was aware of blood running down his neck and put his fingers to the wound, but it was barely a scratch. He turned to see Tao sprawled across the rear seat.

And into his confusion crashed a voice he knew. He turned, still in shock, and saw a face. A jaw chewing on a flavourless piece of gum.

'Shit, Chief,' Wu said. 'I only came to see how Doc Campbell and the baby were. I'd have handed in the gun last night, only you weren't there to sign for it.' He looked at Tao with disgust. 'Bastard,' he said, with something like relish in his voice. 'At least I won't have to put any more money in the swear box.'

PETER MAY

At twenty-one, Peter May won the Scottish Young Journalist of the Year Award; just four years later, his first novel was published. Since then he has gone on to become one of Scotland's most successful and prolific television dramatists, creating several major television series, among them *The Standard* and *Squadron*.

In the mid eighties, while on a visit to Hong Kong, he decided to take a day trip to China. It was a decision that would change his life. 'I was absolutely blown away by the place,' May remembers. He resolved that one day China would be the setting for a new novel, and that he would go back there to research it.

However, it wasn't until 1996 that May was able to set aside his television commitments and return to China. By then he was clear about his objectives and his storyline. 'I wanted to show people China as it is today, and I thought it would be great to bring somebody from the West and put them in a Chinese setting where both sides were learning and sparking off one another.' The result was the winning combination of Li Yan, a Beijing detective, and Margaret Campbell, a Chicago pathologist—first brought to life in May's novel *The Firemaker* (1999).

Through the character of Li Yan, May aimed to give an unprecedented close-up view of the Chinese police. 'I was very fortunate because I made contact with an American criminologist who had visited China many times and who had trained the top five hundred police officers there. He gave me introductions that really, as an outsider, I could never have achieved.'

May has since returned to China every year and is amazed by the generosity he has been shown and the changes he has seen. He is now an honorary member of the Chinese Crime Writers' Association and a Chinese production company are negotiating for the television rights of his first four 'China thrillers'. The author was delighted to see *The Runner,* the fifth in the series, featured in a recent *China Daily* weekend supplement. 'The Chinese love crime fiction. Thousands of policemen write crime stories and young detectives are encouraged to attend courses in western detective fiction.'

the cruellest miles

The heroic story of dogs and men in a race against an epidemic

Gay Salisbury & Laney Salisbury

With temperatures at 50° below zero, 'Wild Bill' Shannon and his nine-dog crew headed out into the night and a ferocious blizzard. He was the first of a relay of courageous drivers and their dog sleds who were attempting to reach the isolated Alaskan outpost of Nome.

As they battled their way across one of the most forbidding and dangerous landscapes on earth, they were driven on by the knowledge that the fate of the whole town lay in their hands.

Prologue

'We are prisoners in a jail of ice and snow. The last boat may be justifiably considered to have gone and this little community is left to its own resources, alone with the storms, alone with the darkness and chill of the North.'

Nome Chronicle

Curtis Welch was the only doctor for hundreds of miles along this forgotten edge of the Bering Sea, and for the past eighteen years he had watched winter descend suddenly, as it tends to do up in the far north. There were just two seasons here, they said: winter and the Fourth of July. Winters were at least seven months long in Nome, and the other seasons came and went within a few short weeks.

From July to October, the Bering Sea was free of ice and the town was open to steamboats and schooners that sailed in from Seattle, the closest major port, about 2,400 miles and fourteen days away to the south. By early November, the Bering Sea would be frozen over and the light nearly drained from the sky. The *Victoria*, usually the first passenger ship to arrive in spring and the last to leave in the fall, would have unloaded its cargo and headed south, leaving the town cut off from the world save for one route: a dog-sled trail that linked the town to the interior of Alaska.

The unrelenting cold came on suddenly and violently, with blizzards that lasted for days and brought about an extreme isolation that could sap the determination of the hardiest soul. Each fall, nearly half the town's population left aboard the last ships of the season and stayed away until spring. And yet Curtis Welch stayed behind. He had done so each year, except once when he left on a short stint to work as a stateside doctor during the Great War. Welch had fallen for Alaska from the moment he arrived in 1907, and his fondness had grown over the years. He was fifty now, the golden blond hair white, standing up in shocks. He looked forward to the town's annual exodus, and to his solitude.

At any time of year, Nome was a distant place, a speck on the map of America's last frontier, that vast territory of Alaska stretching out over nearly 600,000 square miles. At one end, in the southeast, were the capital, Juneau, and the territory's year-round ice-free ports. At the other end, to the northwest, was Nome. In all its parts, Alaska defied exaggeration. To the west, active volcanoes spewed smoke over a rugged north Pacific coast, and to the east, glaciers the size of Rhode Island hovered over fjords. In the interior, the heart of the territory, North America's tallest peak, Mount McKinley, reached up through the clouds over an endless expanse of timber.

In the early 1920s, Nome was the northwesternmost city in North America, a former gold-rush boom town that had lost its glitter. It sat two degrees south of the Arctic Circle on the southern shore of the Seward Peninsula, a windswept fist of land that jutted 200 miles out into the Bering Sea. It was closer to Siberia than to any other major town in Alaska, and a little farther north, on a clear day one could see across the Bering Strait to Russia.

From the second floor of his modest corner apartment above the Miners & Merchants Bank on Front Street, Welch and his wife Lula had front-row seats to the town's winter preparations. The *Victoria* was gone and the last ship of the fall season of 1924, the *Alameda*, sailed in with the town's winter supplies. It sat heavy in the water a mile and a half off the coast, as near as a ship could get to shore without running aground. Nome had neither dock nor safe harbour, and the lighters and launches had to manoeuvre through the surf and out to the great ship before turning back to shore with their precious cargo.

On Front Street, which ran parallel to the sea, gangs of Eskimo longshoremen unloaded the cargo, which they stacked up along the waterfront and readied for storage. There were boxes of fruit and frozen turkeys, mountains of coal and crates of butter and tea. The work went on all day and into the night. Horse carriages and wheelbarrows moved down Front Street to the hulking wooden warehouses along the shore of the Snake River on the west side of town. There was room enough to store supplies for Nome's 1,400-odd residents, as well as for many of the 10,000 other Alaskans living in the scattered villages and small mining camps of the Seward Peninsula and beyond.

The town had become the region's commercial hub, and many Alaskans travelled here through the winter to buy everything from hardware to curtains and coal. If they took ill, they ended up in the care of Welch and his four nurses at Maynard Columbus Hospital, which had twenty-five beds and was the best-equipped medical institution in northwestern Alaska.

Front Street was never busier than in the days before the last ship sailed out. Its wooden planks creaked and its sidewalks sagged from the human traffic that headed down to the waterfront.

Children came home from the tundra with buckets filled with the last of the season's wild berries; these would be turned into preserves or, better still, into cordials, which were technically illegal since Prohibition was the law of the land. Miners who had spent the summer prospecting for gold in the hills beyond Nome returned in knee-high rubber boots and woollen breeches and waited in the hotels and coffee shops to ship out. Those who stayed behind traded in their boots for warm, waterproof native footwear called mukluks.

Nome's permanent Eskimo population lived a mile and a half west of town on a sandbar across the mouth of the Snake River called the Sandspit, and they readied for winter as they had for centuries. Those without jobs as labourers in Nome travelled down the Bering coast with their nets to fish for a last batch of salmon or char, and the women would go to work with their curved steel knives, or *ulus*, and hang the fish up on drying racks to cure in the cold sea air.

If they came upon a seal on one of their frequent trips up north, they would shoot it, load it onto their wide, skin-covered boats (*umiaks*), and, after a rough ride over the waves, bring it home. There it would be skinned to make mukluks, and its blubber would be cut, eaten or rendered into oil for food or fuel.

WINTER WOULD BE LATE this year but the pace nevertheless quickened on Front Street and along the waterfront and in the shops. Men hammered loose boards into place and lashed down the buildings, anchoring them against the wind. The Moon Springs Water Company turned off the town's only plumbing, two crude pipes running down from Anvil Creek. Holes in the wall were patched up in preparation for the blizzards, and the surfmen from the local US Coast Guard station prepared to move down to the beach to haul up Nome's fleet of skiffs, schooners and lighters.

The Arctic ice pack was inching ever closer to the narrow Bering Strait and ice was forming along the shores of the Bering Sea. The sea became 'an ocean of slush rolling ponderously up on the sands, crashing and splattering an icy enamel on everything it touched', said naturalist Frank Dufresne, a town resident.

On the deck of the *Alameda,* the captain knew he would have to retreat south soon or risk being crushed by the encroaching ice. It was time to batten down the crates and send out a clear message: get on board or stay behind for the winter.

When the sound of the whistle echoed across the shore, the last lighter raced out to the ship, picked up its cargo and returned to shore. Black smoke rose from the *Alameda*'s stacks as it built a head of steam, and the anchor went up. Finally, the bow of the ship began its slow turn southwards and all of Nome took a deep breath.

They were on their own, at least until spring.

'It seemed to me that half of the people of Nome had managed to stow aboard the old steamer,' said Dufresne. 'I had the feeling of being deserted on an ice floe . . . It was the worst day I ever spent in Alaska.'

In a few weeks the tundra's rivers and creeks would freeze and the frozen surface would become smooth and transparent. In town, hoar-frost would coat every object, and out on the Bering Sea the waves would flatten out as the sea turned into thickening sheets of ice that might stretch as far south as the Pribilof Islands, 550 miles away.

As the weeks passed, the sun would sink lower beneath the horizon and the fields of ice and snow would be transformed from the purest white to a wash of gold and then to a violet twilight. The days were shorter now, just four hours of sunlight, and the temperatures plunged. Then the blizzards descended, choking gusts of snow that one resident said draws 'the breath out of you, then fills your nostrils and drives it back again down your throat'.

It was as if the Great Ice Age had returned.

DR WELCH HAD GONE through his checklist more than once in the final days before the *Alameda* left that fall. While most of the medical supplies he needed had arrived safely, one item was missing. Earlier that year, in the summer of 1924, Welch had noticed that the supply of diphtheria antitoxin had expired, and he had made a point of ordering up a fresh batch through the health commissioner's office in Juneau. In all his eighteen years practising medicine on the Seward Peninsula, he had not seen a single confirmed case of diphtheria. There was only the slimmest chance that he would ever need the antitoxin, yet he could never be too sure.

But now the waterfront was silent, and Welch reckoned that the order had either been ignored or misplaced. He would have to do without until next spring.

AT ABOUT THE TIME the *Alameda* left town, an Eskimo family with four children arrived from Holy Cross, a village near the mouth of the Yukon River. The youngest child, a two-year-old, had taken ill and refused to eat. When Welch examined the toddler he found him 'very much depleted and emaciated', and noticed that he had extremely foul breath. The mother told Welch that the child had been treated for tonsillitis in Holy Cross, but the diagnosis hardly explained his weakened state. Welch asked the parents whether other children in their village had tonsillitis or severe sore throats—symptoms that resembled those of diphtheria. The parents assured him they had not.

To Welch's relief the child's three siblings appeared healthy, and he set aside his concerns; diphtheria was highly contagious, and if the siblings were infected they would have shown clear symptoms. He guessed the child might be suffering from a less severe infection.

'Many cases have come under my observation in these eighteen years that looked very suspicious, but time had always before proved that they were one of the various forms of inflammatory diseases of the throat,' Welch would note in his medical records.

By the following morning, the child was dead.

Gold, Men and Dogs

There were few worse places on earth to build a town, but Nome had gone up almost overnight after two Swedes and a Norwegian found a nugget the size of a small rock in a creek near the beach. The men came to be known as the 'Three Lucky Swedes', and their discovery in 1898 would set off a stampede.

Nome was not the first town in the far north to have sprung into life on the prospects of finding gold. In the summer of 1896, prospectors had found gold in a creek near the Klondike River, just east of the Alaskan border in Canada's Yukon Territory. The Klondike was a rich find, and newspapers and magazines ran sensational stories about the millions of dollars in placer gold discovered there. Invariably, they failed to list the perils of northern travel. Of the more than 100,000 men and women who set off from all over the world on the months-long trek, fewer than 30,000 would reach Dawson City, the boom town that served as a gateway to the Klondike gold field. Fewer still would strike it rich.

But gold mining was a powerful addiction and, even with the odds stacked against them, prospectors kept coming to the Klondike. Then, in the winter of 1898, word travelled to the region that gold had been discovered on the Seward Peninsula, clear across Alaska, a distance of 800 miles as the raven flies. Thousands of prospectors in the Klondike district decided to abandon their barren claims and make their way to the next shining prospect.

Several hundred miners arrived in Nome in the winter of 1898. How many didn't make it or turned back will never be known. What is clear is that those who did arrive were mostly tough and experienced trail veterans and prospectors. They were known as 'sourdoughs', because they often kept a supply of yeast in crocks held close to their chests. This was used to make bread on the trail and it ensured that the miner would never go hungry.

During the winter of 1898–99, the sourdoughs settled along Anvil Creek, some five miles up from the beach where the Lucky Swedes had discovered gold. When the ice on the Bering Sea melted that summer, a new group of prospectors from the states began arriving by boat. Before long over 1,000 more had set up their tents in what was then known as the Cape Nome Mining District. The sourdoughs called the new arrivals 'cheechakoes', a combination of native Indian words meaning 'newcomer'.

Early that summer, an ageing Idaho prospector named John Hummel decided to try out his luck on the beach. He talked a younger man into doing the physical work for him, and soon the beach was yielding $100 a day. The news went out that Nome's beaches were made of gold and that there were enough nuggets for anyone who could bend down and pick one up. Gold, they said, came in with the tide. Geologists would later discover that there had been only a limited supply of 'Hummel's gold' on the beach, trace deposits left in the sand by aeons of erosion. The real gold lay in the creeks and rivers outside of town.

More than 20,000 cheechakoes arrived in the summer of 1900, and propped up their white camp tents along the beach. There were Norwegians and Frenchmen, Russians and Americans, a babel of languages above the pounding of the surf. Along the shore stood a line of wooden rockers. The tall, unsteady devices had a narrow rectangular sluice box lined with copper plating and quicksilver to catch the gold. There were other, more elaborate mechanical contraptions with wheels, engines and pulleys.

On Front Street, above the beach, they built gambling halls and saloons. By the end of summer the town had risen on the tundra. There were sixteen law offices open for business along Front Street, as well as twelve general stores, four real-estate offices, an equal number of drugstores, five laundries, four bathhouses, three fruit and cigar stores, as many watchmakers and a masseuse. One section of the street, called the 'stockade', was for the bordellos. This was the first stop for the miners who came up from the beach or hiked down from the creeks.

The town sat just 150 miles south of the Arctic Circle, and stayed open around the clock. The sun stayed up for twenty hours and the drinking and brawling went on for ever in the sixty-odd bars that sprang up. There was enough money and time to go around for ever—or so it seemed. Coal sold for $100 a ton, eggs were $4 a dozen, and miners doled out pokes of gold dust without a second thought. Gold dust was used as money because there was not enough currency in circulation. Bars, hotels and stores had scales to measure out the gold, sometimes honestly and sometimes not.

Within weeks, many of the miners had gone bust and ended up destitute on the beach. Crime was up: on the creeks, miners armed with guns and knives jumped claims; down on the beach, thieves would creep up to the tents and lower chloroform-drenched rags through the flaps and onto the mouths of sleeping miners. Then they would grab the gold and vanish. 'The greed of man went farther here than in any other place I have ever known,' one miner recalled.

Federal soldiers managed to establish peace, but they were overwhelmed by the sheer numbers in Nome—or by the lure of gold. Half of them deserted and fled up the creeks with panning trays.

Nome was well on the road to perdition when, on the afternoon of

September 12, 1900, a strong gale blew in from the south with seventy-mile-an-hour winds and lifted up the sea. Massive waves fell on shore and battered the town for twenty-four hours. Prospectors who had stayed behind in their tents were said to have been swept out to sea, and, as the ocean rose, the waves crashed all the way up to Front Street and beyond. The storm splintered buildings and hurled lighters and boats onto the street, smashing whatever was in the way.

As the waves receded and debris piled up on the shore, thousands of prospectors who had survived months of lawlessness, drunkenness and poverty decided they'd had enough. They stood quietly in long lines on the beach and waited for the next ship out. They were called the 'cold feets'. By late October, most of the 20,000 men and women who had arrived a few months earlier had shipped out. Someone would later comment that 'even God leaves on the last boat' out of Nome. This would bear repeating every fall.

The storm marked the end of the rush to Nome. As far as the rest of the world was concerned, the town had vanished from the headlines and no longer existed. But as the last boat left in October 1900, roughly 5,000 miners chose to stay and build up from the ruins. Some had fallen in love with the north; others had taken a shine to the unpretentious ways of Alaskan society. Others simply had nowhere else to go.

THE KLONDIKE and Nome stampedes transformed Alaska. With the near doubling of Alaska's population between 1890 and 1900, new trails were cleared and existing ones widened and improved. The federal government set up military posts in Nome and the deepwater port of St Michael, and soldiers strung up telegraph wires so the forts and towns could communicate with each other and with the states. By 1903, Nome had become part of an impressive telegraph system operated by the US Army Signal Corps, and the territory's isolation was significantly reduced. In addition, the federal government established a mail delivery service, which in winter relied upon dog teams.

The arrival of the mail team was among the most exciting events to watch in Nome. It was not uncommon for the driver to have twenty-five dogs pulling two sleds with a 1,500-pound load. No other animal was more suited for travel in the north. From the beginning, Nome depended on its dogs. Teams were drafted into service as mail trucks, ambulances, freight trains and taxis. The demand for sled dogs was so high, particularly during the northern gold rushes, that the supply of dogs ran out and a black market for the animals sprang up in the states. Any dog that looked as if it could pull a sled—whether or not it was suited to withstand the cold—was kidnapped and sold in the north. 'It was said at the time that no dog larger than a spaniel was considered safe on the streets' of West Coast port towns, according to one sled dog historian.

Drivers liked to work with large dogs because they often carried loads one and a half times heavier than their teams. Newfoundlands, and St Bernards were popular imports, and they were crossbred with the indigenous dog population. In Nome, the imports were bred with malamutes, named after the Eskimo Mahlemiut people. For several hundred years, the Eskimos had used and bred their dogs to freight heavy loads for relatively short distances. When miners crossbred the native dogs with Newfoundlands and St Bernards, the outcome was sometimes astonishing: mutts weighing as much as 125 pounds. The malamute nearly disappeared, yet its name lived on; miners in Nome as well as in the interior often called their mixed-bred dogs malamutes.

Alaska's most skilful drivers and trainers were well known throughout the territory. Nome resident Scotty Allan, who had trained horses and dogs since he was twelve years old, acquired a reputation early on for being able to subdue even the most reprobate of canines and transform them into hard-working, loyal sled dogs. With his soft Scottish accent and patient temperament, Allan could 'gentle anything on four legs'.

Putting together a team took time and skill: each member was selected for its relative speed, strength and gait so that it would match the other dogs in the string. The animals were taught directional commands and to move and think in unison. But each had its own personality, and it was not always easy to bring them in line.

Generally, the dogs were set up in pairs on either side of the main line, or gang line, attached to the front of the sled. The lead dog, or 'leader', was the smartest of the team. Behind the leader were several pairs of 'swing dogs', and closest to the sled were the 'wheel dogs', the biggest and strongest of the team. Sleds were generally between nine and fourteen feet long and made of hickory or birchwood. They were lashed together with rawhide for greater flexibility, and had a curved piece in front called a brush bow, which acted like a bumper and protected the sled against shrubs or trees. If the driver, who stood on runners extending out from the back, was carrying a heavy load or driving uphill, he could help the dogs along by pedalling with one leg as if he were on a scooter or pushing from behind at a jog.

On the Alaskan trail, the sled dogs became partners in a game of survival. Drivers depended on their dogs in order to make a living as freighters, mailmen and trappers, and relied on the animals' skill and intelligence to get them safely across the rough, dangerous terrain. In return for their labour, the dogs required care and protection.

The majority of Nome's residents owned their own team, and the dogs seemed to rule the streets. At one point, dogs became such a hazard that the town passed a law requiring them to wear bells. There were more dogs than people, and their howls, known as 'the malamute chorus', could always be heard throughout the night.

Owners bragged endlessly about their teams and detailed the courage and skill of their lead dogs. They would fight anyone who dared to criticise their faithful companions, and they bet on who had the strongest, fastest and smartest animal.

In the fall of 1907, around the wood-burning stove at the Board of Trade Saloon, Albert Fink, Scotty Allan and a few friends established the Nome Kennel Club with the intention of organising a dog-sled race. Over the following weeks, Fink and his colleagues devised a long-distance race like no other. The 408-mile round-trip trek through every imaginable terrain would test the mettle, intelligence and endurance of dog and driver. The route ran between the ice hummocks of the Bering Sea, up mountains, over the tundra and through a blizzard-swept chute called Death Valley.

The race became known as the All Alaska Sweepstakes, and the inhabitants of Nome, tired of the dullness of the seven-month-long winter, welcomed it with enthusiasm. They donated time and money to preparations for the first race. It took place in April 1908 and was such a success that it became an annual event until 1917, when World War I intervened.

The All Alaska Sweepstakes transformed the isolated town. Each April, Nome became a frenzied festival. In the first few years, Scotty Allan won most of the races. But miners from the Seward Peninsula came down and soon every dog team owner dreamed of winning the thousands of dollars in prize money. News of the event was covered yearly across Alaska and in the states, and Nome, now 'Dog Capital of the World', was once again in the headlines. There was no other race like it; as the official race pamphlet said, it 'easily towers above all other contests of physical endurance, for both man and beast'.

WITH THE END of the All Alaska Sweepstakes, Nome settled into a quiet routine. By 1925, the population was significantly lower than in the years after the first of the cold feets had fled. There had been storms and fires, and the war had led to an inflation that tripled the cost of mining. The town's population was reduced to 975 whites and 455 Eskimos or interracial residents.

Gold remained a principal industry in Nome, but now it was controlled by Hammon Consolidated Gold Fields, a conglomerate from the states. The company had bought up all the claims and water ditches of the Pioneer Mining Company, the firm started by the Lucky Swedes. But the glamour of the gold-rush days and the excitement of the sweepstakes era were gone, and many of the buildings were vacant or decaying. It was still possible to make out a faded advertisement for a lawyer or a saloon left over from the gold rush. Mining equipment sat rusting on the tundra and along the beach.

From a purely Alaskan perspective, however, Nome was a smart and bustling outpost. Lula Welch, arriving with her husband in 1919 from the Candle mining camp on the northern side of the Seward Peninsula, felt an immediate charge of excitement. 'It was so big and bright, I felt it must be New York City,' she said.

It was the first time in twelve years that the Welches had seen an electric light. They had landed in northwestern Alaska in 1907, disembarking from the *Victoria* at Nome. They headed straight for the rough inland mining camp of Council, where Dr Welch had bought a private practice just months after the clinic he and Lula ran in Oakland was destroyed by the San Francisco earthquake. They had intended to stay for a year, but remained in Council for eight years. Welch worked with a portable operating table in a three-bed ward lit by a kerosene lamp. Then in 1915 the couple had moved to Candle, an outpost even more remote and primitive.

Nome felt like a luxurious new beginning for them. It had its own weekly newspaper, the *Nome Nugget*, bakeries, two restaurants, a library, a US Marshal's office and the Dream Theatre. There was a jeweller and a dressmaker. Despite its location and ramshackle surroundings, there was a remarkable array of services available in Nome, and its residents managed to maintain a sort of windswept cosmopolitanism. Strangers and misfits mixed easily. The children took singing lessons and their parents put on plays and dances at Eagle Hall and the Arctic Brotherhood Hall. It was like living in a close-knit island community.

Nome relied on a spirit of cooperation and good citizenship, a surprising transformation in light of the town's sordid history. It seemed as if every citizen had an unofficial duty, and each took it very seriously. The trails were maintained in part by volunteers, who made sure that the wooden stakes marking the route were in place, and the widow Rattenburg, who worked as a dressmaker, sewed the red cotton pennants that marked the trail for miners heading out to Hammon's dredging sites. Shopkeepers kept their stoves well stoked in case a traveller needed to warm up, and Dr Welch treated his patients whether or not they could afford to pay.

Over the years, several people had wandered out into the tundra and frozen to death, so the town fathers built an eight-foot electric cross on the steeple of St Joseph's Church as a beacon for lost travellers.

It remained an inauspicious place to build a town, but Nome functioned much like any other American community of the 1920s. There were contentious school board meetings and internecine civic squabbles of one sort or another. Nome's residents knew exactly how much coal, food and medical supplies they needed for winter. They knew how to plug up their keyholes to protect against blizzards, and how to reach the doctor if their children became ill. But Nome's residents enjoyed a false sense of security, for the town's isolation could quickly turn an average crisis into a catastrophe. If the weather turned suddenly, or there was a fire, or if a cargo ship sank, they might as well be on the dark side of the moon.

Outbreak

Dr Welch remembered each year according to whom he'd treated and how they'd fared; some memories were stronger than others, and some years stood out. One summer there was an infection attributed to mosquitoes; another year there were a number of minor injuries out at the mining camps. No doctor could forget the 1918–19 influenza pandemic, though Welch should have been thankful he had seen only the tail end of it in Nome. He had felt useless as a physician and was unable to keep many from dying.

This year, ever since the *Alameda* sailed off, there had been one tonsillitis case after another, including the strange case of the young

Eskimo child from Holy Cross. And just this morning, December 24, Welch had another sick child on his hands. She was a seven-year-old Eskimo Norwegian girl named Margaret Solvey Eide, who had a severe sore throat and a slight fever. Welch thought she might be suffering from follicular tonsillitis, but her mother wouldn't let him examine her. Her husband had gone Outside—beyond the territory—on a business trip.

Welch told the girl to stay in bed for the holidays and rest, and afterwards he walked home through town. For weeks, the shop windows along Front Street had been filled with skates and sleds, dolls and Erector sets for Christmas. But Welch had been out on so many house calls that he wasn't feeling in much of a holiday mood.

Other residents were in jollier spirits. It was, after all, a special time of year, and in the mid-1920s the highlight was Christmas Eve, when every year many of the town's 200 children filed into the cavernous wooden structure of Eagle Hall. Nome tried its best to celebrate the holiday in the traditional way, trees and all, which was no mean feat given that the nearest evergreen was ninety miles away—at least a two-day trip—to the northeast near the village of White Mountain. Nome's volunteers headed out on their dog sleds with axes and saws; they brought back a little tree for the hospital, another for the school and a third for Barracks Square. The best was reserved for the Christmas Eve celebration at Eagle Hall.

Set up centre stage, the Christmas tree was 'asparkle with tinsel, aglow with lights', and red and green crepe paper billowed down from the balcony. The fireplace crackled, and stockings hung from the mantel bulging with Cracker Jacks, candy canes, pencils, and fresh oranges and apples—delicacies that had arrived on the last ship in the fall and were set aside for the holiday.

The choir from the Eskimo church came down the aisle, candles in hand, and sang carols in their native tongue, and the other children came onto the stage and re-enacted the story of Christmas. Towards the end, they could hear the faintest jingle of sleigh bells outside, and soon the heavy double doors of Eagle Hall swung open and there was Fire Chief Conrad Yenney in his Santa suit, driving a black cutter sleigh pulled along by two skittish reindeer wearing red and green pompoms and silver bells. Yenney leapt off the sleigh, bounded up to the stage and handed out the stockings. When he was done, he drove back out into the night. Coffee and cake were served and 'the whole town was alive, gossiping and carrying on'.

When the bells of St Joseph's Church rang out at midnight, they all walked to the service through the newly fallen snow, and when it was over they headed home along Front Street, which stretched out before them in drifts of snow that had been hardened by the wind and constant traffic of dog sleds and mukluks. Some of the drifts were as high as the second-storey apartments above the shops. Tomorrow, Nome would become a giant playground.

In the days that followed, between Christmas and the New Year, they would play the games they always played during winter. They would put on their double-runner ice skates and go out on the Snake River and Bering Sea, or slide down the steep banks of Front Street on their sleds and mukluks. Jean Summers-Wolf, the daughter of the superintendent of Hammon Consolidated Gold Fields, would always remember a game of 'crack the whip' that ended with her sailing out over the ice for what seemed forever and landing unhurt in an Eskimo fishing hole.

But one little girl missed the festivities that year. Margaret Eide's condition deteriorated as the days passed, and on December 28 Welch received notice that the young girl had died. He asked her mother if he could perform an autopsy, but she refused to let him examine the body. The case bothered him. 'Death from tonsillitis is rare, but nevertheless sometimes does occur,' he wrote.

By January 1925, there was more disturbing news: two other Native children out on the Sandspit had reportedly died. Welch began to suspect the worst.

Then, on the afternoon of Tuesday, January 20, it all came to a head. As he was making his rounds at Maynard Columbus, Welch checked in on a three-year-old boy named Billy Barnett, whom he had admitted almost two weeks earlier after the boy developed a sore throat, swollen glands, fever and fatigue. Within days of entering the hospital, Billy had presented a disturbing new symptom: thick greyish lesions in his throat and nasal membranes.

The grey and bloody ulcers on Billy's tonsils and in his mouth cavity were characteristic of an ancient and dreaded malady, a centuries-old killer of young children which, for good reason, was often referred to as 'the strangler'. Its official name is diphtheria.

Though Welch and his nurses suspected that the child was suffering from this disease, they had decided to keep their tentative diagnosis to themselves, fearing it might send the community into a panic.

Diphtheria is caused by an airborne bacillus that thrives in the moist membranes of the throat and nose and releases a powerful toxin that makes its victims tired and apathetic. In two to five days, other symptoms appear: a slight fever and red ulcers at the back of the throat and in the mouth. As the bacteria multiply and more toxin is released, the ulcers thicken and expand, forming a tough, crusty, almost leathery membrane made up of dead cells, blood clots and dead skin. The membrane colonises ever larger portions of the mouth and the throat, until it has nowhere left to go and advances down the windpipe, slowly suffocating the victim.

It was a slow, painful and frightening way to die. The majority of victims were young children between the ages of one and ten years, and the 'anxious, struggling, pitiful expression of impending suffocation' in child after child infected during one epidemic, as a doctor described it, deeply affected physicians. Before the advent of antitoxin at the turn of the century, they could offer little comfort but their presence and prayers.

Antitoxin, made from the serum of immunised horses, was the sole cure. In the absence of the new shipment, Welch had only a limited supply and it was old. He feared it might have become unstable. For days he contemplated administering the serum, but decided that it was too risky. There was still a slim chance in his mind that Billy had not contracted the disease, and Welch wanted to take every precaution against further weakening the boy. 'I didn't feel justified in using the [antitoxin]', Welch would write a few weeks later in his medical report. 'I had no idea what effect it might have.'

Instead, Welch had rummaged through his pharmacy and pulled out all the old-fashioned remedies doctors had used to treat diphtheria before the invention of antitoxin in 1891. He gave Billy stimulants to strengthen his heart against the onslaught of any toxin that might be circulating in the bloodstream. He swabbed the child's throat with chloride of iron, an astringent that effectively broke up the lesions. These were not sure-fire cures, but in conjunction with the body's own immune system, they might provide a fighting chance.

The treatment had seemed to work for a while: just hours after Welch swabbed the child's throat, the lesions had sloughed off and the colour had returned to his cheeks. He was sleeping more comfortably and appeared stronger by the hour.

Then, by around 4 p.m. on Tuesday, Billy had taken a turn for the worse. Looking in on his patient, the doctor faced his worst fears. It was diphtheria, clear and simple. The child was the very picture of the advanced stages of the disease: sunken eyes, an expression of unrelenting despair, dark lips the colour of wild berries. Each time Billy Barnett tried to draw air into his lungs, he coughed up blood.

At 6 p.m. the nurses called Welch back to the boy's bedside. Billy was turning blue from a lack of oxygen and labouring ever harder for breath. He was in a state of collapse. Without using the antitoxin, there was nothing Welch could do. By now, it was questionable whether an injection even of fresh serum could save the child, given the advanced stage of the disease. Welch had no alternative but to stand by and watch the boy shut down. Billy stared back up at him in fear. As the end approached, the child's windpipe clogged up and they could hear a faint, high-pitched trill, as if someone was slowly letting the air out of a balloon.

It was over. Welch made arrangements for the body's disposal, and went home. There was little else he could do that night, but in the morning he would have to make a full report to the town fathers.

IN 1925, MOST DOCTORS relied on visual aids to diagnose diphtheria. If there was any doubt, they performed a throat culture, which could identify the rod-shaped diphtheria bacilli and determine the presence of toxin. Welch had little first-hand experience of diagnosing diphtheria and even less of making throat cultures. While Maynard Columbus may have been the best-equipped hospital in the region, its technology was basic and its resources limited. Electricity was unreliable and there was neither a laboratory nor an incubator for cultures. It had been years since Welch had done this type of work and, as he himself would admit, 'I hardly feel competent.'

Through his medical journals, Welch had access to information about the symptoms of diphtheria and its various outbreaks. Before antitoxin, diphtheria was one of the major causes of death in the United States as well as a leading killer of young children. Doctors tried every salve, but most of these served only to prolong patients' suffering or hasten their deaths. Then, in the early 1820s, doctors began trying out a new procedure called tracheotomy, cutting through the muscles of the neck and into the airway. This was often as fatal as the disease, and the practice was discontinued in the 1880s after a New York doctor, Joseph O'Dwyer, developed small hollow tubes that could be inserted through the mouth into the windpipe. The O'Dwyer tube reduced the mortality of laryngeal diphtheria, a severe form of diphtheria, from virtually 100 per cent to 75 per cent.

A 75 per cent mortality rate, however, was small comfort. The tubes were difficult to use, and a child who could breathe with the use of the tube could still suffer from the shutdown of the renal, respiratory and eventually pulmonary systems caused by circulating toxin.

Finally, a Prussian army surgeon named Emil Behring, building upon the work of the Pasteur Institute in Paris, developed an 'antitoxic' that could neutralise the diphtheria toxin. It was first used on a child in 1891, and it saved the child's life.

Epidemics of diphtheria continued to occur in the 1920s, though at a much slower pace than before, infecting about 150,000 people annually and claiming around 15,000 lives.

WELCH KNEW THE ODDS were stacked against him if he did not find a fresh supply of serum. The disease was highly contagious. The bacteria were resilient and could survive for weeks on a piece of candy, a countertop or a mitten. With a single touch, the bacteria could move from one warm body to the next; a sneeze or a cough could carry the disease through the air; and a simple inhalation could mean death.

Welch also realised that the disease could move beyond the town's boundaries and on to other coastal villages. As acting assistant surgeon of the US Public Health Service and the territory's assistant commissioner of health, he was responsible for the welfare of some 10,000 people in northwest Alaska, with jurisdiction reaching as far north as the Arctic coast and as far south as the Yukon River delta.

Most northwestern Alaskans were Eskimo, and they were at greatest risk. They had little natural resistance to any of the bacterial or viral illnesses brought in by seafarers or miners, and over the past one and a half centuries—since the first contact with Europeans—an astonishingly large portion of the population had been wiped out by measles, tuberculosis and influenza.

Welch had witnessed the flu pandemic of 1918–19, which had obliterated entire villages and settlements throughout the Seward Peninsula. 'The Natives showed absolutely no resistance,' said the then Alaskan governor, Thomas Riggs. By the time the scourge was over, 8 per cent of the total Native population in Alaska and 50 per cent of the Native population in Nome had died. Those who survived continued to suffer from weakened immune systems.

During earlier epidemics of smallpox, measles and typhoid fever, Welch's predecessors had set up quarantines and pesthouses to monitor and care for sick Natives. Native Alaskans had a well-grounded and paralysing fear of disease. Eskimos believed in the spirit of death and feared that if a person died in their home that spirit would claim them next. A death often caused family members to panic and flee, and this only served to spread the disease.

Welch worried that Nome's native population would react in the same way and that, in their attempts to flee, they would spread the bacteria through the town and down the coast.

THE FOLLOWING MORNING, Wednesday, January 21, Welch was shaken from his troubled sleep well before dawn. The daughter of Henry Stanley, an Eskimo on the Sandspit, was very sick and needed immediate attention. The family lived a mile and a half away; Welch decided it might be faster to walk than to hitch up the dogs and drive there. Gathering up his medical kit and his squirrel-skin parka and white cotton anorak, he ran down the stairs and out onto the street.

The Sandspit was a long, thin strip of beach that ended at the mouth of the Snake River on the west side of town. Most Natives lived in single-room houses, or igloos, made of driftwood, whalebone, sod, scraps of tin and whatever else they could salvage from the beach. Some of the homes were still lit by seal-oil lamps, and the air inside was thick with the smell of seal, dried salmon, sweat and damp fur.

Seven-year-old Bessie Stanley lay in the back of the igloo, dark eyes peering out from a hollow-cheeked face, her chest heaving beneath an invisible weight. Welch took her temperature and found that the girl was feverish. As soon as Welch prised open her mouth, he could smell the stench. The inside of Bessie's mouth had become 'one mass of fetid, stinking membrane', and when he touched the membrane it bled profusely.

By late evening, the girl would be dead, and there was little doubt in Welch's mind that they were face to face with a catastrophic epidemic: the town was hovering on the edge of the abyss.

He reached the apartment just as Lula was preparing lunch, and he sat down and covered his face with his hands. It took him a moment or two to gather up his thoughts and regain his professional composure. He told Lula what was happening, then picked up the phone and asked the operator to get the mayor, George Maynard, on the line as quickly as she could. Then he told Maynard to gather up the town council, every one of them, and immediately head on up to the hospital. There was no time to lose.

Quarantine

It was a comfortable office by Nome's standards, with a big bay window, a row of potted plants, tenderly cared for by Head Nurse Emily Morgan, and shelves filled with the well-thumbed volumes of Welch's medical library. The room faced south onto the street, and Welch often sat there and watched the whole town go by.

He knew every member of the town council. He had treated each of them, and their families as well, and on several occasions he and Lula had been invited to their homes for dinner. Most of them had children and none of them realised what was about to happen.

George Maynard was there, the burly publisher of the *Nome Nugget* and the town's mayor, and so was Mark Summers, superintendent of the Hammon Consolidated Gold Fields. Summers had shut down operations over at the Hammon mining camps so that his employees could take the day off to mourn young Billy's death and pay their respects to the child's father, who was a company employee. The attorney Hugh O'Neil was also present, along with G. J. Lomen, the former mayor of Nome and now a judge.

Welch took a deep breath and began to explain what had taken place over the past few months, beginning with the numerous cases of sore throat he had begun to notice after the *Alameda* had sailed off, moving to the Eskimo child from Holy Cross, then on to the death of Margaret Eide. He had come to the conclusion that all of Nome's children were at risk. Billy Barnett had died of diphtheria, and there was every indication that out on the Sandspit Bessie Stanley was suffering from the same illness. It was clear to Welch that Nome had an epidemic on its hands.

Given the contagious nature of the disease, Welch fully expected that new cases would begin to appear within twenty-four hours. The only treatment available for diphtheria was serum, he told them, and he had only enough for about six patients. To make matters worse, those estimated 80,000 units were already six years old. Welch had ordered a fresh supply over the summer, but it had failed to arrive, and he could not expect another delivery until spring. To fight the epidemic properly, Welch said, he needed at least 1 million units.

Welch did not need to argue his case. Everyone at the council meeting had vivid memories of the devastation caused by the flu epidemic of 1918, particularly among the Eskimos. Mayor Maynard immediately asked Welch to take charge of the situation. The doctor declined, suggesting that a temporary Board of Health, with the power to act independently of the town council, be established instead. The council approved, and Maynard, Welch and Mark Summers became the principal members of the board. Without further prompting from Welch, they all agreed on a course of action: to lock down the town straight away. Welch suggested that every school, church, moviehouse and lodge be shut down, and that travel along the trails be strongly discouraged and banned outright for children.

One council member remembered that a card party was in full swing over at Pioneer Hall, and they agreed that someone should go over and shut it down. Then, in an effort to break the news gently to his fellow citizens and keep panic down to a minimum, Mayor Maynard decided to print up a circular detailing the facts of the epidemic as well as the first suggested steps to a total quarantine.

The meeting was over. The town leaders stood up and the health board made plans to meet every evening until the danger had passed. It was late afternoon by the time Welch headed out. He made his way to the radio telegraph station and asked the US Signal Corps officer in charge to send out two urgent bulletins. One, to be coded for all points in Alaska, would alert every major town and official, including the governor in Juneau, to Nome's desperate need for serum.

The other would go to Washington, DC, to Welch's colleagues at the US Public Health Service, which regulated the production of antitoxins and vaccines:

> AN EPIDEMIC OF DIPHTHERIA IS ALMOST INEVITABLE STOP I AM IN URGENT NEED OF ONE MILLION UNITS OF DIPHTHERIA ANTITOXIN STOP MAIL IS ONLY FORM OF TRANSPORTATION STOP I HAVE MADE APPLICATION TO COMMISSIONER OF HEALTH OF THE TERRITORIES FOR ANTITOXIN ALREADY

In less than a week, Nome's plight would make the front pages of nearly every newspaper in America.

THE QUARANTINE BEGAN almost immediately. The Dream Theatre was closed, all social gatherings disrupted and schoolchildren ordered to go home. Jean Summers-Wolf remembered much later that she and the other children knew right away that something was radically wrong. 'I remember holding my breath real tight and running past any building I encountered with that big red sign QUARANTINE. KEEP OUT.'

Mayor Maynard finished composing his notice and sent it out to be posted all over town, then headed for his office at the *Nome Nugget* to make sure it made the next edition.

> An epidemic of diphtheria has broken out in Nome and if proper precautions are taken there is no cause for alarm. On the other hand, if parents do not keep their children isolated from other children, the epidemic may spread to serious proportions.

Despite their attempts to contain the disease, the health board had acted too late. Soon after Bessie's Stanley's death, her sisters, Dora and Mary, had developed membranes in their throats, and their parents also appeared to have developed related symptoms. Welch treated them all 'vigorously with the old serum'.

By Saturday, January 24, the fourth day of the crisis, the death toll stood at four, by conservative estimates, and still there was no word of any available serum from Fairbanks, Anchorage or Juneau, Alaska's major towns, or from Washington, DC.

The phone in Welch's office began to ring with one parent after another calling in about a sick child or a loved one. Lars Rynning, the young superintendent of schools, called to say he had a sore throat and a fever of 99.6°, and that he was particularly worried about an ulceration that had begun to form in his throat. His wife also complained of a bad sore throat, and both were worried about their two-month-old son.

Welch went over and examined the infant and told the Rynnings that, as near as he could tell, their son was in good health. Mother's milk contains a natural immunity to diphtheria and very young infants stand a 90 per cent chance of fighting off the disease without medication. Welch was convinced that the Rynnings had been exposed to the virus, however, and placed them under quarantine. But he decided against giving them any of the serum. Lars and his wife were young and strong and he felt they stood a better chance of survival than most others. The medicine had to be saved for the worst cases, and there would be many more.

There was one other detail about Lars Rynning that bothered Welch: Rynning was not only the school superintendent but a teacher as well, and the chances were high that he had already come into contact with nearly every school-age child in Nome.

Welch was already feeling overwhelmed and exhausted, and there was no one around to replace him. The nearest doctor was 400 miles away, a ten-day journey by dog sled. 'My nurses are the only consultants I have,' he noted in his medical report.

EMILY MORGAN was without doubt the most efficient and outstanding nurse in Welch's employ, and she had already proved her worth. She had had a long career in nursing. For three years she had served with the Red Cross in a mobile hospital on the western front in France, working amid the chaos of bombs and the arrival of the dying and wounded. When the war ended she returned home to Wichita, Kansas, to continue her practice.

Morgan was forty-seven when she arrived in Nome the previous fall from Unalaska, on the Aleutian Chain, where she had provided medical care to the Native community. She was nearly a foot taller than Welch and provided a cheerful, easy-going counterpoint to her boss. She also had first-hand experience with diphtheria: she had been infected with it back in Wichita, and by the time she'd recovered she knew every twist and turn of the disease's terrible progression.

At Welch's suggestion, the health board had appointed Morgan as Quarantine Nurse, and she would go out in her heavy woollen sweater, fur parka and knee-high fur boots to find and treat the most severe cases. She soon found herself putting up more and more of the red and black QUARANTINE signs, which hung over the doorways and stood out against the white of the snow.

Morgan focused on the Sandspit, where teams of volunteers handed out food, fuel and water. She had learned to work in the crudest and most insalubrious environments and thought nothing of roughing it out in the cold. But Nome was particularly tough. In Kansas 'we had plenty of doctors and hospitals', she said, but here she often worked alone, with Welch only occasionally at her side.

Morgan always took along her medical bag, which contained a clinical thermometer, tongue depressors, several tubes of antitoxin, some candy to tempt the children, and a flashlight. She checked on her patients constantly and took care to see that the antitoxin was working, but often found she could offer only her sympathy.

Once, on her rounds, Morgan returned to the home of an Eskimo family where earlier she had been disturbed by the condition of one of the five children, a young girl named Mary, whose symptoms were extreme: the child's tonsils were covered with a membrane, the darkest Morgan had ever seen. As Morgan approached the igloo, a young Eskimo boy came running out.

'You are too late,' he told her. 'Mary has gone to heaven.'

Inside, Morgan found the father hewing a coffin out of rough boards while his two other daughters looked on. Morgan could do little to ease their grief, so she knelt beside the father and 'did all I could toward finishing the crude box'. When they were done, the man lined the box with his daughter's parka, placed her inside, nailed it shut and buried her in a nearby snowdrift. A proper burial would have to wait until spring, when the ground had thawed out.

During a house call to a family named Blackjack, Morgan noticed that, while the parents sat cross-legged in the middle of the room eating dried fish dipped in seal oil, their young daughter, Vivian, lay under the covers in her bunk. 'Her sharp black eyes stared at me defiantly; her lips were compressed tightly. I knew by the redness of her face that her temperature was high,' Morgan remembered. She tried to open Vivian's mouth but the girl resisted. 'I smiled at her and in a low tone told her mother I would not force her. But with a temperature of 104 something had to be done . . . [T]hen in a pleading voice [Vivian] said, "Mother, let us pray."' Morgan prayed with the mother and child, and when Vivian 'looked straight at me and opened her mouth . . . her throat showed all the indications of diphtheria'.

Morgan gave the child a shot of serum, and her condition improved. But both Morgan and Welch estimated that at the current rate of infection, their stock of serum would not last through the week. Without a new supply, many would die.

Late on Saturday evening, Morgan and Welch went to the health board to summarise their findings. Between them, they said, they had twenty confirmed cases, with at least fifty others still at risk.

The board had been briefed on Welch's desperate message to Washington, and while all knew there was nothing they could do to help the government to find serum, there was another problem they might solve—how to get serum to Nome once it was located. The Bering Sea was icebound, so a sea trip direct from Seattle was out of the question. At this time of year, mail and supplies were shipped by boat to the ice-free port of Seward in southeast Alaska, then travelled north for 420 miles to Nenana on the only major railroad in Alaska. From there it took about twenty-five days for the mail teams to travel the 674 miles west to Nome. It was a start-and-stop route, divided up among several drivers, with time built in for overnight rests. The board had to come up with a faster alternative.

Mark Summers had a plan: if a shipment of serum could be brought to Nenana, a mail driver could carry it halfway and then hand it over to a fast dog team sent from town. They needed someone they could depend on, someone who could make the trip in record time. Summers knew that the only man who could do it was a cheerful Norwegian named Leonhard Seppala.

Seppala was the gold company's main dog driver. He supervised the 110 miles of ditches that supplied water to the gold fields, freighted supplies and passengers out to the mining camps and ferried officials on trips to other towns in Alaska. Seppala's record was legendary, earning him the nickname 'King of the Trail'. Tireless and disciplined, he was undoubtedly the fastest musher in Alaska. He had won most dog races he entered in Nome and in the interior, and with his favourite lead dog, Togo, had toppled a number of long-distance records. Seppala knew every turn of the trail from Nome to Nenana and had once reached Fairbanks—the interior capital seventy miles northeast of Nenana—in thirteen and a half days with the added weight of a passenger. It had taken him just four days to reach Nulato, halfway on the Nenana-to-Nome trail, and he had averaged an exhausting eighty-one miles per day.

After listening carefully to Summers's suggestion, the health board's approval was unanimous. But Maynard suggested that the board members also consider one other option: to fly in the serum.

The mayor had long been an advocate of Alaskan aviation. It was a fledgling industry in the territory, but he was certain that planes would eventually end the crippling isolation of many Alaskan towns and allow them to thrive.

While flying the serum in would be quicker, board members were sceptical: winter flights were extremely dangerous, the cockpits were wide open, and it would be a tough trip in the cold and the wind.

The previous year, a former army pilot had been the first to fly through the Alaskan winter. The experimental flights, which were airmail runs between Fairbanks and McGrath, were considered a great success and proved that winter flight in Alaska was possible. But they had been short compared to the projected flight to Nome, and had taken place in much warmer weather.

The board members were almost convinced that Nome's fate lay in Seppala's hands, and so that very evening Summers paid his employee a visit to tell him to prepare for the run of his life.

Meanwhile, Maynard sent a telegram to the one man who had the power and political clout to make an air rescue possible: Alaska's delegate to the US Congress, Dan Sutherland.

> SERIOUS EPIDEMIC OF DIPHTHERIA HAS BROKEN OUT HERE STOP NO FRESH ANTITOXIN HERE STOP INTERVIEW SURGEON GENERAL DEPARTMENT OF PUBLIC HEALTH AND TELL HIM TO DISPATCH MILLION UNITS ANTITOXIN TO NOME IMMEDIATELY . . . AIRPLANE WOULD SAVE TIME IF FEASIBLE STOP

Sutherland had been working to bring aviation to Alaska for the past three years and had lobbied hard for the experimental air-mail runs. Now, as he sat in his office near Capitol Hill and read the message from Nome's mayor, Sutherland saw a perfect opportunity to herald the cause of aviation once again.

LEONHARD SEPPALA was forty-seven and by rights he should have been slowing down. But he was as strong as the day he arrived in Nome to search for gold in the summer of 1900, and, even after a quarter of a century living and working in the cold, he was as agile and graceful as a gymnast. At five foot four and about 145 pounds, the King of the Trail didn't quite look the part. He had a rugged, youthful face and light brown hair with boyish waves that rode back over his head, as if perpetually blown by Nome's northern winds.

He was a rare natural athlete, and a man of unusual strength and endurance. While the majority of the dog-sled drivers would have considered thirty miles to be a hard day's drive, Seppala often travelled fifty, sometimes even a hundred miles, weather permitting, logging twelve hours on the trail with a full load. One winter alone he covered 7,000 miles by dog sled.

'Sepp', as his friends called him, was something of a show-off, known to flip double back handsprings just for laughs and land with a somersault. He would walk down Front Street on his hands, his back arched and his boots almost brushing his tousled head, and the schoolchildren would laugh and clap their hands.

Ever since Mark Summers's call for help, Seppala had been training with the team in the treeless hills that stretched away to the Sawtooth Mountains. There had been relatively little snow this year, so the dogs were not in their usual prime condition. If the serum could be located, Seppala would have to travel more than 300 miles to Nulato, almost midway between Nome and Nenana. It would be a long haul.

Seppala had decided to train with twenty of the thirty-six Siberian huskies in the kennel. This was a relatively large string for such a light load, but the dogs could turn sore-footed on the hard run to Nulato and some might even tire out. Seppala planned to drop several off at the villages along the trail, so that he could have fresh replacements for the return.

The trail between Nulato and Nome was one of Alaska's most hazardous. Much of it ran along the windswept, blizzard-prone coast of Norton Sound, and the most dangerous stretch was a forty-two-mile short cut across the Sound. Depending on the conditions under which the Sound froze, the short cut could be either a long stretch of glare ice—a slippery sheen that had been ground down by wind and blowing sand—or a course littered with giant pieces of ice rubble, crevices and long avenues of tiny spears of ice that could shred a dog's paws into bloody ribbons. The biggest risk in taking the short cut was getting separated from shore: with little warning, the ice could break up and carry a team away into the Bering Sea.

On and off the trail the dogs required constant attention, and Seppala poured time and money into them. He had raised each one from a pup and knew them as well as he knew his wife and child.

'The dogs always came first in importance,' Constance, his wife of fifty-two years, told a newspaper reporter in 1954. 'Our living room was often a place of utter confusion, littered with mukluks, harnesses, dog sleds, tow lines, ropes and other equipment being repaired and spliced and generally worked over.'

Food was a constant concern for the drivers of Alaska. The dogs' diet had to include enough protein and fat to keep them healthy and warm for winter travel, and the drivers had to stock huge quantities. The most common food was salmon. A musher would build traps out of wood and wire and lay them out in the river to catch the salmon runs. Then he would cut up the fish and hang them to dry on racks. The job could take a whole summer; each year the driver would stock about 5,000 pounds of the vitamin-rich meat.

Mushing was the easiest part of the job. The dogs' health had to be monitored daily, whether the animals ran or not; an unchecked virus could spread and wipe out an entire kennel. On the trail, every dog's paws had to be checked and, when necessary, treated. A good driver put his dogs' needs ahead of his own. After a ten-hour day on the trail, the animals were the first to eat, and preparations could take two or three hours. Wood had to be chopped and holes hacked through the ice for water, which was then hauled up to the camp pail by pail—a gallon for each dog. If there was no water, a driver had to go through the tedious process of melting snow in a pot; it took four quarts of snow to produce a single quart of water.

Along the coast, the driver would feed the dogs strips of dried salmon, bones included, and if there was enough wood around he would cook up a thick fish soup (some drivers preferred beaver meat, which was also rich in fat) with rice or oatmeal. On the trail, each of Seppala's dogs was given a pound of dried salmon and a third of a pound of seal blubber a day.

Once the feeding was over, the animals' sore muscles were massaged and boughs of spruce were cut down for their bedding. The smell and feel of it was a comfort to the dogs, and they relaxed and settled down after their meal. This was followed by a ritual the mushers referred to as 'the thankyou howl'.

It began with a single dog's high-pitched wail, which was picked up by a second and then a third dog. Soon, every dog had its nose up, joining in a full-throated cacophony. The singing would end as suddenly as it began, and the dogs would turn in ever-tightening circles, pawing at their bedding until they were comfortable. Then they would cover their noses with their tails and fall asleep. Finally the driver would have a few moments to take care of his own needs.

Seppala had loved the work from the moment he first stepped behind a sled in his early twenties, during his first winter in Nome. Jafet Lindeberg, one of the Three Lucky Swedes, had lured him to Alaska to work for his mining company, and had sent him out to look into rumours of a gold strike ninety miles northeast of town.

Seppala had a clear recollection of that first run: he had been mesmerised by the sway of the sled and the feel of runners gliding through the snow. 'The birchwood runners of my sled make tracks so deep in my memory I can see them to this day,' he once said. 'All [the dogs] asked at the end of a grueling day was to be fed.'

The first rule of survival was to hang on to the team, because without the dogs you were dead.

SEPPALA WAS ONE of few Alaskan drivers who depended almost exclusively on Siberian huskies. As far as Seppala was concerned, no other dog could equal their speed and stamina. He may have seen his reflection in the dogs: they were just as driven and competitive as he was, and they were smaller and lighter than their peers.

The present-day Siberian husky came from east of the Lena River in Siberia, where Natives had used dog teams to hunt for fur-bearing animals, seal and polar bear for centuries. In the late seventeenth century, when the Siberian Natives were forced to pay taxes to the Russians, trading fairs began to play an important role in the economic life of the region, and many villagers had to travel distances of more than 1,000 miles with loaded sleds to barter for goods. Travelling over mountain ranges, rivers and tundra, the dogs grew stronger and faster. Many of the Native groups practised selective breeding, and by the late nineteenth century the Siberian had become a tough cross-country dog, bred to cover long distances.

The Siberian dog was twice as fast and could travel at least twice as far as its cousins on the other side of the Bering Strait. During a race between a merchant and a Russian officer in the Kolyma River region in 1869, one team covered 150 miles in fifteen hours; the other made it in sixteen hours. The malamute teams of Nome, bred for freighting heavy cargo, rarely went faster than five miles an hour.

Huskies, malamutes and other native sled dogs of the north survived in the cold because of an extraordinary combination of physical features. They had two coats—an outer one made of long, coarse guard hairs that protected the skin against water, snow and sun, and an undercoat of soft, dense and woolly fur for warmth, which was shed during the summer. The ability of northern sled dogs to retain heat is considerable: because dogs sweat through the pads of their feet, the chance of heat radiating through their skin and two thick coats is virtually nil. The tail is well furred and bushy, and curls over the dog's nose while he sleeps, providing protection from the cold. (The tail also protects the groin area, the one place on a husky where there is little fur.) The eyes tend to be almond-shaped, so there is less exposure to the wind and snow, and the ears are pricked and covered with soft fur on the inside to keep heat loss to a minimum. The paws are slightly oval and the pads tough and compact to minimise the build-up of ice, which can lacerate and cripple a dog. These dogs can withstand temperatures of –80° Fahrenheit.

Seppala's lead dog was a Siberian husky named Togo. At the age of twelve, the black and grey leader had become Seppala's favourite. The relationship was based on friendship as much as on partnership and mutual need. They were 'inseparably linked', a friend said. 'One does not speak of one without mention of the other.'

Now, as Seppala led the dogs through their drills in the Sawtooth

Mountains, he felt lucky to have Togo with him for the round trip to Nulato. Togo had accompanied his master on every important journey, and together they had covered nearly 55,000 miles of trail. They had saved each other's lives many times crossing the frozen Norton Sound, and despite Togo's advanced age, Seppala still felt that, wherever they went together, he travelled 'with a sense of security'.

Flying Machines

On January 26, six days after the outbreak, on a bitterly cold Monday morning more than 700 miles northeast of Nome, a messenger from the local Signal Corps office knocked on the door of William Fentress Thompson's home on Eighth Avenue between Lacey and Noble streets in Fairbanks. Thompson, the publisher and editor of the *Fairbanks Daily News-Miner*, was barely out of bed when he took the urgent message, which was from Dan Sutherland, Alaska's delegate to the US Congress:

> COULD AVIATOR AT FAIRBANKS PUT PLANE IN COMMISSION WITHIN 48 HOURS TO CARRY SUPPLY OF ANTITOXIN TO NOME FOR RELIEF OF DIPHTHERIA EPIDEMIC THERE? ANSWER QUICK COLLECT STOP

Thompson dressed quickly. This was the first he had heard of an epidemic, and his mind raced for a lead for his evening newspaper. Thompson was in his early sixties and had been a newspaperman on the frontier for most of his life. He never shied away from controversy, and made a point of standing his ground, a trait that had earned him his fair share of critics and the nickname 'Wrong Font', a play on his first two initials and the printer's symbol for the wrong typeface. Throughout his career, Thompson had seen gold towns boom and bust across the Yukon Territory and Alaska as the easy gold ran out in the creeks and rivers and the miners fled. For the past decade he had watched his own town of Fairbanks teeter on the edge of a similar fate—one he was no longer willing to accept.

Built on the banks of the Chena River, a tributary of the Tanana, Fairbanks had been known as 'the biggest log cabin city in the world' in the years following the discovery of gold in 1902. A bustling city and a main distribution point for the interior, it linked the settlements with Alaska's ice-free ports to the south, by trail and now by railroad. But as the placer gold diminished and the interior villages emptied, Fairbanks's population dwindled, and by 1925 the town was struggling to keep economic ruin at bay. So, by extension, was Thompson. His readership had been nearly halved, and he wrote, edited and published each edition of the *News-Miner* almost single-handedly. He made it his personal mission not only to inform readers but also to keep up their 'flattened spirits', as one reader described it.

Thompson practised a sort of booster journalism, hunting down and supporting schemes he thought could bring money into the town. In 1925, he was working on the fledgling business of the Fairbanks Airplane Corporation. With the telegram in hand from the Alaskan delegate, he realised that a successful air rescue could energise the airline and help to lure business back to town. Thompson was not a mere opportunist. He had a sincere desire to help the people of Nome, and if he could arrange a mercy mission, well, he would be doing all of Alaska a favour.

Thompson walked around the house with Sutherland's telegram. It was 50° below zero outside and there were very few people on the street. He reread the message as he considered the news from Nome and all its implications. This would be his last great campaign.

OVER THE PAST THREE YEARS, Thompson had become obsessed with the development of an Arctic airline industry. Since the end of World War I the territory had become a beacon for former army pilots seeking adventure, and in 1923 Thompson and a group of businessmen formed the Farthest-North Airplane Company and hired a former army pilot from North Dakota named Carl Ben Eielson.

Eielson and Thompson became fast friends. Together, they persuaded a banker to put up money for a plane, and they soon had sufficient funds to build a crude runway, a 1,200-foot-long, 600-foot-wide stump-ridden strip at one end of the local baseball field. It was good enough, and by the summer of 1923 Eielson was flying passengers on the company's single airplane, a Curtiss-built 'Jenny'. Just a few months later Farthest-North Airplane merged with its only rival, the Alaska Aerial Transportation Company and was renamed the Fairbanks Airplane Corporation.

The company now had three planes and two pilots, Eielson and a former barnstormer named Noel Wien. It was barely an airline, but the aircraft were up and flying, and they were the only ones in Alaska. Business was good in 1923 and 1924; the company flew everything from gold to supplies, and it ferried passengers from one city to the next. With few exceptions, everything arrived safely.

The two pilots quickly built up reputations as courageous and capable men. Wien became the first pilot in North America to fly north of the Arctic Circle, and in February 1924 Eielson made the first winter flight in Alaska, a 260-mile trip from Fairbanks to McGrath on one of ten experimental air-mail runs scheduled by the US Post Office for that winter. On two of those runs a makeshift flying ambulance had been set up and Eielson transported two patients back to the hospital in Fairbanks. Thompson had great faith in the company's future.

About a month before the Nome epidemic broke out, Fairbanks Airplane sold around $15,000 worth of stock to raise money for a fourth plane: an eight-passenger aircraft with an enclosed cabin. At Thompson's urging, dozens of Fairbanks residents bought stakes in the company. Among those investors was Dan Sutherland.

Thompson was convinced that Nome could be saved with a single flight out of Fairbanks. All they needed was a pilot. And this was a problem. Eielson was in Washington trying to lobby the government to develop northern flight and authorise permanent air mail, and Wien had gone in search of the company's new aerial limousine.

Thompson began to consider other options. Just a few days earlier he had met a Justice Department agent named Roy Darling, who was in Fairbanks on business. The special investigator seemed like an even-tempered and responsible fellow, and Thompson remembered that he had flying experience.

Before joining the Justice Department, the thirty-eight-year-old Darling had learned to fly and handle weaponry at the Royal Aeronautical School and the Royal School of Infantry in Canada, and had joined the US Navy as an ordnance specialist in 1917. He was based at the Indian Head proving grounds in Maryland, where he had tested guns, bombs and other weapons. He was quickly promoted to senior lieutenant but his naval career had been cut short in May 1919. While en route from Washington, DC, to Indian Head, the seaplane in which he was travelling malfunctioned and plunged 500 feet into the water. Darling broke his right femur, fractured his jaw, lacerated his lower lip and broke the arches on both feet. A series of operations had left him with one leg shorter than the other

—NOTICE.—

DO NOT ENTER ! This house contains a case of

DIPHTHERIA.

When the danger from contagion has passed this card will be removed. Until further order this house is under hospital regulations, in accordance with Sec. 29, Chap. 14, R. S.

Per Order, **BOARD OF HEALTH.**

Any person removing or interfering with this card without authority is liable to a fine of Fifty Dollars.

OPPOSITE (top): the Quarantine Nurse, Emily Morgan, posted these diphtheria notices on homes where there were suspected or confirmed cases of the disease.
OPPOSITE: a photograph of Carl Ben Eielson's plane, taken in 1924 and captioned 'Alaska's Mail Service: Yesterday and Today'.
OPPOSITE (bottom): Dr Curtis Welch and the nurses who worked with him: Anna Carlson, Emily Morgan and Bertha Saville.

ABOVE (top): a team of dogs with their driver.
ABOVE: a dog team crossing Norton Sound.
RIGHT: passengers boarding the last boat out of Nome before the town becomes icebound.
BOTTOM: the diphtheria outbreak leaves Front Street deserted.

and a severe limp. He was forced to walk with a cane, wore a built-up shoe and had a limited range of motion in one knee.

With his severe limp and his scarred face, Darling cut a relatively rugged figure, even by Alaskan standards. Courage and stoicism were much admired in the territory, as was a measure of self-sacrifice. Thompson felt that this remade man, wounds and all, might just be the one for the job. He was tough and daring. From the point of view of an inveterate newshound like Thompson, Darling was the mother lode, a made-to-order hero.

THOMPSON TOO HAD a bad leg from an old accident, and he picked up his cane as soon as he finished his coffee and hobbled across the frozen town to see the 'broken flyer'. Darling was still in bed, so Thompson sat him up, plied him with coffee, and began to tell him the sad story of Nome's children. It didn't take long to convince the man: despite his accident six years earlier, Darling was eager to fly.

There were a few conditions, Darling explained. He would have to keep the news from his wife, Caroline, who had settled into a new home in Anchorage, and he had to get permission from the Justice Department. He would also need clearance from the US Navy so that, if he crashed, Caroline would be eligible for benefits. (Darling was technically on medical leave from the navy because of his injuries, and he was not due for official retirement with honours and benefits until June 1925.)

Darling was ready to go to Nome even if he 'had to go hanging on to the tail of a kite'. So Thompson asked him to examine the three planes stored in a warehouse on Third Avenue and report back.

Early that afternoon, Darling walked over to the warehouse with a mechanic named Farnsworth and another man, Fred Struthers, the manager of Fairbanks Airplane, and the three of them rolled open the heavy doors. It was nearly dark. One of them turned on a flashlight and in the middle of the warehouse they saw the two dilapidated aircraft, surplus training planes from World War I. There was a third plane outside, and it was hardly in better shape.

The aircraft had been sitting in the makeshift hangar since the flying season ended in October, and their wings had been dismantled. The fabric coverings, which had once stretched taut over the wooden frames, had become weak from the rough landings and the wind and rain, and the machines were badly in need of an overhaul.

The men examined each plane and agreed that only one was fit for the job. It was the *Anchorage*, a World War I surplus Standard J-1 biplane previously used to train army pilots. Its name was stencilled in red and black letters on the fuselage and its tail still carried the faded red, white and blue insignia of the Army Air Service. The engine looked to be in fairly good shape; there was even an extra thirty-gallon tank welded beneath the centre of the upper wing.

Struthers, Farnsworth and Darling walked over to Thompson's office to give him a complete report. The *Anchorage* could be put back in flying shape and would be ready to 'hit the air for Nome, rain or shine' within three days, the men told Thompson. The flight itself would take no more than six hours. It was all the editor needed to hear. When they left, he headed for his desk and began to type. A few hours later, Thompson had his story.

That evening, the *News-Miner* carried the tale of Nome's plight. It read like a rallying cry for help and featured Roy Darling, whom Thompson had described as Nome's 'Forlorn Hope'.

'The atmosphere is not right for flying, no flier would fly on a bet on such days as these . . . EVERYTHING is AGAINST the "game",' the lead story in the paper shouted. 'Yet the emergency undoubtedly exists, and Fairbanks [is] in the eyes of the Flying World, and Nome is our neighbor and our pal. What you goin' to do? The answer is GO.'

Before calling it a night, Thompson sent word of the plane's condition to Sutherland and asked him to get official permission for Darling to fly.

MORE THAN 3,000 MILES away in Washington, DC, Dan Sutherland went to work. A supporter of home rule for Alaska and an advocate for breaking the West Coast's grip on the territory's lucrative fishing, shipping, mining and lumber industries, Sutherland was a scrapper. He had recently startled Washington by appearing in the centre of the business district wearing neither jacket nor waistcoat. 'I am allowing the dust of Washington to blow off me,' he told a reporter, 'so that I will be in finer trim to go after the gentlemen who are looting Alaska of its salmon and timber, and get quicker results when Congress convenes again.' His persistence on Capitol Hill had earned him the nickname 'Fighting Dan' back home.

Sutherland had a personal stake in Nome. He had been one of the first to step foot on its beach in the summer of 1900. When the others left, he stayed on as a miner and part owner of one of Nome's freight companies. He knew the Alaskan winters well. When he turned to politics in his late thirties, he stumped thousands of miles across the interior on foot and by dog sled to win a seat on Alaska's first legislature after it became a territory in 1912. He was a popular representative, and in 1921 Alaskans voted him to be the territory's congressional delegate in Washington, DC.

Soon after receiving Thompson's message, the now fifty-five-year-old delegate approached the Public Health Service and its chief, Hugh Cumming, the US Surgeon General, and told him that Fairbanks was prepared to launch an air rescue of Nome. A single flight would take just a few hours, Sutherland said, but a dog sled would take weeks. By then, many children would be dead.

When Cumming told Sutherland he was open to the idea, Sutherland immediately cabled Mayor Maynard in Nome:

> HEALTH DEPARTMENT WILL TAKE IMMEDIATE ACTION TO RELIEVE THE CONDITIONS AT NOME STOP THEY ARE TRYING TO GET AN AIRPLANE STOP WILL KEEP YOU ADVISED STOP

Sutherland's other telegram, to Thompson, earlier that Monday morning, had been triggered by a wonderful discovery. The day before, a doctor in Anchorage had come across a supply of 300,000 units of antitoxin. When Dr John Bradley Beeson, chief surgeon of Anchorage Railroad Hospital, heard about Nome's epidemic, he had headed straight for the Signal Corps office next to the railroad tracks and fired off a telegram to Alaska's governor, Scott C. Bone:

> 300,000 UNITS OF SERUM LOCATED IN RAILWAY HOSPITAL HERE . . . PACKAGE CAN BE SHIPPED BY TRAIN TO NENANA . . . COULD SERUM BE CARRIED TO NOME BY MAIL DRIVERS AND DOG TEAMS?

At about the same time, the Public Health Service had found 1.1 million units of antitoxin in various hospitals along the West Coast, and these were to be sent to Seattle, where they could be forwarded to Alaska. But the next available ship north, the *Alameda*, was still out at sea and would not dock until Saturday, January 31, several days away. Worse still, the boat would take six or seven days to reach the port at Seward, and by the time the serum had made its way to Nome, many more children would be dead.

Beeson's serum would have a two-week head start. Although not sufficient to wipe out the epidemic, it could keep it in check for a while longer. Governor Bone directed Beeson to prepare the serum at once and send it north to the interior by train. In the twelve hours it took for the serum to reach the interior, he would decide whether to allow an airplane rescue or to rely on the dogs.

Dr Beeson was somewhat of a celebrity in Alaska. Four years earlier, he had been in the local papers after a house call of more than 500 miles to the small town of Iditarod, where a banker was in urgent need of treatment. An impromptu relay of dog teams was set up along the route to carry Beeson to the interior gold town, and they travelled at such speed and over such rough terrain that the drivers had to lash the doctor onto the sled.

At one point, the sled had broken through the ice and Beeson was plunged into the water. As he struggled to free himself, he felt the sled lurch. He could see up through the surface of the water and so was a witness to his own rescue as the dogs skilfully pulled the sled safely onto the bank. There were other mishaps along the route: one of the drivers' toes froze and another driver was hurt, and Beeson had had to drive a sled for the very first time.

In retrospect, he was astonished he had made it all the way, and equally surprised that his patient, who was in the advanced stages of pulmonary tuberculosis, was still alive when he arrived. There was little Beeson could do but try to get the patient back to Anchorage, where he could receive round-the-clock care.

Unable to set up a relay for the return journey, Beeson set off with one driver and little hope. By fortunate coincidence, he met up along the route with Leonhard Seppala, who was headed to Anchorage with two officials of the Alaska Road Commission. Seppala was travelling with four teams and forty-three dogs, and he agreed to break away with Beeson and his patient. Seppala drove a strong, fast team and they made it back to the hospital without incident.

Beeson's house call had taken a month from beginning to end.

Now, as Beeson looked at the amber-coloured glass vials of serum on the main floor of Anchorage's four-storey hospital, he recalled every mile of that unbearably cold trip, and each jolt of the sled. If the shipment had to be carried by dog team all the way to Nome, it would need protection, so Beeson padded the inside of a container and placed the vials inside. He took a heavy quilt and wrapped it round the container, then placed it into a wooden crate, covering it with thick brown cloth. When he was done, he pinned a note to the cloth instructing whoever would be carrying the serum to warm the container up for fifteen minutes after each stop on the trail. By the time he was through, the package weighed twenty pounds.

Beeson carried the serum over to the railway station where the locomotive stood by and handed the package to the conductor, Frank Knight. Knight placed it in a snug corner of the baggage car. As the engineer blew the whistle, the train jolted forward. Beeson sent a message to Governor Bone telling him the serum would be arriving in Nenana by the following night, Tuesday, January 27.

'Appreciate your prompt action for Nome relief,' Bone replied.

BACK IN HIS OFFICE, Scott Bone considered his options. The decision would be his whether to send the serum by dog team or by plane. With his slight paunch and bushy grey eyebrows, the sixty-four-year-old governor had a kind and warm way about him. He made friends easily, and was relatively broad-minded. Bone had been a journalist most of his life and worked his way up the pressroom ranks to become editor of the *Seattle Post-Intelligencer*. Then, after a brief time as publicity director for the Republican National Committee, in 1921, he became the tenth governor of Alaska.

The governorship, a position appointed by the US president, was a tough and in many ways a thankless job. The salary was a pittance; a previous governor had once complained that he spent $10,000 annually in office, $3,000 more than he was earning. Many Alaskans resented the fact that they did not even have the right to elect their own leader, and some viewed the position as a branch of the meddlesome federal government.

While Bone may have been the highest official in a region more than twice the size of Texas, he exercised little executive control. Most decisions about the territory's development, the allocation of resources and taxes, were in the hands of conflicting and often uninformed bureaucrats in Washington.

For nearly every decision, Bone had to wade through a swamp of federal bureaucracy, and he knew that the issue of transporting the serum could get bogged down in red tape. Delegate Sutherland and *News-Miner* editor Thompson were pushing hard for an air rescue, and while Bone leaned towards the idea, he wanted to make sure that his was a responsible choice. The final decision was his alone, and no amount of pressure, political or otherwise, could sway him.

Bone was familiar with the debate surrounding the potential for an Alaskan airline industry, and he had no doubt that air routes would play an important role in the territory's future. However, he began to question the wisdom of a mercy flight to Nome.

The weather had turned bitterly cold. For over a week, an Arctic high-pressure system had pushed temperatures in the interior to their lowest in nearly twenty years. The cold grew as the days wore on, stealing what little solar heat had been stored in the ground.

The low temperatures had been front-page news in nearly every newspaper in the interior. In Fairbanks, the post office had closed because there was not enough heat to keep the employees warm. Farther east in Canada's Yukon Territory, temperatures of –70° forced a halt to the delivery of water and mail in Mayo and Dawson City.

Meanwhile, an entirely different system was harassing Juneau and the other towns of southeastern Alaska. The average January temperature is close to freezing, relatively warm compared to the interior, but the amount of snowfall is high and the storms from the Gulf of Alaska frequent. From his new offices in the Goldstein Building—by far the tallest in Juneau—Bone could see the town digging out from beneath a snowstorm as twenty-five-miles-per-hour winds whipped down the streets, creating ten-foot-high drifts and traffic jams of cars and horse-drawn buggies.

The recent snowstorms and gales had also created havoc in the shipping lanes. The steamer *Admiral Watson* limped down the Gastineau Channel into port that morning, listing dangerously from the layers of ice that coated its pilothouse, rails and bow. It had been the stormiest voyage in memory, 'an almost continuous succession of snowstorms and gales', the captain remembered. If strong winds and temperatures of 10° above zero could do such damage to a stalwart of the Seattle-to-Juneau service, one could only imagine the dangers of flying a plane during an Alaskan storm.

The three aircraft in Fairbanks each had open cockpits, and Bone questioned whether any pilot, let alone an injured man like Darling, could survive any flight in temperatures of –50°. Until now, most flights in Alaska had taken place during the summer or the warmer winter months. Eielson's experimental air-mail runs had been a success, but he had never flown in temperatures colder than –10°, some forty degrees warmer than the temperatures in Fairbanks that week.

In the course of the mail runs, during which he'd spent less than fifty hours in the air, Eielson had crash-landed a few times, coming close to destroying his plane, and had gone through a large crate of spare parts. The US Post Office refused to send more and, with none available in Fairbanks, they called a halt to the two remaining runs. Of the ten scheduled runs, Eielson completed eight.

Eielson's flights had become famous. In a cabinet meeting in Washington, someone had read out an account of Eielson's adventures, and the story so captured the imagination of President Calvin Coolidge that he sent Eielson a congratulatory note.

US Post Office officials, however, felt the territory was not yet ready for a regular air-mail service, and they asked for their crippled plane back.

Eielson had been flying a government-issue De Havilland, which was far sturdier than the flimsy biplanes owned by Fairbanks Airplane. Even if Thompson's 'Forlorn Hope' could overcome the wind, the cold and the mechanical limitations of the time, there was one factor that Thompson, Dan Sutherland and Mayor Maynard were overlooking. The days were short in January, and Darling would have a limited number of daylight hours in which to fly safely. Flying at night was a risky proposition, and the *Anchorage* had no navigational tools save for a magnetic compass, which was unreliable given the proximity to the North Pole. Any pilot taking off from Fairbanks for Nome would find himself in the dark, in every sense, without a light to guide him along the route or a radio to warn him of an approaching blizzard.

To make matters worse, the territory had been mapped out in haphazard fashion. When the Post Office and other territorial officials organised the experimental mail runs in 1924, they had to consult three maps because each one showed a different topographical outline of the route. The pilots thus learned the terrain the hard way. A mountain measuring 1,000 feet on a map would loom up at 5,000 feet, and a river bank that had been considered as an emergency landing spot would turn out to be a tiny creek in a forest.

Even if Darling made it across the interior, all the daring in the world could not help him up the Bering Sea coast. He knew none of the local landmarks—the big rock of Besboro Island off the coast of Unalakleet or the lopsided Topkok Mountain east of Cape Nome—signposts that might have helped guide him if he were blown off course. Further, it would be difficult for any plane, let alone the *Anchorage*, to survive the coast's sudden snowstorms and gusts of up to seventy-five miles per hour.

Anchorage's engine, while a model of modernity by the standards of the early 1920s, was in one respect like any other motor of its time—cooled by water and therefore unreliable in severe cold. Antifreeze had not yet been invented and pilots had experimented, with limited success, with various mixtures of alcohol. Further, the oil turned viscous at about 10° above zero, and whenever a pilot landed he would have to set up a fire pot beneath the engine to keep it warm while the passenger or a local mechanic drained the oil into a pan and warmed it over the coals.

Water-cooled engines shook so hard in the air in those days that bolts and screws would sometimes come loose. Water lines were broken, radiators were loosened, steam spouted from cracks and spark plugs fouled. The engines sputtered and cut out, and the quiet, eerie hum of the wind through the guy wires would suddenly replace the roar of the engine. In the 1920s, an engine failure usually meant death or, at the very least, serious injury. If a plane lost flying speed, it would go into a tailspin followed by an uncontrolled dive, and if the engine remained idle, there would be no possibility of recovery.

The aircraft had hardly been designed with Arctic travel in mind.

IT WAS CLEAR to Governor Bone that flying to Nome would be a hazardous undertaking. In his opinion, the equipment was inadequate to handle the rigours of the northern winter, and, although Darling had a deep supply of courage, he lacked the necessary experience. If he went down, the serum would go down with him, and so would Nome's chance to fight the epidemic.

On the other hand, a mail drive was not without risks. If Bone were to trace the mail trail from Nenana to Nome on a map, his finger would follow the course of the Tanana River to the point where it converged with the Yukon, 137 miles to the west at the village of Tanana. It would continue on or along the river for another 230 miles to the village of Kaltag. The Tanana and Yukon rivers cut through the heart of the interior, a land Jack London once described as a 'pitiless' expanse of 'the bright White Silence'. One could travel for days in the interior and never see another soul.

From Kaltag, the trail left the Yukon River and rose into the mountains and along a ninety-mile portage of plateau, forest and river that tumbled out at the Bering Sea coast. The coast was often stormy and treacherous, and offered an entirely different riding experience from the deep cold and nearly windless interior. The snow was icy and hard, the wind blew unimpeded for miles, and there were few trees to dip behind for protection or to cut down for fuel.

The trail followed the coast of the Bering Sea along Norton Sound for 208 miles, and travelled across its shifting fields of ice. It traversed lagoons and river deltas and passed through 'blowholes' or wind tunnels. There was nowhere to hide along the coast during a blizzard or a gale, so drivers holed up in roadhouses whenever they could find one. When they could not, they would huddle behind a pressure ridge, ice hummock or boulder, and in the absence of any natural protection, they made do with climbing into the sled.

The 674 miles between Nenana and Nome held every kind of danger. A driver caught unaware or without sufficient preparation risked serious injury or death.

Roadhouses were the rough equivalent of small inns, simple log cabins insulated with mud and moss, or, in the more remote areas, just a canvas tent with a large barrel stove. On the more popular trails, they were separated by about a day's travel—a distance of thirty to fifty miles—and provided a modest place to rest, eat and warm up. Meals generally cost between one and two dollars, and wild game was often the speciality of the week. There was freshly baked bread and local vegetables, and if a traveller was lucky he could find a basin of water and a towel to rub across his grimy face.

Each roadhouse had its own particular character. The innkeepers were tough, independent sorts on the whole, but they knew the value of a cup of coffee or a free meal for the wanderer who stumbled in wet and cold. On more than one occasion, a roadhouse operator would go out into the cold in the middle of the night to bring in a lost traveller. Alaskans depended on this kind of 'bush hospitality'. One never knew when one might need a helping hand.

BY LATE in the afternoon on January 26, Governor Bone had made his decision. He had weighed the risks of the new technology against the old and now he knew what had to be done. The serum would be taken to Nome on dog sleds. But instead of sending one team to meet Leonhard Seppala midway on the trail, he would set up a relay of the best and fastest drivers in the interior. The teams would travel night and day with no rest, no matter how bad the conditions, until they met up with Seppala at the halfway mark.

The most respected travellers on the trails were the mail drivers. They were usually the best dog drivers around, and experts at surviving in almost all weather conditions. It was a tough job and carried huge risks, and this was reflected in their pay, which was about $150 a month, one of the highest in Alaska. They took their oath seriously and went out on the trail at times when no one else dared.

They braved blizzards, rain and bitter cold, and sometimes became the only contact between the isolated miner and the outside world.

Bone sent off one message to Dan Sutherland telling him of his decision and another to Edward Wetzler, the US Post Office inspector in Nenana who had maintained daily contact with the drivers.

> PLEASE ENGAGE RELAY DOG TEAMS TO CARRY [ANTITOXIN] TO TANANA AND THENCE TO RUBY THERE TO BE MET BY TEAM FROM NOME STOP PLEASE EXPEDITE SITUATION REPORTED SERIOUS STOP TERRITORY WILL MEET EXPENSE STOP

The governor dictated a separate message to Dr Welch informing him of the decision to go with the dogs:

> INSPECTOR WETZLER INSTRUCTED TO HIRE DOG TEAMS BY RELAY TO RUBY STOP YOU WILL PLEASE HIRE DOG TEAM IMMEDIATELY AND START IT TO RUBY STOP THIS OFFICE DOING ITS UTMOST TO EXPEDITE DELIVERY STOP

The Northern Commercial (NC) Company was the main trading concern in Alaska, with posts in every town along the territory's major rivers. The company had the mail delivery contract between Fairbanks and Unalakleet and was the only operation in Nenana capable of locating drivers in the interior at such short notice. Wetzler walked over to the home of Tom Parsons, the local NC Company agent, and asked him to get the best drivers up and onto the trail.

The call went out across the interior by telephone and telegraph, and the men in the Signal Corps cabins put down their coffee mugs and set out to find the boys of the NC Company.

At the roadhouse in Minto, a tired twenty-one-year-old Athabaskan Indian named Edgar Kallands was resting after a long haul. He had been en route to Nenana, thirty-one miles away, and now he was being ordered to turn back to Tolovana to take his station there and prepare for the journey to the village of Manley Hot Springs. He had been looking forward to seeing 'the big city' and taking a long rest. But before the sweat on his gloves had dried, he was up again and ready for the call.

Fifty-nine miles to the west, another Indian by the name of Johnny Folger was instructed to take the serum to Tanana, the geographical centre of Alaska, where the Yukon and Tanana rivers converged. From there, the message was relayed down the line to the villages along the Yukon—Kallands, Nine Mile Cabin, Kokrines, and Ruby—where other men were ordered to prepare. Sam Joseph, a stocky Athabaskan, hitched up his dogs and moved out to take up his post. Harry Pitka, a mail driver born in a spruce bow tent and raised by a medicine man, learned of the relay as he sat watching his wife make a new pair of moccasins. His job would be to cover the thirty-mile leg to Ruby, and he hooked up his string of seven dogs without a moment's hesitation. Pitka was twenty-seven, and he had had a tough life. He was severely short of money, but he did not think twice about this volunteer mission.

WHILE THE MUSHERS made hurried preparations to reach their stations, 'Wrong Font' Thompson learned of Bone's decision and was furious. Marching off to his typewriter, he banged out a shrill editorial for the January 27 issue of the *News-Miner*:

> Governor Bone has evidently taken charge. Fairbanks is standing by, ready with airships and men, to cut Nome's waiting time in half if Washington wires the orders 'go' . . . Fairbanks, only four hours away by airship . . . must sit by the fire and vision [*sic*] the Nome babies and their pioneering parents strangling and dying most horrible deaths, and no help for them. It almost makes a pioneer 'see red'.

Thompson geared up for a protracted fight, determined not to let any official or politician stand in his way. He took aim at Bone in particular, regarding him as a traitor to the pioneering Alaskan spirit. By deciding in favour of a musher and his dogs and against an air rescue, Bone had chosen to bet against the modern age.

At a time when American innovation and ingenuity were changing the world with production lines and radio communication, Bone had put his faith in the folk wisdom of Alaska's Natives. The vast majority of mushers who would have to risk their lives were Athabaskan Indians and Eskimos, and the rest were white men who had taken almost all their survival cues directly from the Natives.

By 1925, most Native Alaskans had made their pact with the modern age. They still hunted, fished and traded on occasion, but their bread and butter was in hauling supplies and carting the US mail along the trails.

The machine had not yet been built that could match the endurance, speed and reliability of men and dogs. The airplane might be the way of the future, but for the people of Nome the dog team was the only hope for the present. And if the serum could rescue Nome from the ravages of an ancient plague, then its safe arrival by dog sled would be a testament to the hard-learned survival skills and spirit of Athabaskans and Eskimos.

The 'rule of the 40s'

Six hundred and seventy-four miles east of Nome, 'Wild Bill' Shannon waited impatiently inside the two-room railroad station at the interior town of Nenana. It was Tuesday, January 27, just shy of 9 p.m., and he had been awaiting the serum from Dr Beeson in Anchorage. The locomotive had left Anchorage almost twenty-four hours earlier and it was due to arrive at any moment.

Nenana was the second-to-last town on the 470-mile-long railroad, which started at the southern port of Seward on a bay off the Gulf of Alaska and ended in Fairbanks. It had been picked for the start of the serum run because it was at the junction where the railroad met the mail trail to Nome. The serum's 300-mile journey by train from Anchorage would shorten the trip by days, but once the serum arrived in Nenana it would still have to travel the 674 miles west to Nome, clear across the territory.

Lanky and fair-haired, Wild Bill was a jack-of-all-trades and, like so many other men in the territory, master of quite a few of them. He was a mail driver, miner, trapper and fearless dog driver, who was known to have the fastest dog team in the area. His skills as a driver, combined with a combustible mixture of hot temper, sharp wit and willingness to take risks on the trail, no doubt accounted for his nickname. Tonight, his hard-acquired knowledge and skills would be tested, perhaps as never before.

On his way to the railroad station, Shannon had sensed that the temperature was dropping well below the –30° to –40° range that was typical for that time of year. When it was this cold, your breath formed into ice crystals and the air pinched your nostrils as you drew it in. It was like the sting of a bee, and the pain cut short every deep breath. Even inside the railroad station he stayed bundled up, his bearskin parka down nearly to his knees.

Had the decision been left to Edward Wetzler, the governor's man in charge of overseeing the relay, Shannon would not have set off until daybreak. By then the sunlight would have warmed the trail slightly and given the driver a clear view of it. Even so, Shannon would still be violating a rule of survival that many mushers were reluctant to challenge, but often did. Wild Bill Shannon was about to break the 'rule of the 40s'.

The rule warned against running a dog team in temperatures below –40° and above 40°. At 40° and over, a husky can get overheated and suffer from dehydration. At –40° there is little room for error. Even the US Army stationed in the interior village of Tanana had forbidden its soldiers from going out on patrol when the temperature dropped so low. Tonight, it was 50° below zero.

At this temperature, Alaska was a different world, a land with its own peculiar physics. A cup of boiling water flung into the air, for example, would become a ghostly cloud of vapour. Steam rose from every finger on a bared hand as the vapour that passes continually through the pores became more visible. Opening the door to a warm cabin was an invitation to the phantoms. As the cold air rushed inside, moisture on the walls and floors would form into a chain of ice crystals, like tiny chandeliers. Outside, where the supercooled air sucked out any lingering moisture, the landscape took on a fragile, glasslike quality.

Ahead of Shannon lay fifty-two miles of rough terrain over a frozen river and along steep banks to the roadhouse in Tolovana, where another dog driver would be waiting. Normally, the Nenana–Tolovana run took two days, with an overnight stop at Johnny Campbell's roadhouse in Minto. Shannon was told to cover the route in a single spurt. This would have been a challenge for any musher at any time, but in Shannon's case it was especially dangerous, because he would be working with a team of relatively inexperienced dogs.

The leader in Shannon's nine-dog crew was Blackie, a five-year-old husky with a white cross on his chest. Shannon had adopted Blackie after leaving the army, where he had served time as a blacksmith in the Alaskan interior. Over the past few years, the dog had helped him to deliver the mail, carry goods and supplies to his copper claims and run the traplines in the nearby woods. Shannon knew the dog's quirks, strengths and weaknesses as well as the animal knew Shannon's.

But the eight other members of the team, all two-year-olds, were a different story. There was Solly, a Siberian husky with ice-blue eyes; Jimmy, the grandson of Blackie; also Princess, Cub, Jack, Jet, Bear and Bob. They were all good, strong dogs and Shannon had raised and trained them, but they were young, and this was their first twelve-hour run in such cold temperatures. Shannon knew that the animals could become a danger to him as well as to themselves. They would need close monitoring.

It would have been wiser for Shannon to wait until morning, as Wetzler had argued, especially given the falling temperatures. But in these parts, a man did not carry the name 'Wild Bill' without having earned it, and he was prepared to risk all. Across the river from the Nenana railroad station, on the steep river bank, stood the white crosses of forty-six Athabaskan Indians who had died here during the influenza pandemic seven years earlier, a quiet reminder of how vulnerable Native Alaskans were to the white man's diseases.

'Hell, Wetz,' Shannon had told the Post Office inspector. 'If people are dying . . . let's get started.'

The distant chugging of the steam locomotive could be heard well before Shannon and the dogs saw the train. When it emerged from the darkness, steam gusted from the locomotive. A small crowd had gathered on the platform, among them Shannon's wife, Anna, who had come to see him off.

The crowd's excitement was infectious, and the dogs strained and leapt in their padded leather harnesses, tugging at the sled. Even before the train came to a complete stop, conductor Frank Knight jumped onto the platform with the twenty-pound package of serum and ran over to Shannon.

Shannon took the precious cargo and tied it down in his sled. He double- and triple-checked the harnesses and lines and made certain the emergency supplies were in order. Satisfied, Shannon mounted the runners, released the sled and took off, bolting along the tracks, down the bank to the Tanana River and into the cold, dark interior. He had never had such a large audience watch him start a run, but tonight there was no time to think about anything but the job ahead.

High above the spires of spruce and birch, the stars shone with cold brilliance and the moon was a sliver, less than a quarter full.

THE ROUTE WOULD FOLLOW the Tanana River northwards in three long, meandering curves for the thirty miles to Minto, an Athabaskan village in the lowlands, and then curve sharply to the west to Tolovana. As they crossed the Tanana to the trail on the east bank, the dogs surged forward in their collars, panting heavily and leaving behind wisps of steam that hung for a moment like ghosts. The route was in atrocious shape. A few days earlier, a horse team dragging heavy freight had punched deep holes in the trail. Horses could wreak havoc on a trail, and had been the bane of the dog rigs for years.

Shannon's team fought to keep its footing, but finally Shannon accepted that the trail was too broken up to be of use. Shouting, 'Haw!' he ordered Blackie to turn left and lead the team onto the Tanana River. The temperature would be several degrees colder on the frozen river than on the steep bank, but at least the path had not been broken up by the horses.

Shannon was taking a big risk. In any type of weather, travelling over a frozen river can be extremely dangerous. River ice is in a constant state of transformation. It can be smooth along one stretch and a jumble of craggy ice sculptures on the next. The large frozen peaks are strong enough to support a truck, but the narrow valleys in between can easily crack underfoot.

It was nearly pitch dark, and though Shannon was fighting the numbing cold, he had managed to stay alert, and was watching for hazards along the river. He was particularly worried about overflow, which occurs when water bursts through the surface and seeps over the top of the ice. The pent-up water can be under such pressure that it forms a geyser sometimes three or four feet high and the slick may spread for miles across the ice.

In temperatures below zero, overflow refreezes rapidly, forming a fragile shell that will crack loudly or flex like rubber underfoot, either of which are clear signals for the traveller to get off. But once the overflow has frozen to a hard sheen, it can be as slippery as glass.

The other risk of riding over frozen rivers is from drum ice, the opposite of overflow. Drum ice occurs when the water beneath a frozen river recedes, leaving behind a deep ice cavern. It appears ordinary on the surface, but when a team drives over it the sled begins to make a hollow sound, like a drum. If the team doesn't get off quickly the ice could cave in and the driver fall ten to twenty feet down to the dry riverbed.

So far, Shannon had been lucky. His team had avoided any drum ice or overflow and the pups were working well together. But as the hours passed, a chill crept deeper into Shannon's bones. It was becoming harder and harder, he realised, to warm his extremities. He began to swing his arms violently downwards and started pedalling more frequently on the runners, hoping to drive the blood back into his fingers and toes. His focus began to move from the trail and the dogs to his own inability to stay warm.

Suddenly, Blackie made a sharp turn. The swing dogs followed in unison and the sled veered off. Shannon lost his balance but managed to hold on to the handlebars and regain his footing. His first thought was that Blackie's behaviour had been odd, but then he pieced together what had happened: Blackie had avoided a black hole, an opening in the ice that had been eaten away by the current below and was 'large enough to drag down the entire team'. Blackie had either seen the steam rising off the river or heard the rush of current against the hard-packed ice. Either way, he had reacted quickly.

But something was wrong with four of the pups. Bear, Cub, Jack and Jet were no longer running steadily. Sled dogs, at their best, will place their back leg inside the print of their forepaw, and many of them will be in step with each other. But as dogs tire, they fall out of rhythm. A pair of hind legs will be slow on the uptake. Another dog will begin crabbing, leaving paw prints at the edge of the trail as he stumbles, lags and has to be dragged forward by the other dogs. Cub, Jack and Jet were clearly exhausted. They had nothing left to draw on but heart, the sheer will to keep moving forward with the other dogs. And Bear was not much better. Shannon had been on the trail for four or five hours now. The temperature was still dropping, and the colder it became, the slower time seemed to pass.

Shannon's own physical problems had not resolved themselves, and his attempts to get blood down to his extremities no longer seemed to be paying off. If he did not do something quickly to get more heat to his legs, he knew he would die, along with his dogs, and perishing with them would be any hope of getting the serum to Nome. His body was simply losing heat faster than he could produce it. In an attempt to protect against the cold, his body was shunting blood from its extremities to its core vital organs. Already his face was growing numb, and one of his big toes had frozen. As sluggish as he felt, he knew what he had to do.

Shannon stopped the team and got off the sled. He raced to the front, just ahead of Blackie, and began to jog. The dogs matched their pace to Shannon's. When finally he felt the blood returning to his limbs, Shannon knew he had warmed up enough to go back to the sled and ride the runners.

This worked, but only for a while. Shannon was getting tired again, and, as he would recall, was becoming 'fairly stupefied by the cold'.

Soon it would be difficult for him to hold on to the sled, let alone lean forward and pedal from the runners.

Shannon knew that he was becoming hypothermic. A human being can shiver for just so long. The process is exhausting. It makes the muscles tense from the build-up of lactic acid and carbon dioxide. With the loss of muscle control, the skin grows pale, numb and waxy. The shivering fits lead to stumbling, then slurred speech, then mental lapses: moments of time unaccounted for, a wandering of the mind, odd behaviour. Finally, apathy and exhaustion set in. A person no longer cares about reaching his destination. All he wants to do is to sleep. This feeling nags him every step until at last he gives in to the desire, curls up in the foetal position, and closes his eyes.

At this stage, the body shuts down. All blood flow to the extremities stops, the breathing rate slows and the pulse becomes shallow and weak. The victim is in a hibernation mode. The skin becomes bluish-grey and the limbs grow rigid. As the internal temperature continues to drop towards 86°, the body becomes a metabolic icebox. Although death by hypothermia is relatively painless, the 'long conscious fight' against a relentless chill can be agony.

With the fear building inside him, Shannon pushed on, knowing he had to reach Minto before he lost control of himself and his team.

At around 3 a.m., the door to Johnny Campbell's roadhouse opened. Campbell took one look at Shannon and his dogs and it was clear to him that something terrible had happened. Parts of Shannon's face had turned black from severe frostbite. Blood had stained the mouths of Bear, Cub, Jack and Jet. Helping Shannon inside, Campbell placed him near the sheet-iron stove and poured him a cup of hot black coffee. Shannon was too tired and cold to eat. As he attempted the first sips from his coffee, he took a look at the thermometer outside: it was –62°.

Along the Yukon River

For four hours, Bill Shannon sat huddled at the stove in Campbell's roadhouse, drinking coffee and allowing the heat to wash over him. Finally, he was ready to take some food to give him the strength to continue the journey. Despite all that had happened,

Shannon had not lost his resolve. He would complete the remaining twenty-two miles to Tolovana. He had given his word that he would.

As Dr Beeson in Anchorage had instructed, Shannon had taken the serum inside so it would not freeze, unwrapping the layer of fur and canvas and dangling the container from the rafters to share the warmth of the stove. The cabin was probably no warmer than 50°, but in comparison with the temperature outside it felt tropical.

Just before seven o'clock on Wednesday morning, Wild Bill took a last pull from his sixth cup of coffee and went outside to check on his dogs. Although by the clock it was morning, it would be several more hours before dawn finally drove out the Alaskan night.

Earlier that night, after helping Shannon into the roadhouse, Johnny Campbell led the dogs to a lean-to, where he fed them and let them rest. But one look suggested that they needed far more than an hour or two of downtime. Several were suffering from what mushers in those days described as 'lung scorching', a condition in which they believed a dog's lungs were turned black as coal from frostbite. Lung scorching was more conjecture than proven fact. Mushers did not perform autopsies on their dogs. Modern veterinary medicine tells us that a dog suffering from working too hard in the severe cold more probably has a pulmonary haemorrhage. The lungs do not turn black, but fill up with blood. Although the dog finds it harder and harder to breathe, he will keep running, spurred on by his teammates, until eventually he drowns in his own blood or passes out from oxygen deprivation. In either event, he will soon be dead. The initial warning signs are bleeding from the mouth and nose, where the lining of mucous membrane becomes brittle and cracks in the cold.

When Shannon checked on the dogs, Cub, Jack and Jet could barely struggle to their feet. The trip to Tolovana was at least another three to four hours and Shannon knew that these three dogs would not make the distance. He would leave them behind. It was questionable whether they would ever run again, but at least for now he could take comfort in the fact that Campbell would take good care of them until he returned.

Down to six dogs, Shannon could only hope there would be no further mishaps on the trail. But Bear, too, was looking weak. Shannon decided to let him try to make the rest of the run. If he had to, he would take Bear off the team and put him in the sled basket. After readying the dogs, Shannon released the sled brake. The drive to Tolovana had now resumed.

THAT SAME MORNING, more than 600 miles away, the telephone rang at Leonhard Seppala's cabin at Little Creek, near Nome. It was the call he had been waiting for. On the other end was Mark Summers, Seppala's boss at the Hammon Consolidated Gold Fields and the man who had suggested Seppala for the western half of the relay. It was time, he was told, to head out.

Seppala was not a man to leave things to the last minute. Salmon for the dogs had already been stacked and tied down in the sled. Earlier in the week, his wife Constance had wrapped and frozen individual servings of cooked beans, ground beef and hardtack that he could warm up on the trail for his own nourishment. All in all, he was travelling light; he had to if he wanted to make good time.

Seppala hung up the phone and put on his fur parka and mukluks. Out in the kennel, the dogs had heard the phone and were keyed up by the time Seppala stepped outside. When he headed towards them, they exploded in a frenzy of howls and yelps. They knew that it was time to run.

Seppala not only had the longest leg to travel—315 miles to Nulato and 315 miles back, a journey of about six days—but one of the most difficult: the windswept ice of Norton Sound. There was also the probability of a blizzard delaying his journey, or worse: the ice breaking up and carrying him out to sea.

The uproar in the kennel could be heard for miles around, and by the time Seppala had hooked up all the dogs, a small group from Little Creek had gathered to see the driver off. Seppala said goodbye to his wife and his curly-haired daughter Sigrid, mounted the runners, released the brake and clucked. The temperature was –20° with winds in a rare state of calm, perfect conditions for mushing. The dogs burst down the main trail in a sprint for Nome, three miles away.

Dog teams were hardly uncommon in a town where the mail was delivered by dog sled on a regular basis, but this twenty-dog team was an extraordinary sight. As they raced towards Nome with their light load, the dogs barely skimmed the surface of the snow. They moved with a smooth, elegant gait, each tug line pulled taut, the gang line nearly strumming from the pressure.

Seppala shouted out commands from the back of the sled; with twenty dogs running at stop speed, he could have been on the verge of losing control, but Togo responded to the commands as if he were attached to invisible reins. A crowd had gathered to watch Seppala run through town and it cheered as he approached. Stray dogs darted up to the team and added to the clamour, barking and nipping at each other's heels. The team careered round the sharp bend onto Front Street, with the sled bouncing and the bells on the handlebars jingling. When Togo reached the east end of the street, he darted through a passageway of shacks and out onto the beach trail. Soon, Seppala's diminutive outline faded into the distance and the crowd fell silent in the midmorning chill.

The weight of what lay ahead had begun to sink in.

EVER SINCE Billy Barnett's death eight days earlier, both Dr Welch and his nurse Emily Morgan had had little time for sleep. Billy's five-year-old sister Katherine had also developed symptoms and, even after receiving 15,000 units of the old antitoxin, showed few signs of improvement. Over on the Sandspit, the Stanleys were struggling to keep the remainder of the family intact after the tragic loss of Bessie. The parents, Henry and Anna, and another daughter, Mary, had improved after receiving serum, but Dora had not. And now a neighbour, Minnie Englestad, was ill. She was given 2,000 units of serum. In town, both Mr Cramer and Mr Hillodoll had raw sore throats, but Welch thought it wise to see whether there was any improvement before using up more of his dwindling supply.

Welch and the other town elders knew there was good reason to be hopeful. The mushers had come through before and, with Seppala's aid, surely they would come through again. But never before had so much been at stake, and it was difficult to keep up one's spirits knowing that the coldest weather in twenty years had already shut down regular mail service in Fairbanks and parts of the Yukon Territory. It was only a matter of time before the bad weather reached Nome.

For Seppala and his team, there were no distractions yet. Now that they were out on the trail, the adrenaline was pumping and the rush that the dogs set out in would not wear off until they stopped for the night. On day four, Seppala and his dogs would be at Isaac's Point, and there they would have to make what might well turn out to be the most important decision of the run: whether to cut across Norton Sound, running the team over the dangerous sea ice, or take the safer coastline route round the inlet that was at least twice as long. The end point of both routes was the settlement of Shaktoolik, located on the western coast of Norton Sound. From there, Seppala would pick up the mail trail to Unalakleet and then head over the Nulato Mountains to the Yukon River.

Time was important, but so was safety. The Sound was known throughout Alaska for its treachery; many drivers avoided it. The ice was prone to sudden breakups and over the years it had taken more than its fair share of victims. Mark Summers had warned Seppala not to risk crossing it.

Seppala had not given Summers his word. When he reached Isaac's Point, he would have to read the ice carefully and make his decision. And much of that decision would depend on the actions of Togo, who, like many lead dogs, had a sixth sense when it came to danger.

A good lead dog is the brain behind every team. He (or she) is the smartest dog in a master's kennel as well as among the fastest and hardest working. The lead dog sets the tone. He has the power to demoralise a team by allowing his tug line to run slack or to inspire it by pulling hard and steadily through a dangerous spot on the trail. It takes a large measure of courage, strong will and an almost Zen-like quality of mind for a dog to make a good leader. They are the ones who must keep a straight course along featureless sea ice that seems to have no horizon, or face a blizzard head-on. They are also the ones who must make the decisions in an emergency and, maybe most important, know when to disobey a bad command, no matter how forceful a driver may be.

In Alaska, trail-hardened lead dogs had become the stuff of legends. And Togo was a living one.

By 1925, Togo was as well known in Alaska as Seppala. He had been the driver's leader for at least the past seven years and had travelled across every terrain imaginable.

On the face of it, Togo did not look like a great leader. He was small, about forty-eight pounds, with a black, brown and greyish coat that made him look mottled, even dirty. He had won speed races and led the team on nearly every important expedition made by Seppala. At twelve years of age, Togo was still surprisingly fast, strong and alert. He was the best dog Seppala had at navigating sea ice and would often run well ahead of the team on a long lead in order to pick out the safest and easiest route across Norton Sound or other parts of the Bering Sea.

Born in October 1913, Togo was the only pup in the litter. His mother, Dolly, was one of the original female Siberians brought to Alaska. His father was Suggen, Seppala's leader during the 1914 All Alaska Sweepstakes. Seppala paid little attention to Togo when he was born. He was small and had developed an ailment that caused his throat to swell, so he spent much of his infancy in the arms of Seppala's wife, who applied hot rags to soothe the dog's pain. Despite the close attention from Constance, or perhaps because of it, Togo became difficult and mischievous. Whenever Seppala tried to harness the team, Togo would dash out and nip the ears of the working dogs, sending them into paroxysms of frustration. He was, as one reporter once wrote, 'showing all the signs of becoming a full-fledged canine delinquent'.

By the time Togo was six months old, Seppala had given him away to a woman who wanted a house pet when she returned to the states. Togo, who had been named after the Japanese admiral who won the Russo-Japanese War, rebelled at his civilised surroundings and became more and more irascible. Within a few weeks, Togo had escaped, leaping through a windowpane and running several miles back to his mates at the kennel. Seppala took him back. 'A dog so devoted to his first friends deserved to be accepted,' he would later observe.

For several weeks Togo continued to get loose and harass Seppala's team when they hit the trail. His antics amused, infuriated and intrigued Seppala. He noticed that whenever Togo met an approaching team on the trail, he would dart up to its leader and jump at him, as if he were trying to clear the way for his master. This behaviour almost cost him his life. One day he ran up to a team of trail-hardened malamutes, got mauled and had to be rushed by dog sled back to Little Creek. The experience would make Togo an even more valuable racing dog. One of the most difficult skills to teach a lead dog is how to pass another string without getting distracted and possibly lured into a fight. For the rest of his life, whenever he passed another team going in the same direction, Togo would lean into his harness, yelp and speed ahead, leaving the opponent in his wake. 'Like a lot of humans,' Seppala said, 'Togo had learned the hard way.'

Togo was about eight months old when he finally found the opportunity to show his worth, not only as a great sled dog but as a leader. One morning Seppala set out to a mining camp outside Nome. He tied Togo up and instructed that he be kept secure for two days after his departure. He was in a rush. There had been a gold strike at Dime Creek 160 miles from Nome, and a prospector had hired Seppala to get him there quickly. Seppala could not afford to have Togo hassling his team. The dog hated being locked up, and the night Seppala left he broke free from his tether and jumped the seven-foot-high fence surrounding the kennel, catching his hind leg in the top wire mesh.

Hanging by his leg on the outside of the fence, Togo was 'squealing like a little pig' until a kennel hand came out and cut the dog loose. Togo dropped to the ground, rolled over and ran off after Seppala.

The dog ran through the night, followed Seppala's trail to the roadhouse at Solomon, and rested quietly outside.

When Seppala left the next morning, he noticed his team was off to an unusually quick start. He attributed it to the scent of reindeer somewhere ahead. But when he looked far off down the trail, he saw a dog running loose. It was Togo, up to his usual tricks. Throughout the day, he led charges against reindeer and bit playfully at the leader's ears. When Seppala finally caught Togo, he had no choice but to put him at the back of the team in the wheel position where he could keep a close eye on him. As he slipped the harness over Togo's neck, the dog settled down and became serious. He kept his tug line taut and his attention focused on the trail. Seppala was astounded. He finally understood what Togo had been wanting all those months: to be a member of the team.

As the day wore on, Seppala kept moving Togo up the line. By the end of the day, the eight-month-old shared the lead with a veteran named Russky and had travelled seventy-five miles on his first day in harness. It was a feat unheard of for an inexperienced puppy. This was no canine delinquent but an 'infant prodigy', Seppala said. 'I had found a natural-born leader, something I had tried for years to breed.'

On Wednesday, January 28, the first full day of the relay, the sun finally came up some 650 miles east of Nome at the roadhouse at Tolovana, Shannon's final destination. There was still no sign of Shannon. Among the regulars waiting at the roadhouse and warming themselves by the three big stoves was twenty-one-year-old Edgar Kallands. Half Athabaskan (on his mother's side), half Newfoundlander, Kallands, like many of the drivers in the interior, had been forced since boyhood to rely on his own wits for survival. Kallands would take the serum from Shannon as soon as he arrived.

By his own definition, Kallands was a loner, and dogs had played a large role in his life. Growing up in a small village in the interior, his best friend had been a puppy. There was simply no one else around. 'He was my dog, or I was his dog. One or the other,' he once said. 'He was raised up with me.' As he grew up, his affection for dogs became even greater. While most teams would run into the woods when let loose, Kallands's dogs always stayed close, certain as they were that they would receive his affection: '[W]hen I go away and come back and they're waiting for me, I pet them all right away. I wouldn't just pet one and go on. I pet the whole bunch. Anytime I got up amongst them, they were all right around me.'

At around eleven o'clock in the morning, when the stillness outside the Tolovana roadhouse would usually be broken only by the occasional crack of a tree splitting in the cold or the extended clang of ice cracking under pressure, Kallands heard the pattering of dogs' feet and the rustle of runners gliding through the snow.

It was Wild Bill Shannon. As the team approached, Kallands and the roadhouse owner and his family all went out to help.

Shannon's face was still creased and black with frostbite, and his dogs looked done in. Even the coming of daylight had done little to raise the temperature, which was now running at around –56°. For Wild Bill, the relay was finally over. He had done his part against tough odds, and done it well.

After allowing the serum to warm up at the roadhouse, Edgar Kallands was ready to start the next leg of the relay. He hopped on his sixteen-foot mail sled, released the brake and took off. His share of the relay, thirty-one miles to Manley Hot Springs, would be overland through thick woods on a trail that cut across a wide bend of the Tanana River. It was as difficult a part of the trail as any. Years later, in an interview with a reporter, he recalled his memory of the day and what had driven him: 'It was 56 below, but I didn't notice it. We were dressed warm. We didn't have down, but I had a parky. It went below my knees, so the heat couldn't get out. You was always running or moving; your feet never got cold . . . But what the heck? What do you notice when you're twenty years old? You don't notice a thing. I think about it now. How did I survive?'

Behind the roadhouse at Tolovana, the Signal Corps operator dashed off a message to Ed Wetzler in Nenana, the governor's man in charge of overseeing the relay: ANTITOXIN DEPARTED TOLOVANA 11 AM. The relay was on its way again.

SHANNON TRIED TO REST in Tolovana, but he had the fate of Cub, Jack, Jet and now Bear on his mind. In a few days, he would return to Nenana with all four dogs in his sled. Cub, Jack and Jet would die not long after his return. Shannon's own frostbite had been so severe that it would be weeks before he would be able to shave.

He told a reporter that he had done nothing out of the ordinary, that his animals deserved all the praise. 'What those dogs did on the run to Nome is above valuation. I claim no credit for myself. The real heroes of that run . . . were the dogs of the teams that did the pulling, dogs like Cub, and Jack and Jet that gave their lives on an errand of mercy. I can't tell you yet whether I'll be able to save Bear or not. He's in pretty bad shape, and it looks like I may lose him.'

No record exists of Bear's fate. He may have survived, but in all likelihood he never ran again—a horrible fate for an animal that lived and breathed solely to run with its pack down a moonlit trail.

THE TEMPERATURE at Nome was –20°, with a ten-knot wind blowing in from the north. In the dim purple light of the arctic morning, Emily Morgan and the other nurses gathered in the breakfast nook at Maynard Columbus Hospital could see the cross above St Joseph's Church light up the sky. Usually at this time of day, the staff would be finishing their breakfast and taking the report of the night nurse coming off duty. But on this Thursday morning, January 29, the second day of the relay, there seemed little time for routine. The epidemic had taken a turn for the worse and Welch needed all the help he could get over at the Sandspit and in town.

Yesterday had been another exhausting day, yet by that evening, after Welch and Morgan had examined their findings in preparation for their daily report to Mayor Maynard, there seemed some hope. Welch had been able to report that no new cases had developed. Had the town turned the corner on the crisis even without new serum?

Unfortunately, it had not. Between late Wednesday evening and Thursday morning, at least two more children had come down with diphtheria. One of them, Daniel Kialook, a Native on the Sandspit, had membrane covering both sides of his throat and a temperature of 99.6°; another child in town was also ill with diphtheria, while several others were complaining of sore throats. Welch and Morgan now had some twenty confirmed cases on their medical list and almost double that number of suspected cases.

Welch had no way of telling how many more cases would develop by the end of the day or in which quarter of town. It was not the town population's fault. Everyone had obeyed the quarantine and each full-blown case, as well as those suspected of having been infected, had been kept away from the general population. But the strain of diphtheria affecting Nome was too virulent for these basic precautions to make enough of a difference, and the lack of modern medical equipment to fight the disease was finally getting to Dr Welch.

If only he had the means to perform the Schick test. A little more than a decade earlier, in 1913, the Schick test, named after the Hungarian-American pediatrician Béla Schick who created it, had been developed to identify those who had a natural immunity to the diphtheria toxin, probably as a consequence of an earlier exposure that they survived. It was a simple test: an injection of diluted diphtheria toxin between the layers of the skin. If the skin turned red, the person was susceptible. With this information, Welch and Morgan would have been able to identify and take steps to shield those residents who were vulnerable and reassure those who were not.

Even without Schick tests, Welch and Morgan could have reduced the epidemic's severity and possibly brought it under control if they had throat swabs, a microscope and an incubator for making cultures and determining whether the bacteria were present. Although a person can be immune to the toxin the bacteria produces, he or she can still carry the bacteria and communicate it to others. In addition, some people may take longer than others to develop symptoms or have such mild symptoms that their infection goes undetected for days. Welch had no way of reliably distinguishing a child with a nascent case of diphtheria from one who had a plain old sore throat. Nor did he have a way of identifying healthy carriers and preventing them from travelling freely, thereby spreading the contagion, even beyond town.

Without these basic tools, the job of stemming the epidemic was all the more difficult. Each sniffle and cough had to be treated as if it were the start of the disease. And the one tool Welch did have—antitoxin, weak at six years old—was now down to 21,000 units. From this point on, Welch and Morgan would have to play God and determine who would receive the life-saving medicine and who would not.

By early that Thursday afternoon, Welch passed on the news to Mayor Maynard that his earlier, more positive assessment had been premature. If the epidemic continued to spread at this new rate, there could be several more deaths before the drivers carrying the 300,000 units reached Nome. 'The situation is bad,' a panicky Maynard wrote in a telegram to Thompson in Fairbanks and Sutherland in Washington; '. . . the number of diphtheria cases increasing hourly.' According to reports from the Signal Corps operator, the serum was about 180 miles west of Nenana and was expected to reach Ruby at around eight o'clock that evening. It was another 400 miles from

Ruby to Nome; if all went well, it would be a further eight days at least before new antitoxin reached Nome.

Or would it? Maynard had never really given up on the idea of an air rescue. Governor Bone had overruled him, not changed his mind. With Welch's latest report and certain information he had recently received from the governor, Maynard wondered if the time was ripe to put in a second bid for a dramatic air rescue.

The previous day, Maynard had received a message from Bone that more serum had been located in several towns near Juneau and was being consolidated for shipment. This batch weighed about twelve pounds. Bone was planning to send it by scheduled steamer from Juneau to the port town of Seward. From there it would travel up the rail line to Nenana and wait for the next mail run.

The Juneau batch had seemed minuscule compared to the 300,000 units en route and the 1.1 million units scheduled to depart by boat from Seattle on Saturday. But with the epidemic escalating, prompt delivery of even a twelve-pound package might mean the difference between life and death for four to six children at risk of slow strangulation. Now was the moment to turn up the heat on Bone and on the federal authorities in Washington for an air rescue, and Maynard knew just the men to start the ball rolling—Thompson and Sutherland. Thompson, in particular, understood that, if you wanted to get the full attention of Washington's politicians and officials, there was no better way than through the American press.

It had been easy to get their attention when the story first broke. From the day the Associated Press first reported the diphtheria epidemic in Nome and the dearth of antitoxin, the morning and afternoon papers, from San Francisco to Chicago to New York, had covered it without hesitation and in increasingly bold type. In a matter of days, Nome, Alaska, had once again captured the world's imagination, this time through a race of Alaska's dogs against the grim reaper. DOGS PITTED AGAINST DEATH IN NOME RACE, read the headline in the *San Francisco Bulletin*. DOGS CARRY ANTITOXIN TO SNOW BOUND ALASKAN CITY, wrote the *Washington Herald*.

Editors fired off telegrams to Welch and Governor Bone, requesting interviews and personal accounts. Welch, with no time to spare, angrily declined. 'I am a physician, not a press agent,' he snapped. Bone, on the other hand, had been a press agent. He typed out energetic reports for the International News Service praising the dog drivers, 'who suffered for the sufferers' as they headed towards Nome.

The story soon jumped to radio. Audiences across the country began to reach for the dial to tune in to the 'Race Against Death' taking place out there in the vast northern reaches of the continent.

Soon it was not just Nome in the limelight. Towns forgotten since the end of the Alaskan gold rushes once again became household names: Fairbanks, Tanana, Manley Hot Springs and Ruby. Men like Wild Bill Shannon, Edgar Kallands and Curtis Welch became symbols of America's thirst for adventure and for heroes.

And then, just as the relay was starting, snowstorms and gales that had been battering Juneau for days headed for the states, hitting the Midwest and the Northeast from Maine to Georgia, pushing temperatures in New York to record lows.

It was 1° below zero outside the warm apartments of New York, and those looking out of their windows were being given a small taste of what living in the Arctic was all about. Manhattan had, ironically, found itself icebound. The Hudson River had frozen solid, trapping barges and ferries in ice floes. At the West 60th Street piers, two separate cargoes of live cattle were unloaded and herded down Twelfth Avenue to an early slaughter. The cows aboard were freezing to death where they stood. City and county workers in the thousands were trying to break up the ice and clear city streets.

A northeasterner unable to keep warm in zero-degree weather in New York could now begin to fathom what dog sledding in temperatures of –50° degrees might be like, alone and mostly in the dark. In living rooms across America, readers began drafting letters and poems in honour of the men and dogs taking part in the relay.

Maynard understood the intrinsic appeal of this man-against-nature story. He understood that the mushers were worthy of every bit of the praise and attention they were getting. But he also understood that Alaska needed to move into the modern age. It needed modern communication and transportation, so that the next time an Alaskan town found itself under threat it would not have to rely upon native technology older than anyone could calculate.

And there was something else driving Maynard, Thompson and Sutherland. They were simply tired of being ignored by the federal government. After all, a good argument could be made that the federal authorities, having acquired Alaska from the Russians in 1867, had in the end paid it little attention. Welch had asked for serum the previous summer. His request had been ignored.

If it had to be a crisis in Nome that focused the nation on Alaska's plight, so be it. In an aggressive campaign of telegrams and exclusive dispatches, Maynard employed a no-holds-barred approach in the pleas he sent to wire services, newspapers and institutions across the states, from the venerable Associated Press and the *New York World* to the Seattle Chamber of Commerce.

'Help immediately!' Maynard begged in a cable to the AP.

> HELP BY AIRPLANE WITH ANTITOXIN SERUM IS THE APPEAL OF NOME, NOT FOR SOURDOUGHS BUT ESPECIALLY FOR CHILDREN OF YOUNG AMERICA . . . PLEASE GET UNCLE SAM TO SEND A PLANE FROM FAIRBANKS WHERE . . . MEN HAVE VOLUNTEERED TO FLY TO NOME IN FOUR HOURS TO BRING RELIEF TO THE DANGEROUS SITUATION PREVAILING HERE. ANTITOXIN SHIPPED FROM JUNEAU WOULD ARRIVE IN NENANA ON FEB 3 WHICH IF SENT BY AIRPLANE FROM THERE TO NOME WILL BEAT THE DOG TEAMS BY SEVERAL DAYS WHICH MAY MEAN THE SAVING OF MANY LIVES. EVERYTHING LOOKED FAVORABLE YESTERDAY BUT TODAY CONDITIONS HAVE BEEN REVERSED . . . DR WELCH . . . HAS ONLY ONE GOOD DOSE LEFT AND THIS IS SIX YEARS OLD STOP

Soon, nearly every American newspaper printed Maynard's broadcast for help, publishing it on their front pages and giving it a prominent headline. The *Washington Post* urged: EPIDEMIC GROWS GRAVER, CITY BEGS OFFICIALS HERE TO SEND AID BY AIR. The *New York Sun* suggested that an air rescue would be 'the greatest humanitarian service ever rendered by a flier in peace time'.

Washington immediately began to reconsider its stance on the proposed mercy flight.

DELEGATE SUTHERLAND was the first politician to move into action. With the snow still thick on the ground in Washington, DC, Sutherland approached the Justice and Navy departments for official permission for Roy Darling to fly a plane out of Fairbanks. Permission was granted. He then urged officials at the US Surgeon General and the Public Health Service to review the possibility of an air rescue to Nome. They seemed open to the idea, and Sutherland then wired Thompson and Mayor Maynard the good news.

The news from Sutherland, however, did little to calm Maynard. By the following day, Friday, January 30, the mayor's anxiety had escalated. Apparently there had been another death overnight, bringing the toll to five since the outbreak began on January 20.

Dr Welch and Nurse Morgan were now monitoring twenty-two patients and thirty suspected cases. At least fifty-five people, according to his medical records, had been in close contact with someone who had the disease. Among the seriously ill was the young daughter of a miner named John Winters. She had membrane on both sides of her throat and a 102° fever. Welch gave her 6,000 units of serum, bringing his supply down to 13,000.

After hearing the day's tolls from the doctor and his staff, Maynard again hurried to the Signal Corps office, this time with a much more audacious plan. The chances were high, he knew, that even with the epidemic worsening, Governor Bone could not be persuaded to allow a plane to fly in the twelve pounds of Juneau serum. So Maynard decided to turn up the pressure a notch. He addressed his next telegram to his colleagues at the Chamber of Commerce in Seattle. He wanted them to use their influence in Washington to prepare a plane to leave from Seattle with the 1.1 million units of serum scheduled to leave on board the steamship *Alameda* the next day bound for Alaska's ice-free port of Seward. A plane could get the serum to Nome within seventy-two hours.

The Seattle businessmen moved on the suggestion and wired the Chamber of Commerce's representative in Washington, J. J. Underwood, asking him to secure a meeting with Major General Mason Patrick, chief of the US Air Service.

The year before, the air service, with the help of the navy, had launched the first successful round-the-world flight on planes built for long-distance flying. The planes, Douglas World Cruisers with fifty-foot wingspans and cruising speeds of ninety miles per hour, had been built by a torpedo-plane manufacturer, Donald Douglas.

The Chamber of Commerce wanted one of those fliers, Lieutenant Erik Nelson, to fly the serum to Nome. Nelson had been a member of the Black Wolf Squadron, which had flown from New York to Nome via Fairbanks in 1920, and his chances of succeeding in a Douglas World Cruiser were far greater than Darling's chances in a flimsy aircraft of the Fairbanks Airplane Corporation.

The proposed flight, taking off from the Sand Point federal aviation field north of Seattle, would be a ground-breaking event: a rescue attempt that was also the longest air-mail flight in US history.

The press understood the significance of the proposed flight and called in experts to debate the possibility. Sand Point Commander Lieutenant Theodore Koenig, reached by the *Seattle Union Record* and the *Post-Intelligencer,* confirmed for reporters that a properly equipped plane with a large flying radius leaving from Sand Point could reach Nome before one of the smaller planes in Fairbanks. 'Even so,' Koenig said, 'the flight from Seattle presents grave difficulties as the opportunity to make favorable landings and replenish the fuel supply en route to the northern city is practically nil.'

While the experts debated the merits of the flight, one reader in New York and the general manager of a major US wire service were working on an entirely different plan. The reader was Carl Lomen, son of the former Nome mayor, who was in the city on business. The wire service general manager was Loring Pickering of the North American Newspaper Alliance. Lomen and Pickering wanted the government to send a cruiser with a plane on board up the Pacific coast as far north as the Bering Sea ice line so that, when the plane took off, it would have the shortest possible trip to Nome.

In a telegram to the US Surgeon General, the Alliance offered to find and pay for a bacteriologist, culture tubes, swabs, an incubator and other emergency laboratory supplies at any point on the Pacific coast if Washington would dispatch a 'cruiser carrying airplane and crew' to the edge of the ice pack of the Bering Sea. According to the telegram, the ice pack reached as far as Nunviak Island that winter, only some 300 miles south of Nome.

The telegram arrived at the office of the US Surgeon General and got pushed all the way up to the desk of President Coolidge, who instructed his health tsar to provide Nome with whatever it needed.

Sutherland, meanwhile, was continuing to pressurise the War Department and the Surgeon General's office on the Newspaper Alliance's proposal.

The navy had less than twenty-four hours to make its decision and, by the close of day, they had decided that the trip was too risky. A cruiser would not be able to get close enough for a plane carrying serum to make a nonstop flight to Nome without itself risking being crushed by the Bering Sea ice. The best the navy could offer, it said, was to place its minesweeper *Swallow*, which operated along the northwest Pacific coast as well as in Alaskan waters, on high alert to rush any bacteriologist and lab supplies found by the Alliance to the ice-free port of Seward.

At least one expert disagreed with the navy's decision: the renowned explorer Roald Amundsen happened to be in New York, attempting to drum up support for his 1925 aerial assault on the North Pole. A cruiser was entirely feasible, he told reporters; 'from what I know of the Western Coast of Alaska at this time of year, I am convinced that a cruiser or destroyer could get within firing range of Nome'. Despite this strong endorsement, the navy would not commit.

Sutherland kept up his lobbying efforts to fly the Juneau serum. Over the past two days he had kept one card close to his chest—William Thompson in Fairbanks. Sutherland had cabled Thompson to begin preparations for a flight, in the event that the War Department declined Maynard's plea for a plane. 'SUGGEST AVIATOR DARLING HAVE SOURDOUGH PASSENGER WHO KNOWS THE TRAIL,' he told Thompson.

Thompson gathered up the crew of volunteer mechanics and ordered them to begin assembling the plane. He then went on a hunt for a mechanic to assist Darling during the flight and found Ralph Mackie, a resident of Anchorage who had flown with the Royal Flying Corps in Canada. Meanwhile, a former war pilot who had been travelling in the interior learned of the epidemic, and sent a telegram to Thompson that he was heading to Ruby, a town along the mail route, where he would wait to help Darling to refuel when he landed. Ruby had a depot of aviation fuel that had been left behind by the army for the pilots of the 1920 New York–Nome aerial expedition. The former war pilot could decant the fuel into canisters and be ready for a quick turnround.

For the first time, the plane seemed a real possibility: the craft was being assembled and Darling now had a copilot who knew the country. Even the temperature had warmed by ten degrees, to –39°. But they still needed to get control of the serum.

Thompson and Sutherland kept up the pressure on Governor Bone, urging him to approve the flight. Bone refused. They then turned to Edward Wetzler, the point man for the relay in Nenana, and pestered him to hand over the Juneau serum as soon as it arrived by train. Wetzler adamantly declined. His loyalties remained with the governor. Even the Surgeon General's office, which appeared to question Bone's decision, baulked at ordering him around, requesting solely that Bone 'use his discretion'.

Once again, the *News-Miner* editor was livid. 'Nome looks to Fairbanks for LIFE, and if there is not too much Red Tape interfering, Fairbanks will be in Nome in less than almost no time,' Thompson wrote in his paper. 'Fairbanks is standing by, lashed to the mast . . . beating its Sourdough wings off trying to rush to the help of its friends, and restrained from doing it.'

BONE REFUSED TO BUDGE. Despite immense pressure and a rising tide of calls from the press for a dramatic air rescue, he stuck with his decision. He wired Wetzler, ordering him not to release the twelve-pound package of serum from Juneau to anyone under any circumstances. The serum would stay in Nenana until a mail team could pick it up.

But if Bone understood anything, as an ex-reporter and ex-PR man, he understood public opinion. To do nothing but stay the course would subject him to accusations of stubbornness at best and a callous disregard for human life at worst. Doing nothing might also hurt Nome. If the epidemic was gaining ground at the speed Maynard had warned, the relay, Bone realised, had to be speeded up.

Bone summoned his aide. He told him he wanted to call in more drivers for the final part of the run between Nulato and Nome for the 300,000 units of serum. And for this he needed the help of Mark Summers, the superintendent of the gold company in Nome.

The decision was shocking. In effect, Bone risked cutting out the most important man of the relay—Leonhard Seppala. And he was asking Mark Summers, Seppala's sponsor, to do the cutting.

The argument for the change made sense. Although Seppala was the fastest driver in Alaska, under the original plan he had a 630-mile round trip to cover. As fast as he was, no one man could beat fresh recruits who had to travel only a short distance before they turned the serum over to someone else.

On the other hand, Seppala was still the best man to take the serum across Norton Sound, a dangerous short cut that could save a day of travel. To preserve that part of the original plan, Seppala had to be informed that, instead of driving all the way to Nulato, he should wait for the serum somewhere near Shaktoolik, on the western coast of the Sound, for the oncoming driver.

The problem was that there was no longer any way to communicate with Seppala. The telephone lines in Nome went only as far as Solomon, fifty miles east of town, and the Signal Corps system bypassed the villages along the coast by shooting across Norton Sound to St Michael, where a relay station conveyed messages to Unalakleet and then over the Nulato Mountains to the interior and beyond. While the new plan still assumed that Seppala would make the dangerous run back across Norton Sound, it relied upon the driver heading north to find Seppala. Two oncoming drivers could easily miss each other in blizzard-force winds.

Still, Bone's order had to be followed. Summers tracked down Ed Rohn, a dog driver whose claim to fame was that he had once beaten Seppala in a race, and ordered him to drive twenty-one miles to Port Safety and wait there at the roadhouse for further instructions. He then called out to the kennels at Little Creek, got Gunnar Kaasen, another Hammon dog driver, on the phone, and requested that he put together a dog team and drive to the mining village of Bluff, about thirty miles east of Safety.

Kaasen went to the kennels, looked over the team, and began to harness up the dogs that had been left behind. Before he left, Seppala had made it clear that, if Hammon needed a team for company business, Fox, a brown and black husky, should be the leader. Kaasen, who worked closely with Seppala at the gold fields in the summer, had always admired another dog. The dog was stocky for a Siberian, black as night except for a white right foreleg. His name was Balto. One by one, Kaasen brought the dogs to the gang line. When it came time to clip in the leader, he ignored Seppala's direction and brought Balto to the position.

It was a decision that would leave a strain in the relationship between the two colleagues.

When Kaasen reached Bluff, he was to enlist roadhouse keeper Charles Olson, a bachelor and old-time sourdough, and tell him to hitch up his rig, drive twenty-five miles farther east to the trading post at Golovin and wait for the serum.

While the drivers prepared to take up their positions, Summers reached the storekeeper in Unalakleet via the Signal Corps system and told him to 'spare no expense' in posting more teams on the trail. At least two more teams were placed, one in Unalakleet and another thirty-eight miles up the coast at Shaktoolik.

All told, twenty men and about 150 dogs would now be taking part in the race to save Nome. As for Seppala, all that could be done was to warn the new men on the route that they should keep a lookout for the Norwegian and his team of Siberian dogs. Should they meet up with Seppala, they were to stop him and hand the serum over to him. Summers had already calculated that the most likely place for a hand-over would be somewhere near Shaktoolik.

With the new plans in place, there was little more that Bone could do but wait. It was probably clear to him that if the dogs failed there would surely be hell to pay, given his stubborn refusal to allow a daring air rescue.

TWO DAYS EARLIER, on Wednesday, January 28, the young Edgar Kallands, who had taken the 300,000 units of serum from an exhausted Wild Bill Shannon, completed his run to Manley Hot Springs with relatively few mishaps. The weather had been a brutal 56° below zero and, according to one newspaper report, Kallands's gloved hands froze to the sled's handlebar; the trip from Tolovana had taken more than five hours and the roadhouse owner had to pour boiling water on the birchwood bar to pry him loose. Kallands stayed overnight in Manley, and he and the dogs finally got the rest they needed. Then they began the fifty-four-mile journey to their home in Tanana. At Tanana, Kallands and his fellow townsfolk would listen to the progress of the serum run by telephone over the old telegraph line between Tanana and Ruby that the Corps had abandoned when it went to wireless communications.

Names of fellow Athabaskans like Sam Joseph, Titus Nickolai, Dave Corning, Harry Pitka, and George and Edgar Nollner would crackle across the wire over the next two days as each continued the westward relay across the interior to meet Seppala.

AT 3 A.M. on Friday morning, January 30, Charlie Evans, the twelfth driver in the relay, was waiting at Bishop Mountain when he heard a dog team in the distance. The driver was George Nollner, Evans's close friend, and he was humming an Athabaskan love song, thinking of the woman he'd married a few days earlier. George had split his run, between Whiskey Creek and Bishop Mountain, with his older brother, Edgar, in order to speed the serum down the trail. When George arrived, he unwrapped the package and the two went inside the cabin to sit by the stove and warm the serum. They stayed inside for nearly an hour, worried that the deepening cold would freeze the medicine and render it useless.

The temperature had warmed slightly over the past day. But it had been only a brief reprieve. By early morning, a troubling cold had begun to set in. Outside the cabin, when Evans looked up at the sky, the green and white lights of the aurora borealis danced a slow, graceful waltz. Like so many of the mushers, Evans was half Athabaskan on his mother's side. For many Athabaskans, the northern lights were the torches of spirits to guide travellers on their journey to heaven. All one had to do was whistle and, according to their legend, the spirits would come down out of the sky to one's aid. But Evans knew not to be lulled into a false sense of security. The temperature was –62°.

Evans's run would begin at Bishop Mountain, a fish camp on the north bank of the Yukon River. He knew every twist and turn of this stretch of the river, because in the summer he piloted a riverboat, navigating the Yukon and the nearby Koyukuk tributary. The two rivers meet ten miles west of Bishop Mountain at Evans's home village of Koyukuk. His father, John Evans, a gold miner from Idaho, ran a store there, and in winter Charlie helped out his dad transporting merchandise and furs by dog sled.

It was about 4.30 a.m. when Evans finally started off on the thirty-mile trip to Nulato. He had been up all night waiting for George and was already tired. Just ten miles into his run, he ran into trouble. The suppressed waters of the Koyukuk had broken through the ice where the river converged with the Yukon and covered the trail for half a mile with overflow. The dogs managed to avoid the open water, but the relative warmth of the vapour rising up off the river created a thick, cottony wall of ice fog. The fog rose to Evans's waist and swallowed the dogs and the sled.

Evans drove blind through the thick mist, grateful when it lowered enough ahead of him to reveal the tips of the dogs' tails and the bobbing tops of their heads. All he could do was stand on the runners, hold on for bumps and 'let the dogs go'. Many dogs would baulk in the blinding whiteness, but Evans's dogs 'had a sixth sense, seemed to know what I was thinking'. A light breeze had begun to blow, creating a wind chill, and Evans began to stiffen up with the cold. The wind was blowing sand off the exposed portions of the steep bank; under such conditions the sand could feel like shards of glass when it hit a driver's face.

Evans neared the village of Koyukuk where his father was waiting, straining for any sounds of his son. John Evans heard the squeak of the runners against the cold snow and ran out to the bank to urge his son to stop, to come inside and warm up.

'I can't stop,' Charlie shouted back from the river. 'Them dogs would be hard to wake up.'

Five miles past Koyukuk, the river swung ninety degrees to the south-southwest and ran along a ridge of densely wooded trees that rose 1,000 feet above the river. Nulato was about ten miles away.

Some time after Charlie left his father behind, the legs of his two lead dogs turned blue and became swollen, burnt raw by the cold where the harnesses had cut away the skin and fur. They had severe frostbite. The dogs stumbled on, until suddenly one of the lead dogs dropped to the ground. Then the other went down. The team stopped and Evans staggered up to the front. Both dogs were crippled and Evans had to put them in the basket of the sled. According to one report, he moved to the front of the team, where he strapped a harness over his shoulder and helped the remaining dogs pull the sled over the last stretch of the trail to Nulato.

A little before 10 a.m., Evans could see the outline of Nulato Island in the middle of the river, and a little way beyond, off to the right, was Nulato. As Evans pulled in to the village, he carried the lead dogs into the cabin and slumped by the stove. Both dogs were dead. When asked about the run some fifty years later, Evans simply recalled: 'It was real cold.'

THE SERUM had been on the trail now for three days and had travelled 356 miles. But there were still 318 miles to go, and the job of moving the serum thirty-six miles closer to Nome now rested in the hands of an Athabaskan Indian called Tommy Patsy, who had made a name for himself a few summers earlier when he had taken part in one of the last hunts of a grizzly bear by spear.

About half an hour after Charlie Evans arrived, Patsy secured the serum in his own sled and with the fastest dogs in the village set out on the trail, which followed the river southwest to Kaltag, a village that sat on a bluff overlooking the Yukon. The trail then left the Yukon River and headed over the mountains, where the weather grew worse. Kaltag was the start of the ninety-mile-long portage linking the interior with the Bering Sea coast. At the other end of the portage, at the Native settlement of Unalakleet, the relay would leave the relatively calm but cold interior and enter the unpredictable conditions of the coast. The serum had yet to face its greatest challenge—the crossing of Norton Sound.

The Ice Factory

Alaskans called it 'the ice factory'. Norton Sound, a forbidding inlet of the Bering Sea some 150 miles long and 125 miles across at its widest point, appeared from afar to be an endless expanse of solid ice that stretched until it met the sky. But the distant view was deceptive, for the closer you got to the Sound, the more conscious you became that the ice was in a constant state of change. Huge tracts would suddenly break free and drift out to sea or a long narrow lead of water would open up and widen. Depending upon the temperature, wind and currents, the ice could assume various configurations—five-foot-high ice hummocks, a stretch of glare ice or a line of pressure ridges that looked like a chain of mountains across the Sound. Even among people whose valour on ice had been proven, Norton Sound was considered the most perilous kind of terrain to cross.

Then there was the wind. It was a given that on Norton Sound the wind howled and that life along these shores would be a constant struggle against a force that tried to beat you back at every step of every task. But when the wind blew from the east, people took special note. These winds were shaped into powerful tunnels, and gusts barrelled down mountain slopes and through river valleys, spilling out onto the Sound at speeds of more than seventy miles per hour. They could flip sleds, hurl a driver off the runners and drag the wind chill down to –100°. Even more terrifying, when the east winds blew, the ice growing out from shore often broke free and was sent out to sea in large floes.

EARLY SATURDAY MORNING on January 31, the fourth day of the relay, two men—Myles Gonangnan, a full-blooded Eskimo, and the Norwegian Leonhard Seppala—stood on opposite sides of Norton Sound, unaware of each other's location, and studied the ice and the wind. Each had a decision to make. He could take an over-water route, cutting a great deal of time, or could follow the safer onshore trail that skirted the Sound. For neither man would the decision be based on courage or even stamina—but solely on which way the wind blew.

Over the past few days, the wind had been blowing onshore, pushing water in from the Bering Sea and raising the level of the Sound, which had weakened the ice. As long as the wind continued to blow from that quarter, there would be little cause for alarm. The ice would continue to break up, as always, but it would merely drift towards shore. Sometime during the night, however, the wind's direction had shifted. It was now blowing offshore, from the northeast, and getting stronger.

A little before five that morning, Gonangnan had received the serum at Unalakleet from his fellow Eskimo and townsman, Victor

Anagick, who had travelled down from the Old Woman shelter cabin on the portage. Leaving it inside Traeger's store to warm near the heat of his iron stove, Gonangnan set out to examine conditions on Norton Sound. He had to decide whether to take the trail route northeast into the foothills or the short cut over the ice, which ran several miles out from shore, under the shadow of Besboro Island.

The shortest route of all would have been to cut straight across the Sound, heading northwest in a direct line to Nome. But in the middle of the Sound was a large body of open water called a polynya, which was kept free of ice most of the season by a constant eddying. As ice formed in the area of the polynya, wind and current pushed it towards the edge, where it compacted and was then driven into the southerly moving ice pack of the Bering Sea. It made a terrifying grinding noise, like giant bulldozers dragging their metal buckets against concrete.

Gonangnan studied the giant field of ice as it creaked and sighed, and by the light of the moon he could see the whole body slightly rise and fall. The sea was rolling in from beneath. Somewhere out in the distance there was open water, spray exploding off whitecaps and floes rumbling and fragmenting. In the cavernous sky above, the stars twinkled with unusual clarity, and behind him the wind was growing stronger. The signs were clear: a storm was brewing and could well land full force on the coast in twenty-four to forty-eight hours. The question was no longer whether the sea would break up but when. He would not risk taking the short cut.

Gonangnan returned to the store, picked up the serum and tied the package down in his sled. It was about 5.30 a.m. when he took off for the foothills behind Unalakleet. A few hours later, across the Sound, Leonhard Seppala, unaware that the relay had changed, made his decision. He would cross the Sound.

For the first twelve miles from Unalakleet, the inland trail ran parallel to the coast, up and down a series of hills with bared slopes and sharp turns, before coming back briefly to shore. In the rising wind, Gonangnan headed over the slippery surface of the lagoon behind Unalakleet and then turned inland and climbed a 300-foot rise into the hills. It was a steep ascent that required alternating between pushing the sled from behind at a jog and pedalling from the runners. Drifts created by the wind and a recent snowfall had built up on the trail and the dogs punched their way through. But the wind had had too much of a head start on Gonangnan. The trail soon became too heavily drifted with snow for the dogs. They wallowed in it, unable to get traction. Gonangnan had to stop the team and strap on his snowshoes in preparation for breaking trail.

Breaking trail was a laborious process. A driver had to anchor the sled, take off his own gloves to put on snowshoes and then jog back and forth over the trail until he had packed down enough snow for the dogs to get through. Whenever there was an easy stretch, he would get back on the sled and ride the runners to catch his breath. A trailbreaker could easily go over a bad stretch of trail three times before the ground was tamped down enough for the dogs.

It took Gonangnan several hours before he finally reached the abandoned fish camp at the point where the trail came back down to the shore. He had been on the trail for about five hours and had managed only twelve miles. It was dismal progress. He built a small fire in one of the abandoned huts and set the serum nearby. He knew the worst was yet to come. The wind outside was blowing harder with each passing hour.

From the fishing camp, the trail ran for five miles up and down over steep ridges until it reached thc Blueberry Hills. The Blueberry Hills' summit is 1,000 feet high and the ascent to its exposed ridge top is considered one of the most difficult climbs on the trail to Nome for dogs and driver. At the end of the ridge, the trail makes a sharp turn to the west and heads down a steep three-mile descent to the beach for the final stretch to Shaktoolik.

After warming himself and the serum for about fifteen minutes, Gonangnan headed back out on the trail and began the exhausting climb. For the next several hours he alternated between running behind the sled and riding the runners. The varied terrain required him to be constantly on the move and on the alert. As a team climbs, the sled skids sideways and downhill. The driver must constantly fight gravity. With knees bent and hands locked tightly to the sled, he pedals vigorously, trying to kick the sled back up into line with the dogs. When on the sled, he puts all his weight over the uphill runner to create a little friction. The dogs, too, struggle against the drift of the sled, and the wheel dogs take the brunt. Each time the sled slips downhill, the force nearly jerks the wheel dogs off their feet and they must dig into the snow with their claws to regain footing.

As Gonangnan battled up to the summit, the wind came at him nearly head-on, picking up walls of snow and dumping them across the trail. Gonangnan later recalled that 'eddies of drifting, swirling snow passing between the dogs' legs and under the bellies made them appear to be fording a fast running river'.

Suddenly, the world closed in on him. It was a whiteout. The horizon ahead had been swallowed up between the overcast sky of the growing storm and the endless white line of the Blueberry Hills. He could not make out the jumbled ice of the Sound below. Every point of visual reference had vanished. It was a northern vertigo, a physical experience unlike any other, where one loses one's sense of balance in the absence of shadows and edges. A dog driver on the trail could no longer tell whether there was a dip or a bump ahead, or whether the dogs had made a wrong turn and were heading off the edge of the ridge.

The team veered sharply to the west and the sled picked up speed. They had begun the descent back to the beach. This section of the trail, although protected from the wind, is notoriously icy and most drivers usually prepare before heading down. They will unhook a few dogs from their tug lines and begin the descent with their foot on the brake to slow down the sled. To add friction, some will wrap chains called roughlocks round the runners, and, if they have to, they will inch down the slope in stretches of controlled speed, stopping whenever they begin to accelerate too rapidly.

There would be no such preparation time for Gonangnan. In the whiteout, he did not even realise he had reached the edge until he flew off it like a runaway locomotive. On a steep gradient, a sled picks up speed faster than the team and can run right over the wheel dogs. If the runners catch an edge, the sled may flip, tumbling the entire team and the driver hundreds of feet down to the beach.

That day, Gonangnan was lucky. As he neared Norton Sound, the whiteout conditions cleared and he could see the beach below. The sled began to slow down. He had made it safely down the descent. But as he well knew, the final miles once he returned to the shoreline would provide a different yet equally unnerving challenge. Out in the open on the Sound there was nothing to block the wind, which shot down the Koyuk River valley and across the Sound, slamming into the low-lying spit of Shaktoolik in a noise like thunder. The headwinds can be in excess of fifty miles per hour, the gusts even more.

By 11 a.m., the wind was blowing at gale force, about forty miles per hour. The wind chill was down to at least –70°, for the air that feeds the gusts comes down from the Arctic. Gonangnan and his dogs had been travelling for about nine hours, but Gonangnan mushed on. Drifting particles of snow and sand hurtled towards him like a white wall. Four gruelling hours later, Shaktoolik appeared on the horizon.

It was about 3 p.m. when Gonangnan arrived at Shaktoolik, and still there was no sign of Seppala. No one knew where he was. He could have been delayed or he might have already come across the Sound, passed through Shaktoolik without resting, and was on his way to Unalakleet. Gonangnan, however, had not seen him on the trail.

Mark Summers had prepared for this eventuality, asking Henry Ivanoff, a Russian Eskimo who captained a schooner on the Sound in the summers, to be ready to take the serum. Ivanoff sat in the store waiting for the serum to warm while Gonangnan gave him the last few details about the weather outside. While he might not have been the ideal man for the job, Ivanoff would do his best. And so he set off along the shore ice of Norton Sound, bound for Ungalik.

THAT SAME Saturday afternoon, Dr Welch and Head Nurse Morgan continued their vigilance. For the past eleven days, they had been monitoring and caring for an increasing number of patients. Today, three more children had come down with the disease, pushing the case load to twenty-seven. There were thirty suspects and at least eighty people who had come in contact with the bacteria, and now there was no more antitoxin. A new fear had taken hold of Welch. Among his patients was Margaret Curran, whose father ran the roadhouse out at Solomon. Margaret had recently gone out there to help her father to cook for guests. Had she spread the disease beyond Nome? Welch was not taking any chances. 'Would advise keeping all government nurses at their stations as they are all I have to depend on outside of Nome and it seems inevitable that diphtheria will occur at some of these stations in near future,' he wired to the authorities in Washington.

A freelance reporter in Nome working for the Universal Service press agency captured the town's mood. 'The situation in diphtheria stricken Nome is extremely critical,' E. R. Hyldahl wrote in a story picked up by the Seattle press. 'There is nothing left to stop the ravages of the disease . . . All hope is in the dogs and their heroic drivers.'

Later that day, Welch was given an update: Gonangnan had left Unalakleet early that morning and all the mushers on the line had been told to keep an eye out for Seppala. With or without Seppala, it was hoped that the serum would reach Nome the next day.

Welch heard the news with relief. In a telegram to the Public Health Service, he wrote:

> HAVE RECEIVED INFORMATION THAT 300,000 UNITS ANTITOXIN WILL ARRIVE TOMORROW AT NOON STOP IF YOU COULD BE HERE ALONE YOU COULD REALIZE WHAT THIS MEANS TO ME STOP

AROUND THE SAME TIME Seppala, too, was feeling confident. Earlier that morning, just a few hours after Gonangnan had set off on the inland route, Seppala had thrown off the cautions of Summers and others and chosen the short cut across the northern section of Norton Sound to Ungalik. It was a good move. He had made the crossing.

The wind was behind him now and he was grateful. A storm was clearly brewing and the wind continued to blow hard. The snow was lifting up off the ground in an explosion of hard, fine crystals, but he was moving with the wind so it did not matter much to him. In fact, the tail wind had made for a fast journey. He had just left the fishing camp of Ungalik and the dogs were speeding towards Shaktoolik over the last twenty-three miles of shorefast ice.

Seppala had covered nearly 170 miles in the past three days and so far he had been lucky with the weather and the ice. Although he could not see the town through the haze of snow, Seppala knew that Shaktoolik was only minutes away.

Suddenly, Togo and the dogs picked up speed. They were racing but after what? And then he saw it. There was another sled-dog team up ahead. It wasn't moving. Instead, the driver was standing in the middle of the team, flailing his arms. A reindeer had wandered out on the trail and his dogs were fighting to get at it, all snarled up in a tangle of lines and flying fur. Now Seppala's dogs wanted to join the pursuit and they put on a burst of speed. Seppala held on tight.

When the other driver saw the Siberian huskies coming towards him, he knew he had more important things to do than get his dogs away from the reindeer. There was only one man who could be out on the trail today with a team of Siberians heading in the opposite direction. He began to wave his arms frantically, determined to catch Seppala's attention. But Seppala, who could not make out what the driver was shouting above the whistling of the wind, had no intention of stopping to help. He could not afford the delay.

Togo was approaching the team rapidly. Henry Ivanoff ran towards Seppala as he raced past: '*The serum! The serum! I have it here!*'

Seppala at first did not believe what he had heard. He slammed on the sled brake. The brake made little purchase against the snow and only after some distance did he manage to stop the dogs and turn them round. By the time Seppala made his way back to Ivanoff, the driver had stopped the fight. He ran over to Seppala with the serum and told him of the change of plan. It was Seppala's job now to carry the serum back across Norton Sound and on to the roadhouse at Golovin, where Charlie Olson was waiting for the hand-over.

Alarmed by the news that the epidemic had spread rapidly, Seppala started off at once for Ungalik, twenty-three miles to the north. He had to decide what to do. The route back across Norton Sound had become much more dangerous since the morning. The wind was building and it was beginning to get dark, so he would not be able to see or hear the ice. He could take the long route round the shore, but neither he nor Nome could afford the extra day of travel. Seppala had his own daughter to worry about. Sigrid was only eight years old, his only child, and he had no way of knowing if she was on Dr Welch's growing list.

Seppala may have had his doubts about recrossing Norton Sound but the rest of the world did not. In the states that same Saturday afternoon, former residents of Nome were regaling the press with tales of the courageous musher who would save the town.

'There isn't any quit in him,' said a former mayor of Nome, George Baldwin. 'There isn't any quit to any of those chaps, for that matter—Kaasen, Wild Bill Shannon—he's an Irishman—Edgar Kallands or any of 'em. Those dogs of theirs will get them there quick.'

The kind of confidence these Alaskan sourdoughs had in Seppala, Seppala had in his lead dog, Togo. When he saw the huts of Ungalik up ahead, Seppala turned left without hesitation and headed out across Norton Sound. It was now dark. The temperature, as he would later estimate, was –30° and the gale was in his face. With the wind chill, it was a brutal 85° below zero. There was nothing Seppala could do but drive as if he were in a race.

Seppala had been out on the Sound with Togo once before in a northeast gale. He had been just a few miles offshore when, in a lull between gusts, he heard an ominous crack. He ordered Togo to 'haw', but the leader had already felt the crack and was heading at top speed towards the nearest point on land. He was closing in to shore when Togo inexplicably reared up and somersaulted back onto his teammates. Seppala shouted angrily. This was no time for circus stunts. He ran up to Togo to see what was the matter, and as he neared the dog he saw why he had stopped. No more than six feet ahead was an open channel of water. The lead was growing wider before Seppala's eyes. He was on a floe, drifting out to sea. He skirted the edges of the floe, looking for an opportunity to escape, but there was none. It had been noon when he set out from Isaac's Point and now night was falling and the temperature dropping. There was nothing he could do but curl up with his dogs, conserve his strength and warmth, and hope for a shift in the wind.

Several hours later, no such shift had occurred and Seppala's anguish grew. His dogs sensed the change in his mood and let out a long and low plaintive cry. Then Togo gave a short yelp.

The leader had sensed a shift: the wind was beginning to blow onshore. Seppala hitched his team back up and waited. He drifted for nine more hours until he could see the shoreline only a few hundred yards ahead. The ice raft was closing in on a floe that had jammed up against the shorefast ice. Seppala mushed along the perimeter to find a place to jump off. The closest point on the raft to the floe was about five feet—too wide for Seppala to jump. But if he could get Togo to the other side, the dog could pull the two floes together. Seppala tied a long towline to Togo's harness, picked him up and hurled him across the open channel.

Most dogs would have run away after a stunt like that but, as Seppala later reported, 'Togo seemed to understand what he had to do.' Once on the other side, Togo dug his nails into the floe and lurched towards shore. The line snapped. Togo spun round and looked back across the chasm at Seppala. The line slipped into the water. Seppala was speechless. He had just been given a death sentence.

Animal psychologists have a phrase for the ability to find solutions. It is called 'adaptive intelligence'. The icy lead separating Togo from Seppala was keeping the dog from his reward: reuniting with his master and his team. As Seppala stood staring across the lead at Togo, the dog dived into the water, snapped the line up into his mouth and struggled back out onto the jammed-up floe. Holding the line tightly in his jaws, Togo rolled over the line 'until it was twice looped about his shoulders' and began to pull. The floe started to move and Togo continued to pull until it was close enough for Seppala and his teammates to jump safely across.

Now, as Seppala and Togo crossed Norton Sound in the late afternoon of Saturday, January 31, Seppala had no choice but to put his faith in Togo one more time. As Seppala feared, it was already too dark for his own eyes to see anything. The wind was deafening. Occasionally, he leaned out over the sled, listening for any clue that the ice was cracking up. The Sound was holding, and Togo seemed unfazed by the wind, covering the miles of trail with his head low and his body level in deep concentration. He kept a straight course, despite the hummocks and slippery patches of ice in his path.

At eight o'clock that evening, Seppala and Togo pulled up the bank at Isaac's Point on the other side of Norton Sound. The dogs had travelled an incredible eighty-four miles that day, half of it against the wind, and they were worn out. Togo and the team had averaged eight miles per hour. They were hungry and needed a rest before battling the wind for the next fifty miles to Golovin. Seppala unhooked the dogs and fed them salmon and seal blubber. They wasted no time in curling up their tails and going to sleep.

With the dogs cared for, Seppala drew his sled into the roadhouse and unlashed the package. He undid the wrappings of fur and canvas down to the paper cartons enclosing the serum. From the appearance of the cartons, Seppala was certain that the serum inside had frozen, so he placed it as close to the fire as he dared. While the serum warmed, Seppala slid into his reindeer sleeping-bag and took a few hours of rest. At this point, he could only hope.

Cold Glory

At 2 a.m. on Sunday, February 1, the fifth day of the relay, Nichuk, the owner of the roadhouse at Isaac's Point, shook Seppala awake. The storm that had been heading up from the south over the past two days had arrived, and it was time for Seppala to leave. Removing the serum package from its spot near the stove, Seppala wrapped it inside his sleeping-bag, covered it with a sealskin robe and tied it down with a blanket in his sled. As an extra precaution, he covered it with additional animal skins. With a storm like this, he was taking no chances. He pushed the sled out of the door.

The wind was howling and the ice on Norton Sound hissed and cracked. While Seppala harnessed the last dogs to the gang line, an old Eskimo emerged from the roadhouse and headed towards him.

'Maybe you go more closer shore,' he said quietly. Eskimos did not take unnecessary chances on the trail, and this time even Seppala understood that he had to be cautious.

The trail between Isaac's Point and Golovin, where according to the new plan Seppala would hand the serum over to Charlie Olson, was a few miles offshore, bypassing a number of craggy points that jutted out from the coast. Although the trail would be rougher, Seppala decided to stay within a few hundred feet of the land.

It was about –40° now, and as he edged down the bank at Isaac's Point he could feel the wind building in strength. The Eskimo had been right: this was no time to be out over water. The ice he had crossed a day earlier had already broken up, and around him he saw cakes of ice threatening to come loose. The cracks seemed to be getting closer, and in some places open water was just a few feet away. Togo zigzagged round the weak spots and several times put on a burst of speed towards shore. At times, blizzard conditions obscured Seppala's vision. Once the last bay had been crossed, the team turned towards the mainland, putting the ice floes behind them, and Seppala breathed a little easier.

A few hours later, the entire section of ice over which they had come broke up in chunks and blew out to sea.

Once firmly on shore, Seppala stopped the team and rubbed the dogs down, brushing off a layer of ice and snow that had formed over their faces, drying off their paws and tending to any cuts on their feet. Although the most dangerous part of the run was behind them, the most physically challenging part was just starting. They would have to climb a series of ridges to the 1,200-foot summit of Little McKinley, which overlooks Golovin Bay.

Many mushers consider that climb to be the toughest part of the trail to Nome. The exposed ridges stretch out over eight miles. The downgrades are steep and the dogs and drivers have little time to recover from one ridge before they have to charge up the next. By the time the summit of Little McKinley is reached, the teams have climbed about 5,000 feet. Seppala's dogs were being asked to make the climb with less than five hours of rest, and after they had travelled for four and a half days and covered 260 miles of trail. With few reserves to call on, the team began to stumble from exhaustion. But they did not stop, and strained up the final ascent, then raced three miles down to Dexter's roadhouse in Golovin.

Some thirteen hours after the start at Isaac's Point, the team arrived at its destination and Seppala passed the serum to Charlie Olson. Since he had picked it up from Ivanoff on the shore ice of Norton Sound, he and his dogs had travelled 135 miles, more than two and a half times the distance covered by any of the other drivers. And this was done at top speed, in blizzard conditions over heaving ice. They were ready for a rest.

The time was a little before 3 p.m. Now, all that stood between Golovin and Nome was a stretch of seventy-eight miles.

THE STORM was making itself felt beyond Golovin. On the same day, a Sunday, Nome awoke to the sound of the wind rising. It had been nearly two weeks since Billy Barnett's death. The streets were empty; not a single parishioner was heading up to Sunday mass and there were no children skating on the Snake River. Earlier in the week, some boys had been allowed out to throw snowballs at each other, albeit at a safe distance. Now even they had retreated to their cabins.

Out on the Sandspit, Nurse Morgan struggled against the wind, visiting as many families as possible before the cold became unbearable. Since the death of Bessie Stanley, the first Eskimo to die from diphtheria, the Sandspit had been under a strict lockdown.

Across town, Dr Welch went through the medical reports, visited patients and did what he could to keep up with the number of victims. Another case had been identified and there were now twenty-eight cases in Nome. As Welch told the local United Press reporter, Robert McDowell, 'even if the dogs manage to arrive with the supply there will be sufficient antitoxin to care for only 30 people'.

As dire as that sounded, the more serious concern was that the drivers might not make it to Nome. This was already shaping up as an extraordinary blizzard. Even experienced mushers wouldn't want to tempt fate under these conditions. If just one driver in the relay got lost or blown off course by the storm and could not reach the warmth of a roadhouse, the ampoules of serum would eventually freeze, expand and crack, thus ruining the supply.

Caught between the need for serum and the possibility that a heroic attempt to mush through the storm could result in the loss of the first shipment, Curtis Welch called a meeting of the Board of Health to ask them to stop the relay. The loss of a few hours or even a few days, he explained, was not as important as the safety of the shipment. Twenty-eight lives were now depending on the antitoxin reaching Nome intact. The health board members agreed.

In an attempt to reach the mushers, Mayor Maynard picked up the phone and requested the operator to put him through to Pete Curran, the roadhouse keeper at Solomon. Maynard told Curran that when Gunnar Kaasen arrived from Bluff with the serum, he should be ordered to remain in Solomon until the storm abated and it was safe to resume travel. A call was also sent out to Port Safety, where Ed Rohn, the last driver in the relay, was informed that the rescue attempt had been temporarily halted.

No one in the room knew if these calls would have any effect: the exact location of the serum was unknown. The last update had been Gonangnan's departure from Unalakleet yesterday morning. It was not even clear whether Gonangnan had met up with Seppala.

Out at Port Safety, twenty-one miles from Nome, Rohn received the telephone call from Nome. He could not have agreed more with the decision of the health board. From the window of the roadhouse, he could see the ice beyond the lagoon that separated Port Safety from the Bering Sea. It was, as he described it, in 'constant motion from a heavy groundswell'. Rohn unhooked the dogs, fed them and put the sled away. Before settling in for a long rest, he telephoned Nome with a message: the wind was blowing eighty miles per hour, 'whirling the snow so that it was impossible for man or beast to face the storm . . .' As the message came through, the connection crackled and the line went dead. Nome lost what little communication it had with the drivers and it could only pray that the message would reach Kaasen.

It would not.

FIFTY MILES EAST, on the other side of Cape Nome, Gunnar Kaasen sat in the roadhouse at Bluff. He had no inkling of the meeting in Nome or the decision to hold off the relay. Bluff was a tiny mining village of fewer than forty people, named after the surrounding grey bluffs that towered over the coast. It was situated well east of the telephone lines to Nome.

Kaasen had arrived at the roadhouse sixteen hours earlier, and at five o'clock on Sunday evening he was still sitting by the glowing iron stove, alert for any sounds indicating Olson's arrival. He occasionally opened the door and looked out into the swirling snow.

All Kaasen could hear was the wind as it moaned through the buildings abandoned after the gold rush. It had been years since he could remember such a strong wind, and for a moment he worried that Olson had been pinned down by the storm somewhere out on the trail. He had no way of knowing when or if Charlie Olson would arrive, and so he had to stay ready to move out at any moment.

The dogs needed to be fed. There were thirteen of them staked outside in a line. Kaasen struggled out of the door and fed each one of them salmon and a chunk of tallow. This would provide the necessary calories to keep the dogs warm.

Kaasen had taken a chance in choosing Balto as his lead dog. He was relatively inexperienced and Seppala considered him second-rate. Too slow to make the first string, he was used principally to haul freight on short runs. Kaasen thought more highly of Balto. The dog may not have been fast, but he was steady and strong.

By 1925, Kaasen and Seppala had already been working together for years organising Hammon Consolidated's water irrigation system of the gold fields. Kaasen often used the dogs for company and personal trips. The two men came from the same region of Norway, but they could not have been more different. Kaasen was a towering and tough man, six feet two, gruff and introverted. He had a quiet, no-nonsense way about him.

'Either you listened to him or you got thumped on the head,' one of his relatives said fondly. Fondly, because the driver had a gentle side, which came out more in acts of kindness than in words. He had a passion for vanilla ice cream and loved to share it with anyone who had an appetite, and he kept the door open to any boy or girl hungry for his wife's famous cinnamon rolls.

At around 7 p.m., Kaasen heard a faint shout outside. It had to be Olson. Kaasen pushed open the door. It was clear that Olson had had a bitter ride. His hands were too numb from frostbite to unlash the serum, and his seven dogs, short-haired for sled dogs, were stiff in the groin. Kaasen helped the musher inside the roadhouse and sat him down. Then he went back outside to retrieve the serum and bring the team inside. Olson had tied rabbit-fur blankets round each dog's groin, but this was not enough protection. All seven limped into the cabin and lay down stiffly on the floor. 'They couldn't have gone much further,' Kaasen observed.

It had taken Olson nearly four and a half hours to travel the twenty-five miles from Golovin to Bluff. Putting on the dog blankets had nearly cost him his fingers. In the warm cabin, Olson pulled off his gloves. His fingers were white and hard as stone; at best it would be days before their full use would be restored.

As they sat in the roadhouse, Olson warned Kaasen to hold off. However much Nome needed the serum, this was not the weather to travel in. Kaasen looked around the room: Olson's fingers were burning with pain; the dogs lay crippled, ragged and exhausted on the floor. It was good advice. Kaasen would heed it, but only to a point.

Two hours later, the wind still had not died down. If anything, it had risen and it was getting colder. It was ten o'clock and the temperature was –28°, without the wind chill. Snow was coming down fast and being blown by the wind. If he didn't leave now, the trail to Port Safety, thirty-four miles away, would be impassable with drifts. Kaasen stepped outside. In all his twenty-four years in Nome he had never felt such a blast. One report put the wind's speed in excess of seventy miles per hour. 'I had seal mukluks on my feet. They go up to the hips. And I had sealskin pants over them. On my head I had a reindeer parka and hood and a drill parka over that. But the wind was so strong that it went right through the skins.'

Kaasen made his decision: he would head out.

When all thirteen dogs were hooked up to the gang line, he went back inside and got the serum. With his heavy parka reaching below his waist and his face hidden deep inside the fur ruff of his hood, Kaasen loomed in the doorway like some mythological giant of the north. He said a brief goodbye to Olson, opened the door and stepped back out into the night.

Few drivers had the courage, the know-how and the dogs to face a blizzard head-on. No amount of movement can keep a musher warm in such conditions. Most travellers caught out in a blizzard stop and make camp. Yet even that can be dangerous, for on this coast there are few trees to fuel a fire. A driver has only the sled to hide behind and his sleeping-bag, fur robes and dogs to help to keep him warm.

A blizzard attacks a musher by causing confusion. His eyelashes freeze shut, his face is pounded by snowy blasts every way he turns and he loses his sense of direction. Stumbling through a blizzard, 'you don't know whether to pray, curse or cry. You generally do all three together,' the All Alaska Sweepstakes racer Scotty Allan once said. 'But after a while the blizzard becomes a hated thing with a personality. You get that back to the wall feeling, and like a man in the heat of battle, you forget to feel afraid. You grow to glory in the fight with the damned thing.'

Five miles into the run, Kaasen's worst fears materialised. Since he left the roadhouse, the wind had sanded the trail down to a hard and fast crust, but here by a ridge a towering drift had formed, blocking the trail. Balto tried to run his way through, but he and the other dogs quickly became mired in the snow. Kaasen waded in after them to clear a path, but he, too, floundered as the snow rose up to his chest. There was no way the team could get to the other side except by retreating and then going round the ridge. Kaasen had to turn the dogs round. He grabbed Balto's harness and together they dragged the team in a tight arc through the drift and back out the way they had come. Getting round the ridge would be difficult. Balto had worked largely on the trails to the various dredge sites beyond Nome, and Kaasen was asking the dog to find an unfamiliar trail in unfamiliar territory in the pitch dark of the blizzard.

Kaasen could barely see a hundred feet ahead of him. Balto lurched forward and tentatively ploughed his way through the snow along the back of the ridge. He understood that he had to regain the trail, to find the faint scent of dogs that had pattered before him that winter. Balto kept his nose low to ground, his ears flattened against his head to keep out the wind, as he moved slowly over the snow.

A dog's sense of smell is at least 600 to 700 times more powerful than that of a human, and Balto was capable of smelling the tracks left behind by other dogs several feet beneath the snow. A canine's paws are sensitive too, which would help Balto to feel the hard-packed surface of a trail that had been covered by new snow. Minutes passed like hours. They were beyond the ridge and still Balto searched. Suddenly, the dog lifted his head and broke out into a run. They were back on the trail.

A few miles farther on, the trail turned hard again as Kaasen entered a valley. It was Topkok River, its frozen surface wiped clean of snow by the wind. Kaasen's right cheek began to sting with frostbite. Crossing the river, as he neared the west bank, Balto stopped. Kaasen went to the head of the team and saw a large stretch of overflow. Balto had run right into it and now refused to go farther. It was shallow, but deep enough to have soaked the dog's feet. Kassen turned the team off the river, dried Balto's feet, then moved on.

With the overflow behind them, the team charged over a series of ridges that ran perpendicular to the shore. Each dropped sharply down to a creek, and Kaasen found a momentary reprieve from the wind. The last and highest of the ridges was Topkok Mountain, the brutal 600-foot climb with a long, exposed summit. As Kaasen approached the base of Topkok, he stopped for a few minutes and caught his breath. Then, pushing from behind, he urged the dogs on as he charged up the mountain. It seemed that for every step they took forward, the storm pushed them back two. The dogs crawled on their bellies as they fought their way up. Kaasen's right cheek went numb from the cold. 'Topkok is hell when it's storming,' Kaasen would later recall. 'It was storming some when I got up there.'

Upon reaching the summit, Kaasen jumped back onto the sled and held on as the dogs raced along the ridge. He strained his eyes in the darkness to make sure they were not heading towards the edge. If it had been daytime and calm, Kaasen would have been able to see clear across the coast to Cape Nome, but it was well after midnight now and the storm continued to rage. At the end of the ridge, the team picked up speed and began to race down the far slope of Topkok. They were on the six-mile stretch of flats after Topkok, and the wind was coming across the sloughs and lagoons, picking up snow in such thick veils that Kaasen could barely see his hand in front of his face. He could only guess at his position each time Balto crossed another lagoon or creek. He had given control of the team over to Balto and his job now was to hold on.

'I didn't know where I was,' Kaasen would later recall. 'I couldn't even guess.' Then, in a lull between gusts, Kaasen recognised a vast depression in the land up ahead as the Bonanza Slough. He was well beyond Solomon. It was two miles back. He had missed the roadhouse, which was just north of the trail. It was then that he made a decision, the most controversial of the entire race. He would push on to Port Safety. He could rest later.

It was about ten more miles to Port Safety, where Ed Rohn was to take the serum into Nome. As Kaasen headed over across Bonanza Slough, he entered a long blowhole and the wind hit him. It takes a wind of sixty to seventy miles per hour to flip a sled, and throughout his journey Kaasen had struggled to keep the rig down. Finally, he was overwhelmed. Entering the blowhole, Kaasen did not have enough strength or weight to keep the sled upright. Several times the sled was hurled off the trail, dragging the dogs with it. Each time, Kaasen had to take off his gloves, untangle the team and right the sled.

Before crossing to the other side, a final gust slammed into the sled. Kaasen found himself buried in a drift. He crawled in the darkness back to the sled, righted it and fumbled with the dogs' harnesses. He patted the sled to make sure the serum was still in place. He worked his hands up and down the basket, first methodically and then frantically. It was gone. His stomach tightened. The worst had happened. Kaasen dropped to the ground and crawled around in the snow, probing in the darkness with his bare hands for the serum. His right hand hit against something hard. He grabbed it. It was the serum. He lashed it back to the sled, gave it a few extra turns with the rope and fled this devilish stretch of land.

The gust that flipped Kaasen's sled marked a turn in the musher's luck. At the end of the slough, the trail curved to the southwest and the wind was now at his back. In his own words, the going was better and 'boosted' him along over the last few miles to the Port Safety roadhouse in a little over an hour.

When he arrived, it was about three o'clock in the morning and the roadhouse was dark. After sending the storm warning to Nome earlier that evening, Ed Rohn had gone to sleep, assuming that Kaasen would be waiting at Solomon for the storm to abate before heading on to Port Safety.

Kaasen stared up at the roadhouse from the trail. He contemplated waking Rohn. But it would take time for the driver to harness and hitch up his dogs. The wind appeared to be easing, and although he and his dogs were cold, they were still moving fast down the trail. He figured he would make better time if he continued on to Nome.

For the last twenty miles, the trail ran along the beach. The wind continued to die down, but travel was slow and difficult because of heavy drifts. Although his fingers ached with frostbite and several of his dogs were stiffening up, Kaasen was grateful at least to be able to see the path ahead.

Around 5.30 a.m. on Monday, February 2, Kaasen could make out the outline of the cross above St Joseph's Church. Within a few minutes he pulled up onto Front Street and stopped, exhausted, his eyes stinging from the cold, dry air, outside the door of the Miners & Merchants Bank of Nome.

Witnesses said they saw Kaasen stagger off the sled and stumble up to Balto, where he collapsed, muttering: 'Damn fine dog.'

THAT MONDAY, February 2, within minutes of Kaasen's arrival, Welch began to unwrap the package. The serum was frozen solid but the vials did not appear to be broken, a testament to the care Dr Beeson in Anchorage had taken in packing them. The serum would have to be thawed before it could be used, and that would take time. Welch took it to the hospital and put it in a warm room (by Alaskan standards), at 46°. By nine o'clock, the serum in the vials had been partially liquefied and not a single bottle was broken. By 11 a.m., the serum was clear and was ready for use.

News of the serum's arrival had spread through town, and the first order of business was to treat the most severe cases. Welch went first to the Winters and McDowell households. John Winters's wife was very ill; she had contracted the disease from her daughter two days earlier, on January 31, and her condition had deteriorated over the past few hours. Now her husband had come down with the disease.

Robert McDowell, the United Press reporter, had also developed symptoms. His throat was red and swollen and there were the beginnings of a membrane, so Welch gave McDowell an initial shot of 5,000 units. The newsman's reports had played an important role in getting the Nome story out to papers across the globe. But now, with his twenty-four-year-old wife and infant daughter under quarantine, he had become the story.

Nurse Morgan, meanwhile, headed over to the Sandspit to give each member of the Stanley family several thousand units of antitoxin. She went on to visit other families and immunised each of them.

By early afternoon, more than 10 per cent of the 300,000 units had been used up. Many of the same patients would receive a second round of injections, and later that evening several thousand more units of serum were gone. The 300,000 units would be exhausted long before the arrival of the second shipment of 1.1 million units.

Of all the cases that had developed since the start of the relay, Margaret Curran's frightened Welch the most. She had developed symptoms earlier in the week, several days after her return to town from her father's roadhouse in Solomon. If she had contracted diphtheria, then every traveller who passed through the roadhouse would have been exposed to the disease. In a matter of days, reports of new infections could come in from communities along the coast. The 1.1 million units en route to the ice-free port of Seward had to reach Nome a lot faster than officials had planned.

The shipment had left Seattle by ship on Saturday and it still had to travel by rail from Seward to Nenana before the regular mail could take it to Nome by dog sled. The medicine was expected to arrive in Nenana around February 8, in six days. The regular mail route journey from Nenana to Nome typically took about twenty-five days. Time was not on Nome's side, especially if Welch's worst fears about the Curran case turned out to be justified.

At a meeting of the Board of Health that Monday, Welch took a position he had not taken before. It was time, he conceded, to try to deliver at least half of the next shipment of serum by air—a dangerous gamble. 'I should feel much safer if I knew that I would get additional shipment not more than ten days from date,' Welch wrote in a telegram that was read by Surgeon General Cumming.

As news of Welch's plight spread, it seemed that everyone now agreed that half the shipment should be diverted farther up the railroad to Fairbanks, where a plane would be waiting to carry it to Nome. Everyone, except Governor Bone.

With Welch's assent, Mayor Maynard brought Thompson and Sutherland up to date on the situation. Thompson must have gone right to work on it, for the following day Roy Darling and Ralph Mackie were in the cockpit of the biplane, taking it for a test drive down the main street of Fairbanks in –14° weather beneath clear skies.

The test run was proof enough to everyone in town that the plane could take off at a moment's notice. Volunteers began to pack the aircraft with supplies. The excitement was growing in Fairbanks, and, in Nome, Welch and the others heard the news with relief.

There was even greater cause for relief when news spread that the 300,000 units that had been brought by dog-sled relay seemed to be working. The repeated thawing and freezing did not seem to have damaged the serum's efficacy, and on February 3 it looked as if even those who were seriously ill would recover.

The members of the Winters family were improving, and Robert McDowell was on the mend just hours after receiving the medicine.

'I'm carrying on,' McDowell said in a dispatch to colleagues in San Francisco. 'My case is not considered serious.' The reporter had to dictate the message to a friend because he was still under quarantine.

But it was not all good news. Later that afternoon, McDowell's daughter developed a greyish-white spot in her throat, and his wife, Vera, also appeared to be ill. At seven o'clock that evening, Vera drew her final breath, apparently the sixth victim of the epidemic.

Vera McDowell was a prominent woman in Nome. She was the first white girl to be born during the gold-rush days, delivered on March 16, 1900, and her loss was felt by many of the townsfolk. Some newspapers attributed her death to diphtheria, but Nome's death records stated the cause as venous air embolism and miscarriage. (Vera had been four to five months pregnant.) An air embolism is an infrequent complication of pregnancy, and since she had no symptoms of a sore throat, Vera McDowell probably did not have diphtheria. But in the chaos of the epidemic, Vera's death was reported across the states, and officials in Washington and the public at large shuddered at the news. The *San Francisco Chronicle*'s headline read: SIX DEAD AS PLAGUE GAINS ADDED FORCE.

On Friday, February 6, Vera's parents and close friends got permission to hold a private funeral and led a small procession by horse-drawn hearse to the Belmont Point Cemetery, where the body was placed in a vault until proper burial could be made after the ground had thawed in the spring.

By Friday afternoon, about one-third of the serum had been used. Mayor Maynard, Hammon executive Mark Summers, and 'Wrong Font' Thompson again bombarded Bone with messages demanding that he authorise an air flight from Fairbanks.

'If this rate continues you can see how long this shipment will last,' Summers said in his telegram.

Bone acknowledged their concern but held his ground. To Mayor Maynard it seemed as though Juneau and Washington simply did not care enough to act decisively and sanction such a bold new move.

Maynard lost no time taking his complaints to the press. The headline for the *Washington Post* that day read: NOME MAYOR ATTACKS CAPITAL FOR INACTIVITY. Maynard was quoted as saying:

> This bureaucracy stands idly by while our people suffer and die and while red-blooded men are willing to fly airplanes to our relief. If Nome is compelled to wait until the Governor of Alaska considers that conditions here are really serious, Nome might as well abolish its Public Health Board, to govern our life and death from Juneau.

Bone's health official, Harry DeVighne, bristled at the attack: 'Alarming reports sent out from Nome in criticism of official agencies are wholly unjustified,' he told reporters. 'The territory is alertly watching the situation and while I believe that the delivery of the larger supply from Seattle would be safer by dog team than by any airplane available in the territory, the flight will be authorized if warranted by a crisis.'

The governor's office also sent a message to Wetzler directing him to round up more drivers for a second relay. Meanwhile, the train at Seward was ordered to idle at the station and wait for the serum, due to arrive on board the *Admiral Watson* the next day, Saturday.

The US Army, the US Navy and the airplane executives in Fairbanks, however, acting on an initiative begun by Maynard, continued to prepare for the flight. There was nothing the governor could do to stop them.

In Fairbanks, mechanics fitted skis to the plane and tuned the motor. Pilots Darling and Mackie stowed an extra propeller on board, along with 'as many spare engine parts as weight will permit', sleeping-bags, rifles, snowshoes and camp equipment.

'If forced down,' they told the North American Newspaper Alliance in an interview, 'we will mush over the trail and connect with the dog teams [of the second relay] . . . The antitoxin will not freeze unless we do. We will carry it in containers next to our bodies.'

The two may have known a great deal about airplanes, but they knew very little about travelling even short distances in the Alaska wilderness without dogs.

In Seattle, at the behest of Washington officials, Commandant J. V. Chase of the Navy Yard at Bremerton ordered the minesweeper *Swallow* to prepare once again to head to the edge of the ice pack to aid the fliers in case they hit trouble on their way to Nome.

'It is most gallant of Darling,' said another official, Dr George Magruder, head of the Public Health Service in Seattle, who coordinated the shipment of the 1.1 million units to Alaska. 'The flight under the best of conditions is extremely hazardous. With an old plane . . . and in the dead of winter it is a perilous venture.'

In addition, the army ordered the men of the Signal Corps to prepare fires along the route to guide the fliers, and in Nome, Captain Thomas Ross and his colleagues in the US Lifesaving Crew began to hack out a landing field on the Bering Sea in front of Nome. As far as Maynard, Sutherland and Thompson were concerned, everything was in place for a flight—except Governor Bone's authorisation.

ON SATURDAY, February 7, with the serum due to arrive by ship late that evening, Bone reversed himself and sent a message to Wetzler authorising him to divert half of the 1.1 million units when it arrived by train the next day. It was clear that he was taking the action under duress, most likely as a consequence of a report of yet another diphtheria case. The officials in Nome were in 'hysteria', Bone said in his message to Wetzler. 'There is no emergency that justifies such a hazard. However, I sincerely trust that nothing will go wrong.'

Early Sunday afternoon, as the second batch of serum headed by train towards Nenana and then on to Fairbanks, Darling and Mackie went to the hangar where the *Anchorage* was stored to make last-minute preparations for the flight. They were both wearing several layers of fur clothing, and on their faces they had smeared petroleum grease to protect them from the cold. They wore close-fitting chamois helmets, with peepholes for their eyes and nostrils, and between them they had a single parachute—a problem, one newspaper reported, that would be 'solved between themselves'.

Finally, they packed two Thermos bottles of hot water, a bar of chocolate, bouillon cubes, beans, rice, flour, an axe and extra fur robes. It was time to start the engine. The serum was due soon.

Mackie and Darling heaved themselves into the open cockpit. A crowd had gathered to watch them. A volunteer mechanic by the name of Richard Lynch moved towards the front of the plane to spring the propeller. It was about 40° below zero. Lynch, who had borrowed Mackie's new overcoat to help to keep him warm, stepped up to the propeller, swinging the blade down hard. The propeller caught on the first try and the engine sprang to life.

Caught off guard by his success, Lynch slipped on the snow and got Mackie's overcoat caught in the first revolution of the blade. He was hurled ten feet into the air. Luckily, the coat ripped and Lynch came crashing to the ground, injuring his knee.

The engine kept roaring. Mackie spent several minutes trying to idle it down but he could not. A mechanic standing at the back of the plane, holding down the tail while the engine ran at full speed, began to suffer from frostbite on his face. The slipstream created by the propeller was causing air to condense, forming a coat of ice on the fuselage and the tail, as well as on the mechanic's face.

In the cockpit, Darling's feet grew numb while Mackie, fiddling with the engine, lost feeling in his hands. The problem preventing them from regulating the engine was a broken radiator shutter, which caused the engine to overheat.

They would have to improvise another shutter, but that would take time, and the light in the sky was fading. The decision was made to call off the flight for the day. As the pilots and mechanics unloaded the provisions from the plane and began to work on a new shutter, a musher by the name of A. C. Olin left Nenana at 5 p.m. by dog team, headed for Tolovana. Packed in his sled were half of the 1.1 million units of antitoxin.

Despite the day's fiasco, Mackie and Darling were not dismayed.

The two men told reporters that evening that they would be ready to take off the next day and land in Nome before Wednesday.

On Monday morning, the radiator again was troublesome. Not enough alcohol and glycerine had been added to the water in the radiator and it had frozen.

Mackie remained confident. 'Our plane will pass the dogs before we have been in the air for two hours,' he predicted. But on Tuesday the pilots again failed to get off the ground.

Finally, *News-Miner* editor Thompson, for whom the daring air rescue had meant so much, faced the truth. There would be no air rescue. And in that decision, Governor Bone was vindicated.

In defeat, Thompson was neither defiant nor dismissive of the great accomplishments of his opponents. To his credit, he struck just the right tone. 'We believe in the airship and we believe in the dog . . . ,' he would write in a *News-Miner* editorial that evening:

> We know that even an ordinary airship can make 60 miles an hour and we know that a dog cannot. Where the dog has it over the airship is that the dog . . . knows nothing about horizons, visibilities, temperatures, gasoline—all he knows is to obey his master's voice and marche . . . The burden of proof is today on the airship. The dogs are running and every hour getting closer to the goal. The airship will go when it can, but the dog seems to go whether he can or not. We take our hat off to the dog.

Indeed, by the time Thompson's editorial appeared, the second relay—which included many of the drivers from the first—had already left the town of Ruby, a little over a third of the way to Nome.

The second run was also difficult, with heavy snowstorms. The drivers were forced to break trail for much of the way. Finally, on February 15, in the middle of a blizzard, Ed Rohn brought the second shipment of serum to Nome after a ninety-mile run.

Thompson could be magnanimous in defeat because the setback could only be temporary. The day of the dogs would soon pass into history. The race to save an Arctic town did for Alaska what he could never have done with all his harangues—it focused the attention of the entire country on his territory.

ON FEBRUARY 2, the same day that Gunnar Kaasen drove his team into Nome, President Coolidge signed the Airmail Act of 1925, otherwise known as the Kelly Act. The legislation, which had been

TOP LEFT: the mouth of the Snake River, with Nome's Sandspit—home to many of the town's Eskimo population—in the background. TOP RIGHT: Leonhard Seppala sets up camp for the night beside a frozen lake.

MIDDLE: a team of howling sled dogs are ready to run. LEFT: Togo, Leonhard Seppala's valiant lead dog, on the Nome Serum Run.

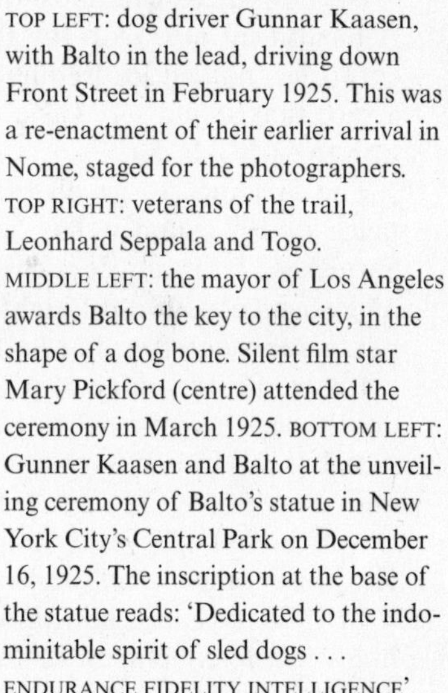

TOP LEFT: dog driver Gunnar Kaasen, with Balto in the lead, driving down Front Street in February 1925. This was a re-enactment of their earlier arrival in Nome, staged for the photographers. TOP RIGHT: veterans of the trail, Leonhard Seppala and Togo. MIDDLE LEFT: the mayor of Los Angeles awards Balto the key to the city, in the shape of a dog bone. Silent film star Mary Pickford (centre) attended the ceremony in March 1925. BOTTOM LEFT: Gunner Kaasen and Balto at the unveiling ceremony of Balto's statue in New York City's Central Park on December 16, 1925. The inscription at the base of the statue reads: 'Dedicated to the indomitable spirit of sled dogs . . . ENDURANCE FIDELITY INTELLIGENCE'.

introduced three years earlier by Representative Clyde M. Kelly of Pennsylvania, had accelerated through Congress in the past few weeks. Private air companies would now be allowed to compete against the dog teams for mail contracts.

Within a decade of the serum run, there were several permanent airmail runs. By 1941, planes covered fifty-six routes while dog teams covered ten, and by the early 1960s only a single dog route remained in Alaska: on St Lawrence Island, about 150 miles off the Bering coast. The postman was Chester Noongwook, who drove his team fifty miles to the landing strip where the airmail plane touched down. His last run took place in January 1963.

The death knell for the heritage of dog sledding in Alaska came in the late 1950s, when the modern snowmobile was invented. The vehicles quickly became popular in Alaska and the dog teams became almost a novelty in many villages. By the 1960s, the sled-dog population in most Alaskan villages was smaller than the number of 'iron dogs', according to one sled-dog historian.

By 1970, travel over most of Alaska's trails was a thing of the past. A local historian, Dorothy Page, had joined forces with a sled-dog enthusiast named Joe Redington, and together they decided to create a race that would serve as a tribute to the dogs and their contribution to early Alaska.

The first race to go all the way from Anchorage to Nome took place in 1973, and it has since been held every year on the first Saturday of March. It is called the Iditarod. The race covers what had once been a vital freight route between Anchorage and Nome, passing through the old Iditarod Mining District.

Iditarod is the name of a river on which the town was built when gold was discovered in 1907, and the word comes from an Athabaskan Indian term that has been translated as 'a distant place' and 'clear water'. The exact definition has never been clear. The race travels across the westernmost portion of the serum route: from Ruby to Nome in even years and from Kaltag to Nome in odd years.

In 1975, Alaska again showed its enthusiasm for dog sledding by holding a re-enactment of the serum run. Many of the sons of the original drivers took part in the relay, which took six days longer than in 1925.

Today, the Iditarod is a $4 million industry. It enjoys the support of a number of corporate sponsors and uses high-tech equipment along a trail that is broken out every year by volunteers on snowmobiles.

Where once it had taken a front-runner three weeks to reach Nome, it now takes between eight and ten days. Today, a team of Siberians would not even place in the running. The sled dogs that run in the Iditarod are mostly Alaskan huskies, which are even smaller and swifter than the Siberian. The Alaskan husky is not a registered breed but a bloodline of racing dogs, a hybrid bred for speed. The winning dogs of the Iditarod are generally crossbreeds of Siberian huskies and other native dogs mixed in with speedier Irish setters, English pointers and German shorthairs. According to Raymond Coppinger, professor of biology at Hampshire College, '[W]hen the distance is over ten miles, modern racing sled dogs are the fastest animals in the world.' With a person and sled attached, these dogs can run 3.2-minute miles for nearly twenty-five miles over a varied terrain that includes hills, curves, and woods.

Epilogue

On Saturday, February 21, two weeks after Kaasen reached Nome with the serum, the quarantine was lifted. The Dream Theatre celebrated by inviting everyone in town over twelve to a free double bill of the Harold Lloyd comedy *Grandma's Boy*, and *Shirley of the Circus*, a Shirley Mason five-reeler. James Clark, who ran the moviehouse, decided to wait a few more weeks before letting the younger kids in.

Beyond Nome, the celebration began much earlier. Within hours of Kaasen's arrival, local stringers for Associated Press, International News Service, Pathé News and other news organisations had sent out dispatches over the radio and telegraph announcing the victory of man and dog over the worst that nature could throw at them.

'Science made the antitoxin that is in Nome today,' cheered the *New York Sun* in an editorial, 'but science could not get it there. All the mechanical transportation marvels of modern times faltered in the presence of the elements . . . Other engines might freeze and choke, but that oldest of all motors, the heart, whose fuel is blood and whose spark is courage, never stalls but once.'

From the White House, President Coolidge sent out letters of commendation, while the Senate stopped its work to pay tribute to 'that classic, heroic dog team relay that carried the life-saving antitoxin to the suffering, dying people of the little town of Nome, way out there on the bleak coast of the Bering Sea', as Washington senator Clarence Cleveland Dill inserted in the record.

The pharmaceutical firm H. K. Mulford gave out twenty gold medals, one for each driver on the first relay. The Alaskan government also gave each of them twenty-five dollars as well as a citation stamped with the territorial gold seal.

Public response was overwhelming. The *Seattle Times* ran a public subscription fund to raise money for the drivers and the dogs, and the proceeds were divided equally among them. Dozens of letters and poems addressed to 'Balto' began to pour into Nome's post office. Local schoolchildren did their best to reply to most of them; the *Nome Nugget* received more poems than it could print.

The media realised that there was even more money to be made from the courage of others. The wire photo service Pacific & Atlantic arranged for a driver to deliver the first photographs and newsreel footage of the relay. They were, in fact, re-enactments of Kaasen's arrival in Nome.

Within days of the run, offers also began to pour in from the movies, as well as from showmen and publicists of every kind. Because Kaasen was the first driver to reach Nome, the newspapers rushed to describe his and Balto's experience on the trail. Kaasen and his team became instant celebrities, and by late February 1925 they had a movie deal and a tour lined up and were on their way to the states. With Balto and the other dogs, Kaasen and his wife, Anna, travelled south to Seward, where they boarded the steamship *Alameda* for Seattle. It was the first time in twenty-one years that the quiet musher had left Nome, and by the time the ship reached Seattle, a hero's welcome awaited him. Moments later, Kaasen was lost in the crowd.

'We've been here only ten minutes and I've lost my husband already,' Anna Kaasen complained. 'I could start back to Nome right now and not feel so badly about it.'

Weeks later, Kaasen and the dogs began their brief movie career. Hollywood producer Sol Lesser, who would later make Rin Tin Tin and Tarzan pictures, shot the dogs and driver for a thirty-minute film called *Balto's Race to Nome*. Lesser wasted no time hiring Kaasen and his team to promote the movie, and soon they were touring venues on the West Coast. In Los Angeles, Mary Pickford sat with

Balto on the steps of City Hall as the mayor placed a wreath of flowers round the dog's neck.

While Kaasen and the dogs were touring the West Coast, the parks commissioner of New York City announced that a statue of Balto would be erected in Central Park. It was a rare honour, normally accorded only to such luminaries as Christopher Columbus, William Shakespeare and Alexander Hamilton. Donations poured in to build the statue and the sculptor Frederick Roth began to design it.

Kaasen finished up his Hollywood commitments and, under the auspices of another promoter, went on a nine-month-long vaudeville circuit of the states. (A pay dispute between Kaasen and Lesser had led to the sale of the team to the new promoter.) The tour ended in New York, where on December 16, Kaasen, dressed in a squirrel-fur parka and timber-wolf-fur trousers, attended the unveiling of the statue. Balto stood quietly by his side, displaying no interest in the ceremonies until two northern sled dogs brought back from the Yukon Territory broke from the crowd and tried to join them. Kaasen managed to prevent the dogs from getting into a fight.

After the unveiling, Kaasen reluctantly left the dogs behind with the promoter who had bought the team, and travelled back to Alaska through Canada. He arrived in Nenana by train and immediately returned to his job hauling supplies.

It had been almost a year since Kaasen had left Nome, and when he returned in February 1926 he found his small town transformed. While he was away, a bitter feud had developed over the attention he had received from the press.

At first, Leonhard Seppala chose to stay out of the fray. He praised Kaasen for making the tough trek to Nome, but he was less generous when Togo's contribution failed to be as celebrated as Balto's. He was outraged that several newspapers had attributed Togo's trail achievements to Balto, and devastated when he learned that New York was about to put up a bronze effigy of the wrong dog.

Seppala had once said that 'in Alaska, our dogs mean considerably more to us than those "outside" can appreciate, and a slight to them is as serious a matter to their drivers as if a human being's achievements were overlooked'. The lack of recognition afforded Togo was a serious and heart-wrenching blow to him.

'It was almost more than I could bear when the "newspaper" dog Balto received a statue for his "glorious achievements",' Seppala wrote in his memoirs.

For the next several years, Seppala would go out of his way to remind the public that he and Togo had travelled farther than any of the other teams, and that their section of the route had been by far the most dangerous.

By fall 1926, Seppala had made his own plans to take his Siberian dogs on tour, with the ultimate goal of racing in the Northeast. In October, he left Nome with Togo and forty-two other dogs on one of the last steamships sailing before the winter set in. At last Togo would receive the national recognition he deserved. Seppala and his Siberians made an astonishing number of promotional appearances. He posed for photographs with Togo and the whole team in department stores and he appeared in a national ad campaign for Lucky Strike cigarettes.

In town after town, Seppala paraded the whole team down Main Street. Wherever he went, he drew crowds so huge that the police often had to be brought in to maintain control. Oddly, this man, who had spent so much of his life in the company of dogs, turned out to be a natural-born public speaker, combining playfulness with wry humour. He told one audience that his secret for staying in shape at the late age of fifty was that he neither smoked nor drank. Then, as he was turning somersaults and handsprings, two cigars fell out of his pocket. The crowd roared. 'They probably considered it all part of the show,' a friend had said.

New York City was the last stop on the tour. With Togo at the lead, Seppala drove the serum run team to the top of the steps of City Hall, then up Fifth Avenue, and finally on a circuit through Central Park. There was a series of appearances at Madison Square Garden. Before thousands of spectators, Seppala drove the team round the ice hockey rink, and the dogs were so excited they sped round the turns at top speed, crashing into the walls. During half time at one game, the explorer Roald Amundsen went out on the ice to give a speech honouring Togo, and presented the animal with a gold medal. There was thunderous applause from the 20,000 spectators. It was a fitting end to the tour, and when it was over Seppala was free to return to his great love, racing.

At the invitation of the Chinook Kennels in Wonalancet, New Hampshire, Seppala headed up to New England in January 1927 to participate in the burgeoning race circuit. He and his Siberians blew the competition away. In his first race in Poland Springs, Maine, in January, Seppala beat out his host and the other competitors by more than seven minutes. A Poland Spring socialite named Elizabeth Ricker was so impressed with Seppala's dogs that she not only replaced her dog team with a team of Seppala's Siberians but bought most of the remaining Siberians Seppala had brought with him from Alaska. Then, with Seppala as co-manager, Ricker opened up a kennel at the resort, and the two began to breed and sell the Siberians.

For the next few years, after opening the kennel with Ricker, Seppala divided his time between Alaska and Maine. In March 1927, he made his first trip back to Alaska after his tour of the states. Togo had aged considerably since the serum run, and his vigour was now less pronounced. Seppala thought the trip back would be too much for the dog, so he decided to leave him behind with Ricker.

The serum run had been Togo's last long-distance race, one in which 'he had worked his hardest and his best', and the dog was put into retirement to live out his final years. He spent most of his time by the fire in the living room of Ricker's home. 'It was a sad parting on a cold gray March morning when Togo raised a small paw to my knee as if questioning why he was not going along with me,' Seppala remembered.

On December 5, 1929, Seppala finally found the courage to put Togo to sleep. The dog was sixteen years old.

Years after Togo's death, Seppala kept the dog's spirit alive. One reporter, writing about Seppala many years later, said that 'in the depths of his keen gray eyes—lives a dog who will never leave'.

'While my trail has been rough at times,' Seppala wrote in his journal when he was eighty-one, 'the end of the course seems pretty smooth, with downhill going and a warm roadhouse in sight. And when I come to the end of the trail, I feel that along with my many friends, Togo will be waiting and I know that everything will be all right.'

Togo's body was placed on exhibit at the Yale Peabody Museum in New Haven, Connecticut, where it remained for decades. Finally, it was returned to Alaska. It can still be seen in a glass case at the Iditarod Trail Sled Dog Race Museum outside Anchorage.

For the most part, the other drivers in the serum run returned to their everyday lives once the publicity faded. Wild Bill Shannon continued to drive the mail, hunt, and run his traplines. His hands and face were still blackened and scarred by the cold, and he once said during a visit to the states: 'This hero business is big blah . . . I want to get back [home] where they shake hands and know how to fry bacon.'

A few years later, he was attacked and killed by a bear.

Relatively little is known about the Native drivers who covered nearly two-thirds of the run. Few reporters or moviemakers wanted to hear their story. For the most part, Alaska's Natives were considered a part of the landscape, regardless of the fact that they spoke the same language, held down jobs and contributed to the economy.

For many of the Natives, a simple thankyou was sufficient. 'I got more in gratitude from one lady at Nome City than I ever would have got in money from that race,' said Charlie Evans, who ran through the ice fog and lost two dogs in the sprint from Bishop Mountain to Nulato.

In the 1970s, during a surge in interest to preserve Alaska's history, stories about the Native drivers' heroism emerged. By then, many of them had died and the memories of those still alive had faded. Nevertheless, their role in the run was acknowledged, and they began to gain the recognition that had eluded them for so many years.

In the early years of the now-famous annual Iditarod race, reporters sought out the original drivers, and race officials bestowed on them the honorary 'Number 1' position.

In 1985, on the sixtieth anniversary of the serum run, President Ronald Reagan sent each of the three surviving drivers a letter of recognition: honours went to Charlie Evans, Edgar Nollner and Bill McCarty, an Athabaskan-Irish driver who travelled the route between Ruby and Whiskey Creek.

> Together with 19 others, you traveled across some of the world's cruelest miles to accomplish the impossible—and you did it in the name of humanity.

Edgar Nollner was the last survivor of the drivers on the first serum run. On January 18, 1999, he died of a heart attack at the age of ninety-four. He was survived by twenty-three children and more than 200 grandchildren. In 1995, he told the Associated Press that he was surprised at all the attention and had never expected to become famous.

'I just wanted to help, that's all,' he said.

GAY AND LANEY SALISBURY

Co-authors Gay and Laney Salisbury explain what led them to write *The Cruellest Miles*: 'Most of us find impossible to resist the face of a friendly dog, or a good dog story, and the story of dogs and men racing serum to save the children of Nome from diphtheria in 1925 is the greatest dog story ever told.

'Proof of this can still be found in Central Park in New York, where there is a larger-than-life-size bronze statue of a dog named Balto. He lead the last relay team into Nome under blizzard conditions, and became, next to the movie star Rin Tin Tin, the world's most famous dog. We are first cousins, who both grew up in the New York area, and were among the millions of children who loved to climb atop Balto whenever we played in Central Park. A plaque dedicates the statue to the "indomitable spirit" of the sled dogs, their "endurance, fidelity and intelligence".

'The inspiration for this book came when we read the obituary of Edgar Nollner, the last surviving 1925 musher, who died in January 1999 at the age of ninety-four. Although the headline read "Hero in Epidemic", Nollner always claimed that the twenty-four-mile stretch he mushed, in a blizzard so thick he could not even see his dogs, was "simply a day's work". The article said he had helped to "carve a legend in the snow", and we were keen that the story was not forgotten.

'Numerous children's books have been written about Balto and the serum run—it was even the subject of an animated movie by Steven Spielberg—yet there was only one previous history of the events and that was written nearly forty years ago. We spent over four years travelling across Alaska and the rest of the USA, and unearthed diaries, letters and photographs, interviewed survivors, pored through old newspapers, telegrams and medical notes, to faithfully reconstruct the events of those six fateful days.

'Writing and researching *The Cruellest Miles* has been the adventure of a lifetime. We hope you have as much fun reading it.'

Source notes accompanying *The Cruellest Miles* may be found on our website: *readersdigest.co.uk/cbmoreinfo*

ACKNOWLEDGMENTS AND PICTURE CREDITS: *Pompeii*: pages 6–8: Roman head: Antonio M. Rosario/Getty Images/The Image Bank/; aqueduct: Grant Faint/Getty Images/The Image Bank; skyline: Getty Images/National Geographic. *Shutter Island*: pages 148–150: silhouette of man: Michael Prince/Getty Images/Stone; barbed wire: Walter Bibikow/Getty Images/Taxi; page 289: © Sigrid Estrada. *The Runner*: pages 290–292: Barry Patterson/Illustration. *The Cruellest Miles*: pages 434–436: Reul Griffin Collection, Accession #59-845-783. Alaska and Polar Regions Dept., Ramuson Library; 468–469: middle left and top right: Anchorage Museum of History and Art; bottom left: reprinted from the Boston Evening Transcript, Feb 3, 1925; top middle right: photograph by Jeff Schultz; bottom middle right: Courtesy of Terence Cole; bottom right: Authors' Collection; 530–531: top left: Courtesy of Terence Cole; top middle left: Courtesy of Bill Hawks and Sigrid Seppola Hawks; middle left: Anchorage Museum of History and Art; bottom left: Reul Griffin Collection. Accession # 59-845-783. Alaska and Polar Regions Dept., Ramuson Library; top right: Carrie M. McLain, Memorial Museum, Nome, Alaska; top middle right: Authors' Collection, middle right; Courtesy of Matt Morgan; bottom right: Courtesy of Brown Brothers: page 539: © Margaret Peters.

DUSTJACKET CREDITS: Spine from top: Roman head: Antonio M. Rosario/Getty Images/ The Image Bank; aqueduct: Grant Faint/Getty Images/Image Bank; barbed wire: Walter Bibikow/Getty Images/Taxi; Barry Patterson/Illustration; Reul Griffin Collection, Accession # 59-845-783. Alaska and Polar Regions Dept., Ramuson Library.

Printed by Maury Imprimeur SA, Malesherbes, France
Bound by Reliures Brun SA, Malesherbes, France

227AX